NAVY BLUES by Del

"I'm sorry to wake you, honey, but I've got to get to the sub."

Carol was surprised to see that he was dressed and prepared to leave. "You'll be back, won't you? Will you . . . could you stop off and see me one more time, before you leave?"

His dark gaze caressed her. "Honest to God, Carol, I don't think I could stay away."

RED TAIL by Lindsay McKenna

"Don't like the shoe on the other foot, eh, Travis?"

Glaring at him, she muttered, "It's likely to be the other way around real soon, mister."

"Not if I have my way. Come tomorrow morning, I'm going to be in that captain's office asking for a section change. No offense, Lieutenant, but I'd much rather ask you out for a date than have you as my Air Commander."

DEMON LOVER by Kathleen Creighton

"I have pretty good self-control, but I'm not dead. You wanted me to kiss you, didn't you?" Chayne demanded.

"Yes," she whispered.

"You know, I can't decide if you're foolish, or much smarter than I give you credit for. But I think—" he slowly stroked his thumb in the palm of her hand "—I'm going to find out."

DEBBIE MACOMBER

hails from the state of Washington. As a busy wife and mother of four, she strives to keep her family healthy and happy. As the prolific author of dozens of bestselling romance novels, she strives to keep her readers happy with each new book she writes.

LINDSAY McKENNA

spent three years serving her country as a meteorologist in the U.S. Navy, so much of her knowledge about the military people and practices featured in her novels comes from direct experience. In addition, she spends a great deal of time researching each book, whether it be at the Pentagon or at military bases, extensively interviewing key personnel. She views the military as her second family and hopes that her novels will help dispel the "unfeeling machine" image that haunts it, allowing readers glimpses of the flesh-and-blood people who comprise the services. Lindsay is also a pilot. She and her husband, both avid rock hounds and hikers, live in Arizona.

KATHLEEN CREIGHTON

is a fifth-generation Californian, recently transplanted to rural South Carolina. She has a huge and loving family, a wide range of interests and an eclectic assortment of friends, many of whom would probably have to be considered eccentric. Being quite an ordinary person herself, she has a special appreciation for those who march to a different drummer.

MEN IN UNIFORM

Debbie Macomber
Lindsay McKenna
Kathleen Creighton

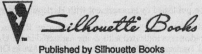
Silhouette Books

Published by Silhouette Books
America's Publisher of Contemporary Romance

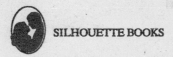 SILHOUETTE BOOKS

by Request

MEN IN UNIFORM

Copyright © 1994 by Harlequin Enterprises B.V.

ISBN 0-373-20100-1

The publisher acknowledges the copyright holders
of the individual works as follows:
NAVY BLUES
Copyright © 1989 by Debbie Macomber
RED TAIL
Copyright © 1985 by Lindsay McKenna
DEMON LOVER
Copyright © 1985 by Kathleen Modrovich

CONTENTS

A Note from Debbie Macomber

Dear Reader,

I've always been a sucker for a man in uniform, and from the reception my navy books received, I believe a lot of other women feel the same way.

The idea for the first navy book came when my good friend Linda Lael Miller and I were walking around the track at the local high school. We noticed several news helicopters in the area and wondered what was happening.

Then we saw it. The USS *Nimitz* was heading toward Bremerton, its new home port. Three thousand men in their dress-white uniforms manned the rails. In all my life I'd never witnessed such a scene. The waters of Sinclair Inlet were filled with small boats weaving in and out of the giant ship's wake. Wives and girlfriends frantically waved, their excitement and joy filling my heart with a surge of patriotism so strong that tears blurred my eyes.

The sight of that mighty ship and the anticipated reunion of the sailors with their families soon set me to weaving the fabric of my NAVY series.

I hope you enjoy Carol and Steve's love story. It's one of my all-time favorites.

Warmest regards,

Debbie Macomber

NAVY BLUES

Debbie Macomber

Dedicated to
Mary Magdalena Lanz,
July 2, 1909 to May 1, 1988
Beloved Aunt

Special thanks to:
Rose Marie Harris, wife of MMCM Ralph Harris,
retired U.S. Navy; Debbie Korrell,
wife of Chief Steven Korrell, USS *Alaska*;
Jane McMahon, RN

Chapter One

Seducing her ex-husband wasn't going to be easy, Carol Kyle decided, but she was determined. More than determined—resolute! Her mind was set, and no one knew better than Steve Kyle how stubborn she could be when she wanted something.

And Carol wanted a baby.

Naturally she had no intention of letting him in on her plans. What he didn't know wouldn't hurt him. Their marriage had lasted five good years, and six bad months. To Carol's way of thinking, which she admitted was a bit twisted at the moment, Steve owed her at least one pregnancy.

Turning thirty had convinced Carol that drastic measures were necessary. Her hormones were jumping up and down, screaming for a chance at motherhood. Her biological clock was ticking away, and Carol swore she could hear every beat of that blasted timepiece. Everywhere she turned, it seemed she was confronted with pregnant women, who served to remind her that her time was running out. If she picked up a magazine, there would be an article on some aspect of parenting. Even her favorite characters on television sitcoms were pregnant. When she found herself wandering through the infant section of her favorite department store, Carol realized drastic measures needed to be taken.

Making the initial contact with Steve hadn't been easy, but she recognized that the first move had to come from her. Getting in touch with her ex-husband after more than a year of complete silence had required two weeks of nerve building. But she'd managed to swallow her considerable pride and do it. Having a woman answer his phone had thrown her for a loop, and Carol had visualized her plans swirling down the drain until she realized the woman was Steve's sister, Lindy.

Her former sister-in-law had sounded pleased to hear from her, and then Lindy had said something that had sent Carol's spirits soaring to the ceiling: Lindy had claimed that Steve missed her dreadfully. Lordy, she hoped that was true. If so, it probably meant he wasn't dating yet. There could be complications if Steve was involved with another woman. On the other hand, there could also be problems if he wasn't involved.

Carol only needed him for one tempestuous night, and then, if everything went according to schedule, Steve Kyle could fade out of her life once more. If she failed to get pregnant . . . well, she'd leap that hurdle when she came to it.

Carol had left a message for Steve a week earlier, and he hadn't returned her call. She wasn't overly concerned. She knew her ex-husband well; he would mull it over carefully before he'd get back to her. He would want her to stew a while first. She'd carefully figured the time element into her schedule of events.

Her dinner was boiling on the stove, and Carol turned down the burner after checking the sweet potatoes with a cooking fork. Glaring at the orange-colored root, she heaved a huge sigh and squelched her growing dislike for the vegetable. After she became pregnant, she swore she would never eat another sweet potato for as long as she lived. A recent news report stated that the starchy vegetable helped increase the level of estrogen in a woman's body. Armed with that information, Carol had been eating sweet potatoes every day for the last two weeks. There had to be enough of the hormone floating around in her body by now to produce triplets.

Noting the potatoes were soft, she drained the water and dumped the steaming roots into her blender. A smile crowded the edges of her mouth. Eating sweet potatoes was a small price to pay for a beautiful baby... for Steve's baby.

"Have you called Carol back yet?" Lindy Callaghan demanded of her brother as she walked into the small kitchen of the two-bedroom apartment she shared with her husband and Steve.

Steve Kyle ignored her until she pulled out the chair and plopped down across the table from him. "No," he admitted flatly. He could see no reason to hurry. He already knew what Carol was going to tell him. He'd known it from the minute they'd walked out of the King County Courthouse, the divorce papers clenched in her hot little hands. She was remarrying. Well, more power to her, but he wasn't going to sit back and blithely let her rub his nose in the fact.

"Steve," Lindy insisted, her face tight with impatience. "It could be something important."

"You told me it wasn't."

"Sure, that's what Carol said, but...oh, I don't know, I have the feeling that it really must be. It isn't going to do any harm to call her back."

Methodically Steve turned the page of the evening newspaper and carefully creased the edge before folding it in half and setting it aside. Lindy and Rush, her husband, couldn't be expected to understand his reluctance to phone his ex-wife. He hadn't told either of them the details that had led to his and Carol's divorce. He preferred to keep all thoughts of the disastrous relationship out of his mind. There were plenty of things he could have forgiven, but not what Carol had done—not infidelity.

As a Lieutenant Commander aboard the submarine USS *Atlantis*, Steve was at sea for as long as six months out of a year. From the first Carol hadn't seemed to mind sending him off on a three-to-four month cruise. She even used to joke about it, telling him all the projects she planned to complete when he was at sea, and how pleased she was that he would be out of her hair for a while. When he'd returned she'd always seemed happy that he was home, but not exuberant. If anything had gone wrong in his absence—a broken water pipe, car repairs, anything—she'd seen to it herself with barely more than a casual mention.

Steve had been so much in love with her that the little things hadn't added up until later—much later. He'd deceived himself by overlooking the obvious. The physical craving they had for each other had diluted his doubts. Making love with Carol had been so hot it was like a nuclear meltdown. Toward the end she'd been eager for him, but not quite as enthusiastic as in the past. He'd been trusting, blind and incredibly stupid when it came to his ex-wife.

Then by accident he'd learned why she'd become so blasé about his comings and goings. When he left their bed, his loveless, faithless wife had a built-in replacement—her employer, Todd Larson.

It was just short of amazing that Steve hadn't figured it out earlier, and yet when he thought about it, he could almost calculate to the day when she'd started her little affair.

"Steve?"

Lindy's voice cut into his musings, and he lifted his gaze to meet hers. Her eyes were round and dark with concern. Steve experienced a small twinge of guilt for the way he'd reacted to his sister and Rush's marriage. When he'd learned his best friend had married his only sister after a dating period of a mere two weeks, Steve had been furious. He'd made no bones about telling them both the way he felt about their hurry-up wedding. Now he realized his own bitter experience had tainted his reasoning, and he'd long since apologized. It was obvious they were crazy about each other, and Steve had allowed his own misery to bleed into his reaction to their news.

"Okay, okay. I'll return Carol's call," he answered in an effort to appease his younger sibling. He understood all too well how much Lindy wanted him to settle matters with Carol. Lindy was happy, truly happy, and it dismayed her that his life should be at such loose ends.

"When?"

"Soon," Steve promised.

The front door opened, and Rush let himself into the apartment; his arms were loaded with Christmas packages. He paused just inside the kitchen and exchanged a sensual look with his wife. Steve watched the heated gaze and it was like throwing burning acid on his half-healed wounds. He waited a moment for the pain to lessen.

"How'd the shopping go?" Lindy asked, her silky smooth voice eager and filled with pleasure at the sight of her husband.

"Good," Rush answered and faked a yawn, "but I'm afraid it wore me out."

Steve playfully rolled his eyes toward the ceiling and stood, preparing to leave the apartment. "Don't tell me you two are going to take another nap!"

Lindy's cheeks filled with crimson color and she looked away. In the past few days the two of them had taken more naps than a newborn babe. Even Rush looked a bit chagrined.

"All right, you two," Steve said good-naturedly, reaching for his leather jacket. "I'll give you some privacy."

One glance from Lindy told him she was grateful. Rush stopped Steve on his way out the door and his eyes revealed his appreciation. "We've decided to look for a place of our own right away, but it doesn't look like we'll be able to move until after the first of the year." He paused and lowered his gaze, looking almost embarrassed. "I know this is an inconvenience for you to keep leaving, but . . ."

"Don't worry about it," Steve countered with a light chuckle. He patted his friend on the back. "I was a newlywed once myself."

Steve tried to sound casual about the whole matter, but doubted if he'd succeeded. Being constantly exposed to the strong current of love flowing between his friend and his sister was damn difficult, because he understood their need for each other all too well. There'd been a time when a mere look was all that was required to spark flames between him and Carol. Their desire seemed to catch fire and leap to brilliance with a single touch, and they couldn't get to bed fast enough. Steve had been crazy in love with her. Carol had appealed to all his senses and he'd ached with the desire to possess her completely. The only time he felt he'd accomplished that was when he was making love to her. Then and only then was Carol utterly his. And those times were all too brief.

Outside the apartment, the sky was dark with thick gray clouds. Steve walked across the street and headed toward the department stores. He didn't have much Christmas shopping to do, but now appeared to be as good a time for the task as any.

He hesitated in front of a pay phone and released a long, slow breath. He might as well call Carol and be done with it. She wanted to gloat, and he would let her. After all, it was the season to be charitable.

The phone rang just as Carol was coming in the front door. She stopped, set her purse on the kitchen counter and glared at the telephone. Her heart rammed against her rib cage with such force that she had to stop and gather her thoughts. It was Steve. The phone might as well have been spelling out his name in Morse code, she was that sure.

"Hello?" she answered brightly, on the third ring.

"Lindy said you phoned." His words were low, flat and emotionless.

"Yes, I did," she murmured, her nerves clamoring.

"Do you want to tell me why, or are you going to make me guess? Trust me, Carol, I'm in no mood to play twenty questions with you."

Oh Lord, this wasn't going to be easy. Steve sounded so cold and uncaring. She'd anticipated it, but it didn't lessen the effect his tone had on her. "I . . . I thought we could talk."

A short, heavy silence followed.

"I'm listening."

"I'd rather we didn't do it over the phone, Steve," she said softly, but not because she'd planned to make her voice silky and smooth. Her vocal chords had tightened and it just came out sounding that way. Her nerves were stretched to their limit, and her heart was pounding in her ear like a charging locomotive.

"Okay," he answered, reluctance evident in every syllable.

"When?" Her gaze scanned the calendar—the timing of this entire venture was of primary importance.

"Tomorrow," he suggested.

Carol's eyes drifted shut as the relief worked its way through her stiff limbs. Her biggest concern was that he would suggest after the Christmas holidays, and then it would be too late and she would have to reschedule everything for January.

"That would be fine," Carol managed. "Would you mind coming to the house?" The two bedroom brick rambler had been awarded to her as part of the divorce settlement.

Again she could feel his hesitation. "As a matter of fact, I would."

"All right," she answered, quickly gathering her wits. His not wanting to come to the house shouldn't have surprised her. "How about coffee at Denny's tomorrow evening?"

"Seven?"

Carol swallowed before answering. "Fine. I'll see you then."

Her hand was still trembling a moment later when she replaced the telephone receiver in its cradle. All along she'd accepted that Steve wasn't going to fall into her bed without some subtle prompting, but from the brusque, impatient sound of his voice, the whole escapade could well be impossible... this month. That bothered her. The one pivotal point in her plan was that everything come together quickly. One blazing night of passion could easily be dismissed and forgotten. But if she were to continue to invite him back one night a month, several months running, then he just might catch on to what she was doing.

Still, when it had come to interpreting her actions in the past, Steve had shown a shocking lack of insight. Thankfully their troubles had never intruded in the bedroom. Their marriage relationship had been a jumbled mess of doubts and misunderstandings, accusations and regrets, but their love life had always been vigorous and lusty right up until the divorce, astonishing as it seemed now.

*   *   *

At precisely seven the following evening, Carol walked into Denny's Restaurant on Seattle's Capitol Hill. The first year she and Steve had been married, they'd had dinner there once a month. Money had been tight because they'd been saving for a down payment on the house, and an evening out, even if it was only Saturday night at Denny's, had been a real treat.

Two steps into the restaurant Carol spotted her former husband sitting in a booth by the window. She paused and experienced such a wealth of emotion that advancing even one step more would have been impossible. Steve had no right to look this good—far better than she remembered. In the thirteen months since she'd last seen him, he'd changed considerably. Matured. His features were sharper, clearer, more intense. His lean good looks were all the more prominent, his handsome masculine features vigorous and tanned even in December. A few strands of gray hair streaked his temple, adding a distinguished air.

His gaze caught hers and Carol sucked in a deep, calming breath, her steps nearly faltering as she advanced toward him. His eyes had changed the most, she decided. Where once they had been warm and caressing, now they were cool and calculating. They narrowed on her, his mistrust shining through as bright as any beacon.

Carol experienced a moment of panic as his gaze seemed to strip away the last shreds of her pride. It took all her willpower to force a smile to her lips.

"Thank you for coming," she said, and slipped into the red upholstered seat across from him.

The waitress came with a glass coffeepot, and Carol turned over her cup, which the woman promptly filled after placing menus on the table.

"It feels cold enough to snow," Carol said as a means of starting conversation. It was eerie that she could have been married to Steve all those years and feel as if he were little more than a stranger. He gave her that impression now. This hard, impassive man was one she didn't know nearly as well as the one who had once been her lover, her friend and her husband.

"You're looking fit," Steve said after a moment, a spark of admiration glinting in his gaze.

"Thank you." A weak smile hovered over her lips. "You, too. How's the Navy treating you?"

"Good."

"Are you still on the *Atlantis*?"

He nodded shortly.

Silence.

Carol groped for something more to say. "It was a surprise to discover that Lindy's living in Seattle."

"Did she tell you she married Rush?"

Carol noted the way his brows drew together and darkened his face momentarily when he mentioned the fact. "I didn't realize Lindy even knew Rush," Carol said, and took a sip of the coffee.

"They were married two weeks after they met. Lord, I can't believe it yet."

"Two weeks? That doesn't sound anything like Rush. I remember him as being so methodical about everything."

Steve's frown relaxed, but only a little. "Apparently they fell in love."

Carol knew Steve well enough to recognize the hint of sarcasm in his voice, as if he were telling her what a mockery that emotion was. In their instance it had certainly been wasted. Sadly wasted.

"Are they happy?" That was the important thing as far as Carol was concerned.

"They went through a rough period a while back, but since the *Mitchell* docked they seem to have mended their fences."

Carol dropped her gaze to her cup as reality cut sharply into her heart. "That's more than we did."

"As you recall," he said harshly, under his breath, "there wasn't any fence left to repair. The night you started sleeping with Todd Larson, you destroyed our marriage."

Carol didn't rise to the challenge, although Steve had all but slapped her face with it. There was nothing she could say to exonerate herself, and she'd given up explaining the facts to him more than a year ago. Steve chose to believe what he wanted. She'd tried, God knew, to set the record straight. Todd had been her employer and her friend, but never anything more. Carol had pleaded with Steve until she was blue with exasperation, but it hadn't done her any good. Rehashing the same argument now wasn't going to help either of them.

Silence stretched between them and was broken by the waitress who had returned to their booth, pad and pen in hand. "Have you decided?"

Carol hadn't even glanced at the menu. "Do you have sweet-potato pie?"

"No, but pecan is the special this month."

Carol shook her head, ignoring the strange look Steve was giving her. "Just coffee then."

"Same here," Steve added.

The woman replenished both their cups and left.

"So how is good ol' Todd?"

His question lacked any real interest, and Carol had already decided her former boss was a subject they'd best avoid. "Fine," she lied. She had no idea how Todd was doing, since she hadn't worked for Larson Sporting Goods for over a year. She'd been offered a better job with Boeing and had been employed at the airplane company since before the divorce was final.

"I'm glad to hear it," Steve said with a soft snicker. "I suppose you called this little meeting to tell me the two of you are finally going to be married."

"No, Steve, please, I didn't call to talk about Todd."

He arched his brows in mock consternation. "I'm surprised. What's the matter, is wife number one still giving him problems? You mean to tell me their divorce hasn't gone through?"

A shattering feeling of hopelessness nearly choked Carol, and she struggled to meet his gaze without flinching. Steve was still so bitter, so intent on making her suffer.

"I really would prefer it if we didn't discuss Todd or Joyce."

"Fine. What do you want to talk about?" He checked his watch as if to announce he had plenty of other things he could be doing and didn't want to waste precious time with her.

Carol had carefully planned everything she was going to say. Each sentence had been rehearsed several times over in her mind, and now it seemed so trite and ridiculous, she couldn't manage a single word.

"Well?" he demanded. "Since you don't want to rub my nose in the fact that you're marrying Todd, what could you possibly have to tell me?"

Carol gestured with her hand, her fingers trembling. "It's Christmastime," she murmured.

"Congratulations, you've glanced at a calendar lately." He looked straight through her with eyes as hard as diamond bits.

"I thought . . . well, you know, that we could put our differences aside for a little while and at least be civil to each other."

His eyes narrowed. "What possible reason could there be for us to have anything to do with each other? You mean nothing to me, and I'm sure the feeling is mutual."

"You were my husband for five years."

"So?"

She rearranged the silverware several times, choosing not to look at Steve. He wore his anger like a tight pair of shoes and sitting across from him was almost too painful to bear.

"We loved each other once," she said after a drawn-out, strained moment.

"I loved my dog once, too," he came back. One corner of his mouth was pulled down, and his eyes had thinned to narrow slits. "What does having cared about each other have to do with anything now?"

Carol couldn't answer his question. She knew the divorce had made him bitter, but she'd counted on this long time apart to have healed some of his animosity.

"What did you do for the holidays last year?" she asked, refusing to argue with him. She wasn't going to allow him to rile her into losing her temper. He'd played that trick once too often, and she was wise to his game.

"What the hell difference does it make to you how I spent Christmas?"

This wasn't going well, Carol decided—not the least bit as she'd planned. Steve seemed to think she wanted him to admit he'd been miserable without her.

"I...I spent the day alone," she told him softly, reluctantly. Their divorce had been final three weeks before the holiday and Carol's emotions had been so raw she'd hardly been able to deal with the usual festivities connected with the holiday.

"I wasn't alone," Steve answered with a cocky half smile that suggested that whoever he was with had been pleasant company, and he hadn't missed her in the least.

Carol didn't know how anyone could look so damned insolent and sensuous at the same moment. It required effort to keep her chin up and meet his gaze, but she managed.

"So *you* were alone," he added. The news appeared to delight him. "That's what happens when you mess around with a married man, my dear. In case you haven't figured it out yet, Todd's wife and family will always come first. That's the other woman's sad lot in life."

Carol went still all over. She felt as though her entire body had turned to stone. She didn't breathe, didn't move, didn't so much as blink. The pain spread out in waves, circling first her throat and then her chest, working its way down to her abdomen, cinching her stomach so tightly that she thought she might be sick. The whole room seemed to fade away and the only thing she was sure about was that she had to get out of the restaurant. Fast.

Her fingers fumbled with the snap of her purse as she opened her wallet. Her hands weren't any more steady as she placed several coins by the coffee cup and scooted out of her seat.

Mutely Steve watched Carol walk out of the restaurant and called himself every foul name that he could come up with from his extensive Navy vocabulary. He hadn't meant to say those things. Hadn't intended to lash out at her. But he hadn't been able to stop himself.

He'd lied, too, in an effort to salvage his pride. Lied rather than give her the satisfaction of knowing he'd spent last Christmas Day miserable and alone. It had been the worst holiday of his life. The pain of the divorce had still ached like a lanced boil, while everyone around him had been celebrating and exchanging gifts, their happiness like a ball and chain shackling his heart. This year didn't hold much prospect for happiness, either. Lindy and Rush would prefer to spend the day alone, although they'd gone out of their way to convince him otherwise. But Steve wasn't stupid and had already made other plans. He'd volunteered for watch Christmas Day so that a fellow officer could spend time with his family.

Gathering his thoughts about Carol, Steve experienced a healthy dose of regret about the way he'd behaved toward his ex-wife.

She'd looked good, he admitted reluctantly—better than he'd wanted her to look for his own peace of mind. From the moment they'd met, he'd felt the vibrant energy that radiated from her. Thirteen months apart hadn't diminished that. He'd known the minute she walked into Denny's; he'd felt her presence the instant the door opened. She wore her thick blond hair shorter than he remembered so that it fell forward and hugged the sides of her face, the ends curling under slightly, giving her a Dutch-boy look. As always, her metallic blue eyes were magnetic, irrevocably drawing his gaze. She looked small and fragile, and the desire to protect and love her had come at him with all the force of a wrecking ball slamming against his chest. He knew differently, but it hadn't seemed to change the way he felt—Carol needed him about as much as the Navy needed more salt water.

Sliding out of the booth, Steve laid a bill on the table and left. Outside, the north wind sent a chill racing up his arms and he buried his hands into his pants pockets as he headed toward the parking lot.

Surprise halted his progress when he spied Carol leaning against the fender of her car. Her shoulders were slumped, her head hanging as though she were burdened by a terrible weight.

Once more Steve was swamped with regret. He had never learned the reason she'd phoned. He started walking toward her, not knowing what he intended to say or do.

She didn't glance up when he joined her.

"You never said why you phoned," he said in a wounded voice after a moment of silence.

"It isn't important . . . I told Lindy that."

"If it wasn't to let me know you're remarrying, then it's because you want something."

She looked up and tried to smile, and the feeble effort cut straight through Steve's resolve to forget he'd ever known or loved her. It was useless to try.

"I don't think it'll work," Carol said sadly.

"What?"

She shook her head.

"If you need something, just ask!" he shouted, using his anger as a defense mechanism. Carol had seldom wanted anything from him. It must be important for her to contact him now, especially after their divorce.

"Christmas Day," she whispered brokenly. "I don't want to spend it alone."

Chapter Two

Until Carol spoke, she hadn't known how much she wanted Steve to spend Christmas Day with her—and not for the reasons she'd been plotting. She sincerely missed Steve. He'd been both lover and friend, and now he was neither; the sense of loss was nearly overwhelming.

He continued to stare at her, and regret worked its way across his features. The success of her plan hinged on his response and she waited, almost afraid to breathe, for his answer.

"Carol, listen..." He paused and ran his hand along the back of his neck, his brow puckered with a condensed frown.

Carol knew him well enough to realize he was carefully composing his thoughts. She was also aware that he was going to refuse her! She knew it as clearly as if he'd spoken the words aloud. She swallowed the hurt, although she couldn't keep her eyes from widening with pain. When Steve had presented her with the divorce papers, Carol had promised herself she would never give him the power to hurt her again. Yet here she was, handing him the knife and exposing her soul.

She could feel her heart thumping wildly in her chest and fought to control the emotions that swamped her. "Is it so much to ask?'' she whispered, and the words fell broken from her lips.

"I've got the watch."

"On Christmas..." She hadn't expected that, hadn't figured it into the scheme of things. In other words, the excuse of Christmas wasn't going to work. Ultimately her strategy would fail, and she would end up spending the holiday alone.

"I'd do it if I could," Steve told her in a straightforward manner that convinced her he was telling the truth. She felt somewhat less disappointed.

"Thank you for that," she said, and reached out to touch his hand, in a small gesture of appreciation. Amazingly he didn't draw away from her, which gave her renewed hope.

A reluctant silence stretched between them. There'd been a time when they couldn't say enough to each other, and now there was nothing.

"I suppose I'd better get back." Steve spoke first.

"Me, too," she answered brightly, perhaps a little too brightly. "It was good to see you again...you're looking well."

"You, too." He took a couple of steps backward, but still hadn't turned away. Swallowing down her disappointment, Carol retrieved the car keys from the bottom of her purse and turned to climb into her Honda. It dawned on her then, hit her square between the eyes. If not Christmas Day then...

"Steve," she whirled back around, her eyes flashing.

"Carol." He called her name at the same moment.

They laughed and the sound fell rusty and awkward between them.

"You first," he said, and gestured toward her. The corner of his mouth was curved upward in a half smile.

"What about Christmas Eve?"

He nodded. "I was just thinking the same thing."

Carol felt the excitement bubble up inside her like fizz in a club soda. A grin broke out across her face as she realized nothing had been lost and everything was yet to be gained. Somewhere in the distance, Carol was sure she could hear the soft, lilting strains of a Brahms lullaby. "Could you come early enough for dinner?"

Again, he nodded. "Six?"

"Perfect. I'll look forward to it."

"I will, too."

He turned and walked away from her then, and it was all Carol could do to keep from doing a war dance, jumping up and down around the car. Instead she rubbed her bare hands together as though the friction would ease some of the excitement she was feeling. Steve hadn't a clue how memorable this one night would be. Not a clue!

"Your mood has certainly improved lately," Lindy commented as Steve walked into the kitchen whistling a lively Christmas carol.

His sister's words stopped him. "My mood has?"

"You've been downright chipper all week."

He shrugged his shoulders, hoping the action would discount his cheerful attitude. " 'Tis the season."

"I don't suppose your meeting with Carol has anything to do with it?"

His sister eyed him skeptically, seeking his confidence, but Steve wasn't going to give it. This dinner with his ex-wife was simply the meeting of two lonely people struggling to make it through the holidays. Nothing less and certainly nothing more. Although he'd been looking for Carol to deny that she was involved with Todd, she hadn't. Steve considered her refusal to talk about the other man as good as an admission of guilt. That bastard had left her alone for Christmas two years running.

If Lindy was right and his mood had improved, Steve decided, it was simply because he was going to be out of his sister and Rush's hair for the evening; the newlyweds could spend their first Christmas Eve together without a third party butting in.

Steve reached for his coat, and Lindy turned around, her dark eyes wide with surprise. "You're leaving."

Steve nodded, buttoning the thick wool jacket.

"But . . . it's Christmas Eve."

"I know." He tucked the box of candy under his arm and lifted the bright red poinsettia he'd purchased on impulse earlier in the day.

"Where are you going?"

Steve would have liked to say a friend's house, but that wouldn't be true. He didn't know how to classify his relationship with Carol. Not a friend. Not a lover. More than an acquaintance, less than a wife.

"You're going to Carol's, aren't you?" Lindy prompted.

The last thing Steve wanted was his sister to get the wrong impression about this evening with Carol, because that's all there was going to be. "It's not what you think."

Lindy raised her hands in mock consternation. "I'm not thinking a single thing, except that it's good to see you smile again."

Steve's frown was heavy with purpose. "Well, don't read more into it than there is."

"Are the two of you going to talk?" Lindy asked, and her dark eyes fairly danced with deviltry.

"We're going to eat, not talk," Steve explained with limited patience. "We don't have anything in common anymore. I'll probably be home before ten."

"Whatever you say." Lindy answered, but her lips twitched with the effort to suppress a knowing smile. "Have a good time."

Steve chose not to answer that comment and left the apartment, but as soon as he was outside, he discovered he was whistling again and stopped abruptly.

Carol slipped the compact disk into the player and set the volume knob so that the soft Christmas music swirled festively through the house. A small turkey was roasting in the oven, stuffed with Steve's favorite sage dressing. Two pies were cooling on the kitchen counter—pumpkin for Steve, mincemeat for her. To be on the safe side a sweet-potato-pecan pie was in the fridge.

Carol chose a red silk dress that whispered enticingly against her soft skin. Her makeup and perfume had been applied with a subtle hand. Everything was ready.

Well, almost everything.

She and Steve were two different people now, and there was no getting around the fact. Regretting the past was an exercise in futility, and yet Carol had been overwhelmed these past few days with the realization that the divorce had been wrong. Very wrong. All the emotion she'd managed to bury this past year had seeped to the surface since her meeting with Steve and she couldn't remember a time when she'd been more confused.

She wanted a child, and she was using her ex-husband. More than once in the past week, she'd been forced to deal with twinges of guilt. But there was no going back. It would be impossible to recapture what had been between them before the divorce. There could be no reconciliation. Even more difficult than the past, Carol had trouble dealing with the present. They couldn't come in contact with each other without the sparks igniting. It made everything more difficult. They were both too stubborn, too temperamental, too obstinate.

And it was ruining their lives.

Carol felt they couldn't go back and yet they couldn't step forward, either. The idea of seducing Steve and getting pregnant had, in the beginning, been entirely selfish. She wanted a baby and she considered Steve the best candidate... the only candidate. After their one short meeting at the restaurant, Carol knew her choice of the baby's father went far beyond the practical. A part of her continued to love Steve, and probably always would. She wanted his child because it was the only part of him she would ever be able to have.

Everything hinged on the outcome of this dinner. Carol pressed her hands over her flat stomach and issued a fervent prayer that she was fertile. Twice in the past hour she'd taken her temperature, praying her body would do its part in this master plan. Her temperature was slightly elevated, but that could be caused by the hot sensation that went through her at the thought of sharing a bed with Steve again. Or it could be sheer nerves.

All day she'd been feeling anxious and restless with anticipation. She was convinced Steve would take one look at her and instantly know she intended for him to spend the night. The crux of her scheme was for Steve to think their making love was *his* idea. Again and again, her plans for the evening circled her mind, slowly, like the churning blades of a windmill stirring the air.

The doorbell chimed, and inhaling a calming breath, Carol forced a smile, walked across the room and opened the door for her ex-husband. "Merry Christmas," she said softly.

Steve handed her the poinsettia as though he couldn't get rid of the flower fast enough. His gaze didn't quite meet hers. In fact, he seemed to be avoiding looking at her, which pleased Carol because it told her that the red dress was having exactly the effect she'd hoped for.

"Thank you for the flower," she said and set it in the middle of the coffee table. "You didn't need to do that."

"I remembered how you used to buy three and four of those silly things each year and figured one more couldn't hurt."

"It was thoughtful of you, and I appreciate it." She held out her hand to take his coat.

Steve placed a small package under the tree and gave her a shy look. "Frangos," he explained awkwardly. "I suppose they're still your favorite candy."

"Yes. I have a little something for you, too."

Steve peeled off his heavy jacket and handed it to her. "I'm not looking for any gifts from you. I brought the flowers and candy because I wanted to contribute something toward dinner."

"My gift isn't much, Steve."

"Save it for someone else. Okay?"

Her temper nearly slipped then, but Carol managed to keep it intact. Her smile was just a little more forced when she turned from hanging his jacket in the hall closet, but she hoped he hadn't noticed.

"Would you like a hot-buttered rum before we eat?" she offered.

"That sounds good."

He followed her into the kitchen and brought the bottle of rum down from the top cupboard while she put water on to boil.

"When did you cut your hair?" he asked unexpectedly.

Absently Carol's fingers touched the straight, thick strands that crowded the side of her head. "Several months ago now."

"I liked it better when you wore it longer."

Gritting her teeth, she managed to bite back the words to inform him that she styled her hair to suit herself these days, not him.

Steve saw the flash of irritation in his ex-wife's eyes and felt a little better. The comment about her hair wasn't what she'd wanted to hear; she'd been waiting for him to tell her how beautiful she looked. The problem was, he hadn't been able to take his eyes off her from the moment he entered the house. The wisecrack was a result of one flirtatious curl of blond hair that swayed when she moved. He hadn't been able to look past that single golden lock. Neither could he stop staring at the shape of her lips nor the curve of her chin, nor the appealing color of her china blue eyes. When he'd met her at Denny's the other night he'd been on the defensive, waiting for her to drop her bombshell. All his protective walls were lowered now. He would have liked to blame it on the Christmas holidays, but he realized it was more than that, and what he saw gave him cause to tremble. Carol was as sensuous and appealing to him as she'd always been. Perhaps more so.

Already he knew what was going to happen. They would spend half the evening verbally circling each other in an anxious search for common ground. But there wasn't one for them . . . not anymore. Tonight was an evening out of sequence, and when it had passed they would return to their respective lives.

When Carol finished mixing their drinks, they wandered into the living room and talked. The alcohol seemed to alleviate some of the tension. Steve filled the silence with details of what had been happening in Lindy's life and in his career.

"You've done well for yourself," Carol admitted, and there was a spark of pride in her eyes that warmed him.

Steve didn't inquire about her career because it would involve asking about Todd, and the man was a subject he'd sworn he would avoid at all costs. Carol didn't volunteer any information, either. She knew the unwritten ground rules.

A half hour later, Steve helped her carry their meal to the table.

"You must have been cooking all day."

She grinned and nodded. "It gave me something to do."

The table was loaded with sliced turkey, creamy potatoes, giblet gravy, stuffing, fresh broccoli, sweet potatoes and fruit salad.

Carol asked him to light the candles and when Steve had, they sat down to eat. Sitting directly across the table from her, Steve found he was mesmerized by her mouth as she ate. With all his might he tried to remember the reasons he'd divorced Carol. Good God, she was captivating—too damn good to look at for his own peace of mind. Her hands moved gracefully, raising the fork from her plate to her mouth in motions as elegant as those of a symphony director. He shouldn't be enjoying watching her this much, and he realized he would pay the price later when he returned to the apartment and the loneliness overtook him once more.

When he'd finished the meal, he leaned against the shield-back dining-room chair and placed his hands over his stomach. "I can't remember when I've had a better dinner."

"There's pie . . ."

"Not now," he countered quickly and shook his head. "I'm too full to down another bite. Maybe later."

"Coffee?"

"Please."

Carol carried their dishes to the sink, stuck the leftovers in the refrigerator, and returned with the glass coffeepot. She filled both their cups, returned it to the kitchen and then took her seat opposite him. She rested her elbows on the table, and smiled.

Despite his best intentions through a good portion of the meal, Steve hadn't been able to keep his eyes away from her. The way she was sitting—leaning forward, her elbows on the tabletop—caused her breasts to push together and more than amply fill the bodice of her dress. His breath faltered someplace between his lungs and his throat at the alluring sight she made. He could have sworn she wasn't wearing a bra. Carol had fantastic breasts and Steve watched, captivated, as their tips beaded against the shiny material. They seemed to be pointing directly at him, issuing a silent invitation that asked him to fondle and taste them. Against his will, his groin began to swell until he was throbbing with painful need. Disconcerted, he dropped his gaze to the steaming cup of coffee. With his hands shaking, he took a sip of his coffee and nearly scalded the tender skin inside his mouth.

"That was an excellent dinner," he repeated, after a moment of silence.

"You're not sorry you came, are you?" she asked unexpectedly, studying him. The intent look that crowded her face demanded all Steve's attention. Her skin was pale and creamy in the muted light, her eyes wide and inquiring, as though the answer to her question was of the utmost importance.

"No," he admitted reluctantly. "I'm glad I'm here."

His answer pleased her and she smiled, looking tender and trusting, and Steve wondered how he could ever have doubted her. He knew what she'd done—knew that she'd purposely destroyed their marriage—and in that moment, it didn't matter. He wanted her again. He wanted to hold her warm and willing body in his arms. He wanted to bury himself so deep inside her that she would never desire another man for as long as they both lived.

"I'll help you with the dishes," he said, and rose so abruptly that he nearly knocked over the chair.

"I'll do them later." She got to her feet as well. "But if you want to do something, I'd appreciate a little help with the tree."

"The tree?" The words sounded as foreign as an obscure language.

"Yes, it's only half decorated. I couldn't reach the tallest limbs. Will you help?"

He shrugged. "Sure." He could have sworn that Carol was relieved, and he couldn't imagine why. The Christmas tree looked fine to him. There were a few bare spots, but nothing too noticeable.

Carol dragged a dining-room chair into the living room and pulled a box of ornaments out from underneath the end table.

"You're knitting?" Steve asked, hiding a smile as his gaze fell on the strands of worsted yarn. Carol had to be the worst knitter in the world, yet she tackled one project after another, seeming oblivious of any lack of talent. There had been a time when he could tease her about it, but he wasn't sure his insight would be appreciated now.

She glanced away as though she feared his comment.

"Don't worry, I'm not going to tease you," he told her, remembering the time she'd proudly presented him with a sweater she'd made herself—the left sleeve had been five inches longer than the right. He'd tried it on and she'd taken one look at him and burst into tears. It was one of the few times he could ever remember Carol crying.

Carol dragged the chair next to the tree and raised her leg to stand on it.

Steve stopped her. "I thought you wanted me to do that?"

"No, I need you to hand me the ornaments and then stand back and tell me how they look."

"Carol...if I placed the ornaments on the tree, you wouldn't need the chair."

She looked at him and sighed. "I'd rather do it. You don't mind, do you?"

He didn't know why she was so determined to hang the decorations herself, but it didn't make much difference to him. "No, if you want to risk your fool neck, feel free."

She grinned and raised herself so that she was standing on the padded cushion of the chair. "Okay, hand me one," she said, tossing him a look over her shoulder.

Steve gave her a shiny glass bulb, and he noted how good she smelled. Roses and some other scent he couldn't define wrapped gently around him. Carol stretched out her arms and reached for the tallest branch. Her dress rose a solid five inches and exposed the back of her creamy smooth thighs and a fleeting glimpse of the sweet curve of her buttocks. Steve knotted his hands into fists at his sides to keep from touching her. It would be entirely plausible for him to grip her waist and claim he was frightened she would tumble from her perch. But if he allowed that to happen, his hands would slip and soon he would be cupping that cute rounded bottom. Once he touched her, Steve knew he would never be able to stop. He clenched his teeth and inhaled deeply through his nose. Having Carol standing there, exposing herself in this unconscious way, was more than a mere man could resist. At this point, he was willing to use any excuse to be close to her once more.

Carol lowered her arms, her dress fell back into place and Steve breathed normally again. He thought he was safe from further temptation until she twisted around. Her ripe, full breasts filled the front of her dress, their shape clearly defined against the thin fabric. If he'd been guessing about the bra before, he was now certain. She wasn't wearing one.

"I'm ready for another ornament," she said softly.

Like a blind man, Steve turned and fumbled for a second glass bulb. He handed it to her and did everything within his power to keep his gaze away from her breasts.

"How does that one look?" Carol asked.

"Fine," Steve answered gruffly.

"Steve?"

"Don't you think that's enough decorations, for God's sake?"

His harsh tone was as much a surprise to him as it obviously was to Carol.

"Yes, of course."

She sounded disappointed, but that couldn't be helped. Steve moved to her side once more and offered her his hand to help her down. His foot must have hit against one leg of the chair because it jerked forward. Perhaps it was something she did, Steve wasn't sure, but whatever happened caused the chair to teeter on the thick carpet.

With a small cry of alarm, Carol threw out her arms.

With reflexes born of years of military training, Steve's hands shot out like bullets to catch her. The chair fell sideways onto the floor, but Steve's grip on Carol's waist anchored her firmly against his torso. Their breathing was labored, and Steve sighed with relief that she hadn't fallen. It was on the tip of his tongue to berate her, call her a silly goose for not letting him place the glass bulbs on the tree, chastise her for being such a fool. She shouldn't put herself at risk over something as nonsensical as a Christmas tree. But none of the words made it to his lips.

Their gazes were even, her haunting eyes stared into his and said his name as clearly as if it were spoken. Carol's feet remained several inches off the floor, and still Steve held on to her, unable to release her. His heart was pounding frantically with wonder as he raised a finger and touched her soft throat. His gaze continued to delve into hers. He wanted to set her back on the carpet, to free them both from this invisible grip before it maimed them, but he couldn't seem to find the strength to let her go.

Slowly she slid down his front, between his braced feet, crimping the skirt of her dress between them. Once she was secure, he noted that her lower abdomen was tucked snugly in the joint between his thighs. The throbbing in his groin began again, and he held in a groan that threatened to emanate from deep within his chest.

He longed to kiss her more than he'd ever wanted anything in his life, and only the greatest strength of will kept him from claiming her sweet mouth with his own.

She'd betrayed him once, crippled him with her deceit. Steve had sworn he would never allow her to use him again, yet his arguments burned away like dry timber in a forest fire.

His thumb found her moist lips and brushed back and forth as though the action would be enough to satisfy either of them. It didn't. If anything, it created an agony even more powerful. His heart leaped into a hard, fast rhythm that made him feel breathless and weak. Before he could stop himself, his finger lifted her chin and his mouth glided over hers. Softly. Moistly. Satin against satin.

Carol sighed.

Steve groaned.

She weakened in his arms and closed her eyes. Steve kissed her a second time and thrust his tongue deep into her mouth, his need so strong it threatened to consume him. His hand was drawn to her breast, as if caught by a vise and carried there against his will. He cupped the rounded flesh, and his finger teased the nipple until it beaded and swelled against his palm. Carol whimpered.

He had to touch her breasts again. Had to know for himself their velvet smoothness. Releasing a ragged sigh, he reached behind her and peeled down her zipper. She was as eager as he when he lowered the top of her dress and exposed her naked front.

Her hands were around his neck, and she slanted her mouth over his, rising to her tiptoes as she leaned her weight into his. Steve's mouth quickly abandoned hers to explore the curve of her neck and then lower to the rosy tips of her firm, proud breasts. His moist tongue traced circles around the pebbled nipples until Carol shuddered and plowed her fingers through his hair.

"Steve . . . oh, I've missed you so much." She repeated the sentence over and over again, but the words didn't register in his clouded mind. When they did, he went cold. She may have missed him, may have hungered for his touch, but she hadn't been faithful. The thought crippled him, and he went utterly still.

Carol must have sensed his withdrawal, because she dropped her arms. Her shoulders were heaving as though she'd been running in a heated race. His own breathing wasn't any more regular.

Abruptly Steve released her and stumbled two paces back.

"That shouldn't have happened," he announced in a hoarse whisper.

Carol regarded him with a wounded look but said nothing.

"I've got to get out of here," he said, expelling the words on the tail end of a sigh.

Carol's gaze widened and she shook her head.

"Carol, we aren't married anymore. This shouldn't be happening."

"I know." She lowered her gaze to the carpet.

Steve walked to the hall closet and reached for his jacket. His actions felt as if they were in slow motion—as if every gravitational force in the universe was pulling at him.

He paused, his hand clenching the doorknob. "Thank you for dinner."

Carol nodded, and when he turned back, he saw that her eyes had filled with tears and she was biting her bottom lip to hold them back. One hand held the front of her dress across her bare breasts.

"Carol . . ."

She looked at him with soft, appealing eyes and held out her hand. "Don't go," she begged softly. "Please don't leave me. I need you so much."

Chapter Three

Carol could see the battle raging in Steve's tight features. She swallowed down the tears and refused to release his gaze, which remained locked with her own.

"We're not married anymore," he said in a voice that shook with indecision.

"I . . . don't care." Swallowing her pride, she took one small step toward him. If he wouldn't come to her, then she was going to him. Her knees felt incredibly weak, as though she were walking after being bedridden for a long while.

"Carol . . ."

She didn't stop until she was standing directly in front of him. Then slowly, with infinite care, she released her hold on the front of her dress and allowed it to fall free, baring her breasts. Steve rewarded her immediately with a swift intake of breath, and then it seemed as if he stopped breathing completely. Carol slipped her flattened hands up his chest and leaned her body into his. When she felt his rock-hard arousal pressing against her thigh, she closed her eyes to disguise the triumph that zoomed through her blood like a shot of adrenaline.

Steve held himself stiffly against her, refusing to yield to her softness; his arms hung motionless at his sides. He didn't push her away, but he didn't welcome her into his embrace, either.

Five years of marriage had taught Carol a good deal about her husband's body. She knew what pleasured him most, knew what would drive him to the edge of madness, knew how to make him want her until there was nothing else in their world.

Standing on the tips of her toes, she locked her arms tightly around his neck and raised her soft lips to gently brush her mouth over his. Her kiss was as moist and light as dew on a summer rose. Steve's lashes dropped and she could feel the torment of the battle that raged in his troubled mind.

Slightly elevating one foot, she allowed her shoe to slip off her toes. It fell almost silently to the floor. Carol nearly laughed aloud at the expression that came over Steve's contorted features. He knew what was coming, and against his will, Carol could see that he welcomed it. In a leisurely exercise, she raised her nylon-covered foot and slid it down the backside of his leg. Again and again her thigh and calf glided over his, each caressing stroke moved higher and higher on his leg, bringing her closer to her objective.

When Steve's hand closed, almost painfully, over her thigh, Carol knew she'd won. He held her there for a timeless moment, neither moving nor breathing.

"Kiss me," he ordered, and the words seemed to be ground out from between clenched teeth.

Although Carol had fully intended to comply with his demand, she apparently didn't do it fast enough to suit her ex-husband. He groaned and his free hand locked around the back of her head, compelling her mouth to his. Driven by urgency, his kiss was forceful and demanding, almost grinding, as if he sought to punish her for making him want her so much. Carol allowed him to ravage her mouth, giving him everything he wanted, everything he asked for, until finally she gasped for breath and broke away briefly. Steve brought her mouth back to his, and gradually his kisses softened until Carol thought she was sure her whole body would burst into flames. Sensing this, Steve moved his hand from the back of her head and began to massage her breast in a leisurely circular motion, his palm centering on her nipple. Her whole torso started to pulsate under his gentle touch.

Carol arched her spine to grant him easier access, and tossed back her head as his fingers worked their magic. Then his hand left her breast, and she wanted to protest until she felt his fingers slip around her other thigh and lift her completely off the carpet, raising her so that their mouths were level, their breath mingling, moist and excited.

They paused and gazed into each other's eyes. Steve's were filled with surprise and wonder. Carol met that look and smiled with a rediscovered joy that burst from deep within her. An inner happiness that had vanished from her life the moment Steve had walked away from her, returned. She leaned forward and very gently rubbed her mouth across his, creating a moist, delicious friction. Gently her tongue played over the seam of his lips, sliding back and forth, teasing him, testing him in a love game that had once been familiar between them.

Carol gently caught his lower lip between her teeth and sucked on it, playing with it while darting the tip of her tongue in and out of his mouth.

The effect on Steve was electric. His mouth claimed hers in an urgent kiss that drove the oxygen from her lungs. Then, with a strength that astonished her, he lifted her even higher until his mouth closed over her left breast, rolling his tongue over her nipple, then sucking at it greedily, taking in more and more of her breast.

Carol thought she was going to go crazy with the tidal wave of sensation that flooded her being. She locked her legs around his waist and braced her hands against his shoulders. His mouth and tongue alternated from one breast to the other until she was convinced that if he didn't take her soon, she was going to faint in his arms.

Braced against the closet door, Steve used what leverage he could to inch his hand up the inside of her thigh. His exploring fingers reached higher and higher, then paused when he encountered a nylon barrier. He groaned his frustration.

Carol was so weak with longing that if he didn't carry her voluntarily into the bedroom soon, she was going to demand that he make love to her right there on the entryway floor.

"You weren't wearing a bra," he chastised her in a husky thwarted voice. "I was hoping..."

He didn't need to finish for Carol to know what he was talking about. When they were married, she'd often worn a garter belt with her nylons instead of panty hose so their lovemaking wouldn't be impeded.

"I want you," she whispered, her hands framing his face. "But if you think it would be best to leave...go now. The choice is yours."

His gaze locked with hers, Steve marched wordlessly across the living room and down the long hallway to the bedroom that had once been theirs.

"Not here," she told him. "I sleep there now," she explained, pointing to the room across the hall.

Steve switched directions and marched into the smaller bedroom, not stopping until he reached the queen-size bed. For one crazy second, Carol thought he meant to drop her on top of the mattress and storm right out of the house. Instead he continued to hold her, the look in his eyes wild and uncertain.

Carol's eyes met his. She was nearly choking on the sadness that threatened to overwhelm her. Tentatively she raised one hand and pressed it to the side of his face, her eyes wide, her heart pounding so hard she was sure the sound of it would soon bring down the walls.

To her surprise, Steve tenderly placed her on the bed, braced one knee against the edge of the mattress and leaned over her.

"We aren't married.... Not a damn thing has been settled between us," he announced, as though this should be shocking news.

Carol said nothing, but she casually slipped her hand around the side of his neck, urging his mouth down to hers. She met with no resistance.

"Make love to me," she murmured.

Steve groaned, twisted around and dropped to sit on the side of the bed, granting her a full view of his solid back. The thread of disappointment that wrapped itself around Carol's heart was followed by a slow, lazy smile that spread over her mouth as she recognized his frantic movements.

Steve was undressing.

Feeling deliciously warm and content, Carol woke two hours later to the sound of Steve rummaging in the kitchen. No doubt he was looking for something to eat. Smiling, she jerked her arms high above her head and stretched. She yawned and arched her back, slightly elevating her hips with the action. She felt marvelous. Stupendous. Happy.

Her heart bursting with newfound joy, she reached for Steve's shirt and purposely buttoned it just enough to be provocative while looking as if she'd made some effort to cover herself.

Semiclothed, she moved toward the noise emanating from her kitchen. Barefoot, dressed only in his slacks, Steve was bent over, investigating the contents of her refrigerator.

Carol paused in the doorway. "Making love always did make you hungry," she said from behind him.

"There's hardly a damn thing in here except sweet potatoes. Good grief, woman, what are you doing with all these leftover yams?"

Carol felt sudden heat rise in her cheeks as hurried excuses crowded her mind. "They were on sale this week because of Christmas."

"They must have been at rock-bottom price. I counted six containers full of them. It looks like you've been eating them at every meal for an entire week."

"There's some pie if that'll interest you," she said, a little too quickly. "And plenty of turkey for a sandwich, if you want."

He straightened, closed the refrigerator and turned to face her. But whatever he'd intended to say apparently left him when he caught sight of her seductive pose. She was leaning against the doorjamb, hands behind her back and one foot braced against the wall, smiling at him, certain he could read her thoughts.

"There's pumpkin, and the whipped topping is fresh."

"Pumpkin?" he repeated.

"The pie."

He blinked, and nodded. "That sounds good."

"Would you like me to make you a sandwich while I'm at it?"

"Sure." But he didn't sound sure of anything at the moment.

Moving with ease around her kitchen, Carol brought out the necessary ingredients and quickly put together a snack for both of them. When she'd finished, she carried their plates to the small table across from the stove.

"Would you like something to drink?" she asked, setting their plates down.

"I'll get it," Steve said, apparently eager to help. "What would you like?"

"Milk," she responded automatically. She'd never been overly fond of the beverage but had recently made a habit of drinking a glass or two each day in preparation for her pregnancy.

"I thought you didn't like milk."

"I . . . I've acquired new tastes in the past year."

Steve grinned. "There are certain things about you that haven't changed, and then there's something more, something completely unexpected. Good God, woman, you've turned into a little she-devil, haven't you?"

Carol lowered her gaze and felt the heated blush work its way up her neck and spill into her cheeks. It wasn't any wonder Steve was teasing her. She'd been as hot as a stick of dynamite. By the time he'd undressed, she'd behaved like a tigress, clawing at him, driven by mindless passion.

Chuckling, Steve delivered two glasses of milk to the table. "You surprised me," he said. "You used to be a tad more timid."

Doing her best to ignore him, Carol brought her feet up to the edge of the chair and pulled the shirt down over her legs. With feigned dignity, she reached for half of her sandwich. "An officer and a gentleman wouldn't remind me of my wicked ways."

Still grinning, Steve lounged against the back of the chair. "You used to be far more subtle."

"Steve," she cried, "stop talking about it. Can't you see you're embarrassing me?"

"I remember one time when we were on our way to an admiral's dinner party and you casually announced you'd been in such a rush that you'd forgotten to put on any underwear."

Carol closed her eyes and looked away, remembering the time as clearly as if it had been last week instead of several years ago. She remembered, too, how good the lovemaking had been later that same evening.

"There wasn't time for us to go back to the house, so all night while you strolled around, sipping champagne, chatting and looking sedately prim, only I knew differently. Every time you looked at me, I about went crazy."

"I wanted you to know how much I longed to make love. If you'll recall, you'd just returned from a three-month tour."

"Carol, if *you'll* recall, we'd spent the entire day in bed."

She took a sip of her milk, then slowly raised her gaze to meet his. "It wasn't enough."

Steve closed his eyes and shook his head before grudgingly admitting, "It wasn't enough for me, either."

As soon as it had been socially acceptable to do so, Steve had made their excuses to the admiral that night and they'd hurriedly left the party. The entire way home, he'd been furious with Carol, telling her he was certain someone must have known what little trick she was playing. Just as heatedly, Carol had told Steve she didn't care who knew. If some huffy admiral wanted to throw a dinner party he shouldn't do it so soon after his men return from deployment.

They'd ended up making love twice that evening.

"Steve," Carol whispered with ragged emotion.

"Yes?"

"Once wasn't enough tonight, either." She dared not look at him, dared not let him see the way her pulse was clamoring.

Abruptly he stopped eating, and when he swallowed, it looked as if he'd downed the sandwich whole. A full minute passed before he spoke.

"Not for me, either."

Their lovemaking was different this time. Unique. Unrepeatable. Earlier, it'd been like spontaneous combustion. This time was slow, easy, relaxed. Steve led her into the bedroom, unfastened the buttons of the shirt that she was wearing and let it drop unheeded to the floor.

Carol stood before him tall and proud, her taut nipples seeming to beg for his lips. Steve looked at her naked body as if seeing her for the first time. Tenderly he raised his hand to her face and brushed back a wisp of blond hair, his touch light, gentle. Then he lowered his hands and cupped the undersides of her breasts, as though weighing them in a delicate measure. The velvet stroke of his thumbs worked across her nipples until they pebbled to a throbbing hardness. From there he slid the tips of his fingers down her rib cage, grazing her heated flesh wherever he touched her.

All the while, his dark, mesmerizing gaze never left hers, as though he half expected her to protest or to stop him.

Carol felt as if her hands were being manipulated like a puppet's as she reached for his belt buckle. All she knew was that she wanted him to make love to her. Her fingers fumbled at first, unfamiliar with the workings of his belt, then managed to release the clasp.

Soon Steve was nude.

She studied him, awed by his strength and beauty. She wanted to tell him all that she was feeling, all the good things she sensed in him, but the words withered on her tongue as he reached out and touched her once more.

His hand continued downward from her rib cage, momentarily pausing over her flat, smooth stomach, then moving lower until it encountered her pelvis. Slowly, methodically, he braced the heel of his hand against the apex of her womanhood and started a circling, gyrating motion while his fingers explored between her parted thighs.

Hardly able to breathe, Carol opened herself more to him, and once she had, he delicately parted her and slipped one finger inside. Her eyes widened at the stab of pleasure that instantly sliced through her and she bit into her lower lip to keep from panting.

She must have made some kind of sound because Steve paused and asked, "Did I hurt you?"

Carol was incapable of any verbal response. Frantically she shook her head, and his finger continued its deft movements, quickly bringing her to an exploding release. Wave upon wave of seething spasms, each one stronger, each one more intense, overtook every part of her. Whimpering noises escaped from deep within her throat as she climaxed, and the sound propelled Steve into action.

He wrapped his arms around her and carried her to the bed, laying her on top of the rumpled sheets. Not allowing her time to alter her position or rearrange the sheets, Steve moved over her, parted her thighs and quickly impaled her.

His breathing was ragged, barely under control.

Carol's wasn't any more even.

He didn't move, torturing her with an intense longing she had never experienced. Her body was still tingling in the aftermath of one fulfillment and reaching, striving toward another. Her whole person seemed to be filled with anxious expectancy... waiting for something she couldn't define.

Taking her hands, Steve lifted them above her head and held them prisoner there. He leaned over her, bracing himself on his arms on either side of her head. The action thrust him deeper inside Carol. She moaned and thrashed her head against the mattress, then lifted her hips, jerking them a couple of times, seeking more.

"Not yet, love," he whispered and placed a hand under her head, lifting her mouth to his. Their kiss was wild and passionate, as though their mouths couldn't give or take enough to satisfy their throbbing need.

Steve shifted his position and completely withdrew his body from hers.

Carol felt as if she'd suddenly gone blind; the whole world seemed black and lifeless. She started to protest, started to cry out, but before the sound escaped her throat, Steve sank his manhood back inside her. A shaft of pure light filled her senses once more and she sighed audibly, relieved. She was whole again, free.

"Now," Steve told her. "Now." He moved eagerly then, in deep, calculated strokes, plunging into her again and again, gifting her with the sun, revealing the heavens, exploring the universe. Soon all Carol knew was this insistent warm friction and the sweet, indescribable pangs of pleasure. Her body trembled as ripple after ripple of deep, pure sensation pulsed over her, driving her crazy as she remembered what had nightly been hers.

Breathless, Steve moved to lie beside her, bringing her into the circle of his arms. An hour passed, it seemed, before he spoke. "Was it always this good?"

The whispered question was so low Carol had to strain to hear him. "Yes," she answered after a long, timeless moment. "Always."

He pressed his forehead against the top of her head and moaned. "I was afraid of that."

The next thing Carol was aware of was a muffled curse and the unsettling sound of something heavy crashing to the floor.

"Steve?" she sat up in bed and reached for a sheet to cover her nakedness. The room was dark and still. Dread filled her— it couldn't be morning. Not yet, not so soon.

"I'm sorry. I didn't mean to wake you."

"You're leaving?" She sent her hand searching for the lamp on the nightstand. It clicked and a muted light filled the room.

"I've got the watch today," he reminded her.

"What time is it?"

"Carol, listen," he said gruffly, "I didn't mean for any of this to happen." All the while he was speaking, Steve's fingers were working the buttons of his shirt and having little success in getting it to fasten properly. "Call what happened last night what you will—the holiday spirit, a momentary slip in my better judgment...whatever. I'm sure you feel the same way." He paused and turned to study her.

She leaned forward, resting her chin on her raised knees. Her heart was in her throat, and she felt shaken and miserable. "Yes, of course."

His mouth thinned and he turned his back to her once more. "I thought as much. The best thing we can do is put the entire episode out of our minds."

"Right," she answered, forcing some enthusiasm into her voice. It was working out exactly as she'd planned it: they would both wake up in the morning, feel chagrined, make their apologies and go their separate ways once more.

Only it didn't feel the way she'd anticipated. It felt wrong. Very wrong.

Steve was in the living room before she moved from the bed. Grabbing a thin robe from her closet, she slipped into it as she rushed after him.

He seemed to be waiting for her, pacing the entryway. He combed his fingers through his hair a couple of times before turning to look at her.

"So you want to forget last night?" he asked.

"I . . . if you do," she answered.

"I do."

Carol's world toppled for a moment, then quickly righted itself. She understood—it was better this way. "Thank you for the poinsettia and candy." It seemed inappropriate to mention the terrific lovemaking.

"Right." His answer was clipped, as though he was eager to be on his way. "Thanks for the dinner...and everything else."

"No problem." Stepping around him, Carol opened the door. "It was good to see you again, Steve."

"Yeah, you, too."

He walked out of the house and down the steps, and watching him go did crazy things to Carol's equilibrium. Suddenly she had to lean against the doorjamb just to remain upright. Something inside her, something strong and more powerful than her own will demanded that she stop him.

"Steve," she cried frantically. She stood on tiptoe. "Steve." He turned around abruptly.

They stared at each other, each battle scarred and weary, each hurting. Each proud.

"Merry Christmas," she said softly.

"Merry Christmas."

Three days after Christmas, Carol was convinced her plan had worked perfectly. Thursday morning she woke feeling sluggish and sick to her stomach. A book she'd been reading on pregnancy and childbirth stated that the best way to relieve those early bouts of morning sickness was to nibble on soda crackers first thing—even before getting out of bed.

A burning sense of triumph led her into the bathroom, where she stared at herself in the mirror as though her reflection would proudly announce she was about to become a mother.

It had been so easy. Simple really. One tempestuous night of passion and the feat was accomplished. Her hand rested over her abdomen, and she patted it gently, feeling both proud and awed. A new life was being nurtured there.

A baby. Steve's child.

The wonder of it produced a ready flow of emotion and tears dampened her eyes.

Another symptom!

The book had explained that her emotions could be affected by the pregnancy—that she might be more susceptible to tears.

Wiping the moisture from the corners of her eyes, Carol strolled into the kitchen and searched the cupboard for saltines. She found a stale package and forced herself to eat two, but she didn't feel any better than she had earlier.

Not bothering to dress, she turned on the television and made herself a bed on the sofa. Boeing workers were given the week between Christmas and New Year's off as part of their employment package. Carol had planned to spend the free time painting the third bedroom—the one she planned to use for the baby. Unfortunately she didn't have any energy. In fact, she felt downright sick, as though she were coming down with a case of the flu.

A lazy smile turned up the edges of her mouth. She wasn't about to complain. Nine months from now, she would be holding a precious bundle in her arms.

Steve's and her child.

Chapter Four

With his hands cupped behind his head, Steve lay in bed and stared blindly at the dark ceiling. He couldn't sleep. For the past hour he hadn't even bothered to close his eyes. It wouldn't do any good; every time he did, the memory of Christmas Eve with Carol filled his mind.

Releasing a slow breath, he rubbed his hand down his face, hoping the action would dispel her image from his thoughts. It didn't work. Nothing did.

He had never intended to make love to her, and even now, ten days later, he wasn't sure how the hell it had happened. He continued to suffer from a low-grade form of shock. His thoughts had been in utter chaos since that night, and he wasn't sure how to respond to her or where their relationship was headed now.

What really distressed him, Steve realized, was that after everything that had happened between them, he could still want her so much. More than a week later and the memory of her leaning against the doorjamb in the kitchen, wearing his shirt—and nothing else—had the power to tighten his loins. Tighten his loins! He nearly laughed out loud; that had to be the understatement of the year.

When Carol had stood and held out her arms to him, he'd acted like a starving child offered candy, so eager he hadn't stopped to think about anything except the love she would give him. Any protest he'd made had been token. She'd volunteered, he'd accepted, and that should be the end of it.

But it wasn't.

Okay, so he wasn't a man of steel. Carol had always been his Achilles' heel, and he knew it. She knew it. In thinking over the events of that night, it was almost as though his ex-wife had planned everything. Her red dress with no bra, and that bit about placing decorations on the tree. She'd insisted on standing on the chair, stretching and exposing her thigh to him...his thoughts came to a skidding halt.

No.

He wasn't going to fall into that familiar trap of thinking Carol was using him, deceiving him. It did no good to wade into the muddy mire of anger, bitterness, regret and doubt.

He longed to repress the memory of Carol's warm and willing body in his arms. If only he could get on with his life. If only he could sleep.

He couldn't.

His sister, Lindy, had coffee brewed by the time Steve came out of his bedroom. She sat at the table, cradling a cup in one hand while holding a folded section of the *Post-Intelligencer* in the other.

"Morning." She glanced up and greeted him with a bright smile. Lately it seemed his sister was always smiling.

Steve mumbled something unintelligible as a means of reply. Her cheerfulness grated against him. He wasn't in the mood for good humor this morning. He wasn't in the mood for anything...with the possible exception of making love to Carol again, and that bit of insight didn't suit him in the least.

"It doesn't look like you had a good night's sleep, brother dearest."

Steve's frown deepened, and he gave his sister another noncommittal answer.

"I don't suppose this has anything to do with Carol?" She waited, and when he didn't answer, added, "Or the fact that you didn't come home Christmas Eve?"

"I came home."

"Sure, sometime the following morning."

Steve took down a mug from the cupboard and slapped it against the counter with unnecessary force. "Drop it, Lindy. I don't want to discuss Carol."

A weighted silence followed his comment.

"Rush and I've got almost everything ready to move into the new apartment," she offered finally, and the light tone of her voice suggested she was looking for a way to put their conversation back on an even keel. "We'll be out of here by Friday."

Hell, here he was snapping at Lindy. His sister didn't deserve to be the brunt of his foul mood. She hadn't done anything but mention the obvious. "Speaking of Rush, where is he?" Steve asked, forcing a lighter tone into his own voice.

"He had to catch an early ferry this morning," she said, and hesitated momentarily. "I'm happy, Steve, really happy. I was so afraid for a time that I'd made a dreadful mistake, but I know now that marrying Rush was the right thing to do."

Steve took a sip of coffee to avoid looking at his sister. What Lindy was actually saying was that she wanted him to find the same contentment she had. That wasn't possible for him now, and wouldn't be until he got Carol out of his blood.

And making love to her Christmas Eve hadn't helped.

"Well, I suppose I should think about getting dressed," Lindy said with a heavy dose of feigned enthusiasm. "I'm going to get some boxes so Rush and I can finish up the last of the packing."

"Where's your new apartment?" Steve had been so preoccupied with his own troubles that he hadn't thought to inquire until now.

As Lindy rattled off the address Steve's forehead furrowed into a brooding frown. His sister and Rush were moving less than a mile away from Carol's place. Great! That was the last thing he needed to hear.

Steve's day wasn't much better than his sleepless night had been. By noon he'd decided he could no longer avoid the inevitable. He didn't like it, but it was necessary.

He had to talk to Carol.

He was thankful the apartment was empty when he arrived home shortly after six. Not willing to test his good fortune, and half expecting Lindy or Rush to appear at any minute, he walked directly to the phone and punched out Carol's number as though punishing the telephone would help relieve some of his nervousness.

"Hello?" Carol's soft, lilting voice clawed at his abdomen.

"It's Steve."

A pregnant pause was followed by a slightly breathless "Hi."

"I was thinking we should talk."

"All right." She sounded surprised, pleased, uncertain. "When?"

Steve rotated his wrist and looked at the time. "What are you doing right now?"

She hesitated. "I . . . nothing."

Although slightly awkward, their conversation to this point had felt right to Steve. But the way she paused, as though searching for a delaying tactic, troubled him. Fiery arrows of doubt hit their mark and he said, "Listen, Carol, if you're 'entertaining' Todd, I'd prefer to stop by later."

The ensuing silence was more deafening than jungle drums pounding out a war chant.

It took her several seconds to answer him, and when she did, the soft voice that had greeted him was racked with pain. "You can come now."

Steve tightened his hold on the phone receiver in a punishing grip. He hated it when he talked to her like that. He didn't know who he was punishing: Carol or himself. "I'll be there in fifteen minutes."

Carol replaced the telephone in its cradle and battled down an attack of pain and tears. How dare Steve suggest Todd was there. Suddenly she was so furious with him that she could no longer stand in one place. She started pacing the living room floor like a raw recruit, taking five or six steps and then doing an abrupt about-face. And yet she was excited—even elated.

Steve had taken the initiative to contact her, and it proved that he hadn't been able to stop thinking about her, either.

Nothing had been right for her since Christmas Eve. Oh, she'd reached her objective—exceeded it. Everything had gone according to plan. Only Carol hadn't counted on the doubts and bewilderment that had followed their night of loving. Their short hours together brought back the memory of how good their lives had once been, how much they'd loved each other and how happy those first years were.

Since Christmas Eve, Carol had been crippled with "if on-lys" and "what ifs," tossing around those weak phrases as though she expected them to alter reality. Each day it became more difficult to remember that Steve had divorced her, that he believed her capable of the worst kind of deception. One night in his arms and she was fool enough to be willing to forget all the pain of the past thirteen months.

Almost willing, she amended.

It took vindictive, destructive comments like the one he'd just made to remind her that they had a rocky road to travel if they hoped to salvage their relationship.

Before Steve arrived, Carol had time to freshen her makeup and run a brush through her thick blond hair. She paused to study her reflection in the mirror and wondered if he would ever guess her secret. She doubted it. If he couldn't read the truth in her eyes about Todd, then he wasn't likely to recognize her joy, or guess the cause.

Thinking about the baby helped lighten the weight of Steve's bitterness. Briefly she closed her eyes and imagined holding that precious bundle in her arms. A little girl, she decided, with dark brown eyes like Steve's and soft blond curls.

The mental picture of her child made everything seem worthwhile.

When the doorbell chimed, Carol was ready. She held the door open for Steve and even managed to greet him with a smile.

"I made coffee."

"Good." His answer was gruff, as though he were speaking to one of his enlisted men.

He followed her into the kitchen and stood silently as she poured them each a cup of coffee. When she turned around, she saw Steve standing with his hands in his pockets, looking unsettled and ill at ease.

"If you're searching for traces of Todd, let me tell you right now, you won't find any."

He had the good grace to look mildly chagrined. "I suppose I should apologize for that remark."

"I suppose I should accept." She pulled out a chair and sat. Steve claimed the one directly across from her.

Neither spoke, and it seemed to Carol that an eternity passed. "You wanted to talk to me," she said, after what felt like two lifetimes.

"I'm not exactly sure what I want to say."

She smiled a little at that, understanding. "I'm not sure what I want to hear, either."

A hint of a grin bounced from his dark eyes. "Forgiving you for what happened with Todd..."

Carol bolted to her feet with such force that her chair nearly fell backward. "Forgiving me!" she demanded, shaking with outrage.

"Carol, please, I didn't come here to fight."

"Then don't start one. Don't come into my home and hurl insults at me. The one person in this room who should be seeking forgiveness is *you*!"

"Carol..."

"I should have known this wouldn't work, but like a love-sick fool I thought... I hoped you..." She paused, jerked her head around and rubbed the heels of her hands down her cheeks, erasing the telltale tears.

"Okay, I apologize. I won't mention Todd again."

She inhaled a wobbly breath and nodded, not trusting her voice, and sat back down.

Another awkward moment followed.

"I don't know what you've been thinking, or how you feel about... what happened," Steve said, "but for the past ten days, I've felt like a leaf caught in a windstorm. My emotions are in turmoil... I can't stop remembering how good it was between us, and how right it felt to have you in my arms again. My instincts tell me that night was a fluke, and best forgotten. I just wish to hell I could."

Carol bowed her head, avoiding eye contact. "I've been thinking the same thing. As you said when you left, we should chalk it up to the love and goodwill that's synonymous with the season. But the holidays are over and I can't stop thinking about it, either."

"The loving always was terrific, wasn't it?"

He didn't sound as though he wanted to admit even that much, as if he preferred to discount anything positive about their lives together. Carol understood the impulse. She'd done the same thing since their divorce; it helped ease the pain of the separation.

Grudgingly she nodded. "Unfortunately the lovemaking is only a small part of any marriage. I think Christmas Eve gave me hope that you and I might be able to work everything out. I'd like to resolve the past and find a way to heal the wounds." They'd been apart for over a year, but Carol's heart felt as bloodied and bruised as if their divorce had been decreed yesterday.

"God knows, I want to forget the past . . ."

Hope clamored in her breast and she raised her eyes to meet Steve's, but his gaze was as weary and doubtful as her own.

His eyes fell. "But I don't think I can. I don't know if I'll ever be able to get over finding Todd in our bedroom."

"He was in the shower," Carol corrected through clenched teeth. "And the only reason he was there was because the shower head in the other bathroom wasn't working properly."

"What the hell difference does it make?" Steve shouted. "He spent the night here. You've never bothered to deny that."

"But nothing happened . . . if you'd stayed long enough to ask Todd, he would have explained."

"If I'd stayed any longer, I would have killed him."

He said it with such conviction that Carol didn't doubt him. Long before, she'd promised herself she wouldn't defend her actions again. Todd had been her employer and her friend. She'd known Todd and his wife, Joyce, were having marital troubles. But she cared about them both and didn't want to get caught in the middle of their problems. Todd, however, had cast her there when he showed up on her doorstep, drunk out of his mind, wanting to talk. Alarmed, Carol had brought him inside and phoned Joyce, who suggested Todd sleep it off at Carol's house. It had seemed like a reasonable solution, although she wasn't keen on the idea. Steve was away and due back to Seattle in a couple of days.

But Steve had arrived home early—and assumed the worst.

The sadness that settled over her was profound, and when she spoke, her voice was little more than a whisper. "You tried and found me guilty on circumstantial evidence, Steve. For the first couple of weeks, I tried to put myself in your place . . . I could understand how you read the scene that morning, but you were wrong."

It looked for a moment as though he was going to argue with her. She could almost see the wheels spinning in his mind, stirring up the doubts, building skyscrapers on sand foundations.

"Other things started to add up," he admitted reluctantly, still not looking at her.

Carol could all but see him close his mind to common sense. It seemed that just when they were beginning to make headway, Steve would pull something else into their argument or make some completely ridiculous comment that made absolutely no sense to her. The last time they'd tried to discuss this in a reasonable, nonconfrontational manner, Steve had hinted that she'd been Todd's lover for months. He'd suggested that she hadn't been as eager to welcome him home from his last cruise, which was ridiculous. They may have had problems, but none had extended to the bedroom.

"What 'other things' do you mean now?" she asked, defeat coating her words.

He ignored her question. His mouth formed a cocky smile, devoid of amusement. "I will say one thing for ol' Todd—he taught you well."

She gasped at the unexpected pain his words inflicted.

Steve paled and looked away. "I shouldn't have said that—I didn't mean it."

"Todd did teach me," she countered, doing her best to keep her bottom lip from quivering. "He taught me that a marriage not based on mutual trust isn't worth the ink that prints the certificate. He taught me that it takes more than a few words murmured by a man of God to make a relationship work."

"That's not what I meant."

"I know what you meant. Your jealousy has you tied up in such tight knots that you're incapable of reasoning any of this out."

Steve ignored that comment. "I'm not jealous of Todd—he can have you if he wants."

Carol thought she was going to be sick to her stomach. Indignation filled her throat, choking off any possible reply.

Steve stood and walked across the kitchen, his hands knotted into fists at his sides. He closed his eyes briefly, and when he opened them, he looked like a stranger, his inner torment was so keen.

"I didn't mean that," he said unevenly. "I don't know why I say such ugly things to you."

Carol heard the throb of pain in her voice. "I don't know why you do, either. If you're trying to hurt me, then congratulations. You've succeeded beyond your expectations."

Steve stood silently a few moments, then delivered his untouched coffee to the sink. His hesitation surprised Carol. She'd assumed he would walk out—that was the way their arguments usually ended.

Instead he turned to face her and asked, "Are Todd and Joyce still married?"

She'd gotten a Christmas card from them a couple of weeks earlier. Until she'd seen both their names at the bottom of the greeting, she hadn't been sure if their marriage had weathered better than hers and Steve's. "They're still together."

Steve frowned and nodded. "I know that makes everything more difficult for you."

"Stop it, Steve!" This new list of questions irritated her almost as much as his tireless insinuations. "All the years we were married, not once did I accuse you of being unfaithful, even though you were gone half the time."

"It's difficult to find a woman willing to fool around 400 feet under water."

"That's not my point. I trusted you. I always did, and I assumed that you trusted me, too. That's all I've ever asked of you, all I ever wanted."

He was quiet for so long that Carol wondered if he'd chosen to ignore her rather than come up with an appropriate answer.

"You didn't discover another woman lounging around in a see-through nightie while I showered, either. You may be able to explain away some of what happened, but as far as I'm concerned there are gaping holes in your story."

Carol clenched her teeth so tightly that her jaw ached. She'd already broken a promise to herself by discussing Todd with Steve. When the divorce was final, Carol had determined then that no amount of justifying would ever satisfy her ex-husband. Discussing Todd had yet to settle a single problem, and in the end she only hurt herself.

"I don't think we're going to solve anything by rehashing this now," she told him calmly. "Unless our love is firmly grounded in a foundation of trust, there's no use even trying to work things out."

"It doesn't seem to be helping, does it? I wanted us—"

"I know," she interrupted softly, sadly. "I wanted it, too. The other night only served to remind us how much we'd loved each other."

They shared a discouraged smile, and Carol felt as though her heart was breaking in half.

He took a few steps toward the front door. "I'll be leaving in less than three weeks."

"How long will you be away?" For a long time she hadn't felt comfortable asking him this kind of question, but he seemed more open to discussion now.

"Three months." He buried his hands in his pockets and Carol got the impression that the action was to keep him from reaching for her and kissing her goodbye. He paused, turned toward her and said, "If you need anything . . ."

"I won't."

Her answer didn't appear to please him. "No, I don't suppose you will. You always could take care of yourself. I used to be proud of you for being so capable, but it intimidated me, too."

"What do you mean?"

He hedged, as if searching his reserve of memories to find the perfect example, then shook his head. "Never mind, it isn't important now."

Carol walked him to the front door, her heart heavy. "I wish it could be different for us."

"I do, too."

Steve stood, unmoving, in the entryway. Inches from him, Carol felt an inner yearning more potent than anything she'd ever experienced engulf her, filling her heart with regret. Once more she would have to watch the man she loved walk away from her. Once more she must freely allow him to go.

Steve must have sensed the intense longing, because he gently rested his hands on the curve of her shoulders. She smiled and tilted her chin toward him, silently offering him her mouth.

Slowly, without hurry, Steve lowered his face to hers, drawing out each second as though he were relaxing a hold on his considerable pride, admitting his need to kiss her. It was as if he had to prove, if only to himself, that he had control of the situation.

Then his mouth grazed hers. Lightly. Briefly. Coming back for more when it became apparent the teasing kisses weren't going to satisfy either of them.

What shocked Carol most was the gentleness of his kiss. He touched and held her as he would a delicate piece of porcelain, slipping his arms around her waist, drawing her close against him.

He broke off the kiss and Carol tucked her forehead against his chest. "Have a safe trip." Silently she prayed for his protection and that he would come back to her.

"If you want, I'll phone when I return. That is...if you think I should?"

Maybe she could tell him about the baby then, depending on how things went between them. "Yes, by all means, phone and let me know that you made it back in one piece."

His gaze centered on her mouth and again he bent his head toward her. This time his kiss was hungry, lingering, insistent. Carol whimpered when his tongue, like a soft flame, entered her mouth, sending hot sparks of desire shooting up her spine. Her knees weakened and she nearly collapsed when Steve abruptly released her.

"For once, maybe you could miss me," he said, with a sad note of bitterness.

The following morning, Carol woke feeling queasy. It'd been that way almost since Christmas morning. She reached for the two soda crackers on the nightstand and nibbled on them before climbing out of bed. Her hand rested lovingly on her flat stomach.

She'd wanted to schedule an appointment with the doctor, but the receptionist had told her to wait until her monthly cycle was a week late. She was only overdue by a day, but naturally she wouldn't be having her period. As far as Carol was concerned, another week was too long to wait, even if she was certain she bore the desired fruit from her night with Steve.

In an effort to confirm what she already knew, Carol had purchased a home-pregnancy test. Now she climbed out of bed, read the instructions through twice, did what the package told her and waited.

The waiting was the worst part. Thirty minutes had never seemed to take so long.

Humming a catchy tune, she dressed for work, poured herself a glass of milk, then went back to the bathroom to read the test results.

She felt so cocky, so sure of what the test would tell her that her heart was already pounding with excitement.

The negative reading claimed her breath. She blinked, certain she'd misread it.

Stunned, she sat on the edge of the bathtub and took several deep breaths. She started to tremble, and tears of disappointment filled her eyes. She must be pregnant—she had to be. All the symptoms were there—everything she'd read had supported her belief.

Once more she examined the test results.

Negative.

After everything she'd gone through, after all the sweet potatoes she'd forced down her throat, after the weeks of planning, the plotting, the scheduling . . .

There wasn't going to be any baby. There never had been. Her plan had failed.

There was only one thing left to do.

Try again.

Chapter Five

It took courage for Carol to drive to Steve's apartment.
Someone should award medals for this brand of lionhearted-
ness, she murmured to herself—although she was more interested in playing the role of a tigress than a lion. If this second
venture was anything like the first, Steve wouldn't know what
hit him. At least, she hoped he wouldn't guess.

She straightened her shoulders, pinched some color into her
cheeks and pasted on a smile. Then she rang the doorbell.

To say Steve looked surprised to see her when he opened the
door would be an understatement, Carol acknowledged. His
eyes rounded, his mouth relaxed and fell open, and for a moment he was utterly speechless. "Carol?"

"I suppose I should have phoned first ..."

"No, come in." He stepped aside so that she could enter the
apartment.

Beyond his obvious astonishment, Carol found it difficult to
read Steve's reaction. She stepped inside gingerly, praying that
her plastic smile wouldn't crack. The first thing she noticed was
the large picture window in the living room, offering an unobstructed view of the Seattle waterfront. It made Elliott Bay

seem close, so vivid that she could almost smell the seaweed and feel the salty spray in the air. A large green-and-white ferry boat plowed its way through the dark waters, enhancing the picture.

"Oh…this is nice." Carol turned around to face him. "Have you lived here long?"

He nodded. "Rush had the apartment first. I moved in after you and I split and sort of inherited it when Rush and Lindy moved into their own place recently."

The last thing Carol wanted to remind him of was their divorce, and she quickly steered the conversation to the reason for her visit. "I found something I thought might be yours," she said hurriedly, fumbling with the snap of her eel-skin purse to bring out the button. It was a weak excuse, but she was desperate. Retrieving the small gray button from inside her coin purse, she handed it over to him.

Steve's brow pleated into a frown and he stiffened. "No…this isn't mine. It must belong to another man," he said coldly.

A bad move, Carol realized, taking back the button. "There's only been one man at my house, and that's you," she said, trying to stay calm. "If it isn't yours, then it must have fallen off something of my own."

Hands in his pockets, Steve nodded.

An uneasy pause followed.

Steve didn't suggest she take off her coat, didn't offer her any refreshment or any excuse to linger. Feeling crestfallen and defeated, Carol knew there was nothing more to do but leave.

"Well, I suppose I should think about getting myself some dinner. There's a new Mexican restaurant close to here I thought I might try," she said with feigned enthusiasm, and glanced up at him through thick lashes. Steve loved enchiladas, and she prayed he would take the bait. God knew, she couldn't have been any more obvious had she issued the invitation straight out.

"I ate earlier," he announced starkly.

Steve rarely had dinner before six. He was either wise to her ways or lying.

"I see." She took a step toward the exit, wondering what else she could do to delay the inevitable. "When does the *Atlantis* leave?"

"Monday."

Three days. She had only three days to carry out her plan. Three days to get him into bed and convince him it was all his idea. Three miserable days. Her fingers curled into impotent fists of frustration inside her coat pocket.

"Have a safe trip, Steve," she said softly. "I'll . . . I'll be thinking of you."

It had been a mistake to come to his place, a mistake not to have plotted the evening more carefully. It was apparent from the stiff way Steve treated her, he couldn't wait to get her out of his apartment. Since it was Friday night, he might have a date. The thought of Steve with another woman produced a gut-wrenching pain that she did her best to ignore. Dropping by unexpectedly like this wasn't helping her cause.

She'd hoped they could make love tonight. Her temperature was elevated and she was as fertile as she was going to get this month.

Swallowing her considerable pride, she paused, her hand on the door handle. "There's a new spy thriller showing at the Fifth Avenue Theater. . . . You always used to like espionage films."

Steve's eyes narrowed as he studied her. It was difficult for Carol to meet his heated gaze and not wilt from sheer nerves. She was sure her cheeks were hot pink. Coming to his apartment was the most difficult thing she'd done in years. Her heart felt as if it was going to hammer its way right out of her chest, and her fingers were shaking so badly that she didn't dare remove them from her pockets.

"Why are you here?" His question was soft, suspicious, uncertain.

"I found the button." One glance told her he didn't believe her, as well he shouldn't. That excuse was so weak it wouldn't carry feathers.

"What is it you *really* want, Carol?"

"I...I..." Her voice trembled from her lips, and her heart, which had been pounding so furiously a second before, seemed to stop completely. She swallowed and forced her gaze to meet his before dropping it. When she finally managed to speak, her voice was low and meaningful. "I thought with you going away. . . ." Good grief, woman, her mind shouted, quit playing games. Give him the truth.

She raised her chin, and her gaze locked with his. "I'm not wearing any underwear."

Steve went stock-still, holding his jaw tight and hard. The inner conflict that played over his face was as vivid as the picturesque scene she'd viewed from his living-room window. The few feet of distance between them seemed to stretch wider than a mile.

It felt as if an eternity passed as Carol waited for his reaction, and she felt paralyzed with misgivings. She'd exposed her hand and left her pride completely vulnerable to him.

She saw it then—a flicker of his eyes, a movement in the line of his jaw, a softening in his tightly controlled facial features. He wanted her, too—wanted her with a desperation that made him as weak as she was. Her heart leaped wildly with joy.

Steve lifted his hand and held it out to her, and Carol thought she would collapse with relief as she hurried toward him. He crushed her in his arms and his mouth hungrily came down on hers. His eager lips smothered her cry of happiness. Equally greedy, Carol returned his kiss, reveling in his embrace. She twined her arms around his neck, her softness melding against the hardened contours of his body.

His hands tightened around her possessively, stroking her spine, then lowered over the rounded firmness of her buttocks. He gathered her pelvis as close to him as was humanly possible.

"Dear God, I've gone crazy."

Carol raised her hands to frame his face and gazed lovingly into his eyes. "Me, too," she whispered before spreading a circle of light kisses over his forehead, chin and mouth.

"I shouldn't be doing this."

"Yes, you should."

Steve groaned and clasped her tighter. He kissed her, plunging his tongue into the sweet softness of her mouth, exploring it with a desperate urgency. Carol met his tongue with her own in a silent duel that left them both exhausted.

While they were still kissing, Steve unfastened the buttons of her coat, slipped it from her shoulders and dropped it to the floor. His hands clawed at the back of her skirt, lifting it away from her legs, then settled once again, cupping her bare bottom.

He moaned, his breath seemed to jam in his throat, and his eyes darkened with passion. "You weren't kidding."

Carol bit her lower lip as a wealth of sensation fired through her from the touch of his cool hands against her heated flesh. She rotated her lower body shamelessly against the rigid evidence of his desire.

His hands closed over her breasts and her nipples rose as though to greet him, to welcome him. His eager but uncooperative fingers fiddled with the fastenings of her blouse. Smiling, content but just as eager, Carol gently brushed his hands aside and completed the task for him. He pulled the silk material free of her waistline and disposed of it as effectively as he had her coat. Her breasts sprang to life in his hands and when he moaned, the sound of it excited her so much that it throbbed in her ears.

The moist heat of his mouth closed over her nipple and she gasped. The exquisite pleasure nearly caused her knees to buckle. Blood roared through her veins, and liquid fire scorched her until she was certain she would soon explode. She lifted one leg and wrapped it around his thigh, anchoring her weight against him.

Steve's fingers reached for her and instinctively she opened herself to him. He teased her womanhood, toyed with her, tormented her with delicate strokes that drove her over the brink. Within seconds, she tossed back her head and groaned as the pulsating climax rocked through her, sending out rippling waves of release.

By the time Steve carried her into his bedroom, Carol was panting. He didn't waste any time, discarding his clothes with an urgency that thrilled her. When he moved to the bed, his features were keen with desire.

Carol lifted her arms to welcome him, loving him with a tenderness that came from the very marrow of her bones.

Steve shifted his weight over her and captured her mouth in a consuming kiss that sent Carol down into a whirlpool of the sweetest oblivion. Anxious and eager, she parted her thighs for him and couldn't hold back a small cry as he sheathed himself inside her, slipping the proud heat of his manhood into her moist softness.

He waited, as though to prolong the pleasure and soak in her love before he started to move. The feelings that wrapped

themselves around her were so incredible that Carol had to
struggle to hold back the tears. With each delicious stroke the
tension mounted and slowly, methodically began to uncurl
within her until she was thrashing her head against his pillow
and arching her hips to meet each plunging thrust.

Steve groaned and threw back his head, struggling to regain
control, but soon he, too, was over the edge. When he cried out
his voice harmonized with hers in a song that was as ageless as
mankind.

Breathless, he collapsed on top of her. Her arms slipped
around his neck and she buried her face in the hollow of his
throat, kissing him, hugging him, needing him desperately.
Tears slipped silently from the corners of her eyes. They spoke
the words that she couldn't, eloquently telling him of all the
love buried in her heart—words Carol feared she would never
be able to voice again.

When Steve moved to lift himself off of her, she wouldn't let
him. She held him tightly, her fingers gripping his shoulders.

"I'm too heavy," he protested.

"No...hold me."

With his arms wrapped around her, he rolled over, carrying
her with him in one continuous motion until their positions
were reversed.

Content for the moment, Carol pressed her ear over his chest,
listening to the strong, steady beat of his heart.

Neither spoke.

His hand moved up and down her spine in a tender caress as
though he had to keep touching her to know she was real. Her
tears slid onto his shoulder, but neither mentioned it.

In her soul, Carol had to believe that something this beautiful would create a child. At this moment everything seemed
perfect and healed between them, the way it had been two years
before.

Gently Steve kissed her forehead, and she snuggled closer,
flattening her hands over his chest.

He wrapped his arms around her and his thumb tenderly
wiped the moisture from her cheek. Tucking his finger under
her chin, he lifted it enough to find her mouth and kiss her.
Sweetly.

"I tried, but I never could stop loving you," he whispered in a voice raw with emotion. "I hated myself for being so weak, but I don't anymore."

"I'll always love you," she answered. "I can't help myself. This year has been the worst of my entire life. I've felt as if I was trapped in a freezer, never able to get warm."

"No more," he said, his eyes trapping hers.

"No more," she agreed, and her heart leaped with unleashed joy.

They rested for a full hour, their legs entwined, their arms wrapped around each other. Every now and again, Steve would kiss her, his lips playing over hers. Then Carol would kiss him back, darting her tongue in and out of his mouth and doing all the things she knew he enjoyed. She raised herself up on her elbows and brushed a thick swatch of dark hair from his brow. It felt so good to be able to touch him this freely.

"What's the name of that Mexican restaurant you mentioned earlier?" Steve asked.

Carol smiled smugly. "You are so predictable."

"How's that?"

"Making love never fails to make you hungry!"

"True," he growled into her ear, "but often my appetite isn't for food." His index finger circled her nipple, teasing it to a rose-colored pebble. "I've got a year's worth of loving stored up for you, and the way you make me feel tonight, we may never leave this bedroom."

And they didn't.

Carol woke when Steve pressed a soft kiss on her lips.

"Hmm," she said, not opening her eyes. She smiled up at him, sated and unbelievably happy. She wore the look of a woman who loves wisely and who knows that her love is returned. "Is it morning yet?"

"It was morning the last time we made love." Steve laughed and leaned over to kiss her again, as if one sample wasn't nearly enough to satisfy him.

"It was?" she asked lazily. They'd slept intermittently, waking every few hours, holding and kissing each other. While asleep, Carol would roll over and forget Steve was at her side. Their discovery each time was worth far more than a few semiprecious hours of sleep. And Steve seemed equally excited about her being there with him.

"Currently," he said, dragging her back to reality, "it's going on noon."

"Noon!" She bolted upright. She'd been in her teens the last time she'd slept this late.

"I'm sorry to wake you, honey, but I've got to get to the sub."

Carol was surprised to see that he was dressed and prepared to leave. He handed her a fresh cup of coffee, which she readily took from him. "You'll be back, won't you?"

"Not until tomorrow morning."

"Will you . . . could you stop off and see me one more time, before you leave?"

His dark gaze caressed her. "Honest to God, Carol, I don't think I could stay away."

As Steve walked away from his parked car at the Navy base in Bangor, less than ten miles north of Bremerton, he was convinced his strut would put a rooster to shame. Lord, he felt good.

Carol had come to him, wanted him, loved him as much as he'd always loved and wanted her. All the world felt good to him.

For the first time since they'd divorced, he felt whole. He'd been a crazed fool to harp on the subject of Todd Larson to Carol. From this moment on, he vowed never to mention the other man's name again. Obviously whatever had been between the two was over, and she hadn't wanted Todd back. Okay, so she'd made a mistake. Lord knew, he'd committed his share, and a lot of them had to do with Carol. He'd been wrong to think he could flippantly cast her out of his life.

In his pain, he'd lashed out at her, acted like a heel, refused to have anything to do with her because of his foolish pride. But Carol had been woman enough to forgive him. He couldn't do anything less than be man enough to forget the past. The love they shared was too precious to muddy with doubts. They'd both made mistakes, and the time had come to rectify those and learn from them.

Dear God, he felt ready to soar. He shouldn't be on a nuclear submarine—a feeling this good was meant for rockets.

* * *

Carol found herself humming as she whipped the cream into a frothy topping for Steve's favorite dessert: French pudding. She licked her index finger, grinned lazily to herself and leaned her hip against the kitchen counter, feeling happier than she could remember being in a long time.

Friday night had been incredible. Steve had been incredible. The only cost had been her bruised pride when she'd arrived at his apartment with such a flimsy excuse. The price had been minor, the rewards major.

Not once during the entire evening had Steve mentioned Todd's name. Maybe, just maybe, he was ready to put that all behind them now.

If she was pregnant from their Friday night lovemaking, which she sincerely prayed she was, it would be best for the baby to know ''her'' father. Originally Carol had intended to raise the child without Steve. She wasn't sure she would ever have told him. Now the thought of suppressing the information seemed both childish and petty. But she wasn't going to use the baby as a convenient excuse for a reconciliation. They would settle matters first—then she would tell him.

Steve would make a good father; she'd watched him around children and had often been amazed by his patience. He'd wanted a family almost from the first. Carol had been the one who'd insisted on waiting, afraid she wouldn't be able to manage her job, a home and a baby with her husband away so much of the time, although she'd never admitted it to Steve. She knew how important it was for him to believe in her strength and independence. But this past year had matured her. Now she was ready for the responsibility.

Naturally hindsight was twenty-twenty, and she regretted having put off Steve's desire to start a family. The roots of their marriage might have been strong enough to withstand what had happened if there'd been children binding them together. But it did no good to second-guess fate.

Children. Carol hadn't dared think beyond one baby. But if she and Steve were to get back together—something that was beginning to look like a distinct possibility—then they could plan on having a houseful of kids!

*   *   *

It was early afternoon by the time Steve made it to Carol's house. A cold wind from the north whistled through the tops of the trees and the sky was darkening with a brewing storm.

Carol tossed aside her knitting and flew across the room the minute she heard a car door close, knowing it had to be Steve. By the time he was to the porch, she had the front door open for him.

He wore his uniform, which told her he hadn't stopped off at his apartment to change. Obviously he was eager to see her again, Carol thought, immeasurably pleased.

"I'm glad to see you're waiting for me," he said, and his words formed a soft fog around his mouth. He took the steps two at a time and rubbed his bare hands together.

"I can't believe how cold it is." Carol pulled him inside the house and closed the door.

His gaze sought hers. "Warm me, then."

She didn't require a second invitation, and stood on the tips of her toes to kiss him, leaning her weight into his. Steve wrapped her in his embrace, kissing her back greedily, as if they had been apart six weeks instead of a single day. When he finished, they were both breathless.

"It feels like you missed me."

"I did," she assured him. "Give me your coat and I'll hang it up for you."

He gave her the thick wool jacket and strolled into the living room. "What's this?" he asked, looking at her knitting.

Carol's heart leaped to her throat. "A baby blanket."

"For who?"

"A . . . friend." She considered herself a friend, so that was at least a half-truth. She'd been working on the blanket in her spare time since before Christmas. It had helped her feel as if she was doing something constructive toward her goal.

Suddenly she felt as if she had a million things to tell him. "I got energetic and cleaned house. I don't know what's wrong with me lately, but I don't have the energy I used to have."

"Have you been sick?"

She loved him for the concern in his voice. "No, I'm in perfect health . . . I've just been tired lately . . . not getting enough vitamins, I suppose. But it doesn't matter now because I feel fantastic, full of ambition—I even made you French pudding."

"Carol, I think you should see a doctor."

"And if he advises bed rest, do you promise to, er...rest with me?"

"Good heavens, woman, you've become insatiable."

"I know." She laughed and slipped her arm around his waist. "I was always that way around you."

"Always?" he teased. "I don't seem to recall that."

"Then I'll just have to remind you." She steered him toward the bedroom, crawled onto the mattress and knelt there. "If you want French pudding, fellow, you're going to have to work for it."

The alarm went off at six. Carol blindly reached out and, after a couple of wide swipes, managed to hit the switch that would turn off the electronic beeping.

Steve stirred at her side. "It's time," she said in a small, sad voice. This would be their last morning together for three months.

"It's six already?" Steve moaned.

"I'm afraid so."

He reached for her and brought her close to his side. His hand found hers and he laced her fingers with his. "Carol, listen, we only have a little time left and there's so much I should have said, so much I wanted to tell you."

"I wanted to talk to you, too." In all the years they were married, no parting had been less welcome. Carol yearned to wrap her arms around him and beg him not to leave her. It was times like this that she wished Steve had chosen a career outside the Navy. In a few hours he would sail out of Hood Canal, and she wouldn't hear from him for the entire length of his deployment. Other than hearsay, Carol wasn't even to know where he would be sailing. For reasons of national security, all submarine deployments were regarded as top secret.

"When I return from this tour, Carol, I'd like us to have a serious talk about getting back together. I know I've been a jerk, and you deserve someone better, but I'd like you to think about it while I'm away. Will you do that for me?"

She couldn't believe how close she was to breaking into tears. "Yes," she whispered. "I'll think about it very seriously. I want everything to be right . . . the second time."

"I do, too." He raised her hand to his mouth and kissed her knuckles. "Another thing . . . make an appointment for a physical. I don't remember you being this thin."

"I lost fifteen pounds when we were divorced; I can't seem to gain it back." The tears broke through the surface and she sobbed out the words, ending in a hiccup. Embarrassed, she pressed her fingertips over her lips. "I've been a wreck without you, Steve Kyle . . . I suppose it makes you happy to know how miserable and lonely this past year has been."

"I was just as miserable and lonely," he admitted. "We can't allow anything to do this to us again. I love you too damn much to spend another year like the last one." His touch was so tender, so loving that she melted into his embrace.

"You have to trust me, Steve. I can't have you coming back and even suspecting I'd see another man."

"I know . . . I do trust you."

She closed her eyes at the relief his words gave her. "Thank you for that."

He kissed her then and, with a reluctance that tore at her heart, pulled away from her and started to dress.

She reached for her robe, not looking at him as she slipped her arms into the long sleeves. "If we do decide to make another go at marriage, I'd like to seriously think about starting a family right away. What would you say to that?"

Steve hesitated. Carol turned around to search out his gaze in the stirring light of early morning, and the tender look he wore melted any lingering doubts she harbored.

"Just picturing you with my child in your arms," he whispered hoarsely, "is enough to keep me going for the next three months."

Chapter Six

A week after Steve sailed, Carol began experiencing symptoms that again suggested she was pregnant. The early morning bouts of nausea returned. She found herself weeping over a rerun of *Magnum, P.I.* And she was continually tired, feeling worn-out at the end of the day. Everything she was going through seemed to point in one direction.

Self-diagnosis, however, had misled her a month earlier, and Carol feared her burning desire to bear a child was dictating her body's response a second time.

Each morning she pressed a hand over her stomach and whispered a fervent prayer that her weekend of lovemaking with Steve had found fertile ground. If she wasn't pregnant, then it would be April before they could try again, and that seemed like a thousand years away.

Carol was tempted to hurry out and buy another home pregnancy test. Then she would know almost immediately if her mind was playing tricks on her or if she really was pregnant. But she didn't. She couldn't explain—even to herself—why she was content to wait it out this time. If her monthly cycle was a week late, she decided, then and only then would she make an

appointment with her doctor. But until that time she was determined to be strong—no matter what the test results said.

The one thing that astonished Carol the most was that in the
time since Steve's deployment she missed him dreadfully. For
months she'd done her utmost to drive every memory of that
man from her mind, and sometimes she'd succeeded. Since
Christmas, however, thoughts of Steve had dominated every
waking minute. Until their weekend, Carol had assumed that
was only natural. Steve Kyle did play a major role in her scheme
to get pregnant. But she considered having a baby more of a
bonus now. The possibility of rebuilding her marriage—which
she had once considered impossible to do—claimed prece-
dence.

Missing Steve wasn't a new experience. Carol had always felt
at loose ends when he was aboard the *Atlantis*. But never had
she felt quite like this. Nothing compared to the emotion that
wrapped itself around her heart when she thought about Steve
on this tour. She missed him so much that it frightened her. For
more than a year she'd lived in the house alone; now it felt like
an empty shell because he wasn't there. In bed at night her
longing for him grew even more intense. She lay with her eyes
closed, savoring the memory of their last two nights together.
A chill washed over her at how close they'd come to destroy-
ing the love between them. The only thing that seemed to lessen
this terrible longing she felt for her ex-husband was construct-
ing dreams that involved him to help ease the loneliness as she
drifted off to sleep.

Friday morning Carol woke feeling rotten and couldn't seem
to force herself out of bed. She pulled into the huge Boeing
parking lot at the Renton plant ten minutes later than usual and
hurriedly locked her car. She was walking toward her building, trying to find the energy to rush when she heard someone
call out her name.

She turned, but didn't see anyone she recognized.

"Carol, is that you?"

"Lindy?" Carol could hardly believe her eyes. It was Steve's
sister. "What are you doing here?"

"I was just about to ask you the same thing."

Lindy looked fantastic. It had been nearly two years since
Carol had last seen her former sister-in-law. Lindy had been a
senior in college at the time, girlish and fun loving that sum-

mer she and Steve had visited his family. Had that been only two summers ago? It felt as though a decade had passed. Lindy had always held a special place in Carol's heart, and she smiled and hugged her close. When she drew back, Carol was surprised at the new maturity Lindy's eyes revealed.

"I work here," Lindy said, squeezing Carol's fingers. "I have since this past summer."

"Me, too—for over a year now."

Lindy tossed the sky a chagrined look. "You mean to tell me we've been employed by the same company, working at the same plant, and we didn't even know it?"

Carol laughed. "It looks that way."

They started walking toward the main entrance, still bemused, laughing and joking like long-lost sisters...which they were of sorts.

"I'm going to kick Steve," Lindy muttered. "He didn't tell me you worked for Boeing."

"He doesn't know. I suppose he assumes I'm still at Larson's Sporting Goods. I quit...long before the divorce was final. We haven't talked about my job, and I didn't think to mention it."

"How are you?" Lindy asked, but didn't give her more than a second to respond. "Steve growls at me every time I mention your name, which by the way, tells me he's still crazy about you."

Carol needed to hear that. She grinned, savoring the warm feeling Lindy's words gave her. "I'm still crazy about him, too."

"Oh, Carol," Lindy said with a giant sigh. "I can't tell you how glad I am to hear that. Steve never told any of us why the two of you divorced, but it nearly destroyed him. I can't tell you how happy I was when you phoned last Christmas. He hasn't been the same since."

"The divorce was wrong.... We should never have gone through with it," Carol said softly. Steve had been the one who had insisted on ending their marriage, and Carol had been too hurt, too confused to fight him the way she should have. Not wanting to linger on the mistakes of the past, Carol added, "Steve told me about you and Rush. Congratulations."

"Thanks." Lindy's eyes softened at the mention of Rush's name, and translucent joy radiated from her smile. "You met Paul didn't you?"

Carol nodded, recalling the time she had been introduced to Lindy's ex-fiance in Minneapolis. She hadn't been overly impressed by him and, as she recalled, neither had Steve.

"He married...someone else," Lindy explained. "I was devastated, convinced my life was over. That's how I ended up in Seattle. I'm so happy I moved here. Paul did me the biggest favor of my life when he dumped me; I found Rush and we were meant to be together—we both know it."

Hold on to that feeling, Carol mused, saddened that she'd been foolish enough to allow Steve to walk away from her. It had been a mistake, and one they'd both paid for dearly. "I'm really pleased for you, Lindy," she said sincerely.

"Thank you...oh, Carol, I can't tell you how good it is to see you again."

They paused once they passed the security gate, delaying their parting. "What area are you working in?" Carol asked, stopping. The others flooding through the entrance gate walked a wide circle around them.

"Section B."

"F for me." Which meant they were headed in opposite directions.

"Perhaps we could meet for lunch one day," Lindy suggested, anxiously glancing at her watch.

"I'd like that. How about next Tuesday? I can't until then, I'm involved with a special project."

"Great. Call me. I'm on extension 314."

"Will do."

Steve walked past the captain's quarters and through the narrow hallway to his stateroom. Tired, he sat on the edge of his berth and rubbed his hand across his eyes. This was his favorite time of day. His shift was complete, and he had about an hour to kill before he thought about catching some sleep. For the past several days, he'd been writing Carol. His letter had become a journal of his thoughts. Chances were that he would be home long before the letter arrived. Because submarines spent their deployment submerged, there were few opportunities for the pickup or delivery of mail. Any emergencies were handled by radio transmission. There were occasions when they could receive mail, but it wasn't likely to happen this trip.

Steve felt good. From the moment his and Carol's divorce had been declared final, he'd felt as if he'd steered his life off course. He'd experienced the first turbulent storm and, instead of riding it out as he should have, he'd jumped overboard. Ever since, he'd felt out of sync with his inner self.

In his letter, he'd tried to explain that to Carol, but putting it in words had been as difficult as admitting it had been.

He didn't know what had happened between Todd and Carol. Frankly he didn't want to know. Whatever had been between them was over and Steve could have her back. Lord knew he wanted her. He was destined to go to his grave loving that woman.

When he'd sailed out of Hood Canal and into the Pacific Ocean, Steve had felt such an indescribable pull to the land. He loved his job, loved being a part of the Navy, but at that moment he would have surrendered his commission to have been able to stay in Seattle another month.

Although he'd told Carol that they should use this time apart to consider a reconciliation, he didn't need two seconds to know his own mind: he wanted them to remarry.

But first they had to talk, really talk, and not about Todd. There were some deep-rooted insecurities he'd faced the past couple of weeks that needed to be discussed.

One thing that had always bothered Steve was the fact that Carol had never seemed to need him. His peers continually related stories about how things fell apart at home while they were deployed. Upon their return, after the usual hugs and kisses, their wives handed them long lists of repairs needed around the house or relayed tales of horror they'd been left to deal with in their husband's absence.

Not Carol. She'd sent him off to sea, wearing a bright smile and greeted him with an identical one on his return. The impression she gave him was that it was great when he was home, but was equally pleasant if he wasn't.

Her easy acceptance of his life-style both pleased and irritated Steve. He appreciated the strength of her personality, and yet a small part of him wished she weren't quite so strong. He wasn't looking for a wife who was a clinging vine, but occasionally he wished for something less than Carol's sturdy oak-tree character. Just once he would have liked to hear her tell him how dreadful the weeks had been without him, or how she'd wished he'd been there to take care of the broken dryer or to change the oil in the car.

Instead she'd given him the impression that she'd been having a grand ol' time while he was at sea. She chatted about the classes she took, or how her herb garden was coming along. If he quizzed her about any problems, she brushed off his concern and assured him she'd already dealt with whatever turned up.

Steve knew Carol wasn't that involved in the Navy-wife activities. He figured it was up to her whether or not she joined. He hadn't pressed her, but he had wished she would make the effort to form friendships with the wives of his close friends.

Carol's apparent strength wasn't the only thing that troubled Steve, but it was one thing he felt they needed to discuss. The idea of telling his ex-wife that the least she could do was shed a few tears when he sailed away from her made him feel ungrateful. But swallowing his pride would be a small price to pay to straighten matters between them.

What she'd said about wanting a baby right away made him feel soft inside every time he thought about it. He'd yearned for them to start a family long before now, but Carol had always wanted to wait. Now she appeared eager. He didn't question her motivation. He was too damned grateful.

A knock on his door jerked his attention across the room. "Yes?"

Seaman Layle stepped forward. "The Captain would like to see you, sir."

Steve nodded and said, "I'll be right there."

Carol sat at the end of the examination table, holding a thin piece of tissue over her lap. The doctor would be in any minute to give her the news she'd been waiting to hear for the past month. Okay, so her period was two weeks late. There could be any number of reasons. For one thing, she'd been under a good deal of stress lately. For another . . .

Her thoughts came to a grinding halt as Dr. Stewart stepped into the room. His glasses were perched on the end of his nose and his brow compressed as he read over her chart.

"Well?" she asked, unable to disguise the trembling eagerness in her voice.

"Congratulations, Carol," he said, looking up with a grandfatherly smile. "You're going to be a mother."

Chapter Seven

Carol was almost afraid to believe what Dr. Stewart was telling her; her hand flew to her heart. "You mean, I'm pregnant?"

The doctor looked up at her over the edge of his bifocals. "This is a surprise?"

"Oh, no... I knew—or at least I thought I knew." The joy that bubbled through her was unlike anything she had ever known. Ready tears blurred her vision and she bit her lower lip to hold back the tide that threatened to overwhelm her.

The doctor took her hand and gently patted it. "You're not sure how you feel—is that it?"

"Of course I do," she said, in a voice half an octave higher than usual. "I'm so happy I could just..."

"Cry?" he inserted.

"Dance," she amended. "This is the most wonderful thing that's ever happened to me since..."

"Your high-school prom?"

"Since I got married. I'm divorced now, but... Steve, he's my ex-husband, will marry me again...at least, I think he will. I'm not going to tell him about this right away. I don't want him to marry me again just because of the baby. I won't say a word about this. Or maybe I should? I don't know what to do, but thank you, Doctor, thank you so much."

A fresh smile began to form at the edges of his mouth. "You do whatever you think is best. Now, before we discuss anything else I want to go over some key points with you."

"Oh, of course, I'll do anything you say. I'll quit smoking and give up junk food, and take vitamins. If you really think it's necessary, I'll try to eat liver once a week."

His gaze reviewed her chart. "It says here you don't smoke."

"No, I don't, but I'd start just so I could quit if it would help the baby."

He chuckled. "I don't think that will be necessary, young lady."

Carol reached for his hand and pumped it several times. "I can't tell you how happy you've made me."

Still chuckling, the white-haired doctor said, "Tell me the same thing when you're in labor and I'll believe you."

Carol watched as Lindy entered the restaurant and paused to look around. Feeling a little self-conscious, she raised her hand. Lindy waved back and headed across the floor, weaving her way through the crowded tables.

"Hi. Sorry, I'm late."

"No problem." The extra time had given Carol a chance to study the menu. Her stomach had been so finicky lately that she had to be careful what she ate. This being pregnant was serious business and already the baby had made it clear "she" wasn't keen on particular foods—especially anything with tomatoes.

"Everything has been so hectic lately," Lindy said, picking up the menu, glancing at it and setting it aside almost immediately.

"That was quick," Carol commented, nodding her head toward the menu.

"I'm a woman who knows my own mind."

"Good for you," Carol said, swallowing a laugh. "What are you having?"

"I don't know. What are you ordering?"

"Soup and a sandwich," Carol answered, not fooled. Lindy wasn't interested in eating, she wanted answers. Steve's sister had been bursting with questions from the moment they'd met in the Boeing parking lot.

"Soup and a sandwich sounds good to me," Lindy said, obviously not wanting to waste time with idle chitchat.

Shaking her head, Carol studied Lindy. "Okay, go ahead and ask. I know you're dying to fire away."

Lindy unfolded the napkin and took pains spreading it over her lap. "Steve didn't come home Christmas Eve. . . . Well, he did, but it was early in the morning, and ever since that night he's been whistling 'Dixie' ". She paused and grinned. "Yet every time I said your name, he barked at me to mind my own business."

"We've seen each other since Christmas, too."

"You have?" Lindy pinched her lips together and sadly shook her head. "That brother of mine is so tight-lipped, I can't believe the two of us are related!"

Carol laughed. Unwittingly Lindy had pinpointed the crux of Carol and Steve's marital problems. They were each private people who preferred to keep problems inside rather than talking things out the way they should.

"So you've seen Steve since Christmas," Lindy prompted. "He must have contacted you after Rush and I moved."

"Actually I was the one who went to him."

"You did? Great."

"Yes," Carol nodded, blushing a little at the memory of how they'd spent that weekend. "It *was* great."

"Well, don't keep me in suspense here. Are you two going to get back together or what?"

"I think it's the 'or what.' "

"Oh." Lindy's gaze dropped abruptly and she frowned. "I don't mind telling you, I'm disappointed to hear that. I'd hoped you two would be able to work things out."

"We're heading in that direction, so don't despair. Steve and I are going to talk about a reconciliation when he returns."

"Oh, Carol, that's wonderful!"

"I think so, too."

"You two always seemed so right together. The first time I saw Steve after you were divorced, I could hardly recognize him. He was so cynical and unhappy. He'd sit around the apartment and watch television for hours, or stare out the window."

"Steve did?" Carol couldn't imagine that. Steve always had so many things going—he'd never taken the time to relax when they were living together. Another problem had been that they didn't share enough of the same interests. Carol blamed herself for that, but she was willing to compromise now that her marriage was about to have new life breathed into it.

"I wasn't joking when I told you he's been miserable. I don't know what prompted you to contact him at Christmastime, but I thank God you did."

Carol smoothed her hand across her abdomen and smiled almost shyly. "I'm glad I did, too."

Steve's letter to Carol was nearly fifty pages in length now. The days, as they often did aboard a submarine, blended together. It felt as if they were six months into this cruise instead of two, but his eagerness to return to Carol explained a good deal of this interminable feeling.

Carol. His heart felt as though it would melt inside his chest every time he thought about her mentioning a baby. The first thing he was going to do after they'd talked was throw out her birth control pills. And then he was going to take her to bed and make slow, easy love to her.

Once he had her back, he wasn't going to risk losing her again.

In the past two months, Steve had made another decision. They needed to clear the air about Todd Larson. He'd promised her that he wouldn't mention the other man's name again, but he had to, just once, and then it would be finished. Laid to rest forever.

Finding Todd in their shower hadn't been the only thing that had led Steve to believe Carol and her employer were having an affair. There had been plenty of other clues. Steve just hadn't recognized them in the beginning.

For one, she'd been working a lot of overtime, and didn't seem to be getting paid for it. At first Steve hadn't given it much credence, although he'd been angry that often she couldn't see him off to sea properly. At the time, however, she'd seemed as sorry about it as he was.

His return home after a ten-week absence had been the real turning point. Until that tour, Carol had always been eager to make love after so many weeks apart. Normally they weren't in the house ten minutes before they found themselves in the bedroom. But not that time. Carol had greeted him with open arms, but she'd seemed reluctant to hurry to bed. He had gotten what he wanted, but fifteen minutes later she'd made some silly excuse about needing groceries and had left the house.

None of these events had made much sense at the time. Steve had suspected something might be wrong, but he hadn't known how to ask her, how to approach her without sounding like an insecure schoolboy. Soon afterward he'd flown east for a two-week communication class. It was when he'd arrived home unexpectedly early that he'd found Carol and Todd together.

The acid building up in his stomach seemed to explode with pain and Steve took in several deep breaths until the familiar ache passed. All these months he'd allowed Carol to believe he'd condemned her solely because he'd discovered another man in their home. It was more than that, much more, and it was time he freed his soul.

*   *   *

"Carol? Are you here?"

Carol remained sitting on the edge of the bathtub and pressed her hand over her forehead. "I'm in here." Her voice sounded weak and sick—which was exactly how she felt. The doctor had given her a prescription to help ease these dreadful bouts of morning sickness, but it didn't seem to be doing much good.

"Carol?" Once more Lindy's voice vibrated down the hallway and Carol heard the sound of approaching footsteps. "Carol, what's wrong? Should I call a doctor?"

"No . . . no, I'll be fine in a minute. My stomach has been a little queasy lately, is all."

"You look awful."

"I can't look any worse than I feel." Her feeble attempt at humor apparently didn't impress Lindy.

"I take it the sale at the Tacoma Mall doesn't interest you?"

"I tried to call," Carol explained, "but you'd already left. You go ahead without me."

"I'll do no such thing," Lindy answered vehemently. "You need someone to take care of you. When was the last time you had a decent meal?"

Carol pressed her hand over her stomach. "Please, don't even mention food."

"Sorry."

Lindy helped her back into a standing position and led her down the hallway to her bedroom. Carol was ashamed to have Steve's sister see the house when it looked as if a cyclone had gone through it, but she'd had so little energy lately. Getting to work and home again drained her. She went to bed almost immediately after dinner and woke up exhausted the next morning.

No one had told her being pregnant could be so demanding on her health. She'd never felt more sickly in her life. Her appointment with Dr. Stewart wasn't for another two weeks, but something had to be done. She couldn't go on like this much longer.

The April sun seemed to smile down on Steve as he stepped off the *Atlantis*. He paused and breathed in the glorious warmth of afternoon in the Pacific Northwest. Carol wouldn't be waiting for him, he knew. She had no way of knowing when he docked.

But she needn't come to him. He was going to her. The minute he got home, showered and shaved, he was driving over to her house. He was so ready for this.

They were going to talk, make love and get married. Maybe not quite that simply, but close.

He picked up his mail and let himself into the apartment. Standing beside the phone, he listened to the messages on his answering machine. Three were from Lindy, who insisted he call first thing when he returned home.

He reached for the phone while he flipped through his assorted mail.

"You rang?" he asked cheerfully, when his sister answered.

"Steve? I'm so glad you called."

"What's wrong? Has Rush decided he's made a terrible mistake and decided to give you back to your dear, older brother to straighten out?" His sister didn't have an immediate comeback or a scathing reply, which surprised him.

"Steve, it's Carol."

His blood ran cold with fear. "What happened?"

"I don't know, but I wanted to talk to you before you went to see her," she said and hesitated. "You were planning on going there right away, weren't you?"

"Yes. Now tell me what's the matter with Carol."

"She's been sick."

"How sick?" His heart was thundering against his chest with worry.

"I... don't think it's anything... serious, but I thought I should warn you before you surprise her with a visit. She's lost weight and looks terrible, and she'll never forgive you if you show up without warning her you're in town."

"Has she seen a doctor?"

"I...don't know," Lindy confessed. "She won't talk about it."

"What the hell could be wrong?"

The line seemed to vibrate with electricity. "If you want the truth, I suspect she's pregnant."

Chapter Eight

"Pregnant?" Steve repeated and the word boomeranged against the walls of his mind with such force that the mail he'd been sorting slipped from his fingers and fell to the floor. He said it again. "Pregnant. But...but..."

"I probably shouldn't have said anything." Lindy's soft voice relayed her confusion. "But honestly, Steve, I've been so worried about her. She looks green around the gills and she's much too thin to be losing so much weight. I told her she should see a doctor, but she just smiles and says there's nothing to worry about."

The wheels in Steve's mind were spinning fast. "The best thing I can do is talk to her, and find out what's happening."

"Do that, but for heaven's sake be gentle with her. She's too fragile for you to come at her like Hulk Hogan."

"I wouldn't do that."

"Steve, I'm your sister. I know you!"

"Okay, okay. I'll talk to you later." He hung up the phone but kept his hand on the receiver while he mulled over his sister's news. Carol had said she wanted to have a baby, and she knew how he felt about the subject. He'd longed for a family since the first year they were together.

However, they weren't married now. No problem. Getting remarried was a minor detail. All he had to do was talk to the chaplain and make the arrangements. And if what Lindy said was true, the sooner he saw the chaplain, the better.

Without forethought he jerked the receiver off the hook and jabbed out Carol's number with his index finger. After two rings, he decided this kind of discussion was better done in person.

He showered, changed clothes and was halfway out the door when he remembered what Lindy had said about letting Carol know he was coming. Good idea.

He marched back over to the phone and dialed her number one more time.

No answer.

"Damn." He started pacing the floor, feeling restless, excited and nervous. He couldn't stay in the apartment; the walls felt as if they were closing in on him. He'd spent the last three months buried in the belly of a nuclear submarine and hadn't experienced a twinge of claustrophobia. Twenty minutes inside his apartment, knowing what he now did, and he was going ape.

He had to get out there even if it meant parking outside Carol's house and waiting for her to return.

He rushed out to his car and was grateful when it started right away after sitting for three months.

He was going to be a father! His heart swelled with joy and he experienced such a sense of elation that he wanted to throw back his head and shout loud enough to bring down brick walls.

A baby. His and Carol's baby. His throat thickened with emotion, and he had to swallow several times to keep from breaking down and weeping right there on the freeway. A new life. They were going to bring a tiny little being into this world and be accountable for every aspect of the infant's life. The responsibility seemed awesome. His hands gripped the steering wheel and he sucked in a huge breath as he battled down his excitement and fears.

He was going to be a good father. Always loving and patient. Everything would be right for his son...or daughter. Male chauvinist that he was, he yearned for a son. They could have a daughter the second time, but the thought of Carol giving him a boy felt right in his mind.

But he had so much to learn, so much to take care of. First things first. Steve tried to marshal his disjointed thoughts. He had to see to Carol's health. If this pregnancy was as hard on her as Lindy implied, then he wanted Carol to quit her job. He made good money; she should stay home and build up her strength.

The drive to Carol's house took less than fifteen minutes, and when Steve pulled up and parked he noticed her car in the driveway with the passenger door opened. His heart felt like it was doing jumping jacks, he was so eager to see her.

The front door opened and Carol stepped outside and to her car, grabbing a bag of groceries.

"Carol." She hadn't seen him.

She turned abruptly at the sound of her name. "Steve," she cried out brokenly and dropped the brown shopping bag. Without the least bit of hesitation, she came flying across the lawn.

He met her halfway, and wrapping his arms around her waist, he closed his eyes to the welcome feel of her body against his. His happiness couldn't be contained and he swung her around. Her lips were all over his face, kissing him, loving him, welcoming him.

Steve drank in her love and it humbled him. He held her gently, fearing he would hurt her, and kissed her with an aching tenderness, his mouth playing over the dewy softness of hers.

His hands captured her face and her deep blue eyes filled with tears as she smiled tremulously at him. "I've missed you so much. These have been the longest three months of my life."

"Mine, too." His voice nearly choked, and he kissed her again in an effort to hide the tide of emotion he was experiencing.

Steve picked up the scattered groceries for her and they walked into the house together.

"Go ahead and put those in the kitchen. Are you hungry?"

She seemed nervous and flittered from one side of the room to the other.

"I could fix you something if you'd like," she suggested, her back braced against the kitchen counter.

Steve's eyes held hers, and the emotion that had rocked him earlier built with intensity every minute he was in her presence. "You know what I want," he whispered, hardly able to speak.

Carol relaxed, and blushed a little. "I want to make love with you so much."

He held his hands out to her and she walked toward him, locking her arms around his neck. She pressed her weight against him and Steve realized how slender she was, how fragile. Regret slammed into his chest with all the force of a wrecking ball against a concrete wall. She was nurturing his child within her womb, for God's sake, and all he could think about was getting her into bed. He hadn't even asked her how she was feeling. All he cared about was satisfying his own selfish lusts.

"Carol..." His breath was slow and labored. Gently he tried to break free, because he couldn't think straight when she was touching him.

"Hmm?" Her hands were already working at his belt buckle, and her mouth was equally busy.

He felt himself weakening. "Are you sure? I mean, if you'd rather not..."

She released his zipper and when her hands closed around his naked hardness, he thought he would faint. His eyes rolled toward the ceiling. "Don't... don't you think we should talk?" he managed to say.

"No."

"But—"

She broke away and looked up at him, her eyes hungry with demand. "Steven Kyle, what is your problem? Do you or do you not want to make love?"

"I think... we should probably talk first. Don't you?" He didn't know if she would take him seriously with his voice shaking the way it was.

She grinned, and when her gaze dropped to below his waistline, they rounded. "No. Because neither one of us is going to be able to say anything worth listening to until we take care of other things...."

It wasn't possible to love a woman any more than he did Carol at that moment, Steve thought. She reached for his hand and led him out of the kitchen and into the bedroom.

Like a lost sheep, he followed.

* * *

The newborn moon cast silvery shadows on the wall opposite the bed, and Steve sighed, feeling sated and utterly content. Carol slept at his side, her arm draped around his middle
and her face nestled against his shoulder. Her tousled hair fell
over his chest and he ran his fingers through it, letting the short,
silky length slip through his hands.

Gently he brushed a blond curl off her cheek and twisted his
head so that he could kiss her temple. She stirred and sighed in
her sleep. He grinned. If he searched for a hundred years he
would never find a woman who could satisfy him the way Carol
did.

They hadn't talked, hadn't done anything but make love until they were both so exhausted that sleep dominated their
minds. They may not have voiced the words, but the love between them was so secure it would take more than a bulldozer
to rock it this time. Steve may not have had a chance to say the
words, but his heart had been speaking them from the minute
Carol had led him to bed.

Bringing the blanket more securely over her shoulders, he
wrapped his arm around her and studied her profile in the fading moonlight. What Lindy told him was true. Carol had lost
weight; she was as slender as a bamboo shoot, and much too
pale. She needed someone to take care of her and, he vowed in
his heart, he would be the one.

He almost wished she would roll over so that he could place
his hand on her abdomen and feel for himself the life that was
blossoming there. He felt weak with happiness every time he
thought about their baby. He closed his eyes at the sudden
longing that seared through his blood.

Carol hadn't yet told him that she was pregnant but he was
sure she would in the morning. Until then, he would be content.

He closed his eyes and decided to sleep.

Steve woke first. Carol didn't so much as stir when he
climbed out of bed and reached for his clothes. Silently he tip-
toed out of the room and gently closed the door. She needed her
sleep.

He made himself a pot of coffee and piddled around the
kitchen, putting away the groceries that had been sitting on the
counter all night. He pulled open the vegetable bin and care-

lessly tossed a head of lettuce in there. The drawer refused to close and he discovered the problem to be a huge shriveled up sweet potato. He took it out and, with an over the head loop shot Michael Jordan would have envied, tossed it into the garbage.

Carol and sweet potatoes. Honestly. The last time he'd looked inside her refrigerator, it had been filled with the stuff in every imaginable form.

He supposed he should get used to that kind of thing. It was a well-known fact that women often experienced weird food cravings when they were pregnant. Sweet potatoes were only one step above pickles and ice cream.

Just a minute! That had been last Christmas . . . before Christmas.

Steve's heart seemed to stop and slowly he straightened. Chewing on the inside of his lip, he closed the refrigerator door. Carol had been stuffing down the sweet potatoes long before he'd accepted her dinner invitation. Weeks before, from the look of it.

His thoughts in chaos, he stumbled into the living room and slumped into the chair. An icy chill settled over him. No. He refused to believe it, refused to condemn her on anything so flimsy. Then his gaze fell on a pair of knitting needles. He reached for her pattern book and noted the many designs for infant wear.

His heart froze. The last time he'd been by the house, Carol had been knitting a baby blanket. When he'd asked her about it, she'd told him it was for a friend. His snort of laughter was mirthless. Sure, Carol! More lies, more deceit.

And come to think of it, on Christmas Eve she'd pushed her knitting aside so that he couldn't see it. She'd been knitting the *same* blanket for the *same* friend then, too.

He was still stewing when Carol appeared. She smiled at him so sweetly as she slipped her arms into her robe.

"Morning," she said with a yawn.

"Morning."

His gruffness must have stopped her. "Is something wrong?"

Such innocent eyes . . . She'd always been able to fool him with that look. No more.

"Steve?"

"You're pregnant, aren't you?"

She released her breath in a long, slow sigh. "I wondered if you'd guess. I suppose I should have told you right away, but . . . we got sidetracked, didn't we?"

He could hardly stand to look at her.

"You're not angry, are you?" she asked, her eyes suddenly reflecting uncertainty.

Again such innocence, such skill. "No, I suppose not."

"Oh, good," she said with a feeble smile, "you had me worried there for a minute."

"One question?"

"Sure."

"Just whose baby is it?"

Chapter Nine

"Whose baby is it?" Carol repeated, stunned. She couldn't believe Steve would dare to ask such a question when the answer was so obvious.

"That's what I want to know."

His face was drawn extremely tight—almost menacing. She moved into the room and sat across from him, her heart ready to explode with dread. She met his look squarely, asking no quarter, giving none. The prolonged moment magnified the silence.

"I'm three months pregnant. This child is yours," she said, struggling to keep her voice even.

"Don't lie to me, Carol. I'm not completely dense." The anger that seeped into his expression was fierce enough to frighten her. Steve vaulted to his feet and started pacing in military fashion, each step precise and clipped, as if the drill would put order to his thoughts and ultimately to his life.

Carol's fingernails dug into the fabric on the sides of the overstuffed chair and her pulse went crazy. Her expression, however, revealed none of the inner turmoil she was experiencing. When her throat felt as if it would cooperate with her tongue, she spoke. "How can you even think such a thing?"

Steve splayed his fingers and jerked them through his hair in an action that seemed savage enough to yank it out by the roots. "I should have known something was wrong when you first contacted me at Christmastime."

Carol felt some color flush into her cheeks; to her regret it probably convinced Steve she was as guilty as he believed.

"That excuse about not wanting to spend Christmas alone was damn convenient. And if that wasn't obvious enough, your little seduction scene should have been. God knows, I fell for it." He whirled around to face her. "You did plan that, didn't you?"

"I...I..."

"Didn't you?" he repeated, in harsh tones that demanded the truth.

Miserable and confused, Carol nodded. She had no choice but to admit to her scheme of seducing him.

One corner of his mouth curved up in a half smile, but there was no humor or amusement in the action. The love that had so recently shone from his eyes had been replaced by condemnation.

"If only you would let me explain." She tried again, shocked by this abrupt turn of events. Only a few hours before, they'd lain in each other's arms and spoken of a reconciliation. The promise that had sprung to life between them was wilting and she was powerless to stop it.

"What could you possibly say that would change the facts?" he demanded. "I was always a fool when it came to you. Even after a year apart I hadn't completely come to terms with the divorce and you, no doubt, knew that and used it to your advantage."

"Steve, I—"

"It's little wonder," he continued, not allowing her to finish speaking, "that you considered me that perfect patsy for this intrigue. You used my love for you against me."

"Okay, so I planned our lovemaking Christmas Eve. You're right about that. I suppose I was pretty obvious about the whole thing when you think about it. But I had a reason. A damn good one."

"Yes, I know."

Carol hadn't realized a man's eyes could be so cold.

"What do you know?" she asked.

"That cake you're baking in your oven isn't mine."

"Oh, honestly, Steve. Your paranoia is beginning to wear a little thin. I'm doing my damnedest to keep my cool here, but you're crazy if you think anyone else could be the father."

He raised his index finger. "You're good. You know that? You're really very good. That fervent look about you, as though I'm going off the deep end to even suspect you of such a hideous deed. Just the right amount of indignation while keeping your anger in check. Good, very good."

"Stop that," she shouted. "You're being ridiculous. When you get in this mood, nothing appeases you. Everything I say becomes suspect."

His hand wiped his face free of expression. "If I didn't know better, I could almost believe you."

She hated it when Steve was like this. He was so convinced he was right that no amount of arguing would ever persuade him otherwise. "I'm going to tell you one last time, and then I won't say it again. Not ever. We—as in you and I, Steve—are going to have a baby."

Steve stared at her for so long that she wasn't sure what he was thinking. He longed to believe her—she could recognize that yearning in his eyes—and yet something held him back. His Adam's apple moved up and down, and he clenched his jaw so tightly that the sides of his face went white. Still the inner struggle continued while he glared at her, as if commanding the truth—as if to say he could deal with anything as long as it was true.

Carol met that look, holding her gaze as steady and sure as was humanly possible. He wanted the truth, and she'd already given it to him. Nothing she could say would alter the facts: he was her baby's father.

Steve then turned his back on her. "The problem is, I desperately want to believe you. I'd give everything I've managed to accumulate in this life to know that baby was mine."

Everything about Steve, the way he stood with his shoulders hunched, his feet braced as if he expected a blow, told Carol he didn't believe her. Her integrity was suspect.

"I . . . my birthday—I was thirty," she said, faltering as she scrambled to make him recognize the truth. "It hit me then that my childbearing years were numbered. Since the divorce I've been so lonely, so unhappy, and I thought a baby would help fill the void in my life.''

He turned to look at her as she spoke, then closed his eyes and nodded.

Just looking at the anguish in his face was almost more than Carol could bear. "I know you never believed me about Todd, but there's only been one lover in my life, and that's you. I figured that you owed me a baby. I thought if I invited you to spend Christmas with me and you accepted, that I could probably steer us into the bedroom. None of the problems we had in our marriage had extended there.''

"Carol, don't—this isn't necessary. I already know you were—''

"Yes, it is. Please, Steve, you've got to listen to me. You've got to understand.''

He turned away from her again, but Carol continued talking because it was the only thing left for her to do. If she didn't tell him now, there might never be another chance.

"I didn't count on anything more happening between us. I'd convinced myself I was emotionally separated from you by that time and all I needed was the baby...''

"You must have been worried when I didn't fall into your scheme immediately.''

"What do you mean?'' Carol felt frantic and helpless.

"I didn't immediately suggest we get back together—that must have had you worried. After Christmas Eve we decided to leave things as they were.'' He walked away from her, but not before she saw the tilt of righteous indignation in his profile. "That visit to my apartment...what was your excuse? Ah yes, a button you'd found and thought might be mine. Come on, Carol, you should have been more original than that. As excuses go, that's about as flimsy as they get.''

"All right, if you want me to admit I planned that seduction scene, too, then I will. I didn't get pregnant the way I planned in December ... I had to try again. You had to know swallowing my pride and coming to you wasn't easy.''

He nodded. "No, I don't suppose it was.''

"Then you believe me?''

"No.''

Carol hung her head in frustration.

"Naturally only one night of lovemaking wasn't enough," he said with a soft denunciation. "It made sense to plan more than one evening together in case I started questioning matters later. I'm pleased that you did credit me with some intelligence. Turning up pregnant after one time together would have seemed much too convenient. But twice... Well, that sounds far more likely."

Carol was speechless. Once more Steve had tried and found her guilty, choosing to believe the worst possible scenario.

"Fool that I am, I should have known something was up by how docile and loving you were. So willing to forget the past, forgive and go on with the future. Then there was all that talk about us starting a family. That sucked me right in, didn't it? You know, you've always known how much I want children."

"There's nothing I can say, is there?"

"No," he admitted bleakly. "I wonder what you would have told me next summer when you gave birth—although months premature, astonishingly the baby would weigh six or seven pounds and obviously be full term. Don't you think I would have questioned you then?"

She kept her mouth shut, refusing to be drawn into this kind of degrading verbal battle. From experience she knew nothing she could say would vindicate her.

"If you don't want to claim this child, Steve, that's fine, the loss is yours. My original intent was to raise her alone anyway. I'd thought...I'd hoped we could build a new life together, but it's obvious I was wrong."

"Dead wrong. I won't let you make a fool of me a second time."

A strained moment passed before Carol spoke, and when she did her voice was incredibly weak. "I think it would be best if you left now."

He answered her with an abrupt nod, turned away and went to her bedroom to retrieve his shirt and shoes.

Carol didn't follow him. She sat, feeling numb and growing more ill with each minute. The nausea swelled up inside her until she knew she was going to empty her stomach. Standing, she rushed into the bathroom and leaned over the toilet in a ritual that had become all too familiar.

When she'd finished, she discovered Steve waiting in the doorway, watching her. She didn't know how long he'd been there.

"Are you all right?"

She nodded, not looking at him, wanting him to leave so that she could curl into a tight ball and lick her wounds. No one could hurt her the way Steve did. No other man possessed the power.

He didn't seem to believe she was going to be fine, and slowly he came into the bathroom. He wet a washcloth and handed it to her, waiting while she wiped her face. Then, gently, he led her back into the bedroom and to the bed. Carol discovered that lying down did seem to ease the dizzy, sick feeling.

Steve took his own sweet time buttoning his shirt, apparently stalling so that he could stick by her in case she was sick a second time, although she knew he would never have admitted he cared. If she'd had the energy, Carol would have suggested he go, because for every minute he lingered it was more difficult for her to bear seeing him. She didn't want him to care about her—how could he when he believed the things he did? And yet, every now and again she would find him watching her guardedly, his eyes filled with worry.

"When do you see the doctor next?" He walked around the foot of the bed and resumed an alleged search for his socks.

"Two weeks." Her voice was faint and barely audible.

"Don't you think you should give him a call sooner?"

"No." She refused to look at him.

Steve apparently found what he wanted. He sat on the edge of the mattress and slowly, methodically put on his shoes. "How often does this sort of thing happen?" he asked next.

"It doesn't matter." Some of her energy returned, and she tested her strength by sitting up. "Listen, Steve, I appreciate your concern, but it just isn't necessary. My baby and I are going to be just fine."

He didn't look convinced. His brooding gaze revealed his thoughts, and when he looked at her, his expression softened perceptibly. It took a moment for his eyes to drop to her hand, which rested on her abdomen.

The change that came over him was a shock. His face tightened and his mouth thinned. A surge of anger shot through her. "You don't want to claim our daughter, then it's your loss."

"The baby isn't mine."

The anguish in his voice was nearly Carol's undoing. She bit her lower lip and shook her head with mounting despair. "I can't believe you're actually saying that. But you'll never know, will you, Steve? All your life you're going to be left wondering. If she has dark eyes like yours and dark hair, that will only complicate your doubts. No doubt the Kyle nose will make you all the more suspicious. Someday you're going to have to face the fact that you've rejected your own child. If you can live with that, then so be it."

He twisted around and his fists were knotted into tight fists. "You were pregnant at Christmas and you're trying to pawn this pregnancy off on me."

"That is the most insulting thing you've ever said to me."

He didn't answer her for a long time. "You've insulted my intelligence. I may have loved you, but I'm not a blind fool."

"They don't come any blinder."

"Explain the milk?"

"What?" Carol hadn't a clue to what he was talking about.

"At Christmas, after we'd made love, we had a snack. Remember?"

Carol did.

"You poured yourself a glass of milk and I commented because you used to dislike it. We were married five years and the only time I can remember you having milk was with cold cereal. You could live your whole life without the stuff. All of a sudden you're drinking it by the glassful."

With deliberate calm Carol rolled her gaze toward the ceiling. "Talk about flimsy excuses. You honestly mean to say you're rejecting your own child because I drank a glass of milk an entire month before I was pregnant?"

"That isn't everything. I saw your knitting Christmas Eve, although you tried to hide it from me. Later, I asked you about it and you claimed it was a baby blanket. It was the same piece you were working on at Christmas, wasn't it?"

"Yes, but . . ."

"That blanket's for your baby isn't it, Carol? There never was any friend."

Frustration mounting in volcanic proportions, she yelled, "All right, it wasn't for any friend—that's what you want to hear."

"And then there were the sweet potatoes. Good God, you had six containers full of yams that night . . . pregnant women are said to experience silly cravings. And that's what it was, wasn't it—a craving?"

Standing, Carol felt the weight of defeat settle on her shoulders. No amount of arguing would change anything now. Steve had reasoned everything out in his own mind and found her answers lacking. There was no argument she could give him that would change what he'd already decided.

"Well?" he demanded. "Explain those things away, if you can."

She felt as if she were going to burst into helpless tears at any second. For six years she'd loved this man and given him the power to shatter her heart. "You're the only man I know who can put two and two together and come up with five, Steve," she said wearily.

"For God's sake, quit lying. Quit trying to make me doubt what's right before my eyes. You wanted to trick me into believing that baby is mine, and by God, it almost worked."

If he didn't leave soon, Carol was going to throw him out. "I think you should leave."

"Admit it!" he shouted.

Nothing less would satisfy him. She slapped her hands against her thighs and feigned a sorrowful sigh. "I guess you're just too smart for me. I should have known better than to try to fool you."

Steve turned and marched to the front door, but stopped, his hand gripping the knob. "What's he going to do about it?"

"Who?"

"Todd."

It took every dictate of Carol's control not to scream that her former employer had nothing to do with her being pregnant. "I don't have anything more to say to you."

"Is he going to divorce Joyce and marry you?"

With one hand cradled around her middle, Carol pointed to the door with the other.

"I have a right to know," Steve argued. "If he isn't going to help you, something should be done."

"I don't need anything—especially from you."

"As much as I'd like to walk away from you, I can't. If you find yourself in trouble, call me. I'll always be there for you."

"If you want to help me, then get out of my life. This baby is mine and mine alone." There was no anger in her words; her voice was low and controlled . . . and sad, unbelievably sad.

Steve hesitated and his lingering seemed to imply that something would change. Carol knew otherwise.

"Goodbye, Steve."

He paused, then whispered, "Goodbye."

The pain in his voice would haunt her all her days, she thought, as Steve turned and walked out of her life.

The loud pounding noise disrupted Steve's restless slumber and he sat up and glared at the front door of his apartment.

"Who is it?" he shouted, and the sound of his own voice sent shooting pains through his temple. He moaned, tried to sit up and in the process nearly fell off the sofa.

"Steve, I know you're in there. Open up."

Lindy. Damn, he should have known it would be his meddling sister. He wished to hell she would just leave him alone. He'd managed to put her off for the past week, avoiding talking to her, inventing excuses not to see her. Obviously that hadn't been good enough because here she was!

"Go away," he said, his voice less loud this time. "I'm sick." That at least was the truth. His head felt like someone had used it for batting practice.

"I have my own key and I'll use it unless you open this door right now."

Muttering under his breath, Steve weaved across the floor until he reached the door. The carpet seemed to pitch and roll like a ship tossed about in a storm. He unbolted the lock and stepped aside so Lindy could let herself in. He knew she was about to parade into his apartment like an angel of mercy prepared to save him from hell and damnation.

He was right.

Lindy came into the room with the flourish of a suffragette marching for equality of the sexes. She stopped in the middle of the room, hands placed righteously on her hips, and studied him as though viewing the lowest form of human life. Then slowly she began to shake her head with obvious disdain.

"You look like hell," she announced.

Steve almost expected bugles to follow her decree. "Thank you, Mother Theresa."

"Sit down before you fall down."

Steve did as she ordered simply because he didn't have the energy to argue. "Would you mind not talking so loud?"

With one hand remaining on her hip, Lindy marched over to the window and pulled open the drapes.

Steve squinted under the force of the sunlight and shaded his eyes. "Was that really necessary?"

"Yes." She walked over to the coffee table and picked up an empty whiskey bottle, as though by touching it she was exposing herself to an incurable virus. With her nose pointed toward the ceiling, she walked into the kitchen and tossed it in the garbage. The bottle made a clanking sound as it hit against other bottles.

"How long do you intend to keep yourself holed up like this?" she demanded.

He shrugged. "As long as it takes."

"Steve, for heaven's sake be reasonable."

"Why?"

She couldn't seem to find an answer and that pleased him because he wasn't up to arguing with her. He knew there was a reason to get up, get dressed and eat, but he hadn't figured out what it was yet. He'd taken a week of leave in order to spend time with Carol. Now he would give anything to have to report to duty—anything to take his mind off his ex-wife.

His mouth felt like a sand dune had shifted there while he slept. He needed something cold and wet. With Lindy following him, he walked into the kitchen and got himself a beer.

To his utter amazement, his sister jerked it out of his hand and returned it to the refrigerator. "From the look of things, I'd say you've had enough to drink."

He was so stunned, he didn't know what to say.

She pointed her index finger toward a kitchen chair, silently ordering him to sit. From the determined look she wore, Steve decided not to test her.

Before he could object, she had a pot of coffee brewing and was rummaging through the refrigerator looking for God knew what. Eggs, he realized when she brought out a carton.

She insisted he eat, which he did, but he didn't like it. While he sat at the table like an obedient child, Lindy methodically started emptying his sink, which was piled faucet-high with dirty dishes.

"You don't need to do that," he objected.

"Yes, I know."

"Then don't . . . I can get by without any favors from you."
Now that he had something in his stomach, he wasn't about to
be led around like a bull with a ring through his nose.

"You need something," she countered. "I'm just not sure
what. I suspect it's a swift kick in the seat of the pants."

"You and what army, little sister."

Lindy declined to answer. She poured herself a cup of coffee, replenished his and claimed the chair across the table from
him. "Okay," she said, her shoulders rising with an elongated
sigh. "What happened with Carol?"

At the mention of his former wife's name, Steve's stomach
clenched in a painful knot. Just thinking about her carrying
another man's child produced such an inner agony that the oxygen constricted his lungs and he couldn't breathe.

"Steve?"

"Nothing happened between us. Absolutely nothing."

"Don't give me that. The last time we talked, you were as
excited as a puppy about her being pregnant. You could hardly
wait to see her. What's happened since then?"

"I already told you—nothing!"

Lindy slumped forward and braced her hand against her
forehead. "You've buried yourself in this apartment for an
entire week and you honestly expect me to believe that?"

"I don't care what you believe."

"I'm to blame, aren't I?"

"What?"

"I shouldn't have said a word about Carol and the baby, but
she'd been so sick and I've been so concerned about her."
Lindy paused and lightly shook her head. "I still am."

Steve hated the way his heart reacted to the news that Carol
was still sickly. He didn't want to care about her, didn't want
to feel this instant surge of protectiveness when it came to his
ex-wife. For the past week, he'd tried to erase every memory of
her from his tortured mind. Obviously it hadn't worked, and
the only thing he'd managed to develop was one hell of a
hangover.

"I shouldn't have told you," Lindy repeated.

"It wouldn't have made one bit of difference; I would have
found out sooner or later."

Lindy's hands cupped the coffee mug. "What are you going to do about it?"

Steve shrugged. "Nothing."

"Nothing? But Steve, that's your baby."

He let that pass, preferring not to correct his sister. "What's between Carol and me isn't any of your business. Leave it at that."

She seemed to weigh his words carefully. "I wish I could."

"What do you mean by that?"

"Carol looks awful. I really think she needs to see her doctor. Something's wrong, Steve. She shouldn't be this sick."

He shrugged with feigned indifference. "That's her problem."

Lindy's jaw sagged open. "I can't believe you. Carol is carrying your child and you're acting like she got pregnant all by herself."

Steve diverted his gaze to the blue sky outside his living-room window and shrugged. "Maybe she did," he whispered.

104   DEBBIE MACOMBER

Chapter Ten

Carol sat at her desk and tried to concentrate on her work. This past seven days had been impossible. Steve honestly believed she was carrying another man's child, and nothing she could ever say would convince him otherwise. It was like history repeating itself and all the agony of her divorce had come back to haunt her.

Only this time Carol was smarter.

If Steve chose to believe such nonsense, that was his problem. She wanted this baby and from the first had been prepared to raise her daughter alone. Now if only she could get over these bouts of nausea and the sickly feeling that was with her almost every day and night. Most of it she attributed to the emotional upheaval in her life. Within a couple of weeks it would pass and she would feel a thousand times better—at least, that was what she kept telling herself.

"Hi."

A familiar, friendly voice invaded Carol's thoughts. "Lindy!" she said, directing her attention to Steve's sister. "What are you doing here?"

"Risking my job and my neck. Can we meet later? I've got to talk to you; it's important."

As fond as Carol was of her former sister-in-law, she knew there was only one subject Lindy would want to discuss, and that was Steve. Her former husband was a topic Carol preferred to avoid. Nor was she willing to justify herself to his sister, if Lindy started questioning her about the baby's father. It would be better for everyone involved if she refused to meet her, but the desperate worry in Lindy's steady gaze frightened her.

"I suppose you want to ask me about Steve," Carol said slowly, thoughtfully. "I don't know that any amount of talking is going to change things. It'd be best just to leave things as they are."

"Not you, too."

"Too?"

"Steve's so closed mouthed you'd think your name was listed as classified information."

Carol picked up the clipboard and flipped over a page, in an effort to pretend she was exceptionally busy. "Maybe it's better this way," she murmured, but was unable to disguise the pain her words revealed.

"Listen, I've got to get back before someone important—like my supervisor—notices I'm missing," Lindy said, scribbling something on a pad and ripping off the sheet. "Here's the address to my apartment. Rush is on sea trials, so we'll be alone."

"Lindy..."

"If you care anything about my brother you'll come." Once more those piercing eyes spelled out his sister's concern.

Carol took the address, and frowned. "Let me tell you right now that if you're trying to orchestrate a reconciliation, neither one of us will appreciate it."

"I..."

"Is Steve going to mysteriously arrive around the same time as I do?"

"No. I promise he won't. Good grief, Carol, he won't even talk to me anymore. He isn't talking to anyone. I'm not kidding when I say I'm worried about him."

Carol soaked in that information and frowned, growing concerned herself.

"You'll come?"

Against her better judgment, she nodded. Like her ex-husband, she didn't want to talk to anyone, and especially not to someone related to Steve. The pain of his accusations was still too raw to share with someone else.

Yet she knew she would be there to talk about whatever it was Lindy found so important, although she also knew that nothing Lindy could say would alter her relationship with Steve.

At five-thirty, Carol parked her car outside Lindy's apartment building. She regretted agreeing to the meeting, but couldn't see any way of escaping without going back on her word.

Lindy opened the door and greeted her with a weak smile. "Come in and sit down. Would you like something cold to drink? I just finished making a pitcher of iced tea."

"That sounds fine." Carol still wasn't feeling well and would be glad when she saw her doctor for her regular appointment. She took a seat in the living room while Lindy disappeared into the kitchen.

Lindy returned a couple of minutes later with tall glasses filled with iced tea.

"I wish I could say you're looking better," Lindy said, handing Carol a glass and a colorful napkin.

"I wish I could say I was, too."

Lindy sat across from her and automatically crossed her long legs. "I take it the medication the doctor gave you for the nausea didn't help?"

"It helped some."

"But generally you're feeling all right?"

Carol shrugged. She'd never been pregnant before and had nothing to compare this experience to. "I suppose."

Lindy's fingers wiped away the condensation on the outside of her glass. She hedged, and her gaze drifted around the room. "I think the best way to start is to apologize."

"But what could you have possibly done to offend me?"

Lindy's gaze moved to Carol's, and she released a slow breath. "I told Steve I suspected you were pregnant."

"It's true," Carol answered with a gentle smile. She would be a single mother, and although she would have preferred to be married, she was pleased and proud to be carrying this child.

"I know... but it would have been far better coming from you. I left a message for Steve to call me once he returned from his deployment. I was afraid he was going to come at you with his usual caveman tactics and you've been so ill lately... It's a weak excuse, I know."

"Lindy, for goodness' sake, don't worry about it. This baby isn't a deep, dark secret." Remembering the life she was nurturing in her womb was what had gotten her through the bleakest hours of this past week. Steve might choose to reject his daughter, but he could never take away this precious gift he had unknowingly given her.

"I don't know what's going on with my brother," Lindy muttered, dropping her gaze to her tea. "I wish Rush were here. If anyone could talk some sense into him, it's my husband."

"Get used to him being away when you need him most. It's the lot of a Navy wife. The Navy blues doesn't always refer only to their dress uniform, you know."

Lindy nodded. "I'm learning that; I'm also learning I'm much stronger than I thought I was. Rush was involved in an accident last year in the Persian Gulf—you probably read about it in the papers—well, really that doesn't have anything to do with Steve, but he was with me the whole time when we didn't know if Rush was dead or alive. I can't even begin to tell you how good he was, how supportive. In a crisis, my brother can be a real trooper."

"Yes, I know." Carol paused and took a sip of her tea. On more than one occasion in their married life, she had come to admire Steve's levelheadedness in dealing with both major and minor emergencies. It was in other matters, like trust and confidence in her love, that he fell sadly short.

"I don't understand him anymore," Lindy admitted. "He was ecstatic when I mentioned my suspicions about you being pregnant... I thought he was going to go right through the ceiling he was so excited. He was bubbling over like a little kid. I know he drove over to your place right after that and then we didn't hear from him again. I phoned, but he just barked at me to leave him alone, and when I went to see him... well, that's another story entirely."

Carol stiffened. It was better to deal with Lindy honestly since it was apparent Steve hadn't told her. "He doesn't believe the baby is his."

Lindy's brow folded into a dark, brooding frown. "But that's ridiculous."

Carol found it somewhat amazing that her former sister-in-law would believe her without question and her ex-husband wouldn't.

"I . . . can't believe this." Lindy pressed her palm over her forehead, lifting her bangs, and her mouth sagged open. "But, sadly, it explains a good deal." As if she couldn't remain sitting any longer, Lindy got up and started walking around the room, moving from one side to the other without direction. "What is that man's problem? Good grief, someone should get him to face a few fundamental facts here."

Carol smiled. It felt good to have someone trust and believe her.

"What are you going to do? I mean, I assumed Steve was going to remarry you, but . . ."

"Obviously that's out of the question."

"But . . ."

"Single women give birth every day. It's rather common-place now for a woman to choose to raise a child on her own. That was my original intention."

"But, Steve . . ."

"Steve is out of my life." Her hand moved to her stomach and a soft smile courted the edges of her mouth. "He gave me what I wanted. Someday he'll be smart enough to calculate dates, but when he does it'll be too late."

"Oh, Carol, don't say that. Steve loves you so much."

"He's hurt me for the last time. He can't love me and ac-cuse me of the things he has. It's over for us, and there's no going back."

"But he does love you." Lindy walked around a bit more and then plopped down across from Carol. "When he wouldn't talk to me on the phone, I went over to the apartment. I've never seen him like this. He frightened me."

"What's wrong?" Carol was angry with herself for caring, but she did.

"He'd been drinking heavily."

"That's not like Steve."

"I know," Lindy said heatedly. "I didn't know when he'd eaten last, so I fixed him something, which was a mistake because once he had something in his stomach he got feisty again and wanted me to leave.''

"Did you?''

"No.'' Lindy started nibbling on the corner of her mouth. "I kept asking him questions about you, which only made him more angry. I soon learned you were a subject best avoided.''

"I can imagine.''

"After a while, he fell asleep on the sofa and I stayed around and cleaned up the apartment. It was a mess. Then . . . I heard Steve. I thought at first he was in the middle of a bad dream and I went to wake him, but when I came into the living room, I found him sitting on the end of the davenport with his hands over his face. He was weeping, Carol. As I've never seen a man weep before—heart-wrenching sobs that came from the deepest part of his soul. I can't even describe it to you.''

Carol lowered her gaze to her hands, which had begun to tremble.

"This is the first time I've seen my brother cry, and his sobs tore straight through my heart. I couldn't stand by and do nothing. I wanted to comfort him and find out what had hurt him so badly. I'm his sister, for heaven's sake—he should be able to talk to me. But he didn't want me anywhere near him and ordered me out of the apartment. I left, but I haven't been able to stop thinking about it since.''

A tear spilled out of the corner of Carol's eye and left a moist trail down the side of her face.

"By the time I got home I was crying, too. I don't know what to do anymore.''

Carol's throat thickened. "There's nothing you can do. This is something Steve has to work out himself.''

"Can't you talk to him?'' Lindy pleaded. "He loves you so much and it's eating him alive.''

"It won't do any good.'' Carol spoke from bitter experience.

"How can two people who obviously love each other let this happen?''

"I wish I knew.'' Carol's voice dropped to a whispered sob.

"What about Steve and the baby?''

"He doesn't want to have anything to do with this pregnancy. That's his decision, Lindy.''

"But it's the wrong one! Surely you can get him to realize that."

She shook her head sadly. "Once Steve decides on something, his mind is set. He's too stubborn to listen to reason."

"But you love him."

"I wish I could deny that, but I do care about him, with all my heart. Unfortunately that doesn't change a thing."

"How can you walk away from him like this?"

Carol's heart constricted with pain. "I've never left Steve. Not once. He's always been the one to walk away."

Chapter Eleven

"I'd do anything I could to make things right between me and Steve," Carol told Lindy, "but it isn't possible anymore."

"Why not?" Lindy pleaded. Carol knew it was hard for Lindy to understand when her own recent marriage was thriving. "You're both crazy in love with each other."

The truth in that statement was undeniable. Although Steve believed her capable of breaking her wedding vows and the worst kind of deceit, he continued to love her. For her part, Carol had little pride when it came to her ex-husband. She should have cut her losses the minute he'd accused her of having an affair, walked away from her and filed for the divorce. Instead she'd spent the next year of her life in limbo, licking her wounds, pretending the emotional scars had healed. It had taken Christmas Eve to show her how far she still had to go to get over loving Steve Kyle.

"You can't just walk away from him," Lindy pleaded. "What about the baby?"

"Steve doesn't want anything to do with my daughter."

"Give him time, Carol. You know Steve probably better than anyone. He can be such a stubborn fool sometimes. It just takes awhile for him to come to his senses. He'll wake up one morning and recognize the truth about the baby.''

"I have to forget him for my own sanity.'' Carol stood, delivered her empty iced-tea glass to the kitchen and prepared to leave. There wasn't anything Lindy could say that would change the facts. Yes, she did love Steve and probably always would, but that didn't alter what he believed.

Lindy followed her to the front door. "If you need something, anything at all, please call me.''

Carol nodded. "I will.''

"Promise?''

"Promise.'' Carol knew that Lindy realized how difficult it was for her to ask for help. Impulsively she hugged Steve's sister. From now on, Lindy would be her only link to Steve and Carol was grateful for the friendship they shared.

Steve had to get out of the apartment before he went crazy. He'd spent the past few days drowning his misery in a bottle and the only thing it had brought him was more pain.

He showered, shaved and dressed. Walking would help clear his mind.

With no real destination in mind, he headed toward the waterfront. He got as far as Pike Place Market and aimlessly wandered among the thick crowds there. The colorful sights of the vegetable and meat displays and the sounds of cheerful vendors helped lift his spirits.

He bought a crisp, red Delicious apple and ate it as he ambled toward the booths that sold various craft items designed to attract the tourist trade. He paused and examined a sculpture made of volcanic ash from Mount Saint Helens. Another booth sold scenic photos of the Pacific Northwest, and another, thick, hand-knit Indian sweaters.

"Could I interest you in something?'' a friendly older woman asked. Her long silver hair framed her face, and she offered him a wide smile.

"No thanks, I'm just looking.'' Steve paused and glanced over the items on her table. Sterling silver jewelry dotted a black velvet cloth—necklaces, earrings and rings of all sizes and shapes.

"You can't buy silver anywhere for my prices,'' the woman said.

"It's very nice."

"If jewelry doesn't interest you, perhaps these will." She stood and pulled a box of silver objects from beneath the table, lifting it up for him to inspect.

The first thing Steve noticed was a sterling-silver piggy bank. He smiled recalling how he and Carol had dumped their spare change in a piggy bank for months in an effort to save enough for a vacation to Hawaii. They'd spent it instead for the closing costs on the house.

"This is a popular item," the woman told him, bringing out a baby rattle. "Lots of jewelry stores sell these, but no one can beat my prices."

"How much?" Steve couldn't believe he'd asked. What the hell would he do with a baby rattle—especially one made of sterling silver.

The woman stated a reasonable price. "I'll take it," he said, astonished to hear the words come out of his mouth.

"Would you like one with blue ribbon or pink?"

Already Steve regretted the impulse. What was he planning to do? Give it to Carol? He'd decided the best thing for him to do as far as his ex-wife was concerned was to never see her again.

"Sir? Blue or pink?"

"Blue," he answered in a hoarse whisper. For the son he would probably never father. Blue for the color of Carol's eyes when she smiled at him.

By the time Steve walked back to the apartment, the sack containing the silver baby rattle felt like it weighed thirty pounds. By rights, he thought, he should toss the silly thing in the garbage. But he didn't.

He set it on the kitchen counter and opened the refrigerator, looking for something to eat, but nothing interested him. When he turned, the rattle seemed to draw his gaze. He stared at it for a long moment, yearning strongly to press it into the hand of his own child.

Blood thundered in his ears and his heart pounded so hard and fast that his chest ached. He would save the toy for Lindy and Rush whenever they had children, he decided.

Feeling only slightly better, he moved into the living room and turned on the television. He reached for the *TV Guide*, flipped through the pages, sighed and turned off the set. A second later, he rushed to his feet.

He didn't know who the hell he was trying to kid. That silver rattle with the pretty blue ribbon was for Carol and her baby, and it was going to torment him until he got rid of it.

He could mail her the toy and be done with the plaything. Or have Lindy give it to her without letting Carol know it had come from him. Or... or he could just set it on the porch and let her find it.

The last idea appealed to him. He would casually drive by her neighborhood, park his car around the block and wait until it was dark enough to sneak up and leave the rattle on the front step. He was the last person she would ever suspect would do something like that.

With his plan formulated, Steve drove to Carol's house. He was half a block away from her place when he noticed her car. She was leaving. This would work out even better. He could follow her and when she got where she was going, he could place the rattle inside her car. That way she would assume someone had mistaken her car for their own and inadvertently set the rattle inside. There wasn't anything she could do but take it home with her.

Carol headed north on Interstate 5, and her destination was a matter of simple deduction. She was going to the Northgate Mall. Lord, that woman loved to shop. The minute she steered onto the freeway on-ramp, Steve knew exactly where she was headed. They'd been married for five years, and their year apart hadn't changed her. The smug knowledge produced a smile.

But Carol exited before the mall.

Steve's heart started to pound. He was three cars behind her, but if she wasn't going shopping, he didn't know what she was planning. Maybe she was rendezvousing with Todd. Maybe all those times she'd told him she was shopping Carol had actually been meeting with her employer. The muscles in his stomach clenched into a knot so tight and painful that it stole his breath.

If there'd been any way to turn the car around, Steve would have done it, but he was trapped in the center lane of traffic and forced to follow the heavy flow.

It wasn't until they'd gone several blocks that Steve noticed the back side of the mall. Perhaps she'd found a shortcut and had never bothered to tell him about it.

Carol turned onto a busy side street, and against his better judgment, he followed her. A few minutes later, when Carol turned into the large parking lot at Northgate Mall, Steve felt almost giddy with relief.

She parked close to the J.C. Penney store, and Steve eased his vehicle into a slot four spaces over. On a whim, he decided to follow her inside. He'd always wondered what women found so intriguing about shopping.

He was far enough behind her on the escalator to almost lose her. Standing at the top, he searched until he found her standing in women's fashions, sorting through a rack of dresses. It took him a minute to realize they were maternity dresses. Although she'd lost several pounds, she must be having difficulty finding things that fit her, he realized. According to his calculations, she was five months pregnant—probably closer to six.

He lounged around while she took a handful of bright spring dresses and moved into the changing room. Fifteen minutes passed before she returned, and to Steve it felt like a lifetime.

When she returned, she went back to the rack and replaced all but one of the dresses. She held up a pretty blue one with a wide sailor's collar and red tie and studied it carefully. Apparently she changed her mind because she hung it back up with the others. Still she lingered an extra minute, continuing to examine the outfit. She ran her fingers down the sleeve to catch the price tag, read it, shook her head and reluctantly walked away.

The minute she was out of sight, Steve was at the clothing rack. Obviously she wanted the dress, yet she hadn't bought it. He checked the price tag and frowned. It was moderately priced, certainly not exorbitant. If she wanted it, which she apparently did, then she should have it.

For the second time in the same day, Steve found himself making a purchase that was difficult to rationalize. It wasn't as if he had any use for a maternity dress. But why not? he asked himself. If he left the rattle in her car it shouldn't make any difference if he added a dress. It wasn't likely that she would tie him to either purchase. Let her think her fairy godmother was gifting her.

From his position at the cash register, Steve saw Carol walk through the infant's department. She ran her hand over the top rail of a white Jenny Lind crib and examined it with a look of such sweet anticipation that Steve felt guilty for invading her privacy.

"Would you like this dress on the hanger or in a sack?" the salesclerk asked him.

It took Steve a moment to realize she was talking to him. "A sack, please." He couldn't very well walk through the mall carrying a maternity dress.

Carol bought something, too, but Steve couldn't see what it was. Infant T-shirts or something like that, he guessed. His vantage point in the furniture department wasn't the best. Carol started to walk toward him, and he turned abruptly and pretended to be testing out a recliner.

Apparently she didn't see him, and he settled into the seat and expelled a sigh of relief.

"Can I help you?" a salesclerk asked.

"Ah, no, thanks," he said, getting to his feet.

Carol headed down the escalator, and Steve scooted around a couple of women pushing baby strollers in an effort not to lose sight of her.

Carol's steps were filled with purpose as she moved down the wide aisle to women's shoes. She picked up a red low-heeled dress shoe that was on display, but when the clerk approached, she smiled and shook her head. Within a couple of minutes she was on her way.

Feeling more like a fool with every minute, Steve followed her out of the store and into the heart of the mall. The place was packed, as it generally was on Saturday afternoon. Usually Steve avoided the mall on weekends, preferring to do his shopping during the day or at night.

He saw Carol stop at a flower stand and buy herself a red rosebud. She'd always been fond of flowers, and he was pleased that she treated herself to something special.

She'd gone only a few steps when he noticed that her steps had slowed.

Something was wrong. He could tell from the way she walked. He cut across to the other side, where the flow of shoppers was heading in the opposite direction. Feeling like a secret government agent, he pressed himself against the storefront in an effort to watch her more closely. She had pressed her hand to her abdomen and her face had gone deathly pale. She was in serious pain, he determined as a sense of alarm filled him. Steve could feel it as strongly as if he were the one suffering.

Although he was certain she had full view of him, Carol didn't notice. She cut across the streams of shoppers to the benches that lined the middle of the concourse and sat. Her shoulders moved up and down as though she were taking in deep breaths in an effort to control her reaction to whatever was happening. She closed her eyes and bit her lower lip.

The alarm turned to panic. He didn't know what to do. He couldn't rush up to her and demand to know what was wrong. Nor could he casually stroll by and pretend he just happened to be shopping and had stumbled upon her. But something needed to be done—someone had to help her.

Steve had never felt more helpless in his life. Not knowing what else he could do, he walked up and plopped himself down next to her.

"Hi," he said in a falsely cheerful voice.

"Steve." She looked at him, her eyes brimming with tears. She reached for his hand, gripping it so hard her nails cut into his flesh.

All pretense was gone, wiped away by the stampeding fear he sensed in her.

"What's wrong?"

She shook her head. "I . . . I don't know."

Her eyes widened and he was struck by how yellow her skin was. He took her hand in both of his. "You're in pain?"

She nodded. Her fear palatable. "I'm so afraid."

"What do you want me to do?" He debated on whether he should could call for an ambulance or contact her doctor and have him meet them at the hospital.

"I...don't know what's wrong. I've had this pain twice, but it's always gone away after a couple of minutes." She closed her eyes. "Oh, Steve, I'm so afraid I'm going to lose my baby."

Chapter Twelve

Restless, Steve paced the corridor of the maternity ward in Overlake Hospital, his hands stuffed inside his pants pockets. He felt as though he were carrying the world on his shoulders. Each passing minute tightened the knot in his stomach until he was consumed with worry and dread.

He wanted to see Carol—he longed to talk to her—but there wasn't anything more for him to say. He'd done what he could for her, and by rights he should leave. But he couldn't walk away from her. Not now. Not when she needed him.

Not knowing what else to do, he found a pay phone and contacted his sister.

"Lindy, it's Steve."

"Steve, how are you? I'm so glad you phoned; I haven't stopped thinking about you."

She sounded so pleased to hear from him, and he swallowed down his guilt for the way he'd treated her. He'd been rude and unreasonable when she'd only been showing concern for him.

"I'm fine," he said hurriedly, "Listen, I'm at Overlake Hospital..."

"You're at the hospital? You're fine, but you're at Over-lake? Good God, what happened? I knew it, I just knew something like this was going to happen. I felt it . . ."

"Lindy, shut up for a minute, would you?"

"No, I won't shut up—I'm family, Steve Kyle. Family. If you can't come to me when you're hurting, just who can you go to? You seem to think I'm too young to know anything about emotional pain, but you're wrong. When Paul dumped me it wasn't any Sunday-school picnic."

"I'm not the one in need of medical attention—it's Carol."

"Carol!" His blurted announcement seemed to sweep away all his sister's pent-up frustration. "What's wrong?" she asked quietly.

"I don't exactly know; the doctor's still with her. I think she might be losing the baby. She needs a woman—I'm the last person who should be here. I didn't know who else to call. Can you come?"

"Of course. I'll be there as fast as I can."

It seemed as though no more than a couple of minutes had passed before Lindy came rushing down the hall. He stood at the sight of her, immensely grateful. Relief washed over him and he wrapped his arms around her.

"The doctor hasn't come out yet," he explained before she could ask. He released her and checked his watch. "It's been over an hour now."

"What happened?"

"I'm not sure. Carol started having some kind of abdominal pains. I phoned her gynecologist, and after I explained what was happening, he suggested we meet him here."

"You said you thought Carol might be having a miscarriage?"

"Good Lord, I don't know anything about this woman stuff. All I can tell you is that she was in agony. I did the only thing I could—I got her here." The ten minutes it took to get Carol to the emergency room had been emotionally draining. She was terrified of losing the baby and had wept almost uncontrolla-bly. Through her sobs she'd told him how much she wanted her baby and how this pregnancy would be her only opportunity. Little of what she'd said had made sense to Steve. He'd tried to find the words to assure her, but he hadn't really known what to say.

Just then Steve noticed Carol's physician, Dr. Stewart, push open the swinging door and walk toward the waiting area. He met him halfway.

"How is she?" he asked, his heart in his throat.

The gynecologist rubbed his hand down the side of his jaw and shook his head. His frown crowded his brows together. "She's as good as can be expected."

"The baby?"

"The pregnancy is progressing nicely... thus far."

Although the child wasn't his and Carol had tried to trick him into believing otherwise, Steve still felt greatly relieved knowing that her baby wasn't in any immediate danger.

"I'm sorry to keep you waiting so long, but quite frankly Carol's symptoms had me stumped. It's unusual for someone her age to suffer from this sort of problem."

"What problem?" Lindy blurted out.

"Gall bladder."

"Gall bladder," Steve repeated frowning. He didn't know what he'd expected, but it certainly hadn't been that.

"She tells me she's been suffering from flulike symptoms, which she accepted as morning sickness. There wasn't any reason for either of us to assume otherwise. Some of her other discomforts can be easily misinterpreted as well.

"The most serious threat at the moment is that she's dangerously close to being dehydrated. Predictably that has prompted other health risks."

"What do you mean?" Lindy asked.

"Her sodium and potassium levels have dropped and her heart rate is erratic. I've started an IV and that problem should take care of itself within a matter of hours."

"What's going to happen?"

Once more, Dr. Stewart ran a hand down the side of his face and shook his head. His kind eyes revealed his concern. "I've called in a surgeon friend of mine, and we're going to do a few more preliminary tests. But from what I'm seeing at this point, I don't think we can put off operating. Her gall bladder appears to be acutely swollen and is causing an obstruction."

"If you do the surgery, what will happen to the baby?" For Carol's sake, Steve prayed for the tiny life she was carrying.

Dr. Stewart's sober expression turned grim. "There's always a risk to the pregnancy when anesthesia is involved. I'd like to delay this, but I doubt that we can. Under normal conditions gall-bladder surgery can be scheduled at a patient's convenience, but not in Carol's case, I fear. But I want you to know, we'll do everything I can to save the child."

"Please try." Carol had looked at him with such terror and helplessness that he couldn't help being affected. He would do everything humanly possible to see that she carried this child to full term.

"Please do what you can," Lindy added her own plea. "This child means a great deal to her."

Dr. Stewart nodded. "Carol's sleeping now, but you can see her for a couple of minutes, if you'd like. One at a time."

Steve looked to Lindy, who gestured for him to go in first. He smiled his appreciation and followed the grandfatherly doctor into Carol's room.

As Dr. Stewart had explained, she was sleeping soundly. She looked incredibly fragile with tubes stretching down from an IV pole to connect with the veins in her arm.

Steve stood beside her for several minutes, loving her completely. Emotion clogged his throat and he turned away. He loved her; he always would. No matter what had happened in the past, he couldn't imagine a future without Carol.

"How is she?" Lindy asked when he came out of the room.

He found he couldn't answer her with anything more than a short nod.

Lindy disappeared and returned five minutes later. By then Steve had had a chance to form a plan of action, and he felt better for it.

As Lindy stepped toward him, he held her gaze with new-found determination. He and Carol were both fools if they thought they could stay apart. It wasn't going to work. Without Carol he was only half-alive. And she'd admitted how miserable she'd been during their year's separation.

"I'm going to marry her," Steve informed his sister brusquely.

"What?" Lindy looked at him as though she'd misheard him.

"I'm going to get the chaplain to come to the hospital, and I'm going to marry Carol."

Lindy studied him for several moments. "Don't you think she should have some say in this?"

"Yes . . . no."

"But I thought . . . Carol told me you didn't believe the baby is yours."

"It isn't."

Lindy rolled her eyes, then shook her head, her features tight with impatience. "That is the most ridiculous thing you've ever said. Honestly, Steve, where do you come up with these crazy ideas?"

"What idea? That the baby isn't mine, or remarrying Carol?"

"Both!"

"Whether or not I'm the father doesn't make one bit of difference. I've decided it doesn't matter. From here on out, I'm claiming her child as mine."

"But . . ."

"I don't care. I love Carol and I'll learn to love her baby. That's the end of it." Once the decision had been made, it felt right. The two of them had played a fool's game for over a year, but no more—he wouldn't stand for it. "I'm not going to put up with any arguments from you or from Carol. I want her as my wife—we were wrong ever to have gone through with the divorce. All I'm doing now is correcting a mistake that should never have happened," he told his sister in a voice that men jumped to obey.

Lindy took a moment to digest his words. "Don't you think you should discuss this in a rational matter with Carol? Don't you think she should have some input into her own life?"

"I suppose. But she needs me—although she isn't likely to admit it."

"You've had just as difficult a time recognizing that fact yourself."

"Not anymore."

"When do you plan to tell her?"

Steve didn't know. He'd only reached this conclusion in the last five minutes, but already he felt in control of his life again.

"Well?" his sister pressed.

"I haven't figured out when. . . . Before the surgery, I think, if it can be arranged."

"Steve, you're not thinking clearly. Carol isn't going to want to be married sitting in a hospital bed, looking all sickly and pale."

"The sooner we get this settled the better."

"For whom?" Lindy prompted.

"For both of us."

Lindy threw up her hands. "Sometimes the things you say utterly shock me."

"They do?" Steve didn't care—he felt as if he could float out of the hospital, he was so relieved. Carol would probably come through the surgery with flying colors and everything would fall into place the way it should have long ago. This had certainly been a crazy day. He'd bought a sterling silver rattle, followed Carol around a shopping mall like an FBI agent, driven her to the hospital, then made a decision that would go a long way toward assuring their happy future. Steve sighed deeply, feeling suddenly weary.

"Is there any other bombshell you'd care to hit me with?" Lindy asked teasingly.

Steve paused and then surprised her by nodding. Some of the happiness he'd experienced earlier vanished. There was one other decision he'd made—one not as pleasant but equally necessary.

"Should I sit down for this one?" Lindy asked, still grinning. She slipped her arm around his waist and looked up at him.

"I don't think so."

"Well, don't keep me in suspense, big brother."

Steve regarded her soberly. "I'm leaving the Navy."

Chapter Thirteen

Carol opened her eyes slowly. The room was dim, the blinds over the window closed. She frowned when her gaze fell on the IV stand, and she tried to raise herself.

"You're in the hospital." Steve's voice was warm and caressing.

She lowered her head back to the pillow and turned toward the sound. Steve stood at her bedside. From the ragged, tired look about him, she guessed he'd been standing there all night.

"How long have you been here?" she asked hoarsely, testing her tongue.

"Not very long."

She closed her eyes and grinned. "You never could tell a decent lie."

He brushed the hair from her cheek and his fingers lingered on her face as though he needed to touch her. She knew she should ask him to leave, but his presence comforted her. She needed him. She didn't know how he'd happened to be at Northgate Mall, but she would always be grateful he'd found her when he did.

Her hand moved to her stomach, and she flattened it there. "The baby's all right?"

Steve didn't answer her for a moment, and a sickening sense of dread filled her. Her eyes flew open. The doctor had repeatedly assured her that the baby was safe, but something might have happened while she had slept. She'd been out for hours and much of what had taken place after they arrived at the hospital remained foggy in her mind.

"Everything's fine with the pregnancy."

"Thank God," she whispered fervently.

"Dr. Stewart said you were near exhaustion." He reached for her hand and laced his fingers with hers. His thumb worked back and forth on the inside of her wrist.

"I think I could sleep for a week," Carol said, her voice starting to sound more sure. It seemed as though it had been years since she'd had a decent rest. Even before her pregnancy had been confirmed she'd felt physically and emotionally drained, as if she were running on a treadmill, working as fast as her legs would carry her and getting nowhere.

"How do you feel now?"

Carol had to think about it. "Different. I don't know how to describe it. I'm not exactly sick and I'm not in any pain, but something's not right, either."

"You should have recognized that weeks ago. According to Dr. Stewart, you've probably been feeling ill for months."

"They know what's causing the problem?" Her heart started to work doubly hard. Not until the severe attack of pain in the shopping mall had she been willing to admit something could be wrong with her.

"Dr. Stewart thinks it could be your gall bladder."

"My what?"

"Gall bladder," he repeated softly. "I'm sure he can explain it far better than I can, but from what I understand it's a pear-shaped pouch close to the liver."

Carol arched her brows at his attempt at humor and offered him a weak smile. "That explains it."

Steve grinned back at her, and for a moment everything went still. His eyes held such tenderness that she dared to hope again—dared to believe he'd discovered the truth about her and their baby. Dared to let the love that was stored in her heart shine through her eyes.

"I never thought I'd see you again," she said, and her voice quivered with emotion.

Steve lowered his gaze briefly. "I couldn't stay away. I love you too much."

"Oh, Steve, how could we do this to each other? You think such terrible things of me and I can't bear it anymore. I keep telling myself the baby and I would be better off without you, and then I feel only half alive. When we're separated, nothing feels right in my life—nothing is good."

"When I'm not with you, I'm only a shell." He raised her hand to his lips and kissed her knuckles.

Carol felt the tears gather in her eyes and she turned her head away, unwilling to have Steve witness her emotion. No man would ever be more right for her, and no man could ever be so wrong.

She heard the sound of a chair being pushed to the side of the bed. "I want us to remarry," he said firmly. "I've thought it over. In fact, I haven't thought of anything else in the past fifteen hours—and I'm convinced this is the right thing for us to do."

Carol knew it was right, too. "But what about the baby?" she whispered. "You think—"

"From this moment on, the child is mine in my heart and in my soul. He's a part of you and that's the only important thing."

"She," Carol corrected absently. "I'm having a girl."

"Okay...whatever you want as long as we're together."

Carol's mind flooded with arguments, but she hadn't the strength to fight him. The intervening months would convince Steve that this child was his far better than any eloquent speeches she could give him now. By the time the baby was born, his doubts would have vanished completely. In the meantime they would find a way to settle matters—that was essential because they were both so miserable apart.

"Will you marry me, Carol, a second time?"

"I want to say yes. Everything within me is telling me it's the right thing to do...for me and for the baby. But I'm frightened, too."

"I'm going to be a good husband and father, I promise you that."

"I know you will."

"I made another decision yesterday—one that will greatly affect both our lives." His hand pressed against the side of her face and gently brushed the hair from her temple. "I'm leaving the Navy."

Carol couldn't believe her ears. The military was Steve's life; it had been his goal from the time he was a teenager. His dream. He'd never wanted to be or do anything else.

"But you love your work."

"I love you more," he countered.

"It's not an either-or situation, Steve. I've lived all these years as a Navy wife, I've adjusted."

A hint of a smile touched his face. "I won't be separated from you again."

For Steve's sake, Carol had always put on a happy face and seen him off with a cheerful wave, but she'd hated the life, dreading their months apart. Always had and always would. The promise of a more conventional marriage seemed too good to be true. Her head was swimming at the thought of him working a nine-to-five job. She wanted this—she wanted it badly.

"You're the most important person in my life. I'm getting out of the Navy so I can be the kind of husband and father I should be."

"Oh, Steve." The joy that cascaded through her at that moment brought tears to her eyes.

"I can't think of any other way to show you how serious I am."

Neither could Carol. Nevertheless his announcement worried her. Navy life was in Steve's blood, and she didn't know if he could find happiness outside the only career he'd ever known.

"Let's not make such a major decision now," she suggested reluctantly. "There'll be plenty of time to talk about this later."

Steve's eyes filled with tenderness. "Whatever you say."

Humming softly, a nurse wandered into the room and greeted them. "Good morning."

"Morning," Carol answered.

The room was bathed in the soft light of day as the middle-aged woman opened the blinds.

"I'm sorry, but there won't be any breakfast for you this morning. Dr. Stewart will be in later, and I'm sure he'll schedule something for you to eat this afternoon."

Carol didn't feel the least bit hungry. Her appetite had been almost nonexistent for months.

"I'll check on you in an hour," the woman said on her way out the door.

Carol nodded. "Thank you." She was filled with nagging questions about what was going to happen. Naturally she hoped Dr. Stewart could give her a prescription and send her home, but she had the feeling she was being overly optimistic.

Steve must have read the doubt in her eyes because he said, "From what Dr. Stewart told me, he's going to have you complete a series of tests this morning. Following those, we'll be able to make a decision."

"What kind of tests? What kind of decision?"

"Honey, I don't know, but don't worry. I'm not leaving you—not for a minute."

Carol hated to be such a weakling, but she was frightened. "Whatever happens, whatever they have to do, I can take it," she said a little shakily.

"I know you can, love. I know you can."

As promised, for the next few hours Carol underwent several tests. She was pinched, poked and prodded and wheeled to several corners of the hospital. As Steve promised, he was with her each time they took her into another and waiting when she returned.

"Quit looking so worried," she told him, when she'd been wheeled back to her room once more. "I'm going to be fine."

"I know."

She slept after that and woke late in the afternoon. Once more Steve was at her bedside, leaning forward, his face in his hands.

"Bad news?" she asked.

He smiled and Carol could tell by the stiff way his mouth moved that the action was forced.

"What's wrong?" she demanded.

He stood and came to stand beside her. She gave him her hand, her eyes wide with fear.

"Dr. Stewart assured me that under normal conditions, gall bladder surgery is optional. But not in your case. Your gall bladder is acutely swollen and is causing several complications to vital organs. It has to be removed, and the sooner the better.''

Carol expelled her breath and nodded. She'd feared something like this, but she was young and healthy and strong; everything would be fine.

"He's called in a surgeon and they've scheduled the operating room for you first thing tomorrow morning.''

Carol swallowed her worry. "I can handle that.''

"This isn't minor surgery, Carol. I don't think you'd appreciate me minimizing the risks.''

"No...no, I wouldn't.''

"Dr. Stewart and his associate will be back later today to explain the details of what they'll be doing. It's major surgery, but you have several things in your favor.''

She nodded, appreciating the fact that she would know precisely what the medical team would be doing to her body.

"What about the baby?''

Steve's expression tightened and he lifted his eyes from hers. "The pregnancy poses a problem.''

"What kind of problem?''

"If the surgery could be delayed, Dr. Stewart would prefer to do that, but it can't be. Your life is at risk.''

"What about the pregnancy?'' Carol demanded. "I'm not agreeing to anything until I hear what will happen to my baby.''

Steve's eyes revealed myriad emotions. Worry and fear dominated, but there was something else—something that took her an extended moment to analyze. Something that clouded his features and ravaged his face. Regret, she decided, then quickly changed her mind. It was more than that—a deep inner sorrow, even remorse.

When Steve spoke, it was as if each word had to be tugged from his mouth. "I'm not going to coat the truth. There's a chance the anesthesia will terminate the pregnancy.''

"I won't do it,'' she cried automatically. "The whole thing's off. I'm not doing anything that will hurt my baby.''

"Carol, listen to reason...''

"No.'' She twisted her head so that she wouldn't have to look at him. As long as she drew a single breath there was no way she would agree to do anything that would harm her daughter.

"Honey," he whispered. "We don't have any choice. If we delay the surgery, you could die."

"Then so be it."

"No." He almost shouted the word. "There's a risk to the baby, but one we're both going to have to take. There's no other choice."

She closed her eyes, unwilling to argue with him further. Her mind was made up.

"Carol, I don't like this any better than you do."

She refused to look at him and pinched her lips together, determined not to murmur a single word. Nothing he could say would change her mind.

The silence in the room was magnified to deafening proportions.

"I love you, Carol, and I can't allow you to chance your life for a baby. If the worst happens and the pregnancy is terminated, then we'll have to accept it. There'll be other children—lots more—and the next time there won't be any question about who the father is."

If Steve had driven a stake into her heart, he couldn't have hurt her more. No words had ever been more cruel. No wonder he was so willing to tell her he'd decided to accept this child as his own. She would likely lose the baby, and believing what he did, Steve no doubt felt that was for the best.

Carol jerked her head around so fast she nearly dislocated her neck. "The next time there won't be any questions?" she repeated in a small, still voice.

"I know this is painful for you, but—"

"I want *this* baby."

"Carol, please . . ."

"How long have you known about this danger?"

Steve looked stunned by her anger. "Dr. Stewart told me about the possibility after I brought you to the hospital yesterday."

Exactly what she'd expected. Everything Steve had done, everything he'd said from that point on was suddenly suspect. He wanted them to remarry and he was going to leave the Navy. His reasoning became as clear as water to her: he didn't really long for a change in their life-style, nor had his offer to leave the Navy been a decision based on his desire to build a strong marital relationship. He didn't dread their separations as she always had—he'd thrived on them. But if he wasn't in the military, then he could spend his days watching her. There would be no opportunity for her to have an affair. And when she became pregnant a second time, he would have the assurance that the baby was indeed his. His offer hadn't been made from love but from fear rooted in a lack of trust.

It amazed her, now that she thought about it, that he would be willing to give up such a promising career for her. He really did love her, in his own way, but not enough. Ultimately he would regret his decision, and so would she. But by then it would be too late.

"I'm probably doing a bad job of this," he said, and rammed his fingers through his hair. "I should have let Dr. Stewart explain everything to you."

"No," she said dispassionately. "What you've told me explains a good deal. You've been completely up-front with me and I appreciate what it cost you to tell me this. I...I think it's my turn to be honest with you now."

A dark frown contorted his features. "Carol..."

"No, it's time you finally learned the truth. I hesitated when you asked me to marry you and there's a reason. You don't need to worry about me, Steve. You never had to. My baby's father has promised to take care of me. When my plan to trick you didn't work, I contacted him and told him I was pregnant. He thought about it for a couple of days and has decided to marry me himself. I appreciate your offer, but it isn't necessary."

Steve looked as if she'd slipped a knife into his stomach.

"You're lying."

"No, for once I'm telling you the truth. Go back to your life and I'll go on with mine. We'll both be far happier this way."

He didn't move for several minutes. His hands curved around the raised railing at the side of the bed and she swore his grip was strong enough to permanently mark the bars. His eyes hardened to chips of glacial ice.

"Who is the father?" he demanded.

Carol closed her eyes, determined not to answer.

"Who is he?"

She looked away, but his fingers closed around her chin and forced her face back toward him.

"Todd?"

She was sick of hearing that name. "No."

"Who?"

"No one you know," she shouted.

"Is he married?"

"No."

A pounding, vibrating silence followed.

"Is this what you really want?"

"Yes," she told him. "Yes...."

A year seemed to pass before she heard him leave the room. When he did, each step he took away from her sounded like nails being pounded into a coffin.

It was finished. There was no going back now. Steve Kyle was out of her life and she'd made certain he would never come back.

Carol felt as if she were walking through a thick bog, every step was hindered, her progress painstakingly slow. A mist rose from the marsh, blocking her view, and she struggled to look into the distance, seeking the light, but she was met instead by more fog.

A soft cry—like that of a small animal—reverberated around her, and it took her a minute to realize she was the one who had made the sound.

She wasn't in any pain. Not physically anyway.

The agony she suffered came from deep inside—a weight of grief so heavy no human should ever be expected to carry it. Carol couldn't understand what had happened or why she felt this crippling sense of loss.

Then it came to her.

Her baby... they couldn't delay the surgery. The fog parted and a piece of her memory slipped into place. Steve had walked away from her, and soon after he'd gone she'd suffered another attack that had doubled her over with excruciating pain. The hospital staff had called for Dr. Stewart and surgery had been arranged immediately. The option of waiting for even one day had been taken out of her hands.

Now Steve was out of her life and she'd lost her baby, too.

Moisture ran down the side of her face, but when she tried to lift her hand, she found she hadn't the strength.

A sob came, wrenched from her soul. There would be no more children for her. She was destined to live alone for the rest of her life.

"Nurse, do something. She's in pain."

The words drifted from a great distance, and she tossed her head to and fro in an effort to discover the source. She saw no one in the fog. No one.

Once more the debilitating sense of loneliness overtook her and she was alone. Whoever had been there had left her to find her own way through the darkness.

More sobs came—her own, she realized—erupting in deafening sound all around her.

Then she felt something—a hand she thought—warm and gentle, press over her abdomen. The weight of it was a comfort she couldn't describe.

"Your baby's alive," the voice told her. "Can you feel him? He's going to live and so are you!"

It was a voice of authority, a voice of a man who spoke with confidence; a voice few would question.

A familiar voice.

The dark fog started to close in again and Carol wanted to shout for it to stop. She stumbled toward the light, but it was shut off from her, and she found herself trapped in a black void, defenseless and lost. She didn't know if she would ever have the strength to escape it.

A persistent squeak interrupted Carol's sleep. A wheel far off in the distance was badly in need of oil. The irritating ruckus grew louder until Carol decided it would be useless to try to ignore it any longer.

She opened her eyes to discover Steve's sister standing over her.

"Lindy?"

"Carol, oh, Carol, you're awake."

"Shouldn't I be?" she asked. Her former sister-in-law looked as if she were about to burst into tears.

"I can't believe it. We've been so worried…. No one thought you were going to make it." Lindy cupped her hands over her mouth and nose. "We nearly lost you, Carol Kyle!"

"You did?" This was news to her. She had little memory. The dreadful pain had returned—she remembered that. And then she'd been trapped in that marsh, lost and confused, but it hadn't felt so bad. She had been hot—so terribly hot—she recalled, but there were pleasant memories there, too. Some-one had called out to her from there, assured her. She couldn't place what the voice had said, but she remembered how she'd struggled to walk toward the sound of it. The voice hadn't al-ways been comforting. Carol recalled how one time it had shouted at her, harsh and demanding. She hadn't wanted to obey it then and had tried to escape, but the voice had fol-lowed her relentlessly, refusing to leave her alone.

"How do you feel?"

"Like I've been asleep for a week."

"Make that two."

"Two?" Carol echoed, shocked. "That long?"

"All right, *almost* two weeks. It's actually been ten days. You had emergency surgery and then everything that could go wrong did. Oh, Carol, you nearly died."

"My baby's okay, isn't she?" From somewhere deep inside her heart came the reassurance that whatever else had hap-pened, the child had survived. Carol vividly remembered the voice telling her so.

"Your baby is one hell of a little fighter."

Carol smiled. "Good."

Lindy moved a chair closer to the bed and sat down. "The doctor said he felt you'd come out of it today. You made a turn for the better around midnight."

"What time is it now?"

Lindy checked her watch. "About 9:00 a.m."

Already her eyes felt incredibly heavy. "I think I could sleep some more."

"As well you should."

Carol tried to smile. "So my daughter is a fighter.... Maybe I'll name her Sugar Ray Kyle."

"Go ahead and get some rest. I'll be here when you wake up."

Already Carol felt herself drifting off, but it was a pleasant sensation. The warm black folds closed their arms around her in a welcoming embrace.

When she stirred a second time, she discovered Lindy was at her bedside reading.

"Is this a vigil or something?" she asked, grinning. "Every time I wake up, you're here."

"I wanted to be sure you were really coming out of it," Lindy told her.

"I feel much better."

"You *look* much better."

The inside of her mouth felt like a sewer. "Do you have any idea how long it'll be before I can go home?"

"You won't. You're coming to live with Rush and me for a couple of weeks until you regain your strength. And we won't take no for an answer."

"But—"

"No arguing!" Lindy's smile softened her brook-no-nonsense tone.

"I don't deserve a friend as good as you," Carol murmured, awed by Lindy's generosity.

"We should be sisters, and you know it."

Carol chose not to answer that. She preferred to push any thoughts of her ex-husband from her mind.

"This probably isn't the time to talk about Steve."

It wasn't, but Carol didn't stop her.

"I don't know what you said to him, but he doesn't seem to think you want to see him again. Carol, he's been worried sick over you. Won't you at least talk to him?"

A lump the size of a goose egg formed in her throat. "No," she whispered. "I don't want to have anything to do with Steve. We're better off divorced."

Chapter Fourteen

"I'm not an invalid," Carol insisted, frowning at her ex-sister-in-law as she carried her own breakfast dishes to the sink.

"But you've only been out of the hospital a week," Lindy argued, flittering around her like a mother hen protecting her smallest chick.

"For heaven's sake, sit down," Carol cried, "before you drive me crazy!"

"All right, all right."

Carol shared a knowing smile with Rush Callaghan, Lindy's husband. He was a different man than the Rush Carol had known before his marriage to Lindy. He smiled openly now. Laughed. Carol had been fond of Rush, but he'd always been so very serious—all Navy. The military wouldn't find a man more loyal than Rush, but loving Lindy had changed him—and for the better. Lindy had brought sunshine and laughter into his life and brightened his world in a wide spectrum of rainbow colors.

"Come on, Lindy," Rush said, "you can walk me to the door and kiss me goodbye."

With an eagerness that made Carol smile, her good friend escorted Rush to the front door and lingered there several minutes.

When she returned, Lindy walked blindly into the kitchen, wearing a dazed, contented grin. She plopped herself down in a chair, reached for her empty coffee cup and sighed. "He'll be gone for a couple of days."

"Are you going to suffer those Navy blues?"

"I suppose," Lindy said. She lifted her mug and rested her elbows on the table. "I'm a little giddy this morning because Rush and I reached a major decision last night." She smiled and the sun seemed to shine through her eyes. "We're going to start a family. Our first wedding anniversary is coming up soon, and we thought this would be a good way to celebrate."

"Sweet potatoes," Carol said, grinning from ear to ear. "They worked for me."

Lindy gave her a look that insinuated that perhaps Carol should return to the hospital for much-needed psychiatric treatment. "What was that?"

"Sweet potatoes. You know—yams. I heard a medical report over the news last year that reported the results of a study done on a tribe in Africa whose diet staple was sweet potatoes. The results revealed a higher estrogen level in the women and they attributed that fact to the yams."

"I see."

Lindy continued to study her closely. Carol giggled. "I'm not joking! They really work. I wanted to get pregnant and I couldn't count on anything more from Steve than Christmas Eve, so I ate enough sweet potatoes for my body to float in the hormone."

"One night did it?" Lindy's interest was piqued, although she struggled not to show it.

"Two actually—but who knows how long it would have taken otherwise. I ate that vegetable in every imaginable form—including some I wouldn't recommend. If you want, I'll loan you my collection of recipes."

A slow smile spread over Lindy's face, catching in her lovely brown eyes. "I want!"

Carol rinsed her plate and stuck it inside the dishwasher.

"Let me do that!" Lindy insisted, jumping to her feet. "Honest to goodness, Carol. You're so stubborn."

"No, please, I want to help. It makes me feel like I'm being useful." She never had been one to sit and do nothing. This period of convalescence had been troubling enough without Lindy babying her.

"You're recovering from major surgery for heaven's sake!" Steve's sister insisted.

"I'm fine."

"Now, maybe, but a week ago...."

Even now Carol had a difficult time realizing how close she'd come to losing her life. It was the voice that had pulled her back, refusing to let her slip into the darkness, the voice that had urged her to live. Something deep within her subconscious had demanded she cling to life when it would have been so easy to surrender.

"Lindy, I need to ask you something." Unexpectedly Carol's mind was buzzing with doubts about the future.

"Sure, what is it?"

"If anything were to happen to me after the baby's born—"

"Nothing's going to happen to you," Lindy argued.

"Probably not." Carol pulled out the kitchen chair and sat down. She didn't want to sound as though she had a death wish, but with the baby came a responsibility she hadn't thought of before her illness. "I don't have much in the way of family. My mother died several years ago—soon after Steve . . . soon after I was married. She and my father were divorced years before, and I hardly know him. He has another family and I rarely hear from him."

Lindy nodded. "Dr. Elgin, the surgeon, asked us to contact any close family members and Steve phoned your father. He . . . he couldn't come."

"He's a busy man," Carol said, willingly offering an excuse for her father, the way she had for most of her life. "But if I were to die," she persisted, "there'd be no one to raise my baby."

"Steve . . ."

Carol shook her head. "No. He'll probably marry again and have his own family someday. And if he doesn't, he'll be so involved in the Navy he won't be much good for raising a child." It was so much to ask of anyone, even a friend as near and dear as Lindy. "Would you and Rush consider being her guardians?"

"Of course, Carol," Lindy assured her warmly. "But nothing's going to happen to you."

Carol smiled. "I certainly plan on living a long, productive life, but something like this surgery hits close to home."

"I'll talk it over with Rush, but I'm sure he'll be more than willing for us to be your baby's guardians."

"Thank you," Carol said, and impulsively hugged Lindy. Steve's family had always been good to her.

"Okay, now that that's settled, how about a hot game of gin rummy? I feel lucky."

"Sure..." Carol paused and her eyes rounded. Her hand moved to the slight curve of her stomach as her heart filled with happiness.

"Are you all right?"

"I'm fine. The baby just moved—she does that quite a bit now—but never this strong."

"Does it hurt?"

Carol shook her head. "Not in the least. I don't know how to describe it, but every time she decides to explore her little world, I get excited. In four short months I'll be holding my daughter. Oh, Lindy, I can hardly believe it...I can hardly wait."

"Have you ever considered the possibility that *she* might be a *he*?"

"Nope. Not once. The moment I decided to get pregnant, I put my order in for a girl. The least Steve could do was get that right." His name slipped out unnoticed, but as soon as it left her lips, Carol stiffened. She was doing her utmost to disentangle him from her life, peeling away the threads that were so securely wrapped around her soul. There was no going back now, she realized. She'd confirmed every insulting thing he'd ever accused her of.

The mention of Steve seemed to subdue them both.

"Have you chosen a name for the baby?" Lindy asked a little too brightly in an all too apparent effort to change the subject.

Carol dropped her gaze. She'd originally intended to name the baby Stephanie, after Steve, but she'd since decided against that. There would be enough reminders that Steve was her baby's father without using his name. "Not yet," she answered.

"And you're feeling better?"

"Much." Although she was enjoying staying with Lindy and Rush, Carol longed to go back to her own home. Now that Steve was completely out of her life, living with his sister was flirting with misery. Twice Lindy had tried to casually bring Steve into their conversation. Carol had swiftly stopped her both times, but she didn't know who it was harder on—Lindy or herself. She didn't want to hear about Steve, didn't want to think about him.

Not anymore. Not again.

"So how are you feeling, young lady?" Dr. Stewart asked as he walked into the examination room. "I'll have you know you gave us all quite a scare."

"That's what I hear." This was her first appointment to see Dr. Stewart since she'd left the hospital. She'd been through a series of visits with the surgeon, Dr. Elgin, and everything was progressing as it should with the post-surgery healing.

"And how's that little fighter been treating you lately?" he asked with an affectionate chuckle, eyeing Carol's tummy. "Is the baby moving regularly now?"

She nodded eagerly. "All the time."

"Excellent."

"She seems determined to make herself felt."

"This is only the beginning," Dr. Stewart said chuckling. "Wait a few months and then tell me what you think."

The nurse came into the room and Carol lay back on the examination table while the doctor listened for the baby's heartbeat. He grinned and Carol smiled back. Her world might be crumbling around the edges, but the baby filled her with purpose and hope for a brighter future.

"You've returned to work?"

She nodded. "Part-time for the next couple of weeks, then full-time depending on how tired I get. Despite everything, I actually feel terrific."

He helped her into an upright position. "It's little wonder after what you went through—anything is bound to be an improvement." As he spoke he made several notations in her file. "You were one sick young lady. I don't mind telling you," Dr. Stewart added, looking up from her chart, "I was greatly impressed with that young man of yours."

Carol's smile was forced and her heart lurched at the reference to Steve. "Thank you."

"He wouldn't leave your side—not for a moment. Dr. Elgin commented on the fact just the other day. We both believe it was his love that got you through those darkest hours. He was determined that you live." He paused and chuckled softly. "I don't think God Himself would have dared to claim you."

Carol dropped her gaze, not knowing how to comment.

"He's a fine young man. Navy?"

"Yes."

"Give him my regards, will you?"

Carol nodded, her eyes avoiding his.

"Continue with the vitamins and make an appointment to see me in a couple of weeks." He gently patted Carol's hand and moved out of the room.

From the doctor's office, Carol returned to work. But when she pulled into the Boeing parking lot, she sat in her car for several moments, mulling over what Dr. Stewart had told her.

It was Steve's voice that called to her in the dark fog. Steve had been the one who'd comforted her. And when she'd felt the pull of the night, it was he who had demanded she return to the light. According to Dr. Stewart, he'd refused to leave her side.

Carol hadn't known.

She was stunned. She'd purposely lied to him, wanting to hurt him for being so insensitive about the possibility of the surgery claiming their baby's life. She'd been confused and angry because so much of what he wanted for her revealed his lack of faith in her integrity.

She'd sent him away and yet he'd refused to leave her to suffer through the ordeal alone.

Before she returned to her own job section, Carol stopped off to see Lindy.

"Hi," Lindy greeted, looking up from her desk. "What did the doctor have to say?"

"Take your vitamins and see me in two weeks."

"That sounds profound."

Carol scooted a chair toward Lindy's desk and clasped her purse tightly between her hands. The action produced a wide-eyed stare from her former sister-in-law.

"Something Dr. Stewart did say was profound," Carol stated in even tones, although the information Dr. Stewart had given her had shaken her soul.

"Oh? What?"

"He told me Steve was with me every minute after the surgery. He claimed it was Steve who got me through it alive."

"He was there, all right," Lindy confirmed readily. "No one could get him to leave you. You know how stubborn he is. I think he was afraid that if he walked away, you'd die."

"You didn't tell me that."

"Of course I didn't! If you'll recall, I've been forbidden to even mention his name. You practically have a seizure if I so much as hint that there could be someone named Steve distantly related to either of us."

"But i'd told him the baby wasn't his. . . . I sent him away."

"You told him what?" Lindy demanded, her eyes as round as dinner plates. "Why? Carol, how could you? Oh, good grief—it isn't any wonder you two have problems. It's like watching a boxing match. You seem to take turns throwing punches at each other."

"He . . . didn't say anything?"

"No. Steve never tells me what's going on in his life. No matter what's happened between you two, he won't say a word. I still don't know the reason you divorced in the first place. Even Rush isn't sure what happened. Steve's like that—he keeps everything to himself."

"And he stayed with me, even after I said I wouldn't remarry him," Carol murmured, feeling worse by the moment.

"There will never be anyone else for him but you, Carol," Lindy murmured. Some of the indignation had left her, but she still carried an affronted look, as if she wanted to stand up and defend her brother.

Carol didn't need Lindy's outrage in order to feel guilty. Lying had never set well with her, but Steve had hurt her so badly. She would like to think that she'd been delirious with pain at the time and not herself, but that wasn't the case. When she'd told Steve that she was going to accept another man's marriage proposal, she'd known exactly what she was doing.

"I owe him so much," Carol murmured absentmindedly.

"According to the surgeon and Dr. Stewart, you owe Steve your life."

Carol's gaze held Lindy's. "Why didn't you say something earlier?"

Lindy tossed her hands into the air. "You wouldn't let me. Remember?"

"I know . . . I'm sorry." Carol felt like weeping. Lindy was right, so very right. Her relationship with Steve was like a championship boxing match. Although they loved each other, they continued to strike out in a battle of words and deeds.

It wasn't until after she got home and had time to think matters through that Carol decided what she needed to do—what she had to do.

It wouldn't be easy.

Steve read the directions on the back of the frozen dinner entrée and turned the dial on the oven to the appropriate setting. He never had been much of a cook, choosing to eat most of his meals out. Lately, however, even that was more of an effort than he wanted to make. He'd been reduced to frozen TV dinners.

While they were married, Carol had—

Steve ground his thoughts to a screeching halt as he forced the name of his ex-wife from his mind. It astonished him how easily she slipped in where he desperately didn't want her. Yet he was doing everything he could to try to forget the portion of his life that they'd shared.

But that was more easily said than done.

He hadn't asked Lindy about Carol since she'd been released from the hospital. He wanted to know if Todd Larson was giving her the time she needed from work to heal properly. The amount of control it demanded to avoid the subject of Carol with his sister depleted his energy. He was like a man lost in the middle of a desert, dying of thirst. And water was well within sight, but he dared not drink.

Carol had her own life, and now that she and the baby were safe, she was free to seek her own happiness. As he could—only there would be little contentment in his life without her.

The sound of the doorbell caught him by surprise. He tossed the frozen dinner into the oven and headed to the front door, determined to get rid of whoever was there. He wasn't in any mood for company.

"Hello, Steve."

Carol stood on the other side of the threshold, and he was so shocked to see her that someone could have blown him over with the toot of a toy whistle.

"Carol . . . how are you?" he asked, his voice stiff, his body tense as though mentally preparing for pain.

"I'm doing much better."

She answered him with a gentle smile that spoke of reluctance and regret. Just looking at her tore through his middle.

"Would you like to come in?" he asked. Refusing her entry would be rude, and they'd done more than their share of hurting each other.

"Please."

He stepped aside, pressing himself against the door. She looked well, her coloring once more pink and healthy. Her eyes were soft and appealing when he dared to meet her gaze, which took effort to avoid.

Carol stood in the center of his living room, staring out the window at the panorama of the city. Steve had the impression, though, that she wasn't really looking at the view.

"Would you like something to drink?" he asked when she didn't speak immediately.

"No thanks . . . this will only take a moment."

Now that he'd found his bearings, Steve forced himself to relax.

"I was in to see Dr. Stewart this afternoon," she said, and her voice pitched a little as if she were struggling to get everything out. "He . . . he told me how you were with me after the surgery."

"Listen, Carol, if you've come to thank me, it isn't necessary. If you'd told me who the baby's father is, I would have gone for him. He could have stayed with you, but—"

"I lied," Carol interrupted, squaring her shoulders.

He let her words soak into his mind before he responded. "About what?"

"Marrying the baby's father. I told you that because I was so hurt by what you'd said."

"What I'd said?" He couldn't recall doing or saying anything to anger her. The fact was, he'd done everything possible to show her how much he loved and cared about her.

"You suggested it would be better if I did lose this child," she murmured, and her voice trembled even more, "because next time you could be certain you were the father."

She seemed to want him to respond to that.

"I remember saying something along those lines."

Carol closed her eyes as if her patience was depleted and she was seeking another share. "I couldn't take any more of your insults, Steve."

Everything he said and did was wrong when it came to Carol. He wanted to explain, but doubted that it would do any good. "My concern was for you. Any husband would have felt the same way, pregnancy or no pregnancy."

"You aren't my husband."

"I wanted to be."

"That was another insult!" she cried, and a sheen of tears brightened her eyes.

"My marriage proposal was an insult?" he shouted, hurt and stunned.

"Yes . . . no. The offer to leave the Navy was what bothered me most."

"Then far be it from me to offend you again." There was no understanding this woman. He was willing to give up everything that had ever been important to him for her sake, and she threw the offer back in his face with some ridiculous claim. To hear her tell it, he'd scorned her by asking her to share his life.

The silence stretched interminably. They stood only a few feet apart, but the expanse of the Grand Canyon could have stretched between them for all the communicating they were doing.

The problem, Steve recognized, was that they were both so battle scarred that it was almost impossible for them to talk to each other. Every word they muttered became suspect. No subject was safe. They weren't capable of discussing the weather without finding something to fight about.

"I didn't come here to argue with you," Carol said in weary, reluctant tones. "I wanted to thank you for everything you did. I apologize for lying to you—it was a rotten thing to do."

It was on the tip of his tongue to suggest that he'd gotten accustomed to her lies, but he swallowed the cruel barb. He'd said and done enough to cause her pain in the last couple of years— there was no reason to hurt her more. He would only regret it later. She would look at him with those big blue eyes of hers and he would see all the way to her soul and know the agony he viewed there was of his making. Her look would haunt him for days afterward.

She turned and started to walk away, and Steve knew that if he let her go there would be no turning back. His heart and mind were racing. His heart with dread, his mind with an excuse to keep her. Any excuse.

"Carol—"

Already she was at the front door. "Yes?"

"I . . . have you eaten?"

Her brow creased, as if food was the last thing on her mind. Her gaze was weary as though she couldn't trust him. "Not yet."

"Would you like to go out with me? For dinner?"

She hesitated.

"The last time you were at the apartment, you said something about a restaurant you wanted to try close to here," he said, reminding her. She'd come to his place with a silly button in her hand and lovemaking on her mind. Things had been bad between them then, and had gone steadily downhill ever since.

She nodded. "The Mexican Lindo."

"Shall we?"

Still she didn't look convinced. "Are you sure this is what you want?"

Now it was his turn to nod. He wanted it so much he could have wept. "Yes, I want this," he admitted.

Some of the tiredness left her eyes and a gentle smile touched her lovely face. "I want it, too."

Steve felt like leaping in the air and clicking his heels. "I'll be just a minute," he said hurriedly. He walked into his kitchen and with a quick twist of his wrist, he turned off the oven. He would toss the aluminum meal later.

For now, he had a dinner date with the most beautiful woman in the world.

Chapter Fifteen

Elaborately decorated Mexican hats adorned the white stucco walls of the restaurant. A spicy, tangy scent wafted through the dining area as Carol and Steve read the plastic-coated menu.

Steve made his decision first.

"Cheese enchiladas," Carol guessed, her eyes linking with his.

"Right. What are you going to have?"

She set aside the menu. "The same thing—enchiladas sound good."

The air between them remained strained and awkward, but Carol could sense how desperately they were each trying to ignore it.

"How are you feeling?" Steve asked after a cumbersome moment of silence. His eyes were warm and tender and seemed to caress her every time he looked in her direction.

"A thousand times better."

He nodded. "I'm glad." He lifted the fork and absently ran his fingers down the tines.

"Dr. Stewart asked me to give you his regards," Carol said in an effort to make conversation. There were so few safe topics for them.

"I like him. He's got a lot of common sense."

"The feeling's mutual—Dr. Stewart couldn't say enough good things about you."

Steve chuckled. "You sound surprised."

"No. I know the kind of man you are." Loving, loyal, determined, proud. Stubborn. She hadn't spent five years of her life married to a stranger.

The waitress came to take their order, and returned a couple of minutes later with a glass of milk for Carol and iced tea for Steve.

"I'm pleased we have this opportunity to talk before I'm deployed," he said, and his hand closed around the tall glass.

"When will you be leaving?"

"In a couple of weeks."

Carol nodded. She was nearly six months pregnant now and if Steve was at sea for the usual three, he might not be home when the baby was born. It all depended on when he sailed.

"I used to hate it when you went to sea." The words slipped from her lips without thought. She hadn't meant to make a comment one way or the other about his tour. It was a part of his life and one she had accepted when she agreed to marry him.

"You hated my leaving?" He repeated her words as though he was certain he'd heard her incorrectly. His gaze narrowed. "You used to see me off with the biggest smile this side of the Mississippi. I always thought you were happy to get me out of your hair."

"That was what I wanted you to think," she confessed with some reluctance. "I might have been smiling on the outside, but on the inside I was dreading every minute of the separation."

"You were?"

"Three months may not seem like a long time to you, but my life felt so empty when you were on the *Atlantis*." The first few years of their marriage, Carol had likened Steve's duty to his sub to a deep affection for another woman who whimsically demanded his attention whenever she wanted him. It wasn't until later that she realized how silly it was to be jealous of a nuclear submarine. She'd done everything possible to keep occupied when he was at sea.

"But you took all those community classes," he argued, breaking into her thoughts. "I swear you had something scheduled every night of the week."

"I had to do something to fill the time so I wouldn't go stir crazy."

"You honestly missed me?"

"Oh, Steve, how could you have doubted it?"

He flattened his hands on the table and slowly shook his head. "But I thought...I honestly believed you enjoyed it when I was away. You used to tell me it was the only time you could get anything accomplished." His voice remained low and incredulous. "My being underfoot seemed to be a detriment to all your plans."

"You had to know how I felt, or you wouldn't have suggested leaving the Navy."

Steve lowered his gaze and shrugged. "That offer was for me as much as you."

"So you could keep an eye on me—I figured that out on my own. If you held a regular nine-to-five job, then you could keep track of my every move and make sure there wasn't any opportunity for me to meet someone else."

"I imagine you found that insulting."

She nodded. "I don't know any woman who wouldn't."

A heavy silence followed, broken only by the waitress delivering their meals and reminding them that the plates were hot.

Steve studied the steaming food. "I suppose that was what you meant when you said my marriage proposal was an insult?"

Carol nodded, regretting those fiery words now. It wasn't the proposal, but what had followed that she'd taken offense to. "I could have put it a little more tactfully, but generally, yes."

Steve expelled his breath forcefully and reached for his fork. "I can't say I blame you. I guess I wasn't thinking straight. All I knew was that I loved...love you," he corrected. "And I wanted us to get married. Leaving the Navy seemed an obvious solution."

Carol let that knowledge soak into her thoughts as she ate. They were both quiet, contemplative, but the silence, for once, wasn't oppressive.

"I dreaded your coming home, too," Carol confessed partway through her meal.

Steve's narrowed gaze locked with hers, and his jaw clenched until she was sure he would damage his teeth, but he made no comment. It took her a moment to identify his anger. He'd misconstrued her comments and assumed the worst—the way he always did with her. He thought she was referring to the guilt she must have experienced upon his return. Hot frustration pooled in the pit of her stomach, but she forced herself to remain calm and explain.

"I could never tell what you were thinking when you returned from a deployment," she whispered, her voice choked and weak. "You never seemed overly pleased to be back."

"You're crazy. I couldn't wait to see you."

"It's true you couldn't get me in bed fast enough, but I meant in other ways."

"What ways?"

She shrugged. "For the first few days and sometimes even longer, it was like you were a different man. You would always be so quiet . . . so detached. There was so little emotion in your voice—or your actions."

"Honey, I'd just spent a good portion of that tour four hundred feet below sea level. We're trained to speak in subdued, monotone voices. If my voice inflections bothered you, why didn't you say something?"

She dropped her gaze and shrugged. "I was so pleased to have you back that I didn't want to say or do anything to cause an argument. It was such a small thing, and I would have felt like a fool for mentioning it."

Steve took a deep breath. "I know what you mean—I couldn't very well comment on how glad you were to see me leave without sounding like an insecure jerk—which I was. But that's neither here nor there."

"I wish I'd said something now, but I was trying so hard to be the kind of wife you wanted. Please know that I was always desperately lonely without you."

Steve took a couple more bites, but his interest in the food had obviously waned. "I can understand why you felt the need for . . . companionship."

Carol froze and a thread of righteous anger weaved it's way down her spine. "I'm going to forget you said that," she murmured, having difficulty controlling her trembling voice.

Steve looked genuinely surprised. "Said what?"

Carol simply shook her head. They would only argue if she pressed the subject, and she didn't have the strength for it. "Never mind."

Her appetite gone, she pushed her plate aside. "You used to sit and stare at the wall."

"I beg your pardon?" Steve was finished with his meal, too, and scooted his plate aside.

"When you came home from a tour," she explained. "For days afterward, you hardly did a thing. You were so detached."

"I was?" Steve mulled over that bit of insight. "Yes, I guess you're right. It always takes me a few days to separate myself from the my duties aboard the *Atlantis*. It's different aboard the sub, Carol. I'm different. When I'm home, especially after being at sea several weeks, it takes time to make the adjustment."

"You're so unfeeling ... I don't know how to explain it. Nothing I'd say or do would get much reaction from you. If I proudly showed off some project I'd completed in your absence, you'd smile and nod your head or say something like 'That's nice, dear.'"

Steve grinned, but the action revealed little amusement. "Reaction is something stringently avoided aboard the sub, too. I'm an officer. If I panic, everyone panics. We're trained from the time we're cadets to perform our duties no matter what else is happening. There's no room for emotion."

Carol chewed on the corner of her lower lip.

"Can you understand that?"

She nodded. "I wish I'd asked you about all this years ago."

"I didn't realize I behaved any differently. It was always so good to get home to you that I didn't stop to analyze my behavior."

The waitress came and took away their plates.

"We should have been honest with each other instead of trying to be what we thought the other person wanted," Carol commented, feeling chagrined that they'd been married five years and had never really understood each other.

"Yes, we should have," he agreed. "I'm hoping it isn't too late for us to learn. We could start over right now, determined to be open and honest with each other."

"I think we should," Carol agreed, and smiled.

Steve's hand reached across the table for hers. "I'd like us to start over in other ways, too—get to know each other. We could start dating again the way we did in the beginning."

"I think that's a good idea."

"How about walking down to the waterfront for an ice-cream cone?" he suggested after he'd paid the tab.

Carol was stuffed from their dinner, but did not want their evening to end. Their love had been given a second chance, and she was grabbing hold of it with both hands. They were wiser this time, more mature and prepared to proceed cautiously.

"Are you insinuating that I need fattening up?" she teased, lacing her fingers with his.

"Yes," he admitted honestly.

"How can you say that?" she asked with a soft laugh. She may have lost weight with the surgery, but the baby was filling out her tummy nicely, and it was obvious that she was pregnant. "I eat all the time now. I didn't realize how sick I'd been and now everything tastes so good."

"Cherry vanilla?"

"Ooo, that sounds wonderful. Double-decker?"

"Triple," Steve answered and squeezed her hand.

Lacing their fingers like high-school sweethearts, they strolled down to the steep hill toward the waterfront like young lovers eager to explore the world.

As he promised, Steve bought them each huge ice-cream cones. They sat on one of the benches that lined the pier and watched the gulls circle overhead.

Carol took a long, slow lick of the cool dessert and smiled when she noted Steve watching her. "I told you I've really come to appreciate my food lately."

His gaze fell to the rounded swell of her stomach. "What did Dr. Stewart have to say about the baby?"

Carol flattened her hand over her abdomen and glowed with an inner happiness that came to her whenever she thought about her child. "This kid is going to be just fine."

He darted his gaze away as though he was uncomfortable even discussing the pregnancy. "I'm pleased for you both. You'll be a good mother, Carol."

Once more frustration settled on her shoulders like a dark shroud. Steve still didn't believe the baby was his. She wasn't going to argue with him. He was smart enough to figure it out.

"Do you need anything?" he surprised her by asking next. "I'd be happy to do what I can to help. I'm sure the medical expenses wreaked havoc with your budget, and you're probably counting on that income to buy things for the baby. I'd like to pitch in, if you'd let me."

His offer touched her heart and she took a minute to swallow the tears that burned the back of her eyes at his generosity.

"Thank you, Steve, that means a lot to me, but I'm all right financially. It'll be tight for a couple of months, but nothing I can't handle. I've managed to save quite a bit over the past year."

He stood, buried his hands in his pockets and walked along the edge of the pier. Carol joined him, licking the last of the ice cream off her fingertips.

Steve looked down and smiled into her eyes. "Here," he said and used his index finger to wipe away a smudge near the corner of her mouth.

He paused and his gaze seemed to consume her face. His eyes, so dark and compelling, studied her as if she were some angelic being and he was forbidden to do anything more than gaze upon her. His brow compressed and his eyes shifted to her mouth. As if against his will, he ran his thumb along the seam of her lower lip and gasped softly when her tongue traced his handiwork. He tested the slickness with the tip of his finger, slowly sliding it back and forth, creating a delicate kind of friction.

Carol was filled with breathless anticipation. Everything around them, the sights, the sounds, the smells of the waterfront, seemed to dissolve with the feeling. He wanted to kiss her, she could feel it with every beat of her heart. But he held back.

Then, in a voice that was so low, so quiet, it could hardly be counted as sound, he said. "Can I?"

In response, Carol turned and slipped her arm around his neck. His eyes watched her, and a fire seemed to leap from them, a feral glow that excited her all the more.

She could feel the tension in him, his whole body seemed to vibrate with it.

His mouth came down on hers, open and eager. Carol groaned and instinctively swayed closer to him. His tongue plunged quickly and deeply into her mouth and she met it greedily. He tasted and teased and withdrew, then repeated the game until the savage hunger in them both had been pitched to a fevered level. Still his lips played over hers, and once the urgent need had been appeased, the kiss took on a new quality. His mouth played a slow, seductive rhythm over hers—a tune with which they were both achingly familiar.

He couldn't seem to get enough of her and even after the kiss had ended, he continued to take short, sweet samples of her lips, reluctant to part for even a minute. Finally he buried his head in the curve of her neck and took in short raspy breaths.

Carol surfaced in slow, reluctant degrees, her head buzzing. She clung to him as tightly as he held on to her.

"We have an audience," Steve whispered with no element of alarm apparent in his tone or action.

Carol opened her eyes to find a little girl about five years old staring up at them.

"My mom and dad do that sometimes," she said, her face wrinkled with displeasure, "but not where lots of people can see them."

"I think you have a smart mom and dad," Steve answered, his voice filled with chagrin. Gently he pulled away from Carol and wrapped his arm around her waist, keeping her close to his side. "'Bye," he told the preschooler.

"'Bye," she said with a friendly wave, and then ran back to a boy who appeared to be an older brother who was shouting to gain her attention.

The sun was setting, casting a rose-red hue over the green water.

They walked back to where Steve had parked his car and he opened her door for her. "Can I see you again?" he asked, with an endearing shyness.

"Yes."

He looked almost surprised. "How about tomorrow night? We could go to a movie."

"I'd like that. Are you going to buy me popcorn?"

He smiled, and from the look in his eyes he would be willing to buy her the whole theater if he could.

Chapter Sixteen

Steve found himself whistling as he strolled up the walkway to Carol's house. He felt as carefree as a college senior about to graduate. Grand adventures awaited him. He had every detail of their evening planned. He would escort Carol to the movies, as they'd agreed, then afterward he would take her out for something to eat. She needed to gain a few pounds and it made him feel good to spend money on her.

When they arrived back at the house, she would invite him in for coffee and naturally he would agree. Once inside it would take him ten...fifteen minutes at the most to steer her into the bedroom. He was starved for her love, famished by his need for her.

The kiss they'd shared the night before had convinced him this was necessary. He was so crazy in love with this woman that he couldn't wait another night to take her to bed. She was right about them starting over—he was willing to do that. It was the going-nice-and-slow part he objected to. He understood exactly what she intended when she decided they could start over. It was waiting for the lovemaking that confused him. Good

Lord, they'd been married five years. It wasn't as if they were virgins anticipating their wedding night.

"Hi," Carol said and smiled, opening the door for him.

"Hi." Steve couldn't take his eyes off her. She was wearing the blue maternity dress he'd bought for her the day he'd followed her around like the KGB. "You look beautiful," he said in what had to be the understatement of the year. He'd heard about women having a special glow about them when they were pregnant—Carol had never been more lovely than she was at that moment.

"Do you like it?" she asked and slowly whirled around showing off the dress to full advantage. "Lindy bought it for me. She said she found it on sale and couldn't resist. It was the craziest thing because I'd tried on this very dress and loved it, but decided I really couldn't afford to be spending money on myself. She gave me a silver baby rattle, too. I have a feeling Aunt Lindy is going to spoil this baby."

"You look . . . marvelous."

"I'm getting so fat," she said, and chuckled. To prove her point, she scooped her hands under the soft swell of her abdomen and turned sideways to show him. She smiled, and her eyes sparkled as she jerked her head toward him and announced, "The baby just kicked."

"Can I feel?" Steve had done everything he could to convince himiself this child was his. Unfortunately he knew otherwise. But he loved Carol, and he'd love her baby. He would learn to—already he truly cared about her child. Without this pregnancy there was no way of knowing if they would ever have gotten back together.

"Here." She reached for his hand and placed it over the top of her stomach. "Feel anything?"

He shook his head. "Nothing."

"Naturally she's going to play a game of cat and mouse now."

Steve removed his hand and flexed his fingers. Some of the happiness he'd experienced earlier seeped out of him, replaced with a low-grade despondency. He wanted her baby to be his with a desperation that threatened to destroy him. But he couldn't change the facts.

"I checked the paper and the movie starts at seven," Carol said, interrupting his thoughts.

He glanced at his watch. "We'd better not waste any time then." While Carol opened the entryway closet and removed a light sweater and her purse, Steve noted the two gallons of paint sitting on the floor.

"What are you painting?" he asked.

"The baby's room. I thought I'd tackle that project this weekend. I suddenly realized how much I have to do yet to get ready."

"Do you want any help?" He made a halfhearted offer, and wished almost immediately that he hadn't. It wasn't the painting that dissuaded him. Every time Carol so much as mentioned anything that had to do with the baby, her eyes lit up like the Fourth of July. His reaction was just as automatic, too. He was jealous, and that was the last thing he wanted Carol to know.

She closed the closet door and studied him, searching his eyes. He boldly met her look, although it was difficult, and wasn't disappointed when she shook her head. "No thanks, I've got everything under control."

"You're sure?"

"Very."

There was no fooling Carol. She might as well have read his thoughts, because she knew and her look told him as much.

"I'm trying," he said, striving for honesty. "I really am trying."

"I know," she murmured softly.

They barely spoke on the way to the theater and Carol hardly noticed what was happening with the movie. She'd witnessed that look on Steve's face before when she started talking about the baby. So many subjects were open to them except that one. She didn't know any man more blind than Steve Kyle. If she were to stand up in the middle of the show and shout out that she was having his child, he wouldn't hear her. He'd buried his head so deep in the sand when it came to her pregnancy that his brain was plugged.

Time would teach him, if only she could hold on to her patience until then.

Steve didn't seem to be enjoying the movie any more than she was. He shifted in his seat a couple of times, crossed and uncrossed his legs and munched on his popcorn as if he were chewing bullets.

Carol shifted, too. She was almost six months pregnant and felt eight. The theater seat was uncomfortable and the baby had decided to play baseball, using Carol's ribs for batting practice.

She braced her hands against her rib cage and leaned to one side and then scooted to the other.

"Are you all right?" Steve whispered halfway through the feature film.

Carol nodded. She wanted to explain that the baby was having a field day, exploring and kicking and struggling in the tight confines of her compact world, but she avoided any mention of the pregnancy.

"Do you want some more popcorn?"

Carol shook her head. "No thanks."

Ten minutes passed in which Carol did her utmost to pay attention to the show. She'd missed so much of the plot already that it was difficult to understand what was happening.

Feeling Steve's stare, Carol diverted her attention to him. He was glaring at her abdomen, his eyes wide and curious. "I saw him move," he whispered, his voice filled with awe. "I couldn't believe it. He's so strong."

"She," Carol corrected automatically, smiling. She took his hand and pressed it where she'd last felt the baby kick. He didn't pull away but there was some reluctance in his look.

The baby moved again, and Carol nearly laughed aloud at the astonishment that played over Steve's handsome features.

"My goodness," he whispered. "I had no idea."

"Trust me," she answered, and grinned. "I didn't, either."

Irritated by the way they were disrupting the movie, the woman in the row in front of them turned around to press her finger over her lips. But when she saw Steve's hand on Carol's stomach, she grinned indulgently and whispered, "Never mind."

Steve didn't take his hand away. When the baby punched her fist on the other side of Carol's belly, she slid his hand over there. She loved the slow, lazy grin that curved up the edges of his mouth. The action caused her to smile too. She tucked her hand over his and soon they both went back to watching the action on the screen. But Steve kept his fingers where they were for the rest of the movie, gently caressing the rounded circle of her tummy.

By the time the film was over, Carol's head was resting on Steve's shoulder. Although the surgery had been weeks before, it continued to surprise her how quickly she tired. She'd worked that day and was exhausted. It irritated her that she could be so weak. Steve had mentioned getting something to eat after the movie, but she was having difficulty hiding her yawns from him.

"I think I'd better take you home," he commented once they were outside the theater.

"I'm sorry," she murmured, holding her hand to her mouth in a futile effort to hold in her tiredness. "I'm not used to being out so late two nights running."

Steve slipped his arm around her shoulders. "Me, either."

He steered her toward his car and opened the passenger door for her. Once she was inside, he gently placed a kiss on her cheek.

She nearly fell asleep on the short ride home.

"Do you want to come in for some coffee?" she offered when he pulled up to the curb in front of her house.

"You're sure you're up to this?" he asked, looking doubtful.

"I'm sure."

Carol thought she detected a bounce to his step as he came around to help her out of the car, but she couldn't be sure. Steve Kyle said and did the most unpredictable things at times.

Once inside he took her sweater, and while he was hanging it up for her, she went into the kitchen and got down the coffee from the cupboard. Steve moved behind her and slipped his arms around her waist.

"I don't really want coffee," he whispered and gently caught her earlobe between his teeth.

"You don't?"

"No," he murmured.

His hands explored her stomach in a loving caress and Carol felt herself go weak. "I...I wish you'd said something earlier."

"It was a pretense." His mouth blazed a moist trail down the side of her neck.

"Pretense," she repeated in a daze.

As if he were a puppet master directing her actions, Carol turned in his arms and raised her face to his, anticipating his kiss. Her whole body felt as if it were rocking with the force of her heartbeat, anticipating the touch of his mouth over hers.

Steve didn't keep her waiting long. His hands cradled her neck and his lips found hers, exploring them as though he wished to memorize their shape. She parted her mouth in welcome, and his tongue touched hers, then delicately probed deeper in a sweet, unhurried exploration that did incredible things to her. Desire created a churning, boiling pool deep in the center of her body.

His fingers slipped from her nape to tangle with her hair. Again and again, he ran his mouth back and forth over hers, pausing now and again to tease her with a fleck of his tongue against the seam of her lips. "I thought about doing this all day," he confessed.

"Oh, Steve."

His hands searched her back, grasping at the material of her dress as he claimed her mouth in a kiss that threatened to burst them both into searing flames. With a frustrated groan, he drew his arms around her front, searching. His breath came in ragged, thwarted gasps.

Carol could feel the heavy pounding of his heart and she pressed her open mouth to the hollow at the base of his throat, loving the way she could feel his pulse hammer there.

"Damn," he muttered, exasperated. "Where's the opening to this dress?"

It took Carol a moment to understand his question. "There is none."

"What?"

"I slip it on over my head . . . there aren't any buttons."

"No zipper?"

"None."

He muffled a groan against her neck and Carol felt the soft puffs of warm air as he chuckled. "This serves me right," he protested.

"What does?"

He didn't answer her. Instead, he cradled her breasts in his palms, bunching the material of her dress in the process. Slowly he rotated his thumb over her swollen, sensitive nipples until she gasped, first with shock and surprise, then with the sweet sigh of pleasure.

"Is it good, honey?" he asked, then kissed her, teasing her with his tongue until she was ready to collapse in his arms.

"It's very good," she told him when she could manage to speak, although her voice was incredibly low.

"I want you." He took her hand and pressed it down over his zipper so that she could feel for herself his bulging hardness.

"Oh, Steve." She ran her long fingernails over him.

Exquisitely aroused, he made small hungry sounds and whispered in a voice that shook with desire. "Come on, honey, I want to make love in a bed."

She made a weak sound of protest. "No." It demanded every ounce of fortitude she possessed to murmur the small word.

"No?" he repeated stunned.

"No." There was more conviction in her voice this time. "So many of our discussions end up in the bedroom."

"Carol, dear God, talking was the last thing I had in mind."

"I know what you want," she whispered. "I think we should wait . . . it's too soon."

"Wait," he murmured, dragging in a deep breath. "Wait," he said again. "All right, if that's what you honestly want—then fine, anything you say." Reluctantly he released her. "I'm going to have to get out of here while I still can, though. Walk me to the door, will you?"

Carol escorted him to her front door and his hungry kiss revealed all his pent-up frustration.

"You're sure?" he asked one last time, giving her a round-eyed look that would put a puppy to shame.

"No . . . I'm not the least bit sure," she admitted, and when his eyes widened even more, she laughed aloud at the excitement that flared to life so readily. "I don't like this any better than you do," she told him, "but I honestly think it's necessary. When the time's right we'll know it."

He shut his eyes and nodded. "I was afraid of that."

Chapter Seventeen

Carol woke before seven Saturday morning, determined to get an early start on painting the baby's bedroom. She dressed in a old pair of summer shorts with a wide elastic band and a Seahawk T-shirt that had once been Steve's. A western bandana knotted at the base of her skull covered her blond hair. She looked like something out of the movie *Aliens*, she decided, smiling.

Oh, well, she wouldn't be seeing Steve. She regretted turning down his offer of help now, but it was too late for second thoughts. She hadn't seen him since the night they'd gone to the movies, nor had he phoned. That concerned her a little, but she tried not to let it bother her.

He was probably angry about her not letting him spend the night. Well, for his information, she'd been just as frustrated as he was. She'd honestly wanted him to stay—in fact, she'd tossed and turned in bed for a good hour after he'd left her, mulling over her decision. It may have been the right one, but it didn't take away this ache of loneliness, or ease her own sexual frustration.

For six years the only real communication between them had been on a mattress. It was long past time they started building a solid foundation of love and trust. Those qualities were basic to a lifetime relationship, and they'd both suffered for not cultivating them.

By nine, Carol had the bedroom floor carpeted with a layer of newspapers. The windows were taped and she was prepared to do the cutting in around the corners and ceiling.

She carried the stepladder to the far side of the room and, humming softly, started brushing on the pale pink paint.

"What are you doing on that ladder?"

The voice startled her so much that she nearly toppled from her precarious perch. "Steve Kyle," she cried, violently expelling her breath. "You scared me half out of my mind."

"Sorry," he mumbled, frowning.

"What are you doing here?"

"I...I thought you could use some help." He held up a white sack. "Knowing you, you probably forgot to eat breakfast. I brought you something."

Now that she thought about it, Carol realized she hadn't had anything to eat.

"Thanks," she said grinning, grateful to see him. "I'm starved."

Climbing down the stepladder, she set aside the paint and brush and reached for the sack. "Milk," she said taking out a small carton, "and a muffin with egg and cheese." She smiled up at him and brushed her mouth over his cheek. "Thanks."

"Sit," he ordered, turning over a cardboard box as a mock table for her.

"What about you?"

"I had orange juice and coffee on the way over here." Hands on his hips, he surveyed her efforts. "Good grief, woman, you must have been at this for hours."

"Since seven," she said between bites. "It's going to be a scorcher today, and I wanted to get an early start."

He nodded absently, then turned the cap he was wearing around so that the brim pointed toward his back. Next, he picked up the paintbrush and coffee can she'd been using to hold paint. "I don't want you on that ladder, understand?"

"Aye, aye, Captain."

He responded to her light sarcasm with a soft chuckle. "Have you missed me?" he asked, turning momentarily to face her.

Carol dropped her gaze and nodded. "I thought you might be angry about the other night when you wanted to stay and—"

"Carol, no," he objected immediately. "I understood and you were right. I couldn't call—I've had twenty-four-hour duty."

Almost immediately Carol's spirits lifted and she placed the wrapper from her breakfast inside the paper sack. "Did you miss *me*?" she asked, loving the way his eyes brightened at her question.

"Come here and I'll show you how much."

Laughing, she shook her head. "No way, fellow. I'd like my baby's bedroom painted before she makes her debut." Carol noted the way Steve's face still tightened at the mention of her pregnancy and some of the happiness she'd experienced by his unexpected visit evaporated. He'd told her he was trying to accept her child and she believed him, but her patience was wearing perilously thin. After all, this child was his, too, and it was time he acknowledged the fact.

Pride drove her chin so high that the back of her neck ached. She reached for another paintbrush, her shoulders stiff with frustration. "I can do this myself, you know."

"I know," he returned.

"It isn't like I'm helpless."

"I know that, too."

Her voice trembled a little. "It isn't like you really want this baby."

An electric silence vibrated between them, arcing and spitting tension. Steve reacted to it first by lowering his brush.

"Carol, I'm sorry. I didn't mean to say or do anything to upset you. My offer to help is sincere—I'd like to do what I can, if you'll let me."

She bit into her lower lip and nodded. "I . . . I was being oversensitive, I guess."

"No," he hurried to correct her, "the problem is mine, but I'm dealing with it the best way I know how. I need time, that's all."

His gaze dropped to her protruding stomach and Carol saw a look of anguish flitter through his eyes, one so fleeting, so transient that for a second she was sure she was mistaken.

"Well," she said, drawing in a deep breath. "Are we going to paint or are we going to sit here and grumble at each other all day?"

"Paint," Steve answered, swiping the air with his brush, as if he were warding off pirates.

Carol smiled, then placed the back of her hand over her forehead and sighed. "My hero," she said teasingly.

By noon the last of the walls were covered and the white trim complete around the window and door.

Carol stepped back to survey their work. "Oh, Steve," she said with an elongated sigh. She slipped her arm around his waist. "It's lovely."

"I sincerely hope you get the girl you want so much, because a boy could take offense at all this pink."

"I am having a girl."

"You're sure?" He cocked his eyebrows with the question, his expression dubious.

"No-o-o, but my odds are fifty-fifty, and I'm choosing to think positive."

His arm tightened around her waist. "You've got paint in your hair," he said, looking down at her.

Wrinkling her nose, she riffled her fingers through her bangs. Steve's hand stopped her. His eyes lovingly stroked her face as if he meant to study each feature and commit it to memory. His gaze filled with such longing, such adoration that Carol felt as if she were some heavenly creature he'd been forbidden to touch. He raised his hand to her mouth and she stopped breathing for a moment.

His touch was unbelievably delicate as he rubbed the back of his knuckles over her moist lips. He released her and backed away, his breath audible.

Carol lifted her hand to the side of his face and he closed his eyes when the tips of her fingers grazed his cheek.

"Thank you for being here," she whispered. "Thank you for helping."

"I always want to be with you." He placed his hand over hers, intertwining their fingers. Tenderly, almost against his will, he lowered his knuckles to her breast, dragging them across the rigid, sensitive tip. Slowly. Gently. Back and forth. Again and again.

Carol sucked in her breath at the wild sensation that galloped through her blood. Her control was slipping. Fast. She felt weak, as though she would drop to the floor, and yet she didn't let go of his hand, pinning it against her throbbing nipple.

"How does that feel?" he asked, and he rotated his thumb around and around, intensifying the pleasure.

". . . so good," she told him, her voice husky and barely audible.

"It's good for me, too."

His eyes were closed. As Carol watched his face harden with desire she knew her features were equally sharp.

He kissed her then, and the taste of him was so sweet, so incredibly good. His lips teased hers, his tongue probing her mouth, tracing first her upper and then her lower lip in a leisurely exercise. The kiss grew sweeter yet, and deeper.

Steve broke away and pressed his forehead against hers while taking in huge, ragged puffs of air. "There's something you should know."

"What?" She wrapped her hands around his middle, craving the feel of his body against her own.

"The orders for the *Atlantis* came in. I have to leave tomorrow."

Carol went stock-still. "Tomorrow?"

"I'm sorry, honey. I'd do anything I could to get out of this, but I can't."

"I . . . know."

"I got some Family-grams so you can let me know when the baby's born."

Carol remembered completing the short telegramlike messages while they were married. She was allowed to send a handful during the course of a tour, but under strict conditions. She wasn't allowed to use any codes, and she was prohibited from relaying any unpleasant news. She had forty-six words to tell him everything that was happening in her life. Forty-six words to tell him when his daughter was born, forty-six words to convince him this baby was his.

His hand slipped inside the waistband of her summer shorts and flattened over the baby. "I'll be waiting to hear."

Carol didn't know what to tell him. The baby could very well be born while he was away. It all depended on his schedule.

"I'd like to be here for you."

"I'll be fine. . . . Both of us will." Carol felt as if she was going to dissolve into tears, her anguish was so keen. Her hand reached for his face and she traced his eyebrows, the arch of his cheek, his nose and his mouth with fingers that trembled with the strength of her love.

His hands slid behind her and cupped her buttocks, lifting her so that the junction between her thighs was nestled against the strong evidence of his desire.

"I want to make love," she whispered into his mouth, and then kissed him.

He shut his eyes. "Carol, no—you were right, we should wait. We've done this too often before . . . we . . ."

She hooked her left leg around his thigh and felt a surge of triumph at the shudder that went through him.

"Carol . . ."

Before he could think or move, she jerked the T-shirt off her head and quickly disposed of her bra. Her mouth worked frantically over his, darting her tongue in and out of his mouth, kissing him with a hunger that had been building within her for months. Her fingers worked feverishly at the buttons of his shirt. Once it was unfastened, she pulled his shirttails free of his waistband and bared his chest. Having achieved her objective, she leaned toward him just enough so that her bare breasts grazed his chest.

The low rumbling sound in Steve's throat made her smile. Slowly then, with unhurried ease, she swayed her torso, taking her pleasure by rubbing her distended nipples over the tense muscles of his upper body.

Steve's breathing came in short, rasping gasps as he spoke. "Maybe I was a bit hasty . . ."

Carol locked her hands behind his head. "How long will you be gone?" she asked, knowing full well the answer.

"Three months."

"You were too hasty."

"Does this mean . . . you're willing?"

"I was willing the other night."

"Oh, dear God, Carol, I want you so much."

She rubbed her thigh over his engorged manhood and he groaned. "I know what you want." She kissed him with all the pent-up longings of her heart. "I want you, too. Do you have any idea how much?"

He darted his tongue over one rigid nipple, feasting and sucking at her until she gave a small cry.

He lifted his head and chuckled. "Good, then the feeling's mutual."

With that, he swung her into his arms and carried her into the bedroom. Very gently he laid her atop the mattress and leaned over her, his upper body pinning her to the bed.

He stared down at her and his eyes darkened, but not with passion. It was something more, an emotion she couldn't readily identify.

"Will I . . . is there any chance I'll hurt the baby?" He whispered the question, his gaze narrowed and filled with concern.

"None."

He sighed his relief. "Oh, Carol, I love you so much."

She closed her eyes and directed his mouth to hers. She loved him, too, and she was about to prove how much.

Carol woke an hour before the alarm was set to ring. Steve slept soundly at her side, cuddling her spoon-fashion, his hand cupping the warm underside of her breast.

They'd spent the lazy afternoon making slow, leisurely love. Then they'd showered, eaten and made love again, with the desperation that comes of knowing it would be three months before they saw each other again.

It was morning. Soon he would be leaving her again. A lump of pain began to unflower inside her. It was always this way when Steve left. For years she'd hid her sorrow behind a cheerful smile, but she couldn't do that anymore. She couldn't disguise how weak and vulnerable she was without him.

Not again.

When it became impossible to hold back the tears, she silently slipped from the bed, donned her robe and moved into the kitchen. Once there, she put on a pot of coffee just so she'd be doing something.

Steve found her sitting at the table with a large pile of tissues stacked next to her coffee cup. She looked up at him, and sobbed once, and reached for another Kleenex.

"G-g-good m-morning," she blubbered. "D-did you sleep well?"

Obviously bewildered, Steve nodded. "You didn't?"

"I s-slept okay."

Watching her closely, he walked over to the table. "You're crying."

"I know that," she managed between sobs.

"But why?"

If he wasn't smart enough to figure that out then he didn't deserve to know.

"Carol, are you upset because I'm leaving?"

She nodded vigorously. "Bingo—give the man a Kewpie doll."

He knelt down beside her, took her free hand and kissed the back of it. He rubbed his thumb over her knuckles and waited until she swallowed and found her voice.

"I hate it when you have to leave me," she confessed when she could talk. "Every time I think we're getting somewhere you sail off into the sunset."

"I'm coming back."

"Not for three months." She jerked the tissue down both sides of her face. "I always c-cry when you go. You just never see me. This t-time I can't . . . h-hold it in a minute longer."

Steve knelt in front of her and wrapped his arms around her middle. With his head pressed over her breast, one hand rested on top of her rounded stomach.

"I'll be back, Carol."

"I . . . know."

"But this time when I return, it'll be special."

She nodded because speaking had become impossible.

"We'll have a family."

She sucked in her breath and nodded.

"Dammit, Carol, don't you know that I hate leaving you, too?"

She shrugged.

"And worse, every time I go, I regret that we aren't married. Don't you think we should take care of that next time?"

She hiccuped. "Maybe we should."

Chapter Eighteen

"This works out great," Lindy said, standing in line for coffee aboard the ferry *Yakima* as it eased away from the Seattle wharf, heading toward Bremerton. "You can drop me off at Susan's and I can ride home with Rush. I couldn't have planned this any better myself."

"Glad to help," Steve answered, but his thoughts weren't on his sister. Carol continued to dominate his mind. He'd left her only a couple of hours earlier and it felt as if years had passed—years or simply minutes, he couldn't decide which.

She'd stood on the front porch as he walked across the lawn to his car. The morning sunlight had silhouetted her figure against the house. Tears had brightened her eyes and a shaky smile wobbled over her mouth. When he'd opened the car door and looked back, she'd raised a hand in silent farewell and done her best to send him off with a proud smile.

Steve had stood there paralyzed, not wanting to leave her, loving her more than he thought it was possible to care about anyone. His gaze centered on her abdomen and the child she carried and his heart lurched with such pain that he nearly dropped to his knees. There stood Carol, the woman he loved and would always love, and she carried another man's child. The anguish built up inside him like steam ready to explode out of a teakettle. But as quickly as the emotion came, it left him. The baby was Carol's, a part of her, an innocent. This child deserved his love. It shouldn't matter who the father was. If Steve was going to marry Carol—which he fully intended to do—she came as part of a package deal. Carol and the baby. He sucked in his breath, determined to do his best for them both.

Now, hours later, the picture of her standing there on the porch continued to scorch his mind.

"Lindy," he said, as they reached a table, "I need you to do something for me."

"Sure. Anything."

Steve pulled out his checkbook and set it on the table. "I want you to go to the J.C. Penney store and buy a crib, and a few other things."

"Steve, listen . . ."

"The crib's called the Jenny Lind—at least I think it was." The picture of Carol running her hand over the railing that day he'd followed her came to his mind. "It's white, I remember that much. I don't think you'll have any trouble knowing which one I mean once you see their selection."

"I take it you want the crib for Carol?"

"Of course. And while you're there, pick out a high chair and stroller and whatever else you can find that you think she could use."

"Steve, no."

"No!" He couldn't believe his sister. "Why the hell not?"

"When I agreed to do you a favor, I thought you wanted me to pick up your cleaning or check on the apartment—that sort of thing. If you want to buy things for Carol, I'm refusing you point-blank. I won't have anything to do with it."

"Why?" Lindy and Carol were the best of friends. His sister couldn't have shocked him more if she'd suggested he leap off the ferry.

"Remember the dress?" Lindy asked, and her chest heaved with undisguised resentment. "I felt like a real heel giving her that, and worse, lying about it." Her face bunched into a tight frown. "Carol was as excited as a kid at Christmas over that maternity dress, and I had to tell her I'd seen it on sale and thought of her and how I hoped against hope that it would fit."

She paused and glared at him accusingly. "You know I'm not the least bit good at lying. It's a wonder Carol didn't figure it out. And if I didn't feel bad enough about the dress, the rattle really did it."

Steve frowned, too. He'd asked Lindy to make up some story about the dress and the toy so that Carol wouldn't know he'd been following her that afternoon. Those had been dark days for him—and for Carol.

"Did you know," Lindy demanded, cutting into his thoughts and waving her finger under his nose, "Carol got all misty over that silver rattle?" The look she gave Steve accused him of being a coward. "*I* nearly started crying by the time she finished."

Steve's hand cupped the Styrofoam container of coffee. "I'm glad she liked it."

"It was the first thing anyone had given her for the baby, and she was so pleased that she could barely talk." Lindy paused and slowly shook her head. "I felt like the biggest idiot alive to take credit for that."

"If you'll recall, sister dearest, Carol didn't want to have anything to do with me at the time."

Lindy's eyes rounded with outrage. "And little wonder. You are so dense sometimes, Steve Kyle."

Steve ignored his sister's sarcasm and wrote out a check, doubling the amount he'd originally intended. "Buy her a bunch of baby clothes while you're at it…and send her a huge bouquet of roses when she's in the hospital, too."

"Steve…I don't know."

He refused to argue with her. Instead, he tore off the check, and slipped it across the table.

Lindy took it and studied the amount. She arched her eyebrows and released a soft, low whistle. "I'm not hiding this. I'm going to tell Carol all these gifts are from you. I refuse to lie this time."

"Fine…do what you think is best."

Steve watched as she folded the check in half and stuck it inside a huge bag she called her purse.

"Actually you may be sorry you trusted me with this task later," Lindy announced, looking inordinately pleased about something.

She said this with a soft smile, and her eyes sparkled with mischief.

"Why's that?"

Lindy rested her elbows on the tabletop and sighed. "Rush and I are planning to start our family."

The thought of his little sister pregnant did funny things to Steve. She was ten years younger than he was and he'd always thought of her as a baby herself. An equally strange image flittered into this mind—one of his friend Rush holding an infant in his arms. The thought brought a warm smile with it. When it came to the Navy, Rush knew everything there was to know. Every rule, every regulation—he loved military life. Rush was destined to command ships and men. But when it came to babies—why, Rush Callaghan wouldn't know one end from the other. One thing Steve did know about his friend, though—he knew Rush would love his children with the same intensity that he loved Lindy. Any brother and uncle-to-be couldn't ask for anything more.

"Rush will be a good father," Steve murmured, still smiling.

"So will you," Lindy countered.

Blood drained from his heart and brain at his sister's comment. "Yes," Steve admitted, and the word felt as if it had been ripped from his soul. He was going to love Carol's child; he accepted the baby then as surely as he knew the moon circled the earth. When the little one was born, he was going to be as proud and as pleased as if she were his own seed.

"Yes," he repeated, stronger this time, his heart throbbing with a newly discovered joy. "I plan on taking this parenting business seriously."

"Good," Lindy said, and opened her purse once more. She drew out a plastic dish and spoon. "I take it you and Carol are talking to each other now."

Smiling, Steve took a sip of his coffee and nodded, thinking about how well they'd "communicated" the day before. "You could say that," he answered, leaning back in his chair, content in the knowledge that once he returned they would remarry.

"There were times when I was ready to give up on you both," Lindy said, shaking her head. "I don't know anyone more stubborn than you. And Carol's so damn proud; there's no reasoning with her, either.''

They'd both learned lessons in those areas. Painful ones.

"Take care of her for me, Lindy," he said, his eyes appealing to his sister. "I'm worried about her. She's so fragile now, delicate in body and spirit."

"I don't think she'll be working much longer, but I'll make a point of stopping in and seeing her as often as I can without being obvious about it."

Her job had been an area they'd both avoided discussing, because ultimately it involved Todd. As much as possible, Steve avoided all thoughts of the sporting good store where Carol was employed.

"I'd appreciate that," he murmured.

"If you think it's necessary, I could suggest picking her up and driving her to work with me."

"That's miles out of your way."

"No, it isn't," she returned, giving him an odd look. "Rush's and my apartment is less than a mile from Carol's place. In fact, I drive right past her street on my way to work anyway. It wouldn't be any trouble to swing by and pick her up."

"True, but Larson's is the opposite direction from the Boeing plant."

"Larson's? What's Larson's?"

"Larson's Sporting Goods where Carol works." Even saying it brought an unreasonable surge of anger. It had always bothered him to think of Carol having anything to do with the store.

"Carol doesn't work at a sporting goods store. She works for Boeing," Lindy informed him crisply, looking at him as though he'd recently landed from Mars. "She's been there over a year now."

"Boeing?" Steve repeated. "She works for Boeing? I . . . I didn't know that."

"Is Larson's the place she used to work?"

Steve nodded, wondering how much his sister knew about Carol's relationship with the owner.

"I think she mentioned it once. As I recall, they were having lots of financial troubles. She was putting in all kinds of extra hours and not getting paid. Not that it mattered, she told me. The couple who owned the place were friends and she was doing what she could to help out. I understand they're still in business. Carol never told me why she decided to change jobs."

Steve chewed on that information. Apparently for all their talk about honest communication they'd done a poor job of it. Again.

Lindy removed the lid from the Tupperware dish and started stirring some orange concoction that faintly resembled mashed carrots.

"Good Lord, that looks awful."

"This?" She pointed the spoon at the container. "Trust me, it's dreadful stuff."

"What is it?"

Lindy's gaze linked with his. "You mean you don't know?"

"If I did, do you think I'd be asking?"

"It's sweet potatoes."

"Sweet potatoes?" he echoed, wrinkling his nose. "What are you doing eating them at this time of year? I thought they were a holiday food."

"I just told you."

"No, you didn't." He didn't know what kind of guessing game Lindy was playing now, but apparently he'd missed some important clues.

"Rush and I are trying to get me pregnant."

"Congratulations, you already told me that."

"That's why I'm eating the sweet potatoes," Lindy went on to explain in a voice that was slow and clear, as though she were explaining this to a preschooler.

Steve scratched the area behind his left ear. "Obviously I'm missing something here."

"Obviously!"

"Well, don't keep me in suspense. You want to have a baby so you're eating sweet potatoes."

Lindy nodded. "Three times a day. At least, that was what Carol recommended."

"Why would she do that?"

Lindy offered him another one of those looks usually reserved for errant children or unusually dense adults. "Because she told me how well eating this little vegetable worked for her."

Steve's brow folded into a wary frown.

"Apparently she heard this report on the radio about yams raising a woman's estrogen level and she ate them by the bowlful getting ready for Christmas Eve with you." Lindy reached inside her purse and pulled out several index cards. "She was generous enough to copy down some recipes for me. How does sweet potato and ham casserole sound?" she asked, and rolled her eyes. "I don't think I'll be sampling that."

"Sweet potatoes," he repeated.

Lindy's gaze narrowed to thin slits. "That's what I just got done saying."

If she'd slammed a hammer over his head, the effect would have been less dramatic. Steve's heart felt as if it was about to explode. His mind whirled at the speed of a thousand exploding stars. A supernova—his own. Everything made sense then. All the pieces to the bizarre and intricate puzzle slipped neatly into place.

Slowly he rose to his feet, while bracing his hands against the edge of the table. His gaze stretched toward Seattle and the outline of the city as it faded from view.

"Steve?" Lindy asked, concern coating her voice. "Is something wrong?"

He shook his head. "Lindy," he said reaching for her hand and pumping it several times. "Lindy. Oh, Lindy," he cried, his voice trembling with emotion. "I'm about to become a father."

Chapter Nineteen

An overwhelming sense of frustration swamped Steve as the *Atlantis* sailed out of Hood Canal. As he sat at his station, prepared to serve his country for another tour, two key facts were prominent in his mind. The first was that he was soon to become a father and the second, that it would be three interminable months before he could talk to Carol.

He'd been a blind fool. He'd taken a series of circumstantial evidence about Carol's pregnancy and based his assumption solely on a series of events he'd misinterpreted. He remembered so clearly the morning he'd made his less-than-brilliant discovery. He'd gone into Carol's living room and sat there, his heart and mind rebelling at what he'd discovered ... what he thought he'd learned.

Carol had come to him warm from bed, her eyes filled with love and laughter. He'd barely been able to tolerate the sight of her. He recalled the stunned look she'd given him when he first spoke to her. The shock of his anger had made her head reel back as though he'd slapped her. Then she'd stood before him, her body braced, her shoulders rigid, the proud tilt of her chin unyielding while he'd blasted his accusations at her like fiery balls from a hot cannon.

He'd been so confident. The sweet potatoes were only the beginning. There was the knitting and the milk and a hundred little things she'd said and done that pointed to one thing.

His heart ached at the memory of how she'd swallowed her self-respect and tried to reason with him. Her hand had reached out to him, implored him to listen. The memory of the look in her eyes was like the merciless sting of a whip as he relived that horrible scene.

Dear God, the horrible things he'd said to her.

He hadn't been able to stop taunting her until she'd told him what he wanted to hear. Repeatedly he'd shouted at her to confirm what he believed until she'd finally admitted he was too smart for her.

Steve closed his eyes to the agony that scene produced in his mind. She'd silently stood there until her voice had come in desperate, throat-burning rasps that sounded like sobs. That scene had been shockingly similar to another in which he'd set his mind based on a set of circumstances and refused to believe her.

Steve rubbed a hand wearily across his face. Carol had never had an affair with Todd. She'd tried to tell him, begged him to believe her, and he'd refused.

"Oh, God," he whispered aloud, tormented by the memory. He buried his face in his hands. Carol had endured all that from him and more.

So much more.

Carol was miserable. She had six weeks of this pregnancy left to endure and each day that passed seemed like a year. Next time she decided to have a baby, she was going to plan the event so that she wouldn't spend the hottest days of the summer with her belly under her nose.

She no longer walked—she waddled. Getting in and out of a chair was a major production. Rolling over in bed was like trying to flip hotcakes with a toothpick. By the time she made it from one position to another, she was panting and exhausted.

It was a good thing Steve wasn't around. She was tired and irritable and ugly. So ugly. If he saw her like this he would take one look and be glad they were divorced.

The doorbell chimed and Carol expelled her breath, determined to find a way to come to a standing position from the sofa in a ladylike manner.

"Don't bother to get up," Lindy said, letting herself in the front door. "It's only me."

"Hi," Carol said, doing her best to smile, and failing.

"How do you feel?"

She planted her hands on her beach-ball-size stomach. "Let me put it this way—I have a much greater appreciation of what my mother went through. I can also understand why I'm an only child!"

Lindy giggled and plopped down on the chair. "I can't believe this heat," she said, waving her hand in front of her face.

"*You* can't! I can't see my feet anymore, but I swear my ankles look like tree trunks." She held one out for Lindy's inspection.

"Yup—oak trees!"

"Thanks," Carol groaned. "I needed that."

"I have something that may brighten your day. A preordered surprise."

With an energy Carol envied, Steve's sister leaped out of the chair and held open the front door.

"Okay, boys," she cried. "Follow me."

Two men marched through the house carrying a huge box.

"What's that?" Carol asked, struggling to get out of her chair, forgetting her earlier determination to be a lady about it.

"This is the first part of your surprise," Lindy called from the hallway.

Carol found the trio in the baby's bedroom. The oblong shaped box was propped against the wall. "A Jenny Lind crib," she murmured, reading the writing on the outside of the package. For months, every time she was in the J.C. Penney store she'd looked at the Jenny Lind crib. It was priced far beyond anything she could afford, but she hadn't seen any harm in dreaming.

"Excuse me," the delivery man said, scooting past Carol.

She hadn't been able to afford a new crib and had borrowed one from a friend, who'd promised to deliver it the following weekend.

"Lindy, I can't allow you to do this," Carol protested, although her voice vibrated with excitement.

"I didn't." She looked past Carol and pointed to the other side of the bedroom. "Go ahead and put the dresser there."

"Dresser!" Carol whirled around to find the same two men carrying in another huge box. "This is way too much."

"This, my dear, is only the beginning," Lindy told her, and her smile was that of a Cheshire cat.

"The beginning?"

One delivery man was back, this time with a mattress and several sacks.

Rush followed on the man's heels, carrying a toolbox in his hand. "Have screwdriver, will travel," he explained, grinning.

"The stroller, high chair and car seat can go over in that corner," Lindy instructed with all the authority of a company foreman.

Carol stood in the middle of the bedroom with her hand pressed over her heart. She was so overcome she couldn't speak.

"Are you surprised?" Lindy asked, once the delivery men had completed their task.

Carol nodded. "This isn't from you?"

"Nope. My darling brother gave me specific instructions on what he wanted me to buy for you—right down to the model and color. Before the *Atlantis* sailed he wrote out a check and listed the items he wanted me to purchase. Rush and I had a heyday in that store."

"Steve had you do this?" Carol pressed her lips tightly together and exhaled slowly through her nose in an effort to hold in the emotion. She missed him so much; each day was worse than the one before. The morning he'd left, she'd cried until her eyes burned. He probably wouldn't be back in time for the baby's birth. But even if he was, it really wouldn't matter because Steve Kyle was such an idiot, he still hadn't figured out this child was his own.

"And while we're on the subject of my dim-witted brother," Lindy said, turning serious, "I think you should know he was the one who bought you the maternity dress and the rattle, too."

"Steve did?"

Lindy nodded. "You two were going through a rough period and he didn't think you'd accept them if you knew he was the one who bought them."

"We're always going through a rough period," Carol reported sadly.

"I wouldn't say that Steve is so dim-witted," Rush broke in, holding up the instructions for assembling the crib. "Otherwise, he'd be the one trying to make sense out of this instead of me."

"Consider this practice, Rush Callaghan, since you'll be assembling another one in a few months."

The screwdriver hit the floor with a loud clink. "Lindy," Rush breathed in a burst of excitement. "Does this mean what I think it does?"

Steve wrote a journal addressed to Carol every day. It was the only thing that kept him sane. He poured out his heart and begged her forgiveness for being so stupid and so blind. It was his insecurities and doubts that had kept him from realizing the truth. Now that he'd accepted what had always been right before his eyes, he was astonished. No man had ever been so obtuse.

Every time Steve thought about Carol and the baby, which was continually, he would go all soft inside and get weak in the knees. Steve didn't know what his men men thought. He wasn't himself. His mood swung from high highs to lower lows and back again. All the training he'd received paid off because he did his job without pause, but his mind was several thousand miles away in Seattle, with Carol and his baby.

His baby.

He repeated that phrase several times each night, letting the sound of it roll around in his mind, comforting him so he could sleep.

Somehow, someway, Steve was going to make this up to Carol. One thing he did know—the minute he was back home, he was grabbing a wedding license and a chaplain. They were getting married.

The last day that Carol was scheduled to work, the girls in the office held a baby shower in her honor. She was astonished by their generosity and humbled by what good friends she had.

Because she couldn't afford anything more than a three-month leave of absence, she was scheduled to return. A temporary had been hired to fill her position and Carol had spent the week training her.

"The shower surprised you, didn't it?" Lindy commented on the way out to the parking lot.

"I don't think I realized I had so many friends."

"This baby is special."

Carol flattened her hands over her abdomen. "Two weeks, Lindy. Can you believe in just two short weeks, I'll be holding my own baby?"

"Steve's due home around that time."

Carol didn't dare to hope that Steve could be with her when her time came. Her feelings on the subject were equally divided. She wanted him, needed him, but she would rather endure labor alone than have Steve with her, believing she was delivering another man's child.

"He'll be here," Lindy said with an unshakable confidence.

Carol bit into her lower lip and shook her head. "No, he won't. Steve Kyle's got the worst timing of any man I've ever known."

Carol let herself into the house and set her purse down. She ambled across the living room and caught a glimpse of herself in the hallway mirror as she walked toward the baby's bedroom. She stopped, astonished at the image that flashed back at her.

She looked as wide as a battleship. Everyone had been so concerned about the weight she lost when she'd been so sick. Well, she'd gained all that back and more. She'd become a walking, breathing Goodyear blimp.

Her hair needed washing and hung in limp blond strands, and her maternity top was spotted with dressing from the salad she'd eaten at lunch. She looked and felt like a slob. And she felt weird. She didn't know how to explain it. Her back ached and her feet throbbed.

Tired, hungry and depressed, she tried to lift her spirits by strolling around the baby's room, gliding her hand over the crib railing and restacking the neatly folded diapers.

According to Lindy and Rush, the Atlantis was due into port any day. Carol was so anxious to see Steve. She needed him so much. For the past two years, she'd been trying to convince herself she could live a good life without him. It took days like this one—when the sky had been dark with thunderclouds all afternoon, she'd gained two pounds that she didn't deserve and she felt so...so pregnant—to remind her how much she did need her ex-husband.

The doorbell chimed once, but before Carol could make it halfway across the living room, the front door flew open.

"Carol." Steve burst into the room and slowly dropped his sea bag to the floor when he saw her. His eyes rounded with shock.

Carol knew she looked dreadful.

"Honey," he said, taking one step toward her. "I'm home."

"Steve Kyle, how could you do this to me?" she cried and unceremoniously burst into tears.

Chapter Twenty

Steve was so bewildered by Carol's tears that he stood where he was, not moving, barely thinking, unsure how to proceed. Handling a pregnant woman was not something listed in the Navy operational manual.

"Go away," she bellowed.

"You want me to leave?" he asked, his voice tight and strained with disbelief. This couldn't be happening—he was prepared to fall at her knees, and she was tossing him out on his ear!

With hands held protectively over her face, Carol nodded vigorously.

For three months he'd fantasized about this moment, dreamed of holding her in his arms and kissing her. He'd envisioned placing his hands over her extended belly and begging her and the baby's forgiveness. The last thing he'd ever imagined was that she wouldn't even listen to him. He couldn't let her do it.

Cautiously, as though approaching a lost and frightened kitten, Steve advanced a couple of steps.

Carol must have noticed because she whirled around, refusing to face him.

"I . . . I know the baby's mine," he said softly, hoping to entice her with what he'd learned before sailing.

In response, she gave a strangled cry of rage. "Just go. Get out of my house."

"Carol, please, I love you . . . I love the baby."

That didn't appease her, either. She turned sideways and jerked her index finger toward the door.

"All right, all right." Angry now, he stormed out of the house and slammed the door, but he didn't feel any better for having vented his irritation. Fine. If she wanted to treat him this way, she could do without the man who loved her. Their baby could do without a father!

He made it all the way to his car, which was parked in the driveway. He opened the door on the driver's side and paused, his gaze centered on the house. The frustration nearly drowned him.

Hell, he didn't know what he'd done that was so terrible. Well, he did . . . but he was willing to make it up to her. In fact, he was dying to do just that.

He slammed the car door and headed back to the house, getting as far as the front steps. He stood there a couple of minutes, jerked his hand through his hair hard enough to bruise his scalp, then returned to his car. It was obvious his presence wasn't sought or appreciated.

Not knowing where else to go, Steve drove to Lindy's.

Rush opened the door and Steve burst past him without a word of greeting. If anyone understood Carol it was his sister, and Steve needed to know what he'd done that was so wrong, before he went crazy.

"What the hell's the matter with Carol?" he demanded of Lindy, who was in the kitchen. "I was just there and she kicked me out."

Lindy's gaze sought her husband's, then her eyes widened with a righteousness that was barely contained. "All right, Steve, what did you say to her this time?"

"Terrible things like I loved her and the baby. She wouldn't even look at me. All she could do was cover her face and weep." He started pacing in a kitchen that was much too small to hold three people, one of whom refused to stand still.

"You're sure you didn't say anything to insult her?"

"I'm sure, dammit." He splayed his fingers through his hair, nearly uprooting a handful.

Once more Lindy looked to Rush. "I think I better go over and talk to her."

Rush nodded. "Whatever you think."

Lindy reached for her purse and left the apartment.

"Women," Steve muttered. "I can't understand them."

"Carol's pregnant," Rush responded, as though that explained everything.

"She's been pregnant for nine months, for God's sake. What's so different now?"

Rush shrugged. "Don't ask me." He walked across the kitchen, opened the fridge and took out a beer, silently offering it to Steve.

Steve shook his head. He wasn't interested in drinking anything. All he wanted was for this situation to be squared away with Carol.

Rush helped himself to a beer and moved into the living room, claiming the recliner. A slow smile spread across his face. "In case you haven't heard, Lindy's pregnant."

Steve stopped pacing long enough to share a grin with his friend. "Congratulations."

"Thanks. I'm surprised you didn't notice."

"Good grief, man, she could only be a few months along."

"Not her," Rush teased. "Me. The guys on the *Mitchell* claim I've got that certain glow about me."

Despite his own troubles, Steve chuckled. He paused, standing in the middle of the room, and checked his watch. "What could be taking Lindy so long? She should have phoned long before now."

Rush studied his own timepiece. "She's only been gone a few minutes. Relax, will you?"

Steve honestly tried. He sat on the edge of the sofa and draped his hands over his bent knees. "I suppose I'm only getting what I deserve." His fingers went through his hair once more. If this continued he would be bald before morning.

The national news came on and Rush commented on a recent senate vote. Hell, Steve didn't even know what his friend was talking about. Didn't care, either.

The phone rang and Steve bounced off the sofa as if the telephone had an electronic device that sent a shot of electricity straight through him.

"Answer that," Rush said, chuckling. "It might be a phone call."

Steve didn't take time to say something sarcastic. "Lindy?" he demanded.

"Oh, hi, Steve. Yes, it's Lindy."

"What's wrong with Carol?"

"Well, for one thing she's having a baby."

"Everyone keeps telling me that. It isn't any deep, dark secret, you know. Of course she's having a baby. My baby!"

"I mean she's having the baby *now*."

"Now?" Steve suddenly felt so weak, he sat back down. "Well, for God's sake she should be at the hospital. Have you phoned the doctor? How far apart are the contractions? What does she plan to do about this?"

"Which question do you want me to answer first?"

"Hell, I don't know." His voice sounded like a rusty door hinge. His knees were shaking, his hands were trembling and he'd never felt so unsure about anything in his life.

"I did phone Dr. Stewart," Lindy went on to say, "if that makes you feel any better."

It did. "What did he say?"

"Not much, but he said Carol could leave for the hospital anytime."

"Okay... okay," Steve said, pushing down the panic that threatened to consume him. "But I want to be the one to drive her there. This is my baby—I should have the right."

"Oh, that won't be any problem, but take your time getting here. Carol wants to wash her hair first."

"What?" Steve shouted, bolting to his feet.

"There's no need to scream in my ear, Steven Kyle," Lindy informed him primly.

Steve's breath came in short, uneven rasps. "I'm on my way... don't leave without me."

"Don't worry. Now, before you hang up on me, put Rush on the line."

Whatever Lindy said flew out his other ear. Carol was in labor—their baby was going to be born anytime, and she was styling her hair! Steve dropped the phone to the carpet and headed toward the front door.

"What's happening?" Rush asked, standing.

Steve paused. "Lindy's with Carol. Carol's hair is in labor and the baby's getting washed."

"That explains everything," Rush said, and picked up the phone.

By the time Steve arrived at the house, his heart was pounding so violently, his rib cage was in danger of being damaged. He leaped out of the car, left the door open and sprinted toward the house.

"Where is she?" he demanded of Lindy. He'd nearly taken the front door off its hinges, he'd come into the house so fast.

His sister pointed in the direction of the bedroom.

"Carol," he called. He'd repeated her name four more times before he walked into the bedroom. She was sitting on the edge of the mattress, her hands resting on her abdomen, taking in slow, even breaths.

Steve fell to his knees in front of her. "Are you all right?"

She gave him a weak smile. "I'm fine. How about you?"

He placed his hands over hers, closed his eyes and expelled his breath. "I think I'm going to be all right now."

Carol brushed a hand over his face, gently caressing his jawline. "I'm sorry about earlier...I felt so ugly and I didn't want you to see me until I'd had a chance to clean up."

The frenzy and panic left him and he reached up a hand and hooked it around her neck. Gently he lowered her mouth to his and kissed her in a leisurely exploration. "I love you, Carol Kyle." He released her and lifted her maternity top enough to kiss her swollen stomach. "And I love you, Baby Kyle."

Carol's eyes filled with tears.

"Come on," he said, helping her into an upright position. "We've got a new life to bring into the world and we're going to do it together."

Sometime around noon the following day, Carol woke in the hospital to discover Steve sleeping across the room from her, sprawled in the most uncomfortable position imaginable. His head was tossed back, his mouth open. His leg was hooked over the side of the chair and his arms dangled like cooked noodles at his side, the knuckles of his left hand brushing the floor.

"Steve," she whispered, hating to wake him. But if he stayed in that position much longer, he wouldn't be able to move his neck for a week.

Steve jerked himself awake. His leg dropped to the floor with a loud thud. He looked around him as though he couldn't remember where he was or even who he was.

"Hi," Carol said, feeling marvelous.

"Hi." He wiped a hand over his face, then apparently remembered what he was doing in her hospital room. A slow, satisfied smile crept over his features. "Are you feeling all right?"

"I feel fantastic."

He moved to her side and claimed her hand with both of his. "We have a daughter," he said, and his voice was raw with remembered emotion. "I've never seen a more beautiful little girl in my life."

"Stephanie Anne Kyle," she told him. "Stephanie for her father and Anne for my mother."

"Stephanie," Steve repeated slowly, then nodded. "She's incredible. You're incredible."

"You cried," Carol whispered, remembering the tears that had run down the side of Steve's face when Dr. Stewart handed him their daughter.

"I never felt any emotion more powerful in my life," he answered. "I can't even begin to explain it." He raised her hand to his lips and briefly closed his eyes. "You'd worked so hard and so long and then Stephanie was born and squalling like crazy. I'd been so concerned about you that I'd hardly noticed her and then Dr. Stewart wrapped her in a blanket and gave her to me. Carol, the minute I touched her something happened in my heart. I felt so humble, so awed, that I'd been entrusted with this tiny life." He placed his hand over his heart as if it were marked by their daughter's birth and she would notice the change in him. "Stephanie is such a beautiful baby. We'd been up most of the night and you were exhausted. But I felt like I could fly, I was so excited. Poor Rush and Lindy, I think I talked their heads off."

"I was surprised you slept here."

He ran the tips of his fingers over her cheek. "I had to be with you. I kept thinking about everything I'd put you through. I was so wrong, so very wrong about everything, and yet you loved me through it all. I should have known from the first that you were innocent of everything bad I've ever believed. I was such a fool . . . such an idiot. I nearly ruined both our lives."

"It's in the past and forgotten."

"We're getting married." He said it as if he expected an argument.

"I think we should," Carol agreed, "seeing that we have a daughter."

"I never felt unmarried," Steve admitted. "There's only one woman in my life, and that's the way it'll always be."

"We may have divorce papers, but I never stopped being your wife."

The nurse walked into the room, tenderly cradling a soft pink bundle. "Are you ready for your daughter, Mrs. Kyle?"

"Oh, yes." Carol reached for the button that would raise the hospital bed to an upright position. As soon as she was settled, the nurse placed Stephanie Anne Kyle in her mother's arms.

Following the nurse's instructions, Carol bared her breast and gasped softly as Stephanie accepted her mother's nipple and sucked greedily.

"She's more beautiful every time I see her," Steve said, his voice filled with wonder. The rugged lines of his face softened as he gazed down on his daughter. Gently he drew one finger over her velvet-smooth cheek. "But she'll never be as beautiful as her mother is to me right this minute."

Love and joy flooded Carol's soul and she gently kissed the top of her daughter's head.

"We're going to be all right," Steve whispered.

"Yes, we are," Carol agreed. "We're going to be just fine—all three of us."

* * * * *

A Note from Lindsay McKenna

Dear Reader,

Lieutenant Storm Travis of *Red Tail* was one of the first female helicopter pilots in the Coast Guard and, as such, always had to be ten times better than any male pilot to keep her position and respect within the community. The last thing she needed was a brash, cocky ex-air force chopper jockey assigned as her copilot! And Lieutenant Bram Gallagher didn't exactly see it as good news, either... at least, not at first.

In creating this book, I hoped to salute all the pilots and crews who go out on search-and-rescue missions. The countless number of lives they save is mind-boggling, and the entire Coast Guard is indeed composed of heroes and heroines, whether on the sea or in the air.

Warmly,

Lindsay McKenna

RED TAIL

Lindsay McKenna

Dedicated to

The Coast Guard's brave men and women who
risk their lives daily for all of us in
the line of duty...
and
Commander Bud Breault, a former Red Tail
Taxi Service pilot who did one hell of a job at the
collective and cyclic saving people's lives...
and
LCDR Bill Nettel, Coast Guard black shoe,
whose pride in the USCG is exhilarating...
and
USCG Air Station Miami personnel who made
our visit memorable, impressing on us that their
love and dedication is something
all Americans can be proud of...

One

"**Y**ou shouldn't be here, Lieutenant Travis," her flight mechanic said as she walked up to him.

Storm thrust her hands into the pockets of her light beige slacks in response to Merlin Tucker's growly greeting. The gargantuan helicopter and Falcon jet hangar was semiactive in the muggy Sunday afternoon heat at the Coast Guard Air Station in Miami. The sounds of mechanics working on their helicopters or jets filled the hangar. Only those who pulled duty were around. All except her. Storm drew to a halt, needing the familiarity of the sights, sounds, and smells to give her a semblance of emotional stability.

As she lifted her head and met Merlin's squinty blue eyes, a rueful smile pulled at her lips. "I guess I just wanted to be around something familiar, Merlin," she offered in explanation.

Merlin's triangular-shaped face screwed up into a frown as he observed her drawn features. "Yeah, I know what you mean," he said gruffly. "Come on over here. I'll show you what I'm doing." He looked around to make sure that no one else was near. Five other Search and Rescue H-52 helicopters sat like well-mannered steeds in their assigned positions on the floor of the hangar. Satisfied that no other knowledgeable mechanic was going to accidentally walk by and see his handiwork, he pulled back the cowling.

Storm wandered over, looking up at the turbine engine on the helicopter. "Are you sure you want me to see this, Merlin?" she asked him dryly. There wasn't another Coast Guard chopper pilot who didn't envy Storm when she pulled duty with the flight mech. He was the top mech on the base and everyone knew it. They said he had magic in his fingers. And when Merlin and Dave, her copilot, had been assigned to work together, they had always made an unbeatable team.

Her gray eyes darkened with recent pain. Oh, God, Dave... She had to push away all those nightmare memories. Wrinkling her brow, Storm leaned over Merlin's thin shoulder.

Tucker, who was only twenty-two, compared to her own twenty-eight years, chuckled. Everyone swore it was more like a witch's cackle. "Now, lieutenant, we'll just pretend this conversation didn't happen, okay?" He pointed proudly to the turbine engine on the helicopter. "I'm fine-tuning this bird for your next flight tomorrow morning. She'll pull a couple more RPMs for you when you need them the most." He grinned, the gap between his front teeth showing. It was against regulations to make certain finite engine adjustments because even the most experienced helicopter pilots who flew the 52s could overtorque the transmission and cause control problems. But Storm knew the absolute limits of the helo so he gave her the edge. His grin widened.

Storm turned her back on him. "I didn't see a thing, Merlin."

He cackled, rummaging back into the engine, grease smeared all over his long bony fingers. "That's right, lieutenant, not a thing."

Shaking her head, she gazed across the floor, noticing another person in civilian clothes entering the spacious well-lit hangar. A slight frown knitted her brows for a moment. Who else beside herself would be spending off-duty time here at the base? Everyone else had a family...someone to go home to...share life with. Stop it! You've got to stop this, Storm. It isn't going to do any good brooding about the past. You've got enough to worry about now.

"Why don't you take your day off and go home?" Merlin asked, capturing her attention.

Storm turned back around, resting her shoulder against the clean white surface of the aircraft. "Kinda lonely," she admitted.

Merlin surfaced for a moment, his normally gruff features softening. "Listen, lieutenant," he began, "it wasn't your fault. Lieutenant Walker disobeyed your orders. He should have stayed in the left seat. He had no business leaving the cockpit in that situation."

Tears scalded her eyes as she stared at Merlin, who was a couple of inches shorter than her own five feet eight inches. Her fingers trembled as she rubbed her forehead, a deluge of emotions surfacing. Why couldn't she cry? Get it out once and for all? The bitterness of the answer nearly choked her: because she was still recovering from the death of her husband, Hal, a little over a year ago. "I—I know that, Merlin."

Merlin grimaced and climbed down from the helicopter to rummage around for another tool. He straightened up, resting one greasy hand on his hip as he faced her. "Look, I've been in Search and Rescue for three years, lieutenant," he said, "and it's not uncommon for a drug smuggler to use any ploy or distraction in order to escape. That poor little kid just happened to be the bait. The smuggler was smart. Not only did Lieutenant Walker climb out of the chopper and try to rescue him, but so did those two Customs agents." He lifted his shoulders apologetically. "Lieutenant Walker traded his life for that little kid's. Quit blaming yourself because it happened. Hell, I'll lay you odds that if you had been the copilot instead of the aircraft commander, you'd have done the same thing he did!"

Pain was lapping at her temples again. She always got headaches because the tears wouldn't come. The tears just sat there, clogged in her throat, swimming in her eyes. But none of the animallike grief that clawed within her chest would burst forth, relieving her of the horrible anguish over the loss of her copilot and best friend, Dave Walker. "I went over to see Susan and the boys this morning," she said, her voice cracking.

Merlin's brows rose. "Yeah? How are they doing?" he asked.

Storm tucked her lower lip between her teeth, staring down at the concrete. "Not very well." She closed her eyes, drawing in a ragged breath. "They're like family to me, Merlin."

Merlin's blue eyes filled. "Yeah, I know they are, lieutenant. And you've become a part of everyone's family here at the base." He offered her a coaxing smile meant to raise her spirits. "I've been in the Coast Guard since I was eighteen, and I think the best thing they ever did was bring women pilots into SAR."

Storm looked up. Merlin was an unmerciful tease when he knew she was up for it. But one look at his open features and she knew he was leveling with her. She was one of three women in SAR at the air station. The other two women flew the sleek medium-range Falcon jets while she flew the helicopters. Merlin had been her flight mech off and on for two years and never said a word about this until now.

"What are you talking about?" she mumbled, brushing the unshed tears from her eyes.

Merlin grinned. "Hey, ever since you got assigned here, lieutenant, this place has really become a tight-knit family. You broke the ice, being the first woman pilot here. Not that we didn't have a family feeling before. But having women of your caliber around has made a real difference. We all took pride in our birds before, but when you got assigned to this duty section and I got to fly with you, everyone was dying of jealousy. And I mean envy with a capital *E*."

Storm forced a broken laugh. "Oh, come on, Merlin!"

"No, I'm tellin' you like it is. Now just stand there and hear me out, will you? Maybe I shoulda said something sooner. Maybe you need to hear this so you realize how important you are to all of us poor enlisted slobs. The way a male officer treats a situation is different from how a woman officer treats it. A man might bull his way through a situation that requires a little finesse. A woman seems to automatically sense that a softer word will do it better." Merlin grinned happily. "And I gotta tell you, lieutenant, we all like your touch. There ain't a crewman here at the base that doesn't love flying with you. They all know you're tops."

Storm felt heat rushing to her face. My God, she never blushed! Completely embarrassed by Merlin's sudden praise, she became flustered. "That's strange. I have a reputation for shooting straight from the hip."

"Yeah, you ain't one to mince words, lieutenant. But we all value your honesty. Just listen to me—what happened to Lieutenant Walker wasn't your fault. You're the best pilot here. You got a touch with a helo that no one else has. Why the hell do you think the commander is assigning the new guy to your duty section? He could have given you a seasoned copilot from another section." He gave her a satisfied look. "So there! You just stop and think about that before you start nose-diving again. Commander Harrison wouldn't be giving you a green copilot if he didn't believe you could teach the young pup the ropes of SAR!"

"Excuse me," a male voice interrupted, "I'm looking for Lieutenant Travis. Can you point him out to me."

Both of them turned as if they had rehearsed the synchronized movement a hundred times before. Their looks of surprise were identical as they surveyed the stranger.

Storm had to look up. It was the same man in civilian clothes she had seen at the entrance of the hangar earlier. Her heart took an unexpected beat when she realized he was staring down at her with more than passing curiosity. Myriad impressions cartwheeled across her mind as she took stock of him.

He was tall and broad-shouldered. Or at least taller than she; he was probably around six-one. His massive chest and breadth of shoulders told her he could easily carry the weight of the world around on them if he chose. Her gaze ranged upward from the languid grace of the hands resting on his slim hips to his face. Midnight blue eyes coolly met her inquiring gaze. His face was square, holding a moderately strong chin and a nose with a bump on it that told her, from the looks of him, that he had gotten into a fight at one time and broken it. But it was his sensual mouth with one corner curved into a slight smile that made her pulse race. It was a face molded by experience, with featherlike lines at the corners of his eyes telling her he enjoyed laughing. Lines across his broad brow broadcasted the fact that he concentrated unerringly on given tasks. It was a face hewn from more than thirty years of life and yet, handsome in an unconventional sense.

Merlin chuckled, appraising the stranger dressed in a pale green short-sleeve shirt and a pair of jeans. "Him? This is

Lieutenant Travis right here,'' he said, jerking his thumb in Storm's direction. Merlin chuckled again and gave Storm a merry look, climbing back up on the helicopter to complete the task of tuning up the engine.

Disbelief widened the stranger's eyes as he stared down at her. The sudden thinning of his mouth placed her on guard. Pulling out a set of papers from his shirt pocket, he opened them, the frown becoming pronounced on his brow.

"The Operations officer assigned me to this duty section to be Lieutenant S. Travis's copilot," he growled.

She wanted to laugh but had the good grace to curb her burgeoning smile. It was a commonly made error that she tolerated with ease. She was used to being an oddity among the male populace of SAR. And who was this man assigned to her? Commander Harrison, the Operations officer, had said a green pilot fresh out of helicopter school was going to be assigned to her. She had expected some twenty-four-year-old boy. Her gray eyes became somber as she stared back at him.

"I'm Lieutenant Storm Travis. Who are you?"

His eyes flared with utter disbelief. "There's got to be a mistake," he growled.

If he weren't so upset, Storm would have laughed. But right now his looks were turning thundercloud-black and she had no wish to provoke him further. In a gesture of defensiveness, she crossed her arms. "There's only one S. Travis on this base, mister, and you're looking at her. Now, who are you?"

He swore softly, looking down at the orders in his long spare fingers. "I don't believe this. Somebody's made a mistake."

Merlin peered across his shoulder, then ducked back to his work, realizing it was a safer place to be at the moment. If that big guy thought he was going to start giving Storm a hard time, he'd better watch his step. Grinning, Merlin kept one ear keyed to the deteriorating conversation behind him.

"Mistake on what?" Storm demanded throatily.

He shoved the papers under her nose. "Here are the orders they cut for me out of helicopter school. I'm Lieutenant Bram Gallagher, the new copilot assigned to Lieutenant S. Travis's duty section."

Taking her time, she coolly read the orders and then looked up at him. What an arrogant macho male—

"No one's assigning me to fly with a damn woman."

Storm glared at him. "Too bad, Lieutenant Gallagher. The Coast Guard in all its infinite wisdom has done just that."

Gallagher stared down at her, fists planted on his hips. He had come in a day early before having to check in to find out the lay of the land. At Base Security, he had gotten his new I.D. and decided to wander over the hangar area. This would be his new home for the next three years of his life. A woman? A damn woman was his aircraft commander? Of all the stupid, asinine things! He had heard the Coast Guard was moving to open more slots to females. But he never expected this! His nostrils flared.

"How many women pilots are stationed here?" he demanded.

"Three. And only one in helicopters. Me. Aren't you lucky?" Storm chastised herself. Dammit, she was behaving like a brat toward him. This wasn't the first time she had weathered grief from a stricken male ego bruised by her appearance.

He appraised her coldly. "There's got to be a mistake," he repeated unhappily.

Merlin chuckled and hunched deeper into the engine. Gallagher glared up at the flight mech and then turned back toward her.

"The only mistake is your attitude, Lieutenant Gallagher," she reminded him sharply.

Bram took a step back, trying to adjust to the shock. Under any other circumstance, she would have been worth looking at. When he had been walking up to where she and the mech had stood talking, he thought she had nice well-shaped legs. Like a willow, maybe. And when she had turned toward him, her dove-gray eyes had taken his breath away. They were wide and vulnerable-looking, with a hint of darkness in their depths. He had thought there was an aura of sadness surrounding her, but she had swiftly changed her expression, hiding her real feelings. Her nose was straight and clean; face square, holding a jaw that warned him she was nobody's patsy. Her mouth was decidedly her finest feature, expressive and slightly full. Just right to kiss. But right now her lips were compressed into a stubborn line, and her gray eyes blazed with silver flecks of anger.

In a characteristic gesture, Bram combed his fingers through his short black hair, pushing back several strands that always dipped across his brow.

"Look, I've just finished helicopter flight school in Mobile, Alabama," he stated. "I graduated at the top of my class, lieutenant. And I'm sure as hell not going to be relegated to a woman to help fine-tune my knowledge of flying SAR."

Storm relaxed slightly. At least he was honest. That was in his favor. She was glad to hear that he was at the top of his class. He wasn't a slouch at the stick, then. And judging from his penetrating eyes and aggressive stance, he was cut out for SAR. It took more than a very competent pilot, Merlin often told her, to fly well. It took guts. One wrong touch on the cyclic or pull on the collective, and mere inches could mean the difference between life and death. Storm smiled to herself. She liked Bram Gallagher's hands. They were long and artistic-looking, with large knuckles. Hands that proclaimed his flight ability. Almost every pilot she knew possessed those "flight hands," and she was no exception.

She grinned. Maybe she shouldn't have, but Storm couldn't help herself. "Tell me something, Gallagher. Why aren't you an ensign or a JG, coming out of flight training? You're a full lieutenant according to your transit orders." Besides, he was too old for flight school—past thirty. Her grin widened—two more years and she'd be over the hill herself. Suddenly Storm realized she was actually enjoying herself—at Gallagher's frustrated expense; but he looked as if he could take a few blows to the chin and live to tell about it. And her heart raced every time he gave her that look. It was a look charged with interest, ferreting her out, examining her, stroking her with his midnight blue gaze. She found herself drawn to him for no reasonable explanation she could think of. So far all he'd done was insult her.

His brows knitted. "Not that it matters to you, Lieutenant Travis, but I just happen to be an Air Force Academy graduate, with nine years of fighter pilot flying under my belt." He gave her a warning look. "And I was also a major in the Air Force, one rank above you before I left."

"Then what are you doing here?" she asked, disbelief in her voice. An ex-fighter pilot? This was getting more and more interesting by the moment. Even Merlin popped up and gave

Gallagher an incredulous look and then dived back to his work like an ostrich sticking his head back into the sand.

Bram gave her a bored look, noting the confusion registering on her face. She wasn't pretty in a classic sense. Tall, yes. The ginger hair framed her face in a pageboy that barely brushed her shoulders, and it gave her an outdoorsy look. And she wore no makeup. That wasn't a detriment in his eyes. No, the natural golden tan of her skin made her gray eyes look like beautiful diamonds. Eyes that he could get lost in if he allowed himself to.... Shoving away all those feelings, he capped his torrid thoughts and brought himself back to her tart question.

"I was assigned by the Air Force to do a study on Coasties a couple of years ago. I got involved in your SAR flying and decided you guys had a hell of a lot more action going on saving lives than I did riding an F-16 around in the sky playing fighter pilot. I quit the Air Force and got a direct commission in this service and learned to fly helicopters. I don't know how I did it, but I only lost one pay grade. That's why I'm a full lieutenant and not a JG. It's one step down from major, in case you didn't realize it."

She frowned, immediately disliking his insinuating tone. "I'm not some child that has to be taught military subjects by you, Lieutenant Gallagher."

It was his turn to grin when he realized he had managed to probe beneath her cool unruffled exterior. So, she didn't like to be patronized. Good, he'd keep that piece of information under his hat. "Don't like the shoe on the other foot, eh, Travis?"

Glaring from beneath her dark lashes she muttered, "It's likely to be the other way round real soon, mister."

"Not if I have my way. Come tomorrow morning at 0800; I'm going to be in that captain's office asking for a duty section change. No offense, lieutenant, but I'd much rather ask you out for a date than have you as my AC."

Storm's lips parted and she felt heat rising to her cheeks. The nerve! She met his laughter-filled blue eyes. "Tell me," she spat out, "are all ex-Air Force fighter jocks the same? Overconfident male chauvinist—"

Bram laughed heartily, folding the paper up again and stuffing it back into his shirt pocket. So, she was human after all. Decidedly human. He allowed his eyes to slide across her tense form. Nice full breasts, slender waist, and beautifully curved long thighs. Not bad. Not bad at all except for that vinegar personality of hers. Still, she was interesting. Damned interesting. He'd never run across a woman like her during his service career. Well, maybe after he got his orders changed, he'd make a point of knowing her better. There was no wedding ring on her hand.

"See you later, sweetheart. No offense to you, but I'm going to go find a male pilot to train with. Women should be left to what they do best, and that isn't flying helicopters."

Storm gasped, openmouthed. Before she could find a decent derogatory retort, Gallagher turned on his heel, walking away from them. "Why—" she whispered angrily, "that—"

"I'll add a few more to that list you're making, lieutenant," Merlin said, extricating himself from the engine and watching Gallagher walk away. There was nothing apologetic in the pilot's stride or the way he squared his shoulders and carried himself.

She clenched her teeth, fighting back a few more choice epithets. "Arrogant swelled-headed jock!" she sputtered.

Merlin scratched his curly blond head. "Man, has he got a surprise coming. Old Man Harrison ain't gonna let him swap duty sections." He gave Storm a conspiratorial smile. "Cocky bastard's gonna learn his first lesson of becoming a Coastie— you get put with the best when you're training." He winked. "And that's you."

Storm groaned, pacing back and forth for a moment. "I don't know, Merlin. Maybe Gallagher would be better off with a man. At least he'd have more respect for him. Besides, I don't think I've got what it takes to put up with his brand of chauvinistic brutality right now."

The mech wiped his hands off with the rag he carried in his back pocket. His face was serious. "Look, lieutenant, we'll back you all the way if he tries to pull any smart stuff. It'll be a cold day in hell if that bastard starts aiming for you."

She gave Merlin a weary smile. "Thanks," she whispered, meaning it. "God, when is my string of bad luck going to end?"

Merlin gave a philosophical shrug of his shoulders. "They say things always come in threes, lieutenant. First, your husband dies in an accident, then Lieutenant Walker, and now it looks like you're gonna get saddled with a first-class know-it-all who's ex-Air Force and thinks he's better than all of us put together." He gave a sad shake of his head. "Well, don't worry, lieutenant. We'll be there to help you weather this."

Storm drove slowly down the avenues of Opa-Locka beneath the hot July sun. The city embraced the Opa-Locka airport where the Coast Guard station was situated. She had put down the top on her dark blue MG, needing the fresh air and the wind against her face. Anything that reminded her of freedom. She felt as if she were standing in a square room with the walls moving in on her. A cry uncurled deep inside her and she felt like screaming. But nothing happened. Her gray gaze darkened with anguish and tears pricked the backs of her eyes.

Bram Gallagher filtered back into her mind. She felt a moment's relief from the depressive grief and trauma. His arrogance bordered on the unbelievable. She had worked with pilots from all the various armed forces at one time or another. Fighter jocks all seemed to be cast out of the same mold—that raucous sense of humor, blended with a self-assured ego. Her own brother, Cal Travis, was a Marine Corps fighter pilot assigned to a naval carrier, and he personified those traits. And Gallagher was certainly no exception. Plus, he had the swaggering walk to go with it. Well, Gallagher, you've got a few lessons coming, the hard way.

Still, something had stirred within her dormant heart and Storm couldn't quite identify what it was. But it was a good feeling and, God knew, she needed something to neutralize the past few nightmarish weeks.

"Bram...." The name rolled off her tongue. An unusual name. Different. And so was he. But he was distinctly male in every thrilling sense. A wry smile curved her mouth. "They ought to call you Ram," she muttered and then laughed out loud. "You just lower your head and charge!"

Two

The first statement thrown at Storm occurred the moment she swung through the doors of the Operations Center. It was one fifteen in the afternoon and time for the next duty section to take the next twenty-four-hour alert. Lieutenant Kyle Armstrong was at the forty-cup coffeepot when she walked in. The other eight pilots raised their heads in greeting.

"Hey, Stormie, the Old Man's secretary called over here. He wants to see you right away."

She rolled her eyes heavenward as she joined Kyle, and reached for a heavy glass mug with her name on it. "You really know how to make a woman's day."

"Sorry," he demurred. "Hey, we saw your boy earlier," Armstrong mentioned, a grin lapping at the corners of his mouth.

Storm gave him a dirty look, throwing an extra spoonful of sugar into the coffee as a fortifying measure. "My 'boy'?"

"Yeah. The ex-fighter jock. What's his name? Gallagher?"

"Quit grinning like a damn coon hound hunting fox," she growled, lifting the scalding coffee to her lips. Wrinkling her nose, she took a small sip. Couldn't the day wait even long enough for her to get her customary coffee into her veins and wake up her brain? She had slept poorly throughout the night, finally sleeping soundly at eight A.M. The alarm pulled her out of sleep at noon, and she had rushed through a shower to make it to the station on time.

Kyle, who was twenty-nine and the father of two kids, laughed. The other pilots who were lounging around waiting for the orders of the day to be handed out joined his laughter. "Just a little inside info, Storm," he said. "Gallagher was over here at 1100 nosing around and asking about you."

"Yeah," Jesse Mason chortled. "He wanted to know *all* about you."

Her gray eyes narrowed as she turned around, observing her cohorts. She had been flying with all these men for a long time, and they were like brothers to her. "What'd you tell him, Jess?"

Mason, who was part of the duty section to be relieved, grinned. "Not a damn thing. Told him if he wanted to know anything about you, he should go and ask you. I told him how Coasties stuck together."

It was her turn to smile. "I'll bet he just loved that answer."

"Not exactly," Kyle chuckled.

"Hey," Jesse called as she turned to leave. "We don't want him! If the Old Man decides to transfer him to another section, Stormie, we don't want the bastard. He's too sure of himself. A guy like that can get you killed. I don't care if he was top stick in his class—his attitude sucks."

Chuckling to herself, Storm waved good-bye to them, stepping out into the stifling grip of the hot, humid afternoon. Climbing back into her sports car, she balanced between shifting gears and drinking most of her coffee before she arrived at the Administration building. Now primed with coffee, Storm felt like she could withstand the coming showdown. Taking a deep breath, she entered the air-conditioned building and walked toward the commanding officer's quarters of Captain Jim Greer.

"Lieutenant Travis, come on in," the captain called as he saw her step into the outer office.

Storm entered the large well-appointed office, coming to attention. Out of the corner of her eye she spotted Bram Gallagher. He looked breathtakingly handsome in his flight suit. And he wasn't looking happy.

"At ease, Storm," Captain Greer ordered, looking up from his cluttered desk. "I want you to meet your copilot replacement, Lieutenant Bram Gallagher."

Storm turned, offering her hand. Gallagher's grip was strong and firm but controlled. His eyes were cobalt with veiled anger as he met her mischief-laden gaze.

"A pleasure, Lieutenant Travis," he told her silkily.

Liar, Storm said to herself. Her fingers tingled from his touch as she resumed her at-ease position, hands behind her back. Greer smiled up at her.

"It's all mine, believe me," she murmured, barely able to keep from smiling.

"Lieutenant Gallagher has never worked with women pilots before, Storm. I've informed him that in the Coast Guard we're the least likely of all the services to be, shall we say, chauvinistic." He transferred his attention to the other pilot. "Storm will be responsible for teaching you all the finer points of CG helo operations, Lieutenant Gallagher. It will be up to her and the Operations officer to determine how much you fly or don't fly. She'll help set up a training schedule for you, which will be approved by Commander Harrison, and you'll answer to her if there are any problems."

"And if there are, sir?"

"Then you talk to the Operations officer, Commander Harrison." Greer folded his hands, giving the pilot an icy smile laced with warning. "But I'm confident that if there are any problems, you two can work them out amicably between yourselves."

"We will, sir," Storm assured the captain heartily, flipping Gallagher a venom-laden look.

"Yes, sir," Gallagher mimicked, giving her an equally viperous glance in return.

Once outside the building, Gallagher reached out, pulling her to a halt. "You're enjoying this a little too much, lieutenant."

"Am I?" she asked coolly. Storm forced herself not to react to his firm, arousing touch.

"Yes, and if I didn't know better, so are your shipmates."

"You brought it on yourself, Gallagher."

His features darkened as he regarded her. "I've never seen men so protective of a woman in their ranks before. What'd you do, bed down with each one of them?"

Her response was instantaneous and totally instinctive. Storm's palm caught his cheek in a glancing blow, the slap sounding sharply. Startled, Storm took a step away from him, her face flushed scarlet. She stood there, hands clenched into fists at her side, breathing hard. Gallagher ruefully rubbed his reddening cheek. My God, she had never struck anyone in her life! She began to tremble from the surge of adrenaline flowing through her body.

"How dare you," she quavered.

A slight grin pulled at his mouth and he gave her a sheepish look. "Guess I had that coming, didn't I?" And then his blue eyes darkened. "Storm's a good name for you," he said in a husky voice.

The suggestive tone was overpowering to her shattered senses. Storm was angry at herself for reacting like a woman instead of an officer who was supposed to be in charge. What the hell was the matter with her? Shape up, Travis, she berated herself. Her gray eyes narrowed.

"It's obvious you don't care for me as your superior, Lieutenant Gallagher," she told him through clenched teeth, "but that's something you and I are just going to have to suffer through. I don't like this any more than you do. And what's more, you had damn well better pay attention to my orders when I give them while we're in the air. The first time you even think of disobeying me could cause us to be killed. I won't stand for that. You can hate me on the ground but up in the air, mister, I'm the AC and what I say goes. Do we understand each other?"

Bram stared down at her. He lost his smile, aware of the steel backbone she possessed. The problem was that he liked her as a woman; already she had intrigued him. He had barely slept all last night thinking about her. A new glint of respect shone in his eyes. "Okay, I can buy that, lieutenant. In the air, you're the queen. I won't ever disobey an order you give me—that's a promise."

She eased upright, realizing she had hunched over into an almost attacklike position. She stabbed a finger toward him. "You've got a lot to learn, Gallagher. You jet jocks in the Air

Force are used to one-man shows. Here in the Coast Guard, we work as a close-knit team. In the air, I'm not the queen. I'm just part of the coordinated flesh and blood team that's flying that helicopter toward a rescue. And one more thing. All I want from you is your respect. Hate my guts, but respect the knowledge I've accrued." She marched toward her blue sports car, then spun on her booted heel, glaring at him. "I'll see you over at the Ops center. We're due for our 1330 briefing by the Section Duty officer."

What the hell had she done? Storm groaned, forcing herself to slow down on the way over to the hangar area. Her face was hot with mortification. I'll bet Gallagher thinks I go around slapping men all the time. Why should she care what he thinks? And that look Captain Greer had given her . . . he knew the fur was going to fly. She ran her fingers haphazardly through her ginger hair in an aggravated motion.

The ten Coast Guard pilots sat with their cups of coffee in hand as the SDO, LCDR Mike Duncan passed out the assignments. Storm sat rigidly next to Gallagher. She had endured his stare when he was the last to enter the Operations area. Storm had noticed that all the normal congenial noise died down to silence when he entered. A part of her felt compassion for him. He was new, and an outsider, not only because he was a green helicopter pilot, but because he was from another branch of the service. Grimacing, Storm glanced over at him. His probing blue eyes met hers. She quickly refocused her attention upon Duncan.

"Storm, you get to take those five loads of pallets from supply and drop them over at the staging area." Duncan, a man of forty with prematurely graying hair, gave her a slight smile. "Maybe you can show Lieutenant Gallagher the finer points of sling ops."

She nodded. "Okay." Great, they got the trash run today. Did she have a black cloud hanging over her head or something?

After being dismissed, Bram followed her to the line shack that sat near the Ops building. Bram came abreast of her and slowed his pace. Automatically Storm allowed the rest of the pilots to amble on by them. She glanced up at him.

"What's wrong?" she asked.

"Nothing. Just wanted to apologize for what I said earlier outside Admin to you," he murmured. "It was a cheap shot."

She bit back "You're damn right it was." Instead she shrugged. "Apology accepted, Gallagher."

An elfin grin pulled at his mouth. "You have one hell of a right cross, lady."

It was her turn to smile as they walked down the sidewalk toward the line shack. "I've never slapped a man in my life. You were the first. And you'll be the last," she promised throatily.

Bram pulled the glass door open. The surprised look she gave him told Bram she wasn't used to that kind of help from a man. Too bad, he thought. I'm going to treat you like a lady whether anyone likes it or not.

All the duty section pilots milled around the cramped confines of the line shack. It sat next to the ramp area where serviced and repaired aircraft were parked.

Storm pulled over the maintenance book on CG 1378 and opened it up. Bram moved beside her, squeezing into the small counter space between the other pilots. She was vividly aware of his male strength, his body hard from being physically fit. Collecting her scattered thoughts, Storm pointed down at the log.

"We always check this to mark any discrepancies or problems with the helo, Bram. It's up to us to record them and then sign for the helo we'll be using that day."

The press of bodies, the good-natured gibing and jokes, filled the line shack. After signing out CG 1378, Storm shut the log, handing it back to the warrant officer behind the desk.

"Let's go," she said, giving him a slight smile.

Bram returned it, remaining at her side, and then pushed open the door. The muggy afternoon air hit them as they walked around the corner of the building and onto the concrete ramp.

Storm began to relax. This was her home, the one place where she felt comfortable since the loss of her husband and Dave Walker. Merlin was waiting for them, over by CG 1378, throwing them the customary salute.

"Afternoon, Lieutenant Travis, Lieutenant Gallagher," he said gruffly.

"Afternoon, Merlin." Storm smiled, taking the mandatory baseball cap of dark blue off her head. Unzipping a large pocket on her left thigh, she stuffed it in there. The breeze was light, coming in from the Atlantic Ocean, and she inhaled deeply of the salt-laden air. She made formal introductions between Merlin and Bram Gallagher. Storm smiled to herself as both men eyed each other warily. She stood with one hand resting against the white surface of the helicopter.

"We want to welcome you officially to the Red Tail Taxi Service, Gallagher," she said.

Bram cocked his head. "What?"

Storm gestured to the international orange stripe that adorned the tail of their helicopter. "We're unofficially known as Red Tails."

"The taxi-service part is because you'll be doing anything from hauling groceries to rescuing snowbound families up in Alaska, depending on where you're stationed. Here in the Florida area we don't have to deal with snowstorms, but we fight the hurricanes every year." Her grin widened. "So if somebody calls you Red Tail, you'll know what they're referring to."

He scratched his head. "Relegated to a taxi service, eh?"

"Yes, sir," Merlin cackled. "Oh, one thing we forgot to tell him, Lieutenant Travis."

She gave Merlin a surprised look. "What?"

"Tell him that we're part of the Department of Transportation and not the Defense Department."

"Translated, what does that mean?" Bram asked dryly.

Storm pursed her lips. "It means if you get shot at by a druggie, Gallagher, it's not considered combat or even war. Since the CG is with the Transportation Department, we're an anomaly of sorts."

"A Red Tail and noncombat, eh?"

"You got it right, sir," Merlin responded. "An elite taxi-service with fringe extras like getting shot at." He winked. "When we stalk the druggies, we're in combat."

"Well," Bram said good-naturedly, "I was tired of flying a jet around all day. Looks like the CG is infinitely more interesting in many ways."

Maybe it's going to be all right after all, Storm thought. She went through the rest of preflight inspection with Gallagher, who became an attentive shadow at her left arm as they walked around the helo. He asked intelligent questions, and she was pleased. There was a new eagerness blossoming within her. Suddenly she was seeing Bram in a new light—as a professional pilot. When it came down to work, he was all business. The wisecracking guy with the arrogant chip on his shoulder had disappeared. Breathing a sigh of relief, Storm climbed into the right-hand seat, the AC's seat.

"Okay," Storm called, her voice echoing hollowly within the confines of the helicopter, "so much for social amenities. Let's get this show on the road."

A new palpable tension thrummed through the aircraft. Merlin busied himself in the back as they slipped into their confining shoulder harness and seat belt system after donning helmets.

Bram watched Storm out of the corner of his eye. Her movements were economical and spoke of someone who was confident with a job. He gave a small shake of his head. He was certainly going to have to change his perspective on how he viewed women. Because of the peacetime missions of the Coast Guard, there were women flying jets and helicopters and serving aboard the cutters at sea. A slight smile edged his mouth as he threw her a thumb's up, indicating he was finished with his personal preflight checklist. They began the next phase of checks for the starting of the engine and rotor engagement. Given Storm Travis's fascinating job as his aircraft commander, Bram decided to try and enjoy the time spent with her instead of creating a chauvinistic rift, which would only intensify the friction between them.

Storm adjusted the slender mike close to her lips, glancing over her shoulder to make sure Merlin was secure in his small chair, which was bolted near the entrance door. He was strapped in.

"If you'll call Tower, I'll lift off," she told Gallagher. "We've got five sling loads. I'll do the first couple of loads and you watch. Then we'll let you try your hand at it."

Bram nodded. "Fine with me, lieutenant." A glint of laughter came to his blue eyes as he studied her serious features. "Sure you trust an ex-Air Force fighter jock?"

She grinned back. "As long as you don't think this helo has afterburners, Merlin and I will survive."

Their laughter was drowned out when she flipped the starter button on the cyclic stick, which sat in position near her gloved right hand. The shrill sound rang through the hollow interior of the H-52 Sea Guard Sikorski helicopter. The trembling began and subsided as soon as the engine turbine came up to speed. When ready, she released the rotor brake, and the rotor slowly started moving around and around above their heads. Very soon, the steady noisy beat of the rotor smoothed out, and the 52 sat shuddering and trembling around them, ready beneath her capable hands. After receiving clearance from the tower, Storm placed her right hand on the cyclic stick that sat between her legs, wrapped the fingers of her left hand around the collective and placed her booted feet against the rudder pedals. Pulling gently up on the collective, the rotors punctured the air as pitch was increased and the ship smoothly slipped its hold from the earth.

Bram's respect for her increased as they worked throughout the afternoon carrying the pallets. The 52 could lift a maximum of eight-thousand-three-hundred pounds, including its own weight, so the pallet loads weren't large. He found Storm to be a natural instructor pilot. After watching her lift several loads with impressive ease, he tried his hand at it. The wind was picking up out of the northwest, and the pallets suspended beneath the 52 had a tendency to sway drunkenly from side to side. The helo's movement had to be choreographed with the temperamental load by constant manipulation of the controls. He grew to appreciate Storm's quietly-spoken suggestions with an air of relief. Although he had been at the top of his flight class, six weeks to learn how to fly helicopters did not compensate for the on-the-job experience that all new graduates had to accrue out in the field.

"Anybody ever tell you you're an IP by nature?" he asked, glancing over at her.

Storm gave a distant smile. As always, her feet and hands were near her own set of controls. If Gallagher got into trouble, her lightning reflexes would have to save them. On any mission, the other pilot always maintained that position of readiness. "You mean I'm not yelling and cursing at you like the IP back in flight school did?"

Bram liked her husky voice. Her eyes spoke volumes. Her voice reminded him of a roughened cat's tongue stroking his flesh. It increased the air of mystery surrounding her. He knew nothing of her, and he wanted to know everything—especially now that he had had a chance to see her in action at the controls of a 52. She had what was known in their business as "hands." Another term used was "top stick." Even the IP in flight school didn't have Storm's silken touch with the helicopter, and it made him feel slightly in awe of her. She was a woman doing what he normally assumed to be a man's job better than any man he had seen thus far. He nodded, answering her easy question. "Lady, if you had been my IP back in flight school, chances are I'd have flunked out on purpose, just to get another six weeks with you."

Storm avoided his openly admiring gaze, feeling heat sweeping up her neck and into her face. Oh, God, she was blushing! Compressing her lips, she looked away, forcing herself to concentrate on the task at hand. "You're doing fine, Gallagher," she managed. "Most copilots don't understand cargo sling procedures, but you're doing quite well."

Bram's grin widened. "Business all the way, eh?" he teased.

Storm refused to meet his eyes. He knew he had gotten to her! He had seen her face turn scarlet. "That's right," she informed him coolly, her heart beating traitorously in her breast.

His laughter was deep and exhilarating over the intercom system. "I'll let you have your way for now. But we aren't always going to be sitting in a 52, Lieutenant Travis," he warned her silkily.

Storm absolutely refused to blush again. She willed her body not to respond. Damn his cavalier attitude! Bram Gallagher certainly knew how to get under her skin.

"Hey, lieutenant, I'm starved!" Merlin wailed.

She glanced at her watch. It was almost supper time. Where had time gone? "Okay. We'll pick up this last load and then go eat!"

"Anything the lady wants," Bram murmured innocently, but he looked meaningfully at her.

Storm ignored the implication. After the mission had been completed, they landed the 52 and shut it down, unstrapping themselves from their complicated harness system. Climbing out, Storm placed the dark blue baseball cap back on her head once again as did the others. Merlin and Gallagher joined her and they walked into the line shack. After completing his paperwork, Merlin went to the mess hall for some chow.

"Let's go up to the officer's mess," Bram suggested.

She grimaced, giving him a sidelong glance. "We could grab something from the vending machine. It's quicker."

Again Bram gave her that infuriating smile that threatened to make her blush. "Because I want to sit back and relax a little, Lieutenant Travis. Or are you going to give me an argument on that too?"

Her gray eyes narrowed. "No argument, Lieutenant Gallagher," she informed him lightly. Why did she have the feeling he was stalking her?

Stuffing her cap into one the pockets of her flight suit, she walked through the doors of the officer's mess. They stood out in their olive-green flight suits among the other officers who were dressed in dark blue serge pants and light blue short-sleeve shirts. Storm bridled when she saw Kyle Armstrong and his copilot grinning up at her when they entered. She felt like she had to explain why they were over here and then decided to hell with it. Let them think what they wanted. They went through the cafeteria line, and Storm found a couple of chairs at an empty table to give them some privacy from prying eyes.

Bram sat opposite her, his tray filled. He gave a glance at hers.

"You're not eating much," he noted, pointing disapprovingly at the soup and salad.

Storm ran her fingers through her hair, wishing she had a brush right now. She knew her hair probably looked flattened against her skull after wearing the helmet. And then she laughed at herself—why, all of a sudden, did she worry about how her hair looked? She hadn't before. She met Gallagher's concerned gaze.

"I like staying at one hundred and thirty pounds, that's why. Don't start picking on my eating habits too," she said gruffly, picking up her fork.

His smile was devastating as he paid attention to his plate heaped with slices of hot roast beef. "Am I picking on you?"

"You know you are."

"My, my, aren't we touchy. Are you like this every day?"

"For your benefit, yes."

"My benefit?"

Storm glared up at him. She felt giddy and happy—but why? It was him. Damn! "Yes, yours. And don't give me that innocent look, Gallagher. You know what I'm talking about. We're not boy meets girl. We're adults. And I can see you coming from ten miles away."

He nodded, chewing thoughtfully in the silence afterward, his blue eyes dancing with laughter. "Want to play twenty questions with me?"

Storm gave him a black look. "No."

"What are you hiding from?"

"You."

"Why?"

"Because, lieutenant, you seem to feel it's your right to know me on a personal level."

He gave her a guarded look, continuing to eat. "I think that's fair. After all, we're going to be working together for at least a year."

"Don't remind me."

Bram grinned, knowing she didn't mean it. He saw the confusion and fear in her eyes and suddenly realized that something must have occurred in her personal life to make her so wary. "Okay," he said, easing up on her, "I'll can my twenty questions. Just answer two for me, will you?"

"Two?"

He held up two fingers. "Yeah, two."

She frowned. "I can count, Gallagher, and you don't need to hold up your fingers so everybody can see you."

So, that was it. Bram looked around, noticing a couple of the pilots and watching them with great interest. His face softened and he dropped his hand. "Looks like there's more than a little interest in you and me by your protective friends."

Uncomfortable and yet relieved that he understood, Storm blotted her lips with the napkin. He wasn't as insensitive as she had first thought. "They're worse than women when it comes to me," she admitted unhappily. Kyle Armstrong would tease her mercilessly tonight when they all got together at the Q or alert quarters.

He laughed softly, shaking his head. "What is this, reverse discrimination? Men being protective about you and on guard toward me?"

Storm shrugged. She didn't want to tell him that Armstrong and the rest of the guys wanted to see her married again. They were forever trying to fix her up with some eligible bachelor. Their hearts were in the right place, but it was embarrassing. "They mean well," she told him. "They're like brothers, you know? Sometimes they get in your hair and become an irritation."

Bram nodded. That was good to know—she treated them like brothers, not lovers. "Well," he informed her softly, his voice a vibrating growl, "don't even begin to look at or treat me like a brother, lieutenant."

She toyed with the salad, her pulse skyrocketing. "Don't worry, Gallagher, I'll never make that mistake with you."

His mouth drew into a grin. "Good. I'm glad we finally agree on something."

Storm gave him a warning glare. "I agree with you on very little, Gallagher."

"That'll change," he informed her darkly.

"I doubt it."

Storm didn't want to go inside the Q, which stood outside the ramp and hangar area. Four days had flown by and they were on alert again. It was almost 2100 when she walked outside, heading toward the quiet ramp where the readied helos and Falcon jets sat waiting for the next SAR call. Hands thrust deep in her pockets, she watched the apricot color of the sunset deepening. The colors were spectacular; she had come to love dusk in Florida. Tonight there were a few threatening clouds, mostly towering cumuli, rising like castle turrets in the distance. That meant a few isolated thunderstorms later over the ocean. Bowing her head, she walked slowly along the ramp area, away from the hangar, lost in the world of changing colors that painted the sky. It was lovely, and finally she halted, lost in the display.

"Beautiful, isn't it?" came Bram's voice from behind her.

She turned her head slightly, watching him quietly walk up to her shoulder and halt. The peacefulness of the sunset muted all her suspicions as she saw awe written across his features. He was just as moved as she was. A small smile curved her lips.

"This is my favorite time of day," she confided softly, returning her attention to the sky.

"Mine too. That and dawn. I like to see the colors on the horizon. Best time to fly."

She felt totally at ease with Bram. Four days had worked miracles in dispelling their initial distrust of each other. There was a tender look in his eyes right now. Storm liked the feeling swirling and building quietly between them, a sharing of something far greater than themselves. The apricot hue deepened to an incredible orange that grew paler as it reached toward the darkening cobalt sky.

Bram glanced down at Storm. Her profile was clean, and her skin had a glow to it. There was a faraway look on her face now, and he longed to reach out and touch her. Her lips were slightly parted, her eyes wide, as she continued to watch the spectacle. They stood in silence another ten minutes before he spoke.

"I've been trying to find some time today to talk with you alone, Storm," he said, turning toward her.

Her heart catapulted as he called her by her first name. It rolled off his tongue like a caress, and she responded effortlessly to the tone in his voice. But she also heard the seriousness of it and faced him, a mere twelve inches separating them. Looking guilelessly up into his features, she searched his darkened blue eyes.

"About what?"

"You don't play games, do you?"

Her brows drew downward. "Games? No. Is that what you wanted to talk about?"

He shook his head. "No." He scratched his head furtively, looking toward the sunset again. "I'm having one hell of a time relating to you, Storm. You're not like the women I know. Or have known. They're into their cute, coy games. They don't come out and say what they really feel." He gave her a rueful smile. "You come off differently."

Storm felt defensive about his assessment, crossing her arms. "That doesn't make me any less a woman, you know."

He raised his eyes. "I didn't mean it that way. No, you're a woman in or out of a flight suit; believe me," he said fervently. Then he grinned. "The touch you have with a helo is a woman's touch, not a man's."

"Flying is a matter of finesse and sensitivity, not brute strength," she reminded him.

He held up his hands. "I agree. Listen, we're getting off track, Storm. I need to say something to you,"

She licked her lips, preparing for the worst. "Okay. I always want honesty between us, Gallagher. Even if it hurts, I want the truth."

Placing his hands on his hips, he looked down at the concrete between them for a long moment. Finally he raised his head, an undecipherable expression in his eyes as he met her gaze. "First, I owe you a genuine apology for the way I behaved that first afternoon we pulled alert. I don't normally go around accusing women of going to bed with men." He grimaced, finding it hard to put the rest of it into words because of the avalanche of emotion boiling up within him. "Last Friday, before I left Mobile, Alabama, to move down here, I got my finalized divorce papers." He lowered his gaze, pursing his lips. "A two-day drive down here plus the bitterness of the divorce has made me a little sour on women. And when I met you Sunday and realized it was going to be a woman breaking me into SAR, I damn near came unglued." His blue eyes grew softer as he searched her stunned features. "I was angry at my ex-wife, and I lashed out at you instead, Storm. You represented all women to me in that moment and how much they can hurt a man."

Storm cleared her throat, unable to maintain his gaze. "I see . . ." she whispered. Tears came to her eyes, and it surprised her. Why tears? Her heart contracted with pain for him. "Under the circumstances, I guess I can't blame you for your actions, Bram. I probably would have done something quite similar."

A slight smile edged his sensual mouth. "I'm finding out all kinds of good things about you, Storm Travis. You stand up for what you believe in, but you're equally forgiving of others' mistakes. That's a nice attribute."

She shivered inwardly as his voice soothed her. Tears stung her eyes and she turned away from him. Was she going to cry? My God! "In the past year, I've found out just how human I am," she admitted rawly. Rubbing her brow, she managed a small broken laugh. "Just one thing . . ."

Bram cocked his head, watching her profile silhouetted against the darkening horizon. "Name it."

"Be just as forgiving with me, Bram. I—I'm kind of on an emotional roller coaster right now because—of, well, circumstances. I might shout at you when we're in the cockpit together, or—"

He reached out, placing his hand on her shoulder, turning her toward him. It startled him to realize that her dove-gray eyes were filled with tears, making them appear luminous and vulnerable. He wanted to keep his hand on her shoulder but allowed it to drop to his side instead.

"We got off on the wrong foot the other day because of my attitude, Storm," he told her earnestly. "You showed your professionalism with me, regardless of how badly I made an ass of myself. You didn't let your personal opinion of me interfere with teaching me the ropes. You've earned a big chunk of my respect. I'll never lose my temper with you when you get a little out of sorts."

A quivering smile fled across her lips. His touch had been healing and stabilizing to her torn emotional state. Storm longed to have him put his hand on her once again, to simply step into the circle of his arms. She had been a year without any kind of emotional support—bereft, floating aimlessly. And she yearned for what Bram offered honestly and without games. A newfound respect shone in her eyes for him.

"Okay," she murmured huskily, "truce?"

"Truce," Bram promised thickly.

Three

The Q, the barracks for pilots on alert, consisted of two double bunks to a room in a two-story structure. On retiring to their rooms, the pilots unlaced their boots and left them nearby in case the duty officer called on two or more of them to assist in a search and rescue mission. The room at the end of the hall was a large lounge sporting several comfortable sofas and chairs gathered around a color TV set. Storm had her boots off, dangling her long legs over the arm of the chair. It was almost ten P.M. and she dozed intermittently, the television blaring in the background, providing the stabilizing sound of human voices.

One by one, the on-duty pilots called it a night. Storm was afraid to go to bed. This was her first night back on duty since the loss of Dave Walker. She had been placed on nonduty status and given time to recover from the emotional shock and loss. It was the normal procedure after air crashes or traumatic circumstances. Kyle rose and walked over under Bram's watchful eye, his hands resting on each arm of the chair as he stared down at her.

"Okay, Stormie?" he asked in a low voice.

She nodded, barely opening her eyes. "Yeah, fine, Kyle."

"Sure?"

Kyle knew what she was going through. They had been close friends since she had first been assigned to SAR. "Yeah…" she mumbled, her arms wrapped across her body, head buried against the chair.

"You look real tired."

"I am."

"Why don't you hit the sack? You're gonna end up with a crick in your neck if you don't." He smiled, but his green eyes were solemn as he watched her closely.

Storm shrugged. She didn't want to tell Kyle of the nightmares that stalked her every night. "I'll go in a little while. Thanks…."

He straightened up, giving her knee a pat. "Okay. Good night."

Dozing again beneath the lamplight and the comforting noise of the television, Storm remembered very little after that. At one point, Bram came over and checked on her before he left for his room, which was situated next to hers. He had gently stroked her hair, crouching down beside her, his blue eyes assessing her worriedly. For the first time in a year, she felt protected. Smiling softly, she mumbled good night to him and dozed off again.

Near eleven, Storm roused herself and stumbled blindly into her darkened sleeping quarters. Drunk with exhaustion, she left her flight suit on and wearily lay down on the bunk. Maybe now she was tired enough for sleep to come without a battle. She was lucky if she got three hours of sleep a night since the accident.

"I've got to help him, Storm!"

She shook her head adamantly, gripping the flight controls as the helicopter hovered precariously over the deck of the yacht. The ocean was fairly calm, making the boarding of the ship by the SES drug-busting Coast Guard crew of the *Sea Hawk* relatively easy. The yacht had a helicopter landing pad on the rear deck. When the request came in for them to assist in the mop-up operation, Storm landed the aircraft gently on the pad. It was an unusual request, but she complied. Merlin was out the door, helping to round up the smugglers and their cache of marijuana and coke. But it wasn't over yet. The whine of the turbine engine of the 52 added to the cacophony of shouts and orders. She and Dave watched in horror as one smuggler grabbed a small boy who was part of the crew, holding him hostage at the bow of the ship with a gun held to his head. Two Customs agents armed with shotguns slowly approached the twosome.

"He isn't going to put down the gun," Dave said grimly, giving Storm a sharp glance. He began unharnessing. "Damn!"

"Dave...don't go! Stay here. There's nothing you can do!" she ordered. Her concentration was torn between keeping the helicopter steady on the deck and remaining aware of the chaos taking place around them.

"He's gonna kill that kid, Storm. I know Spanish. Maybe I can get our guys to back off and I'll talk him into giving up the boy."

Before Storm could protest, he was gone. Helplessly she watched as Dave, still in his helmet, climbed out and ran toward the prow of the ship. She bit her lower lip hard, aware of the hatred on the face of the Colombian smuggler. Storm watched as everything in her recurring nightmare slowed to anguished single frames, sending waves of horror through her.

Even above the roar of the 52's rotor blades kicking up gusts of wind, Storm heard the smuggler screaming shrilly in Spanish as Dave placed himself in front of the boarding crew. Her stomach knotted, and her sweaty hands tightened on the controls. The smuggler raised the gun, aiming it at Dave's chest. No! Oh, God, no! He was going to shoot Dave! She watched as the ugly snout of the gun barrel rose level with Dave Walker's chest. She saw the man's finger pulling back on the trigger.

"No!" she screamed again and again. Sobs tore from her throat, and she buried her face in her trembling hands, unable to stop the awful sounds from escaping. She was barely cognizant of someone switching on the overhead light, as well as the mumbling and movement around her. Hands, friendly hands, fell on her shoulder, pulling her around, breaking the spell.

"Stormie?" Kyle whispered anxiously. He pulled her upright so she could sit up. A few of the other pilots, awakened from their sleep by her screams, stumbled out of bed and down the hall, coming to her room and standing near Armstrong.

She sobbed hard, embarrassed, realizing she had awakened almost everyone in the Q. "I—I'm sorry," she cried brokenly. "I didn't mean to wake everyone . . ."

Armstrong smiled understandingly, watching as Gallagher made his way through the assembled pilots, crouching down by Storm's left leg. "It's okay," Bram soothed.

Storm felt Bram's firm grip on her arm. It had an immediate mollifying effect on her turbulent emotional state.

"I'll take care of her," Bram told the others, daring any of them to dispute his right to do so. She was his partner. He was her copilot. It was an unwritten law that they took care of each other, and it didn't matter how new he was. Reluctantly Armstrong released his grip on Storm's other arm. There was a trace of disbelief in his green eyes, questioning Bram's motives. He glanced up at Storm, who was trying to wipe away the tears with her trembling hands.

"Stormie?"

"I—Bram will take care of me," she stammered thickly. "I'm going to get up anyway. You guys don't need me waking you up again. Especially when we're on alert." She rose unsteadily, grateful for Bram's assistance. Grabbing her boots, she stumbled from the room and headed toward the lounge. She found a chair and sat down, pulling on the boots and lacing them up expertly out of habit. Bram joined her moments later, his boots already on. His hair was tousled, his eyes puffy with sleep. She felt a sharp stab of guilt as she met his inquiring blue gaze.

"I'm sorry, Bram," she murmured, standing.

He shrugged his broad shoulders. "Don't be. Come on, let's go for a walk. You need some fresh air."

How did he know that? The confining area was almost suffocating her. She made no protest when he kept his hand on her arm as he led her outside into the muggy night. They walked away from the building toward the ramp in the distance. Once the darkness closed in on her, she felt better. Looking up, Storm lost herself in the beauty of the night sky. They walked for almost ten minutes before she finally came to a stop and turned to Bram.

"You must think I'm crazy."

His craggy features were shadowed by the starlight as he looked down on her. "No. I think something traumatic happened recently. I've known too many good pilots who had to bail out or lost someone in a crash to think you're crazy." A slight smile pulled at his mouth. "You scared the hell out of me, though. I probably rose two feet off that bunk when you started screaming."

Storm shakily pushed her slender fingers through her hair. "God, I feel like a fool," she muttered. "What will the other guys think?"

Bram reached out, placing both hands on her shoulders, his fingers lightly massaging the tenseness out of them. "They were worried for you, Storm. Want to tell me what happened? I'm your copilot, remember? We're a team now."

She was grateful for his gentle demeanor. His hands were strong and coaxing to her taut shoulder muscles, and she longed just to fall into his arms. Hesitantly she told him about Dave Walker. Tears welled up in her eyes again as she repeated the nightmare to him.

Bram released her, then lifted his callused hands and framed her face, forcing her to look up at him. His heart wrenched in his chest as he saw the glittering gray diamonds of her eyes awash with tears.

"Look," he said evenly, "that was a situation where no matter what you said or how you felt, Storm, Dave would have done it anyway. If he loved children that much, you had to expect that of him. He counted on the smuggler giving up the child, not shooting him instead," he told her softly.

Huge tears rolled down her taut cheeks and Bram's features blurred. "But—but I lost my copilot!" she cried hoarsely. "I was responsible! I should have done something more—"

Bram's face tightened, his eyes darkening. "Listen to me, Storm," he said gruffly in a more authoritative voice, "you did all you could. You sat with a helicopter perched on a yacht that was unstable as hell. There was no way you could shut down the 52 and go out there to help him. The helicopter might have slid off into the ocean. You accurately assessed your duties." His lips became a grim line. "Quit blaming yourself. You're human. You did the best you could under some hellish circumstances. You're damn lucky those smugglers didn't start firing at you. Hell, you could have been killed too!"

His touch was excruciating, awakening her dormant senses to an agonizing awareness. What he said was true. She knew

that in her head. But in her heart—her heart was shattered with
the loss of Dave. She had lost two men whom she had loved and
cared for deeply in the span of a year. Dave had been like a replacement for her brother Cal, whom she adored but rarely saw
anymore.

"Oh, Bram . . ." she whispered rawly, "I hurt so much inside for Dave's wife and his children . . ."

"Come here," he ordered sternly, and took her into his arms,
crushing her against his body. He had felt her hesitate initially
but then Storm had fallen against him like a supple willow. He
groaned, feeling her softness yield against the hard planes of his
body. He placed one hand against her silken hair, aware of her
special female fragrance that thrilled all his senses. She buried
her head on his shoulder, crying softly, and he held her, rocking her gently in the darkness, murmuring comforting words of
solace near her ear.

Finally the tears eased and so did the pain she had been carrying in her heart. The feel of being held was overwhelmingly
consoling to her ravaged spirit, and Storm nuzzled into Bram
like a lost kitten beneath his solid jaw, content to remain there.
Other senses were coming to life within her, though, as she became aware of his steady heartbeat, his male scent, and the
strength of his arms around her body, providing her with safety.
It was all so crazy. She had known Bram Gallagher less than a
week, and here she was in his arms. Somehow it seemed right,
and she knew he felt the same way.

Bram stroked her hair. "Better?" His voice was husky.

Storm nodded, not wanting to pull away but knowing she
must. Reluctantly she placed her hands on his chest, looking up
into his shadowed unreadable face. His cobalt eyes gleamed,
sending a shiver of longing coursing through her.

"I'm sure you need this on top of everything else," she said,
her voice hoarse.

A slight smile curved the corners of his mouth. "I don't
consider you a problem, Storm." His arms tightened momentarily against her, and she became wildly aware of his arousal,
her body tingling with an aching fire of its own. "Matter of
fact, if you want the truth, it's nice to be needed again."

Her heart wrenched as she heard the pain reflected in his
voice. He had tried to disguise it with lightness, but she had
heard the inflection. Bram was affecting her sensually, and

Storm fought to maintain a level of lucidity. Stepping out of his embrace, she said, "You don't need me crying on your shoulder."

Again that same smile warmed her heart. "How long has it been since you cried, Storm?"

Touching her flushed cheeks with her palms, she closed her eyes. "A year."

"I'm glad you decided to put those tears on my shoulder, then," he said, pointing to the darkened patch on his flight uniform.

She managed a partial smile. "Masochist."

"You got it. Come on; feel like walking back now?"

Storm hesitated, her eyes widening. "I—I'm afraid I'll wake them up again with my screams."

Bram shook his head. He slid his hand around her waist, pulling her against him and urging her to walk beside him. "It won't come back tonight, Storm."

She stared up at him in a daze. "Promise, Bram?" She felt the unreasonable fear of a little girl. And right now she needed his reassuring strength. He gazed down at her, pulling her close for just a second and then releasing her.

"I promise, princess," he whispered huskily.

At one thirty P.M. the next day, the pilots who would stand the next twenty-four hour alert relieved them. Storm welcomed the transition with bloodshot eyes. All she wanted to do was finish out her day at the office and then get home and relax in a hot tub of water. As Bram had promised, she had had no more nightmares.

But her sleep was light and broken. The next morning each of the pilots had come and talked individually with her, their concern evident. It almost made her cry again. Bram had remained in the background, watching her, their eyes occasionally meeting, but allowing the other men to show their concern toward her. It was this family feeling that had made Storm realize long ago that she would never give up this wonderful career. She gained a sense of achievement when they rescued people from life-threatening situations. And when she needed support, the pilots and crews were there for her—just as she had always been there in the past for each of them and their families.

Bram walked with her toward the parking lot. He glanced down at her. "Why don't you go home and get some rest," he suggested.

"I intend to." Storm gazed up at his strong, confident face. "What will you do this evening?"

He snorted. "Unpack. I just bought a house, and everything is still in boxes."

She frowned. He was alone, without family and friends here at a new duty station. And on top of that, just divorced. Storm remembered what it was like when Hal had died. If it hadn't been for the other pilots' families inviting her over for dinner or just coming to visit, she probably wouldn't have made it.

"W-would you like to come over for a home-cooked meal tonight?" she ventured.

Bram's brows shot up, his eyes mirroring surprise. It made her heart wrench when she realized just how human he was. Seeing usually the bulwark of strength surrounding him, it was easy for Storm to forget that he was a man with vulnerabilities, weaknesses, and strengths like anyone else. His boyish response stole her heart away.

"A home-cooked meal?"

She gave him a genuine smile, halting at her sports car. "Yeah. Real food. Nothing out of a can. Well?"

Bram grinned broadly, excitement shining in his blue eyes. "Sure."

Taking a pen from the pocket on the left arm of his flight suit, Storm dug out a small notepad from her pants pocket, scribbling down her address and phone number. "Here," she said, slipping the paper into his hand. "If you get lost, give me a call. I doubt you will. Opa-Locka is too small to get lost in. Or if you can't make it, call me."

He stared down at the paper and then up at her. There was a newfound gentleness in his expression. "You don't have to do this, Storm."

"You're right. I don't have to do anything I don't want to. See you at six thirty, Bram."

Bram arrived at exactly 1830. The door was open, and he peered through the screen as he knocked.

"Come on in," Storm called.

She dried her hands on a towel, meeting him as he wandered through the foyer on his way to the kitchen. A smile lit up her features when she saw him. He was dressed in a pair of well-worn jeans that hugged his lower body and a pale blue short-sleeve shirt. He smiled, handing her a bottle of wine.

"I didn't know if you were going to have fish or meat, so I compromised on a rosé," he said by way of explanation.

Storm was touched by his thoughtfulness, and she detected a hint of shyness in him. In Bram Gallagher? Maybe she had misread the man behind the brash Air-Force image. He was clean-shaven, his eyes clear and hair still damp from a recent shower. "Actually I thought barbecued chicken was in order. It's easy to fix, and we can stay outdoors until the mosquitoes decide to get their required pint of blood."

"Chicken sounds delicious," he responded with a smile.

"Come on. You can help me make the salad. I assume you eat vegetables?"

"Yeah, I like rabbit food."

Storm laughed, feeling high with happiness. She noticed the way he looked at her, and it sent the blood rushing to her cheeks. Once in the small kitchen, she gave him a cutting board, a knife, and some radishes.

"You cut those up, and I'll slice the green pepper."

Bram raised one eyebrow, casting a look over at her as she worked a few feet away. "Anyone ever suggest you wear shorts and a tank top to work instead of a flight suit?"

Storm shot him a look. "A few people," she admitted.

"I'll bet it was more than just a few," he rejoined, grinning. Damn, she had the most beautiful pair of legs he had seen in a long time. They were long, shapely, and golden-tanned. But more than that, there wasn't an ounce of fat on her. "You jog by any chance?"

"Religiously. And you?"

"Not so religiously. Maybe a couple of miles every second or third day. You?"

Storm squelched a smile, her heart fluttering in her breast. He was good for her badly deflated feminine ego. "Three miles a day whether I want to or not."

"I can tell," he murmured appreciatively. Not only that, but the light pink tank top clung to her like a second skin, revealing nicely rounded breasts.

"Thank you," she said, forcing herself to pay attention to the green pepper. Otherwise she'd end up cutting off her fingers, he affected her so strongly.

"You look better, Storm," he said, looking up from his duties.

"I climbed into a hot tub and soaked for a while. It does wonders, believe me."

"No more dark shadows under those beautiful gray eyes of yours."

"Flatterer."

"You need it."

"Being a chauvinist again?"

Bram grinned boldly. "Hardly. After I got over the initial shock that you were really a pilot, and, to top it off, my AC, I decided to change my attitude and enjoy the scenery."

Storm laughed, shaking her head. "One of these days, Gallagher, all that Irish blarney that comes so trippingly off your tongue is going to get you into trouble," she promised, walking by him. She hesitated at the door, catching the widening smile on his face. There was an incredible naturalness that existed between them no matter where they were. Bram was the first man she had invited into her cloistered existence since Hal's death. And she was glad it was him.

"Usually," he informed her archly, "this quicksilver tongue of mine gets me *out* of trouble, not into it."

"I hope you speak Spanish, then."

"I do. And German. And French. Satisfied?"

"I'm impressed. I can barely speak English fluently."

"Lady, all you have to do is just stand there. Your eyes speak eloquently enough for you," he said throatily, catching her widening gaze.

Flustered, Storm had no quick answer. "When you finish, bring the salad and come join me outside."

Bram cocked his head. "What's the matter, the heat getting to be too much in the kitchen?"

"Wise guy," she taunted. "I'm going to open that bottle of wine. We can sit in the shade drinking it while the chicken gets done."

He grinned. "I'll see you in a few minutes."

The house was a one-story ivory stucco with wooden shutters that could be closed to protect the windows during hurricane season. As Bram wandered through it he decided that he liked the warmth of Storm's home. And it was a home, he decided, admiring the pale peach walls and burnt orange furniture coupled with brass and glass coffee tables and lamps. She had good taste, but then, that was obvious in her personal sense of style and quality.

The backyard was enclosed by a six-foot-high fence. A large cypress tree with hanging moss drooping off its limbs dominated the center of the yard. Storm was busy basting the succulent chicken in spicy sauce when he ambled out the back door with the bowl of salad in his hands. He ducked beneath the spreading arms of the cypress to join her. She had opened the bottle of wine and placed it on the picnic table, two glasses poured and waiting. Picking them up, Bram handed one to Storm when she had completed her duties.

"Let's toast," he said, touching her glass with his, gravely meeting her gray eyes. "To a friendship that will last a lifetime from this day onward."

Her lips parted and for a precious second, Storm lost all coherent thought as she met his midnight blue eyes that touched her aching heart and body. Swallowing, she nodded. "Yes, to friendship. The very best of all worlds combined," she murmured sincerely, taking a sip of the rosé.

Bram watched her intently as he drank. Her face was flushed from working over the barbecue. There was a luminous glow to her features that made her appear eighteen-years-old. Now her gray eyes were lively and not as somber as before. Wispy bangs had been dampened where they touched her brow, her ginger hair curving around her square face, lending her a softness he hadn't been aware of before. Or had he? Bram wanted to say out loud, Stop; don't say another word. Just stand there and let me drink in all of you, Storm. Let me map out your face in my mind's eye so I can carry it with me forever.... Whatever could he be thinking? Disgruntled with his own rampant thoughts, he sat down opposite her, appreciating her long thoroughbred legs.

"You acted surprised when I invited you over for dinner," Storm said, breaking into his thoughts.

Bram roused himself, meeting her curious gaze. "I didn't want you to do it because you felt you had to. Just because I held you and maybe helped you last night doesn't mean you owe me anything."

She warmed to his honesty. "That wasn't the reason, Bram."

"What was?"

"I tried to imagine what it would be like to move to a new base where you knew no one. You have no friends here—" she lowered her lashes "—and without a wife, I figured you had to be awfully lonely."

He took another sip of wine. In a way, he wished he had something stronger to drink right now to numb his mind and body, which were responding to Storm on a physical level. He had to fight himself. "So you felt sorry for me?"

"No. Compassion."

His blue eyes sparkled. "Thanks. I'm glad I'm not here out of pity."

"Pity is the most useless emotion in the world," Storm answered softly, her tone suddenly serious.

"That and guilt."

"Ouch. I'm afraid I'm still carrying around that particular emotion with me."

Bram slid his long strong fingers around the beaded coolness of the wineglass. "Because of Dave's death?"

Storm sobered. "Yes."

"About five years ago I lost my radar-navigator when we had to bail out of the Phantom I was flying," he told her in a softened voice. "Chuck had to go first because if I bailed out, the blast of the ejection would have injured him. Apparently his ejection seat wouldn't work, so he tried to manually bail out, but that didn't work either." He shrugged, resting his arms on his thighs and staring down at the grass. "I bailed out at seven-thousand feet in the dive figuring I'd die, too, because I'd passed all the altitude limits for safe ejection. I thought I'd end up eating dirt before my chute pack ever opened."

Storm grew solemn. "Thank God, you didn't die." The fervency of her hushed words startled them both. She blushed deeply, at a loss for words. She nervously fingered the stem of the wineglass, suddenly rising to busy herself with turning the chicken over on the grill.

Bram sat back, watching her. There was an indefinable magic simmering between them. He had felt it that first day in the hangar when they met. Despite his shock, he had been drawn to Storm. And last night, when she had cried in his arms, his closed, guarded heart had reached out to comfort her. Storm had been like a lost, frightened child in those precious twenty minutes, entrusting herself completely to his protection. And it had brought out a side of him that had rarely surfaced before. Storm was strong-willed, like himself; nevertheless, she had not lost her vulnerability or her femininity. She had not lost the ability to lean on someone when she was weak. A smile played on his mouth as he watched her beneath half-closed eyes. You are rare, he told her in his thoughts. Just as rare as your name. . . .

"How did you end up with a name like Storm?" he asked suddenly.

Storm took a deep breath, thankful to be on safer ground with him. She sat back down, crossing her slim legs. "My mother loves thunderstorms, so, that's how I got the name," she explained. "I guess I howled lustily in the delivery room, and Mom put two and two together and came up with Storm."

He grinned with her. "It's a beautiful name."

"Growing up with it wasn't," she laughed. "It got me into more trouble. The kids all thought I was a scrapper of some sort. Cal and Matt, my brothers, ended up defending me a lot as a consequence."

"You're a lover, not a fighter," Bram interjected.

She shrugged bashfully. "I'll take the fifth on that one."

"Everyone thought you were a cloudburst just ready to rain on somebody's parade?"

"That was about the size of it."

"So tell me, how in the hell did you end up as a Coast Guard helicopter pilot? Was it your name?"

Storm laughed. "No, my father owns a crop-dusting business here in Florida. He uses helicopters instead of fixed-wing aircraft to spray the orchards. They live over in Clearwater, as a matter of fact. He's spent his life dusting orchards all over the state."

"So you were born with a cyclic in the right hand and a collective in the other," he teased.

"Almost." Her gray eyes grew warm with fond memories. "You have to meet my parents to appreciate them, Bram. My mother was a feminist long before the word was even coined. And my father was never one to put women under his foot or in their place. So when I came along, I starting riding in helicopters like Cal did from age seven on. I soloed at age sixteen and flew with my father until I entered Coast Guard flight school. The rest is history—I've been in SAR ever since, one way or another. And I hope to stay in it another ten years before they move me up the chain of command to manning a desk instead.''

He rested his chin against his folded hands, enjoying her openness and warmth. ''I like the confidence you have in yourself,'' he declared. ''You have a career that complements your strengths.''

''And my weaknesses,'' she reminded him. ''I have my Achilles' heel too, Bram.''

''You going to tell me what they are, or do I have to find out for myself?'' he teased.

''I think it would be dangerous to tell you.'' She laughed.

Storm rose and brought over the blue and white china plates. The chicken was done. Ladling out two huge spoonfuls of potato salad onto his plate, she handed it to Bram. ''How many pieces of chicken?''

Bram came around the end of the table, standing next to her at the barbecue. ''Three?''

''Hungry, aren't you?'' she commented dryly.

''When it comes to home cooking, lady, I'll eat more than my fair share.''

Storm smiled, placing the chicken on his plate. She chose a breast for herself and joined him at the table. The tangy salt breeze moved the humid air just enough to make it pleasant beneath the enfolding arms of the huge old cypress tree. Bram dug into the meal as if he were starving and it touched her heart. A softened smile touched Storm's lips, but she said nothing.

Four

After dinner, Storm brought out a fresh strawberry pie replete with whipped cream topping. She laughed as she cut Bram a piece, handing it to him.

"There's no secret in how a woman gets to you."

He grinned appreciatively. "What? Through my stomach?"

"Yes."

"Listen, after struggling through a year of my own cooking, you're probably right." He gave her an arch look. "Why? Are you trying to get my attention?"

Storm grinned merrily, cutting a piece of the pie. "Not at all, Lieutenant Gallagher. Besides, I wouldn't want a man to love me just for my cooking abilities."

He dawdled over the pie, watching her. "What would make you interested in a man?"

Casting a quick look over at him, Storm realized their teasing had turned serious and her heart beat unsteadily in response. She placed both elbows on the table, meeting his curious gaze. "I was married to a wonderful man for five years before he died in an accident, Bram." Her gray eyes darkened with pain. "We were the best of friends. We enjoyed each other's company whether it was sharing a mutual career or just doing housework together."

"So, friendship is important to you?"

She nodded, studying the pie and realizing her appetite had fled. "When we made our toast earlier, I meant what I said about friendship being the very best of all worlds combined." Storm gave him half a smile. "The bedroom scene is important, but lust dies very quickly compared to real love."

"But it can be fun while it's happening."

She grinned with him. "I suppose you're right—if that's all you expect out of it and realize it's not a very sturdy foundation for a relationship."

His blue eyes glimmered with mirth. "What else is important to you in a relationship, Storm?"

"Honesty."

Bram nodded soberly. "I'll drink to that." He paused for a moment. "I gather your husband was in the Coast Guard also?"

Storm took a deep breath. It was the first time she had ever discussed Hal's death. Yet here now with Bram, it seemed right, and she followed her intuition. "Yes. We met at my first assigned station, which was Air Station Clearwater. I was assigned to fly the larger helicopters, the twin-engine H-3Fs."

"So, you were his copilot?"

"Yes. During the following year, we fell in love. Spending so much time together as a crew, we discovered we had a lot in common."

Bram heard the wistful note in her voice and envied her. "I wish I could say my exploration into marriage was as good," he said harshly.

Storm tipped her head, giving him a look full of compassion. "Interesting that you call it an exploration," she murmured.

He finished off the pie, then poured the last of the rosé into their wineglasses. "I was single until I was twenty-six, Storm."

"Wild oats to sow by any chance?"

"Probably. I was having too much fun living it up. Flying hard, meeting the boys regularly over at the Officers' Club afterward for drinks, and enjoying the women who liked to be in the company of fighter pilots."

Storm's eyes glimmered with laughter, and he saw it, giving her a rueful grin.

"Hey, life to me is one nonstop adventure. I don't apologize to anyone for what I did or didn't do. I took full responsibility for my actions. Sometimes I had a great time. Sometimes I crashed and burned."

"Can't you use some other metaphor?"

"Fighter jock talk, that's all," he assured her, smiling.

"So, one of the fast women finally settled her loop around you, and you got married?" Storm asked.

"Maggie had red hair, green eyes, and a temper to match," he told her. "I liked her spunk. There was always excitement wherever she went, and I wanted to be a part of it."

Storm rested her chin on her folded hands, curbing a knowing smile. "So, how long did it last?"

"Five years. And looking back on it, I was kind of proud of the fact that it held together that long." He looked up at Storm. "Maggie didn't like being tied down to one place too long. She said she had nomadic blood in her veins or some such thing. Blamed it on her need to travel and to be in a constant state of motion and animation."

"So, she didn't like being base-bound?" Storm asked, thinking that any woman who married a career officer had to get used to some less than wonderful conditions at air bases.

"You got it."

"Did you really love her, Bram?"

He ran his fingers through his hair. "Honestly? Yes. But it was that romantic lust you were talking about earlier that was the reason I married her. It was great for a year, but after that, things faded fast."

She stared at him intently for a moment. "From the tone in your voice, I'd say you loved her a great deal even though your reasons for getting together were different at first."

Bram refused to meet her knowing gray eyes. "How did you get to be so smart, Travis, and still be under thirty?" he growled.

"I can hear the pain in your voice, Bram. That's not age talking, it's wisdom."

He sat there, resting on his elbows, his face now placid and thoughtful. "I really did fall in love with Maggie during that first year," he admitted. "I liked her spirit, her zest for life."

His voice dropped to a whisper and he shook his head. "The only trouble was, she didn't love me. She was happy for about a year, and then she more or less lost interest in married life. I hadn't. I saw the woman beneath her dazzling facade, and I fell in love with her."

Storm saw the anguish in his eyes when he talked of his ex-wife and reached out and touched his arm to give him solace. "Well, if it makes you feel any better, I've been emotionally crippled by this past year."

Bram smiled gently. "We're some combination, eh?"

Storm nodded thoughtfully. "I guess we've both lived through some hard times," she intoned. She grinned over at him. "Just a couple of sad cases, right?"

Bram raised one eyebrow and gave her that intent look that always thrilled her. "Well, with a pair like us, we have nowhere to go but up from here, right?"

"Right," Storm agreed. "If nothing else, we can make each other laugh when we're crawling around in our individual depressions."

Groaning, he got to his feet. "Don't remind me. I've been through enough hell this past year with Maggie leaving me and fighting my way through flight school."

"Well," she informed him dryly, "things will go better from here on out."

"Is that a promise?"

"Yup. Every dog has its day, Gallagher, and we'll have ours. We'll wind up winners; I promise."

Next morning Storm dressed in her light blue summer uniform to assume her duties as assistant training officer for the air station. Hooking the bright red and blue tie at her throat, she picked up her purse. The morning was beautiful, and she enjoyed driving to work with the top down on her sports car. All her thoughts centered on Bram and the wonderful dinner they had shared together. She liked the fact that Bram could poke fun at himself and admit the mistakes he had made. He was a man with tremendous confidence, but he didn't allow his ego or pride to get him into lasting trouble. That was a commendable trait, she thought. Just thinking about Bram's honest talk and easy laugh made her happy. He'd turned out to be even

more special than she'd imagined. Smiling, she parked the car
and walked into the Administration building.

Her office was located halfway down the passageway, on the
left. LCDR Bob Moody was the training officer, and she was
his assistant. Every pilot and copilot had collateral duties besides flying SAR. She grimaced, knowing the paperwork on her
desk was going to be tremendous by today. The double load
they all carried was awesome. There wasn't an officer around
who didn't acknowledge the pressure of duty combined with a
grueling SAR schedule. Taking off her cap as she walked into
her office, Storm halted, her eyes widening. There, in the center of her neatly kept desk was one red rosebud in a beautiful
cut-glass vase. The beginning of a smile touched her lips as she
stared down at it in disbelief. Placing her purse and hat on the
coat rack, Storm walked over to her desk and sat down, opening the card that was leaning up against the vase.

Dear Princess,
Have lunch with me today at Pondi's Restaurant at 12:30.
I'll buy.

Just another Sad Case

Storm smiled tenderly as she stared down at the scrawled
handwriting. "Bram Gallagher, what am I going to do with
you?" she whispered. Reaching out, she petted the velvety red
bud, which was just beginning to unfold. It smelled heavenly.
She sat back, shaking her head.

"Who's the secret admirer?" Bob Moody stuck his head into
her office.

Storm smiled. "None of your business."

Bob grinned, leaning against the door jamb. "Well, whoever it is, it's about time, Stormie."

Laughing, she tucked the note into her desk. "You're as bad
as Kyle and the gang. Trying to marry me off, Bob?"

"We just want to see you happy again, that's all," he reassured her.

Storm's heart ached with warmth toward him. "I know," she
whispered, losing her smile. "And all you guys have been the
best tonic in the world for me. You know that."

Bob rubbed his slender jaw, his brown eyes alight with enjoyment. "Yeah, but we're all married and can't chase after

you ourselves. Whoever the guy is who sent you that rose had better appreciate what he has.''

Storm pulled out some documents that were begging for her attention from the In file basket. ''Oh, I think he does,'' she answered.

''Not going to tell me who, huh?''

''No.''

''Lucky bastard,'' Bob said, smiling. ''He'd just better damn well appreciate the fact that you're special, that's all.''

Storm tried to quell her feelings of excitement throughout the morning. Every hour dragged by, and she had to force herself to stop watching the clock. My God, she was acting like an eighteen-year-old girl instead of a twenty-eight-year-old woman! Chastising herself, Storm concentrated on her given tasks, refusing to look at the clock anymore. But occasionally she did raise her head to stare dreamily over at the rose, inhaling the fragrant scent that hovered in her office like a delicate perfume.

Everyone else in Admin had left for lunch, so the place was practically deserted when Bram wandered through its doors. Dressed in dark blue slacks and the mandatory light blue shirt, he removed his garrison cap as he walked down the empty hall. He lightened his step as he neared her office and quietly came to a halt at the doorway in order to watch Storm work.

His eyes mellowed with warmth as he saw that she had placed the rose near her left arm, well within reach if she cared to touch or smell it. Out of the flight suit and in the more feminine apparel of her uniform skirt and blouse, Storm looked breathtaking in his eyes. Crossing his arms, he leaned up against the door, a grin playing at his lips as he watched her.

''Do you always work this hard?'' he asked.

Storm jerked her head up with a gasp of surprise. Her heart leapt to a momentary thundering gallop. Closing her eyes, she placed her hand on her breast, leaning back in her chair.

''You scared the hell out of me, Bram!'' she whispered.

''Sorry. Ready to eat?''

Laying down the pen, Storm smiled. ''Sure am. I'm starved.'' Her face softened as she caressed the rose. ''And thank you for this. It was a lovely surprise.''

His smile was genuine. "Roses are always reserved for beautiful women."

She stood, coming around the desk and retrieving her hat and purse, a look of devilry in her gray eyes. "Is that more of the Gallagher malarkey designed to impress the woman he wants?"

Placing his hand beneath her elbow, he guided her out down the hall. "Absolutely." And then he gave her a wicked look. "Well, were you impressed?"

Laughing, she nodded. "Very. I love flowers, and it's been a long time since I've gotten some. It was a lovely thought, Bram," she whispered, becoming serious and meeting his midnight blue eyes. "Thank you."

"No one ever said that two sad cases couldn't make each other smile every once in a while, did they?"

Storm smiled in agreement. "No, they didn't. And you certainly made my day, and then some. No matter what else goes wrong today, it won't faze me. All I have to do is touch that rose's velvet petals or lean over and smell its wonderful fragrance, and all my worries disappear."

Bram nodded, opening the door of his car for her. "You're a romantic at heart, Lieutenant Travis, and that appeals greatly to my instincts."

Storm paused, waiting for him to get in. When he did, she gave him a wicked look in return. "I just wonder which instincts you're referring to, Gallagher."

His glance was almost a leer. "You're just going to have to wait with bated breath to find out, aren't you?"

"You're impossible," she teased.

"Yeah, so I've been told."

Storm cringed inwardly when they entered Pondi's. It was a popular off-base restaurant located near the air station. Many of the pilots ate there as a change of pace from military cooking. Storm saw the looks on her friends' faces. What did they expect? Bram was her copilot! Still, the look on Kyle Armstrong's face and a few others' made her feel embarrassed. She was grateful for Bram's quick appraisal of the situation.

"Why do I get the feeling the rest of these fly boys are intensely protective of you and don't want to see you with another man?" he whispered near her ear.

"They mean well, Bram. They all knew Hal and you're seeing the family attitude at work," she explained lamely, sitting down opposite him in the booth. After ordering a drink and their lunch, Storm relaxed, enjoying Bram's presence. She decided to ignore the speculative looks they had received.

"We're scheduled for a training flight tomorrow morning," he informed her.

"Oh?"

"Yeah, I guess the Ops officer wants me to get my feet wet in a hurry. We have training scheduled every other day for the next month."

"I'm not surprised."

"Is it because I was a jet jockey at one time?" he asked wryly.

Storm shook her head. "No, it's because of hurricane season coming in late August through October, Bram. They don't want any pilot going out with a green copilot in weather situations that arise during that time of year. I imagine Commander Harrison figured you could take the punishment of the training to protect you and me."

"But that means that you're logging in a hell of a lot more time in the cockpit getting me trained."

"I can take it," she assured him, trying not to smile.

She liked his protectiveness toward her. "Are you always this protective?"

Bram shrugged, taking the Scotch and water that the waitress handed to him. "Maggie always accused me of being overprotective. She said it suffocated her. Maybe I am. Just part of my nature."

Lifting the vodka gimlet to her lips, Storm took a sip. Setting it back down, she said, "Well, I find it kind of refreshing."

"Aha, you mean you're not all feminist?" he challenged.

"I think I'm a nice blend of present with past," she defended herself archly. "I don't want any male to tell me what he thinks I can or cannot do. That should be left up to me to decide."

"But you still love flowers and will let a man take you to dinner?"

"You bet."

"Thank God!" Bram countered, raising his eyes heavenward.

Her laughter was full and unrestrained, and Storm didn't realize that the other pilots in the restaurant were smiling in response.

Five

"Storm, wake up!" Bram called, giving her shoulder a gentle shake. He heard her mumble incoherently, turning slowly on her back. Even in the shadowed darkness of the alert quarters, he could see the exhaustion in her features.

"What?" she asked thickly.

"We have a rescue," he explained, gripping her hand and helping her sit up. "Didn't you hear the alarm go off?"

"Uh," she groaned, rubbing her face tiredly. "No—I guess not . . . I'll be out in a second. Just let me get my boots on. . . ."

Bram waited in the silence of the lounge, watching her stumble out of the sleeping quarters. The last month and a half was beginning to tell on both of them, but particularly on Storm. He worried about the paleness of her features. "Come on," he coaxed, putting his hand on her elbow, "The ODO wants to see us right away."

They rode down to Ops in a companionable silence. Lieutenant Kenny Hoffman glanced up as they entered the office.

"Grab a cup of coffee," he told them, pointing to the percolator.

"I'll get it," Bram told her.

Storm gave him a grateful look. "Thanks. Okay, Ken, what do we have?"

He shook his head woefully. "Figure it out—the weather deteriorates to fog so damn thick you can cut it with a knife, and everybody gets into trouble." He went over to a large map that hung on the back wall. "We received word earlier from Communications that a light plane ditched. The source of the call was unknown and came in on a VHF-FM radio."

She took the cup of coffee from Bram, thanking him silently with her eyes. Taking a sip, she sat it down, starting to scribble some necessary information on the briefing form that would be needed for the case. "Any FAA flights through that area?"

"Yeah, one. It appears to be the plane that ditched. It's only twenty miles offshore, so that will give you plenty of on-scene time in the area to try and find them."

"God only knows how in this fog," Bram murmured, gazing out the window at the thick gray curtain.

Ken nodded unhappily and peered over at Storm. "I have a Falcon crew who will be going up in about twenty minutes. They'll use their radar to home in on the ditched plane's debris, and they'll vector you in to where it's located. I've got a cutter on its way. If you can't locate the aircraft, they'll stop every few minutes and listen for people in the water near the crash area."

"Good," she muttered. "If we can't get down in the water to rescue them, then the cutter can get to them instead."

"You got it."

She looked at him, her eyes dark and troubled. "How many people aboard that flight, or don't they know, Ken?"

The officer avoided her look, his mouth becoming a thin line. "It's a family, Storm."

She sucked in a deep breath, chewing on her lower lip. "Kids, too?"

Kenny nodded. "Yeah, two. Parents, two kids, and grandparents, unfortunately."

"Dammit," she whispered rawly, casting a glance up at Bram. Somehow his solid breadth assuaged her. In the past month and a half, they had become an inseparable team, learning to rely on each other during several life and death situations. Bram could be trusted completely, and right now all she wanted to do was lean against him and rest. But rest had evaded them. All they had done was fly, train, and work at their respective desk jobs. There had been little time for personal contact. She saw Bram's blue eyes dim as he held her gaze. He knew she was close to exhaustion.

"I'll get with Merlin on our helo," he said.

"I'll be out as soon as possible," she promised.

Storm was settling the helmet on her head when Bram climbed aboard. He gave Merlin a pat on his thin shoulder by way of greeting and made his way forward into the shaded cockpit. The luminescent red glow from the instrument panel cast eerie shadows across their faces as they worked in unison, strapping into their harness system and going through the necessary instrument checks. Bram brought the microphone close to his mouth, glancing over at Storm.

"You know the Air Force has a good term we ought to use," he said lightly. "All the SAC bomber crews use it."

She tiredly turned her head. "What's that?"

"Ready, ready now."

A slight smile pulled at her lips. "Are we?"

"Sure. Want me to take navigation?"

Flying was the easier of the two. "I'd appreciate it, Bram."

"You got it, princess. Ready, ready now."

She warmed to the nickname he had christened her with that night out on the ramp when she had cried in his arms. Occasionally he would stroke her with the intimate phrase, and it never ceased to lift her failing spirits.

"Flatterer," she accused.

His grin broadened in the darkness, teeth starkly white against his shadowed features. "Until my dying day."

"Dying isn't funny, Bram."

"Come on, Storm, chin up. It was a joke."

After getting clearance for takeoff, Storm listened to the engine's whine increase as she pulled the 52 up into the murky whiteness of the fog. At thirty-five-hundred feet, they climbed far above the white blanket that stretched as far as they could see. Above the fog, the night was clear. It was a beautiful sight as the starlight struck the surface of the fog below them. Merlin busied himself with assembling the items that might be needed for the rescue in case they found the ditched plane before they began the track over the ocean.

"Hey, we get a day off tomorrow," Bram reminded her.

"It's a good thing. I'm going to spend it sleeping," Storm said wearily.

"How about after you wake up? Got any plans for the rest of it?"

She scowled. "Oh, just a week's worth of laundry, the house desperately needs a cleaning, and—"

"Come to the beach with me, Storm. We need time away from everything." He looked over at her, his eyes searching her features. Her skin had an opalescent glow to it, the flesh pulled tightly across her cheekbones, accenting her fatigue. "I'll bring the picnic basket and pick you up at three."

"But we don't even get off until one thirty," she protested. And then she glanced at her watch. "It's almost 0500 now."

"Trying to tell me no?"

"No." She grinned. "It sounds great, Bram, but I'm afraid I won't be much company. I'm beat."

"I'm not asking you along to entertain me, Storm," he returned dryly. "Let me take care of the details and do the worrying for both of us, okay? Just give me an unqualified yes or no."

She smiled softly. "Yes."

"Good."

"Don't gloat about it."

"Was I?"

"You know you were, Bram, so quit playing coy with me."

His laughter filled her earphones, and she grinned at him. She loved his irrepressible spirit. There had been times in the recent past when she had been grouchy and just plain irritable. But he had taken it in easy stride, cajoling her with teasing to bring her back to a better frame of mind. "I don't want to be a killjoy about this, but with the fog as bad as it is, I doubt it'll burn off in time for the beach."

"Killjoy."

"Sorry. Just giving you the facts."

"Where's that romantic streak in you, Travis? You know the sun's going to shine for us when we go to the beach."

She gave him a long look. "I might be a romantic but you're a confirmed idealist, Gallagher."

"And you love me for it. Don't you?"

Shaking her head, Storm muttered, "I give up on you."

"No, you don't. I haven't met a women yet who didn't like a man who challenged her. And you're no exception to that rule."

Their banter provided much-needed relief, and no one appreciated it more than Storm. Bram always had the ability to lighten the atmosphere when things got tense. Well, she thought grimly, it was really going to be tense when they sank back into the fog to fly the mandatory track that would hopefully lead them to where the plane had ditched. Merlin would have to watch for a sign of flares from the ocean—that is, if there were any survivors, and if they were in the area pinpointed by the Coast Guard.

"Better go down," Bram told her. "We're over the track."

"Roger. Merlin, you got your eyes peeled?"

"Sure do, lieutenant."

Compressing her lips, she put the helicopter into a gradual descent, sinking down into the cottony thickness of the fog. Within seconds, they were flying through total whiteness. All her concentration zeroed in on the helicopter instruments. She took the 52 down to a hundred-and-fifty feet off the water's surface. With the fog this heavy, no one would be able to spot a flare or any other kind of light at a higher altitude. If a flare was to be spotted at all . . .

Bram read the altitude to her every few minutes. She held the helicopter steady, thankful that there was barely any wind and the ocean was calm.

They continued their radio and flare search for the survivors. The Falcon jet high above them got a contact on radar. Bram glanced over at her.

"What do you want to do?"

"We'll drop to fifty feet at thirty-five knots of air speed over the area they've pinpointed. Read off the altitude as I descend."

"Roger. Seventy-five feet . . . seventy . . ." He continued to call out the altitude until she hit fifty. "Keep her steady at fifty. Want me to fly some?"

"Not yet." Her eyes ached from the strain of watching the instruments. It was too easy to get disoriented in fog and lose one's sense of direction. Bram knew how to fly on instruments but had little experience flying in this kind of weather. Storm would have to keep flying despite her fatigue.

They worked a track pattern crisscrossing the unseen ocean below them for almost fifteen minutes. Bram had the navigation chart spread across his thighs, calling off coordinates when they had to make another turn and take in a new unexplored part of their search pattern. Somewhere up above them, dawn was occurring, she thought. If only they had some light—anything would help. Glancing at the fuel gauge, they had another twenty minutes before they'd have to go back to base to refuel. It was 0600. The tension was palpable in the cabin; each of them was fully aware of the danger of flying so close to the ocean's surface. One slight move and they could be buying into a chunk of watery real estate.

"Target at four o'clock at twenty yards!" Merlin cried triumphantly. "A red flare!"

"Drop a Datum Marker Buoy," Storm ordered. "We always drop a DMB or a float flare so we can vector back to it, Bram," she explained.

Merlin tossed the DMB out the door seconds after her initial command.

Bram looked out the right window at her right shoulder. "Circle to the right, Storm," he ordered.

She brought the 52 around heading back toward the spot. Their eyes narrowed as they slowly passed over the area again. Storm's hands rested tensely on the controls as Bram tried to probe the fog.

"Why didn't we just fly toward the target Merlin saw?" he asked.

"Because we don't know what the Falcon saw on radar, Bram. Also, Merlin saw a flare. It could be from a sailing ship in distress. If we get in too big of a hurry and are not careful circling back to the object, we just might crash into a ship's mast or something."

He grinned tightly. "I see your point."

"That's right." Storm frowned. "Sure you didn't see spots before your eyes, Merlin?" she asked.

"Swear to God I didn't. I saw the red flicker of a flare. I know I did."

"I hope he did," Bram said.

"Yeah. I'm coming back to the left, Bram. Maybe we should have gone left in the first place."

"Ten lashes with a wet noodle."

She shook her head, a tired smile edging her mouth. "Sorry, I'm no masochist. You are, remember?"

"Oh, yeah, I forgot. Want to play the role of the sadist?"

Storm chuckled as Bram continued to look out the cockpit window. "No, thank you. I like myself just the way I am."

"That makes two of us."

"You're such a—"

"There!" Merlin cried.

Storm saw the feeble glare of a red flare staining the fog. "Merlin may need your help at the door once we set down," she told Bram.

"Right."

Circling the inverted light aircraft, the wash of the rotor blades made the fog swirl and twist into strange patterns as they approached.

"I count four people," Bram said. He called in the necessary information back to base.

Merlin was busy in the back, getting prepared to slide open the door once they landed.

"Okay," Storm muttered, bringing the 52 into a hover. She studied the ocean surface. It consisted of long rolling swells with no waves. Perfect for landing, Storm thought, breathing a sigh of relief. For once, something was with them instead of against them.

"Bram, tell base to stand by in case we need medical assistance."

"Roger."

The next few moments the 52 hovered above the greenish ocean. The wash of the rotor blades spewed up froths of seawater around the survivors clinging weakly to the wreckage of the plane. Storm landed quickly and manipulated the controls to maneuver the helicopter closer so that the door could be opened directly toward the plane.

Merlin slid the door back and locked it into position, then lowered the rescue platform. He looked toward the cockpit.

"Lieutenant Gallagher, I think I could use your help."

"You got it." He glanced over at Storm and winked. "I'll be careful," he told her, seeing the sudden pang of anguish on her face.

"Do. There's only one gunner's belt. For God's sake, don't slip off that grating platform and fall into the ocean."

He grinned, then released the shoulder straps, and carefully extricated himself from the seat. He placed a hand on her shoulder and gave it a squeeze. "You aren't going to lose me," he soothed huskily. Then he was gone.

The rescue took almost twenty minutes. Worriedly Storm watched as the four survivors were brought aboard. The elderly woman fainted once she was safely in the helicopter. The older gentleman was in shock, cradling his wife in his arms. The little boy of six valiantly let go of the plane and swam the short distance so that Merlin could retrieve him from the warm water. Bram had to slip off the grate and rescue the little four-year-old girl who refused to leave the fuselage of the aircraft. Storm watched in silence as he swam the twenty feet, his white helmet with red reflecting tape visible on the dark ocean's surface. Her heart beat frantically in her breast while she watched him disappear into the plane. She knew he was capable, but her fear of losing another copilot only increased her anxiety.

Twisting a look over her shoulder, Storm watched as they got the four survivors huddled into the warming folds of blankets. All were in shock to some degree. Then Merlin locked the door, and Bram clambered forward, soaking-wet. His face was dripping with water as he lowered himself into the seat, strapping back in.

"That's it," he said, removing his flight gloves and dropping them on the deck behind him.

"What about the others? Ken had said six were on board the plane."

"Both parents are dead. I checked them over—no pulse. Both bodies are trapped in the cockpit. When the cutter arrives, they can retrieve them."

Her lips thinned. "You positive?" They never left a rescue until everyone was accounted for.

"I'm afraid there's no question. Looks like they lost consciousness on impact. The old man said they tried to revive them, but it was no go." He cast a glance back toward the hold of the ship. "The rest are all suffering from exposure and shock." He gave her a warming look. "I think Merlin could use my help back there as soon as we lift off," he said huskily. "The grandmother fainted, and the old man isn't in any better shape." The sound of children crying forlornly filled the rear of the helicopter.

Storm nodded. "Okay." She applied power, and the 52 strained skyward, swallowed up into the fog once again. Climbing to fifteen-hundred feet, they broke free, the sunlight almost blinding them. Bram's hand wrapped around her arm, and he squeezed it gently.

"You look pale," he observed.

"I was scared."

"I know. I'm sorry, but the little girl wouldn't come. You saw how she clung to the wreckage."

Storm blinked back the tears. "Yes, I know. Look, go back and see if you can help."

"The kids just need to be held, I think."

"Okay."

"Hey..."

"She looked up after he unstrapped, meeting his melting blue gaze. "What?"

A slight smile crossed his strong sensual mouth. "You're one hell of a woman, you know that?"

A shiver of expectancy raced through her, and she avoided his gaze. Bram eased himself out of the seat, making his way back into the hold of the helo.

The sun was weakly filtering through the layers of fog by the time they arrived at the base around 0700. The ambulance was standing by. The little girl clung mutely to Bram, her arms wrapped tightly around his neck and her face buried beneath his chin. The boy gripped Bram's hand fiercely as Merlin tried to urge him to get up from the seat and walk toward the open arms of the waiting paramedic standing outside the helicopter. Storm came back to the rear and helped Bram out of the helicopter with his two frightened charges.

Storm crouched down on the runway next to Bram to meet the children's frightened looks. The little girl sobbed, throwing herself into her embrace, her small arms wrapped awkwardly around her. Tears streamed down Storm's cheeks as she spoke soothingly to the child. Bram gently guided the boy into her arms and then he and Merlin helped the grandparents down from the helicopter, escorting them to the ambulance. The next ten minutes tore Storm's heart apart. Each of the children eventually left her arms and were taken by the paramedics and placed with their exhausted grandparents. She stood up, a feeling of helplessness overwhelming her as the doors to the ambulance closed.

Bram walked over. Just his nearness allowed all the tension to drain from within her. They were left alone, both standing beside the helicopter.

"Come on," he urged softly. "Let's get over to the line shack and finish the debriefing and then we can go home."

Her gray eyes were wet with tears as she looked up into his strong face and tender gaze. "Home? Do you know how good that sounds?"

He nodded, wanting to reach out and envelop her in a hug. Under the circumstances, it wouldn't have been correct military bearing. He quelled the urge, giving her a squeeze instead. "Come on. You've done enough for one day," he murmured.

The debriefing form blurred before her eyes. Storm forced her fragmented thoughts to fill it out accurately. She felt numb with fatigue and sadness. Ken questioned them at length until finally, by 0830, they were over at the Q, getting cleaned up and ready for their collateral duty. If another SAR case came in, they could again be called to fly. Luckily, however, there was only one case, and the other crews were called to fly it. By the time 1330 came and they were officially relieved of duty, Storm was groggy with exhaustion.

Slats of sun filtered through the gray overcast sky that hung stubbornly two-hundred feet above the air station. Bram walked silently at her shoulder, checking his stride for her sake. Storm waged an inner war, trying to deal with a gamut of emotions. She tried to forget about the two children who had clung to her for comfort after being rescued. She felt Bram's hand on her arm, and she slowly halted and looked up into his face.

"You're not even walking a straight line, Storm," he said, frowning.

"I'm drunk with fatigue," she admitted, not even bothering to try to smile.

One corner of his mouth lifted. "At least you'd pass the Breathalyzer test if the cops stopped you."

She felt the ache of tears in her throat. Bram's concern unleashed the wall of emotion she had been fighting to keep contained. "Please, let me go, Bram," she begged rawly. "Just let me go home. I need to sleep this off."

He looked at her gravely, his eyes concerned. "I'm taking you home. And no argument, Storm. You're in no shape to drive. Having to fly on instruments, combined with two SARs, has done you in."

Miffed, she pulled from his grip, anger tingeing her voice. "Dammit, I just flew on instruments for a couple of hours! I think I can negotiate a twenty-minute drive to my house."

Ignoring her, he gripped her arm and led her to his car, opening the door. "Get in," he ordered tersely, brooking no argument.

She didn't have the strength to protest. Glaring at him, she slid into the car, taking off the baseball cap and stuffing it in the side pocket of the flight suit. Once he was in the car she said in a weary voice, "I just want to be left alone, Bram. Is that too simple for you to understand?"

He rested his arms on the steering wheel, looking over at her. Shadows of exhaustion were beneath his eyes; the shading of his day-old beard made him appear more gaunt. He grimaced slightly as if experiencing momentary pain. "I'm doing this for your own good," he said heavily. "Hell, you couldn't even write one sentence in there this morning without making spelling errors. That isn't like you, Storm."

She felt the backlog of tears building and leaned against the car seat, shutting her eyes tightly. Storm didn't want him to see her cry, and she was angry at him. It was helpless anger, because Bram knew what was needed under the circumstances and she was fighting it. Why? she asked herself. The weight in her chest grew heavier. She felt his hand on hers, gripping it firmly, giving it a squeeze.

"What does the SAR manual say about survivors needing to talk after they're rescued?" he asked, his voice a low vibrating tone. "If you allow survivors to talk about the loved ones they lost, it will speed recovery?"

Tears streamed down her cheeks and tangled in her hair. Storm finally raised her head, turning to look at Bram. "I didn't want you to see me like this," she quavered hoarsely.

His hand tightened on her fingers. "Why? Did you think I'd respect you less?" A slight smile filled with tenderness curved his mouth. "So what if you're a pushover for the children? All of us were equally affected by them, Storm. I looked up once and saw tears in Merlin's eyes."

She bowed her head, her lower lip trembling as tears washed down her face. "I hate missions that involve children, Bram." She said it with such force and agony that she heard Bram groan softly.

"Come here, princess," he coaxed gently, taking her into his arms. "Come here and let it go . . ."

It was so easy to turn and bury her face in the folds of his flight suit and weep. Bram rocked her gently, stroking her hair, whispering soothingly as she released the flood of pent-up anguish for the now-orphaned children. The solid beat of his heart finally brought some semblance of steadiness back to her disordered state as she lay quietly in his arms afterward.

"The children always suffer the most," she whispered, barely opening her eyes. "The adults can take shock better; take the grief. But the children have no defense against it, Bram. No defense . . ."

"This is the part of SAR no one gets used to," he agreed faintly.

Slowly Storm pulled away, peering up into his suffering face. He was no less affected by it than she or Merlin. His blue eyes were suspiciously bright, and her heart contracted with a new emotion. A broken smile fled across her tear-stained lips. "I'm glad you're here, Bram."

He leaned down, placing a warming kiss on her lips, parting them, and taking her tears away. His eyes were a turbulent, stormy blue as he drew away, his hand caressing her cheek.

"I'm finding life's opened up a whole new chapter to me, Storm," he admitted thickly. "Part of it is the Coast Guard. But you're responsible for the rest." His eyes were tender with concern. "Let's get you home."

Storm awoke sometime around five that day, still feeling exhausted. Jogging three miles, then taking a hot shower helped clear her head. Inwardly she felt as if somehow she had been emotionally purged, leaving her empty inside. But that sort of numbness always followed a particularly harrowing SAR mission. Running her fingers through her damp hair, she thought of Bram's tender comforting and she began to feel some of the depression lighten and evaporate.

The phone rang, interrupting her thoughts. Sitting down on the edge of the bed, Storm answered it.

"Hello?"

"Well, did you survive?"

She smiled, closing her eyes, loving the husky tone of Bram's voice. "Partly."

"I tried calling earlier, but you were out."

"I got up at five and went for a run. Figured it was the best way to throw off the depression."

"I could think of better ways to cheer you up," he suggested.

Storm laughed softly. "Will you ever change?"

"No, but I'm working on changing you."

A smile lingered on her lips. "I'm a lost cause, and you know it."

"I never take no for an answer. Hey, how about that picnic?"

"Now? It's almost—"

"Why not roast hot dogs and marshmallows tonight along the shore? Who said we had to go during the day?"

Her brows rose. "Say, that sounds nice. That way there aren't the tourists milling around."

"Yes, ma'am. It also means some privacy, and we can watch the moon rise together. Game?"

A new thread of excitement coursed through her. Suddenly Storm felt as if someone had lifted a hundred pounds from her shoulders. "It sounds wonderful, Bram," she agreed fervently.

"Just what the doctor ordered."

Laughing, Storm said, "Do you ever lose that undeniable sense of humor, Bram?"

"Never. When we quit laughing at ourselves in a bad situation, then the going *really* gets rough."

"I'm all for laughing, then."

"We'll drown our sorrows in a good bottle of wine tonight, trade a few stories around the campfire, and generally relax. How does that sound, princess?"

Storm cradled the receiver to her cheek, closing her eyes. She ached to have time alone with Bram. "You're a good salesperson. I'm sold."

He chuckled. "My mother always did say I could sell ice cubes to Eskimos."

The sun was sinking into the depths of the glasslike ocean as Bram made their campfire. The air was drier than usual, and Storm loved it. She breathed in the warm salty air and spread a well-worn blanket onto the sand nearby. The beach was devoid of human beings, most of them having been sunburnt during the day and retiring to their hotels to nurse their wounds. She sat back, hands resting on her long thighs, watching Bram. He wore a pair of threadbare jeans, almost washed free of their color, and a red T-shirt that outlined his magnificent shoulders and chest. A smile lingered in her eyes—he was beautiful to watch.

As if sensing her stare, he lifted his head. A few unruly strands of dark hair dipped on his brow as he smiled across the fire at her. "You look a-hundred-percent better than this morning," he told her, throwing a few more pieces of dried driftwood onto the licking flames.

"I can say the same for you."

"I guess that means we're a mutual admiration society," he teased, grinning boyishly.

Storm began to unpack the hamper, pulling out the chilled bottle of white wine and two plastic cups. "Must be. After all, if we don't love ourselves first, how can we possibly love others?"

Bram joined her, flopping down on his back and then rolling onto his side, propping himself up on one arm. He arranged the cups, waiting for her to pop the cork on the wine. "You know, that's one of the secrets to life," he said seriously.

"What? Loving ourselves first?"

"Yes. If you can't be content with yourself, forgive yourself, and in general accept yourself as you are, how can you do the same for others?"

Storm smiled distantly, pouring the wine. "Some people might accuse you of being selfish, Bram."

He raised the cup. "Let them." He raised his eyes, meeting hers. "Here's to love of self so that we have the capacity to love others..."

She gave him a guarded look and hesitantly clinked her cup against his, tasting the dry fruity wine. Bram looked supremely contented as he sipped his wine, watching the sun set in a rainbow palette of colors, and occasionally glancing over at her. It was a pleasant half-hour as they sat near each other on the blanket watching the light fade, allowing the silence between them to speak volumes.

A pale lavender stained the horizon, the darkness of night on its heels as Bram broke the silence.

"Why do you apologize for being human, Storm?" he posed softly, startling her with the question.

She stretched out next to him, resting her head in the crook of her arm. The question had been asked gently and without blame. "Explain," she said huskily, feeling the wine steal through her, making her utterly relaxed.

Bram poured the last of the wine into their cups, setting the bottle into the sand beyond the blanket. "This morning," he said. "I've been working with you for three months now, and you always get uptight when children are involved. Why are you so afraid to cry in front of me and not the other pilots?"

She rolled onto her stomach, frowning. "I'm afraid you'll think I'm weak. You never see the guys cry when there's been a bad SAR mission. They've gotten used to me doing it around them."

He snorted softly. "They cry in the arms of their wives when they get home."

Her gray eyes squinted as she recalled the times Hal had held her after highly emotional SAR cases. "Why are you asking me about crying, Bram?"

"Because I happen to think you're a highly sensitive individual who needs to let out what she feels," he explained quietly. "I've watched you bottle up a lot since we started working together."

"I can't sit in the cockpit bawling like a baby when I have to function, Bram."

"I know that."

"Than what do you want from me?"

He placed the cup on the sand, pulling her next to him, fitting her beside his male body. His cobalt eyes were flecked with gold as he searched her grave, pensive face. He traced the line of her brow, from cheek to square jaw with his fingers. "You," he whispered thickly. "I want to experience the full emotional range of Storm Travis. You share parts and pieces of yourself with me, but not all of you. I've stood by for three months watching, sensing, and feeling the woman who climbs into that flight suit and flies SAR. When things are tense, your voice is always calm. Always soothing. You make us all rally around you because we know you care. We know you know your job." A glint registered in his serious look as he caressed her satin cheek. "I've sat in the left seat watching you control that other half of you. I've seen you compress those beautiful lips into a thin line, controlling your emotions. I've watched your wide gray eyes go narrow with pain and anxiety. And I've seen you come off a mission and suppress it all." He stroked her hair, combing his fingers through the silken tresses. "And I've stood there wondering what or how you deal with all you've seen."

Storm trembled beneath his tender touch. His fingers were sure, confident, stoking the fires of her dormant body into brilliant, yearning life. Bram was so overwhelmingly male that an ache spread outward from the lower region of her body. She had been wishing for this moment for over a month now. Yet Bram had never made a move to touch her or hold her again after that first night. It was as if he sensed her need to be approached slowly; he seemed to want to prove to her that his intentions were honorable and not selfishly based. As she stared up into his darkened face, highlighted by the flickering firelight, she knew that he was serious where she was concerned. Despite his joking and teasing, he wasn't the ex-fighter jock out on the make for a one-night stand. No, her instincts had told her from that very first night that he was a man of integrity. Hesitantly she pulled her mind back to focus on his question, her gray eyes widening with vulnerability.

"I don't do anything with it," she admitted slowly.

"Why?"

She gave a painful shrug, laying her head in the crook of his arm. "When Hal was alive, I could talk with him about it, cry on his shoulder..."

Bram took a deep breath. He reached down and gently cupped her face in his hands. "Do you know that I see every emotion register on your face, Storm?"

She gave a shake of her head. "No. If you do, you're the first to tell me that."

A corner of his mouth curved upward, and he leaned down, kissing her temple. She smelled of apricots, and the scent increased his need of her. "You speak with your eyes, Storm. Sometimes I see reflections of pain there, sometimes a wistful look, and..." he placed his finger beneath her chin, raising her lips to his mouth, "...sometimes longing..."

She felt his mouth tremble slightly as it grazed her lips. The featherlike touch incited a string of explosions along her nerve endings and instinctively, she slid her hand upward, caressing his neck and curling her fingers into his dark hair. His male scent was like an aphrodisiac, spurring her hungrily forward to meet his questing mouth. Her lips parted beneath his exploration. His breath was moist against her flesh, and she pressed her body forward, needing further contact with him.

Bram groaned, pulling her possessively against him, his hands on her hips, making her aware of his arousal. Her mouth opened, trusting him, asking him to drink of her honeylike depths. A pounding hunger throbbed through him, and the smoldering spark between them caught and exploded violently to life. Her returning hunger seared him; made him tremble with need of her. All of her. A delicious sense of joy spiraled between them as he unbuttoned her blouse, sliding his hand down across her taut, expectant breast. He felt her stiffen, arching unconsciously to him as his fingertips grazed the hardened peak of her nipple. Part of him wanted to hurry, but another part gloried in the moment with Storm. Never in his life had he wanted to take the time as now to love a woman totally, love her completely. Every cell in his body screamed out for want of Storm. He bent down with agonizing slowness after pulling the lacy bra away to capture the nipple; he wanted her to enjoy the time spent in each other's arms thoroughly.

A gasp escaped her tremulous lips as his mouth settled firmly on her breast, his teeth gently tugging at her nipple, sending frenzied nerve-tingling messages to her wildly aching lower body. Her fingers sank deeply into his shoulder muscles, and Storm cried out his name, begging him, needing him. Each calloused touch of his fingers on her body as he slowly undressed her was a tormenting brand. Her mind was banished, and only her heart dominated, pounding hard with every quickened breath she took. His lips scorched her body, teasing her mercilessly, and a moan of utter necessity clawed deep

within her throat as she pleaded with Bram to take her higher
and higher where there was only loving, giving, and taking. She
felt his well-muscled body settle above her, his knee gently
urging her thighs apart, and she opened her gray eyes, meeting, melting, beneath his fiery gaze tendered with love.

In that instant, Storm knew she loved him as she had never
thought she could love another man. Bram was her match, her
equal. He met her fearlessly on her own ground, coaxed her
beyond it, and urged her to new heights of euphoria in every
sense of the word. His hand slid beneath her hips and instinctively she arched upward, desiring oneness with him. She was
unprepared for the jolting charge of pleasure, coupled with
exhilaration, as he thrust deeply into her, branding her, making her his forever. Her lips parted, a sigh of absolute joy escaping her as she closed her eyes, bringing her arms up, pulling
him down upon her to share the volcanic needs they brought to
each other. Higher and higher the throbbing, fusing sensation
of his body carried her until she felt like dissolving in rapture.
The shattering climax made her freeze, and he held her tightly,
increasing the pleasure, extending it for her, until she nearly
fainted with fulfillment. Seconds later, when she felt his body
tense, his husky voice murmuring her name, she held him close,
wanting to hold him forever.

Six

"Cold?" Bram asked hoarsely, pulling her closer into his arms.

Storm shook her head, kissing his jaw, and tasting the salt of perspiration upon his flesh. "No, just deliriously happy," she murmured, resting weakly against his supporting shoulder.

He smiled, lying above her, his arm protectively thrown across her slender waist. The moon was barely edging the horizon, sending a thin stream of light across the quiet ocean. Only the breakers crashing into a foamy existence upon the sand disturbed the silent world around them. Bram drank in her relaxed face. A slight upward curve of her lips told him how she felt. Words weren't necessary. Running his fingers lightly across her golden skin, he smoothed away the dampness created by their loving.

"When they made you, they must have broken the mold," he told her quietly, marveling at the beauty of her tall athletic body.

Storm barely opened her eyes, relishing the sensations still simmering within her body. A lazy smile touched her lips. "Is that a compliment or an insult?"

Bram grinned. "You'll never hear me run you down, princess. It was a compliment. God, you have the most beautiful legs I've ever seen on a woman." And then a distressed expression came to his face.

"What's wrong?" Storm asked, concerned.

A silly grin spread across his mouth. "Oh, I was just thinking what a crying shame it is that you have to wear those damn baggy flight suits. They hide some nice features about you, lady."

Storm slid her hand upward, marveling at the strength of his arm and shoulder. "You know what I first thought when I saw you?" she asked wistfully, her voice barely above a whisper.

"Besides my being the epitome of an arrogant, sexist bastard at the time, you mean?" he asked, leaning over, brushing the full lips that were begging to be kissed again.

"Mmm," Storm murmured, savoring his strong mouth against hers. She reveled in his ability to excite her with the slightest touch.

Bram drew a half-inch away, his blue eyes alight with tenderness. "You're easy to please, you know that?"

"That's because you know what you're doing," she murmured huskily, opening her eyes to gaze at him. "Do you want to know what else I thought?"

He nodded. "Yeah. We got sidetracked," he said ruefully, "but I'm not apologizing."

She pressed herself to him and snuggled beneath his chin. "I thought you had the broadest set of shoulders I had ever seen. I thought you could carry the weight of the world around on them."

Bram grimaced. "They should have looked short, stubby, and deflated the day I met you, then. I was just coming out of one year of my life that had been a living hell. I didn't feel very strong or broad-shouldered, believe me."

Storm sobered, hearing the pain in his voice. She quickly embraced him. "It's a good thing our physical bodies don't resemble our emotional states, then." She chuckled. "Or else I would have looked like a blob of Jell-O out there at the helicopter this morning."

He nuzzled her, placing playful nibbling kisses along the clean line of her jaw to her delicate ear. "That's why we can be a couple of sad cases, and no one can tell the difference," he said, his breath sending waves of warmth across her slender neck.

Gently she pulled away, searching his eyes. "I don't think we need to refer to ourselves that way anymore, do you?"

Bram slowly sat up, bringing her back into his arms. "No, we don't. You've survived Hal's death, and I've discovered that I'm not the least bit sad."

Storm rested her cheek against his naked chest, the small fine hairs covering it tickling her. "Somehow, Bram," she whispered, "you've helped me rescue myself from my own personal tailspin." Tracing her fingers lightly across his collarbone, she closed her eyes, loving him. "I was so lost without Hal. It was as if half of me had been destroyed in that car accident. I was lonely . . ."

He kissed her hair. "You're a woman who's used to sharing all of herself with her mate, princess. And that's a very rare quality most men would kill for."

She laughed. "Bram!"

He smiled down at her, his eyes telling her he was very serious about his last statement. The smile died on her lips as she looked up at him like a wide-eyed child. He kissed her nose.

"You think I'm kidding?"

"No . . ."

His face grew somber. "The women I've known aren't into sharing any more of themselves than necessary, Storm. Like I said before, they play a game. I'll give this part of myself if you'll give me this." He frowned. "Or they'll blackmail you with their bodies or their emotions."

"And Maggie was like that?"

He nodded. "I don't blame her for it. I understood it. I saw the psychological reasoning behind it. But it wasn't what I wanted or expected. I thought that once we got married, Maggie would begin to trust me with herself. All of herself." He looked out toward the blackened sea. "But I was wrong. She just went on playing her childish emotional games to keep me in line, so to speak."

Storm shivered, the dampness from the ocean beginning to creep inland. Bram gave her a concerned look and reached over, retrieving her blouse and helping her slide it back on. As they dressed she stole a look over at him. He looked virile and irresistible in only a pair of jeans, his chest deep and heavily muscled in the dancing firelight. She turned, sliding her arms about his thickly corded neck, and looked into his eyes.

"Bram," she said softly, her voice barely audible, "I'll always cherish this night with you. I'll never regret it . . ."

He groaned and swept her into his arms, his mouth descending on her lips, stealing her breath, causing her heart to thunder as he claimed her. Gradually he broke their heated kiss, his cobalt eyes burning into her soul, stealing her heart, infusing her with the joy of total love. "You were mine from the moment we met," he told her in a low vibrant voice. "I couldn't take my eyes off you, Storm. I didn't want to. It was just a matter of time until now."

Closing her eyes, she swayed back against him. She felt somehow complete, as she never had before. Her kiss-swollen lips hinted at a smile. "I want now to last forever."

Bram stroked her cheek, his fingers trembling slightly. "It will, princess," he promised.

They sat near the fire roasting the hot dogs, and then later the marshmallows. Storm leaned against Bram's shoulder, the warmth of the fire lulling her into a peace she had rarely felt since Hal's untimely death. Bram gingerly pulled the charred marshmallow off the stick, blowing on it until it cooled, and then held it close to her lips.

"Last one."

Opening her mouth, she allowed him to feed her. There was something satisfying in the simple gesture. "Mmm, I think I'm going to turn into a fat white marshmallow," she said laughingly, wrapping her arms around her knees.

Bram grinned, his arm resting comfortably around her shoulder, allowing her to lean against him. The flames flickered and danced over the whiteness of the sand, the rest of the world dark and shadowy around them except for the carpet of scintillating stars above. "You could stand to put on a couple of pounds. You're a little too skinny."

Storm nestled contentedly against him. "Hurricane season always leaves you short on sleep and a few pounds lighter."

"I'll be glad when we're out of it," he declared. "Then we can lead a more normal life and see each other a little more often."

She laughed. Their duty consisted of alert every fourth day. Then they had regular administrative duties at the base besides flying, training, or being called in for the special exercises required of every available pilot. "You see me twice or three times a week. Aren't you a glutton for punishment?"

"With Merlin watching us with that know-it-all gleam in his eyes? I can't lean over and kiss you; I can't touch you—" There was flat disgust in his voice. "I don't call that 'seeing' one another."

"Speaking of Merlin, he cornered me the other day and asked me what your intentions were toward me."

Bram looked down at her. "What business is that of his?" he growled.

Storm lifted her chin, looking into his narrowed eyes. "You've got to remember, all the guys at the air station are like big brothers watching out for me. Ever since you put that rose on my desk, the word's gotten around." She chuckled.

His scowl deepened. "They're all jealous," he told her. "Every damn last one of them would love to be right here beside you. They're married, and I'm not."

"Boys," she muttered. "Little boys—every last one of you. I feel like a prize marble being fought over."

He gave her a grudging smile. "Of course, I can't blame them."

"That's big of you, Gallagher."

"Don't go getting a smart mouth, Travis."

She pushed away, a glimmer of mischief in her eyes. "Yeah?" she challenged, getting to her knees. "You wouldn't be threatening me, would you?" she taunted good-naturedly. "All right, jet jockey, let's just see what you're really made of!" And with that, Storm leapt lithely to her feet, shoving him backward into the sand. The surprise written on his face was worth the spontaneous gesture on her part. Laughing, Storm whirled away, running down the beach.

"Why, you—" Bram called, shoving himself upright. And then he grinned. She was living up to her name, all right. Okay, if she was that sure of herself, he'd give her a run for her money. "You won't get away with this!" he shouted as she was swallowed up by the darkness. Sprinting through the sand after her, Bram was surprised at her speed and agility. This was a playful side to her he hadn't seen before, and it was tantalizing. His eyes quickly adjusted to the gloom as he left the area of the firelight. Storm was a good distance ahead of him, silhouetted against the thin wash of moonlight. God, she ran like a tireless cheetah, he thought as he ran swiftly to close the distance between them.

He had to run a good half-mile before even getting close to her. Once she had looked quickly across her shoulder and he had seen a smile lingering at the corners of her mouth, her face dampened by perspiration. Bram called on his reserves for a final burst of speed, but just as he got within ten feet of her Storm whirled around to a stop, her long leg arcing out in a graceful kick that barely brushed his chest. Startled, he jerked to a halt, panting hard.

Storm laughed, gulping air, assuming another languid karate position. "Come on!" she teased. "You want me, come and get me!"

He grinned, watching her closely. So, she knew karate. And what a beautifully balanced body she possessed, he thought, watching her. Her limbs gleamed in the moonlight, each movement fluidly melting into the next. "How long have you been doing that?" he asked.

"A long time."

"What color belt are you, show-off?"

Her teeth gleamed against her honey-colored skin. "Fourth-degree black. Come on, want to try and take me?"

Bram made a lunge for her. Instantly, in a breathtaking feat of athletic control, she leapt upward, both feet in the air, her left leg shooting outward, again lightly brushing his chest. Storm landed perfectly balanced, spinning around to face him. Again he tried, but she was deadly with her feet. He got nowhere. Finally he stopped trying, laughing so hard it hurt. Storm joined him, throwing herself into his arms, kissing him repeatedly. Together they fell to the dark sand, inches from the foaming surf, their laughter mingling with the roar of the ocean around them.

He rolled Storm on top of him, running his hands down her long beautifully formed back. "You're something else," he said, smiling up at her. "I'm impressed as hell. Is that what you did to keep all the men away from your door until I came along?"

She tried to struggle out of his arms, laughing. "You conceited jet jockey!" she gasped. "I might have known you'd think that! Let go of me, Bram Gallagher!"

He dodged her flailing hand. "Not on your life, honey. I don't aim to get kicked by one of your lovely feet. Now come here . . ." He slid his fingers through her hair, gently wrapping it in his hand and rolling her down onto the sand, kissing her long and hard. Her lips were salty, her mouth sweet with the taste of marshmallow. Her breasts rose and fell swiftly, and he could feel the birdlike flutter of her heart against his chest as he deepened the kiss. Storm was warm, alive, yielding, and so much woman that it made him tremble with longing for her once again. She was part playful child, but part proud woman who made no excuse for what she was or was not. He knew in that liquid moment that he loved her completely, unequivocally, and forever.

The next five days were a precious interlude with Bram that was interrupted by Hurricane Brian bearing down on them from the gulf with a vengeance. The six H-52 helicopters were in constant use, and the fifty seasoned Coast Guard pilots were being used up faster than any of them were able to get proper crew rest before flying again.

Storm ran for the safety of the hangar, her flight suit soaked before she made it inside. She walked tiredly down the long crosswalk between the busy crews repairing and preflighting the helicopters for coming missions.

Bram was already in the Ops center when she entered. Kyle Armstrong was coordinating the duty schedule that was filled with more SAR cases than they could handle. Storm thought Kyle's lean face looked drawn. But didn't everyone's? Including hers. Bram roused himself from his thoughtful posture as he studied the chart on the wall. His blue eyes warmed with unspoken affection as Storm met his gaze. She mustered a small smile; it was filled with a silent answering tenderness for him alone.

"Coffee?" Bram asked her, already moving over to the pot.

"Please," she replied thankfully, and walked over to the Ops desk.

"You look better than all of us put together, Stormie," Kyle said, handing her the next case they would fly.

Bram ambled over, handing her a cup, a smile lingering in his eyes. He knew why she looked so good, and Storm had trouble covering up her own smile as she slid her fingers around the

mug. Just the slight touch of Bram's long strong fingers made
her heart leap. How could she forget that wonderful night on
the beach? The love they had shared between them had been
pure and honest. It was a complete giving to each other without any games.

"I'd rather fly in a hurricane than have to handle drug
smugglers," she told Kyle, studying the report.

The pilot gave her a commiserating look. "You got one
there," he agreed.

Bram leaned over her shoulder, reading the report. Storm
was acutely aware of his maleness, and she had to make a conscious effort to concentrate on the paper and ignore him. Once
he turned his head, his blue eyes probing, disturbing and sensual. Sipping the coffee, Storm shot him a disgruntled look of
warning. Bram knew how much he affected her—damn him!—
and he was enjoying that bit of power over her a little too much.

"We're going to relieve the 1406?" Bram asked.

"Yes. They're running low on fuel." Kyle glanced up at both
of them. "It's going to be a sector search," he warned them.

Storm groaned. "A sector search?" That meant Bram would
also be busy with navigation duties. Imaginary grid lines were
drawn over the sea in the supposed area of the lost ship and
then followed with the use of instruments and navigation.
While it was one of the most accurate patterns for aircraft
searching alone, it was twice as hard to fly the lines in inclem-
ent weather.

"Sorry, Stormie. This is where we bite the bullet and earn our
wings. We've got a fifty-foot yacht called the *Rambler* adrift
out in this area. He pointed to the large chart behind him.
"We're spread thin and can only allot one helicopter to this
assignment."

Storm rubbed her brow, shifting her weight to one booted
foot. "What about Clearwater air base over at Tampa? Can't
they throw an H-3 our way? It has more search capability than
our 52s."

"No go. They're just as busy on that side of the state as we
are on ours. Research Coordinating Center Miami is asking
some of the northeastern air bases to send all available helicopters and crews down here to try and give us some relief.
Man, this damn hurricane has really caught everyone off guard.

So many boats were out for weekend fishing even though they were warned about Brian."

"Typical mañana mentality," Storm muttered, running her fingers through her drying hair. It was one of their most frustrating problems: Fishermen tended to disregard the seriousness and destructiveness of a hurricane. And when it hit, the boats were stranded at sea, putting an unnecessary burden on Coast Guard personnel. The "mañana mentality" of "oh, the weather will pass and I'll be safe" endangered themselves and their rescuers. She pulled herself back to the present situation. "Okay, a sector search. What else?"

"The *Rambler*'s last report to our station was that there were six people aboard and they were taking in water faster than they could pump it out. The engine aboard the yacht isn't working, so they're at the mercy of the current."

Bram frowned. "I don't think I even want to hear the weather report."

"You won't, Bram. We've got thirty-foot waves out there, and the wind's an erratic bastard at best."

"That means spray coming off the top of those waves," Storm thought out loud. It meant visibility was going to be moderately to severely reduced. She had made rescues where she could not see the outside of the windows of the 52 because of the blinding spray. Her face became grimmer. "The other crew hasn't spotted the *Rambler*?"

"Negative. Okay, let's get down to the brass tacks here so you can get out there," Kyle said briskly.

Storm lifted the 52 off into the buffeting winds around the air station. Hurricane Brian's outer arms were creating sporadic but violent wind shifts and gusts, making the handling of the helicopter constant continuous work. Merlin took his position at the window by the cabin door in the center of the helicopter, assuming lookout position. Once they were on track, they began searching the angry sea below as they followed the imaginary search pattern lines. The tension in the cabin was palpable as Bram kept calling off the coordinates to her. Five-hundred feet below them the sea was a churning gray-green mistress with waves hungrily grasping skyward with wicked intensity.

"Looks bad down there," Storm said to no one in particular.

"Amen," Merlin chimed in. "Man, if that yacht's still floating, it's going to be a miracle."

Storm's arms and fingers ached after the first thirty minutes of flying back and forth on the search pattern track. Meticulously accurate navigation in a situation like this was an absolute must. Even the slightest error in longitude or latitude could carry them away from the search area, and six lives could be lost. Bram bent over the instruments, navigation charts resting on his thighs as he concentrated on the most important task of a rescue mission.

"Target at five o'clock, two-hundred yards!" Merlin cried out excitedly.

Storm slowed and turned the bucking, shuddering 52. Squinting into the gray noontime light, she saw the *Rambler*. She heard Bram curse softly.

"Merlin, get that rescue platform ready. We're going to need it," he said.

Her lips tautened into a thin line as she dropped the 52 closer to the strewn wreckage of the once-beautiful yacht. Five bright-orange life vests were visible, with people clinging to the hull of the overturned boat. Storm's gray eyes narrowed as she jockeyed the 52 into a slow circle around the boat as Bram relayed the vital information to the air station.

"Do you see six people, Merlin?" she asked.

"Negative. Only five."

"Damn."

Bram twisted his head, glancing over at her. "What do you want to do?"

"The wind's erratic, but we've got to try lowering a basket. We've got five people in a concentrated area."

The basket was lowered from the crane hoist attached to the helo fuselage. Only two of the five were able to crawl into the wire basket to be hoisted. The other three were so weakened, they could not even grab the basket. Storm chewed on her lower lip, reviewing a number of alternatives for rescuing the other three. "Let's try to land close enough to pick them up."

"You see those waves?" Bram asked grimly.

"Yeah."

"They're at least forty feet high."

She nodded, tension seeping throughout her body, the adrenaline pouring into her bloodstream, making her heart pound. Oh, God—one wrong movement on the cyclic or collective either while floating in the basin of the troughs or upon lifting momentarily above the waves could kill them all. At the least, she'd lose the 52 to the greedy sea. At worst, they would die. Neither was pleasant to ponder.

"You tell me up or down, Bram. I'm going to have my hands full trying to follow Merlin's instructions. I don't want to divide my concentration between flying and watching those waves coming."

"Roger." He folded the charts up, stuffing them into a pouch behind his seat.

Sweat glistened on her face as she brought the 52 downwind within three-hundred feet of the yacht. Tension thrummed through the helicopter as Merlin donned the gunner's belt, a long nylon harness keeping him tethered to the craft so he wouldn't fall out or off the platform. Storm frowned worriedly. Merlin had been jerked out the door more than once trying to reach a drowning survivor with the long wood pole with a hook at the end of it. Thank God for the gunner's belt, at least.

"Okay, we're going down," she told them stiffly, measuring the last wave as it sloshed a few feet from the bottom of the 52. With a flick of the wrist and a deft touch to the collective, Storm gently set the helicopter on the ocean's wild surface. Spray immediately covered the windows of the cockpit, making it impossible to see. The wind tore at them, trying to throw the tail of the helicopter around, and Storm had to adjust to it by manipulating the foot pedals with her boots.

Merlin slid the door open, releasing the platform so it gave him three more feet for walking out on to try and reach the people who were now screaming frantically for help.

"Up," Bram told her, his voice low.

Storm raised the 52, the wave sloughing by like a predatory animal intent on dragging them downward.

"Down."

And so it went. She had not only to deal with the weather, but to listen to Bram's instructions as well as Merlin's yell above the roar of ocean, rotor blades, and people clinging to the hull only five feet away. Sweat trickled down from her armpits, soaking into her flight suit. Her gloves became damp with sweat, and she held the cyclic and collective more firmly, afraid that if her grip slipped, it would send them all to a watery grave.

"Damn," Bram snarled, watching as Merlin tried to get the first survivor off the hull and onto the platform. The yacht shifted, momentarily trapping the people. Storm brought the helo solidly against the boat, which was now beginning to break up. The survivors crawled across the hull, desperately heading toward them. Merlin leaned out, fingers stretched, yelling at them to crawl closer. "He's going to need help, Storm."

Her gray eyes were troubled. Under such conditions, another helicopter and crew was needed to help in the rescue. But they were all out on individual SAR cases. There was only one gunner's belt. Bram would be back there with no guarantee that he wouldn't fall out into the angry ocean. Her alternatives were limited: Either she left the remaining three people or— No, she couldn't release Bram to go back there and help. As copilot, he was her second set of eyes and ears. Without him up front to help her gauge when to lift off or miss the next wave, it might spell sure death for them. It was suicidal.

What should she do? If she left them and waited for help, the remaining people might drown. If she released Bram, they might all die. But one of the three survivors was a child.... Anxiety surged through her. She didn't want to lose Bram either. God, she couldn't take it! Not again....

"Storm?"

"Be careful, Bram."

He gave her a sudden tender look as he unsnapped his harness. "You bet I will, princess. Think you can handle watching the waves? I'll tell you when to lift off from the platform."

"Okay."

He patted her tense shoulder. "I'll hook up to the intercom when I get back there."

For the next fifteen agonizing minutes, Storm fought to keep the valiant 52 steady amid the turbulent sea around them. Four of the five survivors were now aboard, huddled in shock within the blankets. Sweat trickled down her brow, running into her eyes, making them smart. Hurry, hurry! she screamed silently. It was an incredible game of tag with a merciless ocean that sought to deluge them with murderous waves and a relentless wind that slammed repeatedly into the copter. Sea spray was being whipped into the helo, soaking everyone and everything.

"Closer!" Merlin yelled, standing precariously out on the platform. He extended his arm, motioning for the last woman to let go and crawl the necessary two feet to the helicopter platform. Finally a wave broke her hold on the hull, and she bobbed like a cork swallowed into the sucking grasp of the ocean. Bram grimly watched the woman flail. She was hysterical, her movements jerky and uncoordinated. Instead of striking out with steady strokes toward them, she foundered, at the mercy of the current.

"Close in on her, Lieutenant Travis!" Merlin said. "She's panicking."

Gingerly, with a feather-light touch, Storm allowed the 52 to move sideways, closing the distance between them. "Up!" Bram yelled, warning Merlin to hold on. The 52 moved upward, fighting the screaming wind, trying to crest above the next wave. Seawater slammed into the sponsons below the belly of the copter, making them shudder drunkenly. Dammit! Storm chastised herself. The waves were not a constant uniform height. They ranged anywhere from forty to fifty feet. It was hard to judge their height and simultaneously keep everything else under control.

"Down," Bram shouted. Quickly Storm maneuvered the 52 back toward the woman in the water.

Merlin cursed. "Man, she's outta her head, Lieutenant Gallagher." He tried to motion for her to swim toward them, but it was hopeless. Only five feet separated them.

Bram unsnapped his helmet, setting it on the deck. Quickly he jerked the two cords that inflated the life vest he was wearing. Grabbing the trail line, he tied it around him. Getting out of his boots, he gripped Merlin's arm. "I'll go in after her. Watch the waves for Lieutenant Travis. Just keep a firm grip on this line..."

"She's in a panic, sir," Merlin warned, screaming above the wind and rotors.

"No!" Storm yelled. "Bram—don't do it!"

With his helmet off, he was no longer in communication with her. Merlin started to relay the message, but the officer had already dived into the murky water before he could say anything.

Storm's heart lurched with anger and fear. Bram shouldn't have done it! But another part of her said Yes, he had to. She knew better. More than one crewman had dived into water to save survivors. But this time...this time it was the man she loved. That thought slammed into her, leaving Storm close to tears.

"Up!" Merlin cried.

She wrenched back on the controls. More spray and seawater slapped at the underbelly of the 52. Damn, the waves were getting larger!

Storm's throat ached with unremitting tension as she watched Bram fight his way through the violent water toward the last survivor. Her attention was torn between three separate functions, and she could not risk concentrating on Bram any longer. Merlin would have to orchestrate the rescue of Bram and the woman. An icy fear gripped her as she begged, coaxed, and swore at the 52 under her breath, coordinating the macabre dance on the ocean's surface. Another three minutes passed before Merlin was able to use the long wooden pole to snag Bram's outstretched hand and pull him aboard with the unconscious woman in his arms.

"Get her up!" Merlin cried, slamming the door shut against the howling fury of the hurricane.

Grimly Storm wrenched the 52 skyward with its heavy load. The helicopter strained mightily, the whine of the turbine increasing in screeching protest as she banked, heading upward, away from the hellish sea below them. Radioing in, Storm was too busy for the first five minutes to divide her attention between her duties and the cabin.

"Storm—" It was Bram's gasping voice. "Call base.... Tell them to stand by with an ambulance...."

Swiftly Storm risked a glance back, aware of the anguish in his voice. Merlin and Bram were both kneeling over the last survivor, giving her mouth-to-mouth resuscitation. Storm compressed her lips and returned to the job at hand, forcing the tears back. Her hands tightened around the controls. She silently willed the woman to live. She had probably swallowed too much seawater, her lungs full of the brackish liquid. Thank God, Bram was safe. Forcing all those thoughts aside, Storm cranked up the engine on the 52, keeping an eye on the engine temperature gauge. The needle hovered unsteadily between the safety of the green region and the danger area of the red. The turbine engine of the 52 was actually too powerful for the helicopter transmission, and if a pilot unwisely pushed the engine past its limits, the torque could cause flight control problems.

Storm was so intent on monitoring the performance of the 52, she didn't realize Bram had come forward until his hand settled briefly on her shoulder. A quick glance over at his pale glistening features made her heart wrench with fear.

"How is she?"

"Looks like about a quart of water came from her lungs. She's breathing on her own, but she doesn't look good," he informed her, strapping in.

"And you?"

He glanced over at her, a tight grin pulling one corner of his mouth upward as he wiped his face. "I drank a quart of water just trying to rescue her."

Storm found no humor in the situation. "You could have drowned out there, Bram."

As he pulled the charts from the pocket to help in navigation, he gave her a narrowed look. "That's part of our job."

Chilling anger caused her gray eyes to glimmer like chips of ice. She refused to answer him, burying all her emotions. The twenty-minute flight back to the air station was completed in tense silence.

Storm finished the postflight check and was the last to leave the confines of the helicopter once they had landed. In the meantime, Bram and Merlin had helped the survivors into the two waiting ambulances. Tucking her helmet into her duffel bag, Storm jogged to the line shack.

Bram was soaked and so was Merlin. They all looked like drowned rats. None of them looked particularly dynamic under the circumstances. Walking back into the Ops Center, Kyle's face was grimmer than before.

"All hell's breaking loose here," he told them. "We're getting your aircraft refueled in the hangar right now. We need all available equipment. Merlin, you'd better get in another supply of rescue items."

"Yes, sir." Merlin shook his head dolefully, making an about face and leaving Ops.

Storm felt as if she were about to snap. "What now, Kyle?"

"We've got a freighter in trouble. I've got 1378 on the way. We've got twenty crew members to get off that ship before it sinks."

Swearing softly, Storm rapidly read through the report. It was now 1500 and the day was looking even more bleak and overcast. Though it was midafternoon, it appeared to be dusk. Visibility was quickly deteriorating, and that meant IFR flying in a few hours—just one more overtaxing demand on her and Bram. Her mind was tired, and she felt numb. Stealing a glance over at Bram, she felt a moment's reprieve from the inner turmoil she was experiencing.

"Look, grab some coffee, and I'll have the rest of the info radioed to you while you're on your way to the freighter."

"What's the registry?"

"Panamanian."

Storm sighed heavily. "Could be Colombian drug smugglers who came up the coast to drop their goods off on smaller boats and got caught in this damned hurricane. That's the usual pattern, isn't it?"

Kyle soberly agreed. "RCC says they can barely speak English. I hope Merlin has brushed up on his Spanish."

"Bram can handle it," she told him, scooping up the search briefing papers.

Kyle looked at his watch. "Look, you two have completed four-and-a-half hours of demanding flying. You've done your bit, and you both look pretty beat."

"Thanks a lot," Storm said, feeling more and more tense by the second. She looked up at Bram, who gave her a cup of the lifesaving coffee. "What do you want to do?" He looked like hell, his face drawn and pale. Rescuing the woman in that heavy ocean current had taken a drastic toll on him physically. His blue eyes glimmered with a sudden tender light that made her feel warm and safe within his regard.

"You're the AC. I'm game if you are."

She thought for a moment. He should be left behind, considering his present condition. But the look in his eyes told her he could handle it.

"We'll do it, Kyle."

A look of relief washed across Armstrong's features. "Thank God. Frankly, I don't know what I would have done if you said no."

Reaching out, Storm squeezed Kyle's arm. "Thanks for giving us a choice though..."

Seven

───

They sat in the helicopter, preparing to lift off again. Bram looked over at her.

"Let me fly for a while. You need a break."

"Fine," Storm agreed, pulling the navigation charts out and placing them on her lap.

"What's wrong, Storm?"

Her answer was clipped, emotionless. "Nothing."

Bram stared at her, appraising her unreadable features. He saw the strain in the set of her lips, the look of tension in her eyes. "You're pissed off about something."

Storm snapped her chin up, glaring at him. "I said it was nothing, dammit. Now, let it go at that. We've got work to do."

He studied her grimly, as if not convinced by her anger. "Okay," he responded, "but later you and I are going to talk."

She said nothing, avoiding his piercing look. Damn him. Didn't he realize how worried she was for him when he left the helicopter? He knew she was sensitive to losing another copilot. But this time there was so much more at stake: She loved him. And he didn't know that. Finally she chanced a glance over at Bram. He coolly met her stare.

"Sometimes you're an insensitive rock," she said grimly.

"Yeah?"

"Yes!"

"You're barking up the wrong tree, Storm."

"Bull."

"You hotheaded—"

"Let's cut out the pleasantries, Bram, and get this show on the road. We can call each other names after this damned flight is over with."

"Okay, if that's the way you want to play it. You damn well better be prepared to explain yourself when we get back."

The freighter *Antonia* foundered like a beached whale in the Atlantic Ocean below them. CG 1378 was already on station, using the rescue basket, which was being lowered to the crewman anxiously standing below on the heaving deck of the ship. Storm recognized the voice of Doug Sanders, the pilot of 1378. They circled, watching the problems that were occurring. The wind was whipping in a tight concentric pattern, throwing the rescue basket around like a toy beneath the H-52. If it slammed into one of the waiting Colombian crewmen huddling on the bow of the sinking freighter, it could kill one of them.

"CG 1446," came the call to Storm over the radio.

"Go ahead, CG 1378."

"CG '46…hey, Stormie! Glad to have you out here with us. I thought you were on another SAR."

She smiled thinly. "We just completed it and got sent right back out. Looks like you're having trouble, Doug."

"Roger that. These damn Colombians we've already got on board are crazier than hell. They're hysterical. Already had two or three of them below try to hang on to the basket all at once. My mech's been trying to use hand signals to tell them we'll lift them one at a time. They aren't paying much attention."

"How many do you have on board, Doug?"

"Three. They look like smugglers. I'll bet you my next paycheck on it."

She shook her head, maneuvering the helo in a wide circle above the other 52. She felt Bram's hand on her arm and she turned.

"I speak Spanish fluently. How about if I go down on deck and organize them for the rescue?"

Her eyes widened for a brief second. Come on, Storm, separate work from emotional fears, she told herself. "Think you can manage it? You look tired...."

Bram gave her his devastating grin that always brought a smile to her face. She didn't smile this time, but he saw her gray eyes lighten momentarily. "Sure, as long as a war doesn't break out down there. They don't look like a very trustworthy lot."

"War never determines who's right, Bram—only who is left. Make damn sure you're left."

His grin broadened. "You're a pretty savvy lady, you know that? Yes, I'll be careful. I'll take one of those portable watertight radios with me and stay in contact." He winked and unstrapped, giving her shoulder a gentle squeeze, and left the cockpit for the gloomy interior of the helicopter.

Storm watched him go with misgivings. More than once she had wished mightily for the reassurance of a weapon on board—especially around the drug smugglers, who they had to rescue or round up in coordinated busts with the cutter crews who prowled the sea for them. She radioed Doug, outlining their plan. Relief was evident in the pilot's voice as he agreed to it. Both H-52s were low on fuel and couldn't stay on station much longer. Something had to be done quickly to effect the rescue.

In a matter of minutes, Doug had pulled away from the *Antonia,* allowing Storm to lower her copilot in the basket to the deck of the ship. Waves crashed across the bow, and she worriedly watched as the crewmen clung desperately to the railing, trying not to be washed overboard. Bram's bright-orange flight suit and white helmet stood out among the Colombians, who quickly surrounded him as he got out of the basket. He was tall and huskily built next to the smaller crewmen, and Storm smiled to herself as Bram quickly organized them. It wasn't long before Merlin was hoisting them aboard, one at a time. In fifteen minutes, eight bodies were packed closely together inside the confines of the aircraft. Storm maneuvered the weighted helicopter away from the badly battered *Antonia* so that Doug could move in and pick up the rest. She heard Merlin snapping and yelling at the crew, and she twisted around to find out what was going on.

The largest sailor was gesturing angrily toward Merlin, shouting in Spanish at him. Dammit, she wished Bram were aboard—his bulk could intimidate them into silence.

"Hey, Stormie, I've got my quota," Doug sang through the airwaves. "All you need to do is go back and pick up Bram and we'll have it made. I'm a little overweight, or I'd do it."

"Roger," she said, watching as the 1378 backed out of the area so she could pick up Bram. He looked alone and lost down on the deck awash with debris from the freighter.

"Merlin, stand by to lower the basket—" Her voice froze as the caution panel lit up for a TRANSMISSION OIL HOT indication. Her eyes widened, moving to the gauge. The needle was resting in the red, meaning the transmission was overheating! Anxiously she went through the customary checks to see if it was a real emergency or just the gauge acting up. Merlin came forward, crouching down near her. His face became drawn as he looked at the flight instruments.

"We've got trouble," he warned her, pointing to them.

"Yeah, I know."

"We're slightly overloaded, lieutenant. Beyond our eight-thousand-pound capacity."

Storm twisted around, glaring at the crewmen in the back. "Dammit, we shouldn't be! What the hell are they carrying? Search them, Merlin. We should be able to take one more person on board without this happening."

Her mind feverishly raced over the reasons for the problem. With high humidity and temperature conditions, coupled with high-powered hovering, the helo's engine was laboring. Being overloaded weight-wise was the straw that placed them in a critical situation.

She radioed Doug, asking him to stand by.

"I can't," he told her, "I'm into my half-hour's reserve of extra fuel, Storm. I've got to go. You've got to come with me. If your transmission overheats and you get any other indications that it's coming apart, you're going to have to ditch."

"Bram's down there," she said, desperation in her voice. She heard a disturbance behind her and turned her head. Merlin shoved the only huge Colombian crewman down on the deck of the helicopter, yanking up his voluminous shirt, exposing a belt filled with white plastic pouches strapped around his waist.

"Goddamn thieves," he snarled, "they're all carrying co-caine on them, lieutenant!"

Cursing, Storm radioed the air station, apprising them of the situation. Did any of those idiotic crewmen have a weapon? A cold horror raised the hair on the back of her neck at that thought. It was usual for a smuggler to carry firearms. Anxiously Storm flew over the *Antonia,* watching Bram cling to the safety of one of the masts. Wave after wave inundated the ship, and tears rose in her eyes. The caution light stayed on, compounding the peril.

"I got it all, lieutenant. Man, there must be over fifty pounds of coke on them."

"Dump it!" she ordered.

Merlin slid the door open, the wind and rain whipping into the helicopter. The crewmen yelled and started to lunge forward as he began to kick the drugs overboard in order to lighten the load. Merlin punched the closest one in the jaw, sending the crewman sprawling back among his protesting friends.

"It's out!" Merlin gasped, slamming the door shut once again. He glared at the crewmen and dared them to try anything.

The transmission temperature gauge was still high. Storm's mouth thinned, her eyes narrowing. "No good; we're still riding the red."

"Storm," Doug begged over the radio, "let's go. I'm down to twenty-five minutes of fuel left! We'll refuel and come back to get Bram. He'll be okay down there."

Tears crowded her eyes, but she fought them back. Daylight was dying. Armstrong had informed her that no other helicopters were available to help rescue Bram—every one of them was out on a critical lifesaving mission. She thumbed the button on the cyclic, putting her in touch with Bram down below.

"I can't pick you up, Bram. I've got transmission problems. We're going to have to come back just as soon as we change planes and refuel."

"Roger," he answered.

Storm shut her eyes tightly for a second. God, he sounded so calm and nonchalant about it! That ship could break apart at any given moment. He could be washed overboard by a monster wave. He could drown. He—

"The war's finished and I'm left, Storm. I'll be hanging around here waiting for you."

Swallowing hard, her voice came back, hoarse and raw. "Roger. ETA will be," she glanced at her watch, "one hour and ten minutes."

She heard him laugh. It was a full carefree laugh that sent a spasm of anguish through her. "You got a date, princess. See you in seventy minutes."

"I'll be there," she promised grimly and ordered Merlin to throw out a Datum Marker Buoy. She pulled the 52 up and banked it to the left.

"If you don't, I'll turn into a pumpkin," Bram warned.

It was his last communication. Between the screaming and fighting going on between Merlin and the furious Colombian crew, and limping home on a transmission that she wasn't sure would complete the flight, Storm doggedly flew the helicopter back to the air base. On landing, they were met by Customs authorities who willingly took the crewmen into custody. Storm ran to the hangar. She jerked the door to Ops open. Kyle glanced up.

"We're refueling Doug's helicopter right now," he said by way of greeting.

Storm looked down at him, her face devoid of emotion, her gray eyes dark. "I'm going back after him, Kyle."

"You're in the bag, Storm. I'll send—"

She slammed her hand down flatly on the desk and glared at Kyle face-to-face. "I'm going back for him. Let me be Doug's copilot on this flight. We'll use his mech, Anderson. Merlin fought those Colombians all the way back; he's exhausted."

"Okay, you'll be copilot on this flight," he agreed.

Storm's taut face relaxed slightly. "Thanks, Kyle. I owe you one." Any time a pilot flew six hours of flight time, they were automatically "in the bag" and taken off the duty roster to rest for at least twelve hours before attempting to fly again. Her gray eyes softened as she stared across the desk at Kyle.

"Just be damned careful, Storm. You look like hell. You're tired, and mistakes are real easy to come by when you're in this kind of a bind. My ass is on the line on this one."

"I will."

Doug took one look at Storm and said, "I'll fly, you navigate."

"You've got a deal," she agreed tiredly, quickly strapping in. "How many hours have you been flying?"

He grinned, his lean face breaking the lines of tension around his mouth. "Not as many as you, that's for sure. Did all hell break loose in your helo too?"

"Yeah, Merlin found coke on them."

Doug gave a sorrowful shake of his head. "Dumb bastards. You might have had to ditch because of the excess weight. You should have thrown one of them out. Okay, let's get Bram."

The forty minutes it took to follow the track to the drifting *Antonia* was an agonizing eternity for Storm. The long day was ending, darkness beginning to steal over the sky. The rain and wind slashed relentlessly at the helicopter as Doug tracked outbound one-thousand feet above the ocean surface. Luckily Bram was still in radio communication with a circling U.S. Navy P3B that flew high above him. Storm forced herself to relax and stop worrying; she had to unclench her fists every few minutes. She was sorry for snapping at Bram earlier. It was concern for his life that had made her testy. Please, please, she prayed silently, keep him safe. I love him.

"Target at three o'clock, one-hundred yards," the flight mech sang out.

Storm strained against her harness, craning to get a good look at the darkened shape of the *Antonia* rapidly coming into view. Her heart rate rose to a throbbing pound as they neared the listing vessel.

"Thirteen-seventy-eight, it's about time," Bram called over the radio. "I'm getting soaked down here!"

Relief washed through her, and she shared a smile with Doug.

"You mean you didn't turn into a pumpkin yet?" Storm responded.

Bram's laughter was hearty, uplifting. "No, but I've turned into a toad instead. I need to be kissed by my princess in order to turn back into a handsome prince."

"That guy is something else," Doug said, shaking his head. "You want to fly, Storm?"

"No, not as long as you're feeling okay. I'm getting groggy, Doug."

"Roger. You look like death warmed over."

"Thanks a lot. You really know how to boost a woman's flattened ego."

Doug grinned and directed the 52 until they hovered twenty feet above the *Antonia*. Below, Bram waited for the basket to be lowered, clinging to the same broken mast where they had left him. Doug gave Storm a broad smile. "I think your copilot will have some pretty sweet words for you when he gets aboard."

Storm felt her cheeks warm with color. "Now, what's that supposed to mean?"

"Come on, Stormie, we aren't blind, deaf, and dumb," he chided good-naturedly. "We may be married men, but we can tell when a guy's falling in love with our favorite lady pilot."

She colored fiercely, avoiding Doug's humored blue-eyed gaze. Bram falling in love with her? He was still gun-shy from his recent divorce and afraid of entrusting his vulnerable emotions to any woman's care again. He had told her that in so many words on the beach. Frowning, she was too exhausted to parry Doug's comment. Yes, they had shared wonderful love together. And carefree laughter...and...did he love her? Rubbing her eyes, she shook her head.

There was a sudden blast of wind and rain as Bram struggled aboard, collapsing on the deck. Doug motioned for Storm to unharness and go back to assist. She gave him a grateful nod and unstrapped. Anderson was helping Bram to his feet when she came back. Storm placed her hands beneath his left arm and led him to the canvas and nylon webbed seats along the fuselage wall. His hands trembled as he weakly pulled the helmet off his head, letting it fall from his nerveless fingers onto the deck. He felt Storm close to him, providing him with badly needed support. He allowed his head to tip back against the wall and closed his eyes, water running in rivulets down his exhausted features.

Anderson handed her two towels and got up, placing a heavy wool blanket around Bram's broad sloping shoulders.

"Thanks," he whispered tiredly, giving him a weary smile. Then he turned his head to the left, meeting Storm's serious expression. "God, am I glad you're here. You're a sight for sore eyes, sweetheart."

She took the towel, trying to dry his hair, and wipe his face and neck free of the water. Her heart soared with joy as his blue eyes hungrily drank in her form. "Trite, Gallagher, but effective," she said, a slight smile pulling at her lips.

"Can't be original all the time, princess."

She wrapped the towel around his neck, tucking it into the open V of his flight suit.

"You're an original, all right, you damn ex-fighter jock."

He barely opened his eyes, one brow moving upward. "Hey, haven't I earned being called a Red Tail yet? If the guys back in my fighter squadron could have seen me getting seasick and clinging for dear life from the mast of that freighter, they'd have never believed it. I think I earned my water wings today, Travis."

Storm wanted to reach out and caress his face, but the circumstances didn't permit it. Instead she contented herself with simply remaining close to him. "You're right," she said above the noise, "you are officially a Coastie as of today, lieutenant. Now quit bitching and rest—you're shaking like a leaf."

"You're coming home with me," Storm said, brooking no argument from Bram. With the continuing crisis of the hurricane, all pilots were being given the mandatory twenty-four-hours crew rest before returning to fly SAR missions again.

Bram raised one eyebrow as they left the hangar, then bowed his head against the tempestuous rain. He was wet, cold, tired and hungry. "No argument," he shouted above the wind, following Storm to her sports car. Once inside, he fell back against the seat and closed his eyes.

"What you need is a bath, hot food, and rest," she advised, easing the car out into the rain-soaked street.

"Amen," he agreed. He fumbled for her hand, and on finding it, gave it a squeeze. "You are wonderful, Storm Travis," he sighed.

She worriedly looked over at Bram's pale features. Maybe Kyle had been right—they should have ordered Bram to the dispensary for examination. But he had resisted Kyle's suggestion, and they were all too tired to argue. "Rest, Bram," she murmured.

Just getting away from the air base with its continual strain of flying infused her with a new kind of strength. Bram was far more exhausted than he had originally let on. Getting battered by forty-foot waves for over an hour and a half had depleted even his herculean strength. Storm led him to the bathroom, started running the bathwater, and stripped him of the smelly, damp flight suit. He remained in a weary stupor, even the simple task of unlacing his flight boots proving to be too much. Kneeling down, Storm quickly removed the boots and soaked socks and placed them aside.

"Come on," she urged, gripping his arm and helping him stand, "the water's ready."

She left Bram soaking in the tub. Changing out of her flight suit, she slipped into a robe and moved through the familiar task of preparing a quick meal. It was like being married again. Storm shook her head as a tender smile began pulling at her lips. She heated the rich beef stew she had made a few days earlier. Was she enjoying these domestic tasks because it was familiar or because Bram was with her once again? A little of both, she admitted ruefully to herself.

Reentering the bathroom, she found Bram asleep in the tub. An understanding smile touched her mouth. Getting down on her knees, she rolled up the sleeves on her robe and began to scrub him free of the salty ocean smell. He awoke, groggily opening his eyes and sitting up.

"Here," he mumbled, "I can do that—"

"Just sit there," she told him. "I can do it faster and quicker than you can."

He rubbed his face and then wet his dark hair. "I feel like hell. Where's the shampoo?"

"Here," she said, putting it firmly into his hand.

"Thanks." He began to wash his hair.

"I've got beef stew ready and some garlic bread out in the kitchen. Do you feel like eating?"

"I'm so damned hungry I'm shaky."

She smiled, rinsing off his beautifully muscled chest and shoulders. It was a provocative task, and if they hadn't been exhausted, it might have led to other pleasures. Storm gently put those wishes aside, helping him stand and extricate himself from the tub without falling on his face. He was like a sleepy little boy, fumbling for the towel, his movements slow and uncoordinated. After getting him dry, she took another towel and wrapped it around his waist. Taking his hand, Storm led him into the kitchen.

"You go ahead and eat," she urged, placing the steaming bowl of stew before him.

Bram looked up. She looked beautiful in that pale green robe, and it accented her dark gray eyes. Her hair was smooth and straight from wearing the flight helmet for so long, her bangs hanging near her thick lashes. "What about you? Aren't you—"

Storm leaned over, pressing a kiss to his sandpapery cheek. "I'm desperately in need of a shower first. Eat and then go to bed. I'll join you in a little while," she promised softly.

The wind slammed savagely against the house, with the shutters flapping and banging, awakening Bram from his deep sleep. He felt Storm's warm yielding body next to him move, and he inhaled her apricot scent, forcing his eyes open.

The clamor abruptly abated, and peace settled briefly over the darkened room. He was safe. Memories of almost being swept overboard from the *Antonia* at least five different times had haunted his dreams, but he had slept soundly. Bram blinked, opening his eyes. He felt pleasantly tired, not bone-deep tired as before. Twisting his head, he glanced at the clock. Five o'clock in the morning. He looked over at Storm, gently smoothing her hair on the pillow next to where they lay. Propping himself up on one elbow, Bram grimaced, every muscle in his body painfully screaming in protest.

Storm stirred like a lost kitten, automatically reaching out, her hand sliding down across his chest. He smiled; she missed his nearness. With his fingers, he stroked her pale cheek, noticing the strain still evident on her face. He had heard stories about how Coast Guard people were placed under grueling pressure during life-and-death emergencies, but he had never fathomed something of this continuing magnitude. When he had been in the Air Force, everyone had laughed at the "Coasties," viewing them as more of a civilian agency than a military one, because they ended up protecting the civilian populace more than the other armed services did. He had laughed with them, believing they had a cushy job and didn't deserve the respect he now accorded them. Now he knew better.

He pulled his thoughts back to Storm. He loved the velvet texture of her skin beneath his hand as he explored her neck and shoulder. The wind slammed frenziedly against the house, and the rain pounded at the windows, which where shuttered to protect them from the hurricane's flying debris.

Storm moaned, slowly rolling onto her back. Bram's touch had pulled her from sleep and as she raised her lashes she met his tender gaze. "What time is it?" she asked in a sleepy voice. "0500."

She relaxed, shutting her eyes again, loving his gently stroking touch on her arm and shoulder. "God, I feel like I've been hit by a Mack truck," she muttered thickly. "Are you all right?"

Bram rested his hand against her slender waist. "Not only hit, but run over."

Concern showed in her eyes as she opened them, reaching out and sliding her fingers across his broad shoulder. "Bad?"

He shook his head. "Bruised a little, that's all. How about you?"

Storm struggled into a sitting position, the covers falling away, exposing the white satin nightgown she wore. Her hair had been damp when she had gone to bed, and now it lay about her face in softened waves. "I feel like hell, and I probably look like hell," she admitted. "You look pretty good, Bram."

His cobalt eyes gleamed as he shifted to study her in the muted light. "You look absolutely ravishing," he murmured suggestively. "And if we weren't both so damned exhausted, I'd do something about it."

Storm's eyes widened, and as she wordlessly slid down beside him she placed her arms around his neck and rested her head against his. "Hold me?"

His arms came around her body, pulling her daringly close to his hard length. Storm was aware of his arousal and snuggled further into his strong embrace. "Better?" he asked, kissing her temple, cheek, and finally, her lips.

A new urgency filled her and she hungrily met his questing mouth, wanting, needing, the strength and care he offered.

"Mmm, you taste good," he whispered against her lips. He pressed his mouth against hers more insistently, and felt her lips part beneath his. Fire uncoiled hotly throughout him. Raising his head, he stared down into her pewter eyes, now flecked with the silver flame of desire: "I had a lot of time out on the ship to think," he whispered, pressing small affectionate kisses to her lips.

"I was so afraid for you, Bram," she admitted throatily, her eyes clouding as she searched his strong, handsome face.

A mocking smile settled over his mouth. "I was scared, if you want to know the truth. When I saw you leaving, I thought What the hell have you done, Gallagher? Don't you realize this ship can fall apart on you any second?" He shook his head, and his hands tightened on her body. "I suppose any other co-pilot with an ounce of brains wouldn't have risked it. But I'm a dumb ex-fighter jock, and what the hell do I know about ships and the sea?" he teased.

Storm smiled lovingly and reached up, running her fingers through his hair. "Sometimes what you don't know will save you." She laughed softly. "And what you did, Bram, was to go that extra mile. A lot of the people in the Coast Guard are like that, though. You fit the Red Tail mold well."

He inhaled her special female fragrance, nuzzling her ear, lost in the silken texture of her hair against his cheek. "Too bad I risked my tail for a bunch of drug smugglers." He chuckled. "Somehow, doing it for them took some of the satisfaction out of the gesture."

She leaned upward, kissing him soundly, reveling in his natural strength. "It doesn't matter," she told him, closing her eyes, content to be held by him, "you're made of the right stuff. The Coast Guard couldn't have gotten a better pilot if they'd tried."

Bram grinned. "Is that your professional opinion, Lieutenant Travis?"

"Mine and everyone else's," she confided, growing serious. "You're solid gold, Lieutenant Gallagher, but we've been afraid to tell you that because we figured it would go to that already swelled head of yours."

He gave her a nonplussed look and then broke into a solid laugh as he pinned her to the bed beneath him. She was incredibly alluring right now, the silk of her nightgown providing an inviting sensation against his flesh. With one hand he easily captured her wrists above her head.

"You're awfully impertinent, Storm Travis," he said, running his finger down her clean jawline. Then he sobered, staring down at her vulnerable face. "But I'm finding out that's just one more quality that I like about you," he admitted. "Out there on that freighter I had an hour and a half to wonder if I was going to live or die, Storm..." His voice dropped to a roughened whisper as he stared down at her. "I had plenty of time to think and to weigh what is and isn't important in my life." He outlined her provocative lips with one finger. "You're important to me. And I wanted to tell you that. When I got aboard the 52 all I wanted to do was throw my arms around you and hold you. I couldn't, but I thought you'd see how I felt about you..."

Her heart beat painfully in her chest, and Storm became aware of the tears filling her eyes. "I saw something in your eyes, Bram—I couldn't be sure." She gave him a helpless look. "What I might wish it to be and what it actually was could easily have been different," she added almost inaudibly.

Bram cocked his head, a smile lingering on his lips. "You mean you care a little for me too?"

Tears fled down her cheeks and soaked into the strands of her hair. Storm wanted to blurt out I love you, Bram. I love you so damn much, my heart aches! But she couldn't say it. At least, not yet. Perhaps never. Swallowing the lump forming in her throat, Storm looked above his head into the darkness. "I know you've just come out of a divorce, Bram," she began hoarsely, "and you've made it clear that you don't want any serious relationships right now—"

He released her wrists and cupping her chin, searched her tear-stained face. "I've changed my mind," he murmured, leaning down and kissing her lips. He felt her arms slipping around his shoulders, drawing him down on her warm, yielding body, and he groaned softly against her mouth. "I want to love you."

"Yes..." Storm quavered, losing herself within his sensual, masculine aura. "Please, Bram, I need you so much...I almost lost you..."

"Shh," he remonstrated, running his tongue across her pliant, petal-soft lips. "you'll never lose me, princess. Never."

Eight

"I don't know if I'm ever going to get used to seeing palm trees swaying in seventy-five-degree temperatures at Christmastime," Bram admitted, entering the kitchen, drink in hand. He halted in the doorway and leaned against it, idly watching as Storm put the finishing touches on another tray of appetizers for the party that was in full swing.

Storm glanced up. "Newcomers usually find it strange. You'll get used to it." She smiled, picking up the tray and walking over to where Bram was leaning. "Want to take this in? You'd think those guys had never been fed before."

Bram balanced the tray in his hands along with his drink. "Come on in," he urged. "You throw a party, but your guests never get to see the lady who brought it all about. Come on..."

She frowned. "Well—"

"Look, those chow hounds have plenty to eat and drink in there," he ordered. Then his voice grew tender. "Besides, I'd like to spend some time with you."

Giving him a smile, Storm smoothed the folds of her ivory muslin dress. It had a pink ribbon through the lace of the high collar that fitted around her slender neck. She felt extremely feminine tonight, basking in the light of Bram's sensual gaze. Blushing from the look he gave her, Storm acquiesced. "Okay, I'll join you for a little while. But there're so many other things—"

"Let Betty and Susie help next time." He suddenly grinned, leaning down and catching her full on the mouth, kissing her soundly.

"Aha!" Kyle cried, intercepting them. "Finally caught you two!" A self-satisfied look came to his face as he sauntered up to them.

Storm flushed fiercely, unable to meet Kyle's friendly expression for a moment.

Bram wasn't so easily ruffled by the pilot's exclamation. "Here, Armstrong, you carry this instead of bending your elbow or flapping your jaw."

Kyle laughed and took the tray. "We miss you, Stormie."

"See?" Bram said archly.

"I'm coming!"

The Christmas music mingled with the nonstop laughter and chatter of the twenty couples who had made themselves at home in the living and dining room areas of the house. Bram remained with Storm as she made the rounds as hostess, watching, looking, and listening. A warmth stole over him as his focus rested on Storm—as it always did. He would never tire of looking at her vulnerable, honest features and those wide-set gray eyes that made his body tighten with desire for her again. Had it been five months since meeting and snarling at each other in the hangar on that humid Sunday afternoon?

He smiled, made the appropriate small talk, and continued to walk at Storm's side. Since that night after his rescue from the *Antonia,* their relationship had subtly changed and deepened. Both were frightened. Both had something to lose by loving again. But their days and nights had been full of emotion. He rubbed his jaw, troubled. He had come to love Storm as he had no other woman. The feelings she brought alive in him were new, strong, and binding. Maggie had never evoked those kinds of feelings from him. But Storm was infinitely different from his ex-wife. Storm was steady, loyal, and sincere. A slight smile suffused his features as he watched the light dance off her ginger hair, copper and gold highlights burnishing the silky strands.

The amount of flying hours they had logged as a team between September and December had been staggering. And through it all, Storm had amazed him with the dogged steadiness that made her a beacon of sureness to all those around her. There wasn't a man here who didn't enjoy flying with her. Bram's eyes softened as he watched her laugh as she shared a joke with one of the wives. He loved Storm's ability to relate to everyone: adult or child, friend or lover. Right now, this very instant, he wanted to grip her hand and take her to the beach and make passionate love to her beneath the light of the moon. It was Christmas—a time of giving, of sharing. As he surveyed the room Bram realized how much all of these people had come to mean to him. There was a sense of family unity in the Coast Guard that just wasn't found in the other services. It was like finally coming home.

It was nearly two A.M. before the last couple reluctantly left. Storm flopped down on the nearest couch, giving Bram a pleased look as he came and joined her.

"You know how to throw a successful party," Bram congratulated, meeting her tired smile. "No one wanted to leave."

She reached out, sliding her fingers down his hard, muscular arm, relishing his closeness. "I loved it. Thanks for helping me make it a success."

Bram nodded. "We work well as a team," he agreed, looking over at the brightly lit Christmas tree that stood well over six feet tall in the corner of the living room.

"I'm exhausted," she admitted, leaning back on the couch and closing her eyes. Then she opened them and surveyed the room. "And this place has to be cleaned up...."

"Not tonight," he warned her.

She turned her head toward him, basking in the light of his tender gaze. "Stay over tonight?"

"I was planning on it."

"Good."

He got to his feet and pulled her into his arms.

Storm leaned against him, marveling at his seemingly inexhaustible strength. Nuzzling beneath his chin, she was content to remain there, luxuriating in his touch as he gently massaged her neck and shoulders with his large gentle hands. Their time had been rare precious moments stolen from the fabric of their demanding work. And lately she had craved more time alone with Bram to explore him, his life, and what he wanted from the future. The midnight walks on the beach were their special time with each other and more than once they had made love on the white sands that cradled them lovingly.

"Just think," she said wistfully, "we have Christmas Eve and Christmas off. I can't believe it. In all my years in the service I've never lucked out on major holidays."

Bram chuckled. "Yeah, I was the same way. I knew without a doubt if there was a holiday coming up, I'd get nailed with duty. Never failed." He pulled away, keeping his hands on her shoulders, staring down at her. "Merry Christmas," he said huskily, leaning down and touching her lips in a long exploratory kiss.

Storm drank thirstily of his mouth, reveling in the firmness yet sensitivity conveyed through his touch. Gazing up into his eyes, she implored, "Take me to the beach. I want time alone with you, Bram."

A mirthful glint shone in his eyes. "At two in the morning? It's going to be chilly down there. Do you want to change first?"

She nodded. "Yes, give me a minute." And then she reached up, kissing him soundly. "Thank you," she whispered fiercely.

They walked arm in arm on the darkened sand, watching the ocean spill its foamy life out onto the sloping shore. It was a cloudless night, the stars glittering brightly in the heavens, a dazzling cape thrown across the shoulders of the night. The quarter-moon moved silently through the darkness, casting its pearl luminescence over the earth below. Content as never before, Storm rested her head on Bram's shoulder as they drank in the miracle of life surrounding them. She had changed into a pair of jeans, an apricot sweater, and a lightweight white-canvas jacket with blue piping. A slight offshore breeze brought the tangy scent of salt with it, and she inhaled it deeply.

"I feel like the ocean tonight," she admitted softly to Bram, "moody, restless, changing..."

Bram tightened his arm around her waist momentarily. "You're allowed. Happy?"

Storm nodded. "Very. You?"

"The same."

A smile tinged her lips as she glanced up at him. "Talkative bunch, aren't we? Everything we feel or sense can be boiled down to one or two syllables."

His mouth curved upward as he watched Storm, pulling her to a halt and turning her around to face him. "Okay, what gives?" he asked, resting his hands on her shoulders.

"Nothing. I'm just happy."

Bram leaned down, placing a kiss on her parted lips. "Talk to me," he coaxed against her mouth. "What's going on inside that head of yours? I can see it in your eyes."

She laughed softly. "Remember that time I called you an insensitive rock?"

"Yeah, that and a few other choice expletives," he remarked wryly.

"Well, I was wrong. You aren't, Bram." Storm's eyes grew tender. "Just the opposite really. The last two months I've started to realize how sensitive you are."

He shrugged, giving her a teasing look. "It's your fault, you know," he drawled.

Storm tilted her head, not sure whether he was serious or still teasing her. Her mouth set into a petulant line. "Bram Gallagher, why do you always get silly when I'm trying to be serious?"

"I'm sorry, princess. You're so much fun to tease. You're the straight person on our team and I'm the comic. I love playing off your serious side. Am I forgiven?"

Her gray eyes danced with laughter while she tried to suppress a growing smile. "I don't think you'll ever get rid of that fighter-jock sense of humor."

"Ever want me to?"

"Never. You make me laugh when things get bad."

He ran his hands down her arms. "I know. But we're a good balance for one another. I crack jokes to relieve the tension, and you sit there with your unreadable face, eyes narrowed and lips set. We just have different ways of dealing with stress."

"It's a good thing one of us is serious, or we'd be called the Laurel and Hardy of the air station."

Bram raised an eyebrow at her. "Oh? Am I known as the clown of our fine team efforts?"

Storm chortled, falling back into his arms, savoring his closeness. "You know the guys respect you." Reaching up, she caressed his cheek. "You've added a new dimension to all of our lives, Bram. And we're the better for it."

His eyes became softer as he observed her. "You've added a few new dimensions to my life, lady, in case you hadn't realized it."

"Yeah?"

"Yeah."

"Like how?"

He raised his chin. "Oh, in many small but important ways."

Storm's smile died on her lips as she regarded him in the gathering silence. "Tell me how I've touched you, Bram," she whispered.

Resting his jaw against her hair, he held her tightly within his embrace. "You've taught me a lot about women, Storm. When I first met you, I thought you were going to be one tough broad to deal with, but I was wrong. It was your ability to say Hey, I'm just an average human being doing a job I love to do. No big deal. I don't have to be macho to fly helicopters. I don't have to prove a thing to any man." He kissed her temple. "Normally women in a heavily male-occupied field tend to get defensive and put up all kinds of walls to protect themselves emotionally."

She nuzzled against the rough weave of the jacket he wore, seeking his warmth. "But I didn't have to, Bram. The Coast Guard's attitude toward women working in the supposedly male occupations is vastly different from the other services. Here you're a part of a larger team. A loose-knit family concept."

"Still," he insisted, "you could have been tough with me because of the way I behaved at first. But you weren't. You just persevered, restrained yourself, and let me get all the kinks out of my system." He sobered more. "I was deeply touched by your ability to display your emotions, Storm. On and off the job. I came to realize that when you cried in front of a bunch of pilots or crewpeople, it didn't lessen their respect for you in any way. By your being human, you allowed all of us to let down our barriers and express our feelings more openly too."

She tipped her head, meeting his troubled gaze. "I think one of the worst things that has happened to us in the last decade as men and women is that displaying our emotions was considered wrong or weak." She gave a doleful shake of her head.

"Bram, we never get rid of what we feel inside. I find it infinitely easier to show my vulnerability than to hide it and pretend it doesn't exist."

"But when you show your emotions, it makes me feel like it's all right to show mine." He groped for the right words. "I guess I've learned from you that if you are vulnerable, the other person isn't likely to hurt you."

She nodded. "Show your underbelly and your enemy will slit it open, right?"

"Right. Maggie was like that. She never shared that other side of herself with me. I knew it was there; I felt it, and sometimes I heard it in her voice. But she never trusted me enough with her feelings." He kissed her cheek. "On the other hand, you literally placed yourself in my hands from the day we met. You made no excuses for your feelings, and at first, I found that frightening because I had no idea *what* to do with them or you."

"We had a few stops and starts, Bram, but you've been wonderful."

One corner of his mouth lifted. "Sometimes I feel like a first-class klutz with you, Storm. You know who you are. You know what's right and wrong for you. It's that invisible stability around you that I sense, and see operating on a twenty-four-hour basis. I just shake my head wondering how in the hell you got so together before age thirty."

She shared his smile. "You mean you don't have to be over the hill in order to have developed some maturity?"

Bram ran his hand lightly across her hair, smoothing strands away from her cheek. "I'm thirty-two and I still haven't gotten it together, Storm."

"Yes, you have, Bram. In many ways. Look, I'm not perfect. Far from it. Maybe I reflect an area of weakness that you have right now. But you're aware that being vulnerable isn't all that painful, and you're working on it."

He slid his hands down her back, coming to rest against her hips, rocking her gently in his arms. "You are perfect."

"I am not!"

Laughing, he enjoyed watching the play of emotions across her mobile features. "Tell me where you aren't, then," he challenged teasingly.

Her heart took a painful, aching leap in her chest. She wet her lips, allowing the fear she felt to dissipate beneath his cobalt eyes. "I'm afraid to live, Bram," she admitted thickly.

"What?" He snorted. "That's not true. I don't know what you call it when you hang your rear out the line with these SAR missions. Or experience the pain of losing a survivor. You don't run away from life. You couldn't, and do the job we do."

Sliding her fingers up across his chest, she allowed them to come to rest near his shoulders. "I'm saying it the wrong way." His voice dropped into a softened whisper. "Do you remember the time you volunteered to stay aboard the *Antonia?*"

Bram sensed the change in her and became serious. "Haven't ever forgotten it, Storm. Why?"

Her fingers curved into the material of his jacket and she fearlessly met his questioning eyes. "When we rescued you later, do you remember how upset I was?"

"Yes. But when things are tense, you're always like that, whether I'm involved or not."

That was true. Her gray eyes turned bleak. "I found out that day just how much you meant to me, Bram." Her voice broke. "I was afraid. More than I could ever recall in my life."

Gently he cupped her chin. "Maybe because you cared a little for me?"

Her eyes sparkled with unshed tears. "Maybe..."

Bram studied her in the interim silence, his sensual mouth compressing. "I think what I'm hearing you say, Storm, is that you're afraid to get totally involved with me emotionally. Is that it? You're afraid to live on the razor edge of a commitment again?"

Tears made shimmering paths down her drawn cheeks. "Y-yes..."

He inhaled, deeply touched by her honesty. "I'm not exactly a safe bet," he admitted ruefully. "I'm divorced, and searching around for parts and pieces of myself that I hadn't been aware of before you crashed into my life." His features mellowed. "Tonight, Storm, I watched you as we walked around talking with the guys and their wives. I love watching your mobile expressions, your clear, uninhibited laughter, your ability to reach out and touch others. And I found myself wanting you all to myself. I just wanted to grab your hand, run out of the door, and take you here to the beach."

Storm closed her eyes. "I'm afraid, Bram...afraid that if—if I allow myself to love you like I want, that—that you'll be torn away from me like Hal was...."

"Oh, honey," he murmured thickly, embracing her. He felt her tremble and realized she was crying. His heart wrenched in his chest, and he began to stroke her hair. "Nothing's going to happen to me. I'm too damn mean to die. Heaven certainly doesn't want to punch my ticket yet, and the devil sure as hell doesn't want me either," he playfully teased, "so you're stuck with me."

She gripped the material of his jacket, allowing all her pent-up fears over the last few months to surface. Bram's voice was a soothing balm to her ravaged emotional state.

"And speaking of love, Storm," he reminded her gently, raising her chin so he could meet her eyes, "I have a confession of my own to make. Ever since that day on the *Antonia*, I realized that I loved you." He grimaced, looking up into the night. "And I was just as afraid for different reasons to tell you how I felt." Bram gave a shake of his head, again searching her face. "Now that I've said it, it wasn't so hard after all." He smiled tenderly as he framed her face with his hands. "I think I'll say it again because it felt so good: I love you, Storm Travis. Now that you know that, what are you going to do with that little piece of information?"

Storm uttered a small cry of joy, flinging her arms around his neck. "Oh, Bram," she softly sobbed, "I love you too..."

He chuckled. "Well, don't sound so happy about it."

Their laughter intermingled with the crashing surf, and Bram lifted her off her feet, turning her around in a circle until both of them were so dizzy they lost their balance and fell into an unceremonious heap into each other's arms. Bram cushioned their fall, twisting so that he hit the hard sand first to protect Storm. He grinned, rolling her to his side; holding her; kissing her eyes, nose, and mouth with quick warm kisses. Storm giggled, struggling to sit up but he wouldn't let her.

"Oh, no," he breathed, "you're going nowhere, my lady." He proffered his arm as a pillow for her head, lying above her until she stopped giggling. Her eyes were shining with happiness; her lips were parted, curving into a wonderful smile. "I don't know what's so funny about me admitting I love you, Travis," he said, a bit breathless from all their exertion.

"You're crazy, Gallagher!" she protested, running her slender fingers through his dark hair.

"But you love me anyway?"

"Yes," she admitted huskily, "I love you anyway."

"Still afraid?"

She gave a grave nod of her head.

Bram smiled. "Good. So am I. We'll be scared together, okay?"

"Okay..."

"Misery loves company, you know."

"Trite but true," Storm conceded, loving his warmth, his ability to be emotionally honest with her.

He raised his head, a euphoric smile on his face. "If this is misery, then I'm going to love every second of it with you."

"Does anything ever faze you?" she asked wonderingly as Bram helped her stand. He brushed the sand from her back and rear, enjoying his duty.

"Yes. You did. You walked into my well-ordered life and blew it all to hell. That's what you did, Travis." He gave her a wicked glint, placing his arms around her shoulder and drawing her near as they began the long walk back to the car.

"Poor baby," she taunted. "I suppose you want an air medal for bravery, hanging in there with me through our ups and downs."

"No, but a Purple Heart would be in keeping."

Storm gasped and hit him playfully on the arm. "Purple Heart! When did I ever wound anything more than that swelled-headed ego of yours, Gallagher?"

He tried to appear hurt. "Ugh! The lady has just wounded me in action again!" He threw his hand across his chest, pretending injury.

"Straighten up and fly right, lieutenant," she told him, a glimmer of laughter in her eyes.

Bram feigned hurt. "You'd think an ex-fighter jock would get a fair shake with you, lieutenant. But I can tell you don't love me...."

She smiled. "Just wait until we get home," she urged. "Then you'll find out just how much I love you, ex-fighter jock."

"Yeah?"

"Yeah."

A softened smile touched his mouth as he kissed her hair. "Merry Christmas, princess. I couldn't have gotten a better present than those three words from your lovely lips and beautiful heart."

Storm gave him a warm look. "Merry Christmas, Bram. I've never had a happier one, believe me."

"I believe you," he whispered, losing his smile. "This coming year will be a new chapter in both of our lives," he promised her. "And I can't think of a finer gift than giving our love to one another. Come on; let's get home. We've got two days together, and I don't want to waste one precious second of it."

Christmas morning dawned brightly with the sun burning off the low hanging clouds that had moved inland from the ocean overnight. Storm lingered with Bram over coffee in the sunlit living room. Her body tingled pleasantly from recent lovemaking and she eyed him lovingly. His arm rested around her shoulders as she leaned against him.

"Merry Christmas," she whispered.

Bram's face reflected his unspoken affection. "The best ever, princess."

A knock at the front door startled them both. Storm frowned, setting the cup down on the coffee table.

"You expecting anyone?" Bram asked.

"No..."

Bram watched her move across the living room to answer the insistent knock. Even in a pale pink blouse and jeans she looked incredibly feminine, and his body tightened with desire for her again. Storm opened the door and he heard her gasp.

"Matt! What—"

"May I come in, Storm?"

Her eyes widened and she stepped aside for her brother. "Of course."

Bram rose, watching as Storm threw her arms around a dark-haired man who easily matched his own six-feet-one-inch height. Storm sobbed as she clung to the stranger. Bram walked toward them and waited until they parted.

"Oh, Matt," Storm whispered. "It's been so long since— My God, I'm glad to see you." Then she realized Bram was standing nearby. Trying to wipe the sudden tears that had appeared on her cheeks, she smiled tremulously up at him.

"Bram, I want you to meet my youngest brother, Matt Travis. Matt, this is Bram Gallagher."

Bram extended his hand. "A pleasure," he declared.

Like an excited little girl, Storm placed her hands on her cheeks for just a moment. "Come in, Matt. Have you had breakfast yet?"

He shook his head as Storm led him through the foyer. Wearing a rumpled well-traveled dark suit, he pulled off his coat, allowing it to hang over the back of the couch. "No. I just hopped a flight from D.C. to come down here. Can't stand airline food."

Worriedly Storm searched her brother's face. He looked exhausted, shadows skirting his gray eyes. Matt had always been the best-looking of the three siblings, but now his handsome face was drawn and pale. Taking his arm, she propelled him toward the bathroom.

"You also haven't shaved. Look, you're beat. Did you just get off an assignment?"

Matt ran his fingers through his dark brown hair. "Yeah. I haven't eaten or slept in almost two days."

Bram leaned against the kitchen doorway, hands stuffed in his pockets, watching Storm take command. A smile lingered at the corners of his mouth. She fussed over Matt like a mother—her voice was low and coaxing as she kept a hand on her brother's broad slumped shoulder and led him into the bedroom. It looked like more coffee was in order, and he roused himself, moving to the kitchen to prepare a fresh pot.

Storm joined him ten minutes later, her brow furrowed. Bram took her into his arms.

"You all right?" he inquired, concerned.

She closed her eyes, leaning against Bram's solid chest, his heartbeat soothing her disordered emotional state. "Yes and no," she replied. "My God, I never expected to see Matt."

"Does he always drop in like this?" he asked wryly.

Storm shook her head. "I told you a little bit about Cal, my older brother. He's the jet jockey in the Marine Corps." Her eyes glimmered as she studied Bram's face. "He's a lot like you—brash, brazen, arrogant—"

He grinned. "Okay, I get the picture. And Matt?"

Rubbing her forehead, Storm stepped out of the protective haven of Bram's arms and wandered aimlessly about the kitchen, finally sitting down at the table. "Matt's the young-est. He's twenty-seven." She frowned. "He's an FBI agent, Bram. A year ago his wife was killed by Juan Garcia, a drug smuggler who runs a powerful ring in Colombia and the U.S. Matt had been working as an undercover agent here in Flor-ida, and when Garcia learned that he was responsible for put-ting some of his top men in prison, he put out a contract on Matt's wife."

Bram scowled, joining her at the table. "Damn, that's a tough nut to swallow. I'm sorry, Storm."

"It happened six months before I met you," she began softly, her eyes silver with unshed tears. "Matt was the quietest of the three of us. As brash and outspoken as Cal and I are, Matt just keeps everything inside. And when his wife, Maura, was killed in an unexplained 'auto accident,' Matt lost it." She rubbed her face, staring over at Bram. "He's living life with a vengeance in order to get at the mobster who set the wheels in motion to kill her. Since Maura's death, he's been undercover. I've rarely seen him or been in contact with him." She chewed on her lower lip. "God, he's lost so much weight. He looks terrible."

Bram reached out and gripped her hand. "Is there anything we can do to help him?"

Tears slipped down her cheeks as she met his concerned gaze. "Do you know how much I love you for asking that?" she confided.

His grip on her hand tightened slightly. "Family means a lot to me, Storm. Just like it does to you. He's your brother and I can tell you love him an awful lot."

She wanted to get up and throw her arms around him and simply hold him. "Matt's here for a reason. He said he's got a few days off before the action begins. If I can get a couple of decent meals into him and get him to sleep, I think that's all we can do for him right now."

"He's a man on the run, Storm," he told her quietly. "I rec-ognize the look in his eyes. I used to look like that myself when Maggie wanted to call it quits." His expression grew warm. "But I'm not running anymore. I found a woman who I can love without reservation. Maybe when Matt finds someone else, he'll quite running too."

Storm agreed. "God, when Maura died, Matt came un-glued. Both Cal and I flew up to Clearwater, where it happened. It was the worst nightmare of my life except for Hal's death.''

Bram got up and poured them each a fresh cup of coffee and then sat back down beside her. "Matt's here on an undercover assignment?''

Storm nodded and got up to putter around the kitchen, putting bacon in a skillet to fry. "He mumbled something about working with the Coasties on busting part of Garcia's drug-smuggling operation in the Bahamas this time. He'll probably fly out of here and go down there in a day or two.'' She shook her head, setting a plate and silverware on the table. "I hate the thought of it.''

Bram grimaced. "I don't mind working together with the other agencies on a combined operation, but everyone's got guns except us. We're sitting ducks up in the cockpit of a 52.''

Storm agreed. Getting shot at wasn't her idea of Coast Guard flying. The pilots sitting in the helicopters were clear, unobstructed targets. Not only that, but the fuel rested in the bottom of the 52. One bullet through the tank, and they would explode into flames. Bram had been with her on two combined operations to net smugglers at sea, and each time he had snarled something about at least getting a damned bulletproof vest to wear on these missions.

Matt appeared a half-hour later, freshly showered, his skin now scraped free of a day's worth of beard. His lean face seemed almost gaunt in appearance. Bram invited him to sit down and handed him a hot cup of coffee. Storm placed a plate heaped with three eggs, six strips of bacon, plus a steaming hefty portion of home fries before him. Matt gave his sister a warm look, and the first smile they had seen on his wide expressive mouth.

"Obviously you think I need to eat, sis.''

Storm put her hands on her hips. "No arguments, Matt. You're skinny as hell.''

"That's my sister for you," Matt confided to Bram, a gleam of affection in his charcoal eyes.

"She's that way with everybody," Bram assured him, grinning at Storm.

"Now, don't you two think you can gang up on me," she warned both of them, sitting down.

Matt dug hungrily into the homemade food. "Somehow, Storm, you'll keep us in line."

Bram gave her a fond glance. "I can testify to that."

"Keep it up, guys. I'm warning you..."

Storm studied her brother as he ate. She tried to hide her shock over Matt's condition. He wasn't heavily built like Bram; his body was much leaner and tightly muscled. Now his one-hundred-eighty-pound weight had slipped to less than one-sixty. She noticed that the blue shirt and jeans he wore hung loosely on his body. And his eyes were not only ringed with exhaustion, but bloodshot as well. "What have they been doing, working you to death, Matt?"

He shrugged and reached for a jar of jam. "We're getting closer to busting Garcia. It's taken me a year to set this up, but now it looks like we're going to be able to cut his operation by about forty percent." Matt looked up, a pleased expression on his normally unreadable features. "And that will force the bastard back to the gulf and the Texas connection, where we can pin him down. This is step two we'll be initiating now." He spread some jam on the whole wheat toast. "That's why I decided to drop in on you. According to the operation's plans, two helicopter crews from the Miami Coast Guard air station will fly down to the Bahamas to work with us. We finally got permission from the Bahamian government to do it."

Storm's brows rose and she shifted to observe Bram. "Oh? It must be a big bust."

Matt viewed her and then Bram before he resumed eating. "I've already seen the orders. You and Bram are one of the crews going down with us."

Bram scowled. "There's a good chance of gunplay."

"You'd better believe it." He gave a doleful shake of his head. "As soon as I found out you were assigned, Storm, I tried to influence my superiors to get you off the schedule. But apparently your skills are too good to pass up, and they wanted the two top crews from the Miami station in on this." He reached over and took her hand. "I don't think women should be around an operation of this kind. It's just too damned dangerous."

Bram got up, his mouth compressed into a single line. He walked around the kitchen, hands resting tensely on his hips.

There was no way in hell he wanted Storm in on that operation. He groped for a way to keep her off the forthcoming bust.

"Isn't there some kind of regulation that says the military can't have two members from the same family in a combat zone at the same time?" he queried.

Matt looked up, taking a sip of his coffee. "That's a good argument and would hold water except that I'm working in a civilian agency function and am not considered military. The FBI interfaces with the military in regard to drug smugglers all the time. I've already tried that approach, Bram, and it went over like a lead balloon." He stole a look at Storm's placid features. It never ceased to amaze him how stable she was, regardless of the situation. "Sis, this is one time I wish you weren't so damn good at flying helicopters."

Nine

Bram sat gloomily opposite Storm as Captain Greer waited for Lieutenant Kyle Armstrong and his copilot to enter the briefing room. It was one hell of a post-Christmas present, Bram thought, disgruntled. Present in the room besides the Coast Guard pilots and cutter skippers were three FBI agents, Matt Travis among them, and a few Customs and Drug Enforcement Agency agents. They sat stoically at the oblong mahogany table with their cups of coffee in hand. The bright-orange flight suits of the Coast Guard pilots stood out in contrast to the conservative suits worn by the other agents. An older man of fifty had eyed Storm keenly when she had first walked into the room. Bram hoped the agent would protest her taking part in the bust and get her reassigned.

He hadn't slept well last night. Wasn't Storm worried that she could be killed? She had slept soundly in his arms, head nestled beneath his chin, her free arm and leg thrown across his body. And he had stared up at the ceiling and listened to the clock tick with its phosphorescent red figures glowing in the darkness. He loved Storm fiercely. He didn't want to lose her.

Bram moodily stared down at his half-empty coffee cup. Matt Travis was a shell of a man living inside a body, running away from the grief and loss of his wife. A cold fear snaked through Bram. He'd be the same way if anything ever happened to Storm and he knew it. Suddenly life became precious drops of golden moments with her. Bram swallowed against the anxiety he felt winding its way up to form a lump in his throat. As he stared across the table at Storm, he realized the full impact of just how much he loved her. Matt Travis's sudden appearance into their lives had effectively ripped away any ghostly doubts as to how he felt. Life had taken a perverse turn, and he didn't like it at all. Bram wanted the time to continue cultivating their ever-deepening relationship. And he knew Storm felt similarly. The days and nights they were able to spend in each other's arms were precious and far between, but it kept them going. It kept them anticipating the next time they could share a day off together. Bram glared at Commander Harrison, who had approved the roster of crews to fly for the operation. Storm would be flying into danger. What the hell could he do about it? Nothing, a desperate voice declared inside him. Not a damn thing.

"I believe everyone is present," Commander Harrison averred, shutting the door. He looked over at the FBI agent. "Inspector Preston, you may start your presentation."

Preston was a slender man with long bony hands. He shut off the lights and turned on the projector. "For the past two-and-a-half years we've been infiltrating Juan Garcia's Colombian operation. He peddles mainly coke and grass to the Texas gulf and Florida peninsula. Although Garcia is Colombian, he owns a large estate on Andros Island in the Bahamas, where much of the coke is stored before it is airlifted or dropped by ship along our coast." He flashed a picture of an island clothed in forests of Australian pine, palms, and a chain of hills that looked like welts in the fabric of the pancake-flat island.

"This is Andros Island. It is situated west of Nassau. Andros is an ideal enter for Garcia because it's less popular with tourists and to a certain degree offers natural barriers to prevent us from spying. The island is littered with skeletons of planes carrying drugs that crashed there. We've gotten word through our undercover man that Garcia is planning to send a mother ship loaded with grass and coke out to meet smaller boats." He pointed to a crescent-shaped bay sporting a small strip of white sand, protected by a group of hills overlooking the bay. "He's going to anchor in Chisholm Bay and hoist the drugs over the side to waiting boat customers. Commander Harrison?"

Bram's scowl deepened, but he remained silent. The hooked curve of the bay didn't seem to allow much room to safely maneuver many ships. He cast a glance over at two SES cutter skippers who were also in attendance.

"Thank you, Inspector. The Coast Guard's part in this multiarmed operation is twofold. First we will provide two H-52 helicopters to pick up the combined FBI and Customs teams and drop them on Garcia's mother ship, *La Ceiba*. Then the SES cutters *Osprey* and *Sea Hawk* will close the noose from the sea and shut off any escape attempt out of Chisholm. No craft will be allowed to get by the SES contingent." Harrison looked pleased. "In other words, we're sealing off their only route of escape. They have nowhere to go and will have to surrender."

Storm cast a horrified look over at Matt, who appeared composed and unaffected by the plan. They would drop five men onto the deck of an unfriendly ship? Smugglers always carried a wide array of weapons. The chances of the agents getting wounded or killed would be high! Her throat ached with tears; she felt terror for Matt. He had been through one of the most brutal years of his life, but this was no way to end it! Did he want to die because he had loved Maura so much? Her stomach knotted and reflexively Storm lifted her chin, seeking Bram's reassuring gaze.

Bram saw the silent terror mirrored in Storm's eyes. He grimly turned the coffee around and around in his hands.

After everyone had received detailed information about Operation Stingray, the commander looked down the table. "Are there any questions?"

Bram circumspectly eased out of his slouched position. "What kind of resistance are you expecting aboard the *La Ceiba,* Inspector?"

"Minimal, Lieutenant Gallagher. We feel that the element of surprise will reduce the chance of our teams or your helicopters taking any fire. Most mother ships are used to boardings by the SES cutter crews. We intend to expand the use of your CG helicopters to assume a larger role in catching smugglers.

We realize this mission is setting a precedent, and we have no statistics to report our findings yet. Commander Harrison has picked the best crews for this job, and we have every confidence in your skills.'' He smiled.

Bram didn't. "Look, I know this is an extremely unusual situation, but women in any other service are banned from taking part in combat." His eyes narrowed on Harrison. "And where we're going, it is going to be combat."

Harrison gave a curt nod of his head, his focus latching onto Storm. "Ordinarily you're right, Lieutenant Gallagher. But the Coast Guard is caught in a catch-22. We have women serving in both the enlisted and officers' ranks aboard cutters constantly prowling the ocean for drug smugglers. They carry weapons just like any other member of a boarding crew. As long as war is not declared, our women have to take their chances right alongside the men of the Coast Guard. If war were declared, then the U.S. Navy would have to decide whether the women should remain in combat positions or not. I realize your concern, Lieutenant Gallagher, but Lieutenant Travis happens to be the best when it comes to flying in tight situations. You might as well know she was my first choice."

Bram checked his anger and frustration, lapsing back into silence, but continued to glower at the commander. "I assume since we're going into a combat situation, the 52 crews will get some sort of protection?" he inquired icily.

"Bulletproof vests will be issued before you lift off from Nassau."

"No .45s or .38s?" Bram asked, disbelief in his voice.

Commander Harrison shook his head. "We didn't feel there was a need, quite frankly. Up to now, no CG helicopter has been fired on, and we presume this procedure will continue." He shrugged. "Let's face it, the drug smugglers caught by the Coast Guard will get two years in prison. If they shoot at or kill one of you, the courts will keep them for twenty-five years. They aren't stupid. We feel the smugglers will continue to hold off from firing on Coast Guard personnel. All you have to do is hover, drop the teams, and loiter around until you're told to land back on Andros. Also we'll need you to take the teams back to Nassau along with the high-level prisoners we hope to capture on this trip after the situation is secured."

Bram hunched forward, both hands on the table. "Frankly, sir, when everyone else is provided weapons, I'd think it would be a blanket policy that we're at least issued shoulder holsters. Just in case."

The room crackled with tension. Storm stole a look over at Kyle Armstrong. It was obvious that he wanted a weapon too. Nervously she knitted her fingers in her lap beneath the table, remaining silent.

Harrison's patience was threadbare. "I'll take that suggestion under advisement, Lieutenant Gallagher. If the policy changes, you'll know about it before you fly over. Any other questions? Very well; dismissed. The 52 crews have the rest of the day off. Be here at 1800 to fly to Nassau."

Bram remained ominously silent as Storm walked at his side. They left the Administration building, heading toward her sports car in the parking lot. The sun was shining brightly, the humidity rising with the temperature.

Once inside the car, Storm turned to him. "Let's do something special today, Bram," she begged him. "For us."

His heart contracted as he heard the tremor in her voice. "You feel it too?"

"What?"

"I've got a bad feeling about this one, Storm."

Reaching over, she slid her hand down his arm, entwining her fingers within his. "I know it's hard on you, Bram."

His mouth quirked as if he were experiencing pain. "Hard? Scared would be more accurate. Scared of losing you on some asinine operation where they won't even give us minimal protection in case we need it." Frustration laced his tone, and he shook his head. "I've never felt this helpless before."

"It'll be okay," she reassured him. "Come on; want to go to the beach? Our favorite spot? We don't have to be back here for eight hours." Her gray eyes turned pewter with silent pleading. "Say yes."

Bram lifted her hand to his lips, kissing her palm. "Let's go."

Bram lay moodily on the blanket and watched Storm run into the waves, diving into the turquoise ocean and swimming strongly beyond the breakers. He lay on his side, hand propped against his head, allowing the late-December sunlight to warm him. The beach was crowded as usual for this time of year, but all his attention remained focused on Storm. She was so full of life. Closing his eyes, he pictured her smiling face with those haunting gray eyes glimmering with joy. Grimacing, he turned on his belly. What the hell was he going to do? It was impossible to fight City Hall. He couldn't disobey orders. Even Matt Travis couldn't swing enough weight to get Storm removed from the operation.

Storm jogged back up to the blanket, her body shimmering with droplets of water. Flinging herself down beside Bram, she laughed throatily, sliding her arm around his broad shoulders and placing a wet kiss on his cheek.

"Come on! The water's wonderful, Bram."

He forced a smile. Her dark hair was wet and glistening, her full mouth drawn into a teasing grin, her slender body beautifully outlined by the green suit she wore. "All I want is you," he murmured.

Wiping her face, she plopped herself down, beaming. "You've got me, jet jockey."

"Not like I want."

Storm tilted her head, a gleam in her eye. "I'm afraid the beach is a little too crowded for what you have in mind."

He grinned. She was right—she made his body harden with desire for her. No matter whether she wore a flight suit, civilian clothes, or nothing at all, she was desirable to him. "Come here, wet puppy; I want to talk seriously with you." He reached out, pulling her forward so she fell gracefully beside him. Smoothing several locks of hair still beaded with water from her brow, he leaned over, capturing her smiling lips. Her mouth was warm and salty-tasting, supple and pliant beneath his demands. She pressed herself suggestively against his length, and he groaned.

"You could turn a rock on," he grumbled.

Laughing, Storm traced the solid line of his jaw with her fingertips. "Just you, I hope."

"Always, princess."

Closing her eyes for a moment, she whispered. "I'm so glad we came out here today, Bram. Thank you."

He lost his smile, the blue of his eyes intensifying. "You are a wonderful woman," he declared. "So easy to please . . ."

"It doesn't take much to make me happy," she agreed, re-opening her eyes and responding to the caress of his eyes. "The whole family was bred to the bone on the simple pleasures of life."

"Such as?"

"Oh, just a few innocent notions—like happiness is obtainable. Something that everyone in the world is searching for all their lives." Mirth glimmered in her eyes. "And love. Our family believed that both could be found."

"Two of the most prized, sought-after possessions in the universe," Bram added, caressing her cheek. "Your parents are either idealists or dreamers."

She turned, kissing him delicately on his sensitive palm, watching the effect on him. "One of these days you'll meet my parents. And you'll discover that they're pretty squared away. Not pie-in-the-sky dreamers who filled their children's heads full of the impossible."

"You found happiness and love with Hal," he offered.

Storm became sober. "Yes, yes, I did." She lifted her lashes, meeting his burning azure gaze that sent a tingle of longing through her. "But I've found happiness and love a second time too." She ran her tongue across her lower lip. "With you, Bram."

He brought her into the shelter of his embrace, and she rested her head on his forearm, staring up at him. Her ginger hair was beginning to dry, a few strands lifting in the gentle sea breeze. Her face was a golden tan, her cheeks stained with a faint pink flush of exertion. She looked ageless—so much a child and yet a mature woman who intimately knew herself. He caught those rebellious tresses from her cheek, tucking them behind one ear.

"Marry me, Storm."

Her dove-gray eyes widened. "What?"

He regarded her steadily. "Marry me."

A look of confusion blended with hesitation as she stared up at him. "You serious? Or is this one of your little jokes?"

Bram muttered something under his breath and rolled his eyes. "A joke? How often do you think I go around asking women to marry me? After my track record? A joke! ... Well, I'll be damned."

"Then, you're serious!"

Bram gave her an exasperated look. "Of course I am."

Storm eyed him suspiciously, laughter lurking in the depths of her eyes. "This isn't some masterminded plan of yours to get me taken off that operation, is it?"

Bram uttered another expletive, pulling her up so they sat cross-legged opposite each other, holding her hands. "I'm trying to be serious, Storm."

"Then, you shouldn't be teasing me all the time so I think everything you ask is a joke, Bram Gallagher!"

"Okay, okay." He tried to compose himself. "First you accuse me of playing a joke on you and then of being sneaky enough to get you off that operation. Do you always think I have ulterior motives?"

Storm grinned broadly. "You usually do."

"I had that coming."

"And marrying me? Is there a method to your madness in getting me to be your wife?" she teased saucily.

Bram held her hands within his, sobering. "I sat in that conference room this morning, Storm, and I got scared. Scared like I've never been before. I sat there realizing that if something happened to you, I'd end up like your brother Matt. Lost, lonely, and bitter." His voice became husky as he saw Storm's features grow vulnerable with his admission. "I don't know what Hal was like. I have a feeling he was an easygoing man, compared to me. I do know that if you marry me, we'll have our moments where the sparks will really fly because we're both very headstrong, opinionated people. But we also have the maturity and respect for each other to weather those periods." His azure eyes grew warm. "I've been thinking about asking you to marry me for quite a while, Storm. But I was afraid. Afraid that I'd somehow botch up our chances, and I didn't want to do that. You deserve the very best I can be, and I felt I was still trying to get parts and pieces of me put back together again."

"Oh, Bram—"

"Shh," he admonished gently. "Let me get all of this off my chest and then you can talk." His brow furrowed, and he gazed at her long slender fingers. She was an artist in so many ways, he thought. "Over the last five months, you've taught me that not all women are afraid to entrust themselves to a man's care." He shrugged. "You trusted me. And because of that, I've opened up with you. I've found life's been pretty decent since doing that. I like giving and sharing myself with you and vice versa, I believe.''

Storm waited a moment. Her eyes grew misty with tears as she said softly, ''It was easy to place myself in your hands, Bram. Don't ask me how I knew I'd be safe doing it, I only knew I would be. And you've never taken advantage of me. When two people bare their souls to one another, it has to be one of the greatest compliments to themselves and to each other. It means not only trust between them, but as you said, respecting each other's feelings.''

He kissed each of her hands. ''You've shown me a lot, princess.''

''You gave me back my will to live again, Bram.''

''Then, spend the rest of your life with me, Storm.''

Tears streaked her cheeks as she met his suspiciously bright blue eyes. ''Think you can put up with my moodiness?''

''You're like the ocean—quicksilver. I love that about you. I'll never come home to the same woman two nights in a row.''

She laughed gently. ''You must be a glutton for punishment, then.''

''No, I just prefer a woman with diamondlike facets.'' He slid his hand behind her neck, pulling her slightly forward, his mouth caressing her lips. ''I want to spend the rest of my life discovering all the facets of you, Storm.''

She pressed her lips to his, relishing his strength, his tenderness. ''Discover me,'' she urged against his mouth.

By three P.M. they were back at Storm's house. Bram took the beach bag from her, setting it aside as they entered.

''Come on,'' he said, ''let's take a shower together.''

Storm looked up at him, her heart pounding erratically. On the beach, she had wanted simply to fall into his arms and love him wholly, completely. ''Yes,'' she murmured, taking his hand, allowing him to lead. She ached to be one with him, to seal the love between them on all levels, not just emotionally and mentally. Fear lurked in the recesses of Bram's eyes, and she sensed his silent anguish over the forthcoming operation. He was afraid of losing her. Although she tried not to let it show, Storm had to admit that she was afraid of losing him as well.

"Come here," he entreated, turning her toward him. Slipping his hands beneath the straps of the bathing suit, he eased them away from her shoulders. His callused hands slid downward, gently cupping her taut breasts, and he ran his palms across her hardening nipples.

A small gasp escaped from Storm as she shivered beneath his skillful, provocative touch. The sultry steam rose from the shower as they removed their suits and entered it. The hot water pummeled her body, and Storm closed her eyes, allowing the rivulets to cleanse her hair. Bram picked up the bar of soap in his large hands, running it slowly, arousingly across her shoulders, breasts, and abdomen. She tingled beneath his touch, the water and soap creating even more delightful friction. Turning her around, he lathered her beautifully curved back and hips, and down her long coltish legs. A soft moan slid from her throat, and she turned, placing her arms around his shoulders.

"My turn," she said huskily, kissing his mouth with small teasing nips. She felt his hardness pressing against her lower body and drank hungrily of the taste of his mouth. She was quivering against him, wanting him, needing him. Her fingers moved across the breadth of his chest, the soap a liquid pleasure creating even more tactile sensations than she thought possible. Storm watched him through half-closed eyes as she allowed her hands to trail down across his flat belly to the carpet of thick wiry hair below. He groaned, the sound reverberating in the enclosed space. His mouth plundered her yielding lips, drinking deeply of her as he slipped his hands downward, capturing her waist. Warm water trickled across them in tantalizing streams, further goading them toward unrestrained passion.

Leaning over, he ran his tongue across her nipples, feeling her knees buckle, her body bending like a willow against him. A soaring joy engulfed him as he realized she was easily fulfilled by him. He sucked gently on her taut, hardened nipples; heard her chant his name again and again, her fingers digging convulsively into his shoulders. Lifting his head, he kissed her mouth, branding her as his alone, forever. In one smooth motion, he brought her upward against him, allowing her to slide downward, capturing him with her warm, welcoming body. She froze in ecstasy, her head thrown back, a cry of pleasure escaping her lips. Blood pounded through his aching, hard body,

and he trembled with the knowledge that they loved each other
with a fierceness that left them both breathless in its wake.

Her lashes lifted, revealing languorous gray eyes silvered with
hunger and intensity as Storm felt his need within her inviting
body. The steam curled around and between them, the tiny
fingers of water adding tiny jolts of pleasure for each of them.
Together they drove each other over the edge of oblivion. Moments later Storm rested her head against Bram's shoulder,
fulfilled as never before. A low groan from deep within his
body had told her that he, too, had found the ultimate release
within her—the gift of the love shared between them.

Bram eased her from the shower, wrapped her in a thick
luxurious towel, and then picked her up. She clung weakly to
him, her head nestled against his shoulder as he carried her into
the bedroom. Sunlight filtered through the lace curtains, giving the room a muted glow that matched their mood. Placing
her on the bed, Bram drew Storm into his arms, gently kissing
her swollen lips. Her hair was dark and wet, and he smoothed
it from her cheek and brow.

"I love you," he told her, watching her lashes move upward, revealing breathtaking gray eyes that shone with returned love.

"Oh, Bram," she said shakily, leaning upward to kiss him
reverently.

He drew her close, holding her, feeling the strong beat of her
heart against his chest. Opening his eyes, he stared at the clock
on the bedstand. They had only an hour left before they must
return to base. His grip on her tightened, and he buried his head
against her damp apricot-scented hair, trying to quell the raging fear that palled his happiness. Matt Travis's gaunt face rose
in front of him, and Bram struggled to shake the fear. Would
he end up like Matt? A ghost of a man because the woman he
loved was dead?

Ten

Storm and Bram sat sweating in the cockpit of the helicopter, waiting for the FBI agent with a portable radio in hand to give them the signal to lift off. The two support helicopters sat at the base of the hills in a small clearing ringed by tall graceful palms. Perspiration trickled down beneath Storm's armpits, and she wriggled around, trying to scratch various spots. It was impossible with the uncomfortable bulletproof vest on, and she finally gave up. The sweltering Bahamian sun broiled overhead, sending the temperature in the cockpit well into the nineties.

"Come on," Bram snarled softly under his breath, "let's get this show on the road."

Storm glanced back. Five FBI agents sat silently with shotguns and submachine guns at their sides. Baseball caps were pulled down across their narrowed eyes, and they, too, wore bulletproof vests. They were dressed in the standard Coast Guard apparel of a dark navy shirt and slacks. All appeared blank-faced; all kept their thoughts to themselves. Before boarding, Storm had grabbed an opportunity to draw Matt aside, hugging him and begging him to be careful. Worriedly she turned around and faced forward, catching Bram's blazing blue gaze. Everyone was uptight.

"CG 1446 and 2241, crank it up!" came the orders through the helmets they wore.

"Roger, Kingbird," Bram returned on the radio. He shot a look over to Storm. "Let's get this over with," he said flatly.

The H-52 shuddered briefly when engaging the rotor. The blades began to whirl lazily above them, moving faster and faster until finally the din increased as Storm turned the speed selector toward takeoff power. The plan was to remain hidden behind the hills ringing the bay where the *La Ceiba* lay anchored. The two helicopters would fly low-level, hugging the slopes, and then crest and roar down the other side, surprising everyone in the cove. At that moment, the SES cutters were to come around the corner of the bay at full speed and close the noose around the drug runners' activities.

Storm pulled down the shaded Plexiglas visor, covering the upper two-thirds of her face. Bram did the same, his mouth remaining a grim flat line. On this trip, Merlin had been left behind. Bram would have to be the one to shut the sliding door after the five agents were dropped onto the deck of *La Ceiba*.

She concentrated on flying the 52 close to the hundreds of acres of Australian pine carpeting the chain of hills below them. Trees skimmed below the wheels and sponsons of the 52 as she urged the helo to remain steady. Around the hill, shifting winds created vortexes. Storm monitored the helicopter sensitively, adjusting to allow for the ebb and flow of the air currents around them. Behind them, Kyle Armstrong flew in tight formation with their aircraft. Tension permeated the interior of the ship. Bram reported their position, and Storm heard Kingbird give them the go-ahead on cresting the chain of moundlike hills to commence their airborne ambush of the *La Ceiba*.

"T minus thirty seconds," Bram reported to the one agent who had on a pair of earphones. "We're cresting...*now!*"

The agents locked and loaded their weapons in a simultaneous gesture.

The 52 snaked across the steepest hill. They got their first look at Chisholm Bay, its clear turquoise and emerald waters looking calm and peaceful. The *La Ceiba* lolled at the deepest point in the center of the bay. It was surrounded by more than fifty to seventy-five smaller craft ranging in size from small motorboats to sixty-foot yachts. It reminded Storm of a queen bee paid court by all her drones. The *La Ceiba* was a two-hundred-foot-class vessel with a helicopter landing pad located at the aft end of the ship.

"They see us," Bram warned.

Sure enough, the smaller boats began to move with frenetic activity, as if someone had thrown a rock into a quiet pool and the ripples were surging outward from it. The crewmen aboard the *La Ceiba* frantically pointed skyward, and Storm saw a detachment of them appearing out of the holds, rifles in hand. She broke out in a sweat.

"Sonofabitch," Bram snarled. "Kingbird, this is CG 1446. We're facing a hot landing zone. Crewmen on the *La Ceiba* are armed with M-16s and what appears to be AK-47s."

"Roger, CG 1446, we are apprised of the situation. SES *Osprey* and *Sea Hawk* will draw their fire. Out."

"Like hell they will!" Bram swore, clenching his teeth.

"Bram, just keep your hands and feet close to the controls," Storm pleaded, the anxiety in her voice reflecting the fear she felt. "If one of us gets hit going in or coming out, we've got to get the 52 up and away. We can't crash into the ship."

Bram's nostrils flared, and he gently wrapped his hands around the second set of controls.

Storm's heart pounded heavily in her chest, sweat bathing her tense body as she banked the 52 sharply, aiming for the *La Ceiba*. Matt was going to jump off straight into a withering wall of fire. Dear God, he could be killed! She shut out all those thoughts, concentrating on making a swift, accurate approach. There was nothing she could do when she saw the crew point their rifles at them. Were they going to shoot? Or were they only bluffing? Her throat tightened, squelching the scream that wanted to tear from within her. She heard shouts and orders coming from the rear but was unable to turn and look. She brought the 52 flaring in with the tail dipping, and then set it down quickly on the landing pad. The door slid open, and screaming erupted all around them. Storm heard Bram shout a warning. But it was too late.

Bram had twisted around, watching as the last agent leapt from the helicopter. The earphones were jammed with a mul-

titude of voices and orders. Jesus! This was worse than landing in a combat zone in Nam! As he spun back around, his eyes
widened. He yelled for Storm to take off. The boats all around
the ship were in utter panic. A forty-foot inboard motorboat
careened drunkenly between smaller ones. In an attempt to escape, it lost control, slamming into the aft end of the mother
ship, and exploded into a fiery ball. Then he heard Storm cry
out.

There was no time to wait, look, or try to help her. To his
horror, as he wrenched back on the controls to lift off, Storm
slumped forward in her seat. Blood. God, it was splattered
across her face. He felt the sting of several shrapnel wounds
caused by the shattering glass along his neck and lower jaw. The
52 surged upward to escape the holocaust enveloping the aft
end of the *La Ceiba*.

"Storm!" he yelled, risking a glance over at her. He saw her
move, weakly raise one hand toward her head. Her visor had
been shattered; blood covered the left side of her face.

The 52 suddenly lurched, and Bram heard a high pitched
whine screech through the cockpit, warning him that something was terribly wrong. They were losing power rapidly; the
52 was sinking downward. The helicopter's rotor and tail assembly had taken shrapnel from the explosion and the collision of the boats. The foot pedals felt mushy beneath his
booted feet. Land. They had to land! Bram's eyes narrowed as
he labored to keep them airborne.

"Storm! Wake up!" he yelled, manipulating the controls.

Storm was groggy, pain lancing her left temple. She felt the
uneven motion of the helicopter around her. Something was
drastically wrong. She smelled hot oil burning. The stench acted
like smelling salts on her numbed senses.

"Mayday, Mayday, Kingbird," Bram called hoarsely, "CG
1446, Mayday. We're hit. Going down on the beach. Mayday—"

The engine quit. The 52, which was limping along at one-
thousand feet, suddenly started to drop toward the glistening
white sands of the beach below. Autorotation! Grimly Bram
shoved the collective full down, the pitch flat so that the rotors
would continue to spin and give the copter some lift so they
wouldn't fall like a rock and crash. He had thirty seconds to
react and make lifesaving decisions before the helo would hit

the beach. Glancing around, Bram selected a clear area of beach on which to land, noticing several men coming ashore. Dammit, they were smugglers! First he had to get them down in one piece.

The 52 glided heavily downward, the *whap, whap, whap* of the rotor blades using the cushion of air to ride upon. He jockeyed the 52 into the wind. At one-hundred-forty-feet, Bram pulled the cyclic back. Instantly the nose came up and the ship flared, the tail rotor assembly almost brushing the sand. The flare would slow the forward motion of the helicopter, hopefully easing it down to zero knots. The ground raced up to meet them. At the last second, Bram leveled out the 52 and pulled the collective up to get all the lift he could. The helicopter settled with a shuddering thud on the beach, the rotors slowly circling to a halt above them.

Yanking off the confines of the harness, Bram turned anxiously to Storm. She was semiconscious, eyes half-closed. Nearby voices and shouts approached. Bram cursed richly, jerking around. No more than a half-mile away a band of smugglers was running toward them. Why the hell hadn't they been given weapons to defend themselves! He heard volleys of gunfire all across Chisholm Bay. Shoving the visor up into his helmet, Bram knelt at Storm's side. His mind raced with options: Maybe Armstrong could rescue them, or...

"Storm?" he gasped, breathing hard.

She frowned, putting her hand against her temple. "I—I'm okay, I think," she answered weakly.

Bram pushed the button on the cyclic, calling for Armstrong.

"Roger, CG 1446. I'm on my way," Kyle answered.

"Come on," he told her, unsnapping her harness, "we're getting out of here."

Bram pushed what was left of her shattered visor back up into her helmet and then put his arm around her waist, dragging her back through the cabin toward the opened door. He heard the rapidly approaching 52 in the distance above the gunfire and chaos. Storm could barely stand, and he knelt down, throwing her across his shoulder. The sand was deep, and he sank into it as he slogged his way around the 52 toward a stretch of beach where Armstrong could land.

Just as Armstrong's 52 came within a quarter-mile of where Bram stood waiting with Storm, the drug smugglers opened up with a blistering volley of gunfire. Bram watched in shock as the 52 had to abort its rescue attempt, banking sharply back out toward the bay. This was one time when gunships would have been in order. Storm sagged against him, and he divided his attention between her and the smugglers, who were closing the distance between them.

Their leader, an American with flaming red hair and a neatly kept beard, reached them first. The ugly snout of his pistol lifted toward Bram.

"Don't move or you'll both be dead," he barked.

Bram froze, keeping his arm around Storm.

"Search them!"

"We're unarmed," Bram hurled back.

"Sure, you are," a black-haired man grumbled. He rapidly ran his hands over Bram and then closely examined Storm. "What the hell—" He leaned over to get a better look. "Hey, Frank, it's a woman! I'll be damned!"

The red-haired Frank smirked. "Search her anyway. She's a Coastie."

Bram's arm snaked out. He jerked the smuggler up by the collar just as he reached forward to search Storm. "Don't touch her," he snarled, releasing the smuggler and propelling him backward into the sand. Bram jerked his head toward Frank. "She's wounded. I need to get her to a doctor—"

"Tough luck, Coastie. Ramón, get up! Come on, let's head inland." His brown eyes narrowed on Bram. "This is real Providence. You two are gonna provide us a way out of this situation. Get moving!"

The one named Ramón was small by comparison with Bram. He picked up his gun, glaring at the Coast Guard officer as he approached them. Shoving the gun in Bram's heavily muscled back, he snapped, "Move!"

Storm became aware of jagged motion, her head aching as though someone had slugged her with a baseball bat. It was hot, and she felt the damp stickiness of her flight suit chafing roughly against her skin. Someone was carrying her in his arms. She heard voices, but they blurred in and out as she lingered between levels of consciousness. Finally they halted, and she felt herself being lowered to the ground. Someone was gently removing the heavy helmet from her head. A cooling breeze brought her around, and she forced her eyes open. Bram's grim features danced before her eyes. It took several long minutes to realize he had propped her up against the trunk of a pine tree.

Bram's face drew closer and she blinked, dazed. He drew his handkerchief from his pocket and gently wiped the blood from her cheek and jaw below the wound she had sustained. Every touch hurt, and she tried not to wince.

"Sorry," he whispered gruffly. "Just lie still and don't talk."

Frank and his four fellow smugglers rested under another tree, guarding them. Getting to his feet, the leader wandered over to them. He looked down at the woman, interest in his eyes. A slight smile curved at his thin mouth.

"I didn't know you Coasties were sending women to do your dirty work now," he said.

Bram ignored him, concentrating on Storm's head wound. He picked up her helmet, his heart plummeting. A stray piece of shrapnel had smashed through her visor just above her left eyebrow, glancing off her skull and lodging in the helmet itself. She had come within a centimeter of dying. Sweat dripped from his jaw as he examined the wound. It was a small cut no more than an inch in length, but scalp wounds always bled heavily.

"She ain't bad lookin' once you get her cleaned up. What's her name?"

Bram twisted his head, glowering up at him in silent warning to back off.

Frank simpered and leaned over, reading the black leather patch emblazoned with her name and rank on her flight suit. "Lt. Storm Travis. She live up to her name, Coastie?"

Bram gritted his teeth, sensing that silence was the better part of valor for the moment, and returned his attention to Storm. She was groggy, and he needed water for both of them. Keeping a steadying hand on her arm, he worriedly watched her struggle to become more conscious. Frank finally grew bored and walked away. Drawing in a shaky breath, Bram offered Storm a tense smile.

"How do you feel?"

Storm cleared her throat. "Terrible. I've never had such a splitting headache. What happened?"

He recounted the chain of events for her in a lowered voice. Storm's eyes narrowed with pain. She slowly sat up, cradling her head in her hands.

"Kyle couldn't land?"

"No. These guys started firing."

"Then, we're prisoners."

"Yeah," he said flatly, glaring at the sand. Taking off his helmet, he ran his fingers through his wet hair in disgust.

"What do you think they'll do?"

"The ringleader, Frank, said we're their ticket out of here."

"That's good," Storm said, peering up. "At least they won't kill us yet." Her lips parted when she realized he was wounded also. "Glass?" she asked, reaching over and gently touching his right cheek.

Bram nodded. "Yeah, we both look like pin cushions. That shrapnel from the collision much have ricocheted when it hit the cockpit glass, and then struck you." His voice grew strained. "God, I was never so scared as when I looked over and saw your face covered with blood."

Storm reached out, touching his hand. "I'm sorry, Bram."

Grimacing, he continued to squat by her side. "Nothing to apologize for, princess. I knew something was going to happen today. I could feel it coming."

"I did too," she admitted rawly, "but I didn't want to say anything. There was nothing we could do about it anyway, Bram."

He sucked in air between his clenched teeth. "Next time I do this, I'm going in with a pistol or an M-16. If we had either this time, we might have escaped."

Storm scanned the group. "Not with five rifles staring down our throats, Bram. They would have killed us outright." She took his handkerchief and wiped away the last of the blood on her cheek. "As it stands, we may have a better chance to survive this."

"Maybe," Bram concurred gloomily. "The leader has eyes for you. I'm more worried about that than anything else."

"Let's play it by ear. These guys don't have that kind of time to do much else other than make a run for it, much less think about attacking me."

His eyes glittered dangerously. "They won't lay a hand on you," he promised.

Ramón came over, motioning for them to get to their feet. Storm struggled to stand, momentarily dizzy. She was grateful for Bram's arm around her waist, steadying her. For the next hour, they climbed the slope of the hill, weaving through the pines and palm trees. Storm regained most of her strength during that time and preceded Bram. They came across a small stream. Gratefully Storm knelt down, splashing the cooling water across her face and neck. The water tasted delicious as she scooped it up in her cupped hands, allowing it to trickle down her parched throat. She longed to strip out of the smelly flight suit and cleanse her sweaty body.

"Take five," Frank ordered them. He strode over to where Storm and Bram were sitting. His dark brown eyes narrowed in on Storm, and he halted a few feet from her. Bram rose slowly to his feet, his legs spread slightly apart, hands hanging tensely at his sides.

"Don't try it, Coastie," Frank cautioned menacingly. "Get over there and sit down. I'm just going to talk to your girl-friend here."

Bram hesitated.

"Move," Frank warned.

Storm's eyes widened with silent pleading for Bram to do as he was told. Bram reluctantly walked over to a tree and leaned against it, vigilantly watching them. She returned her atten-tion to the smuggler, who came and crouched near where she was kneeling.

"Just to show you there're no hard feelings, I'm Frank Carter."

"I doubt if you're interested in my feelings, Carter," she snapped quietly, her eyes blazing.

He grinned broadly. "I like a woman with spirit. Storm's a real good name for you. How you feeling?"

"Like hell. How am I supposed to feel?"

He shrugged, pursing his lips. "When you play with the big boys, honey, it gets rough sometimes."

"I don't regret an instant of it, Carter."

His smile faded. "You're the best surprise of this whole miserable fiasco, you know that? I could make it real easy on you, honey. Why don't you join up with us? We're going to es-cape. It's just a matter of waiting for night to fall and then making it to one of the bays and paying for a ride to Nassau."

He reached out, his hand extended to touch her. With blinding speed, Storm struck out, slapping his face. The slap resounded like a shot. Leaping to her feet with practiced ease, Storm watched as Carter slowly rose, his face red.

"Don't touch me," she rasped. "I hate you and I hate your kind, Carter."

He nursed his cheek, sizing her up. "Real spitfire, aren't you, Travis? Well, we'll see what you're really made of tonight."

Bram came over to where she was standing as Carter stalked off. She was trembling from the rush of adrenaline and closed her eyes for a moment. She felt Bram's reassuring hand on her arm.

"Okay?" he asked, worriedly searching her wan features.

"Fine. Just a little shaky. The bastard...."

"What did he say?"

Storm watched as Carter goaded his party back to their feet, swearing loudly at them. "Apparently he has plans for me tonight after we make camp."

Bram's mouth tightened. "We've got to try and escape, Storm."

"Carter isn't the type to attack me in front of everyone. He's too insecure for that. If he leads me off at gunpoint, maybe I can disarm him."

"That's too risky."

"Do you have a better plan?"

Bram shook his head. "Not right at the moment."

By nightfall, they were well on the other side of the hill boundary line and working their way down to Red Bay. What had taken a few minutes by helicopter had taken them half a day on foot to cover. Carter wasn't stupid; he ordered their hands tied in front of them and separated them. There was no opportunity to escape, and when they finally began to make camp, Storm wearily sank to her knees, leaning back against a tree. Her head spun with questions. Was Matt safe? Had Kyle been able to radio back for help and alert the authorities that they had been captured? Would they send a party to try and rescue them? Carter had been giving her insidious looks all afternoon. Storm yearned to be next to Bram. Just his nearness was a source of invisible support to her.

Lying down, Storm closed her eyes, trying to rest. If Carter was going to attack her, she would need every ounce of reserve in a battle of wits and human strength to fight him off. Hot tears pricked the back of her eyes as she lay there. She loved Bram so much, her heart ached with the pain of what he must be feeling right now. She had seen the fear in his eyes for her safety. Swallowing against the lump in her throat, Storm forced herself to rest . . . and wait.

Storm was roughly shaken awake. She blinked, feeling a hand dig harshly into her shoulder, yanking her into a sitting position. It was dark. Only pale slats of moonlight filtered haphazardly down through the pine trees to drive the surrounding pitch blackness away.

"Come on," Carter growled softly, jerking her to her feet, "you and I have some unfinished business to attend to."

Her heart pounded achingly in her chest as she struggled momentarily. Carter's fingers dug deeply into her upper arm, bruising her flesh. Bram! Where was he? Eyes widening, Storm tried to twist around to catch sight of him. Their eyes met for an agonizing split second. Storm saw the terror in Bram's face as he struggled against the ropes that bound him hand and foot. Not only that, but they had gagged him as well. Nausea rose in her throat as Carter shoved her forward into the thick underbrush. She nearly lost her balance, stumbling awkwardly. At the last second, Carter gripped her arm, jerking her upright.

"What's the matter, honey? Scared?"

She had to think! No matter how frightened she was, she had to think! Storm looked around at the dark, shadowed foliage. She needed a small space to operate within. Just a small one! Frank held the gun close to his side, occasionally jabbing it into her ribs as he forced her deeper into the lush forest. Branches and leaves swatted her, and Storm felt their sting against her unprotected face. Her throat was constricted in pain, and her breathing was harsh and labored. Revulsion coursed through her. Bram couldn't help her.

They broke into a small clearing dappled with moonlight. Storm worked frantically at the ropes that bit cruelly into her flesh. If only she could free herself!

"That's far enough," Carter said ominously.

Her heartbeat accelerated, pounding thunderously in her chest. Slowly Storm turned toward him, her nostrils flared, her body tensed.

He grinned, motioning for her to come closer. In that single gesture, Carter had waved his right hand out away from his body for a split second. And it was just such a move that Storm had been praying for. In one unbroken motion, she lifted her right leg, aiming her steel-toed flight boot at Carter's hand. There was a metallic snap as boot met gun. Carter yelped, his fingers torn loose from the gun, the revolver sailing off into the darkness.

Storm completed the spinning circle, planting both feet firmly on the ground, breathing hard. Carter snarled an obscenity, holding his wrist.

"You broke it!" he rasped. "You bitch; you broke my wrist!"

He made a lunge for her. Storm again lifted her leg, her boot colliding solidly with Carter's jaw. There was the distinct sound of bone crunching beneath the power of her kick. Carter was thrown backward, uttering a groan as he crumpled into an unconscious heap.

She had lost her balance with her hands tied. Storm saw the ground coming up fast and tucked her head, allowing her shoulder to take the brunt of the jolt. Hitting the earth, she rolled over on her back. A gasp escaped her. Out of nowhere a man dressed in camouflage fatigues pressed his hand across her mouth to stop her from screaming. Storm's eyes widened in shock.

"Shh! It's me, Matt."

Gradually he eased his hand from her mouth. Storm sobbed for breath as she anxiously looked up at her brother. His face was shaded with green, black and brown tones. The jungle fatigues he wore blended perfectly with the backdrop of the night surrounding them. Miraculously Storm saw four more men melt out of the shadows to kneel by her. One of them handcuffed Carter's arms behind him and placed a gag in his mouth in case he regained consciousness.

Matt unsheathed a Ka-Bar, a knife used in jungle warfare, quickly slicing the ropes binding her wrists. Helping his sister sit up, he held her until she stopped trembling.

"Okay?" he asked in a hoarse whisper.

Storm gulped. "Y-yes. Thank God you're—"

"Bram? Is he still alive?"

She blinked back tears. "Yes." She pointed to her left. "There're four other smugglers with him, Matt. They've got him bound and gagged."

Matt's mouth tautened, his eyes gleaming like obsidian. "Okay, you stay put. We'll do the rest." He silently rose to his full height, giving her a worried look. "You all right?"

Nodding, Storm wiped the tears from her cheeks. "Just scared."

Matt gave a quiet order, and the men blended back into the shadows, melding into forest once again. Storm rose to her knees, unsure whether she could stand. What if there was a gunfight? Bram and Matt could be killed! Tears caught in her throat as she sat there, fists clenched against her thighs, waiting.

Within ten minutes, the smugglers had been captured without a shot being fired. Matt came back to the clearing, his face slightly more relaxed. He held out his hand, helping Storm stand, and led her back along the path.

"Bram's okay," he said in a normal tone of voice. "Angry as hell, but okay."

Storm smiled shakily, her legs wobbly. She leaned against Matt. "This was too close," she whispered, her voice sounding raw.

"I know."

"How did it go aboard the ship?"

"Hotter than hell. One man was wounded, but we captured the number-two man in Garcia's organization besides the largest haul of coke ever." He gave her a bleak smile. "That makes me one step closer to Garcia himself. Now all I have to do is track him down in his lair, which is on the Texas gulf coast."

Storm barely heard her brother's words as she caught sight of Bram. They had just untied him, and he was stiffly getting to his feet. He saw her. She left her brother's protective embrace and flew to him. Bram wrapped his arms tightly around her, drawing her against him. A sob tore from her, and Storm buried her head on his chest, eyes tightly shut.

"Oh, Bram," she cried, "I was so worried—"

He kissed her hair. "I'm okay. Are you?" he asked thickly, assessing her worriedly.

She didn't know whether to laugh or cry. "I'm fine...fine..." Her charcoal eyes were large and vulnerable like a child's. "I was so scared," she sobbed, melting back into his embrace.

Bram groaned, holding her tightly, feeling her warmth, her strength. "Thank God," he whispered rawly. "I've never felt so damned helpless. Never." Tears brimmed his eyes as he buried his head next to hers. The rage and impotence he had experienced when Carter took her into the jungle had nearly strangled him. The smugglers had known he would try to prevent Storm from being taken by Carter. By binding and gagging him, they had taken no chances. In the ensuing moments after she had disappeared into the darkness with Carter, he had wanted to scream. Scream with frustration and pure, unadulterated rage over what Carter could do to Storm.

Hearing someone approach, Bram raised his head. He gave Matt a grateful look.

"I think we're ready to go," Matt told them, giving his sister a solicitous glance. "We've got two helicopters coming in to pick us up in a meadow near here."

"Sounds good. We owe you a lot, Matt."

Matt smiled grudgingly and touched Storm's shoulder. "Couldn't let my big sister down, could I? We have a doctor waiting for you in Nassau. A shower, change of clothes, and a hot meal at a hotel will put you back in order."

"Nassau?" Bram asked, mystified.

"Cutters are overcrowded with prisoners right now. We get the Ritz tonight. Tomorrow we'll be flown back to Miami."

It was almost eleven P.M. before they were medically attended to and then dropped off at a hotel in Nassau. Storm felt the stares of people in the lobby as well as the clerks behind the desk. They must look a sight in their dirtied flight suits and disheveled appearance, she thought tiredly. Bram seemed supremely unaware of it. Getting the key, he guided her to the bank of elevators with his hand resting on her elbow.

"Looks like we'll be the talk of the hotel," he said, smiling slightly as they rode the elevator to the tenth floor.

Storm grimaced. "Ask me if I care at this point."

"Do you care, Lieutenant Travis?"

She warmed to his teasing, following him out of the elevator and down the plushly carpeted hall. "Not in the least, Lieutenant Gallagher. We're paid to do a job, not look pretty."

Bram grinned, his sky-blue eyes glimmering with hungry intensity as he scrutinized her. "You look beautiful no matter what you do or don't wear, lady." He slipped the key into the lock, opening the door. "Grab the bathroom first," he urged. "I'll order us up some food. I'm starved."

Storm shook her head ruefully, a smile touching her lips. "Always thinking of your stomach first," she sighed in mock exasperation.

Bram closed the door and took her into his arms. Leaning down, he gently kissed her lips. "I was thinking first about loving you as soon as we get cleaned up."

The tension surrounding their narrow escape began to subside, and Storm managed a laugh. "You're impossible!"

He molded his mouth to her lips and felt her responding pressure as the heat rapidly escalated between them. She tasted of warmth. They were alive.... Placing a rein on his spiraling desires, Bram drew away, a feral light flaming in his azure eyes. "Get in the tub before I carry you over to the bed," he warned.

Shaken by the intensity of his voice, Storm nodded. They had come very close to death, and the sudden look that shadowed his eyes made her poignantly aware of just how much she loved Bram. "I love you."

Long slanting rays of sun invaded their room. Storm stirred, nuzzling like a lost kitten beneath Bram's chin. Eyes still heavy with sleep, she forced them open. Yesterday's events slowly seeped into her waking state. She automatically slid her arm across Bram's powerful chest, giving him a hug. Last night they had showered, eaten a quick meal, and literally fallen into bed, exhausted. Relishing the hard, warm strength of his naked body against her own, Storm sighed contentedly.

Bram moved his hand downward, lightly stroking her back and hips, sending a liquid message throughout her sensitized nervous system. Automatically Storm pressed the full length of her body against him in reaction. A low purr came from deep within her throat as his skillful hand stroked the sensitive flesh of her inner thigh.

"Good morning," he greeted huskily, raising himself up on one elbow.

A tremulous smile tinged her lips as she opened her eyes, meeting his and stirring beneath his gaze. "It is," she sighed, sliding her hands up across his arms to his well-muscled shoulders, reveling in his masculine strength. He was so alive, so vital, it made her heart sing in unison with her throbbing, waking body.

His face was relaxed, his features almost boyish, a rebellious lock of hair dipping down on his smooth brow. Storm reached up, taming the tendril back in place, luxuriating in the scent of him. Longing burned in the depths of his eyes as he leaned down and caressed her lips as if she were some fragile, delicate rose to be worshipped.

"Mmm, you smell good.... Like apricots and honey," he murmured, nibbling at her lip, placing several tiny lingering kisses at the corners and then allowing her to feel the masculine strength of his mouth as he molded it possessively against her. She was tautly strung, responding to each featherlike graze of his hand. He brushed his palm provocatively across her nipples, hearing her moan with pleasure. Dragging his mouth from her lips, he tasted each one, tugging gently, feeling her stiffen with desire for him.

Bram became lost in the sensuousness of the moment and was aware of her wonderful feminine scent that was an aphrodisiac to his own heightened arousal. She tasted like sweet clover honey to him, and her flesh was warm smooth jade to be tantalized by his exploration. From the day he had met her, Storm had never been any less than all woman to him. She possessed a courage coupled with a sensitivity that left him shaken and in awe. She was life to him in all respects, all ways, and he never wanted to lose her. He loved her. Drawing her beneath him, he parted her thighs, wanting, needing to share the power of his feelings with her alone. A groan came from within him as he plunged into the welcoming depths of her liquid warmth. They were one. She was life—giving, taking, and sharing without reserve—and he guided her through levels of euphoria, leaving them both satiated and breathless in its torrid wake.

Storm trembled deliciously as Bram drew her protectively against him afterward. She kissed him, tasting the salt of perspiration on his cheek. He returned the kiss, his mouth caressing her lips in tender adoration. An ache of joy filled her heart, until she was at a loss for words.

Bram stroked her hair, running the gossamer threads through his fingers. "You're like silk," he told her, his voice laden with spent passion.

Storm smiled contentedly, tilting her head up to bask luxuriantly in the warmth of his love. "I always thought of myself as good old durable cotton—infinitely practical, natural, and something that could be worn forever."

He cocked an eyebrow. "No," he retorted mildly, brushing her flushed cheek lightly, "you're silk. Exotic, unique, beautiful..."

"Hmm, I never saw myself that way before."

"I do. Besides, silk is a natural fiber like cotton, and it wears forever." He traced her brow, nose, and touched her rosy, well-kissed lips. "And like silk, you require special attention in the care and handling department."

She giggled. "You mean you can't just throw me into any old washing machine?"

"Nope. Special treatment for you, my lady."

Her gray eyes shimmered with joy as she rose up on one elbow and imprinted a kiss on his mouth. "I never thought of myself as an expensive cut of cloth, Lieutenant Gallagher. Do you always perceive the world in such an interesting fashion?"

"Is that a pun, Lieutenant Travis soon-to-be Lieutenant Gallagher?"

She braced her arms against his chest, laughter edging up the corners of her mouth. "I'll settle for Travis-Gallagher."

He grinned. "Do it this way—when things are going right, use Travis. But when things are going badly, use Gallagher."

Their laughter filled the room. Bram ran his hands down the length of her long back. He gradually sobered, drowning in her lovely dove-gray eyes. "I love you, Storm," he told her quietly. He struggled with words that normally came easily to his glib tongue. But this morning they didn't. He was overwhelmed with her effortlessness and her ability to share her happiness with him. "When you got injured, I died inside," he admitted, meeting her serious gaze. "I've never felt so torn up. I had a helicopter that was dying on me, and you were leaning forward in the harness with blood streaming down the side of your face." He shut his eyes, fighting to arrest the surge of emotion accompanying that gruesome picture. Releasing a shaky sigh, Bram continued. "Storm, I didn't know what real love was until I met you. I thought I knew. I had based a marriage on those conceptions. But they were wrong. Your honesty, your forthrightness, taught me the happiness of actually sharing my life with you. And it wasn't painful."

Storm swallowed against tears as she caressed his cheek. "Love is always interwoven with pain, Bram. We can't have one without the other. But with the way we feel toward one another, I know our love will outdistance any pain we might cause one another."

He grimaced. "I was scared. Scared that I'd lose you like your brother lost his wife. Matt's haunted. I see it in his eyes: I can see it in his expression. I sat there tied up, watching you sleep while those smugglers were eyeing you. I saw myself in Matt's position. If they had hurt you in any way, I would have hunted every last one of them down and made them pay—"

"Shh," she soothed, placing her fingertips against his mouth. "It didn't happen, Bram. We're alive. We're safe, and we have each other." She rested her brow against his stern, uncompromising jaw. "No one said life was particularly safe either in an emotional or a physical sense, darling. Matt reached out to embrace life by loving Maura. He paid a price for having the courage to live. And we're risk-takers in the same sense, Bram. We're both willing to pay the price, whatever that might be, to reach out and love one another regardless of the emotional or physical cost." She leaned upward, kissing his mouth. "Do you know how many people never live at all? How many are afraid to step out of the familiar and experience things such as placing your heart in someone else's hands?"

He nodded, running his fingers through her ginger hair. "I was like that after the divorce, Storm. I met you and fell like a ton of bricks. And my feelings toward you scared the hell out of me because I was afraid to reach out and live again."

"But you did anyway, Bram. That says something about your caliber as a human being."

"And you? You weren't afraid to love me. Or were you?"

Storm lowered her lashes. "I admitted I was frightened, Bram. And I was. Hal was torn from me. I didn't think I could stand the pain of maybe losing you someday too." She gave a helpless shrug. "But the alternative wasn't acceptable."

He sat up, leaning against the headboard, gathering Storm into his arms. "Sometimes I wonder if our courage to reach out emotionally might be construed as foolhardiness by someone else. Because we won't live half-lives with one another, princess. And the more we give and share with one another, the larger the potential for pain if something happens."

"I know," she responded softly, loving his closeness, nuzzling his cheek. "The physical threat to us is far greater than the emotional one, Bram."

"Tell me about it," he agreed unhappily. "All it takes is one bullet from a drug smuggler's gun—"

"Or a malfunction aboard a helicopter. Or a bad wave.... Bram, in our business there're many chances for disaster. We live with those daily. We both love what we do." She looked up at him. "You wouldn't ask me to give up flying because you're afraid of losing me, would you?"

The silence was heart-stopping as he stared at her. His eyes filled with tears, and he compressed his lips. "No—no, I wouldn't ask that of you, Storm."

She nodded, on the verge of tears herself. "If you had, a huge part of me would have slowly died, Bram. I would have given it up for you, but I would have been unhappy."

He lovingly placed his finger beneath her chin. "Look at me," he commanded huskily.

Raising her head, Storm met his clear azure gaze, her heart contracting. The path of tears down his stubbled cheeks evoked a cauldron of emotions from within her. It stunned her. Hal had never cried; never shared this vulnerable human part of himself with her. But Bram trusted her . . . loved her enough to share this secret side of himself with her. A small cry escaped her parted lips.

"I want you to be yourself, princess. To ask you to give up your career would be like asking me to do the same thing. And I know you'd never do that, Storm. I can do no less for you." He cupped her face, gently drawing her forward until their lips barely brushed. "Part of the reason I love you so much is because you're all that you can be. You haven't let society tell you it's wrong to join the service, fly a helicopter, or even risk your life. And you're woman enough to cry when it's all over. That

makes me feel good, Storm—I cherish your ability to run to my
arms and be held. You're not pretending to be a superwoman.
You're simply yourself, and God, woman, I love you for that
and I always will.''

* * * * * *

A Note from Kathleen Creighton

Dear Reader,

I'm often asked whether I actually visit all the places I write about. Much as writers would all love to do so, of course, sometimes it just isn't possible. I was a very new and unpublished writer when I began researching an idea for a book about a border patrol agent who falls in love with a smuggler. I couldn't justify much in the way of travel expense, but since I lived in Southern California, I was only a few short hours (I thought) from Baja California. And so, after a stop in San Ysidro to interview a U.S. Border Patrol agent, I drove intrepidly and alone into Tijuana, Mexico.

My adventurous spirit quickly deserted me when I found myself in an area that reminded me of pictures I'd seen in *Life* Magazine of war-devastated cities, surrounded by signs that told me only that four years of high school Spanish weren't nearly enough! I finally managed to get myself turned around and headed north, and after a three-hour wait at the border checkpoint, crept ignominiously back into the good ol' U.S.A. Safely home again, I went straight to the public library and checked out every book and *National Geographic* article on Baja California and the fabled Sea of Cortez. With those articles and my own imagination, I created the setting for what would become my very first published novel.

Not long after *Demon Lover* came out, a woman approached me and shyly asked if I might tell her the exact location of the smugglers' camp. Because, she told me, she was certain she and her husband had once been fishing in that very same spot!

I hope you enjoy *Demon Lover*, dear friends. May the people, places and events born in my imagination live once again in yours.

Kathleen Creighton

DEMON LOVER

Kathleen Creighton

Chapter 1

Juliet Maguire awoke amazed at finding herself still alive. For a moment she couldn't think why she should be amazed; but then memory returned in a single sickening rush and instead she couldn't understand why she should be alive.

Coyotes. She had been captured by coyotes.

The cold-blooded smugglers, ruthless traders in human contraband, couldn't possibly have any use for one incredibly clumsy Border Patrol agent. It would have been so easy for them to kill her and dump her body in the desert. Why hadn't they?

And where was she? It was dark, but she seemed to be on a bed, in something that moved. She could feel the rough fabric chafing her cheek, hear the low growl of a powerful engine, feel the occasional lurch and sway of rapid motion. The camper—she was in the camper, of course! And they were on a paved road, probably still in the desert, since the road seemed to be arrow straight.

She lay very quietly, holding her breath and listening for sounds of alien breathing. She heard only the drone of the motor and the sound of her own blood pounding in her aching head. She was alone. That fact gave her very little comfort; they had left her alone because there was was absolutely nothing she could do to escape. Julie wasted no time struggling with her bonds. They were simple and effective—completely professional. He knew his business, that one—the tall one...the one who had caught her.

What was it they had called him? *Demonio Garzo*. Or had she only conjured the name from her nightmares? *Blue-eyed Demon*. Julie shivered in the darkness.

How had it happened? She was a professional, an experienced and well-trained agent. How could she have *let* it happen?

Partly to keep her mind off her physical and emotional discomforts, and partly because it was almost second nature to recap any incidents encountered on patrol, Julie stared into the shadowy darkness and began a painful and meticulous replay of the whole fiasco.

...From her position behind the rocky knoll she watched the camper crawl across the desert floor, dragging a plume of dust behind it like a deflated parachute. She frowned, shading her eyes against the late-afternoon glare. Something about that camper bothered her.

It wasn't anything that could be explained. The extra-wide wheelbase and oversize off-road tires, heavy-duty shocks and four-wheel drive could all just be accommodations of a dedicated off-road enthusiast. But there was something—just a gut feeling, an instinct. Julie didn't question it; after nearly ten years as an agent of the United States Border Patrol she had learned to trust her instincts.

The camper climbed steadily toward her up the narrow dirt road, its engine purring with the throaty growl of power to spare, its gearbox whining in high-pitched overtones. She watched it pass and drop out of sight over the ridge, and then climbed back into her own vehicle, reaching for the radio as she snapped her seatbelt into place. She calmly gave her location and stated her intention to pursue a suspect vehicle, then started the motor and pulled slowly out onto the road.

She kept well back. The desert could easily swallow up a vehicle bent on eluding a pursuer. And if the camper was, as she suspected, carrying smuggled illegals from Baja California, it would probably be heading for a rendezvous sometime after dark, either to pass its human cargo on to another, more innocent-looking conveyance for the last leg of the journey to the urban wilds of Los Angeles, or to deposit them in some remote way station to make their own way north. They might even abandon the whole camperload to die in the desert. It wouldn't be the first time.

Julie tightened her jaw and flexed her fingers on the steering wheel. *Coyotes.* There wasn't an agent in the Border Patrol who didn't loathe and fear the unscrupulous smugglers. Julie considered them the lowest form of life—and the most dangerous. They were usually sky-high on drugs and completely unpredictable. They could turn violent without warning. She considered requesting a backup, but rejected the notion as premature. The camper could turn out to be carrying dirt bikes and beer. Just the same, she reminded herself to use extreme caution.

Just before dark the camper left the road and dipped into a dry wash, where it sat motionless and silent. There were no bustling preparations for camp, and no one emerged from the cab; the camper just sat in the gully, out of sight, waiting.

So Julie did the same. She had left her vehicle hidden behind a clump of scrub juniper a quarter mile or so away and now lay on her stomach at the edge of the ravine. She peered down at the pale glint of the camper shell below, her ears straining for the slightest sound. The warm desert wind rustled through sage and juniper and Joshua trees, masking all the other noises of the lively desert nighttime. There was no moon. In the west the pale glow of the distant city washed out the stars, but directly overhead there were enough left shining to provide a ghostly illumination, turning the land into a surrealistic canvas in silver and indigo....

She had remembered to pull on the dark cap she used on night patrols to hide the pale beacon of her hair. *Where is it now?* She closed her eyes and moved her head against the bed, feeling only the weight of her short platinum curls. *Gone, then.*

It would be lying like an inkblot on the white sand, mute evidence for the chopper crew to find. But they would never find her. Who would it be? Rudy Gomez, probably. Rudy and his wife, Marta, were good friends of hers. She had been an attendant at their wedding. What would he think when he found only her cap? Would he feel sorry? What would they say back at the station? Mel, Jack, Gomez and Franconi, Lupe and Paula, Rasmussen... What an odd thought, after so many years, to think of them all going along exactly as before—only without *her*. Would they miss her, miss the way they used to tease her in a companionable sort of way, calling her "Cottontop" and "Dandelion," always going on about her pale hair, that unruly mop of white gold curls that sat atop her long neck and small, supple gymnast's body like thistledown. The teasing was affectionate and casual, though, a mark of their acceptance. And it hadn't always been that way. She had had to earn that acceptance. She was—*had been*—a darned good agent. She had carried her weight and more.

What would they do? What was the procedure? As far as Julie knew, such a thing had never happened before. How long would they search before they gave her up for dead? When an agent was killed in the line of duty two agents always went together to break the news to the next of kin. Next of kin. Her parents. When they saw two unhappy-looking agents standing on their doorstep they would know without being told.

Julie sniffed, awash in bitter regret and self-pity. Poor Dad. He'd encouraged her to go into law enforcement when her enthusiasm for gymnastics had fizzled out. Would he blame himself? And Mom. She'd really been looking forward to having Julie at home in August. She'd made so many plans, in spite of Julie's warning that she'd be there to work and would not be getting much time off. Being transferred to the Los Angeles station temporarily during the Pan American Exposition had been a break for her: a nice change from desert patrols and midnight raids, and a chance for the first real visit with her family since her last vacation. She had fought hard for that assignment. And now she was going to miss it. It seemed, somehow, the last straw. She wallowed in misery for a while, thinking of all the things she was going to miss. Marta's baby shower, the rest of the baseball pennant race, football season. Colin.

Colin! Would anyone even think to tell Colin? She had a date with him... tonight? What day was it, anyway? Anyway, her date was for Saturday, as always, unless she was on duty. Colin would be annoyed—he disliked tardiness. He would be quite put out when he realized he had been stood up. And when he learned why, he would be sorry. . . .

They'd all be sorry when I'm gone! Julie laughed a little in self-mockery. The fantasy of every misunderstood child! She really *was* being childish, and all of this wallowing in self-pity wasn't going to get her anywhere. She dragged her mind back to that lonely and fateful vigil.

. . . She had picked a new sound out of the restless bustle of night noise. An engine. A new vehicle of some sort was approaching from the east, moving slowly without lights, following the silver ribbon of road through the darker scrub. At the edge of the wash the newcomer stopped. For a long slow ten-count it just sat, a dark hulk against the stars, and then headlights stabbed once, brutally, through the night. In that instant Julie identified the shape as a station wagon—that staid and innocent suburban housewife's standby, incongruous there on the vast and lonely stretch of desert. And then the camper's lights came briefly to life—once, twice—and the wagon slipped into the dark gully like a whale sounding.

Julie's hand went automatically to the holster at her hip, and then she crept over the side of the ravine, using the noise of the car to cover the sounds of her own descent. As always she felt that peculiar twinge deep in her belly that she hated to admit was fear; there was no way of knowing just what she would encounter down in that dark ravine. All the agents felt it, and most of them were honest enough to admit it. The only antidote was to concentrate on the plan of attack.

Julie planned to stay out of sight and use her voice, hoping to throw the smugglers into confusion. The illegals might panic, of course, and would probably scatter into the desert, but they could be rounded up later, and the confusion might help to convince the smugglers that there was more than one of her. If only she had some idea how many of *them* there were!

The station wagon had stopped behind the camper. Two men got out of the passenger side of the camper, shut the door behind them and walked back toward the rear of the vehicle. . . .

* * *

Now, replaying the scene in her mind, she could see her mistake as clearly as if it had been circled in red: both men had come from one side of the cab; the driver had stayed behind. And in the darkness and confusion—but that was later, and this was hindsight. Useless recrimination.

. . . The transfer began. Dark bundles of humanity shuffled from one vehicle to the other, the only sounds the creak of the car door, the scuff of gravelly dirt, an occasional hushed murmur in Spanish. One of the smugglers stood with his back to the camper, smoking, while the other hurried the passengers along. The driver of the station wagon leaned against a fender and kicked nervously at the ground.

Julie chose her moment, waiting until all the passengers had left the camper but had not yet found seats in the station wagon. Then, from her cover in a pile of boulders about twenty yards from the camper, she called out in clear, ringing Spanish, "This is the United States Border Patrol. You are surrounded. Do not attempt to run away. Put your hands on your vehicle where I can see them and remain where you are!"

There was a moment of shocked silence and then a high-pitched but masculine laugh—almost a titter. Julie smiled with grim amusement; it was a common reaction from macho Hispanic males confronted with the unpalatable fact that they had been apprehended by a woman. The laughter was an involuntary reaction of sheer disbelief, and it was usually followed immediately by anger. That anger could be very dangerous. Most Mexicans would rather risk getting shot than admit a mere woman had bested them.

The man with the cigarette threw it to the ground and made a movement toward the cab of the camper. Julie rapped out a warning in Spanish and he froze. There was no reaction at all from the other smugglers, and no panic among the illegals, which was unusual but not unheard of, and so welcome that Julie did not question it. She remained safely under cover, repeating her instructions even as she removed her remote com-unit from her belt and flipped the switch that would automatically activate the "officer in need of assistance" signal. The situation was well under control. As long as the smugglers did not suspect that she was alone she should be able to hold them until the chopper arrived. . . .

In the stuffy warmth of the camper Julie felt herself grow cold and clammy as beads of icy sweat formed on her upper lip. She closed her eyes against a wave of nausea as she relived that first awful moment when she had known she was not alone in that pile of boulders. Some primitive sense fired off alarm signals that stopped her breath and prickled the skin on the nape of her neck, but she only had a fraction of a second's warning—not enough time to react. Arms came around her from behind; one hand grasped her arm and pulled it back and up, while the other closed around the wrist of the hand that held the com-unit. Brutal pressure robbed that hand of all feeling. She heard the unit clatter to the ground at her feet. She was pulled roughly back and off-balance so that her head and shoulders fell heavily against a hard, unyielding chest, and the pressure on her arm became pain so intense that she could not suppress a cry.

It happened so quickly, and in complete silence. Julie knew better than to struggle; thanks to her gymnastics training she was very strong for a woman, but in close combat she was no match for a man—even one more nearly her size. Which this man was *not*. Besides, there was no telling what sort of junk these smugglers might be on—glue or angel dust could turn them lethal in an instant. She relaxed and hastily assured her captor in breathless Spanish of her complete capitulation.

From the chest behind her head came a short gust of laughter, as full of humor as the sound of a bullet slamming into its chamber. Her other arm was bent back and up; both wrists were imprisoned in a single iron grip. She was turned in the circle of one sinewy arm, while the man's free hand dragged the cap from her head and tipped her face toward the starlight. She heard a faint hiss of indrawn breath that was quickly drowned by her own involuntary gasp. Even now she could feel her stomach contract at the memory of that face.

It had been dark, of course, and she had been frightened half to death. Probably she had imbued the harsh lines and planes of that face with a hellishness it would not have in daylight. She had not *really* looked upon Lucifer himself! But surely, surely she could not have imagined those eyes? Blue fire. What Mexican could have eyes like that?

As she stared transfixed into those shocking eyes, a call came from the direction of the camper. *"¡Ay! Demonio Garzo! ¿Qué pasa?"*

A reply rumbled out over her head. "I have her; there is only one."

"Qué bueno," came the response, accompanied by a nasty-sounding laugh.

The man who held her, the man called "Blue-eyed Demon," had not taken his eyes from her face or relaxed his hold on her arms. Julie stared back at his impassive face like a rabbit transfixed by a car's headlights, and a pulse throbbed painfully in her throat. She expected to die now; she only prayed it would happen quickly. She saw a brief flash of white teeth—a smile or a grimace? She heard him whisper, *"Buenas noches, Güerita."*

Good night, little fair one.

And then an arrow of pain shot from her chin back through her head, and the starry sky imploded inside her skull.

But she wasn't dead!

There wasn't even much soreness in her jaw where he had struck her.

He. Who was he?

Julie had been left with a vivid impression of a tall, lean body, much taller than most Mexicans, and as hard and strong as saddle leather. And of course, there had been those eyes. . . .

One thing she knew for certain—he was no ordinary coyote. Most of them were nothing more than petty hoodlums and drug addicts who would sell their own mothers for the price of a bottle of tequila or their next fix. Most often they were recruited from the streets by big-time smuggling rings to run the risks and take the rap, and almost without exception they were clumsy, illiterate and vicious. If she had had the misfortune to fall into the hands of one of them, she would not be waking up with just a headache and a bruise on her chin!

El Demonio Garzo was not clumsy; he had moved like a cat in the night. He could not possibly have known her position until she shouted, which meant that he had been both quick and decisive. His methods of subduing her had been efficient and impossible to defend against, but had employed only the necessary minimum of force. So he wasn't vicious either. In fact . . . his voice had seemed curiously *regretful* when he had said—what was it? *Good night, little fair one. Güerita*—what an odd word to choose. Why not the more common and much less complimentary *gringa?*

Ah, well . . . Julie stirred futilely, trying to ease her cramped position and restore circulation to her bound hands and feet. So this . . . demon . . . was a pro. Why should that surprise her? She had guessed from the first that this was a class operation, well equipped and well organized, the men disciplined and well trained. And whatever their motive for keeping her alive, she would find it out soon enough.

There being absolutely nothing else for her to do in the meantime, Julie retreated gratefully back into the oblivion of sleep.

There were voices close by, speaking Spanish, and not quietly. Julie lay with her eyes closed, listening. As fluent as she was in the language, it was not second nature to her, and it was a few minutes before she began to understand. And then her stomach turned and her body went cold, and she opened her eyes wide and stared up at the ceiling of the camper only a few feet above her head.

The camper had stopped. Outside it must have been broad daylight, but inside it was hot, stuffy and gray, like being under a dirty blanket. And just below the small window in the sleeping loft where she lay bound hand and foot, the smugglers were discussing *her*.

Julie was thirsty; her tongue felt like an old wool sock, and tasted like it, too. She had lost feeling in her extremities; she was very hungry and in critical need of a bathroom; but none of those physical discomforts concerned her very much right now. All her attention was focused on the rough voices and guttural laughter coming through the tiny window, and what she heard sent waves of nausea through her that eclipsed everything else. She had picked up a pretty fair vocabulary of gutter Spanish over the years in the course of her job, but nothing to compare with this.

They had apparently been arguing about her fate. Two—Mexicans—by their accents—had been in favor of killing her back in the ravine and were against taking her any farther. The third—and for the life of her Julie could not place *his* accent—was explaining in incredibly crude but graphic terms exactly why he hadn't killed her and what he intended to do with her in the immediate future. His companions were finding his descriptions highly entertaining, adding colorful suggestions of their own from time to time.

There wasn't much of human depravity that Julie hadn't at one time or another encountered in her job. She had faced death a dozen times over and could not remember ever feeling this stomach-burning, throat-tightening fear. For the first time in her life she could understand how women in an earlier age might have felt about "a fate worse than death." But she didn't want to die. Nothing—no violation or degradation of her body, no matter how disgusting or frightening or painful—was worse than dying. She must remember that. *She wanted to live.*

Taking several slow, steady breaths to quiet the pounding of her heart, she forced herself to listen to the voices with the ears of a law enforcement officer, not a woman. Now she could pick out names—the two Mexicans were Pepe and Geraldo, and the other was apparently called Chain, although Julie was certain she had heard him called by a much more fanciful name last night. And she had been right about one thing, at least: He was not Mexican.

She could hear the soft clink of metal on metal, the hiss of a pop-top can opening, the rasp of a match and the scuff of boots in gravel, but no other sounds. They were stopped in a lonely place—the desert of Baja California, certainly—and were relaxing with cold cans of Mexican beer—*cerveza*—and cigarettes. So they had not reached their destination yet; they would be going on soon, and when they did—what of *her?* How long would they let her lie there without water?

Now! The one called Chain was announcing that, as he had driven all night, it was his intention to take a rest—in the back of the camper. This was met with loud guffaws and a few more crude suggestions as to how he might pass the time. Sounds of masculine camaraderie and departure preparations followed. Cans clanked onto the ground, feet shuffled, car doors opened and shut. Footsteps crunched away toward the rear of the camper. The door opened, letting in a shaft of brilliant light and a tantalizing tidbit of fresh air, and the body of the camper quivered almost imperceptibly under the weight of a heavy body.

Up in her loft Julie braced herself, lifted her head and gazed unflinchingly into the face of the blue-eyed demon.

Except that in the daylight he looked less like a demon and more like what he was—just a low-life criminal. A smuggler of illegal aliens. A *coyote*. A quarter inch of dark stubble and a sinister-looking moustache obscured most of his face, and his hair hung in dark, sweat-damp waves on his forehead and collar. The blue eyes that had seemed so electrifying in the starlight now burned with fatigue.

He stood just inside the door, stripping her with his eyes. She felt amazingly calm—suspended, perhaps, in a state of unreality. When she opened her mouth to say something—she didn't know what—it was a shock to hear *his* voice instead; it gave an even more nightmarish cast to what he said.

Without changing his expression or shifting his cool, possessive gaze, he gave her a clear, precise command of such stark vulgarity that it literally took her breath away.

Even as she gasped in shocked reaction she heard a shout of approval and chortles of laughter from below her window. The smuggler pulled the door shut behind him and casually locked it. The camper's engine fired, and the cabin rocked as the cumbersome vehicle pulled carefully onto the road. And up in the sleeping loft Julie struggled against mindless terror.

The smuggler moved toward her, ducking his head to avoid the low ceiling. She licked her dry lips and said in harsh, breathless Spanish, "Please . . . it won't . . . be necessary to use force. I won't fight you. I don't have . . . anything worth dying for."

A brief spark of amusement flared in the bloodshot eyes. "But why should I want to kill you, *Güerita?*" he replied in a gravelly purr. "You will be so much more entertaining alive."

And in that same harshly sensual voice he described what he expected of her. When his hand came toward her suddenly, Julie gave an involuntary cry and closed her eyes, but to her amazement she found that she had braced her whole body

against a touch that never came. Instead she felt the heat of his
body and a stirring of breath redolent of beer and tobacco,
heard a faint grunt of exertion and the drag and click of the
window behind her head being pulled shut. And then, incredibly, she knew that she was once again alone in the loft.

She opened her eyes and stared dazedly at the ceiling for a
moment, then lifted her head and hitched herself closer to the
edge of the bed. Peering over the side she saw that her reprieve
was only temporary. The smuggler was dragging his sweat-
stained T-shirt up over his head; his back was burned to a dusky
walnut, and the silky ripple and pull of sharply defined muscle
was marred by several small, irregular scars. She must have
made a sound, because he jerked his head to look at her as he
tossed the shirt aside. For a brief moment his eyes burned her,
and then he reached into a cabinet and pulled out a bottle of
tequila and turned his back on her, dismissing her.

Julie watched, unable to take her eyes off him as he took a
swallow, tilted his head back and swished the fiery liquid in his
mouth, then spat into the tiny stainless-steel sink. For a long
time he just stood there with his head bowed and his eyes
closed, and then he straightened, slapped the cap back onto the
bottle and returned it to the cupboard.

He seemed almost to have forgotten she was there. Next he
poured a meager sinkful of water from a plastic five-gallon
container on the counter and began to wash; she watched av-
idly as he took handfuls of the precious water and splashed his
face, his head, his neck and torso. Droplets sparkled like tiny
diamonds in his hair and ran in rivulets into the waistband of
his trousers. Julie licked her lips and tried to swallow, but her
throat felt like sandpaper. At that moment she could have
licked the water right off his skin! She would have been glad to
trade her "virtue" for a drink; she realized with a little chill that
she might have to do just that.

The smuggler turned back to her, his chest glistening with
moisture as he toweled his face and hair. From the folds of the
towel his eyes regarded her thoughtfully, consideringly, as if he
was trying to decide just what to do with her. It occurred to
Julie that there was something puzzling about his behavior. If
it had not been for the language she had heard him use, she

would have thought that her presence discomfited him in some way. She felt her courage come stealing back.

"I'm very thirsty," she croaked, and wondered again at the odd look that crossed his face. Surely not...*guilt?* "If you don't have enough water to spare, I...um...wouldn't object to some of that tequila. Also," she went on emboldened by that strange expression, "is it really necessary to tie up both my hands and feet? You're much bigger than I am, and this vehicle is moving. I'm not *crazy*."

He grunted and gave his head a little shake, but went on toweling himself dry. Julie watched him tensely, wondering whether that was a refusal or merely an acknowledgment of her request. His torso, she noticed uneasily, was scarred even more noticeably than his back—just one irregular weal that slashed diagonally across the washboard muscles of his belly between ribs and navel. She wondered what activity could have produced such an injury. An accident? War? Or just hazards of his profession?

"Please," she croaked, trying again. "May I *please* have a drink of water?" Her voice cracked, and she hated herself for begging. For God's sake, was he mute? Stupid? *Drunk?* But she had heard him speak—much too clearly, in fact—and had seen the gleam of intelligence in those blue eyes. Whatever he was, he was certainly no great talker!

But he was throwing the towel aside and reaching into his pocket, taking out a very ordinary-looking pocket knife and stepping forward to saw at the heavy tape that bound her ankles together. Julie, following his movements with mixed apprehension and hope, noticed for the first time that her feet were bare. For some reason that she didn't have time to analyze, that fact jolted her.

The smuggler reached behind her for her hands, throwing her roughly onto her face as he pulled them closer to him, and a moment later she felt the tension in them give. Still without saying a word, he stepped back, folded the knife and tucked it into his pocket, then turned to take a paper cup from a cupboard over the sink.

Julie rolled over slowly and sat up. The tape hadn't severely impeded the circulation in her hands and feet, but lying for so long in such a cramped position had put them to sleep. She

shifted her legs to allow her feet to dangle over the side of the
loft, rocking slowly back and forth with the waves of pain that
swept her with the return of feeling. She was staring down at the
chunks of wood that her hands had become, when the smuggler wordlessly thrust a cup of water under her nose.

Julie glanced fearfully at his scowling face and lifted one
hand, trying desperately to make the fingers work, but the
whole arm felt hot and cold, hollow and tingly, and its motor
function seemed to have been disconnected from her brain. She
let it drop heavily into her lap and stared miserably at the lovely
cool water. She could actually *smell* it.

"I . . . can't do it," she said in English, her tongue rasping
across her lower lip.

She heard a faint noise of exasperation, and then a hand
closed on the back of her neck, steadying her head as the cup
was raised to her lips. Julie knew she ought to be repelled by his
nearness and his touch, but as she closed her eyes and drank she
was conscious only of profound relief.

"*Gracias,*" she murmured, and opened her eyes to find the
smuggler's dark face only inches away from her own. In spite
of the water she had just drunk, her mouth went dry. How
could she have forgotten, even for a moment.

"Uh . . . look," she began, lapsing into English again. She
rubbed her hands together, trying to work out the numbness,
and started again in slow, deliberate Spanish. "I know what
you want from me. I heard what you told the others. I told you,
I won't fight. You don't have to hurt me. I definitely don't want
to die, so. . ." Her voice trailed off, and she took a deep breath
and blurted, "But please—can I just use the bathroom?"

Again there was that flash of something in his eyes that she
could not identify. He stood back to allow her to jump down
from the loft and waved her toward the lavatory with a bow that
was a parody of courtliness.

How strange it felt to be on her feet again! Julie longed to
indulge in a few limbering and stretching exercises, but the
man's eyes, heavy lidded and insolent, followed her every move,
and she had to be content with shaking her feet, bending her
knees and rubbing the small of her back. Still, it was good to
be able to move at all.

The trip to the lavatory left her feeling better equipped to deal with her captor. She had been thinking. It had occurred to her that this smuggler was not as vicious as he wanted his partners to think he was. Perhaps, if she pretended to be a compliant hostage, even this hardened pro could be outwitted. There was just a chance that, if she bided her time, she might be able to catch him off guard and escape. Maybe. At worst she would buy herself time. And time had suddenly become very precious to her....

He was waiting for her, standing with his elbow propped on the loft, his hand dangling over the edge of the mattress. In the other hand he held a can of beer. His eyes followed her as she approached him, trembling with apprehension.

Julie took a deep breath and asked bluntly, "What are you going to do with me?"

His eyebrows rose, and he took a deep swallow of beer. "That's a damn good question," he muttered indistinctly, but unmistakably in English.

American. Of course. She should have known. But he was very fluent in Spanish, and that accent was good—quite unidentifiable. He must have an excellent ear. And it wasn't that unusual to find American mercenaries involved in international smuggling. Illegal aliens were probably only the *least* that this gang dealt in!

She lifted her chin a little and stared at him, waiting. He was gazing intently at the front of her blouse, at her breasts—or her badge—but he seemed more preoccupied than lustful. "Got to get rid of that uniform," he muttered thickly.

A hiss of indrawn breath gave away her fear; she cut it off by clamping resolutely down on her lower lip with her teeth. *Please God, don't let me scream when he touches me.* But he made no move at all, just went on staring at her chest. Finally, with trembling fingers, Julie reached for the top button.

He stood quietly watching her over the beer can, only his eyes moving as they followed her fingers down the front of her shirt. She pulled it open and tugged it from the waistband of her trousers, noticing as she did that all her paraphernalia had disappeared along with her shoes. She let it drop onto the camper's dusty linoleum floor, then shut her eyes, quickly unhooked her bra and dropped it on top of her shirt.

She couldn't bring herself to look at him—blue-eyed demon!—but she was determined not to cower. She was an agent of the United States government. And she knew her body was nothing to be ashamed of—firm and well conditioned, breasts high and full. But she also knew that as she stripped away her clothes she stripped away the protective plumage that made her an officer of the law rather than a woman. Her shoes, her belt, her gun—all gone. And now her shirt with its badge and insignia—her identity as Agent Maguire of the Border Patrol—lay in a meaningless pile at her feet. She was just plain Julie now—a woman, on the small side, helpless against a bigger, stronger male.

A sudden movement jerked her eyes to his face. He had lowered the beer can; she saw his Adam's apple move convulsively as he swallowed. His eyes rested almost lazily on her breasts.

It was so hot. Julie was half suffocating, and she felt as though her skin was burning where his eyes touched it. *Blue fire.* Last night she had thought of that, even in the middle of the nightmare. Now, as she stared defiantly at that dark, dangerous face, at the wide shoulders and powerful arms glistening with sweat, at the hairy, masculine chest and ragged scar, a pounding began under her ribs, and cold, quivering weakness spread from the pit of her stomach down into her legs.

Butterflies, she said to herself, trying to maintain a hold on her self-control. God, I'm scared to death! Who wouldn't be? But after all, it's only sex. It's not important. Staying alive is.

The smuggler spoke, breaking an interminable silence. "Look," he said in a gravelly voice, "can we dispense with this? I mean—" he gave a crooked smile and gestured toward her with the beer can "—if it's really what you want, I'll do my best to oblige. Just don't expect too much. I'm pretty tired."

As Julie stared at him without comprehension he gave a brief, dry snort of laughter and rubbed at his eyes with the dangling hand. "In fact, I'm damn tired. I've got to get some sleep . . . deal with you later. . . ." He thrust the half-empty can of *cerveza* into Julie's nerveless hand and levered himself into the loft. "Don't think I need to tie you up again, do you?" He unlaced his shoes and let them drop, one at a time, to the floor.

Julie shook her head dumbly.

"This camper is doing . . . oh, I'd say about thirty. At that speed you *might* be able to jump out and survive without serious injury, but then you'd be stuck in the middle of the desert without shoes or water." He swung his legs around and lay back, his head sinking into the shadows. Almost immediately he sat forward again, his eyes burning holes into her before narrowing with wry amusement. "Of course, you could always find a way to dispatch me in my sleep—if you prefer my friends' company to mine. Pepe and Geraldo would probably even be happy to give you a hand if you asked them. Especially if you were dressed like that."

There was a low chuckle and a mumbled *"Buenas noches, Güerita."* And in a very few minutes Julie heard only deep, even breathing, and then, to her complete disbelief, a gentle snore.

Chapter 2

Julie bent slowly and picked up her clothing, bemused to note that her muscles were weak, her joints stiff and creaky. Adrenaline, she supposed; it made you feel like Superman while it was there, but had a way of leaving you unpleasantly sick and trembly after it had deserted you.

Her fingers were still too shaky to deal with bra hooks and buttons, so she put the shirt on and drew it together in the front, hugging it against her body as she eased herself into the dining booth across from the sink. It was one of those clever arrangements that could be converted from two benches and a table into a bed; Julie felt so shaken that she considered making it up, curling into a ball and escaping back into the oblivion of sleep.

But she couldn't afford to sleep—she needed a clear head! She had to think!

It was too hot to think. There was a large window beside the table, tightly shuttered now. Julie cranked open the slatted shades and drew back the pane to let in both light and air. The air was hot, but at least it was fresh, and it stirred her hair, cooling the sweat on her neck and forehead. The view was disappointing—utterly barren and desolate—but Julie didn't really see it, anyway.

She was *unbelievably* shaken.

She had been reacting like a woman, not an agent. From the start, through this whole mess, she'd behaved like a...pathetic, helpless female rather than a responsible, highly trained law officer! Why had she let him get to her on such a...a primitive level? Why?

She pressed her fingers to her lips, staring out at the blurred landscape and listening to the sounds of deep, exhausted sleep. While he was asleep she should be exploring every inch of this camper, looking for ways to regain control of the situation. If only she could find her belt, her shoes.

Her shoes. A perfect example. It had bothered her that he had removed her shoes. And why? Because the loss of her shoes lessened her chances of escape? *No.* She made a derisive noise and rubbed agitatedly at her forehead. Because of the thought that he had touched her...his fingers had touched her bare feet while she slept! She had never felt so terribly vulnerable, so afraid...so utterly at the mercy of a man....

Oh, but that's not true. You have.

"Oh God..." she whispered aloud, stunned by the memory. "I really thought I had forgotten that."

It had been so long ago. She had been just a kid, a nervous, naive sophomore cheerleader on her first real date...with a *senior*. A football player. His name, she remembered, was Carl. Carl Swensen. She had been so thrilled, and all her friends had been so jealous.... And she had been so *stupid*. So inexperienced. No one had told her about people like Carl Swensen. But that had been a very long time ago. She was all grown up now. It *couldn't* be the same...could it?

Julie laughed, a shaky, incredulous little ripple. She had actually forgotten that dreadful night. She had been lucky, she supposed, that her gymnastics training had made her so strong. Carl hadn't expected such determined resistance. But even so, she had been bruised and frightened, too humiliated to reveal what had really happened, too demoralized to cope with the lies Carl had spread about her. And she hadn't trusted any boy enough to accept another date until after she'd been through some police-science classes. Until she had learned a little more about men.

Funny…Colin always told her she was afraid of men. Colin was fond of indulging in amateur psychology. Julie had laughed at that particular diagnosis. "Come on now, Colin," she had said. "I work with men every day. Some of my best friends are men. I've probably arrested hundreds of men—by outtalking, outwitting, outrunning, and even, on a couple of memorable, occasions, outshooting them. Afraid of men? Colin, darling, do you actually think I'm afraid of you?"

And he had smiled in that gently superior way of his, puffed his pipe and replied, "Oh, no—but that's why you like me. You feel safe. You never lose your balance with me."

There had been, she remembered, a puzzling trace of sadness in his eyes. But they had argued the topic all evening, and by the end of it she had forgotten that, too, and so had never asked him what he meant.

Afraid of men. Colin had offered the theory that her entire career was a product of her phobia, that she had sought a field which would put her on an equal footing with men, where she could be "one of the boys" and therefore not have to deal with them on a male-female basis at all. Bunk, she had told him, but using a cruder word. Stick to contracts and courtrooms. If I need a shrink I'll go to a doctor, not a lawyer!

But now… Maybe she should have paid more attention to Colin's half-baked ideas, because even though she wasn't afraid of men in general, she was certainly afraid of this one! And not because he was a smuggler, either; she'd handled dangerous, even desperate, men before. But this man had stripped her of her hard-won status; had dominated her—yes, damn it, admit it!—in that *particular* way that a man dominates a woman. And he had done so almost without laying a hand on her. He was dangerous. He kept her off-balance. She *must* keep her wits about her if she was to have any chance at all of getting out of this mess. It was high time she got back into uniform, got her professional head on straight and got back to work!

There was very little food in the camper. Very little, at least, that Julie felt up to eating. The refrigerator held only *cerveza* and some cornmeal tortillas that looked homemade. The cupboards displayed a variety of cans, but the idea of searching for an opener and refueling on cold refried beans in the hot, swaying camper made her feel nauseated. She settled for a can of beer and a dry tortilla, tearing bite-sized pieces from the latter and chewing absently as she gazed out at the seemingly endless plain of dried mud and sand.

Off in the distance she caught the glimmer of water—a mirage, she supposed. She couldn't imagine what water could be out there in that direction—east, if they were, as she knew they must be, heading south. She had no way of knowing where they were, or how far they had come while she slept. Except for an occasional recreational foray into Tijuana she had never been to Baja California. But surely it couldn't *all* be as empty as this?

With both hunger and thirst assuaged, Julie turned her energies to a thorough search of the cabin. She made no effort to be covert. If the smuggler woke up and caught her at it, what could he do? Or say? He probably expected her to search— which meant, of course, that her chances of finding anything useful were slim to none. Still, she had to look.

Except for the fact that the camper was very dirty, understandable considering that it had recently transported a dozen or so human beings an unknown distance, she discovered nothing useful. Though she did notice something that puzzled her. The lower cupboards were very shallow. There appeared to be a great deal of dead space between the backs of the cupboards and the wall of the camper. Secret compartments? What else did this vehicle transport across international borders? Drugs? Guns? Intrigued, Julie carefully cleared out one cupboard and crawled into it head-and-shoulders deep, painstakingly feeling every centimeter and nail and crack for signs of an opening. She tapped softly with her knuckles. Definitely hollow. The access must be from the outside. She gave up and sat back on her heels.

"Finding anything?"

Julie gave a violent jerk and said, "Oh . . . *God*."

"What's the matter? Did I startle you?" The smuggler was sitting up, legs dangling and upper body hunched forward to accommodate the loft's low ceiling.

"Yes," Julie said tartly, "you did. I thought you were asleep."

"Obviously. Aren't you glad I waited until you'd backed out of there? If you'd jumped like that inside the cupboard you'd have hurt yourself." He yawned, erasing an unrepentant grin. "That was one hell of a guilty start."

"Why should I feel guilty?" Julie muttered, scowling at the dirt on her hands. "You *knew* I'd look." She realized belatedly that her uniform shirt still hung unbuttoned, and that her bra was lying conspicuously on the formica tabletop. Shifting so that her back was turned toward the smuggler, she hurriedly did up her buttons, snatched the bra and wadded it into a ball.

"Yeah, I did." He jumped down lightly from the loft, reminding Julie of nothing so much as a black panther leaving his daytime nest in a tree. "Find what you were looking for?"

She backed into the dining booth, out of his way, tucking the bra into the crack in the upholstered seat. "Of course not. You knew I wouldn't. Is it really necessary to keep my *shoes?*"

The smuggler rubbed his stubbly jaws and regarded her from under half-closed lids. "Why quibble about a pair of shoes? As I recall, a couple of hours ago you seemed ready to shed all your clothes."

Julie was silent. His eyes were so cold . . . so knowing. As if he could see inside her head. She kept her eyes on him and swallowed reflexively.

"You'll get them back," he drawled softly, "when I think you've grasped the realities of your situation."

"You think—" She cleared her throat and tried again. "You think I don't *know* what my situation is? I couldn't very well mistake it, could I? I speak and understand Spanish very well!" Her voice had escalated, and she fought it back down to a more self-possessed level. "I thought I had made it pretty clear where my priorities lie."

"Oh, right. You don't want to die and you aren't crazy." He took a beer from the refrigerator and popped it open, squinting against the misty spray. "Not very stoic for a lawman, are you?"

"I'm not interested in being a hero," Julie muttered, avoiding his eyes.

"Uh-huh." He slid into the seat opposite her, leaning across the table to tap the badge on her chest. She jerked away, and he smiled without humor, his eyes glinting coldly in his dark face. "Let's just say I don't trust anybody wearing a badge."

He sat back, sipping his beer. "Did you finish?" he asked suddenly, startling her with the casual, conversational question.

"I beg your pardon?"

"Your search—did you finish, or would you like to get on with it?"

"No, thank you," Julie said sullenly. "What's the point?" Then she sat forward abruptly. "What *do* you carry in those compartments? Guns? Drugs? They're a little small for illegals—unless you're into smuggling children!"

"Ah, that's better," he said blandly. Julie waited stubbornly, and after a moment he shrugged and said flatly, "Gas."

Julie blinked. "What?"

"Gasoline. There are two reserve gas tanks on this truck. Baja doesn't have a station on every corner. You might keep that in mind when you're plotting your escape."

Julie subsided, feeling foolish, and stared out the window. The smuggler, too, was silent, drinking beer and looking broodingly at the bleak vista unfolding beyond the dusty glass.

After a while he pushed the beer can away and leaned back with a soft sigh. "It might interest you to know," he said, his voice sounding as weary and harsh as it had before his nap, "that I don't want you dead either. With that in common, do you think we can work out some kind of accord?"

Julie's skin felt hot and dry. She dropped her eyes to her hands, folded on the tabletop. Her reprieve, it seemed, was about to end. "I told you I wouldn't try to fight you," she said in a low voice.

"Good," the smuggler said briskly. He put his hands on the table just inches from hers; she stared at them as she would at a coiled rattler.

"First, a few facts. There is absolutely no possible way for you to escape, so I'd advise you not to waste your time trying. As far as anyone else is concerned, you are my prisoner, to do with as I please. Do I make myself clear?"

He had leaned forward, the better to zap her with twin bolts of blue lightning. Julie swallowed painfully and said, "Oh, yes."

He continued to regard her until she again had to look away, then sat back, apparently satisfied. "Okay, Julie Maguire. Do as I tell you—trust me—and I guarantee you won't be harmed."

"Trust you?" Julie said faintly, incredulously.

The smuggler seemed not to have heard. "For the time being you will stay in this camper. When we reach our destination you will, of course, share my quarters."

"Of course," Julie said huskily, forcing her eyes back to his face and lifting her chin slightly. "And your bed?"

"That," said the smuggler softly, "depends on you."

Julie blinked. "On *me?*"

"On how good an actress you are, *Güerita.*"

"I . . . don't understand."

The smuggler leaned back in the booth. Julie again caught a glint of cold steel beneath the heavy lids. Still softly, with a slight smile hovering around his mouth, he said, "You will have to convince everyone that you *are* sharing my bed. And not only that, but make them believe you are happy about it. Make them believe you are no longer a danger to us. Do you understand?"

After a moment of shocked silence Julie shifted in her seat and raked unsteady fingers through her close-cropped hair. "No," she whispered hoarsely, giving her head a sharp shake. "No, I don't understand at all. Why? Do you mean you won't—"

He made a short, rude noise. "I've never had to resort to rape," he said in disgust. "I don't intend to start now. Now—any questions?"

Julie, still reeling from her unexpected reprieve, leaned back and regarded him thoughtfully. What a surprising man this coyote was turning out to be! Intriguing . . . and unexpectedly challenging. She felt more confident now that she seemed to have been released from the paralyzing threat of physical and/or sexual assault, but she had an idea that he might prove much more difficult in other ways than those she had imagined.

"Of course I have questions," she said dryly. "But I doubt very much that you'd answer most of them. Okay . . . so I'm supposed to *pretend* to be your . . . um . . . What do I call you?

Chain, or El Demonio Garzo? Or would you prefer just...Demon for short?''

He gazed at her with distaste. "I assure you that this is not a matter for levity. Or sarcasm. If you can't be convincing with this charade I'll be forced to make it more realistic. The only reason you're alive right now, *lady agent,* is because I have a certain...reputation...with these men, and they are confident of my ability to...shall we say, control you. I told them that you would be of some use to me, something they can understand since they both have their women with them. Don't make it necessary for me to prove my mastery of you in front of them. Make no mistake, *Güerita*—if they think you constitute a threat—you're dead—'' He snapped his fingers, making her flinch, "—like *that.*" He waited, watching her face, and then nodded. "All right. That's better. In answer to your question, my name is Younger. Chayne Younger. That's spelled with a *y* and a silent *e*. The other women call me Señor Chayne, by the way.'' His lips twitched in the beginnings of a grin. "To my face.''

Julie thought she knew what they called him behind his back. He *was* a devil, as smooth-spoken and enigmatic as Lucifer, and certainly as confusing.

"All right,'' she said hoarsely. "Just one more question: *Why?* Why are you doing this? Keeping me alive? Why shouldn't you just...let them kill me if I'm so much trouble?''

For a second or two he glared at her, and then he made that noise of disgust again and looked away, out the window. Julie noticed that he had begun to rub mechanically, unconsciously, at the scar on his belly.

"I'm not a killer," he muttered.

Julie couldn't hold back a snort of derision. "Oh, great—you aren't a killer or a rapist. This must be my lucky day! I've been captured by a *pure* smuggler! I'll bet you're just a softhearted *liberal,* aren't you? You think you're down here helping these poor downtrodden souls to a better life, right? Some kind of Mexican Robin Hood? Oh, brother!''

"Lady,'' the smuggler murmured, an unmistakably dangerous edge to his voice, "you have no idea how lucky you are.''

Suddenly, completely unexpectedly, like a snake striking, his hand shot out and clamped like a vise on the back of her neck. It was pure steel, that arm—Julie had never encountered anyone so strong. She had time for one shocked gasp before he leaned across the table and kissed her hard, ravishing her mouth briefly but thoroughly. As he pulled away, leaving her lips moist and throbbing, he paused to impale her with those devastating eyes.

"Don't press your luck," he rasped, and slid out of the booth.

Julie stared out the window, swallowing repeatedly in an effort to combat something she could only describe as panic. The vista that shimmered before her had changed. Instead of sand flats and undulating mirages she saw a desert jungle, a wilderness of chaparral and cholla cactus so dense that an army could get lost a few feet from the road.

The road was appallingly bad. The camper bumped and lurched over what must have been little more than a track through the fearsome tangle, and Julie, realizing that she had not seen a single sign of human habitation, understood the need for the extra gas tanks and other modifications. What a disaster it would be to suffer a breakdown out here!

The silence in the cabin behind her played on her nerves. She turned back reluctantly to find the smuggler, Chayne, leaning against the kitchen counter, drinking another beer and watching her. He gestured with a second can, muttered, "Catch," and tossed it to her.

She caught it neatly, popped it open and leaned quickly to catch escaping foam.

"Thanks," she said with unwilling courtesy, adding dryly, "What are you, a chain-beer drinker? Don't you know this stuff is bad for your figure?"

"So I've heard." His mouth quirked sideways in a wry smile as he rubbed the hard-muscled contours of his stomach. Julie, following the movement with her eyes, felt her cheeks grow hot. No trace of a beer belly on that body! She worked with well-conditioned men every day, but she had never seen anyone in better shape. From her gymnastics days she knew very well the constant training and effort that went into maintaining such superb physical conditioning. Did a smuggler's life really require such fine-tuned reflexes, such strength and agility? How did he maintain such a body, driving illegals through the desert and drinking beer?

"Get used to it," Chayne said. Julie flushed, thinking for one mad moment that he was referring to his body. His eyes glinted at her over the beer can, as if he knew that very well. "You're in a desert now. This stuff is safer than water—and a whole lot more plentiful."

"What do you do—between runs across the border, I mean?" Julie asked casually, following a previous train of thought. She was becoming more and more curious about this coyote who fit no mold, so unlike any she had ever encountered before. And it had occurred to her that she was going to have to feel a lot more comfortable with him if she was ever going to be able to act the part of his... his what? Bedmate? Doxy? Moll? His... woman?

And then there was the matter of the even more difficult role she had to play.... Somehow she must convince this sharp-eyed demon of her sincere desire to cooperate while she worked out a plan to defeat him.

"Obviously," she murmured, allowing her eyes to crinkle at him over her own beer can, "you don't spend all your time guzzling beer."

There was a sardonic twinkle in his eyes that suggested he knew exactly what she was up to, but he only smiled and shrugged. "I guess you'll be finding out soon enough, won't you?"

"I suppose so." She tried a new tack. "Chayne," she said earnestly, veiling her eyes, "why do you do this? I've arrested a lot of smugglers over the years, and you don't fit the pattern. I'm curious—*do* you think you're on some kind of crusade?"

He snorted.

"All right, then why?"

He shrugged, avoiding her eyes. "Pays well," he said shortly.

"That's it? Just the money?"

The smuggler drank beer and pursed his lips, then wiped away the moisture on them with the back of his hand. "Sure, what else is there?"

"Just a mercenary—no altruistic excuses about unfair immigration laws?"

"Nope—sorry. Would it make you feel better if I had an excuse?"

"There aren't any excuses," Julie snapped. "There's no excuse at all for breaking the law!"

"Spoken like a true lawman." Chayne chuckled. "Not even a bad law?"

"If it's bad, *change it!* But as long as it's a law, it's my job to see that it's enforced; and if you break it, you're doing wrong, mister. You're a criminal, nothing more."

Chayne stared past her, his eyes narrowed. "There are worse things," he murmured, rubbing the scar on his belly.

"Than being a criminal?"

He jerked his eyes, still narrowed and steely, to her face. "There are worse crimes," he said in a harsh voice, "than being a smuggler."

Julie gave a sardonic hoot. "Oh, yes, I'm sure you could manage to aspire to greater lows if you put your mind to it! Tell me—have you ever aspired to an honest line of work?"

There was a faint glimmer of amusement in his eyes. "Honest, or *legal?* There's a difference."

Julie glared at him, frustrated. "I'm serious," she said after a moment. "You seem intelligent, resourceful and, uh..." She coughed and added, "Reasonably presentable," ignoring his soft chuckle. "There must be other lines of work that pay as well."

"Not so many for chewed-up veterans of dirty, unpopular little wars," he interrupted quietly. "At least, not when I came home."

Julie was silent, watching the vivid blue eyes turn inward. So he had come by the scars in a war after all—and how many more that didn't show? Julie was no stranger to the wreckage of Vietnam; she still retained vivid memories of a roommate, a former army nurse who used to scream and sob in the night, and of her cousin Dan, who, according to his wife, was still apt to wake up under his bed after a night of thunderstorms. She fought down feelings of sympathy for her captor—something she knew was a symptom of "hostage syndrome." She must not, for heaven's sake, begin to identify with her jailer!

"Oh, come on now," she said skeptically. "Don't try to tell me a Vietnam vet can't get a decent job—especially these days. Hundreds of thousands of them managed just fine without resorting to unlawful activities."

"You're right." He grinned at her suddenly, white teeth flashing in that dark-stubbled face. The moment of brooding introspection had passed; he was on guard once more, and the blue-eyed demon was back. "I'm just an unrepentant sinner, I'm afraid. A bit too late to change my life-style, don't you think?" His eyes teased her, a soft blue now, the blue of autumn skies.

For some reason she felt her cheeks grow hot. "Not necessarily," she protested, stammering a little. "You could change. You could—" She stopped.

He nodded, chuckling softly. "Could what, Julie Maguire? Surrender? Turn myself in? Now you're talking like a woman. Always trying to straighten a man out, change him, make something of him." He set his beer can in the sink and leaned toward her slowly and deliberately. Julie held her ground, determined not to shrink. "Tell me, Julie Maguire...what would you make of me? As a *woman*." He put a knuckle under her chin and lifted it, studying her face with a look of lazy curiosity, as if she were a mildly intriguing bit of flotsam he'd found on the beach. She stared back, frozen, her eyes fastened on his mouth. After a moment she saw it curve in a tight little smile.

"But you're not a woman, are you? You are an officer of the law. And I, as you put it so succinctly, am a criminal. You'd send me to jail in a minute, wouldn't you, darlin'? No matter what. How did you put that? *No excuses for breaking the law*."

He leaned down and kissed her, a feather's touch this time, just a tickle of his moustache on her cheek, a stirring of warm breath on her lips, and a touch that tingled such remote nerve endings as the back of her neck and the palms of her hands. He drew back only far enough to look into her eyes and whispered, "So I guess it's a damn good thing you're *not* a woman, isn't it, Julie? You'd be in one hell of a dilemma, wouldn't you?"

He straightened, releasing her, then turned his back on her, moving his arms to stretch and massage the muscles in his neck and shoulders. "Well...I've got no intention of going to jail," he grunted with finality. "But I do believe I'll take another little nap." He glanced at his wristwatch and hoisted himself into the loft. "We won't reach the village until tonight. That's a good four or five hours yet."

"What am I supposed to do?" Julie asked, aghast at the quaver in her voice.

"Well . . . ," Chayne said placidly, making no effort to subdue a jaw-popping yawn, "I guess you could get on with your search. Unless you'd care to come up here and do some *research* for your new role. . . . No? Well—*buenas noches,* then, *Güerita. Hasta luego.*"

Until later. A sudden tremor shook her, a chill that raised goose bumps on her arms in spite of the warmth of the cabin. Julie felt another wave of fear—the fear of a small child who finds herself unexpectedly lost in a supermarket, surrounded by large strangers. She wanted to put her head down on her arms and cry, but although she had a tendency to choke up and mist over for such things as Disney movies and choirs of small children and marching bands, she had not *really* cried since she was a child.

Colin, she supposed, would say that her embarrassing sentimentality was a kind of sublimation—a "safe" emotional outlet. Colin could be a pain in the neck, at times.

She did put her head down on her arms; it had begun to ache again, and it felt good to close her eyes. And like that lost child in the supermarket, she thought longingly of her mother.

She should have gone home in May. Both her mother's birthday and Mother's Day were in May.

She'd been on the day shift that month, but she could have gotten away for a day, at least. Canoga Park wasn't that far from San Diego. But she'd been too busy, and anyway, she'd planned to be there in August, during the Exposition. . . .

I'll go as soon as I get back, I promise, she thought fervently, then added a prayerful, If I get back. . . .

Julie was assailed by a wave of homesickness so acute that she could almost smell the verbena that bordered the front walk of her parents' house, hear the wind chimes that hung on the patio off the kitchen. With the window open, she had been able to hear them from her bedroom. How often had she lain there in the dark and dreamed to the music of wind chimes tinkling in the night breeze?

She'd had such an *ordinary* childhood, such a typical Southern California suburban middle-class home, in a neighborhood full of station wagons and children and the racket of lawnmowers on Saturday mornings. What had happened that she, Julie Maguire, only child of doting but sensible parents, ex-Girl Scout cookie pusher and high school cheerleader, should find herself in such a predicament? Bargaining for her life with a smuggler in the wilds of Baja California!

Mom...Dad...I love you, she thought contritely. I didn't mean to stay away so long....

Julie woke up with a crick in her neck and what felt like a permanent dent in her forehead from her wristwatch. It was too dark to see what time it was; she had no idea how long she had slept. The camper was silent and still, but outside the window she could hear a dog barking fitfully, voices calling softly in Spanish, laughter, and, somehow reassuring, music—a plaintive Mexican ballad of love sung to the soft strumming of a guitar.

This must be the village Chayne had spoken of. How big was it? *Where* was it? Would there be someone—anyone—who might help her? Would there be a telephone? A church? How far south had they come? How far away was home...and hope?

Outside the window Julie could see the glimmer of moonlight on water and the dark silhouettes of several boats, but no buildings. A fishing village, then. Perhaps...a boat. She could escape in a boat, make her way along the coastline to a settlement.... She had half risen in her excitement, ready to run to those distant outlines this very minute. Now she sank back and took a deep breath to calm herself.

Easy, Julie. Don't be dumb. They aren't going to let you just walk out of here. And besides, you don't even know which way to go!

Her sense of direction was confused. The water was visible out the window, which didn't seem right, somehow.

Before she could sort out why it didn't, the camper door opened and her captor entered carrying a kerosene lantern and a small bundle of clothing. He gave her a quick, hard glance and set both the lantern and the bundle on the table. The angle of the light cast sinister shadows on his face and gave his eyes an unearthly glow.

"Good—you're awake," he said without preamble. "I've brought you some clothes. There's probably enough water left in the tank for a shower. I suggest you use it. It will be a while before you get another."

"What's the matter with the clothes I have on?" Julie asked sullenly.

"Aside from the fact that you've been sweating in them for two days, the sooner these people forget that you're an agent of the United States government, the better." He gazed down at her somberly, his eyes hooded. "I suggest you forget it, too, if you want to save your pretty neck. It's time for you to get into your role and stay there."

Julie opened her mouth to retort, thought better of it and swallowed. "I'm not sure I know how," she said in a low voice. "What's expected of me? I haven't had much experience being cowed and subservient."

He didn't smile. "Keep your eyes down—unless you can get rid of that speculative, calculating gleam. You haven't a thought of escape, remember? Don't speak to me unless I speak to you first, and don't speak to anyone else unless I give you permission. And no matter what I do, you *take* it. With good or bad grace—I don't care. But don't fight me. Got it?"

Julie was almost choking with rage and could only nod stiffly.

"Geraldo's wife Rita is fixing something for us to eat. I expect you're hungry. I hope you can swallow with all of that pride and anger swelling up your throat. Rita is a very good cook."

Julie looked up, surprised to hear a note of amusement in his voice, but he had turned and was ducking back through the camper door. She sat for a moment, plucking at the soft material of a much-washed and worn cotton shirt and glaring at the space the demon had just vacated. Then, her shoulders sagging with resignation, she held up the articles in the pile, one at a time. The shirt was a man's, but it was clean and would be comfortable. There were faded denim jeans that looked as if they would fit her if she rolled up the pant legs. A pair of *hua-*

raches—sandals. There was a pair of cotton panties, very plain and serviceable and bleached to bone white, but no bra. She would have to do without while she rinsed out her own things, but the shirt was soft, unlike her stiff uniform blouse, which was already chafing her nipples painfully.

There was a bar of soap, used; a comb; even, miraculously, a toothbrush! After the day and night she had just endured it seemed an impossible luxury. She had no qualms at all about the likelihood that it was also used. The bottle of tequila would serve quite nicely as a disinfectant.

Julie picked up the last item and sat pulling it through her fingers and blinking back treacherous tears. It was a belt, handwoven in turquoise, red and black in typical Mexican folk art style, a splash of vivid color in the pile of neutral, bleached-out clothing. Its presence in the pile touched her—proof that somewhere in this desolate place, in the middle of a smuggler's nest, there was a person with enough sensitivity and human insight to know how much she needed this small gesture of kindness, this one tiny touch of beauty. Warmed and strengthened, Julie folded the belt, placed it almost reverently on top of the pile and stood up.

She was dressed and waiting long before Chayne finally came for her, and so hungry that she had to hug her arms across her empty belly to ease its ravenous churning.

"Stand up," he said with typical lack of ceremony after he had shut the door firmly behind him.

Julie eased herself out of the booth and stood up, suddenly overcome by an uncharacteristic self-consciousness. She shifted uncertainly as he studied her in silence, his eyes sliding over her from her bare toes in the brown leather sandals, the light blue jeans rolled to the ankles and fitting smoothly over her thighs, to the soft, blousy shirt, which she had chosen to wear loose and belted, its sleeves rolled to the elbow. The blue eyes rested for a moment on the slash of color at her narrow waist, then continued on upward, sliding over the deep V between the swell of her unbound breasts, the long, tanned column of her neck, and narrowed slightly as they scrutinized her face. He stepped forward, put one hand on her shoulder and, with the other, tilted her face toward the light. At last he nodded.

"Do I pass?" Julie asked unsteadily. She put the hollow, butterfly feeling in her stomach down to acute starvation.

"Your hair's wet."

"I washed it."

The smuggler nodded again, rubbing his chin thoughtfully. "It's all right . . . all right. Gives you a kind of drowned look—along with those big brown eyes. That scared look is good too. Try to hang on to it."

"That shouldn't be too difficult," Julie said dryly.

He reached out to touch her chin with a finger. "That bruise is a nice touch, too."

"Thanks a *lot*." She was beginning to be annoyed by the continuing examination, but the smuggler had begun to frown and shake his head. "What's wrong?"

"You still don't look right."

"Sorry," she muttered acidly. "I'm doing my best."

"You just don't have the look of a woman who's been well and thoroughly bedded."

"No kidding!" Julie exploded incredulously. She gave a short, sarcastic laugh. "I'm sorry, but this is the best I can do! It's really too bad I'm not an expert on that subject, but I'm sure *you* are, so why don't you tell me what I'm supposed to look like?"

He rubbed his chin, his fingers making a dry, rasping sound against the rough stubble. Suddenly he looked at his fingers and then back at her face, and his eyes narrowed. "Come here," he growled softly.

Chapter 3

Julie shook her head no and took a backward step. He came after her and took her by the shoulders.

"Hold still."

"What...what are you doing?" Her voice came out sounding high and frightened, and she put out her hands to ward him off. They came up flat against his chest, and she felt the moist heat of it penetrate the fabric of his shirt.

"I'm putting the finishing touches on your makeup," he said, and, leaning down, drew his whiskery jaw across her cheek.

She gasped and uttered a small, shocked cry, pulling back from the abrasive contact. He let go of her shoulders and moved his hands to her head, holding it still while he rubbed his face against hers, burning her skin with his beard. Then he tilted her head back and she felt the painful rasp on the soft, delicate skin of her neck.

It was so completely unexpected, such a devastating assault on her unguarded senses, that Julie was paralyzed with shock. She gripped his forearms, more for support than with any hope of moving him. Her mouth was open, but no sound came out; she couldn't even breathe. Tears rushed to her eyes, and she squeezed them shut and managed to gasp, "Please—you're hurting me!"

His head tilted away from her cheek. She felt moisture, cool on the hot, abraded skin of her neck, and then a gentle, drawing pressure. After a moment he bent lower, his mouth nuzzling the skin revealed by the deep slash of her shirt, seeking the soft, white top of her breast.

Julie heard herself whimper, "No...," and her hands came up to his head, her fingers tangling in his hair as she tried desperately to pull him away. Her legs were shaky...weak; her knees buckled, and she clutched at his shoulders for support. His mouth closed over the tender flesh, and he sucked gently... then harder, bringing blood to the skin's surface, leaving an indelible mark. *His* mark. His brand of ownership.

He straightened then, and Julie drew a shuddering breath, thinking he had finished with her. He took her hands from his shoulders and held them by the wrists, spreading her arms away from him, surveying his handiwork through half-closed eyes. And then he slipped his arms around her, pulled her close and turned his attention to her mouth.

He kissed her long and hard, his mouth deliberately bruising, intent only on leaving her looking swollen and ravished. Julie made small noises of protest in her throat, but it was impossible to resist such a prolonged and purposeful assault; inevitably she had to open to him. With a deep-throated groan of frustration and defeat, she felt her neck muscles relax and her head fall back.

But something was happening to the kiss—it had altered in intent and execution, so subtly at first that she never knew exactly how or when it began to be something else entirely. His head shifted, finding a new, less punitive melding; her hands touched his shirt collar, the warm skin under the hair on the back of his neck. His hands slid over her back, curving downward over her buttocks to press her into his body, stroking back up along her spine to support her head. His lips were firm but no longer hard; they teased and aroused rather than plundered. His tongue took moisture from their mouths and soothed and bathed her burning, tingling lips, slipping and sliding over the contours of her mouth, drawing responses from her that were as wanton as they were distressing.

And then, abruptly, it ended. He lifted his head, leaving her mouth cold and moist, and for an instant his demon's eyes burned into hers with that blue fire. Then once more he took her wrists and lifted her arms from his shoulders, holding her at arm's length.

"Now," he said harshly, "you'll do fine." He took her hand and led her like a child to the door.

"Wait—" Julie protested, stumbling a little on legs that felt like rubber. "I can't—my hair—"

He gave her a swift, impatient glance. "Perfect—looks like you just got out of bed. Come on. Let's not keep our audience waiting."

His voice was dry and cool, but although he himself appeared completely unaffected, he was not altogether unsympathetic. At the door he slipped an arm around her waist to help her make the long step to the ground, and he kept it there for support as they crossed the uneven ground.

Julie wasn't in any condition to be observant as she stumbled through the dark in the curve of the smuggler's unyielding arm. She had an impression of soft velvety skies, stars glimmering on water, the smell of the sea, and a hundred small unidentifiable night sounds. A beautiful, romantic night, under different circumstances. Few dwellings, and those small and widely spaced, flimsily built, with pale light and soft voices escaping through cracks and unglazed windows. A remote and primitive place. There would be no help for her here.

They stopped at the open door of an adobe not much larger than her parents' garage back in Canoga Park. Good smells drifted out to them through the lighted rectangle, making Julie's stomach turn painfully under her ribs. As he answered a greeting from within, Chayne gave her arm a warning squeeze and stepped across the threshold, pulling her after him.

For a moment she was disoriented; the scene of calm domesticity was so *normal*...so *ordinary*...that it seemed unreal. It was like a dream in which the familiar and commonplace becomes interwoven with the fantastic. Dutiful wife at a small gas stove, lifting her head to cast a look of quickly veiled curiosity before turning back to stir a steaming pot; shirt-sleeved husband at the table sipping coffee, lifting his hand and smiling a welcome. They might have been suburban neighbors getting together for a friendly backyard barbeque.

But the adobe was lit by a kerosene lantern, its floor was hard-packed earth, and sea-scented breezes blew in through the unshuttered windows, setting the lamp swaying so that it cast weird, moving shadows. A child of indeterminate age and sex slept in the middle of a double bed in the corner, arms flung wide and soft lips innocently parted, oblivious to this late-night disturbance in his quarters.

The man—the smuggler Geraldo—could he really be the same man who had stood vigil beside the camper in a starlit desert ravine and later talked of killing her as casually as a suburban husband plots the disposal of a pesky gopher? Here in the presence of his wife and child there was none of the vulgar language Julie had heard him use outside the camper window, though he did subject her to a long stare full of speculation as he traded pleasantries with Chayne and waved him jovially to a chair.

The woman—his wife, Rita—did she know what her husband did when he went away to the north in the camper? Or did she only suspect and try to put the dangerous and worrisome thoughts out of her mind? She seemed like any young housewife of Hispanic ancestry in jeans, sandals, flower print cotton blouse and hair cut in an up-to-date style. She might have been about to dash off to a PTA meeting, or to pick up the children from piano lessons.

Reality and fantasy turned topsy-turvy... and Julie was like a child, lost in a nightmare.

She felt a hand on her shoulder pushing her into a chair and sat woodenly, remembering to keep her eyes lowered. While Chayne and Geraldo made meaningless man-talk across her, ignoring her presence, she covertly watched the woman at the stove through her lashes.

What story has she been told to explain me? she wondered. Or does Señor Chayne often bring home "bedmates"? Will she think me some sort of groupie or camp follower, and hold me in contempt? If she knows the truth, will she hate and fear me as a possible danger to her husband? Or might she, possibly, be a friend? Was it she who sent me the belt? And how will I ever know if I'm not allowed to talk to anyone...?

Why shouldn't I talk to her? What possible harm could it do? Julie thought resentfully as she watched the woman move silently between the stove and the table, bringing plates of crisp fried fish and tortillas and bowls of steaming seafood chowder. The loneliness she had felt earlier in the camper seemed to swamp her; it became desperately important, somehow, that she have a friend in this godforsaken place.

The woman placed Julie's bowl before her. Quickly, before she could turn back to the stove, Julie touched her hand and said clearly, *"Muchas gracias."*

For a brief instant the woman's dark eyes widened and looked directly into hers—a pleasant, open glance—and then she nodded and murmured, *"De nada,"* and turned away.

Julie took a deep, satisfied breath and picked up her spoon. Silence had fallen over the table. She glanced up to find Chayne gazing at her, his eyes flinty, and her heart began to knock painfully against her ribs. She lifted her chin slightly and looked back at him.

"The *señorita* is very quiet tonight," Geraldo said with a smirk. "I think she must be tired—from the long journey."

Teeth flashed white in Chayne's dark face, but the smile did not blunt the cold steel in his eyes. "Yes . . . the *señorita* is *very* tired," he said softly. "So tired I am afraid she has lost her appetite. *¿Es verdad, Güerita?*"

Under the force of his gaze Julie felt her anger and defiance waver. The battle of wills was very brief—no contest, really. She swallowed miserably, dropped her eyes and slowly laid her spoon beside her bowl. Fragrant steam rose to her nostrils as she whispered *"Sí, señor,"* and her stomach rumbled in rude denial.

I hate him.

Geraldo roared with laughter, and Chayne chuckled and picked up his own spoon.

"It sounds as if your appetite is returning," he said pleasantly. "Perhaps by the time Geraldo and I have finished you will have recovered enough to eat. Do you think so, *Güerita mía?* It would be a shame if you could not enjoy this delicious soup. After such an exhausting day you will need to recover your strength."

I really hate him.

Julie felt those terrible eyes on her, and her skin burned hot under his gaze. It burned where his beard had chafed it and where his lips had branded it. Her throat swelled shut until she really couldn't eat a bite. She felt like a child being punished in front of company, only *her* parents had never treated her so cruelly. She thought she would strangle on her rage and frustration, her hatred and humiliation. She wanted to hurl the bowl of hot soup into the devil's face, to rake it with her fingernails . . . to leave *her* mark!

Whatever you do . . . don't fight me.

Julie heard the quiet voice even through the clamor of her own fury, almost as if he had actually spoken. She closed her eyes, breathing evenly and fighting for self-control. She didn't hate him. She was an officer of the law, and he was a breaker of the law. Hate was . . . unprofessional. He had done it to her again.

But she was going to get out of this. She was going to beat him. For the moment she had to go along with this act. An act, that was all it was. He had warned her.

She couldn't do it. She just couldn't.

But she knew she would. All she had to do was consider the alternative.

Around her the masculine small talk had resumed. With her eyes closed, Julie savored the wonderful smells while her stomach gnawed on itself and complained aloud at the ill treatment. This is good for you; a little adversity builds character, she insisted silently.

Presently she heard a spoon clatter against crockery and felt a touch on her chin.

"Feeling better now, *Güerita mía?*"

She opened her eyes, almost drowned in a vivid blue gaze, and quickly lowered them again. She nodded and felt the pressure of his knuckle under her chin, lifting it.

"Do you want to eat now?"

Again she nodded.

"What did you say?" His voice was soft but steely.

"Yes . . . please," she whispered in English.

"Ah-ah . . . where are your manners? Speak Spanish for our hosts."

Julie mentally ground her teeth, but managed to keep her eyes downcast and her tone meek. She was learning fast. *"Sí, señor. Por favor."*

The demon sat back, magnanimous in his victory, beaming at her as she pulled her cooled soup toward her and began to eat. She was hungry enough that she didn't even care that he watched her every bite with a smug, proprietary air. The soup *was* delicious—mildly spiced with green chili peppers that spread warmth through her as the hearty seafood filled her empty belly. She ate in silence, and the rest of the meal passed without incident. Rita had retired to a chair beside the bed, where she sat quietly alert to the needs of the men at the table. Chayne and Geraldo talked of fishing and tides and weather, while Julie ate until she could eat no more.

At last Chayne's chair scraped on the hard dirt and he stood up. Julie obeyed his gesture and got to her feet to stand meekly behind him while he expressed his thanks to Rita and said good night. Julie dared a look at Rita over her shoulder and received a brief smile in return. She knew better than to speak again, but the smile was a small encouragement.

"I'll walk you home," Geraldo said expansively as the two men stood in the doorway lighting cigarettes.

"Bueno." Chayne clapped him on the shoulder, and the two smugglers moved into the night, leaving Julie to stumble along behind. The dogs, the voices and the guitar were silent now, and the only lights still burning were in Geraldo's house and one other, set a little farther inland beyond the parked camper. Another adobe, even smaller than Geraldo's. As they approached it Chayne turned to Julie and said quietly, "Go inside. Geraldo and I have things to talk about."

Julie nodded and went inside the hut, closing the door after her. She was struck immediately by a wave of dismay that almost distracted her from her purpose. *Again.*

I can't stay here with him! She sank limply back against the door.

"Gabriel was here today," she heard Geraldo say in a low voice.

The door was wood but not solid; it seemed to be made of slats or poles nailed to a frame, and the murmuring voices came to her clearly through the cracks. All thoughts of exploring her prison were pushed aside, and she held her breath, listening in earnest.

Chayne's voice said sharply, "Today? Why didn't he wait?"

"He had to get back to La Paz. He was supposed to be in Mazatlán by tomorrow."

"Any news of the shipment?"

A brief silence—perhaps a shrug?—and Chayne's voice again. "It's nearly August. We're running out of time, *amigo*."

A placid chuckle, the scrape of feet on gravel. "You talk like a *gringo, amigo*. Be patient."

"*Time*, damn it. The Exposition—"

Geraldo's soothing murmur cut him off. "Don't worry. You know Gabriel will have the shipment here in plenty of time for the opening. And until he delivers it there is nothing for us to do but wait."

There was a murmur Julie could not quite hear as the two men moved a little distance back down the path, and then Geraldo laughed. "*Mañana, mi amigo. Mañana! Buenas noches....*"

Julie was barely able to spring away to the far side of the hut before the door crashed back and Chayne came in, scowling. He stopped when he saw her, then came on, his frown deepening.

"What are you doing?"

Julie stammered, backing away. "Nothing! I was just... waiting for you."

"Listening?"

"No, I—"

"Of course you were," he muttered, throwing her one more brief look of acute distaste and raking a hand through his hair. "You're an *agent!* You can't help it, I suppose." He seemed out of sorts, upset. Julie swallowed uncertainly, afraid of angering him further.

"You'd have been better occupied getting yourself into bed," he said acidly. "That was as much privacy as you're going to get."

Julie stared at him. "Into what bed? Just where in the hell am I supposed to sleep?"

His back was toward her, his voice an impatient growl. "Don't be stupid."

"I'm not stupid," Julie said tersely. "There is only one bed."

"That's right," he muttered without looking up. He had begun to take things out of his pockets and put them on a low stool beside the bed.

"You said..." That traitorous quaver was in her voice again, and she fought to control it. "You told me I would *not* be sharing your bed. You said—"

"Don't be an idiot," he snarled, turning on her, his eyes shooting sparks. "What do I have to do to make you understand the danger you're in? You're a *cop!* The only reason you're not mummifying in some desert gully right now is because you happen to be both female and pretty, and I have been celibate for what to my compatriots is an unreasonable length of time! How would it look if I asked for another bed?"

"You said it would be up to me," Julie said, breathing hard. "You *lied.*"

He gave an incredulous snort. "In the catalogue of my sins that's hardly a big-ticket item!"

"Why did you bother to lie to me?" Julie said bitterly. "I couldn't have done anything about it anyway. Why did you let me think—"

"Look, damn it, in a manner of speaking I suppose it is up to you. You can always take the floor. Take your chances with the lizards and scorpions!"

They stared at each other in furious silence. Julie gave up first.

"Why are you being so cruel?" she whispered, not trusting her voice. "Why did you bother to save my life?"

He made that sound of annoyance and looked away. Then he looked back at her. "Am I being cruel?" His voice was quiet. "I didn't mean to be."

"Oh, sure. And I suppose you didn't mean to be a while ago, either!"

"At dinner."

"Yes, at dinner. That was cruel. And unnecessary. What did I do that was so terrible that you had to humiliate me like that?"

He tightened his mouth and veiled his eyes, giving his face a cold, hostile look, like a mask. "You disobeyed me."

"*Disobeyed?* What am I? Your chattel? Your slave?"

His voice was cold. "No—just my prisoner. But even if you weren't, you've got to get used to the idea that there is no such thing as women's lib or equal rights here. Either way, I have the power to insist on obedience. In your case, it amounts to the power of life or death. Don't forget that."

"How could I possibly? You don't let me, you *enjoy* it so!"

He gave a short, mirthless laugh and sat down on the bed to take off his shoes. He had already removed his shirt, and Julie eyed the bunching muscles in his scarred back with a curious mixture of fascination and dread. He looked up at her, a little smile tugging at his mouth, and she felt her face grow hot.

"Don't you?" he asked. "Enjoy your life? Is the price really so high? My bed . . . for your life?" He stood up abruptly to unfasten his pants, then sat back down to pull them off. When he stood again wearing only a pair of briefs, Julie gulped, tried to look away and found that she could not. What was it about his body that seemed so . . . threatening? He was only a man, not some strange alien beast; why did she stare at him with that mixture of fear and excitement while her heart pounded primitive warning cadences inside her chest? Primitive . . . savage . . . like a black panther. Perfectly proportioned, beautifully sculpted, marred by the touch of violence. . . Grace and power, passion held in check. Arrogance, sensuality . . . It was all there in that lean, whipcord body.

"Well?" he said softly. "Which will it be?"

Julie gasped, "I'm *thinking!*"

He threw back his head and laughed, the first time she had heard sounds of real humor from him. "You remind me of that old Jack Benny bit where the robber says, 'Your money or your life,' and Benny's reply is a lot like yours."

"It's not funny!" Julie quavered, breathing rapidly.

"No, I suppose it isn't." He folded his arms across his chest and arranged his face in solemn lines, though his eyes still gleamed with amusement. "Julie . . . I'm not going to argue with you all night. And you know you can't stand there all night. You really don't have any choice." He came toward her, stalking her like . . . like a panther, she couldn't help but think. He murmured softly, "Is it really so terrible, so frightening . . . the thought of sharing my bed?"

He was close enough to touch her now, and he did so, the backs of his fingers barely brushing the collar of her shirt, the thin fabric that covered her breasts. She managed to control the gasp that tried to escape from her throat, but not the response of tiny nerve endings that brought her nipples springing into sharp relief under her shirt. Nor could she keep him from knowing; his fingers brushed lightly back and forth across the pebbly tips while his eyes held hers, demanding an answer.

Julie held her ground. The tension between them had become so vibrant that it produced its own kind of calm, like the air just before a thunderstorm. "Why shouldn't I be frightened of you?" she said in a voice that sounded as if it didn't have quite enough air. "The sample I've had of your lovemaking wasn't exactly gentle."

"Sample?" He frowned, then drew aside the neckline of her shirt and touched the mark on her breast. His eyes rested there for a long moment, then came back to touch her lips, her cheeks, and then return to her eyes. "That wasn't lovemaking," he said softly. "Making love is a game for two...." His hand rested warm on the curve of her neck and collarbone, his thumb stroking lightly up and down her throat. His voice was a lazy purr. "If we made love, *Güerita mía,* you would have nothing to be afraid of. You would have as much to say... and do... about it as I would. And you would enjoy it as much as I would."

Julie swallowed, feeling the movement of her throat against his thumb. He dropped his hand suddenly and turned away, and his voice was harsh when he said, "Do what you must to get ready, and come to bed, Julie. Don't make me come after you."

He lit a cigarette, jerked back the woven Mexican blanket and top sheet and lay down on the bed, his head propped on one arm and one leg drawn up. He watched her, eyes narrowed against the smoke, and Julie just looked back at him, frustrated and weary, sick to death of skirmishing with this man and coming out second best, worn out by the strange battle of wits and wills. She drew a deep breath and for the second time in twenty-four hours began to undress before the blue-eyed demon.

"Julie . . ." he sighed, stopping her. "Unless you prefer to sleep in the raw, leave your shirt on."

"I . . . don't . . . understand." Her fingers had begun to shake. The bed, just a mattress on a crude wood frame, looked very small, and the demon seemed to take up a very large portion of it.

"No," he said flatly, "I don't think you do." He crushed out his cigarette on the adobe wall beside the bed and pulled the sheet up to his waist. "I thought I'd made myself clear. I like my women willing. Forcing frightened virgins isn't my idea of a good time."

"I'm not a virgin!" Julie rasped. *Good God, why did I say that!*

He chuckled softly, once again without real amusement. What a strange, almost bitter man he seemed at times! "You might as well be. As I said, making love takes two equal players. Rape—or seduction, for that matter—is too much trouble for too little reward. Turn out the lantern when you come to bed. And relax—you're perfectly safe. I won't lay a hand on you."

"Am I supposed to believe that?" Julie cried, her voice high and incredulous.

Another dry chuckle shook his chest, and he lifted an eyebrow sardonically. "Of course not. I lie, remember?" And he calmly turned on his side, away from her.

Her movements felt wooden and jerky as she turned off the lantern and took off her belt, jeans and sandals, then groped her way to the bed. It was a feeling she seemed to be having a lot lately.

Julie lay stiff as a post, staring wide-eyed at the underside of the thatched roof. She concentrated on matching her breathing to his, as if doing so might be a kind of camouflage.

"Julie . . . stop shivering so we can both go to sleep." His voice was a deep, husky drawl. "You're shaking the whole bed."

She muttered, "I'm sorry," and went right on shaking.

He turned over and raised himself on one elbow. She could feel his presence looming over her in the dark. "Why are you still nervous?"

"Why shouldn't I be?"

"I told you you're perfectly safe. Don't you believe me?"

Safe? Would she ever be safe again? "No. I guess I don't."

A soft chuckle. "Why not? Do you think you're so irresistible I won't be able to control myself?" She was silent, and he settled back with a sigh. "Julie, I'm not an adolescent with overactive glands; and at the risk of bruising your ego, you are *not* irresistible. So unless you have a problem, we should both sleep like babies." He yawned noisily. *"Buenas noches, Güerita."*

Julie lay very still, wondering if that odd little pain she was feeling could possibly come from a bruised ego, and thinking, My God...he's done it again! I've done it again! How does he manage to make me lose my head, damn it? I can't afford it.

She wasn't sleepy. She was keyed up and on edge, and so conscious of the warm body next to her that she hardly dared to breathe for fear she might touch him by mistake. The air around her seemed alive with tension. Where was it coming from? Certainly not from *him*. Already his breathing had taken on the deep, natural rhythm of sleep. Why had she ever doubted *his* self-control? She had certainly seen enough evidence of it already! So it was coming from her. What was she afraid of?

Was she afraid of herself? *Oh...Julie....*

She lay awake, fighting sleep now, afraid to fall asleep lest she gravitate toward that magnetic body in unconsciousness. She tried to think, to concentrate on doing her job.

She forced herself to think about the conversation overheard outside the hut. Gabriel. Someone named Gabriel was bringing a "shipment" to be delivered to Los Angeles in August. And it was important that it be there in time for—

In time for the Exposition. In August. In Los Angeles. They could only mean the Pan American Exposition.

In the darkness, Julie shook her head, wide awake and steeped in the irony of it. Here she was supposed to be transferred to the Los Angeles station for the month of August in order to help control the expected increase in contraband traffic during the Exposition, and through a *blunder*, an accident of fate, she had managed to find her way to the source of that traffic!

She had been given, she realized, a rare opportunity. If she played this game right she could break up what appeared to be a very extensive smuggling operation! Excitement washed over

her and then receded, leaving her feeling frustrated and helpless. Standing in her way was one coyote with the body of a
panther, the eyes of a demon, and the mesmerizing touch of a
sorcerer.

Chapter 4

Somewhere, not too far away, there was a rooster crowing, and closer by a soft, irregular creaking. Julie couldn't identify the source of the creaking, and so it became an irritant that would not let her sleep. She made a querulous sound of protest, and a soft voice answered, "Good morning." A man's voice, husky with amusement.

Julie forced one eye open. A tall, dark man with no shirt on stood beside the bed peering into a small mirror propped on a shelf, shaving by the light of a lantern. The razor made a faint scraping noise.

"Oh . . ." she said fuzzily. "It's you."

He glanced down at her, his eyes a cool, clear blue above dark skin streaked with white. "Who were you expecting?"

"Are you making that noise?"

He raised his eyebrows and lifted his razor interrogatively. Julie shook her head and closed her eyes again. "Uh-uh . . . something's creaking."

There was the sound of water swishing. "The shutter, I guess," he said, his voice muffled. "The wind has picked up today. Sorry it woke you."

"Me, too," Julie murmured, rubbing her eyes. "I'm not a morning person."

Chayne gave a soft chuckle and patted his face with a small white towel. "So I see."

Julie gazed at him, still trying to focus her eyes. "Oh...," she rasped. "You've got one there, too."

"Got what where?"

"A scar. On your chin."

He touched it, smiling lopsidedly. "So I have."

"It looks like a dimple."

His laughter exploded as he turned to reach for a shirt that hung on a nail beside the bed. Julie watched the pull and tug of the muscles in his arm and across his ribs and mumbled sleepily, "You look different."

"I think you'd better either go back to sleep or have some coffee," he said dryly, buttoning his shirt. "Rita should have some ready by now." He had turned to the door when Julie stopped him with a cry of protest.

"What now?"

She sat up, fully awake at last. "Where are you going?"

"To breakfast and then fishing. Why?"

Trying to keep the dismay out of her voice and the blush out of her cheeks, Julie said, "Are you just going to leave me here?"

He leaned against the door and gazed at her quizzically with his head tilted, as if he were having trouble hearing her.

"I mean," Julie stammered, "what about food? Aren't you going to bring me something to eat? *And,*" she cried furiously, "there's not even a bathroom in here! Are you going to walk me to the john, or just put me on a long leash? *Stop laughing,* damn you! Do you think it's *funny* that I have to ask you every time I want to go to the bathroom?"

She was sitting cross-legged in the middle of the bed, quivering with embarrassment and indignation. If she'd had anything more lethal than a pillow she'd have hurled it at his head. When he continued to shake with silent laughter she muttered resentfully, "You really love to humiliate me, don't you?"

"You know, I believe I do. There's nothing quite as entertaining as an embarrassed cop." His voice was dry, but as his gaze slipped almost unintentionally from her flushed cheeks to her throat and then continued on down the deep slash of the shirt's neckline, she saw something kindle in those brilliant eyes that made her wish she could pull the bedclothes up to her chin. He sighed regretfully and straightened, shaking his head. "But you aren't confined to this room, and I've no intention of waiting on you hand and foot. The john is a short walk in that direction, and Rita's house is in the other. And I'm sure she'd welcome a little help with the cooking."

Julie gave her head a bewildered shake. "I don't understand. I thought I was a prisoner here."

His face and voice were bland enough, but his eyes were hard. "Oh, you're a prisoner, all right. But you're free to come and go as you please. And if that seems like a contradiction, just remember that you're bordered on three sides by desert, and that there's no way on earth you could carry enough water to get you to the nearest settlement. And," he added, seeing the thought in her mind, "I've taken the precaution of removing a few vital components from the truck's engine. Of course..." he purred, "there's always the sea. But even if you could manage to launch one of the fishing boats by yourself, I wouldn't recommend it, darling. You're the lady who wants to live, remember?" He waited, but Julie only glared mulishly at him, and after a moment he touched two fingers to his temple in a mocking salute and murmured, *"Buenos días, Güerita,"* and left her.

Buenos días. The Spanish equivalent of "Have a nice day." *Damn* him. And why did he always call her that... *Güerita?* It wasn't an expression she was familiar with. *Güero,* she knew, meant "fair" or "blond," and the diminutive, technically, meant "small blond one." Or... *Blondie.* Well, of course! He was calling her *Blondie!* Not so different from Cottontop or Dandelion. Her father had called her Blondie when she was very small.

She found that she was smiling, inexplicably cheered.

Once her jailer had gone Julie could hardly wait to be up and dressed and out of doors. This freedom might be only an illusion, but after the day and night she had spent confined in that horrible camper, even an illusion was to be savored.

In the doorway of the adobe she stood with her head thrown back, glorying in the feel of the sun on her throat and on her toes, bare in the borrowed huaraches. A warm wind laden with strange, pungent odors whipped around the corner of the hut and ruffled her hair before scurrying on like a mischievous child, raising dust on its way to the water. Julie lifted her arms high in a bone-cracking stretch and almost laughed aloud with delight in being alive, breathing in great gulps of perfumed air, reveling in the aching brilliance of morning sun on the water....

Morning sun?

Julie lowered her arms slowly to shade her eyes as she watched the ripple and sparkle of sunlight on blue water. Of course, she thought. No wonder I felt as if my directions were turned around! She had seen a thousand sunsets over the ocean, but not one sunrise. She wasn't looking over the Pacific Ocean; this was the Gulf of California. The fabled Sea of Cortez!

I know where I am! Julie's spirits took another dizzying leap. Those hazy blue shapes on the horizon were islands; therefore, she had to be somewhere in the "midriff" of the peninsula, south of San Felipe. And not so very far south, either, if they had made it over Baja's appalling roads in one day. He was bluffing! Julie thought exultantly. With a boat and a little luck I can get out of here!

She drew in her breath and looked around guiltily, afraid that the excitement of her discovery might show in her face. But although she could hear far-off sounds of voices raised in Spanish conversation and laughter, the only living things visible were the wheeling seabirds and a thin brown dog jogging aimlessly along the beach. Julie smiled grimly after him and set off to find the latrine.

The adobe hut she shared with her jailer had for some reason been placed away from the others, in a little depression that gave it a certain degree of privacy. Behind it and over a rise was a crude outhouse, and beyond this the terrain rose steeply, an escarpment of granite from which boulder-strewn ridges stretched toward the water like the desperate fingers of a thirst-crazed wanderer. The other huts—some of adobe, some wood and galvanized tin, some no more than crude shelters of poles and brush—were clustered together in the cove to the south, with the fishing boats drawn up on the beach and the tantalizing but useless camper parked between the high-tide line and the rocks.

Julie was desert-wise enough to watch for basking rattlesnakes without being intimidated by the prospect of meeting one, so she clambered over the rocks to the north to see what lay beyond the promontory. A secluded little bay curved away to another promontory of volcanic rock—a lovely beach, pristine and unmarked by a single human footprint. The explanation for its serenity lay in a scattered handful of jagged boulders hurled by the same convulsion that had formed the ridges. They dotted the sands and made treacherous dark smudges beneath the quiet waters of the bay, rendering it inaccessible and useless to man.

Buffeted by the wind, one hand pressing her hair flat to her head in a pointless but habitual gesture, Julie shaded her eyes and turned in a slow circle, gazing toward the horizon.

Freedom! But it was only an illusion, and unbelievably frustrating. In some ways being confined to the stuffy camper had been easier to accept. These seemingly limitless boundaries made her feel vaguely guilty. She thought, I've got to do something! I have to get away from them somehow!

But with those beckoning vistas surrounding her, it was hard even to remember that she was a prisoner, hard to remember that the dark man with the electric eyes and a scar that looked like a dimple on his chin was a smuggler—a coyote—and that she was his captive. And utterly at his mercy....

She was conscious suddenly of a hollow feeling that seemed to extend from her breasts all the way down to her thighs. She turned her back to the wind and stared back across the bay to where the boats lay drawn up on the beach.

Fishing. He had said he was going fishing. But the boats had an abandoned look; pelicans and sea gulls roosted on the gunwales, and as she watched, a child scampered across the wet sand with a scruffy dog at his heels, darted to the water's edge and threw something in. A few of the gulls lifted and circled in a desultory way before settling back to their places.

"So where in the heck is he?" Julie asked aloud, conscious of a curious sense of abandonment, as if she had been brought to a party and then left standing by the punch bowl. Odd, this almost childlike dependence. Odd . . . and very dangerous.

Julie chewed her lips, deliberately biting hard enough to cause pain, using the pain as an anchor to reality. She wanted to throw back her head and shout, "I am Agent Julie Maguire of the United States Border Patrol! I am an officer of the United States government!" So what if she'd been taken hostage and stripped of all the external trappings of her identity? It didn't *change* it, or the fact that she still had her duty. These men—*all* of them—had broken the laws she had sworn to enforce, and it was up to her to do everything in her power to resist them and, if possible, to bring them to justice.

"Step one," Julie whispered grimly. "I'm alive." And the next step . . . was to *escape*.

The distant cry of a seabird made her aware of the silence. Except for the wind and that lonely call there was no sound at all. No footprints on the beach, and no sounds of human voices. She might have been alone on the planet. Swallowing fear and loneliness, Julie turned back toward the village. As she searched the foot and handholds for basking rattlesnakes and listened for the dry whir of a warning rattle, she knew that she *was* alone, and without friends. If she were to escape, it would have to be by her own wits.

The sun was getting higher now, and she was hungry. "I'll go and find Rita. I'll feel better after I've had some coffee and breakfast." Speaking aloud seemed somehow to reassure her. Her hands went absently to the brightly woven belt at her waist. Well . . . maybe not entirely friendless. . . .

It occurred to her as she scrambled back over the ridge that this would be a good time to retrieve her bra from the camper. She would ask Rita where she could wash out her clothes.

As she angled upward across the beach toward the camper, she had to pause every few steps to shake the annoying grit out of her huaraches. Finally she just sat down to take them off, and it was then that she heard the voices. The same voices she had heard discussing her fate while she lay bound hand and foot in the camper loft, except that now there was no bawdy banter, no coarse laughter. The discussion was terse and businesslike, and conducted in low tones Julie had to strain to hear.

Casting a quick glance around, she carefully hitched herself backward on the seat of her pants until she was snuggled right up against the camper's rear wheel, directly under the window.

The discussion was in Spanish, of course, and Julie had to listen hard for a few minutes before she could make sense of it. They were discussing the last smuggling run—the near disaster. And how it might affect their next run—the "big one." Geraldo and Pepe seemed concerned about using the same route again; Chayne was pointing out that using the same route would be like hiding in a place that had already been searched.

"It's the safest route we could possibly use!" Julie heard a muffled thump, as if he had brought his palm down on the tabletop for emphasis. "It's too late to try out a new route. The risks involved in attempting an untried trail through the desert are much greater than the remote possibility that the patrol will pick *that* moment to be in *that* spot. No—" another thump "—we must stay with our plan."

He was so adamant that the others capitulated; the unshakable note of certainty in his voice was a powerful influence. Julie wondered how he could be so sure, and then realized with chagrin that he was quite right. It had been a fluke, her being in that particular place that day. She had missed a turnoff and gone perhaps ten miles beyond her usual patrol range. She had topped the ridge, realized her error, and had been turning her vehicle around when she had spotted the camper's dust. . . .

But how had *he* known that?

"Has Gabriel decided how many?" There was a note of asperity in Chayne's voice. "May we at least know whether we are going to be able to do it with one truck?"

"One squad," Geraldo said promptly. "Six men. Plus the three of us." He gave a dry chuckle. "It won't be first-class accommodations, but this truck is adequate."

"Just six . . . ," Chayne murmured, adding something in a mumble too low for Julie to catch.

A cold, clipped voice answered him. Pepe. "Surely you know that a small force, properly trained and equipped, can accomplish as much as a larger one, and has the advantage of being easier to transport and conceal. With these six men we will make Lebanon seem like a fiesta."

Chayne cut in impatiently. "All right, agreed. Have the targets been set?"

"The convention center will be the primary target, of course. We will be given details of the secondary targets when we arrive at the depot to pick up the rest of the dynamite."

"And the location of the depot?"

Pepe's voice was steely. "That too is something we will learn when it is necessary for us to know."

"Of course." Chayne's voice sounded taut with frustration. "And in the meantime, we just sit here and *wait*."

Geraldo laughed, the same lazy chuckle Julie had heard from him last night outside the hut. "Oh-ho, I know how hard that will be for you—you *gringo*s do not like to wait for anything! Listen, my friend. *Relax* a little. *Fish* a little. Make love... maybe *more* than a little!"

There was more laughter; the business meeting was over. But in any event Julie had heard more than enough. Now she only wanted to get clear away from the camper before she was discovered. If she was discovered she was as good as dead—not even Chayne would be able to save her! She felt cold and sick; her knees were weak and her hands shaky, but she managed to get silently to her feet and back to the beach before collapsing onto the sand beyond the rocky point, out of sight of the camper.

Oh God, she prayed silently, what am I going to do?

It was so much worse than she had imagined. Not coyotes—*terrorists*. Who were they? Leftists? From Central America? Cuba? Not that it mattered. All that mattered was that a squad of guerrillas planned to launch a terrorist attack on the Pan American Exposition in Los Angeles. And she was the only hope of preventing it.

A gust of wind buffeted gently against her back, lifting sand to sting her bare ankles. Julie drew her legs up and wrapped her arms around them, resting her chin on her knees as she gazed broodingly across the little bay toward the beached boats. Dangerous or not, those boats were still her only chance. It was hard to judge from a distance just how big and heavy they were, and she didn't dare go closer. They had outboard motors but didn't look very large. Could one person launch one of them? The surf was very flat; even with the wind kicking up white caps the waves slapped gently at the sand. If she could just get a boat to the water's edge . . .

There was a burst of masculine laughter, and the camper door banged shut. Julie stayed crouched where she was, and after a while the three men appeared on the opposite curve of the bay, making their way down the beach toward the boats. There were shouts, and a fourth man emerged from a wooden hut in the main cluster of dwellings to join them—an older man, this one, with gray hair and a beard. The child Julie had seen earlier skipped at his heels, and several dogs dashed in joyful circles, scattering the seabirds and kicking up sand.

Her heart sinking, Julie watched strong men put their shoulders and backs into the launching, two to a boat. How foolish she was to think she could manage it alone! Once the boats were afloat the men still pushed, wading in the shallows, guiding them through the gentle surf to water deep enough to float the outboard motors. And then at last, perhaps a hundred yards out, the motors were lowered, the men scrambled aboard, and the racket of small diesel engines ricocheted off the rocks at Julie's back. The fishing boats aimed for the hazy island shape on the horizon, followed by a screeching, wheeling cloud of seabirds and the frenzied yipping of the dogs.

Julie got to her feet. Absently brushing sand from her rear end and shading her eyes against the sun as she moved slowly down the beach, she gazed thoughtfully after the disappearing fishermen.

So the bay was shallow. . . . Another reason why it was not a thriving fishing or tourist spot? Not more than knee-deep, even a hundred yards out. It must be low tide now. . . .

Julie moved closer to the beached boats. The child and the dogs had gone back up the beach to disappear among the huts. The seabirds, those too complacent to follow the fishermen, had settled back on the gunwales of the remaining boats and ignored Julie as she wandered among them. Only one or two were discomfited when she bent to put her shoulder against the bow of their roost and give it a hopeless push.

To her surprise and delight, and to the disgust of the birds, it moved!

She pushed harder, and the heavy wooden boat slid a good foot toward the water. Julie knelt and brushed away the sand beneath the boat's keel and discovered a layer of poles—a rolling platform! A launching ramp!

By God, she could do it! It was only a few feet to the water, and with one of those poles as a lever . . . She could do it. She *must* do it—and soon. Tonight. She would need food, drinking water or beer...Rita. She would need to get help from Rita, or at least learn from her where the camp stores were kept. Tonight she would head north, toward San Felipe. . . .

Julie's stomach gave a loud rumble, reminding her of more immediate needs, and she almost laughed aloud with the exhilaration she felt at the thought of finally taking action.

She had no trouble locating Geraldo's hut, where she had suffered such a humiliating defeat the night before. The child was playing in the dust before the doorway, pushing a small wooden truck over highways only he could see and making the uninhibited engine noises only a child can make. At Julie's approach he hopped up, converting the truck instantaneously into an airplane, and ran down to the beach to the accompaniment of a truly amazing jet-engine roar.

After watching him for a moment Julie reached into the hut's dim interior to rap on the open door and call hesitantly, *"¡Hola, Rita! Con permiso..."*

"Buenos días, señorita," a soft voice replied, adding in laborious English. "Please come in." Rita, looking as pretty and normal as she had the night before, came forward, wiping her hands on her blue-jeaned thighs and smiling shyly.

Julie smiled back and held out her hand. *"Yo hablo español,"* she said, and was rewarded by a broad smile of relief.

"That's good—my English is terrible! But you speak Spanish very well for a *norteamericana*. How did you learn such good Spanish?"

Julie murmured evasively, "I need it in my job," and turned to the table. So Rita, at least, had not been told who or what she was.

"Of course," Rita went on with a shrug, bustling ahead of Julie to pull out a chair. "Señor Chayne speaks Spanish like a native." She threw Julie a swift look full of the curiosity she was too reserved to voice.

"I hope it isn't too late for breakfast," Julie said apologetically, changing the subject. "I went exploring this morning and lost track of the time. Anything will be fine—some tortillas, coffee...."

Rita made a clicking noise with her tongue and sternly pushed Julie into the chair. "No, no, no. I will fix you a real *norteamericano* breakfast. I have eggs—fresh eggs from Sebastien."

"Sebastien?"

"*Sí,* the old one, you know, with the beard?" Rita made a gesture as if to stroke invisible whiskers on her own chin. "You haven't met him yet? He and his wife, Juanita, live here all year. They have some chickens, goats—"

Julie interrupted cautiously. "You...don't live here?"

"Oh, no. Geraldo and Carlos and I—"

"Carlos? Your little boy?"

Rita nodded, smiling. "Yes, my little *rascal,* you mean. We live in Guadalajara. We are only here for the summer. But here—" She clapped her hands together. "I stand here talking, and you must be very hungry, *señorita*... Please, I don't even know your name!"

Julie told her her name, and Rita repeated it, making an effort to give the *J* the English pronunciation rather than the Spanish *H*. The result was a soft sound somewhere in between.

"Please," Julie said as Rita stood repeating her name in an experimental way, "I don't want you to go to any trouble for me. I know it's late."

"No, no, it's no trouble! I cook breakfast for Señor Chayne all the time, and I have gotten good at it. For a friend of Señor Chayne," she said with earnest sincerity, "it is no trouble!"

"Then at least let me help you."

"No, no, no. Sit down. I will bring you some coffee." Rita hurried to suit her action to her words, placing a thick mug of fragrantly steaming liquid before Julie, who inhaled, sipped and murmured a heartfelt *"Gracias."* As she watched the dark-haired woman through the rising steam, she was more than ever sure that this was the person she had to thank for the gift of the belt. Rita seemed a little nervous, but it was the nervousness of a shy but lonely person attempting to make friends.

"I really do want to help while I'm staying here," Julie said when Rita seemed at a loss for conversation. "You must tell me what I can do."

Rita threw her a smile as she lit the gas flame under a large cast-iron frying pan. "When the men return from fishing, there will be work to do! We will be glad for your help."

"What kind of fish will they bring back?" Julie asked, visualizing a noxious afternoon cleaning the catch.

Rita shrugged. "*¿Quién sabe?* Who knows? Totuava, grouper, perhaps even lobster—"

"Lobster!"

"Oh, *sí*—it is always so when the men return from the north. There will be a feast—a *fiesta!*" Rita's dark eyes sparkled with a touch of mischief. "You will be sorry you asked to help; Juanita will teach you to make tortillas!"

They laughed companionably, and then Julie asked casually, forestalling the questions she knew the other woman was trying to summon the courage to ask, "Are you here on vacation?"

"Well, yes...and no. I suppose it is a vacation for Carlito and me, but for Geraldo it is a job."

"Job?"

"Yes, of course." Rita glanced up from the stove in surprise. "He works with Señor Chayne and Pepe—you know, helping Sebastien with the tourists."

"Um... tourists?" Julie, at a complete loss, took a stab in the dark. "Fishing?"

A shadow of confusion crossed Rita's face. "Well, yes, that too, but Sebastien usually takes care of that part of it. Geraldo and the others take those who want to explore inland. Into the deserts and mountains—hunting and so on. But didn't you know what Señor Chayne does here?"

"Not...really," Julie said faintly. "I...um...haven't known him very long."

Rita smiled gently and nodded, then said surprisingly, "You don't have to know Señor Chayne very long, do you?" And then, looking embarrassed at herself for having presumed to say such a thing, she hurried on. "They are...guides for the tourists, do you understand? Geraldo brings them here in the seaplane. A few stay to fish with Sebastien, but most go into the interior with Geraldo and Pepe and Señor Chayne."

"I see," Julie murmured, blowing on her coffee. "They take them hunting or exploring, and then bring them back here?"

"Oh, no—this is only a stopover. They are taken on to the west coast, to the next stop. *Comprende?*"

Julie nodded thoughtfully. "So...it is like a...guided tour?"

"Yes, exactly!" Rita said happily. Julie thought she seemed relieved, as if she needed reassurance that it all made sense. She was not a stupid woman. What vague doubts and fears must color her nightmares?

"And the travel arrangements are handled through this . . . Gabriel?" Julie prodded, keeping her voice bland, her face full of polite interest. "Does he have an agency of some kind?"

"Yes, yes—at least . . ." Rita frowned, her busy hands slowing for a moment. "I don't really know. But I think—"

She was interrupted by a rapid burst of Spanish from the doorway. Both women jumped like guilty children and jerked around to stare at the woman silhouetted there. She had struck a pose, one hip jutting, one hand on the curve of her waist, and though Julie could not quite make out the expression on her face, she was certain there had been a note of warning in her voice. In any case, the colloquialism she had used was the crude equivalent of "Shut up!"

Rita's full mouth tightened with dislike. "Linda," she murmured. "Why don't you come in? I don't think you've met Señor Chayne's friend Julie."

The newcomer undulated into the hut, exaggerating her body movements deliberately in a way that could have been either comical or insulting. Julie watched her with impassive interest. She had a small, triangular face, full lips, large dark eyes, a rather frowzy mass of curls left in purposeful disarray, and a voluptuous body in tight white pants and a striped halter top that left her midriff bare. She was at once younger than Rita and much, much older. Julie had encountered her type before—in the streets of Tijuana.

"Linda," Rita said with a careful courtesy, "is a . . . friend of Pepe's."

As Julie nodded her acknowledgment of the introduction,
Linda gave a throaty chuckle and lowered herself into a chair.
She shook a cigarette out of a pack she carried in her hand,
leaned over to light it at the gas flame of a stove burner, then
settled back, exhaling smoke and regarding Julie with narrowed eyes through the cloud.

"Sure—like you are a . . . *friend* of Señor Chayne's," she
murmured.

Julie returned the stare calmly, and after a moment Linda
gave a husky gurgle of laughter and leaned forward to tap her
arm. "You know, I think it's going to be nice, having somebody around here I can *talk* to, *comprende?* Now Rita here is
too good to associate with us—a real nice lady, with her husband and her little boy and her nice house in Guadalajara.
Ha!"

Linda made a rude noise and settled back, breasts jutting,
eyes narrowed against the smoke. Rita tightened her lips as she
turned wordlessly to the stove, and Julie caught a bleak look in
her dark eyes. She felt a surge of pity for the woman stuck in
this place so far from her safe suburban home, friendless and
alone with her vague and frightening suspicions.

Just as she was. Except that Rita had her husband, and Julie
had only a coyote—no, a terrorist—to protect her!

What would Rita, this nice lady with a little son to think of,
do if she knew what was going on? Julie wondered. Would she
help me get away? Or is her first loyalty to her husband? She is
afraid for him, but if I could convince her that stopping him is
the best thing for him, maybe she would give me food and water . . . help me launch the boat . . .

Julie jerked herself out of her musings as Rita set a plate of
bacon and eggs before her. She caught Linda's eyes on her,
glittering with speculation, and wondered whether her thoughts
had been mirrored on her face.

"Señor Chayne *es . . . mucho hombre*," Linda murmured,
smiling a lazy, sensuous smile and letting her eyes slide downward to rest disparagingly on Julie's small bosom, completely
shrouded in the loose-fitting shirt. *Quite a man.* The girl's insolent gaze said plainly that she considered Julie, with her neat
little body and baby-fluff hair, an inadequate consort for the
wonderful Señor Chayne.

The disdain in Linda's eyes was replaced once again by speculation as she sat quietly smoking, watching Julie eat. Julie, trying to think in character for the role she was playing, ate with self-conscious concentration, steeling herself for the questions she sensed were perking just behind those ageless black eyes.

"Where did El Demonio pick you up?"

Julie heard Rita's soft intake of breath. Linda's question was deliberately insulting, thrown out abruptly in the hope of catching her off guard. Julie raised her eyes, wide and candid, and said, "El Demonio?"

Linda smiled, her little pointed face catlike. "Señor Chayne, of course. The demon with blue eyes—it is a good name for him, don't you think? Tell me, is he a demon in bed, too?"

Julie felt Rita wince. She chewed slowly on a bite of tortilla and met the challenge in Linda's eyes with a long, thoughtful gaze. She knew from experience that she was being tested, and that the only way to deal with a street fighter like Linda was to meet her on her own terms. Pushing back her plate, she said with a sweet smile, "Now, that's something you'll never know."

Linda's drawl was equally honeyed. "How do you know I don't already know?"

"Because if you already knew, it wouldn't be necessary to ask. And, dear...if you have any ideas about the future, I think it only fair to warn you . . ."

"Yes?"

Julie lowered her lashes and broadened her smile. "That if you ever try to come close to El Demonio I will—" The phrase she used brought a shocked gasp from Rita and a burst of laughter from Linda.

Julie was just surprised and relieved that she had been able to remember it correctly! Illegal aliens, those who were very young and female, were as often to be found working the streets of San Diego as the tomato fields of the San Joaquin Valley. Julie had had her share of epithets and threats hurled at her by both pimps and madams in the course of her job, and she had chosen the coarsest one she could remember.

It had served its purpose; Linda was looking at her with new respect, still chuckling. Rita was clearing away her dishes, avoiding her eyes. Julie thought she had probably spoiled her chance of a friendship there, but it had seemed important that she establish her cover with the far more dangerous Linda. It was with mixed feelings of victory and regret that she thanked a silent Rita for the meal and left the hut.

Outside, she was not surprised when Linda fell into step beside her. The girl offered her a cigarette, and when she refused, lit one for herself and tucked the pack into the waistband of her trousers.

"That's some mouth you've got, for a *gringa*," she said on her first exhalation. "Where did you learn to talk like that?"

"Tijuana," Julie said shortly.

Linda nodded, eyeing her sideways. "You work in Tijuana, huh? I bet you do okay, with that hair." They walked in silence for a few paces, and then Linda, in another of her blunt thrusts, asked, "What happened to your clothes?"

Julie said with equal rudeness, "You ask too many questions." And then, surprised by a look of vulnerability in the girl's eyes, she relented. "Stolen," she said with a shrug, and looked away, across the water. That, at least, was the truth!

Linda nodded and made a sympathetic sound with her tongue. This was something she could understand. "A bad trick, huh? Did he beat you up, too?"

Julie looked at her in surprise, then followed the direction of the sad, sharp eyes and rubbed the bruise on her chin ruefully. She shrugged, not quite trusting herself to reply. Linda had used the term meaning roughly "bad hombre." It was certainly true that the same person who had stolen her clothes had given her that bruise; and it was also true that he was a "bad hombre."

"And Señor Chayne took you away and gave you clothes," Linda said with certainty, providing her own answers. Julie stifled a snort. She was beginning to wonder how "Señor Chayne" had come to be called El Demonio when he was obviously one step away from canonization in the eyes of both Linda and Rita.

A small brown hand, curiously childlike, touched Julie's sleeve. Julie stopped and turned.

"Hey, if you want, I have some clothes you could borrow," the tough street girl said gruffly. When Julie didn't answer immediately, she withdrew her hand and struck a pose, defiantly hipshot, breasts and chin thrust forward, hair cascading over smoldering eyes. "Look, *gringa*—I don't care if you want to go around in a habit! Maybe you feel safer looking like a little sister! You know what I think? You got a tough mouth, but I think you're afraid of El Demonio after all! I bet you don't have the guts to put on some sexy clothes and wake him up a little bit, do you? You wouldn't even know what to do with him, *gringa!*"

Julie studied the triangular face, set now in hard, derisive lines but betrayed by that elusive vulnerability. "You may be right," she said slowly, smiling. "It seems like a very dangerous thing to do—wake up a sleeping demon."

Linda's mouth twitched with the beginnings of an answering grin. Julie shrugged offhandedly. "Hey, sure, I'd like to have something prettier than this thing to wear. *Gracias.* Can I get something to wear to the fiesta tonight?"

"Okay... sure." The Americanism was tossed off in English, in tandem with a carefully noncommittal shrug. Julie smiled, said, *"Gracias,"* then added, *"Hasta luego,"* and left Linda standing on the beach, huddled against the wind, a defiant and oddly touching figure.

As she plodded back around the bay, Julie had more to think about than the sand in her huaraches. It was that phrase— *sleeping demon*. Linda was right. The last thing she needed was to wake up that particular demon! She shared a bed with him. How could she hope to slip away tonight without waking him? With his panther's body, his predator's reflexes, he was sure to be a light sleeper. Unless...

The thought brought a flush to her cheeks and a hollow feeling to her middle. Unless she could insure that his guard would be down, that he would be completely relaxed...that he would sleep as if drugged. And without access to drugs, she knew of only one way to do that: She would have to seduce the demon.

Chapter 5

"*¿Señor Chayne es mucho hombre, no?*"

Julie felt a nudge in her ribs and looked up to find Linda lounging against a post, smiling lazily through the familiar curtain of smoke. She shrugged a noncommittal reply, but her eyes were pulled as if by a powerful magnet back to the scene on the beach.

The fishermen had returned, heralded by a flock of screeching seabirds. From the ramada, the open-sided shelter that was both communal dining room and kitchen, the women were watching them bring the boats in and beach them, and unload the catch.

He looks more like a pirate than a smuggler, Julie thought.

Like the others, Chayne wore only tattered jeans rolled to the knee. A red scarf had been tied around his head Indian-style, serving to keep both hair and sweat out of his eyes as he worked. Sweat and spray had given his body a metallic sheen, like a tarnished statue of a Greek hero.

Pirate, or tarnished hero? Make up your mind, Julie....

But no statue could possibly capture the sheer power, the wild and savage grace, of that body. Its pulse-quickening beauty was in its characteristic fluidity and economy of motion—

bending, stooping, leaping over the bow, thigh muscles bunching, straining faded denim as they braced against the pull of the heavy boat. If those back and shoulder muscles were cast in bronze, it must be molten still.

There went her stomach again! What was the matter with her?

That awful hollow void yawned inside her whenever she thought about what she intended to do tonight. She told herself over and over that it was just another assignment: escape. A very simple plan, really. No big deal at all. She'd handled more complicated operations. All she had to do was fill up El Demonio with lobster and *cerveza* and take him to bed. Afterward he would sleep like a log, and she would be free to slip away to the boats. Easy as pie.

Sure.

Who was she kidding? She hadn't the least idea how to go about seducing a man; she didn't even know whether she could. And what did she know about men, anyway? *Did* sex make men sleepy? What if...what if she couldn't get him to make love to her? She already had his personal assurance that she was not irresistible! Oh God, what if she couldn't?

She watched in awe as Chayne shouldered a two-hundred-pound grouper, bowing his back while the grizzled and stoic Sebastien helped Pepe and Geraldo steady the load, then strode steadily up the beach toward the shelter amid shouts of encouragement and some good-natured teasing. She bit back a tiny whimper of desperation.

What in heaven's name ever made me think I could?

He was...El Demonio Garzo.

No. Far worse than any demon, he was, as Linda kept pointing out, *mucho hombre*. It never sounded quite right in English, but in any language Chayne Younger *was* a lot of man. And Julie knew at last that Colin was right: she was afraid of men. Afraid, at least, of the kind of raw masculinity Chayne Younger radiated.

She had to do it. She had to just think of it as a tough assignment. She'd been afraid before, and it had never stopped her from doing what she had to do.

But it wasn't just that she was afraid. She really didn't know how to go about deliberately enticing a man. She had spent her entire adult life suppressing her femininity, becoming just another agent—one of the guys. The affair with Colin was something she had just . . . drifted into, almost without realizing it. He was older; he made her feel safe. Once upon a time, long, long ago, before that jerk Carl Swensen, she had known how to flirt. It had come naturally to her, as it would to any pretty teenager blessed with bouncy blond hair and big brown eyes. But that had been another life, a different Julie. . . .

A husky gurgle of laughter drew her gaze back to where Linda lounged against one of the posts that supported the ramada's thatched roof. Linda, she was sure, would know exactly what to do. There was an aura of sensuality about her that was as tangible as steam. It was just *there*, in the lines of her body, the curve of her mouth, in the sleepy, sooty eyes. She seemed to adopt those suggestive poses without conscious thought, and although Julie realized that some of them—the undulating walk, the revealing clothes—were just the tricks of her trade, so to speak, Julie was aware that what Linda had went much deeper than that. She had tried to put a name to it— awareness, confidence. Whatever it was, it was probably innate. She doubted very much that it could be taught.

Julie drew in her breath in a soft sigh. Confidence—that was what she needed. Maybe she was the one who should tank up with *cerveza!*

She couldn't, of course, even if she really believed that beer could make her any less scared. She needed all her wits for this campaign. But the thought did give her an idea; it might not be a bad idea to *appear* to drink too much. It would help make her sudden change in attitude more believable!

Believable. There was a word! Could it be applied to any of this? She had just spent the better part of the day coldly plotting to get a terrorist to make love to her! Surely it would make a lot more sense to begin right this minute to get roaring, stinking, obliviously *drunk!*

She had spent the day making plans, laying the groundwork for her escape. After leaving Linda on the beach, she had gone back to the camper, taking advantage of the men's absence to complete a thorough search of the vehicle, inside and out. The search had failed to turn up anything useful except for the bra she had stuffed into the crack in the booth the day before. She had used the last of the water in the tanks for a tepid wash, scrubbing her underwear clean with a sliver of hand soap.

In the early afternoon hunger had driven her back to Rita's adobe. She felt a certain reluctance to face Rita again after that morning, but she still had to learn where the food and water were stored, and make provisions for securing supplies for her voyage. She had no way of knowing how long she might be at sea.

The hut was empty, but the sound of voices led her to the long, thatched-roofed cooking shelter. There she found Rita standing before one of the wooden tables, up to her elbows in flour and cornmeal, making tortillas. Beside her, her thick coronet of salt-and-pepper braids barely reaching the younger woman's shoulder, stood a tiny round woman with a flat, seamed face, sun-bronzed to the color of adobe clay. The two pairs of floury hands flew, making a dry, slapping rhythm that was punctuated but not interrupted by the laughter and conversation that erupted sporadically.

The busy hands had not paused at Julie's arrival, either—not until the tortillas in progress had achieved the desired thinness and been transferred to the growing pile on the table. Then Rita had filled a plate with cold fish smothered in green chile salsa ladled from a large pot simmering on an open fire, and in a cool, pleasant voice had introduced her to Sebastien's wife, Juanita. Then Rita had gone to stir the pot of pinto beans bubbling aromatically on the fire, giving Julie a look of puzzled compassion that made her feel obscurely guilty.

Old Juanita's eyes had been sharp and shrewd. She had studied Julie with that frank appraisal bordering on rudeness that is the privilege of the very young and the very old. Later, in silence and with infinite patience, she had taught her how to make the cornmeal tortillas that, along with the deceptively simple and delicious frijoles refritas, were the staple of every meal.

As her hands struggled with the rapid motions that, properly executed, would turn a blob of cornmeal paste into a perfectly round and uniformly thin pancake, Julie's eyes roamed the shelter, cataloging the galvanized washtub draped with wet gunnysacks, which was the beer cooler, the airtight plastic barrels that held dry staples, the collection of cooking imple-

ments hanging from nails in the rafters. She hoped to find a
knife, anything that could be used as a weapon, but the closest
thing she could see was a soup ladle that might be employed as
a club. These men would not be so careless, but old habits were
hard to break.

By the time the last tortilla had been placed on the stack on
the table, Julie's arms were aching and Linda still had not put
in an appearance. It didn't surprise Julie that the girl would
manage to avoid the cookshed—it was hard to imagine that
sultry, indolent creature immersed in domesticity—but she really did need to find her if she was going to take her up on her
offer of a more alluring costume. She hated to ask directions
from Rita, knowing how she felt about the other woman, so she
brushed cornmeal from her arms and lap and went in search of
Pepe's cabin.

It wasn't hard to find. Except for Geraldo's cabin, which she
already knew, and the larger and more permanent adobe surrounded by animal shelters and derelict machinery that the old
people shared, it was the only hut with an air of occupancy. She
had found Linda sprawled on a rumpled bed, painting her
nails, squinting through the trail of smoke that snaked upward
from a dangling cigarette.

"So, *gringa* . . ." the girl had drawled, slowly waving her
blood-red fingertips. "I suppose you have come for the
clothes." She blew on her nails, watching Julie from under
straight black lashes. "It takes more than clothes to make a
man wake up and look at you. You don't walk like a woman—
you don't even use your eyes! How you ever made a living I
don't know. No wonder you're so skinny, even for a *gringa!*"

"*You* offered me some clothes," Julie retorted, then added
in bold challenge, "What's the matter? Don't you think you
can work miracles?"

Linda laughed, a husky chortle of approval, and examined
her with mixed skepticism and interest. "Well...you sure don't
have much to work with, but I will see what I can do. Pay attention to me, *gringa,* and I can tell you—El Demonio will not
sleep tonight!"

Julie had smiled, hoping the sudden flip-flop her stomach
had executed did not show in her face. The last thing she
wanted tonight was a wakeful demon!

As the men drew nearer Julie was beset by shyness and uncertainty, a confusing morass of feelings and fears that engulfed her like a thick, impenetrable fog. Outwardly she knew she must appear to the others as just a woman waiting for her man, full of that particular tension and anticipation that was the natural distillation of shared intimacy. It was acknowledged and accepted that Chayne Younger was her man—or, more accurately in this man's world, that she was his woman. Only she and Chayne knew that they were not lovers. He was still a stranger to her in every way, a complete enigma. But whatever else he was, he was certainly a dangerous, even deadly, man. She was afraid of him. And even more, she was in awe of him, which was something she had never said of anyone else in the world. And it didn't help at all that he was the most attractive man she had ever met. Just his presence was enough to turn her wits to wool and her will to gelatin. When he was near her, she didn't even recognize herself!

And that, she realized suddenly, was what frightened her so much: that she might be igniting something in herself that she wouldn't be able to reconcile or control. That she, Julie Maguire, was about to find herself holding a tiger by the tail. A tiger... or a panther.

Or a demon.

Julie hung back, waiting in the shadows, watching the other women for her cue. She had become part of a primitive society, as if she had been dropped in a time machine and hurled backward uncounted centuries. How did one behave toward returning "hunter-providers"? She was as nervous as any bride. What would she say to him? She hadn't spoken to him since that morning, and it seemed much longer—a lifetime. So much had happened since he had walked out of the hut, wishing her a good day and calling her Blondie. Her knowledge of his activities, her own plan to escape—they had all made things different, somehow. It was hard to believe. . . . She had to keep reminding herself of the incredible fact that she had shared his bed last night. That only last night he had kissed her...touched her intimately . . . branded her with his mouth.

Her stomach recoiled, and she lifted trembling fingers to the purple mark plainly visible just above the edge of the neckline of her borrowed red tank top. It had earned a low whistle and smile from Linda, who treated her with more respect from then on. The girl had also expressed admiration for Julie's long, well-muscled legs, and had insisted that she show them to advantage by wearing shorts. Of course the skimpy black garment, which hugged Linda's curves like a second skin, draped over Julie's tautly muscled derriere "like the robes of a nun!" But Linda had agreed grudgingly that the woven belt made her waist look impossibly tiny, and the tank top did mold and define her high, round breasts. And, of course, it showed off that mark. . . .

And now fear had given her skin a satiny sheen of perspiration and brought her nipples into sharp relief under the scarlet jersey. Julie thought wryly that if she didn't look sexy now, she never would!

At first, though, it seemed to Julie that she might have saved herself the effort because, along with the other women, she was completely ignored. The men carried in the enormous fish and deposited it on one of the long wooden tables. The grouper had already been cleaned and the offal thrown to the scavenging seabirds; now Sebastien was left to cut it into fillets while the younger men returned to the boats for the lobsters, which would be kept alive in tubs of seawater for tomorrow's dinner. The little boy Carlos darted about under the feet of the men, and the women hurried to lay the table and prepare the heavy iron skillets.

Once the catch had been secured and turned over to the women, the men trooped back down the beach once more to scrub the fish stink and salt film from their bodies in the quiet waters of the bay.

The wind had dropped; the air was warm and moist and very still. The sun was setting behind the mountains at their backs; off across the violet water the islands had already disappeared in the haze of approaching night. Julie watched in bemusement as the men, even old Sebastien, splashed and cavorted in the water like schoolboys, the last coppery rays of the sun turning the moisture on their bodies to fire.

And behind her in the cookshed the women went quietly and efficiently about their work by the light of cooking fires and lamps.

My God, Julie thought. This is the twentieth century! And I
am a woman of my time. I know that I'm the equal of any man.
I do a man's job as well as a man could. Yet this could be the
Stone Age. How do they tolerate this? And why... why don't
I hate it more than I do?

For the truth was, Julie found it oddly comforting. She supposed there must be a kind of security in knowing what was
expected of you—in having no doubts about the roles of *male*
and *female*. It might be prehistoric, and she would certainly
grow to resent it, just as she had resented the subservient role
she had been forced to play last night at supper. But somehow...for tonight, for this time and in this place...it was right.
Even, in a primitive way, exciting....

As if at some prearranged signal, Juanita moved ponder-
ously to a big iron bell mounted on a post just outside the ramada and gave the clapper several firm tugs. The men came
back up the beach through the deepening twilight, laughing
softly and shaking water from their hair. Rita and Linda began to heap food onto waiting plates, and Julie took the pile of
towels Juanita silently handed her and went to stand beneath
the gently swaying lantern at the entrance to the shelter.

Now an odd constraint came over the men. The lines divid-
ing the realms of male and female cut both ways. These strong,
intensely macho men might be the acknowledged lords and
masters of this tiny universe, but the kitchen was the women's
domain, and the men were inclined to tread softly in it. Julie
received a polite and respectful *"Gracias"* from each one for
the towel she offered, as did Rita and Juanita for each heaping
plate, and Linda for each beer she served. The men ate with
quiet concentration, talking among themselves of the wind and
the tides and the day's fishing. Except for those murmured
"Thank yous," they ignored their women, as Chayne and
Geraldo had ignored Rita the night before. And as Rita had
done, the women moved like shadows among them, anticipating their needs and silently providing. And only when their
menfolk were replete, pushing aside empty plates to reach for
a fresh can of *cerveza*, only then did Juanita fill her own plate
and indicate that the rest of them might do the same. Even
then, as they took their plates and retired to a shadowed table,
their ears were still alert for a call from their masters.

Julie found it impossible to eat anyway. As she chewed mechanically on what might as well have been sawdust, she found it impossible, too, to keep her eye from Chayne Younger. The image of his body, golden planes and dusky hollows rippling in the lantern light, seemed permanently etched on her retinas. Her gaze kept returning to those scars, constant reminders of violence that made an especially disturbing contrast to the hand that rested so gently on a small boy's knee. . . .

Carlito, being a male child, had taken his rightful place with the men. He sat on the tabletop between his father and Chayne, swinging his feet as he showed off the shells he had found that day. Each was a treasure proudly offered up on a small, grubby palm, and Chayne examined them all with the solemn concentration of a diamond broker.

Julie forgot to chew. Her eyes feasted on Chayne, on the lines of his neck and the way the dark hair curled on the nape of it, on the shadowed curve of his jaw, and on his mouth, relaxed and unexpectedly gentle. . . .

And then he looked up, straight into her eyes.

Julie was devastated. Her throat closed, and she couldn't breathe. Her skin felt hot—she was suffocating. And still she couldn't break that contact. Her heart thundered in her ears, blocking out all other sound. Her perspective seemed to be shrinking, narrowing down to those twin beams of blue fire.

Somewhere, in a class on criminal psychology, probably, Julie remembered reading about the meaning and significance of direct eye contact. She knew it was a potent thing. Only modern, civilized man places a value on it and uses it as a measure of a man's character. Animals and primitive people consider a direct stare a threat; some use it to establish dominance. And among some species a direct look alone is grounds for immediate attack. In her own experience she knew that exchanging a mutual stare, even with a close friend or family member, could be intense to the point of discomfort. Even in the most ordinary of circumstances, and with ordinary eyes. Here, with *those* eyes . . .

And then, abruptly, she was released. Chayne's eyes dropped, focused instead on a lower point, on the small purple mark that spoiled the creamy silk of her breast just where its gentle roundness began. And only then did Julie realize that her fingers were touching that brand, that her heart was knocking against them with a slow, drumlike cadence. Chayne's lips curved in a sardonic little smile.

The dying fire settled in on itself with a crackling hiss and a shower of sparks. As if at a signal, the men rose and stretched and rubbed full bellies and moved closer to its warmth. And now, relaxed and mellow, the necessities of life satisfied, they called their womenfolk to them. It was time to look to the fulfillment of more abstract needs.

The old people murmured their good-nights and faded into the night. Geraldo settled himself with his son in his lap and his wife at his knee. At a command from Pepe, Linda produced a guitar, which he took and embraced with the tenderness of a lover, cradling it to his naked chest as he tuned it. Then he struck several chords, rich and heavy as the night air, and throwing back his head, tossed a laughing challenge at Linda.

Pepe had a broad, handsome face, with thick, heavy hair and a moustache that accented the sensuality of his mouth. His eyes could be cruel and cold, but now they were only dusky shadows. His teeth shone white as he picked out the first notes of a folk dance and then cleverly turned the rhythms and harmonies to a more modern beat. Linda, responding to the game and the mood, struck a dramatic flamenco pose and then launched into a parody of an exotic dance that was straight out of a Tijuana strip joint. The girl was not a professional dancer, and her body lacked flexibility and grace, but she had that instinctive sexual magnetism that in these circumstances was as pervasive and discomfiting as smoke.

Geraldo's laughter held a touch of embarrassment, but he began to clap in time to the music. Chayne stood at the edge of the firelight, his arms crossed on his chest, watching with lazy amusement. Julie had moved to stand beside and a little behind him, not quite certain what he would expect of her, not sure what to do next. Everything—the fire, the song, the dance, even the air, heavy and cloying—seemed to conspire to aid her in her planned seduction. But far from feeling in control of events, she felt like a novice on roller skates, off-balance and in imminent danger of a painful tumble.

Chayne spoke softly. She gave a violent start and whispered, "What? I'm sorry...."

It was the first time he had spoken to her since that morning, and the sound of his voice rasped across raw nerves, raising the hairs on the back of her neck. Belatedly remembering that she was supposed to appear to be getting drunk, she took a hasty and ill-advised gulp of beer and erupted in a fit of desperate coughing.

In the midst of her distress she felt Chayne's hands on her waist holding her through the paroxysms. When she had regained a measure of control, he drew her back against his chest and crossed his arms over her breasts. She felt his body jerk with silent laughter. Bending to nuzzle the hollow of her neck, he whispered, "Easy, *Güerita* . . . don't overdo it!"

Still winded by her bout of choking, Julie couldn't have answered anyway. She brought her hands up to cling to the brawny arms across her breasts, sure that without their support her legs would not have held her up. She was completely surrounded by heated, hair-roughened man; he filled all her senses—the unique male scent of him in her nostrils; the sound of his heart reverberating in her ears; silky-crisp hair prickling her naked back; blue denim and sinew chafing the backs of her thighs. He was all around her; in another moment she would be absorbed. . . .

"Hey! *Güerita!*"

Julie stiffened and opened her eyes. The nickname, which she had almost grown to like when it was spoken in Chayne's deep drawl, seemed crude and vulgar on Pepe's lips.

"Come on, Blondie—let's see what you can do. Your turn to dance for us, eh?"

Licking her lips in panic, Julie looked around the half circle of faces like a trapped animal. They were all watching her, Linda waiting expectantly, chest heaving, a sheen of sweat on her body and a devilish gleam in her eyes. Pepe's eyes were hot, his mouth cruel; Geraldo's face held heavy-lidded amusement. Only Rita looked across the head of her sleeping child with dark compassionate eyes. Rita—her only ally. She couldn't see Chayne's face, but surely he would be the first to find enjoyment in her humiliation. How they would all relish reducing their captive cop to such a state!

"*. . . There's nothing quite as entertaining as an embarrassed cop. . . .*"

Julie tightened her grip on Chayne's arms, silently pleading. To her relief and astonishment, his voice rumbled up through his chest and out over her head.

"Sorry, my friends. I don't share my women. This little blond one dances for me alone!"

There was laughter, and some good-natured cajoling, but the steel bands across her chest held tight. Julie knew that she had never felt safer and more protected in her life than she did at that moment, in the circle of those arms, and the thought filled her with confusion and despair. They were demon's arms! Coyote's arms. He was a terrorist, a smuggler, a pirate, a criminal.... Oh, Julie...

Pepe shrugged, accepting defeat, and held out the guitar. "Okay, my friend, *you* play now. I want to play another instrument!" He caught Linda around the knees and tumbled her, laughing and squealing, into his lap. He buried his face against her neck, his hands roaming freely and lasciviously over her voluptuous body. Julie closed her eyes on the uncomfortable sight.

Chayne had released her to take the guitar; now he settled himself on the ground near the dying coals, his back against a post, and drew her down and back into the circle of his arms. He placed the guitar across her chest and leaned his head forward so that his lips were just above her ear. With the first soft chords her head fell backward of its own volition to rest in the warm hollow of his neck.

The night was warm; the wind, which had picked up again, made a lonely, sighing sound in the thatched roof overhead, and the dying fire hissed softly. Chayne's fingers stroked and caressed the strings of the Spanish guitar, making music that seemed a part of the night. At first, while he played old Spanish love ballads, Rita and Geraldo sang along, smiling at each other across the head of their son. When he switched to American folk songs, they hummed softly, nodding now and then over a tune they recognized. At some point Pepe and Linda slipped quietly away. Julie relaxed, lulled by the night and the music and the strange, exotic drug that was Chayne Younger's nearness....

He had been playing the song for some time before she recognized it. Only when he began to whistle the melody, stirring the fine hair on her temple, did she remember the words:

> *Send me a letter,*
> *Send it by mail;*
> *Send it in care of*
> *The Birmingham Jail....*

A chuckle rumbled through Chayne's chest. He set the guitar aside, and Julie reluctantly opened her eyes. Rita and Geraldo had taken their son home to bed. She and Chayne were alone.

The spell was broken. Chayne murmured, "Game's over, *Güerita*—I guess we can go home now," and took her by the arms, easing her away from him. Her back felt chilled where the night wind cooled the perspiration from the conjunction of their bodies. Chayne stretched until his joints popped, then got to his feet and pulled Julie up beside him. Looking down at her through veiled eyes, he drawled, "You did a nice job tonight, for a cop."

Julie bristled automatically and snapped, "Thanks a bunch!" And then she remembered that it was not in her best interests to quarrel with him, and lowered her lashes and murmured, "I'm a fast learner."

"Uh-huh," Chayne said sardonically. "Looks like you've had a few lessons, too."

"What? Oh . . . you mean the clothes." She knew very well what he meant. His eyes were fastened on the place where the soft mounds of her breasts disappeared beneath the clinging fabric. An insidious glow of pleasure blossomed in her chest at the frank admiration on his face, and she shrugged, aware that the gesture would deepen the neckline of the tank top. "Well, Linda was kind enough to offer, and I thought, since I was playing the part . . . Do you like it?"

"It is . . . effective," Chayne said dryly. He moved away from her to pick up the last remaining lantern.

Julie licked her lips and said unsteadily, "Chayne . . ."

He turned, eyebrows raised. "Yes?"

"Do you...are you quite sure we aren't being... watched?"

He was silent for a moment, a quizzical tilt to his mouth. "Why?"

Julie gave another shrug and looked away. Her mouth was so dry—her voice sounded hoarse to her own ears. "Oh...I just wondered if it was safe to stop the playacting until we get back to our—to the hut. Shouldn't we play this out a little longer? Just in case anyone—What if Geraldo came back?"

"Just in case," Chayne said, nodding thoughtfully. "How do we play, Julie Maguire? Like this?" He snaked an arm around her neck and drew her hard against his side. She looked up at him, half-fearful, but his face was hidden in shadow.

"Uh...sure. That...that's fine," she gulped.

"Or is this more than you had in mind?"

The growl in his voice warned her. She gave a faint gasp as he pulled her roughly against him, his mouth coming down to cover hers fiercely, almost angrily. When she gave a tiny sigh and parted her lips, he seemed surprised. He hesitated a moment and drew back a little, and then he gave a throaty growl and found her mouth with a new and deeper union. His tongue flicked at the soft insides of her lips and then thrust deep, a savage penetration almost as shocking as the more intimate one it simulated. Heat shot through her, shattering her reserves and pretenses, tearing a permanent, ragged hole in her pride and self-esteem and settling deep in the core of her body, an aching pool of longing and desire. She answered his primal sound with one of her own—a sound she could never have imagined coming from her own throat—and then gave herself up to him.

She felt his fingers rake through her hair and encase her head, holding it still for the hungry thrusts of his tongue; then she felt his arms shift and his hand press hard on the base of her spine, urging her lower body against the raw desire in his. A tormented whimper escaped from her throat, and she arched convulsively into him as jagged bolts of sensation shot through her body.

And then, somehow, his hands were hard on her arms and her body was left cold and bereft. She stared up at him with eyes that wouldn't focus.

"Was that what you had in mind?" Chayne rasped harshly, breathing like a long-distance runner. "Is that what you wanted?"

Julie could only stare at him, still too shocked to speak. After a moment he touched her moist, swollen lips with his thumb, and said with more control, "You're full of surprises, Julie Maguire. . . ."

He gave a snort of astonishment and tucked her into the curve of his arm, secure against his side. Once more he picked up the lantern, and said dryly, "Just in case anyone's watching. And *now* we're going home!"

It seemed miles through the darkness to the lonely adobe he had called home. And when the door had creaked shut behind them, isolating them in that tiny pool of lantern light, Julie couldn't imagine how they had gotten there so quickly.

While Chayne moved to hang the lantern on its nail in the ceiling beam, Julie stood with her back to him, arms crossed and head bowed, rubbing absently at her upper arms. The silence grew and became ominous. She was acutely conscious of the vulnerability of the nape of her neck; she could almost feel the fine hairs there lift and stir. When at last the tension was broken by the click and hiss of a cigarette lighter, it was almost a relief to turn and face him.

Chayne was half sitting on the windowsill, legs outstretched, arms crossed on his naked chest, squinting at her through smoke. She could see the ice blue glitter of his eyes beneath heavy dark brows. She decided to outwait him and lifted her chin in a silent gesture of challenge.

"All right, Julie," he said, with an exasperated sigh, "now that it's just us—would you mind telling me what the hell you think you're up to?"

Chapter 6

Julie held her breath, afraid even to breathe lest it be the wrong thing to do.

What should she say? Oh God, what should she do now?

She had to convince him that she truly wanted to change the rules of the game they were playing. She had to convince him *now*. But if she said the wrong thing...

He'd said it would be up to her. He'd said she was pretty, and that he'd been a long time without a woman. And he hadn't seemed to mind kissing her. But he was no fool. She had been so afraid of him before; would he ever believe an about-face now? She'd have to be very careful not to make him suspicious....

She licked her lips and began, "I don't—" only to be cut off.

"Those clothes, for starters." His eyes raked down her body, and he made an impatient gesture with the hand that held the cigarette. "Why this cheap trampy stuff?"

Julie stared at him in genuine astonishment. She made a small noise of exasperation and shook her head. "Cheap? *Trampy?* You know, I really don't understand you. If the role you've put me in isn't cheap and trampy, I don't know what is. And it's not exactly something I have experience in. Linda

seemed to think what I was wearing was ... that it lacked ..."
She let her voice trail off, smiled ruefully and looked at him
from under her lashes. She lifted one shoulder in a shrug and
just managed to drop one strap of the tank top over the edge of
her shoulder. "I just thought that for the sake of credibility I
should try to look the part."

Chayne snorted and drew on his cigarette, muttering something unintelligible through his hand. And then harshly, almost angrily, he said, "Playacting's one thing. What was that
all about back there just now? Just what in the hell did you
think you were doing?"

"What *I* was doing? You—"

He snapped the cigarette to the floor and crushed it with his
foot in a gesture of restrained savagery. "I have pretty damn
good self-control, but I'm not *dead!* You wanted me to kiss
you! *Didn't you?*" Julie's mouth had gone dry and she couldn't
answer. "You wanted—*asked*—for it! *Didn't you?*"

Riveted by his eyes, Julie nodded.

"Answer me, damn it!"

"Yes," she whispered. "I ... wanted you to kiss me."

"Why?"

She shrugged helplessly and turned her back on him. His
voice came quietly, brushing across the back of her neck like a
physical touch. "I can't figure out whether you're the world's
biggest tease or just dumb, but for someone who was scared
witless at the thought of sleeping in the same bed with me, you
are walking on dangerous ground."

Julie took a couple of aimless, unsteady steps away from
him. In the confined space of the hut there was no room for
pacing, and her movements took her to the edge of the bed. She
stood hugging herself and rubbing her arms, and after a moment she heard herself say softly, "I ... didn't really sleep much
last night."

"What?"

She cleared her throat and repeated it, just a little louder. "I
said, I didn't sleep last night."

He made a dry sound, an expulsion of breath that could have
been frustration, disbelief, astonishment or all three. She
turned to face him and found his eyes burning with that de-
monic fire. She withstood the gaze unflinchingly, and after a

moment he drew a hand over his face; it made a dry, whispery sound on his day's growth of beard. "Julie . . . what are you telling me? You must know that you are a very tempting morsel, and I am a hungry man. The way I feel right now, if we share that bed tonight, it won't be to sleep! Are you trying to tell me that's what you want?"

Julie had a strange sensation of floating; her bones were hollow, weightless. He hadn't moved, but she seemed to be moving toward him, impelled by some magnetic force outside her control. He watched her come, his face dark and unreadable, then slowly uncrossed his outstretched feet and guided her between them, drawing her close, so that she could reach out and touch the warm resilient bulges of his pectoral muscles with her fingertips. She trailed the sensitive pads of her fingers across one smooth, walnut mound to the darker, rougher furring of hair around a flat brown nipple and traced its circumference. There was a sharp hiss of indrawn breath, and his fingers snatched at her wrist, imprisoning it, holding her hand away from his body.

She opened her mouth to protest, but he gave his head a violent shake and grated, "*No.* I don't buy it." His hand closed like a trap on the back of her neck and exerted a slow, steady pressure. The fingers on her wrist eased, his thumb teasing into her palm, opening her clenched fingers like the petals of a flower. He stared at the hand with hooded eyes and murmured thoughtfully, "You know, *Güerita* . . . I can't decide whether you're just a foolish little girl playing with fire . . . or a much tougher and smarter cop than I gave you credit for. But you know, I'm damned . . ." He slowly raised her hand, stroking his thumb in the hollow of her palm, a lazy, circling motion. " . . . If I don't think . . ." He pressed her palm to his lips and let his tongue assume that delicate torture. . . . "I'm going to find out!"

The trembling began then, but it wasn't fear. That slow, sensuous laving of the nerve endings in her palm touched nerves in points of her body she would never have imagined could explode with such exquisite agony—sharp bursts like sky rockets that melted into sweet, shimmering desire. She closed her eyes and swayed, and his thighs closed tightly on hers.

Just when she thought she would not be able to stand it any longer, when she knew that she was about to whimper with frustrated desire, he slowly withdrew her hand and laid it, open and moist, against his chest. "Convince me, Julie...," he whispered. "Show me who you are: woman... or *cop!*"

Beneath her palm she felt a steady drumming that matched the thunder in her own ears. Her body throbbed to that primitive cadence, pulsing with life-forces too elemental to be questioned or denied. She swallowed cotton and muttered huskily, "I can't... think."

He gave a low chuckle. "Good... I guess that's strike one against the cop." His forefinger traced the skin of her chest along the line of the tank top. When it reached the purple mark he had left there it dipped inside and pulled, slowly easing the material down over the pale hemisphere of her breast. His eyes feasted on the smooth perfection of it as his finger traced its silken underside and his thumb drew tiny circles around its taut rosebud nipple. Her breathing accelerated, making her breast rise and fall beneath his hand. She opened her eyes and focused them on his mouth, staring at it, wanting it *there*.... Her hand crept upward over his collarbone, curved over the vibrant warmth of his neck.

"Please..."

"What, Julie? Tell me."

"I... want..."

"What is it you want?"

The hand on her neck slid down to press firmly against her back; the hand on her breast cradled it while his head came forward to meet it. He touched the rosy tip with his tongue, eliciting a gasp of shock and breathless anticipation, then began gentle, encircling strokes that she felt pulling at the deepest part of her body. *"I want..."*

His mouth opened, lowered with tormenting slowness over that tender peak, closed on it at last and began a gentle, drawing pressure that pulled and tugged at that other place deep within her.

Relief flooded her, relief so acute that she was laughing and crying at the same time. "I want *you*... I want you!"

He drew back to look into her eyes. She tightened her fingers convulsively on the back of his neck. "Do you, Julie? You, a cop, want *me*, a criminal?"

Still laughing and crying, shaking with frustration and desire, she cried, "*No!* Not a cop! Not a cop... just a woman. I want you, Chayne. I don't care what you are... I need you!"

"Strike two," he said softly. His hand slipped down her spine, stopping at the cleft between her buttocks. He pressed her hard into the V of his legs, grinding the sensitive mound of her femininity sharply against the part of him that fit it best. She gave a startled cry, and he responded with a chuckle of triumph. "*Yeah*... that's right, Julie. That's what you're asking for. Better be sure you mean it. No games...no playacting. I'm going to make love to you, *Güerita*."

"I doubt... love has anything to do with this," Julie said breathlessly, burrowing her fingers through the hair on the back of his head. "But it *is* what I want. You believe me, don't you?"

His hands were on her hips, guiding her pelvis in slow, grinding movements against his. His eyes were hooded, smoky with passion. "Close enough..."

"Then... shouldn't that be... strike three?"

He laughed softly, sliding his hands up across her ribs, hooking his fingers in the stretchy jersey of her shirt and tugging it down. Julie untangled her fingers from his hair and drew her arms out of the straps, and he rolled the scarlet material down to her hips.

"Strike three?" he murmured absently. He lifted his hands and placed one over each breast, gently kneading. Her small breasts were completely covered by his hands; he seemed fascinated by the contrast of his darkly tanned fingers splayed across the creamy ivory of her skin. "Oh, no... not yet. Your lips tell me you're a woman, but lips can lie. Bodies don't lie. What will your body tell me?"

Julie shuddered and closed her eyes, arching her back, pushing her aching breasts into his hands. She was still trembling, but a strange calm had settled over her. She had long ago shut off her mind, so she could not think of such abstracts as right and wrong, good and bad, love and hate. There was only the solid reality of his body and hers, male and female, and the desperate need that cried out through every nerve, fiber and sinew of her body.

Under his hands her nipples shivered and pulled hard and tight. He rubbed his palms across them, chafing them intolerably, and she cried out in distress. He uncovered and kissed each one and then whispered, "Do they hurt, Julie? Do you see now what I mean?"

Julie mumbled, "What?" and swayed toward him. She felt groggy...drunk. His hands molded her body, curving over the roundness of her bottom and down the backs of her thighs, then back up again, discovering that the legs of the borrowed shorts were wide enough to allow him access to the warm, resilient flesh beneath. As his big hands reached inside the shorts to grasp and knead her buttocks, he straightened and stood up, arching above her, his mouth descending to cover hers, its heat like a brand on her lips. His hands lifted her up and into his body; her hands clung desperately to his shoulders and then found better support at the back of his neck. Naked chests touched and melded. Her breasts were flattened against hard muscle; his hair rubbed sensitized nipples and set them afire. Her mouth opened, and she welcomed the deep thrusts of his tongue with a fierce, primal growl. There was hunger in the sound, and triumph, too; she could feel the trembling in his muscles, feel the urgency of his passion hard against her.

It couldn't go on forever. Julie tore her mouth away and buried her face in his chest. *"Please..."* Her breath sobbed through her in violent shudders. "Please...I want you...."

He was as winded as she was, but his voice held a touch of wry amusement. "I want you, too, believe me, *Güerita*...but there is the small matter of clothing to be dispensed with.... Hold on a minute. *There*."

He released her long enough to unbutton his jeans, then drew her hands from his neck and guided them to his hips. Julie slipped her hands inside the waistband and over the bones of his hips, lifting her face to nuzzle the warm hollow of his neck, licking the beard-roughened skin under his jaw, marveling at the unexpected silkiness of the skin beneath her hands. Very, very slowly she curved her hands over his hard, masculine buttocks, easing blue denim out of the way.

"The lantern..." she murmured against the pulse at the base of his throat.

"No!" His voice was rough. "I want to see you. No hiding in the dark. I want to see all of you, Julie Maguire...every sweet, sexy inch of you. I've imagined you long enough! I want to watch your skin turn pink and moist with desire. I want to watch your face while I make love to you...."

"Not love..."

"Don't quibble!"

There was an urgency in his movements as he jerked her clothing, all of it, down and off and then stood back to let his gaze sweep her nakedness. His eyes glittered; they seared a trail across her small, sculpted breasts and down, down over the rippling pattern of her abdominal muscles, the smooth, taut skin of her belly with its fine tracing of blue veins, to rest with undisguised hunger on curls of golden brown.

Julie sucked in her breath and stood very still, awed by the look in his eyes. *I am a hungry man....* It frightened her, but it excited her, too. There was a throbbing pressure between her thighs and a vast ache in the depths of her belly. She began to tremble again. Her body was cold; she needed...

"Chayne..." she whispered, pleading.

"Come to me, Julie."

She gave a little sigh and walked into his arms. He scooped her up, held her for a moment while he grafted her to him with a look of scorching intensity, and then laid her on the bed. He lowered himself slowly over her, keeping himself braced on his arms. The taut cords in his neck, the pulse that throbbed in a vein in his temple, the deep lines and rigid planes of his face betrayed strain, but he managed a stiff, rueful smile.

"Julie...you deserve to be pleasured all night long, but I...I am fresh out of self-control. I'm sorry...I hope you're ready for me...."

Julie looked up into the dark face poised above her and felt a pang of fear. Her eyes swept down past his hair-crested chest, and she couldn't restrain a sharp gasp. But it wasn't his overwhelming masculinity that caused that spasm of reflexive fear—it was the jagged weal that slashed across the wall of his belly. That terrible scar...

Jerking her gaze back to his face, Julie saw that his eyes had gone cold and hard, and his mouth had tightened in a grim line that etched the grooves of strain in his cheeks. A wave of inexplicable and unexpected compassion swept away her fear. She reached up to touch his face, letting her small hands rest along his jaws, her thumbs smoothing the lines around his mouth. She didn't trust herself to speak, but she gave him a tremulous smile and opened to him, angling her body instinctively to meet his.

But the penetration wasn't easy. The shock of it drove a sharp involuntary cry from her throat.

Chayne froze and jerked his eyes to her face. "I thought you said—"

"I'm *not!* It's just . . . I'm not very . . ."

A muscle twitched at the corner of his mouth. His eyes were shadowed, unreadable. "Not very experienced," he said gently. "You should have told me. I'll try not to hurt you again."

"You didn't. It was just . . ."

"I know," he said softly.

"I'm sorry. I hope I didn't—"

"Julie . . . hush."

Slowly, slowly he filled her, and then was still. Julie gave a deep sigh and felt the tension in her melt, her body turn to liquid, honeyed and sweet. She felt the warmth of him deep within her, completing her, and moved against him.

"Shhh . . . be still." His body exerted a gentle pressure, holding her motionless. His moustache brushed her lips, and the tip of his tongue traced their outline. He licked her parted lips, leaving them shining with moisture, then drew back a little to survey his work. She closed her eyes and smiled, holding her breath in rapturous anticipation, not quite believing she could feel such delight.

She felt his mouth hovering above hers and tipped her chin up, barely touching her lips to his lower lip, then tracing it with her tongue. He laughed softly; she felt it deep inside her. His laughter whispered against her open mouth for an instant and then was extinguished in it as he thrust his tongue deep, sealing her mouth with his. Her tongue found his, shyly at first, then finally joining in the slow, evocative rhythm.

Slowly he lowered his body, easing his weight onto her belly and chest, still taking part of his weight on his elbows. His hand stroked down the side of her ribs, her waist, her hip, sliding over her thigh and then tracing a path upward on the soft inside of it to the point where their bodies joined. He grasped her leg and pulled gently but firmly upward until she took her cue and wrapped both legs willingly, joyfully, around his body.

And now, at last, he began the primeval rhythm. He kept it slow at first, setting the tempo with his tongue until she had to tear her mouth from his and let her breath escape in harsh gasps. Then his mouth moved to her throat, found the pulse spot and exerted pressure that roared in her ears, taking her completely out of herself and into a realm of pure sensation.

He had lied when he'd said he had no more self-control. He controlled everything; he controlled *her*. She was the one who was out of control. She was molten lava, she was earthquake and flood, raging fire and thunderstorm. She was riding the crest of a tidal wave, carried faster and faster, higher and higher, while its roaring filled her ears and her body swelled and tightened, bracing for the inevitable disaster. When it came, and she felt herself falling, hurtling down into the maelstrom, she cried out in panic and hung on for dear life to the only solid reality in her universe. . . .

Chayne.

His breathing was harsh in her ear; his body was heavy, and his heart knocked erratically against her ribs. He lifted himself a little and looked down into her face with a slow, caressing smile and whispered, "Strike three."

Julie squeezed her eyes shut and began to cry. She didn't mean to; as hard as she tried to prevent them, tears oozed from beneath her lashes and trickled into her ears, and her body shook with suppressed sobs. Chayne stared down at her for a moment, his eyes smudged with spent passion. Then he framed her wet face with his hands and said with devastating gentleness, "Was that a first for you?"

Julie nodded violently and drew in a long, wretched sniff.

Chayne swore softly and wiped her face with his hands. He eased himself away from her, rolled sideways and pulled her over and into his arms, wrapping his arms around her and resting his chin on her hair. He didn't say anything at all until she had quieted, and then he murmured, "Damned if you don't keep surprising me, Julie Maguire."

The wind was making a lonesome, crying sound in the thatched roof. With that same rhythmic creaking that had wakened her that morning, it made the darkness seem crowded, alive with restless spirits and lost souls.

Julie stood alone in the middle of the adobe, shivering convulsively and hugging herself. She felt chilled, and yet she wasn't really cold. Or perhaps the cold was inside her. . . .

She wasn't usually given to such fanciful thinking. She had spent too many years dealing in harsh, ugly realities. It was this place, Baja: the deserts and mountains and seas, all of it . . . prehistoric, abandoned, forsaken, and populated by demons. . . .

She looked almost fearfully toward the bed. He was only a slightly deeper shadow in the darkness, a rhythm of breathing sounds to mingle with all the other disturbing night noises. She was grateful for the darkness, glad she did not have to see his face.

Now and forever . . . my very own demon! Dear God, what have I done?

Julie drew in her breath and held it, then threw back her head and rubbed futilely at the ache in her throat.

Don't be melodramatic, Agent Maguire. The plan worked like a charm, didn't it? You had a job to do and you did it. Now, get the hell out of here before you blow the whole thing!

Why was she standing there grieving over spilled milk? Why did she feel like those wretched souls crying in the rafters? She felt as though she had lost something that meant a lot to her. A part of herself that she had placed a very high value on was irretrievably, irrevocably gone. Whatever happened to her—whatever happened to *any* of them—she would never feel quite the same about herself again.

Julie took another deep breath, mentally shaking herself and squaring her shoulders. She had gone into this knowing the risks. If the only casualties were her self-respect and personal integrity, it was probably a fair price for what was at stake.

She looked around one last time and left the hut, closing the door soundlessly behind her. But as she drew in her first breath of rain-tainted air, she knew she had failed to calculate one thing. She had not expected to take along with her, in a flimsy boat on a windy sea and wherever she went for the rest of her life, a part of a smuggler named Chayne Younger. And she had never thought it would be so hard. . . .

It was not as dark outside as it had been in the hut. Although the sky directly overhead was a roiling mass of clouds, far to the east over the water there was a silver half-circle moon. Julie had spent a good many of her on-duty hours working in darkness without the luxury of a flashlight, so she had little difficulty picking her way across the uneven ground to the rocky ridge beyond the camper where she had left the small bundle she had managed to put together during the day. Nothing more than odds and ends: a stack of tortillas, two cans of *cerveza,* Chayne's razor, her hairbrush and underwear, a tin cup, some matches, all rolled in Chayne's windbreaker. Nothing that could have much bearing on her survival, really. She was making this dash for freedom on faith alone.

A gust of wind bumped her back like an impatient elbow. For the first time Julie felt a creeping uneasiness. She stared intently out across the turbulent blackness, trying to make out the surface of the water. It had grown darker all of a sudden; a boiling cloud had rolled across the face of the moon. Julie shook off her worries, reminding herself that this morning it had been windy and the men had taken the boats out without difficulty. After all, this was only the Gulf of California, not the Pacific Ocean!

She started around the bay, using her night vision, following the slightly paler strip of dry sand. A little flurry of rain struck her cheek like a slap, startling her. It wasn't supposed to rain in Baja, was it? She pushed on, turning her face away from the wind, trying to remember everything she knew about small boats. Colin had taken her out several times in the cabin cruiser he kept moored at Mission Bay, but those sun-dappled waters and elegant toys seemed unrelated to all of this elemental sound and fury.

The boats loomed ahead, dark hulks like a herd of large land animals asleep on the beach. Julie chose the one closest to the shore, tossed her bundle over the gunwale and stood gauging the distance to the water's edge. At that moment the clouds rolled away from the moon.

Julie felt her knees buckle, and she sagged against the boat, limp with shock and dismay. Where this morning she had looked out on sparkling blue water there was now only a gleaming mud flat, rippled and oily-looking in the moonlight. The tide was out. It was at least a hundred and fifty yards to the water. There was no way on earth that she could launch a boat.

She lifted her hands in a gesture of futility and utter despair. Of all the low points she had hit in the last few days, this was the lowest! She thought that she could not possibly feel more desperate than she did at that moment.

A moment later she knew that she was wrong. Tired of staring at that expanse of impassable land, Julie turned her back on it, as if not looking at it could make it go away. And as she did she saw a tall shape detach itself from the shadow of a boat farther up on the beach and move toward her with silent purpose.

She erupted in panic-stricken flight. She turned and bolted back down the beach, running headlong, her feet finding their way with blind instinct born of desperation, running as if her life depended on it, as she was certain it did. It was impossible to hear the pursuer above the fury of the storm and her own tortured breathing, but she knew he was behind her . . . gaining on her!

The rocky promontory loomed ahead. Sharp volcanic rock gashed her knee and she didn't even feel it. She heard her name called above the roar of the rain that had begun to hit her in stinging sheets, but it only galvanized her into a still more frenzied effort as she clawed her way up and over the rocks, bent only on achieving that pristine cove on the other side. Although just where she was going, she didn't know; she was beyond reason, running on sheer will and the instinct for self-preservation, even knowing that it was hopeless.

Julie felt her pursuer close behind her only an instant before she was hit in the back of the knees and dropped, sprawling, face first into the sand.

And still she fought, furiously, mindlessly, rolling and twisting out of her attacker's grasp. But before she could regain her feet she was grabbed around the waist and thrown back to the

ground. A hard, heavy body crushed the breath from her chest.
Her raking fingernails searched for his face, eyes, any point of
vulnerability, but her hands slithered uselessly off wet slippery
flesh. A voice, harsh and guttural with rage and effort, shouted
her name and broke into violent swearing. Hands like iron traps
caught her wrists and bore them up and back, slamming them
into the sand. Just inches from her ear that angry voice snarled,
"Enough! Damn it, Julie—that's enough!"

Julie opened her eyes and stared wildly up into Chayne
Younger's contorted face. And then she arched her back and
wailed into that tumultuous sky, *"Noooh! . . . Not you!"*

She could hardly see him in the swirling maelstrom of blowing sand and driving rain, but the body that crushed hers, the
hands that pinioned hers, the voice that shouted in her ear, all
shook with a fury that made the storm seem like a summer
squall.

"You *fool!* You stupid bloody little *cop!* What did you think
you were going to do, huh? *Stupid—*"

Julie went quite still, except for the breath sobbing through
her lungs. "Go ahead!" she screamed. "Kill me!"

"Kill you! You nitwit, don't you know I've saved your life?
Or the tide did. Where did you think you were going? And
why? What kind of stupid, bloody idiot would try to take a
boat out in this? Don't you know what's going on here? Look
around us! This is a *chubasco!* A typhoon!"

Chubasco. Julie had heard the word at dinner. The men had
talked of the chubasco. She hadn't been listening. She'd been
too preoccupied to try to figure out the meaning of an unfamiliar word. *Chubasco . . .* a Baja typhoon.

"Why, Julie?" His voice rasped in her ear. "What made you
try such a foolish thing? I told you I'd keep you alive. Didn't
you trust me?"

"Trust you?" Julie blinked away the rain that seemed to be
trying to drown her and stared into that dark, angry face.
"Keep me alive? And kill how many others? How many innocent people!"

"What the hell are you—"

"I *had* to get away. I have to tell them! I have to—"

"Julie, for God's sake, what are you talking about?"

"I know who you are! I know what you all are! I know what you're planning to do! I had to... stop you. I had to—"

She was struggling again, twisting from side to side beneath him, sobbing with helplessness and frustration.

His body, his face, his voice had all gone ominously still. "What do you know, Julie?" She could barely hear him above the storm.

"Terrorists!" She sputtered and almost choked on the torrent. "You're terrorists! You're going to sabotage the Expo! Kill—"

"How do you know that, Julie? Who told you?"

"I heard you! I heard you and the others in the camper! This morning!"

"Clever little *cop*." Chayne almost spat the word. "Nothing but a cop after all, is that it, Julie? You've been planning this getaway since this morning?"

Julie nodded, panting, shaking water from her eyes. "Yes. *Yes!* I planned it. The whole thing!"

"'The whole thing?'" His voice was, if possible, even quieter. "Meaning...tonight. That was a setup, is that what you're saying?"

"*Yes!* That's exactly what I'm saying!" Her voice came rapidly, breathlessly, cruelly, trying to do with words what she was unable to do with her hands—wound. "Of course it was a setup. You don't think that was real, do you? What do you think I am? Do you really think I could give myself to a terrorist? I needed you off my back! I needed you off guard! I needed you *asleep!* Yes, I planned it! And you fell for it—*El Demonio!*" She stopped, out of breath. The tension stretched like an elastic band—tension in his hands, in his body, in the air.

It was a shock, almost, when he said with grim amusement, "Yes ... I fell for it. But then ... so did you."

"What—"

"You planned it—and then fell right into your own trap, didn't you, *Güerita!*" He moved suddenly upon her, shifting his legs, thrusting hers apart almost casually and driving his body hard against hers.

She gave a sharp cry as she felt the pressure of him on the part of her that was still sensitive from earlier assaults. "*No!*

It was an act! Playacting! I was lying! It didn't mean *anything!*"

He gave a cold, ruthless laugh and ground himself against her. Not even the layers of clothing between them could keep the pressure from building intolerably, making her ache and throb.

"You just might be right about that—it's too soon to tell. And you might have been lying, *Güerita*—but your body damn sure *wasn't!*"

She began to whimper with fear and frustration—frustration at her inability to fight her need of him; fear of his ability to ignite such a terrible need in her. Fear of that awesome explosion of desire he had just sent boiling through her.

"Yeah . . ." his voice rasped in her ear, "you wanted me to make love to you, Julie. You needed me . . . just like you need me now. This plan of yours was an excuse, wasn't it?"

"No!"

"Just an excuse . . . a justification, so you could have what you wanted without compromising your cop code!"

"No! No, that's your ego; you can't believe—"

"I'll tell you what I believe, *Güerita!* I believe *this!*"

His mouth came down out of the rain and wind and turbulence, savagely, ruthlessly, breaking her lips, forcing her mouth open with sheer brute strength, stabbing deep inside her with his tongue. He drew back, surveyed her rain-and tear-wet face and then renewed the assault. It was less a rape and more a seduction, but no less ruthless. His mouth moved with calculated sensuality over hers, his tongue and lips sliding over every part of her mouth, inside and out, evoking unimaginable intimacies, stripping her of all reason. She was panting, trembling, arching her body unconsciously against him, her head turning from side to side, trying to escape that exquisite torture, trying to keep herself from responding.

But she couldn't. She *couldn't!* She gave a wild moan of despair and surrendered, opening to him, searching for him, lifting her head to meet him. He gave a low, triumphant chuckle and growled against her mouth, "Yeah . . . that's right! *Tell me the truth.*"

He released her hands and she reached for his neck. His own arms encircled her, and he rolled over onto his side, pulling her with him. His hands came between their bodies, tearing urgently at snaps and zippers. And then suddenly it stilled. Stilled and then stroked slowly across her ribs beneath her shirt. His tongue licked gently at the insides of her mouth and then withdrew. His lips soothed her swollen ones, and he gave a long sigh.

"Not here," he said harshly against her ear. "Not here. We'd probably drown!" Easing himself away from her, he sat up, then took her hand and got to his feet, pulling her after him.

"Come on, up! Let's get out of this!" He had to shout to make himself heard against the roar of the *chubasco*. Julie was shocked to realize that she had forgotten the storm; it had faded before the turbulence of her own emotions.

Chapter 7

Julie was a strong person, proud of her physical conditioning and stamina. Her job required it to a certain extent, but it had been a part of her makeup for much longer—ever since her childhood passion for gymnastics. She used her strength and endurance as a means of being competitive with men—she always scored among the highest in the patrol during the annual physical fitness exams.

But she knew when she had reached her limit. The cumulative effects of traumas both physical and emotional had wiped out all her reserves. She had as strong a will as anyone, but her legs simply wouldn't obey it. They buckled, and she sat abruptly back down on the sand.

"Come on, Julie—get up! We've got to get off this beach!"

She stared up at the dark form looming over her, blinked water from her eyes and slowly shook her head. Chayne lifted his hands in exasperation, then leaned down and scooped her up in his arms like a rag doll. The next thing Julie knew she was upside down over his shoulder, held securely by a band of solid muscle across her thighs.

Her dignity was offended—he was treating her like a sack of beans! Under the circumstances, dignity might have seemed a frivolous thing to make an issue of, but Julie was long past being rational. She began to kick and squirm and pound on Chayne's unyielding back with her fists.

"Put...me...down...you bas—" The rest of the expletive was a squawk of outrage as a hard hand connected resoundingly with her bottom. Julie considered the vulnerability of her position and elected to shut up.

Flung over his shoulder that way, it was difficult for her to tell where Chayne was going. She had just assumed he was taking her back to the hut, but instead of going back down the beach and over the rocks, he seemed to be tramping steadily uphill, into the wind.

And then the wind dropped as they came into the lee of a mountain or cliff, and Chayne stooped to lower her feet to the ground. He gave her a gentle swat on the bottom and said crisply, "In you go. Watch your head."

It was a cave—a fearsome, almost tangible blackness in an already stygian night. Julie found herself making little whimpering noises of fear deep in her throat as she slid her hands along cold wet granite, feeling her way. The darkness was like cloth over her face; she kept feeling as though she ought to be able to pull it away. Only the presence of Chayne's hand on her waist and the warmth of his breath on the back of her neck kept her from crying like a child with a nightmare.

They had probably gone only a few yards—though it seemed like a mile—before Chayne gave her a reassuring squeeze and said, "Hold on, Julie, just give me a minute."

When his hands left her waist she began to shiver uncontrollably. "Are there...are there any s-s-snakes in here?" she quavered through chattering teeth.

"I don't know," he drawled, sounding relaxed and amused. "We'll find out in a minute."

Julie heard the hiss of his cigarette lighter—such a tiny feather of light, and yet so brilliant after all that darkness that she blinked and shielded her eyes. Blessed light! And blessed peace and quiet, too—the storm seemed far away. Here it was quiet and warm and safe....

"No snakes," Chayne announced cheerfully. "At least, not in the immediate vicinity. Watch your step and come on in."

The lighter clicked off and Julie gave a little cry of protest. "Can't we...build a fire? Light a torch?"

Chayne gave a dry chuckle. "No, I don't think we'll light any fires in here. But I've got a battery lantern here. Just a minute."

The lantern came on, a harsher light that took some getting used to. Once her eyes had adjusted, Julie saw why there would be no fire, why Chayne had known about this place: Against the granite boulders at the far end of the cave was a neat stack of smallish wooden boxes stamped in large black letters, DANGER—EXPLOSIVES.

"Why did you bring me here?" Julie had her back to Chayne, unable, for some reason, to take her eyes off those boxes. "Instead of back to the hut, I mean."

He snorted, preoccupied with what he was doing. "Right now I wouldn't give even money that there's still a roof on that hut!"

"What about the others?" Julie suddenly had a vision of the little boy, Carlos, sweetly sleeping in his parents' bed. Was he sleeping now? Or huddled in a roofless adobe, frightened and cold.

"The others?" Chayne's voice was sardonic. "Don't tell me you care!"

"The little boy..."

"Geraldo will take good care of him. Rita, too. It's not your concern."

"Not my concern. Well, he's doing a terrific thing for his family, isn't he? Involving them in this?" Julie's voice broke and she flung her arm out to encompass the cave, the stored explosives, Chayne. "He's a *terrorist!* How can a terrorist care for or about anyone?"

"Not a terrorist, Julie," Chayne said quietly. "You're wrong about that. Just...smugglers, that's all."

"Just smugglers who smuggle terrorists! In my book that makes you *all* terrorists! Chayne—" She whirled to face him. "You told me you weren't a killer. How can you say that? How can you do this? How can you... They plan to kill hundreds of people—*children!*"

She was crying again, hating the display of weakness. Chayne was on one knee beside a wooden chest, sorting through what seemed to be emergency stores—blankets, medical supplies. Julie gazed down at his dark head, rain-wet and shimmering through her tear-glaze. She sniffed loudly and said in a small, drowned voice, "Chayne, you're going to have to kill me."

His head jerked up. A little half smile tugged at the corner of his mouth. "That's a bit drastic, isn't it? I'll admit I felt like it earlier tonight, when I found you'd gone, but I'd probably settle for a good spanking."

Julie gazed at him steadily. "I'll keep trying, you know. In order to stop me, you're going to have to kill me. I can't let it happen. I'll keep trying to stop you!"

Chayne dusted his hands and leaned an arm across his knee. He watched the tears chase each other down her cheeks in flinty-eyed silence for a moment and then said softly, "Suppose you do manage to get away, Julie. Suppose you even make it to the authorities. What are you going to tell them? That a bunch of terrorists are going to hit the Pan American Exposition? Can you tell them *where,* Julie? Or when? Which of the different Expo locations will they hit? Which hotel? Which stadium? Which convention center?"

"We'll stop you at the border!"

"Will you? Do you know where the crossing will be? Even if you stopped this squad, don't you know that terrorists never put all their eggs in one basket? Along all of those hundreds of miles of desert border, will you stop them *all?* Julie...don't you think Expo security knows the danger of terrorist attack? They try to plan for just that kind of scenario, but the fact is that suicide squads are almost impossible to combat."

"*Suicide* squads?"

"That's right, Julie. So you see, you really don't know enough to be of much use. There really isn't anything you can do."

She stood silently crying. After a moment he stood up. "Come on, out of those wet clothes," he said gently.

Julie swiped a hand angrily across her face. "Not on your life!"

He chuckled, that dry, humorless sound he made so often. "Come on, don't make me use force—or gentler persuasion. You're soaking wet, and I can't have you getting sick. You take them off or I will. Maybe you'd prefer that...."

"I'd rather die than have you touch me!" Julie said dramatically.

Chayne threw back his head and laughed with real amusement. "I thought we'd disposed of that little fiction down there on the beach."

Julie glared sullenly at him. "Turn off the lantern."

His voice still husky with mirth, Chayne murmured, "Soon, Julie. Soon. When I've got us properly bedded down. But not, *Güerita bonita*, to protect your modesty! I'm going to count to three...."

Julie turned her back and untied her belt, then hung it over a rock. Her clammy shirt followed. And she hesitated, head bowed, hands on the button fly of her jeans.

"One..." Chayne intoned.

Swearing bitterly, Julie skinned off the stiff wet denim, taking her panties with the rest. Better to get it over with. And now she waited, shivering, buttocks clenched.

A blanket came around her—wool, thick, warm and scratchy.

"Here, wrap up." Chayne's arms came with it, crossing over her front, pulling her back against his chest. A hand came up to ruffle through her damp hair. "You look like a drowned kitten. Quit shivering." A gust of laughter stirred across her ear, making her tremble even harder. His hand pressed her head back into the hollow of his shoulder, and his lips found the pulse spot behind her ear. He probed the indentation behind her earlobe with his tongue, then teased at the lobe before nipping it gently with his teeth.

Julie said, "Don't," in a very small voice.

"Why not?"

"Because... I don't want you to!"

"That's not true, and you know it. You want it... and this... and this...." His mouth trailed fire down the cords of her neck, defined her collarbone, then closed on the nape of her neck in a love bite that sent shock waves of seismic intensity through every nerve in her body. Her neck wilted like a week-old rose, dropping her chin onto her chest.

"Please don't," she said brokenly. "You don't understand. I *hate* this... I hate you... I hate myself."

"Julie..." It was a sigh, whispered against her temple. He turned her to face him, taking her head between his hands and wiping tears from her cheeks with his thumbs. "Poor little cop." He lowered his lips to her upturned face, tasting the salt moisture on her lips, her nose, her eyelids. "Don't cry, Julie. Don't you know that it's all right? You can't help this. Somebody made the rules a long, long time before there were cops...or criminals. Way, way back, when there was just a man...and woman. That's all we are, Julie. Just a man and a woman. It's okay to feel the way you do when I touch you *here*...when I kiss you. Kiss me, Julie...trust me...."

She looked up into his eyes. The look in them stopped her breath, twisted something in her chest and belly, a pain so acute that she nearly cried out. She couldn't have defined that look. She only knew what it did to her.

"You...*are* a demon," she whispered, awed.

"No, not a demon; just a man. But..." A twinkle of irony flared briefly in his eyes. "It must have been a devil that put you in my path, Julie Maguire! Here...and now, of all possible times! God help us both!"

He turned off the lantern and thick darkness enveloped them. Phantom light, temporarily seared on her retinas, darted about in the void as she strained to see, rebelling instinctively against the totality of her blindness. She made a sound, just the beginnings of panic, and put out her hand.

"I'm here, Julie."

His hands were on her shoulders, guiding her, pushing her gently down. He had made a bed with blankets on the sandy floor of the cave, with mounds of sand for pillows. Julie dropped to her knees and gave a gasp of surprise at the pain that stabbed through her knee.

"What is it? Did I miss a rock?" Chayne was there beside her in the dark, his hands still supporting her, his presence holding fear at bay.

"No, it's my knee. I think I must have hurt it on the rocks."

"Let me see."

He was speaking figuratively. He didn't turn on the lantern, but eased her firmly back onto the blankets, drawing the one that enveloped her aside. "Which one?"

"The left."

Chayne's warm hand was inserted behind her knee, lifting it. His fingers explored with a feather's touch... and then, incredibly, his mouth.

Julie caught at her lower lip with her teeth and shifted uncertainly. "Chayne, what are you doing?"

"Bathing your wound. Hush, Julie... forget everything except that you are a woman. Let me soothe you with my mouth...."

"But it's not—*please*." She was squirming, pushing ineffectually at his head. It was so *personal;* more intimate, somehow, than anything he had ever done to her before.

"It's all right, Julie. It's natural. The first thing any warmblooded animal does with an injury, if it's possible, is put it in its mouth." He caught her hand and held it against her thigh. She lay back with a little moan of defeat.

"That's right, Julie.... Relax...."

His mouth and tongue gently laved her lacerated knee, cleansing and soothing. There was almost no pain. In fact, that warm, liquid stroking was producing some very pleasant sensations in other parts of her body. She barely noticed when his lips and tongue abandoned the site of the injury and moved down the inside of her knee, but when he darted his tongue into the sensitive hollow behind it, just where his hand still held it, a gasp of surprise burst from her, and she reached again to push him away.

"Julie..."

The breathy sigh was close to her ear; she could feel the heat of his body spread out alongside hers. His arms lifted her, settled her against him, cradling her head in the hollow of his neck. Her legs touched warm satin; she realized with a small shiver of fear and excitement that he was naked. Words began to stir through the hair on her temple—husky, hypnotic words, like liquid amber, as intoxicating as brandy.

"Julie, you have a wonderful body, a beautiful body. I'll bet you think you know all about your body, don't you? You think because you've developed it and cared for it and kept it in perfect condition that you know everything it can do, don't you? But you don't.... You're like a newborn babe with a whole new world to discover. Sweet Julie...I'm going to help you find that new world...show you what your body is capable of giving you."

She was shivering again—not with cold but with a deep-down inner trembling. Chayne's hand had been stroking lightly over her ribs; now it moved up to cup her breast while his thumb and forefinger gently rolled the nipple between them.

"This, now..." he murmured against her ear. "This could just mean you're cold...but these beautiful, sensitive breasts don't *ache* because you're cold, do they? What happens when I do this, Julie?" He drew his fingertips lightly over her taut belly skin. A convulsion shook her, and her nipples contracted to hard, painful pebbles. The palm of his hand brushed them— first one, then the other—and she winced and made a tiny whimpering sound of need. He laughed softly and pulled her over onto his chest, folding her close. Her aching breasts flattened against the furnace heat of his chest, but if anything, the constriction in them only tightened while the pressure within them grew.

"You see? It doesn't help to warm them, does it, Julie? They hurt you, don't they? But they only hurt because you aren't listening to what they're telling you—that you're a *woman*...beautiful, soft, made for loving. Listen to your body, Julie, and that pain becomes pleasure...joy. *Listen*...and let me show you...."

How could he know? How could he know so well what she was feeling? How could he know her body better than she did?

Very gently, but as inexorably as a landslide, he bore her over onto her back. Very gently he lowered his mouth over one throbbing nipple and drew it deep, deep into his mouth, exerting a rhythmic pressure that tugged at something way down in the center of her body. She moaned softly, drawing up her leg and arching against his mouth. He released that breast and took the other, but this time his hand stroked down over the concavity of her stomach to cup the small, moist mound at the conjunction of her thighs. Just cupped it in the warmth of his hand and held it...

Julie gave a sharp gasp and pushed against his hand. Softly, against her breast, he whispered, "Easy...relax now." But she couldn't. She *couldn't*. A deeper, more compelling need throbbed beneath his hand, and her body knew instinctively where fulfillment could be found.

His fingers lay between her thighs, gently stroking, while his mouth resumed that deep, rhythmic pulling on her nipple. And then, slowly, slowly his fingers parted her.

Julie drew in her breath in a long, openmouthed gasp. Chayne's arm tightened reassuringly around her shoulders as his fingers probed deeper and the heel of his hand began to exert a slow, rhythmic pressure. She heard Chayne's hypnotic murmur. "Open up, sweet Julie... relax and *feel*. Don't fight it...."

And then her world spiraled off into a breathtaking kaleidoscope of sensation. The vortex carried her higher and higher and then hurled her, shattered, into Chayne's arms.

"Sweet... sweet Julie," he crooned, stroking the damp hair on her temple with his lips. His hand still housed the moist, pulsating delta of her womanhood, shielding it from the cold. He understood that to withdraw too soon would be to leave her bereft. He held her there until her shaking had subsided into a tremulous, effervescent peace, and then cuddled her close, caressing her hair, her back, her legs with long, calming strokes.

Her hand found its way to the warm, vibrant column of his neck. Shyly, hesitantly, she traced the outline of his jaw until he caught her hand and brought it to his mouth. His moustache brushed her palm, and then his lips, and finally his tongue, making slow, languorous circles.

"Chayne," Julie whispered, "I don't... understand. Why don't you..." Her voice trailed away, squeezed off by the growing ache in her throat. She was bewildered, confused, undone by his tenderness. It was the last thing she would have expected from him. Why had he done that? He seemed to demand nothing of her—his only purpose had been to give her pleasure. Even though she could feel the full, heated strength of him against her, there was no urgency in him. He seemed content to share her sensual lethargy, his tongue making little feathery explorations between her fingers, quivering like a captive moth against her palm. Her fingers curled, responding to the tiny, shimmering currents that radiated from that spot like the ripples on a pond. He chuckled softly and took them one at a time into his mouth, tickling and teasing the sensitive pads with his tongue, pausing between each sally to murmur words of mystery and magic.

"Sweet Julie...we've hardly begun. You are so soft...so beautiful, so responsive. You need to be loved...every part of you. This, and this..." His tongue found the pulse in her wrist and flattened against it.

"I'm going to love you, Julie. I'm going to taste...and touch...and know every part of your body...and you are going to learn with me every secret place...every sleeping desire. Come with me...trust me... There's just you...and me. No sight, no sound...just loving."

His words poured warm oil over her troubled mind as his mouth trailed liquid gold down her arm, pausing to explore the sensuous possibilities of the inside of her elbow, the ridge of her collarbone, the underside of one breast.

"So soft...that's the second-softest place on a woman's body, did you know that, sweet Julie? Shall I show you the softest place?"

Her bones were marshmallows, her muscles warm molasses. So lost was she in the web of enchantment he was weaving that she didn't mind when he drew her legs apart and kissed the silky inside of her thigh. He held her thighs parted but made no move to violate her femininity; instead his hands stroked her belly, her legs, played with tightly curled tendrils of hair, circled her navel oh, so lightly...always coming close but never quite touching her *there*. His tongue described slow, exotic patterns over her skin, the liquid heat of his mouth only teasing, suggesting...never fulfilling the throbbing emptiness at her core.

She began to arch her back beneath his hands, languorously at first, like a cat being petted, but gradually becoming more and more frustrated, tormented by that mushrooming ache. She writhed and squirmed, whimpering in desperation, unable to voice her terrible need.

Chayne's whisper came through the darkness like shivering velvet. "Do you want me to kiss you, Julie? Sweet, beautiful Julie...do you want me?"

"*Ye-es!*" she cried, almost sobbing. "Please, I can't—I want...you!"

"All right, Julie...all right."

She went rigid when his lips touched her, but he waited patiently, lightly stroking the insides of her thighs, her belly, her breasts. Waited . . . a warm, melting pressure . . . until she gave a little sigh and relaxed, opening to him like the petals of a flower.

"Chayne . . ."

The night became a sensual fantasy. Julie Maguire ceased to exist—she had no memory, no dreams, no aspirations. In the all-enveloping darkness there was only Chayne. He possessed her—mind, body and soul—with his hands, his mouth, his voice, and finally with his body—filling her, filling the night, filling her whole world.

Julie opened her eyes and knew that outside it was light. The darkness had a transparent quality—it no longer felt like something thick and heavy covering her face. The long warm presence beside her had form and substance that she could see as well as feel. And except for the quiet breathing of untroubled sleep, it was absolutely still; the storm—the *chubasco*—was over.

It was hard to pull herself away from the warmth of Chayne's body, but even harder to stay. She was wide awake and full of a kind of eager anticipation, like a child on Christmas morning. She couldn't lie still.

Careful not to wake Chayne, Julie slipped out of the blankets and groped for her clothes. They seemed as wet as when she had taken them off, and the thought of putting all that cold clamminess next to her sleep-flushed skin was revolting, but the alternatives were either nakedness or robbing Chayne of his blanket. She didn't know why she balked at the thought of waking him. There was just something—a compulsion, almost—that made her want to go alone into the morning. She was like a child with a secret treasure. She wanted to get herself to a private and well-lighted place and take a good look at what she had found, to see if it could possibly be as wonderful as she thought it might be.

Julie emerged from the cave to confront a scene of almost stunning beauty. The air was cool and the light a pale, effervescent gold, like champagne. The gulf was an improbable turquoise gilded by sunlight streaming through holes in bil-

lowy piles of clouds on the horizon, all that remained of the
night's tempest. And in all that vista, from the purple rocks that
enclosed the debris-strewn cove to the hazy blue of the offshore islands, there was not a single sign of humankind. Julie
might have been the very first woman, emerging from her cave
to a prehistoric dawn.

She made her way down to the beach and walked a little way,
kicking at bits of flotsam with her huaraches: seaweed and
brush, broken shells and sea gull feathers—casualties of the
storm from both land and sea, all mixed together. The sun was
warm on her bare legs; she had put on only the soft loose shirt
and it was already beginning to dry. She walked toward the
water until she reached smooth wet sand and then stopped
hugging herself.

She felt good. She felt wonderful. She knew she shouldn't
feel like this, but she did.

She frowned, puzzling it out. She wasn't a person for whom
mystical or poetic expression came naturally, but she felt as
though she were . . . newly born. As though in the night, in the
storm, in the cave, she had come through some tremendous
struggle and had emerged . . . a different person. She wasn't sure
yet—it was all still too new and confusing—but she thought
perhaps . . .

I think . . . I'm happy. I shouldn't be, but I am. It's a beautiful new day . . . and I'm happy.

Footsteps stirred the sand behind her. Julie turned, gave a
sleepy, sunny smile and went blindly into Chayne's arms. It was
a natural action, one not precipitated by thought; if she had
stopped to think she would have lacked the confidence to be
sure of her welcome. But in a manner as natural as hers,
Chayne's arms enfolded her, and his cheek came to rest on the
top of her head. She put her arms around his waist, lacing her
fingers loosely together at the small of his back, resting her
forehead against his chest and inhaling the warm familiar smell
of his body.

They stood that way, not moving, not speaking, for a long
time. Finally Chayne bumped her head gently with his chin and
said in an odd, gravelly voice, "Good morning."

"Good morning," Julie whispered back.

"It's sure a nice morning."

"It's a beautiful morning!"

"How are you?"

"Fine. I'm fine."

"Sore?"

"No. No, I'm fine. Maybe a little *stiff*..."

"Stiff?"

"From sleeping on the ground."

"Sleeping?" His chest bumped against her cheek as his fingers took her chin and lifted it. Eyes of fierce, crackling blue searched every centimeter of her face, boring deep into her own eyes. And for once she wasn't afraid of that electric contact but clung to it, looking just as far into his soul as he did into hers. And in that long, searching look something passed between them—a covenant, an understanding, an acceptance.

The dark, rather forbidding face relaxed into a grin. "Stiff, huh?" Chayne took her by the shoulders and held her a little way from him, then slid his big hands up to grasp her trapezius muscles. He began to knead gently, moving his hands slowly upward until his fingers were massaging the base of her skull. "I can help that," he said softly. "If you want me to..."

"I...um," Julie mumbled thickly. Her neck had lost its ability to support her head, which rested like a plucked chrysanthemum in the basket of Chayne's hands. "Uh...what?"

He chuckled and kissed her upturned face, brushing her eyelids with his moustache, then her cheeks, the tip of her nose, and finally her breathlessly parted lips. She stood with her hands at her sides and drank from his mouth with the trusting abandon of a thirsty child.

Presently Chayne lifted his head and said huskily, "My God, I've created a monster.... What's this, Julie—are you blushing?"

She tried to pull away and was instead gathered back into his arms. "Well, don't you think I should? All you do is touch me and I behave like a...shameless wanton!"

"How Victorian that sounds. Shameless? Absolutely. And wanton? God, I hope so!"

"Chayne...stop that."

"You don't want me to stop."

"No...I don't. Does this mean I'm addicted?"

"To what?"

"Sex."

"I hope so."

"You've turned me into a junkie!"

"A sex junkie!"

No—a Chayne junkie, she thought, but she didn't voice the words.

They were giggling like kids, foreheads touching, breaths mingling, hands roaming in random explorations. Now the laughter died in a sighing expiration as Julie pulled back a little to let her eyes devour him, beginning with the wild curls of dark hair on the walnut forehead; the fine black brows and heavy lashes; cobalt eyes; craggy features and shadowed jaws; the sensitive, gently smiling mouth she could still feel as a lingering tingle of cooling moisture on her own.

With shy fingers she traced the dimplelike scar in his chin, then let her hands follow her gaze down the whisker-roughened neck, over the ridge of his collarbone and across the furred planes of his chest. And then, inevitably, her eyes were pulled downward to what had been invisible and forgotten in the dark—that terrible scar on his belly. Awed, fascinated, she reached with trembling fingers to touch it.

Chayne sucked in his breath audibly and caught her wrist. He held her hand poised away from his body, and in that frozen silence the sound of distant voices carried on the clear morning air, reminding them both that they were not, after all, alone on the earth.

"We could both use a swim," Chayne said.

Though the gentleness in his voice softened the abruptness of the withdrawal a little, Julie was chilled by the harsh austerity in his face, in his eyes. As they walked to the water he hooked an arm around her neck and drew her close—an awkward gesture of silent apology, an unspoken plea for understanding.

But she didn't understand him. She didn't know him. She didn't understand what he was doing to her.

Even as his fingers moved to the buttons of her shirt she was thinking, Why? Why am I doing this? Am I under some kind of spell? To her body he was no stranger; he knew every inch of it. Removing her clothing and standing before him there in the sunshine brought a warm blush to her cheeks, but it was a blush of excitement, not shame. And just the touch of his eyes was enough to bring her breasts to tingling fullness.

But she didn't *know* him.

He was a strange enigma of a man, this smuggler-terrorist-pirate named Chayne Younger. Was that even his real name? Perhaps, after all, the Spanish nickname was best ... El Demonio Garzo. Something not quite real. Something unknowable.

He had told her that he was just a man...but he wouldn't let her know him. And why did she *want* to know him?

The lazy surf of the Sea of Cortez pushed and pulled at her knees as she watched Chayne step out of his ragged jeans and stride naked into the water. Except for one strip of paler skin, his entire body was that dusky walnut, adorned with the masculine pattern of dark hair that seemed only to accentuate and outline its symmetry. She watched the play of muscles beneath gleaming skin, marveling again at the strength and grace of his body. His awesomely beautiful, flawed body.

The body he will not let me touch....

Because he didn't want her to get close to him—to get to know him. He must be aware, just as she was, that the covenant between them was limited to the here and now. Aware that when they left this place, when the real world intruded upon them, that covenant would be null and void. She would once again be committed only to his destruction, and he—would he eventually have to choose between her life and his own freedom?

Whether they had been brought together as a result of an accident of fate or by a capricious devil, their need for each other had been real and compelling. And out of that mutual need had come an understanding. Someday, when that real world did intrude, U.S. Agent Julie Maguire would have to face the person—this Julie she didn't even know—who had accepted that arrangement. This stranger in her body who had so readily accepted intimacy with a man who was the antithesis of everything she believed in.

Someday....

Chayne's big hands curved over her naked shoulders. He pushed her, laughing and protesting, into the gentle waves. She surfaced, sputtering and aimed a hefty splash at his grinning face.

The specter of the future clutched at her insides like a cold, cruel hand, but if the haunting showed in her eyes he did not notice.

Chapter 8

"It doesn't look too bad—not as bad as I expected."

"It's a good thing the tide was out," Julie murmured, reflecting even as she spoke that the remark was a very good indicator of how much she had changed in the last few hours. How much she had been changed.

They were standing on the rocks that separated the settlement from their private cove, surveying the destruction. The beach below was littered with palm thatch; the only roof still attached to its dwelling was Sebastien's sturdy one of corrugated tin, firmly nailed down. Carlito was scampering up and down amid the wreckage, waving palm fronds and screaming like an Indian on the warpath while the dogs yipped and cavorted about him.

The cookshed had blown down. Rita was stirring through the ruins in a desultory way, salvaging cooking utensils and the watertight canisters of staples and adding them to a growing pile.

Old Juanita was stooped over in the middle of her garden patch, stoically nursing what the *chubasco* and the goats had left of her vegetables. The animal pens had been another casualty of the storm; the goats had already been retrieved and were placidly nibbling whatever they could find at the limits of their tethers. Sebastien, Geraldo and Pepe were chasing chickens, laughing and shouting, making a lark of disaster, like schoolboys on a field trip. Sebastien already had a brace of birds in hand, suspended upside down by the feet and flapping and squawking their outrage. As Julie and Chayne watched, Pepe took a flying leap after an escapee and dove belly first and empty-handed into the sand, to his own disgust and Geraldo's delight.

"I'm surprised there hasn't been a flood down through here," Julie said when the laughter had subsided.

"The flood channel is over there, the other side of the ridge," Chayne told her, pointing toward the south. "In fact, that's why Sebastien came to this cove. There used to be quite a settlement over there—a mission, the whole thing. The ruins of the church are still there—or were before this last storm. If they hadn't washed away, I'll show you sometime."

"What happened to it?"

"Flash flood. Wiped it out. Everyone left except Sebastien and his family. They have a big family—all gone away now, gone to the mainland...to the city. Sebastien built all these houses for his children, but none of them wanted to stay."

"Sad," Julie said softly. But she could sympathize with the young people's flight from this place, even while she understood why the old ones would love it. Baja was as lonely and cruel as it was beautiful.

"I guess we'd better see what we can do about finding a new roof," Chayne said dryly. There was an odd note of reluctance in his voice, and he made no move to descend to the beach. Julie wondered if he was as loath to rejoin the company as she was. The privacy of their little rocky cove seemed precious now.

"Besides, I'm hungry." He put his arm around her and drew her against his side, a gesture that was becoming familiar to her. It brought a curious ache to her chest. "Aren't you?"

"Yes. I guess I am. Starving." Julie looked up at him, waiting.

He grinned down at her. "Ready?"

No. No—can't we stay here forever?

"Sure. Let's go." She took a deep breath, mentally squared her shoulders—and then remembered. There was no longer any reason to be on her guard; the playacting was over.

In spite of the havoc and destruction wreaked upon it by the typhoon, or perhaps because of it, there was an almost pastoral mood in the little settlement. There was a closeness among them that Julie had not felt before; they were no longer a nest of smugglers and outlaws so much as fellow survivors, orphans of the storm. They were too concerned now with the immediate necessities of life—food and shelter—to think beyond the here and now. There was no time for deadly plans and nightmare visions of violence and terror. The sun shone, and the breezes blew warm and sweet, and they all laughed a lot and worked at the tasks of cleaning up and rebuilding in companionable harmony, like good friends on a camping trip.

As usual, though, the division of labor was sharp and clear: The problem of food preparation was left to the women, while the men saw to more weighty matters. They took it for granted that a meal would be provided for them even in the midst of chaos, and so of course it was.

Almost as soon as they reached the camp, Chayne left Julie and went to join the other men, who by this time had completed the chicken roundup and were engaged in a solemn inspection of the roofless adobes. Accustomed to things by this time, Julie went to offer her services to Rita, who welcomed her with a quick, searching glance and then a smile. She looked almost gaunt, with dark smudges around her eyes. Julie thought with a pang of guilt, What a terrible night she must have spent, while I . . .

While she had been in another world, with Chayne.

There was still propane, and the gas stove in Rita's hut was big enough to accommodate the coffee pot and the big iron skillet. Fillets salvaged from the giant grouper were fried with onions, green tomatoes and peppers that Juanita brought from her ravaged garden. The men were served picnic-style on the beach. The women, of course, ate by themselves, indoors.

Linda arrived about the time the work was done, looking sullen and cross, like a child in a temper. Clearly the storm had been a bit more than she had bargained for. Julie had no idea

what her arrangement was with Pepe, but she was sure it had
not included hurricanes and roofless adobe huts! But even she
pitched in, once breakfast was out of the way, to help carry
salvaged supplies from the wreckage of the cookshed to one of
the unoccupied huts.

The tub that had held the lobsters had blown full of sand and
the lobsters had disappeared. No one could imagine what had
become of them, but Julie had a whimsical vision of a conga
line of lobsters dancing through the torrential rain to the sea.
Since dinner had absconded and the men were too busy with
other things to make another fishing trip, two of Sebastien's
chickens were sacrificed and consigned to the cooking pot for
the evening meal.

And then another problem arose: The camp's water supply
dwindled to a trickle and then ceased altogether. Julie was surprised to learn that there *was* a water supply from Chayne's re-
marks about the scarcity of fresh water in Baja California. Now
it struck her as ironic that on the morning after torrents of water had fallen from the sky they should be completely out of it!

"There is a spring," Rita told her. "In the canyon—" she
pointed to the south "—near the old mission. It is an oasis,
with palm trees, really very pretty but too rocky and steep to
build houses in. After the flood destroyed the village and the
church was abandoned, Sebastien built a rock ditch to bring the
water here. It isn't much, just a trickle—and even that dries up
if there is a bad dry spell—but it is enough for the garden and
the animals. But now, after such a rain, there should be plenty.
I don't understand!" She was frowning perplexedly at the little wooden trough that should have carried a precious stream
into a barrel beside the thick adobe wall of Sebastien's house.
The wood was still damp but drying rapidly in the warm sunshine. The barrel itself had been knocked askew by the collapse of the goat shed and was nearly empty.

"We must have water," Rita said, looking worried. "The
animals..."

"The ditch has been washed away," old Juanita said in her
dry, ageless voice. "It has happened before." She rarely said
anything, and when she did it was like wind blowing through
sagebrush; it was hard to believe, sometimes, that she had
spoken at all.

"It must be mended," Juanita announced, and as the three
younger women watched in silent amazement, she turned,

hiked up her voluminous black skirts and waddled off down the beach, looking, Julie thought, like an indignant penguin. After a moment's bemused hesitation, Rita, Linda and Julie looked at each other and followed.

The old woman halted at the edge of the little circle of masculine camaraderie and waited impassively, arms akimbo. Silence fell.

"There is no water."

Three pairs of dark eyes slowly lifted to the broad, seamed face. The fourth pair, clear electric blue, sought Julie's and crinkled in amusement. Julie caught her breath, surprised by a lurch in her stomach, and jerked her eyes away.

Sebastien was stroking his beard and nodding sagely. "*Sí.* The ditch has washed away."

"It must be mended."

"*Sí,*" Sebastien murmured, *"mañana."*

"No," Juanita said in an implacable monotone. "Now. The goats must have water. The ditch must be mended." *And that,* she was saying, *is your job.*

Julie was fascinated. Those male bastions were breachable, it seemed, if the occasion was important enough to warrant trouble. She was beginning to realize that, in spite of all that masculine power and authority, the real strength was there in that patient, implacable little woman.

Sebastien stared straight ahead, stroking his beard and unhappily digesting the unpalatable but inescapable truth in her words. "Ah, well . . ." he said finally, philosophically. "The goats must have water." He began slowly to get to his feet.

Chayne beat him to it without difficulty. "Sebastien must go with Pepe and Geraldo in the camper, to show them where to cut the *cardon, Tía.* I will mend the ditch."

To Julie's utter astonishment, the ancient, lined face split in a nearly toothless smile. Juanita murmured, *"Muchas gracias,* Señor Chayne," and reached up to touch him on the arm.

Good God, Julie thought. Even Juanita! You would think he was some kind of saint!

Sebastien, Pepe and Geraldo restored the missing components to the truck's engine and went bouncing off into the interior to cut cardon cactus.

Alive and growing, the desert giants were fleshy green candelabras reaching fifty feet into the sky. Rita explained to Julie that when they died they left skeletons of hardwood, long poles with the strength of iron. In that treeless land those poles were used to build fences and animal shelters, even houses. They formed the framework for the thatched roofs. The door of poles Julie had noticed that first night in the hut—the door through which she had eavesdropped on Geraldo and Chayne—was made of cardon skeletons.

A kind of lazy, sun-drenched somnolence settled over the camp as the high whine of the truck's powerful engine died away beyond the granite ridges. Julie was on her knees beside a bucket of sand outside Geraldo's hut, scouring dishes. In the open doorway old Juanita sat with her lap full of dried pinto beans still in their crackly yellow pods. She was shelling them largely by feel, half dozing, rocking slightly in the sunshine and crooning to Carlito, who, after the excitement of the night, had fallen asleep with his head propped against her ample hip. Inside the hut, Rita was chopping onions for the stew; Julie could hear her intermittent sniffles. Linda, as usual, had disappeared.

Chayne came around the corner of the hut, a shovel on his shoulder. He had on a shirt for a change—blue chambray—but it did nothing to disguise his wild, almost feline beauty. Once again he had tied a rolled bandana around his head—a dark blue one this time. Beneath it his eyes had a smoky look.

At his sudden appearance Julie felt that peculiar spasm in the area of her diaphragm again and thought, Good heavens, what *is* that?

He stood looking down at her, and she felt her skin grow hot. Her fingers became boneless. She thought wildly, Oh, help.

"Come with me." It was a command, spoken very softly in English, for her ears alone. She wanted to, desperately, and so perversely she shook her head and went on doggedly scrubbing plates with handfuls of clean sand.

"I have to finish. Rita has so much to do. I should stay and help. She needs me."

"I need you."

She couldn't have heard that. It was so softly spoken, and when she looked up his face was impassive, his eyes veiled. She must have been mistaken.

"Finish, then," he said gruffly. "I'll wait." He lowered the shovel and leaned it against the wall, then stooped and hoisted the sleeping Carlito into his arms. The little boy promptly snuggled his face against the chambray-covered chest, gave a small sigh and put his thumb into his mouth. Chayne stood for a moment regarding the tousled dark head and then abruptly disappeared into the hut.

Julie scrubbed blindly at a plate, not at all surprised at the shimmering tears that obscured her vision. It was, she told herself, just the sort of corny, schmaltzy scene that always made her choke up, damn it!

Rita came out of the hut, squeezing past Juanita's oblivious bulk and wiping her hands on a towel. Her eyes were red from the onions, and there was an anxious frown on her forehead.

"Julie," she said earnestly, struggling with the unfamiliar consonant, "you go with Señor Chayne. Leave the dishes. I will finish."

"But . . . I'm nearly finished."

"Leave them." She touched Julie's shoulder. "The dishes are not important. Señor Chayne is important. Go. *Hurry.*" The last word was an urgent whisper accompanied by a little nudge as Chayne came back outside, pausing to say something to Juanita that elicited another sleepy, toothless smile.

Julie took a deep breath and stood up, brushing sand from her hands.

"Ready?" Chayne asked, smiling crookedly down at her.

She started to speak, then cleared her throat and just nodded.

"All right, then—let's go!"

"You didn't seem very anxious to come with me," Chayne said casually. "What's the matter?"

They had left the beach behind and were following the narrow ditch of rock and concrete uphill, angling inland over the low ridge to the south.

"I wanted to come with you," Julie retorted. "I just wasn't sure I should."

"Why not? I told you I'd show you the mission."

"Well, there was Rita. . . ."

"Baloney. What's the real reason?"

"Oh," Julie said lightly, hedging because she really couldn't explain the real reason, even to herself, "I just thought it might be against the rules. You know—a mere woman tagging along on a man's job."

Chayne chuckled and swung the shovel from his shoulder to scoop a bit of brush from the ditch. His laughter had a soft, carefree sound.

"How can you use the term 'mere woman' after Juanita's performance this morning? You have it backwards, you know. It's we men who don't dare intrude in the women's domain."

Julie could have argued that a dozen ways, but she chose not to. Her silence prompted Chayne to say quietly, "It must be pretty hard for you to take. Not exactly what you're used to, I imagine."

It was Julie's turn to laugh without mirth. "No. Not hardly."

"You've adjusted nicely, *Güerita.*" His voice sounded gravelly. "In fact, you've handled this much better than I thought you would."

Julie threw him a startled glance and went back to watching the path for rattlesnakes. "Thank you," she said dryly.

It seemed an odd conversation to be having. There they were, only hours away from a night of shared intimacy beyond anything Julie could have imagined, and he had never seemed more a stranger. But of course they *were* strangers—and were going to remain so. Chayne didn't want to know her, and she couldn't allow herself to know him. But you couldn't have conversations with a person without beginning to know him, so what could they possibly say to each other?

Chayne gave her a long, silent look. Julie saw a shutter blot the light from his eyes and a look of bleak acceptance settle over his dark features. His mouth tightened almost imperceptibly, and he hefted the shovel and walked on. Pain, unexpected and inexplicable, clutched at her throat as she hurried doggedly after him.

What's happening to me? she wondered in anguish.

Chayne became a tour guide, informative, impersonal. Sebastien's rock ditch took them up a narrowing canyon, a steep-walled arroyo that would have been like all the other deep dry scars in the landscape except for the miracle of the spring. Even though the waters had been channeled by the mission padres into cisterns and irrigation ditches long ago, the underground moisture supported cottonwoods and palm trees, and the granite rocks were covered with mosaics of algae in brilliant red, yellow, black and pale bluish gray. There were signs and sounds of life all over—the hum of bees, the mosquitoes' whine, frog song, and the blue flash of a lizard.

The cistern was located in the mouth of the canyon oasis, just where it joined another, wider and shallower valley. By a quirk of random convolutions in the earth's crust, the narrow, rocky gorge that held the spring was flash-flood safe—and uninhabitable—while the adjoining valley was wide, fertile and tempting, its topsoil laid down over countless centuries by floodwaters.

"The padres must have come during a dry spell," Chayne said, pointing out the crumbling fragments of adobe walls from the ridge above the cistern. "They had time to build the church, start a school, channel the spring and plant crops before the big one came. They must have had little floods before that, but nothing they couldn't cope with. Like this one." He gestured with his shovel to where the water had come down the valley, leaving pale fingers of sandy silt on the older, darker soil.

"This was only a little one—the damage isn't bad. I think it's just filled the ditch with sand and plugged the outlet." Chayne was probing around the base of the cistern with his shovel, his voice fading into little grunts of exertion as he began to clean out the half-buried ditch.

Julie watched for a minute and then, feeling superfluous, went to explore, following the shade of the cistern's rock and concrete wall. It was hot this far inland, and the grasses that grew lush and green near the base of the wall were cool on her unprotected toes. She paused to lean against the wall, lulled by the heat and the hum of insects and the steady scraping of Chayne's shovel....

In the next instant her heart, her breathing, her *brain*, stopped cold, quick-frozen by the most chilling sound on earth: the whir of a rattlesnake's warning.

It was so close—but where? She didn't dare move her head, or even her eyes. *There*—a small one, neatly coiled at the base of the wall, seeking shelter from the midday sun. It might have been just another sandy brown rock but for that deadly heart-shaped head and cold yellow eyes, and the tiny movements of flicking tongue and shivering tail.

After the first congealing stab of terror, Julie felt very calm, almost . . . detached. She knew she could not move away—the snake was not more than two feet away from her toes, bare and pink in the open huaraches. There was nothing with which she could defend herself—not even a rock or a stick she could lay her hands on. The next move belonged to the snake.

The ugly brown head swayed slightly; the slender tongue darted in and out, gathering sensory data on this unfamiliar, bewilderingly oversized prey. Julie only hoped her toes would not be mistaken for a nest of pink baby mice. She felt a kind of sympathy for the creature, so hideous that its stare alone could immobilize its prey, so fearsome that just the sound of its warning rattle could freeze the reflexes of self-preservation.

It occurred to her that in her uniform, with her service revolver handy, she'd have killed it without a thought—except, perhaps, of revulsion. Though maybe *not*, on second thought, with her revolver. She remembered vividly the time she and Franconi had disturbed a sleeping rattler while on stakeout and Franconi had chosen that method of dispatching it. The red tape and bureaucratic hassle had been a darned nuisance. She and Franconi had both had to explain in triplicate why a weapon had been discharged while they were on duty!

But here . . . here *she* was the intruder. The snake had only sought a comfortable place, and she, not watching where she was going, had blundered into it. It had every right to be here. She did not. Please, she telegraphed with all her might, please go away; I don't mean you any harm.

After what seemed an age, but was probably only a few seconds, the snake darted its head sideways, folded backward upon itself and began to move slowly away, following the base of the wall. A quick movement at the perimeter of her vision caught Julie's eye. She jerked her head up and cried in a hoarse whisper, "No! *Don't!*" And then intently, urgently, "Please, Chayne, don't kill it—let it go."

He was poised there behind her, the shovel raised ready to cut the fleeing reptile in half. His face was terrible, frightening. Julie found that her heart was beating again; it hammered painfully against her ribs. She touched the sleeve of his shirt, and he lowered the shovel, then turned to look down at her, moving his head slowly, as if his neck were stiff.

The look in Chayne's eyes stunned her. For just an instant it was as if she could see clear to the center of his soul—and then the door slammed shut, too quickly for her to identify what she had seen there. She was left frightened and upset, shattered and fragmented without knowing why. She only knew that she hurt. Everywhere. Her heart, her chest, her throat, her face, her fingers where they touched his sleeve.

"What is it?" Chayne growled hoarsely. "Are you—it didn't bite you, did it?"

"No. It didn't bite me."

"Are you going to pass out? You look—"

"I'm fine."

"You don't look fine. You look like hell!"

"Well, so do you!"

He dropped the shovel and pulled her into his arms. She went without resistance, but her body felt cold and rigid.

"What's wrong, Julie?" Chayne murmured into her hair. "Are you so afraid of snakes?"

"No," she said woodenly. "I'm not afraid of them at all."

"Then *what,* damn it? You looked . . . terrified!"

Julie pulled away from him and wiped a hand across her dry eyes. "I was...I am," she said in a tight, bleak voice. "I don't know who I am anymore."

"Julie—"

"I didn't want you to kill it."

"Julie—"

"I don't know *why!*"

"Because U.S. Border Patrol Agent Maguire would have killed it—is that what you're saying?" Chayne's voice was soft. "Don't worry about it. This place does that to you. You begin to feel like an interloper. Human beings shouldn't be here at all."

"Well, I sure as hell shouldn't!" Julie shouted, angry all at once.

"No," Chayne murmured, unperturbed. "You shouldn't."

"You bring me to this godforsaken place, I'm a prisoner among a bunch of terrorists, I'm a stranger to myself and everybody else—and you ask me what's *wrong?*"

He took her arms and moved closer to her. "I'm not a stranger, am I?"

Julie gave a high bark of desperate laughter and stared at the buttons on his shirt, avoiding his eyes, knowing that to look into them would only make her hurt again. "You're the strangest of all," she whispered. "I don't know who you are. I don't even know who I am anymore."

"Come here." He sat down in the soft grass beside the wall and drew her down with him, settling her between his thighs. His arms enfolded her and held her firmly against his chest. "Now," he said roughly, "tell me why it bothers you so much...."

When she couldn't speak, he bent to nuzzle at the back of her neck, murmuring persuasively, "Come on, Julie...what do you find so reprehensible about being with me?"

"It's *wrong*," Julie said hoarsely, and cleared her throat loudly, angrily.

"What's wrong?"

"It's *all* wrong, damn it—and either you know that perfectly well or you're an insensitive S.O.B.!"

"All wrong?" Chayne said into the hair behind her ear. His voice was very quiet. "Was it wrong to save your life?"

"That's not what I meant and you know it. That was... window dressing—playacting!"

"And when the playacting stopped, you used sex as a weapon against me. Was that wrong, Julie?"

"*No!* Yes. I don't know! I had to—it was the only weapon I had."

"So it's not wrong to use sex as a means to an end, but it's wrong if it feels good?"

"Damn you."

"You say that a lot." He sounded amused.

"I mean it," Julie said between her teeth. And then she abruptly relaxed, letting her head drop forward. "Of course it was wrong," she moaned softly. "But you paid me back in spades, didn't you?"

"What do you mean?"

"Just look at me. I can't even think straight! All you do is *look* at me—"

"And that's wrong too, I suppose?"

"Yes!" She could feel his lips against her skin, his breath warm on her neck.

"Why?"

"You know why—because of who I am, who you are!"

"Cop is cop and crook is crook and never the twain shall meet? I thought you said you don't know who you are—or who I am?"

"Don't mock me, Chayne. And don't confuse me. I told you I can't think straight."

"I'll agree with that. You'd have to be pretty confused to find anything wrong with this. I feel good when I make love—"

"*Not*—"

"Shush! When I make *love* to you. And you feel good—"

"That's what's wrong with it!"

"What?"

"It's wrong to feel like this when I don't—"

"Don't what, Julie?"

"I don't love you!" But her mind had recoiled. She had glimpsed the truth and rejected it with desperate vehemence. I *can't* love you, she added, but only silently.

Chayne held her tightly, holding them both very still, as if listening to the echo of her denial. Then she felt him shrug.

"So it's just a question of morals," he said lightly. "Ah . . . middle-class morality."

"Don't mock my morality just because you have none at all!"

"And how do you know I have no morals? I thought you didn't know me at all." His calm, unruffled voice was a mellow counterpoint to her anger; it irritated her beyond bearing.

"Damn you," she whispered impotently, giving up.

"That was assured a long time ago," Chayne chuckled against her ear. "And if being with me damns you, the damage has already been done, hasn't it?" He kissed the side of her neck and slid his mouth across her collarbone to her shoulder, moving clothing out of the way as he went. Julie moaned softly and turned her head toward him.

"What did you say?" Chayne asked.

"Nothing . . . I didn't say anything. I . . . don't think I like this conversation."

"Neither do I. But I think I know how to bring it to a mutually satisfying conclusion."

"How?"

"Like this..." His mouth came down on hers with gentle fervor.

The truth welled slowly up in her like milk coming to a boil, and before she could stop it, it had spilled over into her consciousness. He felt the tremor in her mouth and drew away. She didn't open her eyes, but felt his hot gaze on her upturned face.

"Julie," she heard him whisper with an odd kind of urgency, "believe me—it's all right...."

They slept that night under stars that Julie never saw. Like an exhausted child, she fell asleep over her plate of chicken stew, and she didn't even know when Chayne took the spoon from her fingers and carried her to a makeshift bed of palm fronds in an adobe hut without a roof.

Chapter 9

Julie woke gradually and with reluctance, acquainting herself with first one sensation and then another, fitting each like a piece of a jigsaw puzzle, missing memories, pieces she had to locate and ease painstakingly into their proper places.

The bed was springy but not soft; it crackled and whispered when she moved. Neither mattress nor sand... Then she remembered. Palm fronds, roof thatch gathered up from the beach where the wind had tossed it. The rain-soaked mattresses were drying out there now; Chayne had helped carry them down to the sand. By midafternoon yesterday the beach had resembled a large rummage sale, with bedding and clothing spread everywhere under the sun. By evening almost everything was dry except the mattresses, so they had gathered up the fallen fronds and made temporary beds of them....

I'm slipping back in time, Julie thought as she rubbed her cheek sleepily on the sheet, listening to the crackle under it. Last night I slept on tree branches, like a gorilla. The night before that I slept in a cave....

There was warmth on her face, and light. Too much of it, in fact. Sunlight. Another puzzle piece accounted for it. The truck had returned in midafternoon with a load of cardon wood, but there had been time and fronds enough to rethatch only one room before dark. Chayne had insisted on doing Geraldo's hut first, for Carlito's sake.

Chayne...

Julie squirmed with irritation. The sun on her face was only one of several discomforts that would soon drive her from her primitive but comfortable nest. She was hungry. And she had to go to the bathroom.

You should have taken care of that before you went to bed. She could almost hear her mother's voice. Funny, she couldn't even recall going to bed. There'd been a fire on the beach; she remembered watching the flames and listening to Pepe's guitar while she ate. She hadn't realized how tired she was; very tired indeed if Chayne had carried her here and put her to bed without waking her!

Chayne, Chayne, Chayne!

He was dead center in her every thought, a part of every puzzle piece, a subliminal essence that lingered in her awakening senses. She could almost feel him on her skin, in her pores.... Had he held her last night while she slept? Beside her the bed was rumpled and tossed, but empty.

She missed him.

Where would he be now? With the other men, of course: fishing, or cutting palm fronds, or fixing roofs. Why should she expect to wake and find him beside her? It was late—he had let her oversleep.

But she missed him.

Impossible. Her mind snapped shut like a trap, keeping the thought locked safely inside. It was just too outrageous and intolerable to look at so early in the morning.

Julie scrambled out of bed, feeling out of sorts and vaguely angry without knowing why. She usually woke on a note of optimism—if a bit slowly—but this morning she felt cross and restless. She knew what she needed—a good, exhausting workout followed by a hot shower.

She just wanted to shampoo her hair...do her nails. She wanted her own underwear, darn it!

The door creaked slowly open. Julie jerked around, her heart out of control, but it was only Rita. The other woman put her sleek dark head tentatively around the corner and then, seeing that Julie was awake, smiled apologetically and entered, carrying a plate covered with a napkin, a thermos tucked under her arm.

"Excuse me, I hope I haven't disturbed you. Señor Chayne..."

"Of course you haven't disturbed me," Julie said quickly, making room on the little table beside the bed. "You didn't have to bring me breakfast in bed! I should have been up hours ago. Why did you let me sleep?"

Rita displayed an unexpected dimple. "Señor Chayne's orders. But I thought you would be hungry—you didn't eat much last night."

"I guess I must have been tired," Julie murmured, yawning. She raked a hand through her white gold curls and sat on the edge of the bed. Rita poured steaming black coffee from the thermos and handed it to her.

"*Gracias.*"

"*De nada....*" Rita hesitated, looking shy and uncertain, then turned to go. As she did, her feet encountered the little pile of clothing Chayne had discarded on the floor beside the bed when he had undressed Julie last night—jeans, huaraches and the brightly colored handwoven belt. He had left her wearing the big, soft shirt and cotton panties. Rita stooped to pick up the clothes, an automatic, habitual housewife's gesture, and laid them carefully across the foot of the bed. She fingered the belt admiringly as she placed it on top of the pile. "This is very nice. Very pretty."

"Um!" Julie swallowed scalding coffee and set her cup down abruptly. "I meant to thank you for that. For all of the clothes you let me borrow, but especially for the belt. It's really beautiful. It meant a lot to me. More than you know. I hope—" She broke off. Rita was gazing at her with a puzzled frown, slowly shaking her head. "What is it?"

"You...want to thank *me* for the belt? I don't understand."

"Didn't you give me the belt? But I thought—then where did it come from?"

"*¿Quién sabe?*" Rita lifted her shoulders. "I have never seen it before. Who knows where Señor Chayne found it?"

"Chayne! But I thought *you*—"

Rita shook her head emphatically. "Señor Chayne came to me the night you arrived to borrow something for you to wear." She showed the dimple again. "'Something pretty,' he said. But not a dress—he thought you wouldn't be comfortable wearing a dress." She lifted her hands apologetically. "But it just happened that I was doing my washing, and there wasn't anything I could give him except some...you know..." She gestured with a hand toward her own body. "Some underthings." The dimple came and went, making her look younger, almost impish. "Señor Chayne couldn't use my bra, he said it would be too big for you. And of course my jeans were too big, too." She patted her round, feminine hips and laughed softly. "So all I could give him were the panties and the sandals. The other clothes are his own. And the belt." She touched it, smiling. "I don't know where he got it, but it *is* 'something pretty.' ¿*es verdad?*"

She went out, leaving Julie silent and motionless. She didn't know why Rita's revelation had rocked her so; she could feel herself slowly growing as cold as the waters of the gulf.

That wretched man...no—demon! Why? Why was he doing this to her? Didn't he know it was killing her inside? What good was it if he saved her life and destroyed everything she was?

Julie rose slowly and walked to the tiny clouded mirror that stood on a crude wooden shelf hung on the whitewashed adobe wall. Eyes like burned holes stared back at her out of a white, pinched-looking face.

I look like a lost child, she thought in amazement. She had seen that look so many times in the glare of a spotlight at a dark and lonely desert checkpoint. A lost, terrified child...

She couldn't be in love with him—she couldn't. Just because the sound of his voice could make her forget what she was... Just because his touch could make her forget *who* she was...

It was just a stupid physical reaction. So he was an attractive man. That was no reason for her to lose her head! Just because she had never met a man with walnut skin and cobalt eyes, a man who moved like a panther and beguiled like a demon; just because in all her life she had never met anyone who could ignite fires with his fingers...

She closed her eyes, rubbing miserably at her upper arms. Nerve endings tingled and shimmered at the memory of his touch. She ached with longing.

He was a criminal! She couldn't love him! She *wouldn't* love him! He was nothing but a filthy, rotten, stinking coyote!

A good many emotions were fighting within her; anger submerged victorious. Compared to the seething mess inside her soul, it felt hot and cleansing.

She jumped up, breathing raggedly, then reached for the huaraches and strapped them onto her feet with stiff, jerky movements. The door crashed against the wall of the hut as she left it, heading blindly, almost instinctively for the beach—for her own rocky cove.

Once beyond the sharp rocks Julie slipped off the clumsy sandals and, carrying them in her hand, began to run. She ran along the waterline where the sand was firm and wet, and the sea soon blurred and then erased her footprints. She ran hard at first, then settled into the long steady stride of the distance runner. How far could she run here? To infinity? In Baja, distances meant nothing at all....

She stopped, bending over with her hands on her waist, breathing hard with emotion rather than exertion. She couldn't, after all, outrun her demons.

What a joke it all was! What a cruel joke! For one wild moment she imagined that the guys at the station had set it up, that any minute now they would all jump out from behind the rocks yelling, "April fool!"

What had happened to Julie the cool, the calm, the complete professional.... Julie, who never got involved, never lost her balance, her objectivity.... Julie, who had never expected to fall in love, who had thought herself incapable of it...? She had even told her parents that she would never marry. She could still see the wistful look on her dad's face when he realized that he would never have a grandchild.

And that, at least, was still true, Julie thought with a bark of half-hysterical laughter. Was it punishment—for arrogance, perhaps—that she should fall in love with a man with whom there could be absolutely no hope of a future?

Julie walked on, kicking wretchedly at the sand. No future...and no past, either. Who *was* Chayne Younger? Where had he grown up, spent his childhood? What kind of boy had he been? Did he have a mother, a father...people who loved him? Whom he loved? Was he *married?* It occurred to her with a sense of shock that she hadn't asked him a single question about himself since...since he had made love to her. At that point, she remembered, she had been so frightened by her physical response to him that she hadn't wanted to know anything about him. And now, if her feelings for him were only physical, why did she suddenly want to know all there was to know about him?

She stopped again, rubbing her neck in bitter frustration. Her body felt stiff and tense, her chest tight and achy. She wanted a good workout. It seemed like forever since she'd been to a gym, though quick mental calculations told her that it could not have been more than a week. Working out could make her forget everything; concentrating on her body, on each and every individual muscle in her body, could make it impossible for her to think. And of course there was nothing in the world like flying through the air, her body supple and free...nothing else that could take her out of herself that way.

But that wasn't true anymore, either. Two nights ago she had been taken out of herself and into a whole new dimension, and now she wasn't the same person anymore.

Swallowing a whimper of anguish, Julie dropped her shoes onto the sand. She began slowly, trying some elementary stretching and limbering exercises, listening to the muscles, ligaments and tendons in her body, pushing them to their limits but always careful not to go beyond.

The first front walk-over felt clumsy; the second was better, and she held it, extending her legs in a slow-motion split, testing her balance and control. The loose-fitting shirt got in her way, so she removed it, working in only the little-girl white cotton briefs. Her body was slippery with perspiration, her hair a tangled mass of damp curls. She worked with total absorption, working through the pain of unused muscles, limiting herself to the graceful dance turns and leaps, knowing she wasn't ready yet to risk the dangerous and demanding tumbles that would lift her beyond pain...beyond fear...beyond reason.

But the wet sand stretched away, smooth and glistening, beckoning; it felt cool and springy beneath her bare feet, as firm and resilient as a mat. Almost before she knew what she was doing she was running with power and purpose, gathering momentum for the hurdle, the spring. She launched her body into the air like a missile—flying, flying—only to dive head-first toward the sand in a flawless forward roll. She came to her feet bursting with exhilaration and turned her whole body into a shout of joy, hurtling into a breathtaking series of cartwheels and handsprings that carried her across the sand like a wind-blown leaf. The sense of power and freedom was electrifying. She hardly felt the sand under her hands, her feet, the rushing air that dried the sweat on her body. Her heart sang, I can fly, I can fly....

The sharp-edged volcanic rock lay half-submerged in the sand. She came down on it with the heel of her hand and the shock of pain tore through her wrist and shot up her arm, turning muscles and ligaments to jelly. Momentum carried her body up and over, but she had no reserves left for the push-off, which would return her to her feet. She landed flat on her back with a force that jarred every bone.

For a few seconds she just lay there, stunned, staring up at a sky of flawless blue. As she lifted her head and gave it a shake to clear the cobwebs, she imagined that she heard running footsteps. But when she listened, all she could hear was the pounding of her own heart and the harsh, agonized sounds of her own breathing.

Slowly raising herself to a sitting position, she gripped the wrist of the injured hand and pulled it between her knees, rocking back and forth, softly cursing her foolishness.

"Are you okay?" The question was casual, mildly concerned.

Julie froze for a moment, then resumed her rocking while effervescence surged through her like an injection of a powerful drug. Without turning, she said tightly, "I will be."

"That was quite an exhibition. You're very good."

"Thank you."

"Quite a finish, too. What happened?"

Julie cast a black, bitter look over her shoulder. Chayne was standing a few yards from her, feet apart, thumbs hooked in the waistband of his jeans. His bare chest moved, because he was breathing hard, but his smile was cool, his voice dry and even.

"I hit a rock," she muttered. Her skin tingled and prickled, as if she were breaking out in a rash.

"Bad luck."

"Bad judgment," Julie corrected in disgust. "I'm so out of shape I should never have tried a tumbling run like that without a spotter."

"I wouldn't say you're out of shape," Chayne drawled softly. "I'm no expert, but those weren't exactly beginner's stunts. Very nice to look at, in fact. I especially like your costume." His smile deepened, and the bottom dropped out of Julie's stomach. She cast one helpless glance down at her naked torso, swore softly and dropped her body forward to hide her hot face against her outstretched legs.

A finger traced lightly down her spine from the nape of her neck to the elastic of her panties and turned her bones to melted butter. "What's this? Come on, *Güerita*, don't curl up like a pill bug on my account. It's a bit late for modesty."

He was squatting on his heels beside her, chuckling softly. Julie gripped her ankles and turned her head sideways to glare up at him. Was it her imagination again, or were his eyes really the same color as the sky? Could anyone's eyes possibly be that color?

"Let me see your hand."

He peeled her fingers from her ankle and turned her palm up. Julie silently turned her face back into the shelter of her knees.

"Hmm. Stone bruise. It'll be sore for a day or two, as your doctor, I advise you to stay off it." There was laughter in his voice as he carried her hand to his mouth, pressed a warm kiss into its palm and returned it to her ankle. Julie tensed, trembled, anticipating his touch, but instead his voice dropped away as he shifted position, stretching out on the sand and propping himself on one elbow with his head near her feet. "Are you showing off," he asked pleasantly, "or meditating? That position makes me hurt just to look at it."

"I'm quite comfortable," Julie lied in a muffled voice. But the position constricted her chest, making it too small for her wildly pumping heart. She finally had to abandon it. She straightened, gave her head a defiant shake and dropped back onto her elbows.

"Ah, that's better," Chayne said with satisfaction, and let his lashes drop, veiling the glitter that might have been amusement—or something more disturbing. Julie stared back at him, wishing he wouldn't look at her at all, conscious of the hot sun on her sensitive breasts and stomach.

"I thought you were building roofs or something," she muttered, hoping ill temper would mask her emotions. "What did you do, follow me? How long have you been there spying on me?"

"I'd just come in with a load of thatch when I saw you tear out of the hut." His voice was lazy, almost drowsy. "I thought you seemed upset, so I followed. I've sort of gotten into the habit of looking after you, I guess."

"You don't have to. I can take care of myself!"

"Right," Chayne said dryly, not bothering to make the obvious rebuttal.

"Well, you might have let me know you were watching."

"I didn't want you to stop what you were doing. I liked looking at you." His soft words were like a physical touch, stirring nerve endings to preconditioned responses. Julie swallowed and didn't answer.

"You're very good, I would guess—not being an expert, you understand." He had changed his tone again to a lighter, more conversational one. "Were you ever in competition?"

"Oh sure, I used to go to meets when I was a kid." She shrugged and looked down at the sand. "Like every little aspiring gymnast, I dreamed of championships . . . gold medals . . . making it to the Olympics."

"What happened to the dream?"

"I grew up."

"Not as much as all that," Chayne drawled, sitting up. Julie, following the direction of his warmly amused gaze, blushed furiously and drew her knees up, hugging them to her chest.

"So I'm no centerfold model," she said tightly, tense with unexpected pain. "For a gymnast, I'm a giant!"

Warm fingers closed on her wrist and drew her hand away from her legs. "Don't hide yourself, *Güerita*," Chayne said softly. "I like the way you look."

Julie swallowed convulsively and looked away, overcome with confusing emotions and unable to tolerate the look in those expressive eyes. Chayne's thumb rubbed back and forth over the tendons in her wrist, just barely touching the bruise on the heel of her hand. After a moment she shook her head and said rapidly, unsteadily, "That's not what I meant anyway. I just meant . . . that other things became more important to me. To be a world-class gymnast you have to be totally dedicated. A fanatic. All you do is eat, sleep and train. And that was all I wanted to do until about ninth grade. High school was—well, I wanted to do all the exciting things you're supposed to do in high school. Have dates, go to dances, football games . . . I discovered that there was a lot more to life than gymnastics."

Julie glanced up at him suddenly, realizing that she was telling him about herself and wondering why he was allowing her to do so. His face was impassive, his eyes intent; he had the knack of listening with stillness and concentration, so that there was no doubt about his interest. Encouraged, Julie cleared her throat, shrugged and continued.

"My mom was on my side. She had always worried that I'd regret missing out on childhood, and she didn't want me to miss high school as well. But I think Dad was a little disappointed. He'd been so proud of me—he was the one who drove me to the meets, stayed with me when we had to go out of town."

"Are you an only child?"

She nodded and saw his mouth quirk sideways in a wry smile.

"Sounds to me like you were more concerned with pleasing Daddy than yourself."

"Oh, no!" Julie jumped to her father's defense, shaking her head emphatically. "It wasn't like that at all. I loved it. I truly did. Of *course* I wanted to please my dad—I loved him. He loves sports. He was a pretty fair shortstop in college; I guess I got my coordination and agility from him. And he loves me, so it's only natural, isn't it, that he would teach me to love sports, too? And since I was hardly cut out to be a ballplayer . . ."

"Wrong sex," Chayne said quietly.

Julie stared at him. "What?"

"You weren't a boy. I'd say you probably tried awfully hard to be one, though."

"No!" Julie winced at the stab of a half-forgotten pain. "I told you—he was very proud of me!"

"I'll bet he was." A strange, cold note had crept into the soft drawl. Julie jerked her hand from his grasp and fought back anger. "You don't know him. You don't know *me*. You have no right to make judgments!"

Chayne gave her a long, considering look, and then a twisted smile. "Oh...Julie Maguire," he whispered, shaking his head. "I know you better than you think." He glanced away for a moment and then leveled a razor-sharp stare at her. "For instance, I'd lay odds you were a cheerleader."

Julie glared at him and balled her hands into fists, hating him.

"You were, weren't you?"

Unwillingly she nodded. "Sure, what's wrong with that? How do you know?"

He went on studying her, veiling his eyes in that way that gave them a smoky, almost sleepy look. His face and his voice were cold, remote. "It fits. I told you—I know your type well."

"What do you mean—my *type?*"

He tipped his head to one side and smiled sardonically. "Good Lord, Julie, was there ever a more typical all-American-California-girl-cheerleader *type?* Only child, Daddy's little girl . . . I'll bet I even know what you looked like. You didn't have short hair, did you? Long, bouncy hair—probably a ponytail." He hadn't raised his voice, but it was suddenly tight with inexplicable anger. He drew a finger slowly along her leg from ankle to hip, raising chills. "You wore your cute little short skirt and did cartwheels and handsprings and flirted with the whole damn football team. Dated only the clean-cut all-American heroes, though, and made darn sure none of them ever laid a hand on this sexy little body. After all, you had your image to consider!"

"Oh...*damn* you, you insufferable—" Julie hurled back at him, slapping at his hand, forcing words through teeth clamped tightly on her rage. She was hurt and bewildered by the bitterness and anger in him—too hurt to recognize then that he had slipped back into his own past and was not seeing her at all. "Well, I know your type, too! I'll just bet you were one of those insufferably macho superjocks—the kind that went around bragging about conquests that never happened, making darn sure I didn't have any 'image' left to protect!''

Her voice had risen to a shout that rang in the silent morning. After a long moment, Chayne drew a breath and let it out in a low whistle. He lowered his head and rubbed at the back of his neck, muttering something that sounded like "touched a nerve."

"Julie . . ." His hand riffled through her hair and closed on the back of her neck. "I'm sorry."

She closed her eyes. The warm pressure on her neck moved to her throat and stroked gently up and down over the ache there.

"I don't know what got into me. I didn't mean to hurt you. It's obvious someone already has. Tell me."

"No." Her voice was like sandpaper, and clearing her throat didn't help. Giving her head a quick, violent shake, she pressed her lips together and reached up to grasp the powerful wrist at her throat. And then somehow, without intending to or understanding how she got there, she was in Chayne's arms, shaking with silent sobs and held tightly against his warm, iron chest. He held her while she fought for control, stroking her hair until she had quieted a bit, and then commanded quietly, "Tell me, Julie."

And incredibly she found herself telling him about Carl Swensen. Incredibly, because it was something she had never told a living soul. She told him in detail what Carl had done to her, dredging up from the dank and shadowy basement of her memory all the half-buried pain and fear and humiliation she had suffered as a naive fifteen-year-old.

By the time she had finished she was sobbing like a child again, crying as she had never cried before in all her memory. She wasn't crying for the relatively minor traumas of a sheltered girl. She wept for the Armageddon in her grown-up woman's heart. The war was over and she had lost. Surrender was unconditional. There would have to be a morning after, and to Julie the aftermath of a holocaust could not have looked bleaker.

She did love Chayne Younger. Coyote, smuggler, terrorist, criminal, demon—whatever he was, he was right. None of those things mattered. He was only a man, and she loved him.

The arms that held her, the hands that stroked her hair, the neck into which she sobbed her anguish, the chest that pressed so hard against hers that she could feel its heartbeat as her own—they all belonged to a *man:* the man she loved. She never wanted to be anywhere but in those arms, ever.

Please, God, she prayed, just let me stay here forever. Don't let there be a tomorrow. Make the real world go away.

Make-believe. Couldn't it all be some sort of illusion? It had begun as a charade; why couldn't the whole mess be make-believe, like a movie set? Chayne wasn't a smuggler at all—he was a movie producer. And the others—all actors. Tomorrow the helicopter would arrive to disgorge cameras and lights and technicians and extras, and Chayne would smile and explain that it had all been set up in preparation for filming an epic about the history of Baja California.

"... And Julie, I'd like you to meet Rita and Geraldo Moreno, two of Mexico's biggest film stars.... You may have heard of them...."

The fantasy shimmered and dispersed. Chayne was saying, "Hush . . . hush, it's all right." *It's all right.* As if he knew the real cause of her tears. *It's all right.* As he had told her more than once before.

Julie drew back, wiping her streaming eyes. "It's all right?" she said incredulously. "It isn't! It is *not!*" She knew she must look like a gargoyle, all red and swollen and stuffed up, but she couldn't help it. "Oh, Chayne—please. Please, why can't you stop it? You don't have to do this terrible thing. You can still get out. We can take the camper and just go away!" She waited, pleading with her eyes, seeing the answer in his even before he spoke.

"I'm sorry, Julie. I can't."

"Why? Is it the money? Oh, God—just tell me why!"

He shook his head slowly, his eyes dark and unreadable, and said simply, starkly, "I can't."

"Damn you! Oh, damn you!" Her hands, doubled into fists, pounded at his chest with futile passion. "You . . . mercenary son of a— You cold-blooded—"

Suddenly she froze, her eyes falling to the weal that slashed across his belly. She moved away from him, slowly lifting her swollen eyes to his impassive face.

"That's it, isn't it?" Julie sniffed, wiping at her face with trembling fingers. "It isn't the money at all, is it? You're in this for the *love* of it! It's in your blood! The thrill, the excitement, the danger." She shook her head in wonder, refusing to see the white, pinched look around his eyes, his twisted mouth. "Oh, I've heard of men like you—men who get a taste of war and become addicted to it. War lovers. That's why you do this, isn't it? You love it! You can't live without it! You're a war lover!"

"*War lover!*" Chayne spat the words back at her. For a moment he looked as if he wanted to strangle her, and then the wild light went out of his eyes, leaving them cold and dead. In a curiously flat, metallic voice he said, "Julie Maguire... shall I tell you what I was doing while you were cartwheeling around your pretty green high school football field?"

The rage in her drained away as quickly as it had filled her, and it was replaced by a nameless dread. She had wanted to know about him, but now she was afraid of that knowledge. There was so much pain in his eyes.

He gave that empty, chilling little laugh he used so often. "I was flying a medevac chopper around the Mekong Delta, sweet Julie, a nice little garden spot complete with some interesting extras like booby traps, pungi pits and Bouncing Bettys. Oh, yeah. And napalm. Do you know what human flesh smells like when it's been cooked from the inside out, Julie?"

She shook her head in stark horror, but it was too late for escape. He had caught her wrist in a numbing grip, and his eyes had turned inward to confront his own private demons. He rubbed mechanically at his scar for a moment and then, realizing what he was doing, gave that short, deadly laugh. "You seem to be fascinated by this little reminder. Shall I tell you how I got it?"

"No," she whispered desperately. "Please—I'm sorry."

As if she hadn't spoken, he went on, his words like bullets, cold and impersonal. "I'd set my chopper down near a village—a unit had taken some friendly fire, with heavy casualties. The medic was just a kid—no more than nineteen—and he'd been hit, too. He was running around with a scalp wound as big as my hand, but he'd stuck a pressure bandage on it and put his helmet on over it to hold it in place, and he was doing what he could. I'd taken on almost a full load—all but the dead and good-as-dead—when a Vietnamese woman came running up, clutching this...bundle to her breast. She wasn't much more than a girl, really...not even as big as you are."

His voice had lost the harshness of anger and had gone soft and faraway. "Just a little bit of a thing. And she kept crying, 'Napalm, napalm,' and holding on to that bundle...." He looked right at her then, but Julie wondered whether he really saw her. His eyes were violet with anguish. "I put her in the chopper. If you'd ever seen what napalm does to human beings, you'd know why I didn't look in that bundle.

"I went back for the medic. He didn't want to leave, but I managed to convince him there wasn't any reason for him to stay. He couldn't even stand up, he'd lost so much blood, so I hoisted his arm over my shoulders and got a good grip on his belt and we started for the chopper.

"We both saw her at the same time—the woman." Chayne's eyes stared sightlessly past Julie; she knew he was seeing it all over again—the stark, numbing horror was there, in his face. "She was V.C. And what she had in that bundle was grenades. She was standing there in the doorway of the chopper, and she just looked us right in the eye and pulled out a grenade. I let go of the medic—there was an M-16 right there on the ground. I picked it up and aimed it at her—had her right there in my sights—but I didn't fire. She pulled the pin on the grenade. And I didn't...couldn't...shoot her."

Chayne's voice trailed off. He released her wrist and lay back, one arm across his eyes. Julie wondered if he would continue, she sensed that the story wasn't finished. After a moment his voice came again, sounding empty and tired.

"The medic bellowed like a wounded bull, put his head down and charged. I don't know where he got the strength...." He fell silent again while Julie's heart pulsed agonizingly in slow motion. "A piece of that boy's helmet tore a hole in my belly. So much," he said woodenly, "for the excitement...the *thrill* of war."

Julie sat absolutely still, beyond tears. In spite of the sun that burned her naked back, she felt cold, and there was an odd humming in her ears, like a high-voltage power line. She focused her eyes on Chayne, staring at him until her eyes burned, seeing the explosion in slow motion and living color.

She knew what he had just done, and what it must have cost him. He had given her a piece of his deepest hidden self, a glimpse of a facet of his personality that she was quite certain he did not allow very many people to see. It was a moment she knew might never come again, even if by some miracle she were to grow old with him.

What a rare and complex man he was! He was like a flower with thousands of petals. She could spend a lifetime pulling them away one by one and still never reach his core. Now he had pulled a handful of those petals from his most vulnerable spot and tossed them into her lap, like a gift. And he waited, tensed and exposed, to see what she would do with them.

She knew what she wanted to do. She wanted to comfort him as he had comforted her, but where she had gone into his arms like filings to a magnet, he lay like an effigy, cold and withdrawn, the arm across his face a barricade against her.

Slowly, slowly, she put out her hand...and drew it back. And then, summoning all her courage, she reached out once more and touched her fingers to the ridge that marred the walnut satin of his belly.

His abdomen jerked convulsively, shrinking reflexively from her touch. And as before, his fingers closed on her wrist, pulling her hand away.

For a moment Julie knew frustration and defeat. Then she lifted her head, set her chin in determined lines and bent to touch her lips to the taut, sun-warmed skin of his torso. Her exploring tongue found the scar ridges and traced them, hesitantly at first, down across the quivering concavity of belly to the soft furring of hair below his navel.

There was the sibilant gasp of indrawn breath and then the suspension of breathing. The fingers on her wrist tightened until they hurt, but beneath her lips his belly muscles quivered like captive butterflies.

"Julie..." he rasped. *"What...are you doing?"*

She lifted her head just far enough to look into his bright, pain-filled eyes, then smiled and licked the salt taste of him from her lips.

"Hush...and let me heal your wound," she said, ducking her head to expel the words in soft puffs against his skin. "In the oldest and most natural way in the world...."

Chapter 10

For one timeless moment there was absolute stillness; the flesh beneath her lips was as rigid as carved walnut. And then several quick tremors shuddered through Chayne's body, and he embraced her head with his hands.

There was so much tension in him! Julie could almost hear it, not with her ears but with a new and special sense that was tuned to him alone. There was a curious restraint, too, as if he were trying to keep himself in check, like a man afraid of his own strength. Was he afraid of hurting her? He was holding her so tightly against him. Or—strong, macho man that he was—was he only afraid of his own emotions?

For Julie, his unexpected vulnerability was the battering ram that shattered the last tattered remnants of her defenses. Emotion burst through her like a supernova—she felt bigger, brighter, more powerful than a thousand suns. So this is love, she thought, dazed, as she tucked her arms around Chayne's waist and held him as tightly as he held her. She felt as fiercely protective as a mother tiger—savage...ruthless. At that moment she knew that she would kill for the man she held in her arms; that she would die for him; and that if he were indeed a demon, she would gladly give him her soul....

"God, Julie—" Chayne's voice was raw, as if it hurt his chest to talk. "I'm sorry...."

"Shh...it's all right."

"Please—forgive me, Julie. I had no right..."

"Yes! Yes, you did!"

"*No*. I had no right to lay all that on you. It was unforgivable."

"Chayne..."

"*Inexcusable!* I'm sorry, Julie, you didn't deserve—*ouch!*" He lifted both his head and hers and gave her a fierce, incredulous glare. "What did you do, *bite* me?"

"Just getting your attention," Julie said serenely, and ducked her head to nuzzle the spot on his abdomen she had just caught—not gently—between her teeth.

"My attention!"

"Hush. And now that I have it, do you suppose you could shut up?"

There was a moment's shocked silence, and then he laughed out loud, an unrestrained, almost boyish peal of delight. The sound of it sent another seismic wave of emotion trembling through her as he hauled her up over his body and wrapped his arms around her, hugging her so hard her bones cracked. And then *she* was laughing and hugging him with all her strength, and for a while they just clung to each other, breathless and shaking.

Presently Julie gave a series of small settling-down sighs and relaxed, her moist cheek pillowed on Chayne's chest. His hair tickled his nose. She twitched it, then turned her face into his chest, located the smooth flat circle of his nipple and kissed it.

Chayne, who had relaxed his arms, squeezed her again and began to stroke her back. "Ah, Julie...," he sighed. "You do heal me."

So this is love, Julie thought again, awed. She wanted to soothe his hurts, take away his pain, protect him, comfort him, give—just *give*—to him. Purely and simply, she wanted to give him love, but since she didn't dare tell him so, either with words or with telltale shining eyes, she gave the only way she could. Stirring within his arms, she nuzzled the hair on his chest, discovering the crisp-silk texture with her lips. Her tongue found his nipple again and began to stroke it, laving it in gentle circles as it contracted and hardened in the warmth of her mouth.

"Julie," Chayne said hoarsely after a moment, "what are you trying to do?"

"I'm trying to..." She hesitated only a fraction of a second and then finished "...make love to you." *He* had used that phrase—insisted on it, in fact—so it was safe for her to do so. "Am I succeeding?"

A chuckle rumbled up through his chest. "Admirably."

"I want to make love to you," she whispered against his skin, and then, swallowing her shyness, lifted her head and said fiercely, "I want to give you pleasure, Chayne."

He caught her head between his hands and held it while his eyes burned and fused with hers. "You *do*," he said huskily. "Believe me." Slowly he pulled her head down.

"No, I mean—"

His lips, already parted for the kiss, curved in a smile of understanding. He stopped, waiting.

Julie lowered her face to his, watching his eyes close before she gave a tiny, inaudible sigh and closed her own. Her lips touched his, felt them move slightly beneath hers, felt his moustache brush and tingle across her upper lip. His hands lightly cupped her head, neither urging nor restricting her, while she traced the outline of his mouth with her tongue.

"Julie..." She felt her name rather than heard it—a soft expulsion of breath. "You're trembling."

"I know. I'm not very good at this."

"You're wonderful. Don't be afraid—kiss me, Julie."

She teased the inside of his lips and was rewarded by a low groan of frustration. Instinct took over as she burrowed her fingers through his hair and melded her mouth to his. His mouth opened to welcome the shy offering of her tongue; she felt him quivering with restrained passion and knew that he was trying not to take the lead away from her. The knowledge that she could affect him so deeply went to her head like champagne, making her brave.

She became aware of her naked breasts flattened against crisp hair and resilient muscle and, without lifting her mouth from his, moved sinuously against his chest. Another deep-throated groan rumbled through him as his hands, vibrant with the strain of self-control, molded the sides of her body from arm-pits to hips, gripped and then smoothed over the mounds of her buttocks.

Lifting her mouth from his at last, Julie licked her lips, cleared her throat and said in a blurred voice, "I want to make it good for you, but, um . . . I'm not—I don't know what—"

"Julie," Chayne said, his voice thick with laughter and pas-sion, "you know all you need to know. Believe me. If you make me feel any better, I may resort to rape after all."

"I thought you said you'd never—"

"There's a first time for everything!"

"Hmmm," Julie murmured, growing confidence dropping her voice to a sultry growl. "Is that a threat?"

"No . . ." he whispered, eyes blazing. "A promise."

"I'll remember that." Julie chuckled deep in her throat and pressed her lips to the triangular hollow at the base of his throat. "Tell me . . . if I do anything wrong."

She kept her voice light, her words playful, knowing that if she wasn't careful she might blurt out the words that sang in her heart: I love you, Chayne. I love you. . . .

In exploring his body she lost herself; she had meant to give to him unselfishly, but as the tide of excitement and passion grew in her, she wondered who was pleasuring whom.

Chayne's hands dipped beneath the elastic of her panties to smooth lightly over the skin of her bottom, and then her waist, her back, the sides of her breasts as she slid downward, blaz-ing a trail of kisses over his chest and across the ripple of his ribs. Finally he cupped her head almost reverently, his fingers burrowing through cotton fluff to trace the bones of her skull while her tongue followed his scar to where it dove beneath the waistband of his jeans.

"Julie, I—" His hands dropped away from her, going to the metal buttons just beneath her chin.

"Shh . . . be still." She pushed his hands away and replaced them with her own, dealing with the last impediment to her ex-ploration while her tongue quivered over his belly, impatient with that denim barricade.

And then she sucked in her breath, surprised by the surge of primitive exultation that swept her as she realized the extent of his arousal. His body was a furnace—she marveled now at the self-control that kept him so still.

"Do you still think you're no good at this?" Chayne rasped, his voice wry. And then he gasped in surprise as she touched him with her lips. "Julie—good God..."

After a moment she lifted her head, and he raised himself on his elbows to look at her. She was awed and a little frightened by the fierce light in his eyes, but she gave him a slow sweet smile and moved sideways, taking her weight off him so that she could help him divest himself of his clothes.

"I think," he croaked when she touched him again, "that I've had about all the 'feeling good' I can stand."

Julie gave him a look of wide-eyed innocence and sat back, demurely folding her hands in her lap. "Oh—do you want me to stop?"

"*Stop?* Come here—I'll show you *stop!*" He caught her around the waist, pulling her against him and deftly stripping the virginal white panties down and off. "You're the demon, Julie Maguire," he growled, sending sharp electric shocks into her ear with the tip of his tongue. "A witch...a sorceress. You don't know what you do to me...."

She gasped and squirmed in his grasp, wriggling even closer into his embrace. He gave a low primal growl and met her mouth with his, driving his tongue deep inside her. The urgent rhythm of his mouth matched the pulses that throbbed through her body, and she clung to him, glad to relinquish the initiative into his experienced and sensitive hands.

"I've always wondered," she gasped as he bore her over onto her back, "how people do this without getting all full of sand."

"Oh, you have, have you?" His belly jerked with laughter. "Is that the sort of thing you wonder about, *Güerita?* No wonder you're such a natural wanton.... It's very simple. Shall I show you?"

"Trust you to know a thing like that," Julie retorted breathlessly, nipping his earlobe.

Chayne chuckled softly, kissing his way along her jaw to her mouth. "Do you want to discuss my past sins right now?"

"No...show me. Please."

"All right, Julie—hang on." He rolled onto his back, pulling her over and astride him. "Now... just relax and let me guide you. Do what I tell you...."

"Don't I always?" Julie whispered weakly, and then gasped as his hands cupped her buttocks, carefully adjusting her to meet the thrust of his penetration. His eyes seared into her soul with blue flames while his body filled hers with fires of another kind. Heat turned her bones to melted honey, and after that it was all she could to to breathe, let alone talk.

"Now then," Chayne whispered, brushing lightly over her back as she lay upon his chest. "See? That worked all right, didn't it? No sand at all."

"Mmm-hmm." Julie settled herself even more comfortably, adjusting her body to the bumps and hollows of his, drowsy and content with the warm sun on her back and the steady cadence of his heart beneath her cheek. "I guess you do know what you're talking about."

"Yeah... I do," Chayne murmured, touching his lips to her temple. "See what happens when you trust me?"

Dear God... please let me remember him just like this.

...Standing in the prow of a boat, feet wide apart and braced on the gunwales, a figure of dark and savage beauty in bold relief against a cerulean sky....

Julie shifted the bucket in her hands and stayed to feast her eyes on Chayne, while Rita, Linda, Juanita and Carlito moved on across the tideflat. They were digging clams this morning, while the men worked to repair the storm-damaged boats.

How wild he looked—how free! Dressed as usual in tattered jeans rolled to the knee, chest bare and gleaming coppery in the sun, dark hair bound by that strip of bandana, he looked like a pirate—no, more primitive still, an aboriginal man unspoiled and ungoverned by civilization.

Wind stirred through her hair as she turned to walk on, her bare feet plopping in cool wet sand. It's this place, Baja, she thought for the hundredth time, swinging the bucket so that it brushed lightly against her bare legs. It was such a harsh and lonely place, so far removed from civilization. It was easy to forget that there was another world out there, easy to fall into a basic pattern of existence as old as mankind, where the only things of any importance at all were food, shelter and human companionship.

Look at me, she thought in amazement. I've gone as native as he has! Her skin was dry and brown, scorched and scoured by sun and salt water, her hair an unruly tangle. She wore a skirt of Rita's, and a flowered shirt knotted under breasts unconfined by a bra. The skirt was too long for her, and she had tucked its hem into its waistband, leaving her legs bare to midthigh.

How far away it all seemed—San Diego, the Border Patrol, her friends at the station, even her family. The things she had considered necessities—refrigerators and telephones, grocery stores and hot running water—none of them seemed to matter here.

I could be happy staying right here like this with him. I could be content just cooking his meals . . . having his babies. . . .

That thought produced an unpleasant jolt under her ribs. A vision came to her with stunning clarity, driving the cobwebs of fantasy from her mind: a packet of small white pills lying on gleaming tile beside a bottle of shampoo and a toothbrush. Symbols of the real world. Baja was a fantasy, full of mirages, of people who weren't what they seemed. Reality was that packet of pills and the possible consequences of not taking them. Reality was a badge and a uniform, and the oath she had taken when she accepted them.

Reality was the unmistakable eggbeater rhythm of a helicopter's rotors, coming steadily closer. . . .

They all heard it and froze, listening. Carlito was the first to acknowledge it, shouting, "Helicopter, helicopter!" as he danced his delight and pointed skyward. Rita, Linda and Julie all shaded their eyes and watched it change from a dot in the southern sky to that characteristic and oddly sinister insect shape. Only Juanita seemed oblivious, plodding on across the tidal flat, probing at the sand with her fork, stubbornly archaic in the face of civilization's intrusion.

Julie looked toward the boats. The entire camp had become a tableau, it seemed, a film frozen in midframe, but all she saw was Chayne. Astride the gunwales of a fishing boat, upper body half-turned, arm raised to shade his eyes—oh yes, she would remember this scene for as long as she lived. What was he thinking? How did he feel? Was adrenaline pumping through his veins, keeping him from feeling anything, keeping him from seeing buildings full of happy families and laughing children reduced to twisted, bloody chaos?

The helicopter settled with ponderous dignity onto the beach, its twin rotors stirring up sand, its racket deafening after the quiet. A small dun-colored figure dropped to the ground and moved quickly out of the rotors' draft. Another followed, and another. Julie counted automatically—three . . . four . . . five . . . six . . . seven. *Seven.* The last one wore a short-sleeved white shirt and blue pants, like a vacationing dentist. Gabriel.

At Julie's elbow Rita sighed and said with characteristic practicality, "We'd better get busy and finish this. We are going to have guests for lunch."

Julie skipped the midday meal, and supper as well. She felt guilty about leaving the work of feeding eleven hungry men to Rita and old Juanita, especially with Linda's doubtful assistance, but the thought of serving meals to a squad of cold-blooded killers made her excuse of an upset stomach all too valid.

Anyone looking at them would have found it hard to believe what they really were, though. They were so young! And, except for a quality of aloofness and a certain dark intensity, completely ordinary. They were a breed apart, these young people so fanatic about a cause that they would die for it and take thousands of innocent people with them. Years of experience with lawbreakers of all kinds had taught Julie the folly of expecting criminals to wear distinguishing marks of some kind, but these men were different. They were beyond her understanding and experience. They made her skin crawl with their very *ordinariness*. Only Gabriel, with his comfortable paunch and shrewd greedy eyes, was recognizable to her. *He* was the mercenary here—a wholesaler of human lives. The quick, intensive once-over she received from those prominent black eyes did not trouble her. It was a familiar look, and he was a known quantity. Seeing him made Julie realize just how far out of that mold Chayne was; he was no mercenary—she'd swear by every instinct she had that he wasn't doing this for the money. But if not for the love of adventure, and not for the cause or for money—then why?

Why. Julie paced the confines of the darkening hut, beating her fists against her thighs in frustration and despair. How could he? He seemed like a decent, even a good person. The women here idolized him, the men respected him, and Carlito...well, she had seen him with Carlito and... Was that the moment she had begun to fall in love with him? He seemed to care about people—the way he had helped the old people with the ditch, and put up a roof for Carlito. The way he had been with *her.*

Yes...with her. He had been remarkably kind, in his way. He had a capacity for sensitivity and understanding beyond anything she had ever encountered in a man—and an equal capacity for ruthlessness.

He had made her fall in love with him, against the opposition of every value and principle she had. He had made love to her with unbelievable skill and genuine passion, but how did he *feel* about her? He seemed to care what happened to her. What possible motive could he have had for saving her life if he didn't care about her? But he didn't care enough to stop this insanity! It just didn't make sense! Chayne Younger was a puzzle.

And I hate him, she thought in desperation. I swear to God I do! I love him, and for that most of all, I hate him!

The door of cardon poles opened and Chayne came in. As an icy calm settled over her, masking the turmoil inside, Julie whirled to face him.

"You haven't eaten all day," he said with typical abruptness. "Don't you feel well?"

She couldn't help the little spasm of pain that knifed through her. His tone of voice, his face, his eyes were once more hard and impersonal, the way they had been during those first few hours in the camper. They had come so far since then. In the last twenty-four hours since that traumatic and revealing episode on the beach, he had seemed almost carefree... younger...lighter...even *happy.* She had begun to think—to hope—that she might be able to persuade him to abort the raid. But that hope was gone now. His face was closed and dark, his eyes cold flames. El Demonio Garzo was back.

Julie cleared her throat and answered in a low voice, "No, as a matter of fact, I don't feel very well."

He studied her impassively. "I hope you're not too sick to travel."

"Travel?" Her heart gave a startled lurch.

"You're coming with us," he said flatly. "If I leave you here, you'll try something foolish before our dust has settled." His mouth twisted in that old, humorless smile. "Besides . . . you might come in handy as a hostage if things go bad."

"I see." Julie swallowed against iron bands of pain. "And when you don't need me anymore—as a hostage—what then?"

There was a moment of silence, and then he swore briefly and violently. "Don't look at me like that! What do you expect from me? I told you I'd keep you alive. I promised you wouldn't be hurt." His voice sounded gravelly; she wished he would clear his throat. "Damn it, Julie. That's all I ever promised you."

Julie nodded. "I know," she said painfully, and went on looking at him.

Silence hummed and crackled between them. And somehow, almost imperceptibly, Chayne's face changed, softened, became human flesh instead of carved wood.

"Damn it, Julie," he whispered.

"Would it—" She swallowed and started again. "Would it do any good to beg you to stop this?"

"I can't stop it, Julie." He sounded tired.

Her throat was tight with tension; her jaws felt stiff and creaky. "You don't have to be a part of it."

"Yes—I do."

"Why?" She would not cry. She wouldn't! "Just tell me—"

"I can't explain." His voice was wooden. "I'm sorry."

Julie drew a long quivering breath and closed her eyes. It was her last shot, and if it failed, nothing mattered anyway. She had nothing to lose. In a barely audible voice that seemed far too loud she said, "Would it . . . make any difference at all if I told you . . . I love you?"

Silence again. And unendurable tension. Her emotions were strung perilously on a thin elastic filament of self-control that was being stretched beyond all reasonable limits. What would happen to her reason and sanity if it snapped? She had to open her eyes finally, if only to break that awful suspense, and when she did she released a soft, involuntary gasp. She had caught Chayne by surprise, and in that one unguarded instant his eyes were transparent, the way they had been the day he had almost killed the rattlesnake beside the cistern. And as it had that day, the brief glimpse inside him both exhilarated and terrified her.

But it was only an instant. Chayne turned away, breaking the silence. "I wish I could make you understand that even if I could opt out—and I can't—my absence will *not* keep the attack on the Expo from happening. Get that through your head once and for all, damn it! There is nothing—repeat, *nothing*—you can do to change things. I told you I'd save your life. When it's too late for you to get in the way I'll see that you get back home. That's the best I can do. I'm sorry."

"Thank you," Julie said stiffly, pride dripping coldly from her words. "You've done...more than enough."

"Oh, for—" He jerked his head up. "What in the hell is that supposed to mean?"

There was danger in the soft steel of his voice, but Julie ignored it. "This has worked out pretty well for you, hasn't it? In exchange for my life, you've had someone to warm your bed for you—a pretty inexpensive whore, wouldn't you say?"

She saw him wince as if she had struck him. Under his breath he whispered what sounded like "...never know how expensive...." Little blue currents of anger glittered in his eyes as he smiled and stepped closer. Her heart had begun a drum roll, but she stubbornly held her ground. "If that's how you see yourself," he drawled softly, reaching without haste to stroke the skin on her upper arms, "then I guess that's what you are. But, *Güerita,* just don't forget who started this."

He held her arms in a light grasp, exerting no pressure at all, and yet she yearned toward him. Incredible—but in spite of her anger and grief, her rejection of all he was and meant to do, he still compelled her...drew her...excited her. In spite of everything, she wanted him!

And he knew it—oh, he knew it! His lashes dropped to veil smoky eyes as he watched her, a sad, bitter smile clinging to his lips. And then slowly, watching her all the while, he lowered his head.

His kiss plunged deep into her; she felt it like a knife in her heart. His hands moved to her exposed rib cage, not to draw her close but to use the space between their bodies to tease and torment her. His hands drew exquisite patterns over her skin, touching lightly, delicately, raising goose bumps and silvery shivers of desire while his mouth and tongue, with a deep, pulsing rhythm, simulated sexual possession....

When at last he withdrew, Julie was shaking so hard she could barely stand. She swayed drunkenly, and Chayne's hands tightened convulsively on her waist. For a moment he glared down at her, his eyes demon bright, and then he muttered under his breath and pulled her roughly into his arms.

Julie's cry of denial was smothered by his mouth. He kissed her deeply, holding her head with his hand, and then drew back and said thickly, "No?" And as she began desperately to shake her head, he claimed her mouth again... and again.

It was a conflagration, the kind that can have only one consequence. Where she found the strength to break away from him, she never knew, but suddenly she was free, shaking her head and breathing in frantic gulps.

"No—please. Oh, please don't. I don't want you—"

"The hell you don't!"

"All right, I do! But I *don't*. I want you. You make me want you; I can't help myself! That's what's so unforgivable. You know how I feel—how I must be feeling right now—and you'd do *this* to me? Damn you, you take away my will! If you make love to me tonight, so help me, Chayne, I...I'll never forgive you! *Never!*"

"That's crazy! You want me, and I need—"

"No, it's not crazy. Don't you have any feelings at all? Oh God, Chayne—if you have any compassion for me at all, you'll just leave...me...alone!"

"Any compassion...?" For a long moment he held her, breathing raggedly, and then he swore savagely and thrust her from him. "All right, I'll leave you alone." His words came in angry spurts as he snatched up a canvas satchel and began throwing odds and ends into it—his razor and shaving cream, a change of clothes, cigarettes. Finally he grabbed a pillow from the bed, tucked it under one arm and turned to where Julie still stood hugging herself and shaking.

"I'll wake you," he said in clipped, angry tones. "We leave at first light." He allowed himself a thin smile. "Somehow or other I don't think you'd manage to get up that early without help."

"Thank you." Julie cleared her throat and repeated it with a deeper meaning. *"Thank you."*

"Yeah. Well, sleep well."

"Chayne—"

"What?"

"Where will you go?"

"Wherever the others are, I suppose, where else?"

"Won't you—will it get you in trouble, not spending the night with me?"

He gave a short bark of ironic laughter. "It'll probably get me *respect*, depriving myself of a woman's company the night before an important mission. These guys are fanatics—probably practice total abstinence! My stock ought to rise considerably. *Buenas noches, Güerita* . . . and thanks a lot!"

Chapter 11

Dawn's early light was something Julie appreciated only when it heralded the end of a long graveyard shift. Dressing in chilly darkness, shivering while roosters crowed and others slept, had never been among her favorite pastimes, and it didn't help having a dangerous-looking man in a dark turtleneck watching her every move, either.

"You don't have to wait for me. I'm *up,* for God's sake!" she muttered crossly. "What do you think I'm going to do? Crawl back into bed?"

Chayne drew deeply on his cigarette and didn't answer. The glowing tip of the cigarette flared briefly, casting sinister shadows across the planes of his face and giving his eyes an unearthly glitter. Julie shuddered and finished dressing in silence.

"Ready?" Chayne asked when she had folded the last of her borrowed clothing into a pile and was looking abstractedly around the tiny hut that had become more home than prison. She nodded, and he dropped a windbreaker across her shoulders. "Let's go."

Outside in the growing daylight Rita waited with a thermos of coffee. She thrust it into Julie's arms, and then hugged her impulsively.

"Adiós, Julie," she whispered. *"Vaya con Dios."*

"Thank you," Julie whispered back. "For everything. I left the clothes in the hut. Please thank Linda for me."

"I will, I will. Don't worry. Good-bye, Julie."

"Good-bye." She couldn't think *why* she should feel like crying.

The camper was already loaded, its motor running. Chayne handed her into the cab and took his place behind the wheel. A short distance away Pepe and Geraldo stood talking; at a short tap on the horn from Chayne, Pepe broke away and came over at a brisk trot, giving Julie a swift, appraising glance as he climbed in beside her. Geraldo moved to his wife's side and slipped an arm around her waist.

"Geraldo's not coming?" Julie asked Chayne in a nervous undertone.

He gave her a sideways glance and put the truck in gear. "There wasn't room," he grunted, leaving unspoken the obvious answer—that *she* had taken Geraldo's place. At least, Julie thought grimly, if nothing else I've done that much for Rita!

The sky was turning pastel pink and mauve and blue as the camper growled over the steep grade, leaving behind the Sea of Cortez, gilded by a rising sun and shining like all the treasures of El Dorado.

Once again Julie managed to be asleep when they crossed the border. She had stayed awake through the long, hot day of grueling travel over bumpy and winding desert tracks, through forests of cardon and weird, twisting cirio trees, dense thickets of cholla and mesquite, and across the endless mud flats of the Colorado River delta. By late afternoon they were passing the cultivated fields and vineyards near Mexicali, where the road was in fairly good condition. After a brief meal and rest stop in Mexicali they were off again, whizzing along on paved roads, and it was then that the monotony finally got to her. She kept jerking her head upright and peering owlishly through the windshield into the sunset, but it was a lost cause. The next time she woke it was dark, and her cheek was resting in the hollow of Chayne's shoulder.

The camper had stopped; it was the sensation of abruptly arrested motion that had wakened her.

After one frozen moment of complete disorientation she realized that they were stopped at a traffic light, and an instant later registered the fact that the street signs were in English. They were home! There were people here, other cars, stores, telephones—police! What if she could cause an accident, or create a disturbance that would attract the attention of a passing patrol car? Pepe was driving. Could she bump his arm . . . pull the keys from the ignition . . . grab the wheel?

As if in answer, Chayne's arm tightened around her shoulders like a steel band. He must have felt the tension in her muscles.

"Don't even try it," he whispered against her hair. "I'll knock you out if I have to."

Julie forced herself to relax, remembering only too vividly the single blow to the chin with which he had so effortlessly neutralized her once before. She began to watch for landmarks and signs, trying to get her bearings. And she soon realized with a surge of excitement and renewed determination that she knew where she was.

She'd been through this little town in the plateau country northeast of San Diego many times, and had once even checked out a report of illegals working on a horse ranch near here. But Ramona was such a small town, just beginning to feel the pressures of urban development; in another minute they'd be beyond its stoplights and fast-food restaurants, its gas stations and phone booths. If she could only get them to stop. . . .

She began to fidget and squirm. "Chayne . . ."

"What?"

"Do you suppose we could—I mean, how much longer will it be before we stop? I really need to . . . um . . . I'm sorry. The coffee, I guess."

"We'll be stopping in a little while. Just a few minutes, as a matter of fact."

"I don't know if I can wait."

"You'll have to," Chayne said coldly. "You didn't really think I'd risk stopping in town, did you?"

Julie subsided, reluctantly—and momentarily—conceding defeat, and went back to studying the road and moonlit countryside with avid concentration.

Several miles north of town they left the highway and turned onto a country road that wound uphill past open pastures studded with spreading oak trees. Here and there a light marked a ranch house nestled in a sheltered valley. This was cattle country.

The camper slowed and turned, rattled across a cattle guard and then lurched up a rutted track that ran alongside a creek. Pepe finally stopped beside a broken wooden fence, set the brake and got out, stretching and shaking his legs one at a time.

"What *is* this place?" Julie asked Chayne, bending to peer out the window. "Why are we stopping here?"

For a minute she thought they were still in Baja after all. The silvery moonlight illuminated a building of whitewashed adobe, a belfry rising with poignant and lonely dignity above its heavy wooden doors.

"It's a *church!*" Julie said incredulously, answering at least part of her own question.

"Abandoned," Chayne said briefly. "We'll rest here till daylight."

"How in the world did you ever find this place?"

"Never mind. Are you getting out? I thought you were dying."

"Look at that—those walls must be three feet thick!"

They had climbed stiffly out of the truck and were both rubbing circulation back into cramped limbs. Behind them the terrorists were emerging from the camper and doing the same, talking softly as they followed Pepe up the short, steep rise to the dark, massive doors.

"There's a creek down there, just over that bank. You can...wash up. Whatever. And Julie—" Chayne put his hands on her shoulders and waited until she raised her eyes to his face. In a curiously urgent undertone he said, "Don't try anything stupid, huh? This time it might not be me who comes after you. Promise me you won't run, Julie, or I *swear* I'll come with you, and I won't let you out of my sight."

"I promise," Julie lied glibly, not even bothering to cross her fingers.

Chayne studied her intently, then sighed and gave her a little shake. "Look," he whispered, "I suppose it's too much to ask, but damn it, you've come this far with me—can't you just bear with me a little longer? Please. Julie, don't cross me up now!" His head moved against the sky and his lips touched hers gently. And then, as if he couldn't help himself, he returned with a low groan and a sigh to claim her mouth with a kind of restrained desperation. *"Promise me."*

She swallowed, then ruthlessly blocked out her trembling response to him. "I . . . promise."

"All right, Julie." He lifted his hands reluctantly. She could feel his eyes on her as she made her way across the silvery ground to the creek bed.

Unlike most Southern California streams in August, this one had water in it. It chattered and chuckled, and its banks were cushioned by a thick carpet of oak mulch that deadened her footsteps. It was a chance—her *only* chance. If only her knees weren't shaking so! If only she couldn't still feel the warmth of Chayne's mouth on her own. *God help me—I've got to do it. It all depends on me!* She hesitated only a fraction of a second more before moving swiftly and soundlessly down the ravine.

She hesitated longer when she came to the place where the creek crossed the paved road, flowing under it in corrugated pipes too small to wade through. She would have to cross in the open. If only it weren't such a bright night! But it had to be done; she was committed now. Like a runner on starting blocks, she got ready . . . set . . . then darted across the pavement in a half crouch.

She was crawling under the barbed wire on the other side when she heard an exclamation in Spanish, an answering oath—Chayne's voice—and heavy, running footsteps.

Julie had a head start and she was fast, but it was a long way across open pasture to those clustered rectangles of light, the windows of the ranch houses. She ran headlong, with grim determination rather than panic, and with all the speed and strength her years of conditioning had given her. But even without panic the sensation was nightmarish; she couldn't feel her feet touch the ground, so she seemed to be flying in slow motion while the lights in the distance came no closer. Whistling wind and the thunder of her heart filled her ears, so she couldn't hear her pursuers, and she didn't dare waste energy looking over her shoulder.

Run. Just run. Don't look back. Only a little farther now.

The lights were gone; there was a little hill between the pasture and the house. All she had to do was get over that hill. She had the strength. Did she have the time? *Oh, please, God— don't let me stumble!*

A barbed-wire fence loomed ahead in the moonlight. For one wild moment she wondered if she could vault it—but reason prevailed. With a whimper and a curse she dropped to her stomach and began to wriggle under the bottom strand.

A heavy weight came down between her shoulder blades, slamming her to the ground and crushing the breath from her lungs. Instinctively she tried to turn to face her assailant; the sneakered foot between her shoulders jammed angrily forward and she froze. A stream of appalling profanity poured from the dark silhouette looming against the sky.

"You had to do it, didn't you?" Chayne spat the words between his teeth, sucking in air in harsh gulps. "Damn bloody little fool—I told you not to try it!"

"What did you expect—"

"*Shut up!* Shut up and lie still! I expect you to have some sense. To use your... Hell, I don't know! Damn it, Julie, you try my resources! I'm running out of subterfuges to keep you alive!"

His words were punctuated with little sounds of effort, Julie strained to see what he was doing, and then went rigid with shock. He had reached into his shirt and pulled a gun from the waistband of his jeans. Julie recognized her own service revolver.

"No! Chayne—"

"*Shut... up!* For God's sake, shut up and lie still!" He inspected the chambers and released the safety. Julie opened her mouth, but before she could even acknowledge terror it was over. The night exploded and echoed and reverberated all around her—and once again, inexplicably, she was still alive. Chayne had fired twice in rapid succession—into the soft turf beyond her head.

While she was still dazed and numb with shock, he dropped swiftly to his knees beside her and rolled her limp body under the fence. Then, tucking the gun back into his shirt, he crawled after her.

"Chayne, what—I thought—"

"Yeah, I know what you thought." His whisper was harsh and bitter. "For the last time, keep your mouth shut. Play dead, damn it! Sound carries on a night like this. I don't know how much they can see, either."

There were a million things she wanted to ask, but she swallowed all of them and forced herself to remain limp as Chayne bent and hoisted her body over his shoulder. *Why does he always carry me like this?* Julie thought with giddy irrelevance, but she couldn't ask him that, either. It was so undignified, with her bottom in the air and her head dangling!

But she had no choice but to do as Chayne told her and play dead, allowing herself to flop lifelessly as he strode rapidly, half running, around the base of the hill and into a grove of oaks that hid them from view of the church across the pasture.

Under one dark and spreading canopy he dumped Julie untidily onto the prickly, spongy oak mulch, then turned away from her, poised and listening. The gun, she noted, was back in his hand.

Half-drunk with fear and confusion, she heard her own voice like the sound track from a very old movie, high and tinny. "Why do you do that? I hate to be carried like that!"

"Hush." He was a shadow among other shadows. A panther crouched and ready to spring. After a long and suspenseful wait he moved again, turning to her and tucking the gun away.

"I won't be carried like a sack of beans!" Julie said in a childish quaver. She was close to real hysterics, but completely unable to do anything about it. She couldn't even seem to control what was coming out of her mouth.

Chayne dropped to one knee beside her. "Easy...easy," he murmured in the tone of voice one would use to quiet a skittish horse. And then, in a calm, matter-of-fact voice, like a professor in a classroom, "I'm sure you know that's the most efficient way to carry a dead weight, and it has the added advantage of leaving me with a hand free. Now—" His fingers brushed the side of her face. "Are you going to be able to pull yourself together?"

"You sh-should have *sh-shot* me," she said jerkily. "I told you—"

"Julie, for God's sake!"

"I told you I'd keep trying. What are you going to do with me now? You know I'll do it again! I'm going to stop you—or die trying! I'm—"

His hands bit into her shoulders, and his mouth chopped off her ragged ramblings. She began to struggle for air, forgetting in her befogged state that she could still breathe through her nose. Blackness had begun to creep in around the edges of her consciousness before Chayne released her. She fell back limply, gasping and sobbing for breath. Chayne caught her shoulders again and gave her a violent shake.

"Now maybe you'll shut up and listen to me! I'll have to leave you here—you've given me no choice about that—and I can't . . . oh, *hell*." His hands dropped away and he sat back. Here under the trees it was dark, and he was only a darker shape—faceless. Julie wished she could see his eyes. His voice sounded so tired. Almost . . . defeated. "Julie . . . why is it that you always seem to drive me to violence? Every time you come near me I want to either strangle you or make love to you! Do you have any idea how you've complicated my life?"

Julie opened her mouth to make a sardonic retort and then closed it again. Something in his tone kept her silent. In the darkness his fingers found her face and traced it, like a blind person trying to memorize the face of a loved one.

"I suppose . . . I have no right to ask this of you. I need you to trust me, Julie. Bear with me. Things won't always be like this. There's so much I'd like to tell you, but I can't. Not now. Please, Julie . . ."

His fingers gauged her response. She closed her eyes tightly and pressed her lips together, holding herself rigid, holding her breath against the shuddering sob that was building inside her chest, and after an eternity his hand dropped away. She heard him whisper, "No. S'pose not."

And then, lightly, his tone wry, he went on. "Would it make any difference at all if I told you I love you?"

He was mocking her. Of course he was. He had to be. *Oh God . . . let him be joking. . . .*

"No," Julie said thickly, gulping down tears. "It wouldn't."

"If you go to the police, you'll probably cost me my life. You know that, don't you?"

"If I *don't* go to the police, you'll cost hundreds of others!"

"Damn it, Julie, I've told you—stopping me won't change that! Why can't you believe me?"

"And why can't *you* understand that as long as I'm alive, I've got to try to stop you!"

Chayne swore with eloquence and ingenuity. He hooked an arm around her waist and pulled her hard against him, so hard that she felt the buttons of his shirt bite into her flesh, felt the rapid rise and fall of his chest betraying the suppressed violence in him. Felt the furnace heat in him running like wildfire along her own nerves.

"Strangle you . . . or make love to you," he whispered, and kissed her with a barely restrained savagery that left her feeling bludgeoned. "Remember *this* while you're dialing your station, *Güerita* . . . ."

His hand was on her neck, fingers tangled in the hair on her nape, thumb forcing her chin up while his mouth ravished hers. How quickly and ruthlessly he stripped away her defenses, pretenses, protestations! His body bore her against the steel barrier of his arm; his hand swept down, plunging inside the neck of her shirt to torment a hardening nipple. Julie heard the helpless whimper deep in her own throat and arched convulsively against him even as her doubled fists braced against his shoulders in a vain effort to push him away.

And then with shocking suddenness he tore her from him. Her breath escaped in a gasping sob of rage and anguish. "Oh . . . you monster! You . . . *bastard!*"

Chayne's only answer was his familiar mirthless chuckle as he stood and, in one swift moment, hauled her up and over his shoulder.

This time he angled up and over the little rise, her weight impeding him no more than if she had been a hiker's pack. His body was heated and damp with sweat, but it was more from emotion than exertion. And now, going downhill, he broke into a half trot as Julie hung on to the belt loops of his jeans and cursed softly when she bumped her chin on his back and bit her tongue.

Where in God's name was he taking her? She had a vague impression of fences and dark buildings, of large moving shapes and some startled woofs and snuffles. A door slammed, and a few seconds later something cold and wet nuzzled her face.

Chayne muttered something that sounded like, "Down, Jack," as a woman's voice called with tentative alarm. "Is someone out there?" And then, "Oh—my goodness!"

"Hello, Maddy," Chayne said.

"Chayne, what a *surprise!*"

Julie felt herself being lowered abruptly and set on her feet. Chayne's hands steadied and turned her. She stood blinking in the light, disoriented, shaken and utterly bewildered.

They were standing on wide steps leading to a veranda, and on the veranda, silhouetted against an open doorway filled with warm yellow light, stood a slender woman in slacks, one hand pressed to her forehead and the other to the front of her shirt.

"What in the world . . . ?"

"Can't talk now," Chayne rapped out, and taking Julie by the arms, pushed her ahead of him up the steps.

Can this awful night possibly get any more nightmarish? It was all Julie could do to keep her balance on legs that had lost all form and substance; the dog kept crowding against her, trying to nuzzle Chayne's hand; Chayne was thrusting her into a strange woman's arms.

"Take care of her for me!" he rasped, and planted a kiss on the woman's incredulous brow. Then he ruffled the dog's fur, snapped, "Stay, Jack!" and was gone.

There was silence. At their feet the dog whined softly. In a pleasantly musical voice, the woman said to the empty night, "Well, it's always *such* a pleasure to have you stop by, dear. Do come again soon!" She gave herself a shake and turned her attention to Julie. "Well—" Dark eyes swept her from head to foot. "I won't apologize for him. If you've had any association with him at all, I expect you're used to his behavior—at least a *little!*" The expressive mouth twitched with amusement; it reminded Julie of something, but she was too befuddled to think what. "Please, come inside, dear. You look like you could use something to drink." A surprisingly strong arm

slid reassuringly around her waist. And that, too, was somehow evocative....

"Are you allowed to tell me your name?"

What an odd question? Dazed, Julie stammered, "Of...of
course. I...my name is Julie Maguire. I'm an—"

"Well, Julie, I'm so pleased to meet you! I'm Madeline
Younger."

Younger. They were moving from the veranda into the house;
Julie had an impression of warm, muted colors, of golden
wood and natural fieldstone and the cool green accent of
plants. She shook her head, gamely trying to collect her scattered wits.

"Younger," she repeated hoarsely. "Are you...Chayne's
sister?" *Not his wife. Please.*

A delightful laugh burst from the woman, and she gave
Julie's waist a squeeze. "Oh, dear, you *are* nice. No—and I can
see that you're as confused as I am by all of this. I'm that terrible man's *mother!* Though I take no responsibility at all for
his manners. Come, let's both have a cup of coffee and re-
group, shall we?"

Julie found herself in a huge kitchen made cozy by the
warmth of quarry tile and copper pots. She was ushered gently
but firmly into a chair at a heavy oak trestle table beside a
fieldstone fireplace, cold now in the dead of summer.

"His mother," Julie mumbled incredulously, eliciting another burst of that musical laughter.

"Afraid so," Madeline Younger said tranquilly as she poured
coffee from a chrome pot into thick mugs. "Atonement for sins
in a former life, no doubt. How do you like your coffee, dear?"

"Hmm? Oh—black, please." Julie's mind was skittering
futilely about like a chipmunk in a maze. Chayne's mother.
This was Chayne's *home.* He had brought her here on purpose; he was just...turning her loose! It didn't make sense!

"Drink this, dear."

Julie reached distractedly for the proffered cup and took a
swallow. Then she coughed desperately and pounded her chest.
"Sorry," she wheezed. "What...?"

"Brandy," Madeline Younger said comfortably, settling into
a chair across from her. "You looked like you needed a belt."

Julie sipped carefully this time and felt the cobwebs begin to clear from her head as the alcohol and caffeine burned their way down into her belly. She sat up suddenly.

"Mrs. Younger—"

"Oh, please call me Maddy! Everyone does—even my children and grandchildren."

"Maddy." Julie cleared her throat, hesitating. It didn't seem quite right, somehow, to ask this lovely, compassionate woman for help in turning her son over to the authorities. But it had to be done, and quickly. Those men wouldn't stay at the abandoned church now—they were probably already on their way. But perhaps an APB... "Listen, I hate to trouble you, but is there a telephone I could use? If you—"

"Oh, certainly! You can use the den; I imagine you'll want privacy. Chayne always does. But do finish your coffee first. There's no hurry."

"I'm afraid there is. You see—"

"Julie—that was your name, wasn't it? Julie..." Madeline reached across the table to take her hand in a firm grasp. "I'm not a doctor, but even I can see that you've been through an ordeal. That you've suffered some sort of shock. I really must insist that you sit here for a few minutes and pull yourself together. I would *not* know what to do with you if you fainted in my parlor. Brandy is the extent of my first-aid capabilities, I'm afraid!"

"Mrs. Younger, I really—"

"*Maddy*. And the telephone will still be there when you've finished your coffee and gotten some color back in your cheeks. Now, drink up!" She fixed Julie with a stern glare, and Julie dutifully raised the steaming mug to her lips.

She sipped the toddy, and through a haze of steam and bemusement she studied the remarkable woman who was Chayne's mother. *Chayne's mother.* Why should it seem so extraordinary? Everyone has a mother. She had even wondered about Chayne's, and now here she was, sitting across the kitchen table from the woman who had given birth to him, nursed him, put bandages on his skinned knees....

"Maddy," she asked slowly, "how much do you know—about what Chayne does?"

"What he does? For a living?" She smiled gently. "Of course I know what he does, dear. In a very general way, at least. There's so much secrecy involved, you know—so much he can't tell me."

"Doesn't it...bother you?" Julie asked faintly, trying to keep her voice casual. Her head was beginning to swim again. Here was this lovely person...beautiful, in a dark, faintly exotic way, and very young-looking to be a grandmother. So down-to-earth, so warm and...nice. How could she condone her son's illegal activities, no matter how much she loved him?

"Bother me? You mean, not knowing?" Chayne's mother gave a short laugh that was remarkably like his humorless bark. "My dear, I'd really rather *not* know everything!"

"No, I mean his...occupation. You know—the danger and...so on."

Madeline studied her for a moment before answering. "Of course it bothers me," she said softly. "Of course I worry." She smiled a wise and gentle smile that made her face look at once softer and older. "Mothers do, I suppose. But I also know that I can't live my son's life for him, or ask him to live his life to suit me. He's not an extension of me, after all, but a grown man, and this is what he's chosen to do. Perhaps it isn't what I'd hoped he would choose, but that isn't for me to judge. Is it?"

Julie shook her head, unable to answer. Madeline sat back with a sigh.

"Having children can be a real pain sometimes—as you will no doubt find out for yourself someday." Her quiet laughter rippled across Julie's lacerated nerves. "Do you know what Chayne wanted to be when he was a boy? You'd never guess, to look at him now, but he wanted to be a doctor! He was actually enrolled in premed at Stanford when he...went to Vietnam." She stood up abruptly and carried both coffee cups to the sink. When she turned back, Julie saw lines of deep sadness etched around her fine dark eyes. "Vietnam changed him," Maddy said simply, and lifted her shoulders in a resigned shrug.

"Well—you look much better now. Come with me, Julie, and I'll show you that telephone."

Alone in a den filled with books and records and cluttered with the dozens of personal oddments that give a room life,

Julie sat on the arm of a fat leather chair and stared at the telephone as if it were a coiled snake.

Damn you forever, Chayne, she thought bitterly. You didn't have to kiss me to make me remember you.... Her mind was reeling through a montage of memories.

Cobalt eyes, demon bright; a deep voice murmuring, *"Buenas noches, Güerita...."* A tiny scar like a dimple in a chin streaked with white lather. Two pairs of hands, one big and callused, the other small and grubby, holding delicate seashells as if they were precious jewels. A mouth drawn with deep lines of strain, hovering above hers...

And the tactile memories...sensual memories. Of sun-warmed skin and the wholly unique texture of hair and scar; a sigh and a whispered *"You do heal me...."* Of hands and mouth and tongue pouring fire over her body; of silken hair, wet with rain and cool on her heated skin; of strong arms holding her tightly while she cried; of words sighed against her temple, her breast, her thigh... *"Sweet, beautiful Julie..."*

This is crazy! Julie reached for the phone with trembling fingers and lifted the receiver to her ear. Her hand brushed her cheek; she discovered that it was wet. *Damn it, Julie!* She drew a long, shuddering breath and dialed a familiar number.

"Border Patrol."

Julie released the breath in a gust. Thank goodness it was Lupe. "Agent Maguire here," she said in her professional monotone. "Get the chief for me. Code three."

"Code *three?*" The flat impersonal voice on the telephone cracked and became human. "Julie? What are you doing with a code three? You're supposed to be on vacation!"

Vacation? "I can't explain right now," Julie said tersely. "Just get me the chief."

"Uh...the chief isn't here right now. Rasmussen's acting chief."

"Fine. Let me talk to him."

"Can't. He's gone home for the day."

Julie closed her eyes and counted slowly to three. "Give me his home number. Please."

She had to wipe her palms on her pant legs before she could dial the number. Tensely she counted rings—four...five...six..."

"Rasmussen."

"Ted, sorry to bother you so late—"

"Who is this?"

"Agent Maguire. I've got a code—"

"Julie? What the hell are you doing in town? You're on vacation!"

"Look, I'm not in town, and I'm not on vacation. I've been in Baja—"

"Baja! Doing some fishing? Hey, I'll bet it's great down there this time of year. What in the hell are you calling at this hour for? I have you down for two weeks' R&R, and according to my calculations you've still got...hell, another whole week!"

"Ted," Julie said, getting a grip on her patience, "I am *not* on vacation. I was..." She stopped. *Kidnapped* sounded so melodramatic and improbable. It would take up valuable time explaining. She began again. "Never mind. Right now I've got a code three. Heading north toward L.A. Last seen on S6 about...five miles west of Highway 78. Ford pickup truck outfitted for off-road, customized camper, silver and white. California plates..."

She listened to her voice drone on, giving a full description of the camper and its occupants with cool detachment. When she had finished there was silence on the other end of the line.

"Ted? Got all that?"

"Yeah...I've got it. Look, Julie, you know we've probably lost them. I'll call the Orange County station and alert them, but unless they happen to go through a checkpoint—"

"They won't be going through any checkpoints," Julie interrupted, her voice clipped. "These aren't ordinary smugglers. This is a well-oiled machine. They aren't carrying ordinary illegals, either."

"What? Maybe you'd better explain."

Julie took a deep breath. "They're carrying a bunch of terrorists. They intend to hit the Expo in L.A. Tomorrow, I think. And they're armed and dangerous."

There was another prolonged silence. And then he asked, "Maguire, is this a joke? Have you been partying it up or something?"

"Ted," Julie said wearily, "have you ever known me to do something like that?"

"No. How in hell did you get onto something like this? You're on vacation!"

Julie shouted out of sheer frustration. "I'm *not* on vacation! Who told you I was on vacation, anyway?"

"Chief Patrol Agent Dalton."

"Dalton..." Julie pressed a hand to her forehead. "Ted, send somebody out here to get me. Please. I've got to get in touch with the chief. I don't know what in the world is going on...."

"Get you? What are you talking about? Julie, the truth now—are you drunk? You sure sound funny."

"I'm not drunk! I'm unarmed, out of uniform, afoot and stranded! I've uncovered a major smuggling operation, not to mention a terrorist plot to blow up the Pan American Expo, and you keep telling me I'm on vacation! You bet I sound funny!"

"Hey, take it easy, Cottontop!"

"Ted." She was almost sobbing with frustration. Why did it have to be Rasmussen? Anybody but Rasmussen! "Listen to me. People are going to get killed here very shortly if something isn't done about this!"

"I'll do what I can, Maguire. And you'd better be on the level about this!"

"*Ted!*"

"Okay, okay. I'll contact the Expo security people—you know we're working with them pretty closely anyway, figuring the possibilities for illegal entry during—"

"I *know,*" Julie said patiently. "I was supposed to be working the Expo myself."

"Funny. I have you down as being on—"

"If you tell me I'm on vacation one more time..."

"Calm down, Maguire. I'll do what I can. But the security is tight for the Expo, and I'm sure—"

"What about the CHP? If they can stop—"

"Julie, you know the Highway Patrol isn't interested in our suspects unless they're exceeding the speed limit. But look— you take it easy, you hear? I promise you I'll get this information to L.A. right away."

"And you'll come and get me? I'm in Ramona."

"Uh . . . well, I'm afraid I can't do that, Julie. See, I'm off duty, and . . . I'm kind of tied up at the moment."

"I take it you're not alone."

"Right."

"Can't you send someone? Please, Ted. I'm stranded."

"Well, you know, Julie, I can't really send a Patrol vehicle when you're technically not even on duty. I mean, I know you keep saying you're not, but I have seen the chief's memo, and it says that Agent Maguire is on *vacation*. And if you want my input, you sound like you could use it! Now, if you don't mind, I'd like to phone in this tip and get back to my own R&R!"

Julie was left staring dumbfoundedly at a dead receiver.

Chapter 12

"Julie? Are you all right?"

"What...?"

Madeline Younger moved hesitantly into the room. "I'm sorry, I hope I haven't disturbed you, but when I knocked and there was no answer I thought—"

"Oh...no, it's all right. I'm finished. And I'm fine. Really."

"I just wanted to ask if you would care for something to eat—a sandwich, maybe?"

"Oh, no. That's very kind of you, but I'm not hungry. Thanks anyway."

"Julie, are you sure you're all right? You look quite shaken. I know I probably shouldn't ask..."

Julie shook herself and pasted a stiff smile on her face. She felt like a gargoyle. "I'm just tired, I guess." *Your son is about to kill people, Mrs. Younger.* "And I really can't intrude on your hospitality any longer. I have to get back to Chula Vista." How? She had no money, no one she could call at midnight on a Friday and ask to drop everything and drive nearly a hundred and forty miles, round trip, give or take a few! What was

she going to do? She couldn't ask this woman for help—she
couldn't!

Mrs. Younger, your son is going to ~~help~~ kill a lot of people
and I'm trying to put him in jail—probably forever. Won't you
please help me out?

Tears stung her eyelids, and she stood up abruptly, knocking the phone askew. "Mrs. Younger..."

"You know, Julie," Madeline said thoughtfully, "I really do
think you'd better stay here tonight. It's too late to do anything tonight anyway, and you do look awfully tired. Why not
stay and get a good rest and do what you have to in the morning?"

"Oh, no! No, I couldn't."

I'm trying my level best to destroy your son, Mrs.
Younger... and you're offering me a bed?

"I'm sure Chayne meant for you to stay here tonight,"
Madeline said softly, giving Julie a long, searching look. "He'd
want you to stay."

Oh yes, he certainly would!

"And *I'd* like it if you would."

"I can't impose like this. You weren't expecting—"

"Nonsense! I have all kinds of space. You can have Dana's
old room. If you'll excuse the decor—she was always silly about
horses. But it's closest to the bathroom. I'd give you
Chayne's—it has its own bathroom—but..." She laughed as
she steered Julie down the hall. "Frankly, I have no idea when
he'll be popping in here again. It would be a little awkward if
he arrived later tonight, wouldn't it? Not that I think he'd mind
finding a lovely young woman in his bed, but as his *mother*..."

Chayne won't be coming back tonight, Mrs. Younger. Maybe
not ever.

She was so tired... so defeated. It was so hard to keep
struggling to stay alert, so easy to just let go, let herself be taken
in hand....

"Here you are, my dear. I think you'll be comfortable in
here. The bathroom is right across the hall. If there's anything
you need..."

Julie stood in the middle of the pleasant bedroom, swallowing hard, but the lump in her throat refused to budge. "Mrs.
Younger—Maddy—" She lifted her hands helplessly. "I'm

afraid I didn't come prepared to spend the night." She gave a strangled laugh and wondered how much longer she was going to be able to hold back the tears. "I don't have any clean clothes, or even a toothbrush, and I'm—"

"Oh, you poor girl. Of course you haven't. Here, I know what you need!" She steered an unresisting Julie across the hall and into the bathroom. "Now, you just... Wait a minute... Here." She bustled about, turning on faucets and opening cupboards while Julie stood as if mesmerized, staring at the cloud of steam rising from the bathtub.

"Bubble bath," Madeline announced, lacing the churning water with a flourish. "Does wonders for you when you're really done in." She beamed at Julie through the fragrant mist. "I guess I have two miracle cures in my medicine chest! Now, you just hop right in here and soak away your troubles while I go find you a nightgown. Towels are right here...shampoo and toothpaste... toothbrush, hairbrush, lotion. Let's see, have I forgotten anything?"

"I can't imagine what," Julie murmured shakily, thinking, My God... yesterday I was bathing in the Gulf of California, drying in the sun, sleeping on palm branches under the stars... in the arms of a smuggler.

Madeline had gone. Julie was alone except for the hollow-eyed stranger in the steam-fogged mirror. She stripped off her clothes—Chayne's clothes—the dirt-smeared jeans and soft blue shirt, the sandals, the beautiful handwoven belt. For just a moment she stood running the belt through her fingers, and then she dropped it onto the pile with the rest and folded the whole lot into a bundle.

She wouldn't be wearing them again. Ever. It was over. The whole terrible ordeal...the whole incredible fantasy. Baja was a mirage, and like a mirage, it was already fading away....

Julie woke in a strange bed, staring at a row of horses dancing across a windowsill. Sunlight poured between dainty hooves, ran down over the sill and into a puddle on the floor.

She was, for once, suddenly and completely awake, and she had no desire to lie in bed. She hadn't expected to sleep at all and wished she hadn't—it had been a sleep filled with nightmares and demons and restless fantasies.

A digital clock radio on the bedside table read 9:47. So she had slept longer than she intended after all. It was Saturday. The Pan American Exposition would be officially opening in downtown Los Angeles in exactly thirteen ... now twelve ... minutes. Julie threw back the light blanket, sat up and swung her feet to the floor. She peered at the radio for a moment, coughed nervously and stretched out a hand. And drew it back.

She didn't want to know. But she *had* to know!

Resolutely she turned on the radio and found a continuous-news station.

Music. A commercial for a Las Vegas hotel. A station break. Julie glanced at the clock and let her breath out slowly.

International news: a bombing in Paris; a plane crash in Japan; an anti-American demonstration in West Germany...

Julie found that she was drumming her fingers on the radio's simulated wood case and stood up to pace restlessly. On the dresser lay a pile of clothing, neatly folded. More borrowed clothes. Very nice clothes—gray linen slacks and a tailored shirt in a very lovely shade of peach. Underwear. No bra, but a lace-edged camisole with a tiny blue bow. All just a little large, but not too bad a fit.

The radio droned on. Commercials again. Julie drew the nightgown Madeline had given her off over her head and began to dress. She was bending over to roll up her pant legs when the local newscast began.

"...Los Angeles police and federal agents today announced that they have broken up a plot to sabotage the opening of the Pan American Exposition. In a daring pre-dawn raid on an East Los Angeles warehouse, federal agents, assisted by an L.A.P.D. SWAT team, arrested an unspecified number of Latin American nationals and large quantities of weapons and explosives. Police believe the Latin Americans to be members of a terrorist organization known as the Central American Liberation Front, or CALF. A police department spokesman indicated that the timely and bloodless roundup was a complete success, and credited the work of undercover agents for preventing—quote—great tragedy and bloodshed—unquote. Meanwhile, at the convention center in downtown Los Angeles, the first Pan American Exposition—"

Julie turned off the radio and sat heavily on the edge of the bed. She discovered that she was trembling and began to rock back and forth, hugging herself.

It's over. It's over. Thank God. He wasn't hurt. Oh...God!
She wanted to cry, but it hurt too much.

After what seemed like a very long time, Julie stood up and began moving distractedly around the room. Her movements had a jerky, uncoordinated feel, as if she were very, very cold.

She had to get back to headquarters and find out what was going on! She hated being so out of things.

She'd leave as soon as possible. Madeline would understand her anxiousness to get home now that she was rested.

Madeline. Chayne's mother. Oh God, how would she ever tell his mother?

She couldn't tell her. She wouldn't. Someone else would tell her eventually—

But how was she going to get home?

Of course. Colin! She'd call Colin.

Pasting a bright smile on her face, Julie went to find her hostess. She found her in the living room, sitting cross-legged on the carpet in front of the television set and eating a peach. In sweat pants and a tee shirt, her hair secured haphazardly atop her head with a rubber band, she looked much younger than Julie figured she must be.

"Julie!" Madeline popped the last bite of peach into her mouth and hastily wiped her fingers on the towel draped around her neck before waving Julie over. "Good morning! You've caught me, I'm afraid. What good it does me to spend time on these ridiculous aerobics if I immediately thereafter stuff my face, I really don't know. Pour yourself some coffee and come join me. The exercise show is over, mercifully—not that you need bother with *that!* No, I mean help yourself to a peach—they're especially delicious this year. My own tree."

Julie accepted a peach from the bowl Madeline extended and sat gingerly on the edge of the sofa. "Maddy..."

"Here, you'll need a napkin. These are so good and juicy." She waved a hand at the television screen. "This is interesting, Julie. They're covering the opening of the Exposition live. I'm quite interested in folk art and dancing, particularly Indian and

Mexican, so I'm finding this fascinating. Are you at all interested in the Expo?"

The peach, heavy with nectar, soft and warm as a small living thing, lay in Julie's hands like a lump of clay. "No," she rasped, clearing her throat. "Not really."

"Oh—now this is really lovely. Watch this, Julie...."

On the screen a group of young girls in folk costumes formed shifting patterns, a colorful swirl of ribbons and flowers and smiling faces. Julie saw only a blur.

The scene became smaller, a monitor in a studio control booth. An announcer turned from it to the camera and intoned, "We will return to our continuing coverage of the Pan American Exposition, coming to you live from the convention center in downtown Los Angeles, but first, this update on the late-breaking story out of East Los Angeles."

"Oh, now what," Madeline cried in exasperation. "I did want to see that dance. Did you know—Julie? Dear, what is it?"

Julie found herself on her feet, hands clasped together and pressed to her lips. The peach rolled away across the carpet.

"...We go now to Rob Rivera at the Federal Building for this live report. Come in, Rob."

"Thank you, and what a story it is, Chris! A story that began in the wilds of Baja California and ended this morning just before dawn in an East Los Angeles warehouse. The daring raid by federal agents and Los Angeles police resulted in the arrest of more than twenty illegal aliens suspected of being members of an international terrorist organization. Also recovered in that raid were large quantities of explosives and weapons, and three vehicles rigged with explosives. In other words, car bombs. Considering the firepower and training of the suspects, many of whom are thought to have been suicide raiders, the bloodless roundup is nothing short of miraculous. Police have been lavish in their praise of federal undercover agents...."

"Julie, dear—are you all right?"

Madeline Younger's concerned face swam into focus as the reporter's voice faded into background noise, garbled and meaningless.

"What...? I...um..." Julie cleared her throat and dropped to her knees to retrieve the peach. "I'm sorry—it's bruised. I hope I haven't made a mess on the carpet."

"Don't worry about the peach! For heaven's sake, come and sit down! You look as pale as it's possible to look with such a gorgeous tan!"

Cool fingers closed on Julie's wrist and drew her gently but firmly to the sofa. "Now," Madeline said firmly, still holding her hand, "tell me. If you can, of course. Is it this terrorist thing they're talking about?"

"Maddy..." Julie said unsteadily, "I have to tell you—"

"Oh, my goodness," Madeline interrupted, dropping Julie's hand and jumping up to reach for the volume knob. "I *see*. Oh, yes—I do see."

The imagine on the screen had become jerky and fragmented as the minicam was jostled by a pushing, shoving crowd of reporters and photographers. Through this gauntlet of cameras and microphones, a phalanx of plainclothes officers escorted a group of dark, handcuffed men.

"...feared that provisions for the safety of the prisoners would be inadequate, I think, Chris. This was a suicide mission, according to our information, so I'm sure they're going to have to provide a twenty-four-hour guard. And until that can be arranged, the terrorists are being held in isolation here at the Federal Building. There will be a press conference—"

The picture lurched wildly and then righted itself. And then, either by sheer chance or perhaps because the cameraman, too, had found himself inexplicably compelled, it zoomed in tight and focused on one dark face. For several blinding, heart-stopping moments a pair of eyes looked straight into the camera. Eyes of shocking blue. Demon's eyes, wild and fierce.

"Oh, dear," said Madeline softly, and covered her mouth with her hand.

Julie was transfixed. It was a blind-side attack for which there was absolutely no defense, and it cut through the ice around her heart like a laser. The television screen blurred and shimmered with rainbow colors and then abruptly went dark.

"Oh, dear," Madeline said again, turning, her hand still on the knob. "Chayne is not going to like that!" And then she gasped, "Why, *Julie!*"

"I'm so sorry," Julie said in a small drowned voice as she pressed the back of her hand to her nose and struggled for control. "I didn't know how to tell you."

Madeline started to say something and then stopped. She gave Julie a long and very thoughtful look and then sat down beside her and picked up her cold, clammy hand.

"Now I see," she said gently. "I've jumped to the wrong conclusion. I just assumed you—oh, well. Oh . . . *damn!*"

She jumped to her feet while Julie wiped her cheeks and stared at her in amazement. Far from being distraught with grief and anxiety, she seemed angry.

"Oh . . . *men!*" That elegant woman, so uncharacteristically and comically attired, with a silly tuft of ponytail quivering on top of her head, raised her clenched fists in an eloquent and ageless gesture of frustration. "Why do they behave like such *jackasses?*"

"Colin," Julie sighed, leaning her head back against the headrest, "it was really nice of you to do this."

"That's the third time you've said that since we left Ramona," Colin Redmond replied. From under her lashes, Julie saw the creases in his cheeks deepen as he smiled wryly.

"I mean it. I'm very grateful. And I'm sorry about your golf game. Did they really beep at you out there on the course?"

"When people tell my service it's a matter of life and death, they usually do that, Julie. They're funny that way."

"Please, Colin, don't be sarcastic. Not now. And I did *not* say that."

He threw her a look but didn't reply. He *was* angry—she could read the signs—but all he said, in that terribly calm lawyer's murmur, was, "Care to tell me what's going on?"

"No," Julie said. And then she repented. He had given up his Saturday in order to bail her out; the least she could do was try to explain. She opened her mouth and then closed it again. "I wish I knew," she said at last.

Colin threw her a look. "You might start with where you've been all week." When she didn't reply immediately, he added, "All your station would say was that you were on vacation."

Julie let out a high bark of laughter and then swallowed it when Colin snapped her another look. "I'm sorry," she murmured, contrite. "Did you really call and ask about me?"

It was Colin's turn to laugh without humor and Julie's to throw him a startled glance.

"Of course I called. You stood me up and then dropped off the face of the earth. What did you expect me to do?" His fine, well-kept hands flexed and shifted on the steering wheel. "I . . . care about you."

"Oh, Colin . . ." Julie whispered. "I know you do." She blinked back tears and turned her head to stare blindly through the window. "I'm sorry. You deserve an explanation, but . . . Look, please don't ask me to talk about this now. I . . . just can't. I haven't figured it out myself yet."

Colin released his breath in an exasperated gust and reached for the buttons on his tape deck. Dvorak's Ninth Symphony swelled through the Cadillac's air-conditioned interior, and Julie put her head back against the plush headrest and closed her eyes.

"Shall I come up?"

Julie blinked and sat up. For a minute she just stared through the windshield at the apartment building that had been her home now for . . . what? Five . . . no, *six* years. She felt as though she had been away for at least that long.

"No . . ." she said vaguely. "That's okay. I'm . . ."

"Julie? Maybe I'd better come with you."

She shook herself and said firmly, "No. Really, Colin, I . . . I need to be alone right now. I'm fine."

"Sure?"

"Positive." She had begun to climb out of the car when Colin touched her arm.

"Will I see you tonight?" There was a curiously wary look in his eyes that she couldn't recall having seen before.

"Not tonight, Colin. I really do need some time. There are some things I have to think about—straighten out in my mind. Do you mind?"

"Of course not. Well . . . yes." He smiled crookedly. "I missed you, you know. Worried about you."

He touched her cheek, an unusual gesture for him. Julie swallowed and whispered, "Colin, I—"

"I know. It's okay." He leaned over to kiss her, and she moved so that his lips brushed her cheek. She heard his soft expulsion of breath as he sat back, shaking his head. "Julie, I don't know where you've been or what's happened to you this past week, but . . . you've changed."

Julie swallowed painfully. "Oh? How?"

"I don't know . . . yes, I do." He smiled suddenly, and this time she didn't miss the sadness in his eyes. "You look like someone who's just taken a tumble off the old balance beam."

Julie's laugh had a brittle sound. "What a thing to say."

"A week ago," Colin said lightly, "you'd have said, 'Colin, that's a bunch of garbage.'" He turned on the ignition. "Call you Monday?"

"Yes. Okay."

"All right, then. Call me if you need me. If you need anything."

"I will. And . . . thank you."

The apartment smelled dusty and abandoned; the dishes she had left in the sink a week ago had become life forms. Julie wrinkled her nose as she gingerly ran hot water over them, then wandered aimlessly around, trailing her fingers over her possessions as if that most concrete of senses, touch, might bring her back to where she had been before.

"Oh, Julie," she sighed, poking a finger into a potted palm's bone-dry soil, "how did you ever get into a mess like this? How could you have gotten your nice neat life so screwed up?"

It had been so unexpected—a routine patrol! Well, all right, she *had* made a mistake, missing that turnoff. But it had only been a *little* mistake! Surely it didn't deserve such terrible retribution.

She had believed in blacks and whites, law and order, right and wrong, but most of all she had believed in *herself*. She had believed in her values, her instincts, her judgment, her integrity. She could have justified sharing an outlaw's bed under the circumstances, but she could never, *never* rationalize falling in love with him. It just couldn't happen.

But it had.

And as a result, as even Colin had observed, she had changed. She didn't know who she was, but she knew she wasn't Border Patrol Agent Maguire anymore. She didn't know whether she was ever going to find herself again, but she did know one thing for sure: She was never going to be able to trust herself again. Ever.

The afternoon and evening stretched ahead. She had wanted to get home so badly, wanted to be alone, but now the apartment stifled and oppressed her. Twice she reached for the phone to call the station, and both times she hung up before she had even finished dialing.

She took a shower. Washed her hair. And then went through everything in her closet trying to find something to wear.

Something pretty...

Why had he said she wouldn't be comfortable in a dress?

Because she didn't even own a dress.

She hated her clothes. Everything. Underwear, pajamas, shoes, everything.

Obeying the kind of rash, angry impulse that had never been part of her emotional makeup before, she rummaged through the top drawer of her desk until she located the credit cards she never used—the department store cards she had been generously offered and had blithely accepted when a new shopping mall opened up the previous year. Then, snatching up her car keys and purse, she slammed out of her apartment, leaving dust motes dancing in the afternoon sun.

At ten o'clock Monday morning Julie walked into Border Patrol headquarters through the front door and swept by the startled receptionist. She was wearing high-heeled sandals, a gray linen skirt and a sleeveless crochet-knit top in peach and gray. She had discovered that she liked peach; after her weekend shopping spree she now had quite a lot of it, including a satin teddy with lace trim.

Her dress uniform, neatly folded, was under one arm. In her hands she held her dress uniform hat and a long white envelope.

She plowed through the swinging lobby doors and down the hall, ignoring all greetings, questions and exclamations, then paused at the chief patrol agent's door just long enough to rap twice before she pushed it open and barged in.

Chief Dalton wasn't alone. Momentum carried Julie past the visitor before she registered his presence.

"Ah! I was just about to call you," the chief said mildly, gesturing past her with his glasses. "Someone here to see you."

But Julie had already turned to stone.

"Hello, Julie," Chayne said.

Chapter 13

Chayne! Here! Not a prisoner, but at ease in the visitor's armchair, one neatly shod foot resting across one razor-creased pant leg. Chayne—wearing the telltale three-piece banker's gray pinstripe suit of the standard issue federal-type agent, hair freshly trimmed, jaws so clean-shaven they looked polished. Chayne! It couldn't be, but it was. There was the little scar on his chin that looked like a dimple, and, of course, those incredible cobalt eyes. . . .

Julie's heart took off, soaring like a sea gull into the sun.

"Agent Maguire," Chief Dalton said with an unmistakable air of satisfaction, "meet Special Agent Chayne Younger."

"We've met." She knew it must have been she who spoke, though she could have sworn her lips never moved. She was caught in the whirlpool of those eyes. Chayne . . . a government agent. Her heart tumbled slowly from the heights and landed in her chest, cold and lifeless.

There was a rushing sound in her ears. She shook her head, but her voice remained distant and tinny. "Not . . . Border Patrol?"

"No," Chayne said softly.

"Mr. Younger is with SAT." The chief sounded oddly disembodied, like a voice from offstage.

"SAT," Julie repeated woodenly.

"Special Antiterrorist Team."

"Justice Department?"

"State," Chayne said carefully, watching her with narrowed eyes. "We're a coalition of international units. We coordinate with the Justice Department from time to time. Like now."

"I see." The world had begun to tilt alarmingly. She put her hand on the desk to steady it and found that she was still holding her hat and the envelope. She stared at them without comprehension.

"Julie," Chayne's voice rumbled, "sit down."

"Yes, sit down, Maguire," Chief Dalton said cheerfully. "We'd like to commend you for your part in the success of this operation. Mr. Younger tells me you handled yourself with . . . uh . . . poise and courage in a difficult situation. And, of course, we'll answer any questions you may have."

The icy shell that had paralyzed her cracked, and then blew into a million pieces. Rage boiled through her, bringing with it warmth and blinding pain. With iron control, enunciating clearly, she said, "You deducted a week's vacation. Is that correct?"

The chief looked startled. He glanced at Chayne, but *his* eyes were still fixed on Julie. "Ah . . . well." The chief cleared his throat and put his fingertips together with careful precision. "We will see what we can do to reinstate it, of course. Please understand that it was the best we could come up with at the time. When Agent Younger told us you'd stumbled into the middle of this—"

"*Told* you?"

"Yes. Well, in a manner of speaking. Left a little note in this . . ." He opened a drawer and took something out, put his fist into it to display it, and then dropped it onto the blotter. It was her cap. The knit cap she had pulled on over her beacon hair that long-night in a starry desert ravine.

"The chopper crew picked it up," Dalton said with an air of restrained triumph. And why not triumph? They all must be hugging themselves with delight over the way it had all come off.

Julie cleared her throat once more, carefully avoiding Chayne's intent gaze. "So . . . you knew where I was?"

"*I* did, yes. And, of course, the chopper crew."

"Why wasn't I told about this operation?" Her voice kept failing her—it felt ancient and rusty.

"Well, Maguire, it was a need-to-know situation, and I'm sure you must be aware that the success of an undercover operation of this nature depends on absolute secrecy. We had no way of knowing that you were going to walk into the middle of it. Agent Younger had spent weeks—months—working out a route that would avoid our patrols. Just how in the hell—"

"A foul-up," Julie snapped, standing up abruptly. "Pure and simple." She dumped her uniform on the desk, added the hat to the pile and topped it off with the envelope. "I just stopped by to give you this—my resignation. You'll find my badge in there, too—along with a lost-weapons report."

Chief Dalton coughed and glanced sideways at Chayne. Julie could feel Chayne's eyes burning into her and steadfastly avoided them.

"Uh . . ." the chief muttered, sounding unhappy, "for Pete's sake, Maguire, this isn't necessary. We all make mistakes, and you acquitted yourself commendably."

And then Julie saw the *other* uniform on the desk. The one in a little pile with a pair of dusty shoes, a heavy leather belt and a gun. Her field uniform. She could see the nametag on the shirt pocket.

It was, somehow, the last straw. She made a strangled sound and headed blindly for the door.

"Maguire," the chief began, "the uniforms are yours."

"*Keep them!*" Julie shouted, and stormed out.

She had reached her car by the time Chayne caught her. He took her arm in a painful grip and whirled her around to face him.

"Julie, we have to talk."

"*Don't touch me!*" She ripped herself from his grasp, breathing like someone who had just run a marathon, doubled over with the struggle to draw air into her lungs. "I don't . . . have anything to say to you! I don't . . . want to hear you. I don't want to see you. *Ever!*"

"Julie—"

"Get . . . away from me and . . . let me go!" She was shaking, her face ravaged by her efforts to hold hysteria at bay. The car door resisted her efforts to open it; her hands didn't seem to be working right.

"Where the hell do you think you're going?"

"*Away!*" The door sprang open, and she scrambled into the driver's seat, fumbling for the keys.

"You're hysterical."

"You think so? This is *calm*. If you don't get away from me, I'll show you *hysteria!*"

His body held the car door open. "You're in no condition to drive!"

"Oh yeah? Watch me!" The engine fired. Chayne leaped out of the way as she threw the stick shift into first gear and peeled out, tires squealing. Before the door slammed itself shut on the turn into the street, she heard him swear violently, "Damned bloody idiot! You're going to kill yourself!"

He was right, of course; she was in no condition to drive home. As soon as she was out of sight of the station she turned into a side street and killed the motor, then sat shivering and shaking, waiting for the shock to subside.

Chayne . . . an undercover agent. Not an outlaw, not a smuggler, not a terrorist . . . but a federal officer. Why hadn't she known? How could she not have guessed? It explained so many things—made sense of all the puzzles. Why hadn't she put it all together?

Because she'd been blinded by a pair of demon eyes. . . .

She could see them even now, as clear and deceiving as a mirage. And they still had the power to twist her heart, fever her skin and send pulses throbbing through her body like jungle drums. . . .

He's not an outlaw! It's all right! It's all right. . . .

The mirage shivered and faded, leaving her cold, aching and empty. For of course it wasn't all right. As far as Julie was concerned, it made no difference at all. It didn't change what *she* had done.

Oh, Chayne . . . why couldn't you have told me? You could have spared me all of this.

But even if she could manage to forgive *him*, she knew that she could never, *never*, forgive herself. . . .

* * *

"Well, Julie—" Ice cubes clinked as Colin drained his glass and leaned forward to set it on the coffee table. "I have to admit, that's quite a story." He clasped his hands together between his knees and fixed her with a steady gaze. "Is that all of it?"

"Isn't that enough?" Julie stood and paced restlessly, rubbing her upper arms.

"Oh, without a doubt...without a doubt. So why do I have this impression you're not telling me everything?"

"Because you're a lawyer," Julie snapped crossly. "That makes you cynical."

Colin shook his head, a little half smile pulling at his mouth. "Julie, knock it off. We've been friends for too long, and I know you too well. You got knocked off your pins down there in Baja, and don't try to tell me it was because of being captured by smugglers, or terrorists. Whatever. You've been in law enforcement for a long time. You've handled yourself in dangerous situations before." He was silent for a long time. Julie moved to the window, keeping her back to him. His voice, when it came, was cautious. "This agent—Chayne. Did you sleep with him?" That was followed by a quickly muttered, "Good Lord, I sound like a prosecutor. Forget that I asked that." He rose abruptly and came to stand behind her, his hands resting lightly on her shoulders. "Come on, Julie. Forget it—put the whole thing behind you. Don't you know the cure for falling off a balance beam? Get right back on."

"I think that's *horses,* Colin."

"You'll be fine once you're back in your groove. Let me take you to dinner—"

"I quit my job."

"*What?*"

"I said, I quit my job. Today. Resigned."

"Oh, Julie. Why?"

She sighed and pulled away. "Oh . . . Colin. I can't trust my judgment anymore. I don't—"

"Don't give me that!"

"All right, then. I just . . . don't want to be a Border Patrol agent anymore. What's the matter with that? I've been an agent for a long time, damn it!"

"I see." Colin's voice was very quiet. After a short, oddly suspenseful silence he asked quietly, "What will you do instead?"

Julie smiled crookedly and lifted her hands. "I don't know. I haven't really thought."

"Have you—" Colin cleared his throat. "Have you considered getting married?"

"Is that a rhetorical question?" As soon as she opened her mouth she was sorry. She closed her eyes and said in a low voice, "God, that was a dumb thing to say. Forgive me."

"It's okay. Have you?"

"Oh . . . Colin." She opened her eyes and looked up into his face. His strong, homely, *trustworthy* face. There was a muscle moving high in the side of his jaw; she lifted her hand and touched it briefly. "I *wish* I loved you. I really do. But I don't. I'm sorry."

"I know you don't. I haven't asked you to. Would you consider marrying me anyway?" His tone was dry. He might have been suggesting to a client that he try for a plea bargain.

Julie smiled gently and shook her head. And in that instant the doorbell rang.

After a moment Colin said, "Expecting someone?"

She shook her head. The bell rang again, impatiently.

"Well, aren't you going to answer it?"

She knew who it was; there was a tension and tightly restrained anger in just the sound of the bell. Her heart felt like a jackhammer trying to dig a way out of her chest. She winced when the bell pealed a third time. When it was followed immediately by a loud, determined banging, Colin gave her a quizzical look and pulled the door open.

"Now look, Julie, you're being child—" Chayne stopped short when he saw Colin. Behind his fist, still raised for its assault on the door panels, his eyes blazed with cold fury.

"Come in," Colin said blandly.

"Who the hell are you?"

"Colin Redmond. A friend of Julie's. And you, I take it, are Chayne Younger." It was his very best attorney's manner, poised and dry. Chayne hesitated, and then warily accepted the proffered hand, while Julie, seething with anger, looked helplessly from one to the other. As the two men took each other's measure, she couldn't help but compare them: Colin, tall and slightly stoop shouldered, sandy hair streaked with gray, immaculately tailored, with that air of quiet competence that had always made her feel so *safe;* and Chayne . . . demon eyes blazing in his dark face, collar undone and tie askew, dangerous-looking even in a three-piece suit, and as full of suppressed violence as a caged leopard. . . .

"I was just leaving," Colin said, startling her. She gulped, and a shudder ran through her body.

"Oh—no, Colin, please. Don't go. I don't want—"

"Don't let me keep you," Chayne said pleasantly, moving past Colin and on into the room. Julie took an involuntary step backward.

"Colin," she grated through clenched teeth, "what about dinner?"

There was an electric silence. Colin looked from Julie to Chayne and back again, a peculiar smile on his lips. "Perhaps another time," he said softly. "Nice meeting you, Mr. Younger. Bye, Julie."

"Colin!"

Chayne rocked on his heels and showed his teeth in a savage smile. "So long, Redmond," he said cheerfully, and then added from the side of his mouth, "Say good night to your friend, *Güerita."*

"Colin—" Julie gasped, but the door had already clicked softly shut behind him. "You . . . unspeakably rude, arrogant bastard!" Julie let go of her self-control in one burst of fury. "How *dare* you treat Colin like that? You damned, insufferable—"

"Colin . . . is he by any chance the one who managed to dispose of your virginity for you without ever making *love* to you?"

"Oooh!" Rage took her breath away. When she regained it she fired off a barrage that included every oath she could call to mind.

Chayne clicked his tongue and smiled. "At least you're talking to me," he said dryly.

"How *dare* you bulldoze your way in here? This isn't Baja— I'm not your hostage! This is my apartment! Get out!"

"Not until we've talked." His voice was very quiet. Julie tilted her head to one side and said, "What?"

"I said, not until we do some serious talking." He paced across the living room, tugging at his necktie. When it came loose, he flung it away and whirled to face her. "Where the hell have you been?"

"Where have I—"

"You peeled out of that lot like an accident looking for a place to happen. And then you never showed up here until an hour ago."

"Until— You've been staking out my place?"

"I was worried, damn it! Where were you?"

"None of your business," Julie seethed. "You have an incredible nerve!"

"And what was that infantile tantrum all about, anyway?"

"Infantile tan—"

"You're behaving like an irrational child instead of a trained professional! All I wanted to do was talk."

"I've got nothing to say to you!"

"Well, I've got a hell of a lot to say to you!"

"Nothing I want to hear!"

"Hear me out, damn it! You *owe* me!"

They had been firing their shots at each other across the width of the room. In the aftermath of the shelling, Chayne's whisper was like an echo. "You owe me, Julie."

In the silence, Julie made a strangled sound that was half hiccough, half sob. "Oh, right—for saving my life!"

He put his hands in his pockets and took a step toward her. "For that—yes." His eyes were shadowed, but his mouth had a familiar bitter twist.

"Are you going to explain why you let me think you were a dangerous criminal?" Julie drew a ragged breath that she thought would tear her throat apart. "Why you let me think my life was hanging by a thread?"

"It was," he said quietly. "Believe me. And so was mine."

At her sides, her hands clamped into fists. "But you knew who *I* was. You had so many chances to tell me . . . later. After. Couldn't you have trusted me?"

"Would it have made such a difference?" he asked gently.

Julie's answer was a cry of pure anguish. "Oh God—*yes!*"

He made an exasperated noise and rubbed a hand over his face. "Look, damn it. The number one commandment of an undercover operative is 'Thou shalt not blow thy cover.' You *never* give yourself away, even to someone you know is on your side. Not unless your mission's success depends on it."

"It seems to me that it darn near did. It was dangerous to keep me in the dark. I kept trying to get away. What if I'd been successful? What if they'd killed me? What if you'd been caught trying—"

Chayne was shaking his head slowly. "No. Your ignorance gave you just the right degree of defiance to enable me to keep my cover intact. If you'd known, you'd have felt too safe...too comfortable. You might have given me away with a simple gesture... or a look."

Julie made a mute gesture of defeat and wiped her cheek—and only then realized that she was crying. Chayne frowned suddenly and reached into his shirt pocket for his cigarettes.

"Look, you don't happen to have any beer around, do you?"

Julie sniffed and shook her head.

"Scotch?"

"Just some... vodka, I think."

"Colin drinks vodka?"

"Yes," Julie whispered. "He does."

"Damn," Chayne muttered.

He tossed the cigarette package onto the coffee table and put his hands into his pockets. "Look... Julie." Another step brought him close enough for her to see that his eyes were hooded, wary. "You asked me a question—down there."

Julie's heart stopped beating. Chayne cleared his throat, rubbed the back of his neck, and then lifted his head and drilled her with twin beams of blue light.

"Something about—would it make a difference if you loved me. Was that a hypothetical question?"

"Um..." Julie cleared her throat and counted heartbeats through an unbearable silence. At last she blurted in desperation, "I asked you first!"

She saw his eyes change, become first startled, then wondering, and finally dark and smoky. She had begun to tremble long before he smiled, long before he growled, "Come here," and closed the space between them in two quick strides.

An arm of tempered steel caught her around the waist and dragged her against his body. She felt his heartbeat against her breast as for one timeless moment he looked deep into her eyes. She caught her breath in wonder.

He took her mouth, then simply took it over, possessed it, overwhelming her with a raging hunger as elemental as fire. Such raw and primal passion might have frightened her if her own hadn't erupted with equal violence. If he was fire, she was earth and wind, and she exulted in the power! She felt as if her life had been aimed at this; all her being had one purpose—to be here, with this man. She had been dormant, now she was awake! Alive! This was what living was all about!

Chayne tore his mouth away, breathing raggedly. He groaned, "God, Julie..." while his hands raked through her hair, cradling her head, his fingertips rasping on her scalp. His lips roamed her face, touching her eyelids, temples, cheeks, chin, nose, and then came back to reclaim her mouth with renewed hunger, as if he had stayed away too long.

Julie whimpered deep in her throat, a whimper not of fear or distress, but of complete surrender. Her hands trembled over his face, renewing their tactile memory of his eyebrows, the roughness of his jaw, the silk of his hair and the newness of the bare nape of his neck.

At last they both tore their lips away, trembling, to cling together like the survivors of a calamity, breathing hard and filled with the miracle of it.

"God...Julie..." Chayne said hoarsely against her hair. "Don't ever...do that again. Don't put me through this. I *need* you. I need to talk to you. There's so much I've wanted to tell you and couldn't."

"I'm here...you can tell me now." She closed her mouth over the leaping pulse at the base of his throat, trying to capture it.

"Later..." he groaned, molding her body to his. "I can't...talk now."

Julie slipped her arms inside his jacket and pressed herself closer, absorbing the heat of his body through his clothing. Her hands roamed over his back, glorying in the hard resilience, the vibrant ripple of his muscles.

Her hands touched something foreign and recoiled. "Chayne, that isn't a...?"

"Shoulder holster. Yes. Don't worry about it now, for God's sake!" He held her away from him, lifting her chin so that she had to look into the dizzying vortexes of his eyes. "I'm crazy with wanting you. Do you want to talk about my damned gun?"

Hypnotized by his eyes, Julie could only shake her head. A tiny hiccough escaped her as he scooped her up in his arms.

"I'm going to make love to you, Julie...here and now. And I'm going to keep making love to you until this craving I have for you is satisfied. And when that's taken care of—in a few thousand years—we'll stop and talk. And after that, I'll make love to you some more!"

"In that case," Julie said huskily, "hadn't you better shut up and begin?"

It wasn't a time for tenderness, for slow, honeyed raptures and sweet expirations. There was too much wildness in them both. Undressing was not a voyage of erotic discovery; clothing was disposed of in haste on floor and furniture, and without regard for its preservation.

Over his shoulder, Julie saw the holstered gun on a corner of her dresser, and even with her blood boiling, desire shivering through all her senses and misting her vision, her heart contracted. She closed her eyes and whispered fiercely, "*Love* me, Chayne!"

"I do...." His hand raked down her body to grasp her thigh. "I am..." His warm breath dewed her parted lips. "I *will*...."

Bodies already heated to the point of combustion touched...fused...and exploded together in a nova of blinding ecstasy that left them both spent, but far from satisfied.

Chayne's hard, warm hands framed her face, holding damp tendrils of hair back from her forehead while his thumbs brushed gently across her cheeks. Julie opened her eyes with great effort and encountered a gaze of fearsome intensity. She laughed a little and murmured, "What?" too steeped in love and drugged with sex to be self-conscious.

"Hush... I just want to look at you." He lowered his head and brushed his lips over her temples. Julie sighed and let her heavy eyelids drop, and a moment later she felt the warm pressure of his mouth touch them like a blessing. "I want to watch you... make sure you're not a mirage."

Mirage! Julie whispered, "Funny you should say that." She tipped her face, searching for his mouth.

"Why?" He found her moist, seeking lips and brought them home.

"Because..." she whispered into his mouth, "I've been thinking a lot about mirages lately."

He kissed her deeply, a slow languid melding that left her feeling like a puddle of melted butter. She felt the muscles in his back tense as he gathered himself to move away from her, and she tightened her arms around him. "Don't go... please."

He ducked his head and drank again from her lips. "I must be heavy."

"No...." Her hands smoothed over the muscles of his back and down his spine, finding the flat plane just above the cleft of his buttocks. "Do you think we could stay like this forever?"

"I'd be happy to try. Though I suspect it may not be practical."

"Mmm. I suppose we'd have to eat sometime."

"Food? Who needs food when I've got you?" He buried his face in the hollow of her neck and nipped her earlobe, her shoulder. "Hold still, you delicious morsel, you...."

Giggling and shivering with delight, Julie gave one hard buttock a playful slap. "I remember the first time you called me that."

"I do, too." He bowed his back in order to bring his lips to her breasts, nuzzling at the place where his mark had been.

"I was scared to death." She gasped as his mouth closed over the tender flesh and began to exert a gentle suction.

"Of me?" He drew back to examine the faint rosiness his mouth had made and then bent to circle her nipple with his tongue.

"No." Julie gasped again and arched convulsively beneath him. "Of *me!*" Chayne's hand had moved to cover her breast, all but the tender, aching tip, which he had drawn deep into his mouth. "Chayne..."

"You know," he murmured thickly when at last he released her, "it just may be possible to stay like this after all." He moved experimentally on her, and she gave a husky gurgle of laughter and rubbed her hands over the base of his spine.

"Do you think the people who keep all those records would be interested?"

"Maybe... shall we call them?"

Julie closed her eyes and began to move with him, slowly and tentatively. "No," she whispered, growing breathless. "Not yet. Let's practice awhile... make sure we've got it...."

"Imp!" he growled, driving deep into her.

"Demon!" she whispered in return. Her head fell back as his mouth silenced them both, and for a while only their bodies spoke.

"Julie," Chayne murmured, burrowing his fingers idly through her hair, "you're *not* a mirage, are you?"

There was a seriousness in his voice that nudged her heart and awakened the pain that had been sleeping there. "No," she said huskily, and couldn't go on.

"There were times..." She felt his throat move convulsively, and he lifted his head to plant a quick kiss on the top of her head. "There were times I couldn't believe you were real. I'd wake up and find you there in my arms and..."

Julie stirred, turning her face to nuzzle his chest, and he gave her a fierce, hard hug. "Do you have any idea what it was like, not being able to tell you anything? Not being able to talk to you?"

Do you have any idea what it was like... falling in love with a criminal? Oh, Chayne...

"I thought it was because you didn't want to get close to me," she whispered around the obstruction in her throat. "I thought you didn't want to get to know me."

"You didn't want to get to know me, did you?" Chayne asked softly, nudging her head with his chin. "At first."

"No. I was afraid."

After a moment, Chayne asked in a low voice, "Was it all bad, Julie? Baja, and being my... being with me?"

"No," she whispered. "You know it wasn't."

"You seemed so...distraught about it. Angry. Like you hated yourself for being with me. Hated me."

"Not you—just myself." *And God help me, Chayne, I still do.*

"You were so miserable—it tore me up, not being able to ease your mind. I kept trying to tell you it was all right, that it was okay to love me. Didn't I tell you?"

"Yes..." *But it wasn't, Chayne; don't you understand? It wasn't.*

"I wanted you to be as happy about it as I was." He gave her bottom a gentle swat. "I told you to trust me."

Julie kept silent, pressing her face into his chest in lieu of a reply. Her hand stroked down across his belly, following the scar ridge, and she noticed that there wasn't the slightest quiver of withdrawal. It occurred to her all at once, and with a spasm of fear, that she had the capacity to hurt this man. This hardened, battle-scarred, *dangerous* man, self-possessed, resourceful and utterly unflappable under fire, *loved* her. It was an absolutely terrifying realization. Loving someone was a new and dizzying experience, and she was still trying to get used to it. But *being* loved was something else again.

I don't want to hurt him!

She cleared her throat and said lightly, "The funny thing is, there were times when I was happy."

"Really?"

"Yes, it was so—oh, I don't know if I can explain. So primitive. Or basic. There's a certain contentment to be found—and if this gets out, I'll be drummed out of the feminist movement."

"*Are* you a feminist?"

"Hush—let me finish. It was like being part of a primitive tribe or something. I thought sometimes that I could be happy just...being there with you. Cooking for you..." *If only... Oh, Chayne, why didn't you tell me who you were?*

"Speaking of cooking..."

"Uh-oh."

"Come on, woman." He gave her bottom another swat, somewhat less gentle than the first. "Since you're thinking along those lines anyway, how about finding your man something to eat?''

"I thought you said you didn't need food."

"A rash statement, made without first consulting my stomach."

"Hmm. Is that what I've been listening to?"

"Yes. Come on. *Up!*" He tumbled her, laughing, out of bed and then lay back, his head cradled on his arm, to watch her.

"Hey, that's nice," he said softly as she slipped into a short kimono of black silk. "Is that what off-duty Border Patrol agents wear?"

She shot him a look as she tied the sash. "I don't know. I bought it after I decided not to be a Border Patrol agent anymore. Are you going to lie there while I wait on you hand and foot? Do you expect me to bring you your meals in bed? What do you think I am?"

Chayne's eyebrows shot up. "What's this—back talk already? How quickly they forget! What do I think you are?" His hand shot out and caught the tie to her wrap. "Come here, *woman...*" His voice was light, but his eyes blazed with familiar fires, and they held hers captive as he drew her to the edge of the bed. When her knees touched the mattress he went on pulling, and the tie came loose with a soft slithering sound.

"What do I think you are?" he repeated very, very softly, still holding her eyes. Then abruptly he sat up and caught her legs between his thighs. "My *woman*." Very slowly he parted the edges of the black silk robe. "*My* woman...." His hands measured the curve of her waist. "Say it, Julie. You... are...*mine*." His fingers splayed across her belly and slid downward, and still his eyes held her enthralled. "*Say it!*"

"Yes..." she whispered, closing her eyes. Her legs had begun to tremble.

"Uh-uh. *Say* it, Julie. I want you never to forget it." The words were whispered against her belly as one hand applied pressure to the base of her spine and the other slipped between her thighs. He cupped her gently, his hands holding the center of her femininity hostage while his tongue circled and probed her navel.

"Yes...I—I can't—" Julie gave a violent shudder and clutched at his shoulders as her knees buckled. "I am...yours," she gasped. "Oh...help."

For a few moments longer the exquisite torture went on, and then he released her and pulled her, breathless and shaking, into his lap. While she hid her hot face in his neck, he stroked her back and legs and murmured, "So...now you know who you are. Don't forget it."

"I don't know," Julie gulped. "You may have to refresh my memory from time to time."

"Wanton," he growled. "Up, now, and into the kitchen!"

"Demon!" she threw back at him—when she was safely out of reach.

Julie heard the shower start as she was emptying the contents of her refrigerator and cupboards onto the counter, and she was surprised by the stirring of warmth the sound produced in her chest. He was here, he was real—no mirage! A certain throbbing pressure between her thighs gave ample testimony to that. And he loved her!

Then the pain returned to nibble at her heart. Oh, Chayne—if only you'd told me...

"I don't suppose you have a razor?" The shower noise had ceased.

Julie called back, "Disposables in the right-hand drawer."

"Thanks. Shaving soap?"

A little chill wafted through her. She opened her mouth, then closed it, lifted her hands and put them back down. When she didn't answer, Chayne's voice came again. "Julie?"

She looked up to find him standing in the doorway, a towel knotted precariously around his narrow hips. "I don't have any," she said in a low voice. "You won't find an extra toothbrush, either. Colin never stayed here."

"Julie..."

"I...um...have to tell you about Colin."

"No, you don't."

"Then why did you ask for..."

His voice was very gentle. "It was thoughtless. I just thought you might have a bar of soap around—something I can work up a lather with. That stuff you have hanging in the shower won't cut it, I'm afraid.''

Julie cleared her throat and muttered, "I think there's a bar in the kitchen."

"Kitchen?"

"I use it for doing my hand washables sometimes."

"Hmm." He turned back into the bathroom while Julie fished the soap out from under the sink. She took it to him and stayed in the doorway to watch him work the soap with his hands. The stark white lather against his dark skin fascinated her—and brought back vividly the first time she had watched him shave, that morning she had discovered his tiny dimple-scar and first realized that he was human.

"Do you . . . always shave in the evening?" A blob of lather fell onto his collarbone; she reached out a finger and wiped it off.

Chayne raised his eyebrows and gave her a quizzical glance. "No," he said. "I don't." Julie tried unsuccessfully to dodge the soapy finger he touched to the tip of her nose. He chuckled and gave her cheek a messy caress. "I marked you with my beard once before," he murmured, smiling at her creeping blush. "But I'm not a sadist."

Julie coughed and studied her bare toes, beset all at once by an inexplicable shyness.

"Julie?" His voice was devastatingly gentle. "What's the matter?"

"I . . . think I need to tell you about Colin."

"Not on my account. I won't hold you accountable for what you did before you met me, if you'll do me the same favor. I'll admit to being possessive, but I'm not—"

"I need to, Chayne."

He scrutinized her carefully for a moment, then abruptly rinsed his face, patted it dry and pulled her against his side. "Okay," he said briskly, meeting her eyes in the mirror. "Tell me."

"I . . . uh . . ." She swallowed and took a deep breath. "I met him in court, actually. Several years ago. He was representing a company we'd raided; I was a witness. Anyway, we . . . became friends. Just friends. We'd go to dinner occasionally; he'd take me out in his boat. He was . . ." She looked down at her hands.

Chayne shifted so that she was in front of him, facing the mirror, wrapped in his arms the way she had been the night at the cooking fire, when Pepe had demanded a dance. She had felt so protected then....

"*Safe*," she finished, realizing that, while Chayne could make her feel safe too, it wasn't the same thing at all. She dragged her eyes reluctantly back to his, searching fearfully for signs of condemnation.

"One time, about a year ago—no, a year and a half, I guess, because it was winter—we'd made plans to go boating and it rained. There were small-craft warnings out, so instead we wound up at his place in front of a fire. We had a few drinks and...got carried away with the atmosphere."

She closed her eyes and dropped her head back against his shoulder, and he lowered his head to press the side of his face to hers. "It wasn't...the best idea in the world. I think both of us were looking for something the other just didn't have to give. But neither one of us knew quite how to go back to where we'd been before. The funny thing is, it didn't seem to affect our friendship.... Chayne, what are you doing?"

"Changing the subject," he said fiercely. "That one is closed, understand?"

He had untied her robe. She could feel it drop open, feel the roughness of the hair on his arms against her skin. Hesitantly she continued, "Um...it's just that...I didn't want you to think..."

"I don't have to think. I *know* what you are."

"But I wanted to be...I'm sorry I wasn't..."

"As far as I'm concerned you were," he whispered. "You *are*. Open your eyes, Julie."

It was a command, and she obeyed it. He slowly drew the black silk away from her body, pulled it over the curves of her shoulders and let it whisper between them to the floor. She had looked upon her own body so many times before, but never like this....

Her body looked so small, almost fragile, superimposed upon that hard, dusky masculinity. But at the same time there was a new voluptuousness...a ripeness. She watched, fascinated, as a rosy glow suffused her skin from her scalp to the delta of her thighs—the point where the mirror image stopped.

"You're blushing," Chayne chuckled softly.

"All over," Julie gulped, chagrined.

"That's *one* reason why I love you, you know. Because you blush. Because you were, are, and always will be...only mine."

The pain in her chest eased.

From beneath heavy eyelids she watched his hands splay over her abdomen and move slowly upward to cup her breasts...dark hands against creamy skin. Her nipples stood out like flowers...roses; his fingertips stroked them into tender buds. The fire in her skin turned inward and raced along her nerves to her core. Her eyelids fluttered and dropped.

"Chayne," she said weakly, "what...about food?"

"Man," he intoned, "does not live by bread alone."

"Are you sure? I wouldn't want you fainting from hunger in the middle of—"

"Listen, you shameless wanton. Wasn't that what you said? 'Shameless wanton'?"

"Don't make fun of me!"

"*Never.* The only hunger I care about right now is the one I have for you!"

He held her tightly against him so that she could feel his need of her, and he slipped his hand between her thighs. She turned her hot face into his neck and whispered, "Chayne...you're all nice and clean. You smell so good. I haven't showered."

"Umm. Good."

"Good?"

Leering playfully at her startled expression, he murmured gleefully, "I'll bathe you."

"Hey, that's not fair," Julie laughed shakily. "You've already had your bath!"

"Hmm. Does seem a shame." Chayne stepped back and reached to turn on the shower. "How's your hot water supply?"

"Adequate. Not unlimited. But you—"

"Hush. Don't worry, I'm not water soluble. Now...come with me. I want to do something about that blush...."

Chapter 14

There was something cooking. Bacon. The smell drifted through layers of sleep and stirred small feelings of guilt.

Poor Chayne, Julie thought. He's given up on getting me to fix his dinner.

She tried to feel guilty enough to get out of bed and investigate, but it was hard when she felt so heavy... Her body ached—a good ache, except for something damp in the vicinity of her ribs. A groping exploration produced a wet towel, the towel Chayne had wrapped her in just before he'd picked her up and carried her to bed.

"Morning, sunshine!" The deep voice carried a warm note of laughter.

Julie gave an interrogative chirp and levered an eye open. "Morning?"

"Morning," Chayne said unequivocally.

Julie groaned and pulled the blanket up over her eyes. Fingers burrowed through her hair to massage her scalp with unsympathetic vigor. She groaned louder and attempted to impersonate a mole.

"Ah-hah!" Chayne's deep voice became a clipped tenor. "The old dig-a-hole-in-the-mattress trick! All right, you leave me no choice!"

His weight shifted as his voice retreated; Julie drifted blissfully, thinking he had given up. And then she gave a yelp of alarm—too late! "Chayne, what are you doing?"

What he had done was dive under the covers at the foot of the bed and capture her feet. She felt his warm breath on the pads of her toes, and then his moustache...his mouth...and his tongue.

"Chayne, that tickles!" She tried to jerk her foot away, but he held it firmly, kissing each toe delicately and deliberately before pressing his mouth into the sensitive arch. "Chayne...cut that out!"

His answer was a villain's laugh as he transferred his attentions to her other foot and then the hollow behind that ankle. Julie could only wriggle helplessly as he kissed his way inch by inch up her legs. She began to struggle in earnest, laughing breathlessly, when he reached the inside of her knees. "Chayne...*please*. That's...terrible."

"I know," he murmured smugly, brushing his mouth up the silky inside of her thigh. "I haf vays to make you surrender!"

"Chayne!"

"Now," he said blandly, sliding up over her quaking body and surfacing at her chin, "how's that for a wake-up call?"

Julie lifted her head and focused balefully on laughing blue eyes. "You," she croaked accusingly, "are a morning person!"

"I know. Aren't you glad?"

"Glad?"

"Yeah...you know what they say about opposites." He kissed her deeply, languidly, savoring the taste and texture of her mouth inside and out, and then stood up, taking the covers with him. "Come on...*up*," he said thickly. "I'm burning the bacon."

He went out, leaving Julie to stretch luxuriously in the middle of the stripped bed, warmed by the fires in his eyes.

"Gee, if I'd known you were capable of this," Julie muttered as she surveyed her tiny kitchen a few minutes later, "I'm not sure I'd have been so willing to wait on you hand and foot down there.'' She yawned unabashedly and wandered into the kitchen to grope for the coffee pot.

Chayne laughed as he took her by the shoulders and steered her firmly to a stool at the counter—a counter now cleared and set for two. ''In Baja? I don't think you had much of a choice, do you?'' He poured her coffee and guided her fingers to a moisture-beaded glass of orange juice. ''Come on, drink up.''

''Umm,'' Julie sighed, following orders. ''I suppose not. There was a definite order to things, wasn't there? Took some getting used to.''

''I'll bet it did!''

She bristled. ''I didn't do too badly!''

''No,'' Chayne chuckled, ''considering your meek and servile nature.''

''You know,'' Julie mused between sips of coffee, ''what amazed me was the way Rita just took it naturally. It seemed as second nature to her as breathing, to always think first of the men, to stay quiet and out of the way.''

''It probably was natural. I'm sure she was raised that way.''

''Yeah . . . it was kind of an awakening, realizing that the whole world hasn't achieved the degree of enlightenment we have.''

''Enlightenment?'' Chayne sounded amused.

''Of course!'' Julie exclaimed, and then peered suspiciously at him. ''You're laughing at me in a very smug and arrogant way. Are you a male chauvinist as well as a morning person?''

''I don't know,'' he said placidly, setting a plate of scrambled eggs and bacon in front of her. ''I don't think I've ever thought of myself in those terms at all.''

Julie took a bite of eggs and blissfully closed her eyes. ''My God...you're a better cook than I am. I hereby absolve you of being a male chauvinist.''

''*And* a morning person?''

''*That* will require a good deal more thought,'' she said severely, and then spoiled it with a gurgle of laughter as Chayne pressed a tickly kiss on the nape of her neck. He was dressed in his slacks and shirt and had shaved again; his skin was fresh and cool and smelled rather poignantly of soap. Julie felt a tremor of love like a small earthquake in her soul.

With his fingers lingering warmly on her neck, Chayne said, "I thought Rita seemed happy enough."

"Happy?" And just like that her own happiness cracked and fear and pain began to seep through, like a sulphurous miasma. Ducking her head, she said in a low voice, "Rita wasn't happy."

"No?" Chayne glanced at her as he took the stool beside her. "What makes you say that?"

"Didn't you notice? She was scared to death for Geraldo. I think she knew, or at least suspected, that he was involved in something." She put down her fork, her appetite gone. It was all black, swirling around her like a suffocating yellow fog—the helplessness and terror, the uncertainty, the frustration . . . the guilt. "Chayne, what—what happened to them? Where are they? Rita and Carlos, I mean."

Chayne raised his eyebrows. "Where are they? Back home in Guadalajara, I should imagine."

"And . . . Geraldo? Did your organization's clean sweep include the entire Baja connection?"

She had tried to keep her voice detached and impersonal, but he heard the little break in it and touched her cheek with a gentle and loving finger. "Where did you get this sudden sympathy for lawbreakers? I seem to recall you saying something about 'no excuse for breaking the law.'"

Where indeed? She suddenly felt so cold that she wondered if he could feel it with the tip of his finger where it traced across her lips. She shrugged, and the hand fell away.

"No," he said with a slight smile. "That's your department—smuggling. As far as Geraldo is concerned, I hope by this time he's back in Guadalajara and planning to be more careful where he moonlights in the future."

"Moonlights? I don't understand."

"Geraldo teaches history at a high school in Guadalajara, Julie. A couple of years ago, presented with a growing family, he decided that his income needed supplementing. He started spending his summers with Sebastien—and running illegals for Gabriel. It made a nice change for his family, and a nice *piece* of change, too. That was okay until this year, when he found there'd been some changes. For one thing, there was Pepe.

Then they got the camper, and Gabriel's deliveries started to include things like guns. And explosives."

Chayne pushed his plate aside and reached for his coffee cup. He wasn't looking at her now, but she caught the cold steel glitter of his eyes, and perhaps for the very first time she felt a visceral awareness of what the man she loved did for a living. It was so much worse than organized law enforcement. He was all alone, fighting a war with no rules, with only his wits for weapons, and no backup if it all went sour.... She shivered involuntarily, and to cover it began to gather up the plates.

"Geraldo got worried," Chayne was continuing. "He managed to get word to the authorities, the Mexican equivalent of the FBI, and they immediately suspected terrorist activity and got in touch with SAT." He shrugged, grinning. "Don't ask me to tell you how I got myself invited to the party. I've told you more than I should as it is."

"It's okay," Julie said vaguely, frowning at her hand as she fiddled with the silverware. "I...um..." She cleared her throat and cast Chayne a quick look. "They won't be in danger, will they? Won't Geraldo be suspected of..."

"Our people are keeping an eye on them," Chayne said quietly. "Just to be sure."

"I see." But would they ever be sure? Julie was silent, seeing all over again the fear in Rita's eyes and wondering if it was still there and how long it would be before it was completely gone. Fear for those you love is so much more terrible than fear for yourself. "Chayne," she said in a low, tense voice, "how did you get into this?"

"Into SAT? I was recruited...after Nam. It was...the right timing, all the way around. World terrorism was on the increase, and I was...at loose ends." For the first time since Baja, Julie heard that short, grim laugh. It made her wince with unexpected pain, and she felt an urge to touch him, just to smooth away those strain lines around his mouth and eyes. As if to do so might help to erase the confusion in her own heart.

Chayne shrugged and added matter-of-factly, "They liked my war record, I suppose, and the fact that I'm a certified pilot. And of course my Latin American upbringing."

"Latin American upbringing?" So that explained his proficiency in Spanish!

He turned to smile at her, and she was relieved to see that his eyes were again a clear cloudless blue. "Yeah. I practically grew up in Mexico and Central America. Spoke only Spanish until I was five. My father was an archaeologist—Mayan civilizations. My mother followed him around, but her interests were in a little more recent era. She's written a couple of books on Mexican and Central American folk art . . . music, that sort of thing." He took out a cigarette and lit it. "I'm surprised she didn't mention it."

"She did," Julie said tightly. Her throat ached with remembering. Would she ever be able to talk about that nightmarish morning? Could she ever tell him what it had been like to watch on television as he was taken away in handcuffs; what she had felt, thinking she would never see him again, knowing she had helped put him away, knowing she was *right* to have done so— and hating herself, *damning* herself, for it?

"What did you think of my mother?"

They were facing each other on the stools, knee to knee, but not touching. Chayne's eyes caressed her, but after one quick, pain-filled glance, Julie avoided them. It was like trying to look at the sun. "She's wonderful."

"She is, isn't she? I thought you'd like her."

Julie swallowed, but the muscles in her throat felt stiff and cramped. Why, in God's name, did she suddenly feel like crying? Was it remembering that night and morning she had spent in Chayne's mother's house? Was she like a child, whose tears are renewed by the retelling of his trauma? And how could Chayne not notice?

Because the tears were all on the inside. Outwardly she was still icily calm. "Your father," she said in a flat voice, striving to retain control. "Where is he?"

"He died several years ago. He was a lot older than my mother, and a lifetime of neglecting his health in tropical jungles finally caught up with him."

"You have sisters. . . ."

"Two. Both a lot younger than I am. Born after my parents settled here in California. Both married."

"Maddy mentioned grandchildren. . . ."

"Right. Three. Two boys and a girl."

"I guess that's why—" Her voice caught, and she coughed to cover it.

"Why what?"

"Why you seemed . . . why you were so good with Carlito."

"Yeah . . . I suppose so." His voice was as quiet as hers now, searching and cautious as he sensed the tension in her.

"I left your clothes at your mother's," Julie said rapidly. If she kept talking trivialities, maybe she could hide the turbulence that was building inside her.

Wary now, and watchful, Chayne murmured, "That's okay."

"I didn't intend to leave them for her to take care of. They were filthy. . . ."

"It's okay." His tone was dry, but concern darkened his eyes. "I expect she's used to that."

"I left the belt there, too, in case you were wondering."

"Belt?"

"Yes, the one you—"

"Oh, yes. The belt."

"I thought you'd want it back. It was so—you must have bought it for . . . someone."

"I did."

"Oh. . . ."

"My mother."

"Oh."

"Julie." She had been staring down at her hands but hadn't really noticed that they had curled into fists until Chayne touched them. "Come on, Julie," he said with a trace of gravel in his voice. "You've been slipping away from me for the last fifteen minutes. Damn it, what's wrong?"

Wrong? Oh God, Chayne, everything's wrong! But how could she tell him, when she was so confused herself? On the one hand, she was frozen stiff with fear—fear for him, fear of losing him to the hazards of his profession, terror of the prospect of life without him. But at the same time her insides were a seething mass of guilt and self-loathing for having fallen in love with him at all!

She sniffed and pulled her hands from his in order to wipe her cheeks. "Nothing," she said thickly. "Just . . . remembering.

Hey, look—" She hopped abruptly off the stool. "It's late. I'll go get dressed."

"Julie!"

But she had already fled to the bedroom, untying her kimono as she ran. She knew he wouldn't let it go at that—knew he would come after her. But at that moment she knew only that she had to get away, if only for a moment, from those intent, searching eyes. Eyes full of wariness and love.

She didn't want to hurt him!

"Julie, you're running away from me again." He stopped in the bedroom doorway, transfixed. "Good Lord...what is that you're wearing?"

She tossed the kimono onto the bed and glared at him over her shoulder. Any other time the look on his face would have made her mouth go dry, but now she lifted her chin and snapped beligerently. "It's a teddy."

Chayne coughed and ran a hand through his hair. "Uh-huh. Well . . . if you don't want me to take it off you, you'd better cover it up—quick!"

"Oh, for God's sake," she grated between clenched teeth, "is that all you can think about?" She shivered, although she wasn't cold.

Chayne's voice was very soft, and very near. "Not so long ago we were thinking along the same lines."

"Please . . . don't. Just . . . don't."

"I see." His voice was light but with a warning edge of anger. "The honeymoon's over already—and we aren't even married yet!"

Julie could feel the warmth of him behind her, his presence wafting across her nerves like fingers on guitar strings. Married? What was he trying to do to her? *"Don't,"* she said again with bitter anguish.

"Julie, for God's sake—don't do this to me again! Don't turn away from me. Don't shut me out! Tell me what the devil is wrong!"

"Wrong?" She turned on him, warding him off with her hands when he would have taken her into his arms. "You're going too fast!"

"Fast . . . ?" He reached as if she had struck him, first with shock and then with anger. "Too *fast?* Don't you have any idea how long I've waited for you? What you mean to me?"

"You? *You?* Don't you know what you did to *me?*" There. He had done it. She was crying again. And yelling again. She hadn't wanted to hurt him, but she knew she was going to, and somehow the anger made it easier. "Don't you know that you *destroyed* me?"

"Destroyed you?" Chayne's voice was cold, his anger razor edged and dangerous. "You like to make melodramatic statements, don't you? Do you want to tell me how I've destroyed you? By loving you? Or making love to you? I know it was a bit tough on your conscience—"

"Tough on my *conscience?* You make it sound like I . . . like I lied about my age, or cheated on my income tax! Chayne, I wiped out every principle I ever believed in—every moral and ethical value I had—when I fell in love with you! When I fell in love with a *smuggler.* A *criminal!*"

"Which you now know isn't true!"

"But it doesn't matter, don't you see that? I didn't know that *then.* Why couldn't you have told me, Chayne? You saw what I was going through—you said you did. How could you do that to me?"

"I couldn't tell you," he said implacably, watching her with hooded eyes. "I explained that. If you can't understand that . . ."

"No! You could have told me. You weren't under orders, were you? You chose not to tell me—chose not to trust me! Even at the end, when you left me with your mother, you let me go on thinking . . . you let me spend a whole night thinking you were going to . . . And then I watched you being taken away in *handcuffs!* You're the one who doesn't understand!"

"What I don't understand is why it should be such a huge problem for you. You love me. I love you. And all the misunderstandings are over and done with. They're in the past. We have—"

"*No.* They're not in the past. They're right *here* . . . inside me." She was pressing her fist to her chest as she faced him with streaming eyes, pleading with him to understand. "It *hurts.* Chayne, try to put yourself in my place. How would you feel if you'd just compromised everything you believed in? Everything you thought was good and decent and right?"

"I have," Chayne said stonily. "I've been there."

"All right, then," Julie gulped, pressing the back of her hand to her nose, "you tell me how long it took *you* to get over it!"

"Years." He sounded unimaginably weary. "In fact, not until I found you. And while we're wearing each other's shoes, you tell me how you'd feel if the person you loved hated himself for loving you."

"How would *you* feel if the person you loved was going to commit a horrible crime and you had the choice of letting him do it—"

"Him?"

"—Or having *her* arrested? How would you feel, watching this person you love carted off in irons!"

"There you go being melodramatic again."

"I'm not being melodramatic, damn it—I'm being *angry*. And I'm hurting!"

"So am I," Chayne grated between his teeth. "Just because I'm not carrying on like you are, don't think *I'm* not hurting, too! What it boils down to then is that my loving you isn't enough, and your loving me isn't enough to heal your shattered self-image. Is that it?"

"No! I don't know! For God's sake, Chayne, give me a little time. This just happened; I'm still reeling. I don't even know which way is up. You can't expect me to just forget everything—the person I used to be, the things I used to stand for—and live happily ever after! I've got to put the pieces back together. Find out who in the world I've become. Please...I need time!"

"Time?" His voice was quiet again, and strained...and sad. "Julie, I've already wasted enough of my life being where you are. You healed me just by loving me exactly as I was. I'm sorry you won't let me do the same for you."

He turned and left her standing there with her hand clamped tightly over her mouth. A moment later, when she hadn't heard the front door open and close, she made a small anguished noise and ran after him. She found him adjusting his shoulder holster.

He cast her one narrow, steely look as he picked up his jacket and shrugged into it. "I'm out of time, Julie," he said softly, and picked up his tie. He looped it around his neck and left without another word, or even a backward glance.

Julie spent the morning crying, though only a week earlier she hadn't been able to remember ever having really cried. Under the circumstances she thought she could be forgiven such a binge, that it might even be considered therapeutic after the strain she had been under lately. She indulged herself without guilt. But being a novice at it, she wasn't prepared for the mess several hours of unrestrained weeping could make of one's head. . . .

She had almost stopped when, at around ten o'clock or so, the florist's delivery boy arrived with a dozen pink roses in a long gold box. The card read cryptically, "I know a real tumble when I see one. Your friend always, Colin. P.S.: Equilibrium is vastly overrated."

That started her crying all over again. At eleven Chief Patrol Agent Dalton called to suggest that she look into psychiatric assistance to help her cope with her "post-hostage depression," and to tell her that he was putting her on sick leave while she "weathered the crisis."

And that made her angry enough to finally stop. It was then that she discovered that two aspirin and a cup of coffee had no effect at all on a head that felt like a fifty-gallon barrel full of steel wool upon which someone was pounding steadily with a pipe wrench.

At two-thirty her mother called, defeating her attempt to take a nap under a cold washcloth, to ask why she hadn't called to tell them that she wasn't coming home for the Expo after all. Listening to her mother's gentle reproach made her feel more lonely than guilty.

"Mother, I'm sorry about the change in plans."

"Your dad and I were both disappointed."

"Yes, I know, and I'm sorry. But I was reassigned at the last minute."

"It was thoughtless of you not to call, Julie. We were worried, especially when we couldn't reach you."

"I know, Mother. I've been working such odd hours."

"You know you can always call us *any* time, Julie. We're always here for you."

"Yes, I know, Mother. I'm sorry."

There were other things she wanted to say—or to ask: Mother, as a matter of fact there are some questions I really do need answers to. A girl is supposed to be able to ask her mother these things, isn't she?

Okay, Mom, here goes. How can I love someone so much and be so miserable? I thought love was supposed to be a good thing!

Oh, Mother—how can it be so good between us, and so bad?

How can he say he loves me and not understand something this important?

She could almost hear her mother saying, Well, maybe it isn't love at all, Julie dear. Maybe it's only a matter of...ahem...*sex*. And if you are only good together in bed, no matter how good, then that's not enough to base a relationship on. Is it?

"Yes, Mother, I'll be up to see you soon, I promise. Yes...I love you too. Give my love to Dad."

Julie hung up feeling more alone than ever. She wished that she could talk to someone—a best friend, perhaps, or a sister. But Colin had been her best friend, and she didn't have a sister. And her mother...she seriously doubted that her mother even had a clue what kind of dangers her job involved.

No, there was no one to help her. She was going to have to work this one out by herself.

She showered and washed her hair, and that made her feel somewhat better physically. If only there weren't reminders of *him* all over the place! They were everywhere, in the kitchen, the bathroom.... The bar of soap and the razor on the sink; damp towels on the floor; ghost images in the mirror of his body and hers entwining in wanton patterns of light on dark; erotic hauntings of fragrant steam and moisture sipped from silken skin, more intoxicating than wine... Of soapy fingers sliding over breasts and buttocks and sliding gently into caverns and hollows... Of herself at last becoming nothing but a warm pulsating part of it all—the water, the steam...and Chayne.

She couldn't even bear to look at the bed. She couldn't stay in the apartment another minute!

The credit cards tempted her; she actually took them out and lined them all up on the desk top before sweeping them back into the drawer. She couldn't very well go on a shopping spree every time she felt depressed and confused, especially since she was probably going to feel that way a lot in the future.

But there was one place she could always escape to, one thing she had always turned to when she needed to work off frustrations or just get away from her own thoughts....

"Julie? How much longer do you think you'll be?"

Julie climbed up out of a fog of concentration, executed a simple dismount from the balance beam and reached for a towel. "My goodness, closing time already? I didn't realize it was so late, Terry; I'm sorry, I'll—"

"No, no, you don't have to go. Just lock up when you leave."

Terry Amato had been a world-class gymnast before an accident had left her with a permanently crippled elbow. Her gymnastics academy was highly regarded on the West Coast; she had already trained one U.S. champion, and at the moment boasted several promising Olympics prospects.

"You're working hard," Terry said with a smile. "Does this mean you're going to take my Wonderkids class next session? We've missed you."

Julie shrugged, smiled and gave a noncommittal answer. She'd taught off and on for Terry for years when she could fit it into her work schedule. For the first time it occurred to her that she no longer had a work schedule. She no longer had a job. She was just realizing that she was going to have to come up with a new career—or at least a way to pay the rent. Maybe Terry could use a full-time instructor.

But this wasn't the time to talk about the future. She had come to the gym tonight to forget about that altogether. So she chatted with Terry for a few minutes, promised to lock up tight when she left, and then listened to the tapping of Terry's heels diminishing as she crossed the cavernous room to the door.

She was alone. The huge building was empty but filled with weird shadows and ghost sounds, like a deserted amusement park.

Alone. Julie loved the gym when it was like this, when she could work with absolute freedom, without self-consciousness, giving in to her creative fancies. . . .

The mat beckoned, as the sand had done that morning in the cove. She selected a cassette at random, punched it into the tape deck and stood with bowed head, eyes closed, listening to the metallic waves of canned music swell to the rafters. She waited, feeling the music seep into her bones and muscles, and then stepped out onto the mat. Bits of old routines and spur-of-the-moment improvisations, technical skills and harnessed passions—she let them all flow through her on a wave of emotion and energy that left her both exhausted and exhilarated.

The music died away, and she settled into a graceful scissor split, arms upraised. Ah, well, not the most imaginative finish, perhaps, but . . .

A sound intruded on the dying echoes—the sound of a single pair of clapping hands.

Julie whole body jerked as quivering muscles received an infusion of adrenaline.

"Nice," Chayne rumbled, stepping out of the shadows near the office door. "Very nice."

"How did you get in?" She was amazed to discover that her voice still worked; amazed, too, at the jolt that had gone through her at just the sound of his voice. She pulled her legs up under her but made no attempt to stand; she doubted very much that she was capable of it.

God, he was beautiful. It hurt to look at him. She had an impulse to shade her eyes with her hand as he sauntered toward her across that airplane hangar of a room. There was a half smile on his lips, but it didn't reach his eyes. She could see the demon glitter of them long before he reached her.

"How did you get in here?" she asked again, her voice cracking with the tension. "The door was locked."

Chayne grinned suddenly, blew on his fingertips and then rubbed them on the front of his jacket. "There are some advantages to my line of work. . . ."

Julie shook her head. "No, you didn't."

"No," he admitted with a shrug, "I didn't. I intended to if necessary, but your friend let me in."

"My friend? Terry?"

"Small lady, dark hair? That's the one."

"You...you've been here all that time?" Julie felt her body grow hot with embarrassment. "Watching me?"

Chayne laughed softly and tugged at his tie. "You're blushing again." His voice was heavy with intimate associations. He took off his jacket and dropped it over the balance beam, then leaned against it and crossed his arms on his chest.

"Do you have any idea what a turn-on it is to watch you do that?" His eyes were hooded and smoky; there was sexual arrogance in every line of his body, in the set of his head, the curve of his mouth, the timbre of his voice. How confident he was, how certain of her response to him!

And how right he was to be so certain. Just the sight of him made her body tremble and grow heavy and sultry with wanting. Forgotten were the questions and doubts, the harsh words and tears. He was there, for whatever reason; he was *there*—and that was all that mattered.

Still... "How did you know I was here?" she asked, not really caring.

"Friend of yours at the station told me I might find you here."

"Who?"

"Lupe, I think her name was."

"Oh." She tore her gaze away and got to her feet, tugging her leotard down over her bottom, moving self-consciously under his steady regard. "Why?"

"Why what?"

"Why did you . . . want to find me?"

Under his breath and in Spanish he muttered, "*Dios mío, Güerita* . . . who knows? Who cares?" And then, with a wry smile and a shake of his head, he added, "It was important enough to bring me here, but after watching you I'm damned if I feel like talking. I wish there was some way you could see yourself . . . some way I could make you know how sexy you are . . . and what it does to me to watch you."

Julie thought, Oh, I know, Chayne! I know because I've felt the same way watching you . . . in a fishing boat under a cobalt sky. . . .

But she couldn't speak; her mouth was parched while the rest of her grew liquid, warm and honeyed. She felt herself melting as she was suffused with desire.

"Your body knocks me out.... It always has, you know that? From the very first time you took off your shirt for me, remember? Every muscle...so perfectly defined, but soft, too, and made for touching. Skin so smooth and sweet...skin that blushes all over..."

She had turned her back and taken several unsteady steps away from him, trying to hide her flushed cheeks and ragged breathing, but he only laughed, a low rumble that whispered sensuously down her spine.

"You have a beautiful back, *Güerita mía*...and a truly delightful bottom. It fits my hands perfectly. But then, you know that, don't you?"

His words were like kisses; she closed her eyes and let his voice move over her body like caressing fingers. She knew the wooing timbre of that voice, knew what he was doing, spinning a silken cocoon all around her, immobilizing her with his love spell. She had heard it before, in the darkness of a cave, and knew how potent was its magic.

"Chayne...," she said thickly, "what are you doing?"

The laughter touched her again with velvet fingers. "Loving you."

"*Seducing* me."

"I haven't touched you."

"No...it seems you don't have to."

"Oh, but I do." And then somehow he was. Instead of words, his warm breath stirred across the nape of her neck, and then his mouth took its place. His hands smoothed over her shoulders and drew her into the curve of his hard, vibrant body, and she was enveloped in his furnace heat. His arms crisscrossed her body, one hand sliding beneath the top of her leotard to cover an aching, swollen breast, the other stroking downward over her belly to cup that part of her that most urgently demanded his touch.

"I want to make love to you," he whispered, pressing her hard against him, showing her the truth in his words. "Now."

"Now? Not...here..."

"Here. And now."

"Chayne..."

"We're locked in here, Julie. The world is locked out. The place is ours." The last word was a growl as he turned her in his arms.

His kiss was designed to dispose of inhibitions, wipe out lingering doubts and cut loose all restraints. She felt herself open to him; she let his passion pour into her and was immediately drunk on it. This time when he growled, "Let me love you, Julie," she could only whisper, "Yes...," so lost in him that she never even knew when he lowered her gently to the mat.

"You know, the erotic possibilities of this place are mindboggling," Chayne said lazily, his fingers drawing random designs along her rib cage and raising goose bumps on her gradually cooling skin.

Julie gave a breathy little giggle and said huskily, "You are incredible. Impossible—incorrigible—insatiable!"

"All of the above," Chayne said easily, and gave her bottom a pat. "Let me up, angel—I need my cigarettes."

She rolled onto her stomach, ducking her head to hide the smile and the glow that was creeping over her. *Angel*. It was the first endearment he had ever used with her, except, of course, for *Güerita*. Ridiculous that it should make her feel so cherished.

She propped her chin on her fists and watched him walk to the balance beam and return with his cigarettes and lighter, as unselfconscious in his nakedness as the panther he so often reminded her of. He gave her a lazy smile as he settled beside her, then lit his cigarette and lay back with his head pillowed on his arm.

"Don't know why I never noticed the erotic possibilities of a gym before," he mused, blowing smoke. "Just never had the right inspiration, I guess."

"You ought to be ashamed of yourself," Julie said, swallowing laughter. And then, with curiosity, "When did you spend time in a gym?"

He chuckled and sat up. "You'd be surprised. I'm no good at cartwheels or standing on my head, but there are certain skills that come in handy in my line of work."

"Yeah?" Julie rolled over and sat up, intrigued. "For instance?"

"A strategic forward roll can be very useful in evading a blow—or a bullet."

"I see," Julie said, her laughter gone. "I never thought of that. It wasn't part of my basic training in self-defense."

"No," Chayne said softly, "I don't suppose it was."

They were both silent. Chayne smoked, narrowing his eyes against the curl of smoke. Julie began to feel chilled and reached for her clothes. Chayne watched her dress without comment, then gave his cigarette a final drag and looked around for a place to dispose of it. He raised his eyebrows interrogatively at Julie. When she only shrugged unhelpfully, he tucked the cigarette between his lips, pulled on his pants and stalked off, muttering something under his breath about a "damned nuisance."

When he came back, he settled himself on a rolled-up mat and fixed Julie with a steady blue gaze. She felt the full electric charge of those eyes and waited, her heart beating in a slow, measured cadence. Suspense built with every heartbeat until Chayne cleared his throat, breaking it.

"You wanted time," he said, his voice harsh. "I came to tell you that you can have it."

Julie stared at him, not understanding. Please, she prayed, don't let him leave me. Oh God, please don't let it be another assignment! She licked her lips and said painfully, "Are you . . . leaving?"

"Yes. I'm flying to Washington."

"When?" She thought her throat would crack.

"In about—" he checked his watch—"four hours."

"And . . . um . . . when will you be back?"

"That," Chayne said softly, "depends on you."

Chapter 15

"I don't understand," Julie said in a low voice, fighting panic.

Chayne got up and walked slowly to the climbing rope. He stood idly running his hand up and down it, staring at the place where it disappeared into the shadows. "I have some decisions to make," he said at last, dropping his hand.

"Decisions," Julie murmured, and held her breath.

"Yeah." He gave his sharp, savage laugh. "It seems I can choose a new line of work—or a new face. You see," he went on the distance between them making him sound cold and remote, "thanks to a certain network cameraman, my usefulness to SAT is over. My face has been flashed around the world via satellite, as they like to say in the media, and..." He smiled crookedly and lifted his shoulders in a shrug of self-deprecation. "My face isn't exactly the kind you forget in five minutes after you've seen it."

"No," Julie whispered.

"I think you can see how that could be a problem for an undercover operative."

"Yes..."

"They want to keep me badly enough to offer me this...new identity. Plastic surgery—" he waved a hand over his naked torso "—to remove all distinguishing marks, a new face, contact lenses ... the works."

"Good God," Julie said faintly.

"Yeah."

"Why—" She cleared her throat and tried again. "Why are you telling me this?"

"Why am I telling you this?" His eyes were narrowed; he sounded tense, almost angry. "Don't you think you figure in this somewhere?"

Julie kept her tone calm with a great deal of effort and ignored the question. "Does the job with SAT mean that much to you?" she asked instead, praying that her voice wouldn't break.

"Damn it, Julie." He gave the rope an angry tug. "I don't know. The question is, could you accept me with a different face? And more important—"

"What a question!"

"And *more* important—could you accept my job?"

Julie swallowed. "Could I ... accept your job?" she murmured evasively.

Chayne gave her a long considering look, and then without a word went hand over hand up the rope. In seconds he was hanging in midair high above the mat.

It took Julie completely by surprise. She clamped a hand over her mouth to stifle a cry and waited, frozen with fear, for him to come down. It seemed an eternity before he was safely back on the ground and walking slowly toward her across the mat, brushing at his hands. There was a grim little smile on his face as he took her chin in his hand and subjected her once more to the full laser blast of his eyes.

"Yes," he said gently, "it's there."

"What?"

"The fear."

He turned away from her as she lied futilely, "I don't know what you mean."

He waved an impatient hand at the rope. "You were afraid I'd fall."

"Of course I was! What did you expect? You took me by surprise. I had no idea—and it doesn't mean—Look, Chayne, I'm not exactly unfamiliar with the kind of job you do, after all!"

"I know," he said softly. "I think that's why you're afraid. You understand better than most people would just what my work entails. Especially after being with me in Baja. The question is, could you live with it?"

The question hung in the air between them. Finally Julie said in a low voice, "Maybe a better question would be, could you live without it?"

Chayne gave a sharp bark of laughter and raked his hands through his hair. "I don't know," he said, lifting his hands and letting them drop. And then he repeated tiredly, as he turned away from her, "I don't know, Julie." He paced a little way off, then came back to her. "You know," he said, smiling ruefully, "you accused me once of being a war lover. I put you through a pretty rough time denying it. But the irony of it is, I've thought about it a lot, and I've decided that you're probably right."

She made a strangled sound of protest, but he shushed her with a gesture. "No—there *is* something . . . addictive about living on the razor's edge. It's like some kind of mind-expanding drug, I guess—a kind of perpetual high. Your senses are heightened; all systems are humming along in overdrive. Every day is a miracle. Hell, Julie, I don't have to explain this to you. You *know* what I'm talking about!" He took Julie's arms and looked deep into her eyes, then gave her a little shake and said quietly, "You do know what I mean, don't you, Julie? About the thrill, don't you, Julie? About the thrill, the excitement, the old adrenaline pumping."

"No! I've never—I don't feel that way at all! And anyway, I've quit my job!"

"Yeah . . . and have you thought about what you'll do instead? A desk job, Julie? How about being a housewife? That appeal to you? Cooking and cleaning and driving a station wagon to the market?" He waited, tense and glaring, for her to answer, then steered her to the vaulting runway and released her. "Do something for me, Julie—take a shot at that horse." When she only stared at him as if he had lost his mind, he gave her a little nudge and said harshly, "Go on. Just a simple flip will do—nothing fancy."

He seemed so tightly strung, like a spring wound to the breaking point. Julie tried to read his dark, set face and then lifted her chin and tossed him a look full of all the pain and confusion that had haunted her for days. And then she took a deep breath, raced down the runway, hurled herself into her spring and hit the horse with a slap that jarred clear to her shoulders. Her body snapped up and over. The landing was clumsy, off-balance; she wobbled, took two steps and regained control. Turning on Chayne, she said shakily, "Satisfied?"

He was breathing almost as hard as she was, and his eyes were very bright. "Now you tell me," he rasped, "what did you feel just now? A thrill? Excitement? Freedom? How about *power?*" He closed the distance between them in quick, angry strides and took her arms again. "*That's* why you do this, Julie—don't kid yourself. And don't kid me. You do it for all those things you can't find in a nice, safe, ordinary nine-to-five existence. You do it for the thrill of it, pure and simple. And you know something else?" He gave a strange laugh full of pain and wonder and shook his head. "Just now, when you made that damned vault, I knew exactly how you felt when I went up the rope. Right then, for the first time, it suddenly hit me that what you do may *look* beautiful and graceful, even sexy, but it's *dangerous*. A wrong move and you could spend the rest of your life dead from the neck down! My God, Julie, I—"

She went into his arms, pressing her face into his heaving chest, and they held on to each other until their breathing had quieted and their trembling had stopped.

"Ah, Julie," Chayne sighed, stroking her hair, "I guess we've both got some decisions to make."

Julie shook her head sharply and stood back, brushing at her cheeks. "No," she said thickly.

"What do you mean, no?"

"Chayne . . . would you ever ask me to give up gymnastics?"

"Of course not—what a question. No more than I'd ask you to stop being a Border Patrol agent. That was your decision."

"Right," Julie said softly. "And this has to be yours. I can't ask you to give up your whole career. I'd never do that."

"Damn it, I know that! It's important to me to know how you feel."

She shook her head, adamant. "You have to make this decision on your own, Chayne. Based on the way *you* feel. And then . . . I guess I'd have to decide . . . whether I could live with it." She'd have to decide whether she could live with him disappearing for weeks and months at a time; never knowing whether or not he was going to come back . . . She managed a tight smile. "I can't imagine you with a different face, so don't ask me how I'd feel about that. Probably it wouldn't matter once I got used to it." He'd still be Chayne, and she'd love him if he had two heads! "But it would matter, to both of us, if *I* was responsible for making you give up something important to you."

"If I make the decision to quit SAT now, you'll think it was your fault anyway, won't you?" Chayne's eyes were sad, his smile ironic.

Julie sniffed and shrugged helplessly. "Probably."

"And if I don't quit SAT, I'll probably lose you."

"I don't *know!* I just don't know! Oh, Chayne," she cried, laughing as tears ran down her cheeks, "I think this is what's known as a dilemma!"

He held her again, pressing his lips to her hair and stroking her back. And saying nothing because, it seemed, there was nothing left to say.

Chayne was gone. When Julie woke in the morning and knew that his plane was at that moment streaking east into the afternoon, the air around her became flat and tepid, and all the colors gray.

She tried hard not to think or feel, and to avoid it she kept busy with trivialities. She took her car in for an oil change, and then, as a special treat, had it washed. She went grocery shopping and organized all her cupboards, sorted clothes and took armloads to the Goodwill collection box. Took Madeline Younger's clothes to the dry cleaners. She would have to send them back, of course. Or take them—it would give her something to do. She made a phone call to Madeline to arrange it and hung up feeling that there *might,* after all, be someone she could talk to.

The next day Julie filled her car with gas, made a stop at the cleaners, and then drove to Ramona.

Madeline Younger greeted her with an impulsive hug while the dog, Jack, pushed his muzzle between them and nudged her leg with restrained impatience.

Madeline laughed, "Oh, go on, Jack," while Julie fondled his ears and was rewarded with a gaze of soulful adoration. "Chayne's dog," his mother said, as if that explained something, and tucked an arm around Julie's waist.

"Oh, I can't tell you how glad I am that you called. Here, dear, let me take those. You really shouldn't have gone to the trouble of having them cleaned! Come in where it's cool. I've got some iced tea, or there's beer if you—"

"Tea sounds wonderful."

Inside the sprawling redwood and fieldstone ranch house it was cool and pleasant and smelled of lemons. It was shady and green now, instead of warm and golden, but to Julie it still had the feeling of home and welcome that had touched her so profoundly that night.

In the big sunny kitchen Madeline poured two tall glasses of tea, topped them with mint and lemon, and joined Julie at the table.

"Do you mind if we sit in here? Isn't it funny? I always seem to visit in the kitchen. The living room is for... what? The television set, I guess, and for exercising. Oh, Julie..." She frowned over the top of her glass. "I'm so glad you're here. I've never forgiven myself for what you must have gone through that night. And I didn't get your address, so I had no idea how to get in touch with you."

"It's all right, really."

"I've thought of you so much. I've just been hoping that Chayne would get in touch so I could ask about you."

"He hasn't called you?"

"Oh, just briefly, to let me know he was all right. But he sounded so rushed and abrupt that I didn't have a chance to chat. Drat the man!" But she was chuckling, not terribly put out. "I suppose he's off again?"

"Yes," Julie murmured, sipping tea. "He...uh...he's gone to Washington."

"I see," Madeline said with calm acceptance. After a moment she went on. "I mistook you for a colleague of Chayne's, you know. I thought you and he were involved together in one of his assignments."

"We were, in a way."

"Yes," Madeline said with a smile, "but obviously not the way *I* thought you were. Here I thought you *knew* ..."

"And I couldn't understand how you could be so cool and unconcerned about it!" Julie was laughing and shaking her head. "I asked if you knew what he did for a living, meaning smuggling illegals—"

"Is *that* what he was doing?"

"Yes, and you said—"

"I said—oh, dear! We were talking right over each other's heads, apparently!"

The laughter died. The tears Julie brushed from her cheeks weren't entirely tears of laughter.

"It was...pretty awful," she said in shaky understatement, struggling against her natural reserve. "I thought he was really a smuggler—a terrorist."

Madeline Younger waited without speaking. Julie saw Chayne in her: in her dusky, faintly exotic coloring, in her expressive mouth, and something about the carriage of the head. But Madeline's eyes were a deep slate that just missed being black, and dark with understanding and compassion. They gave Julie the odd feeling that this woman already knew what she wanted so badly to say.

And so she said it, stiffly and with pain. "And...I loved him, Maddy. In spite of it."

"Loved?" Maddy said with a gentle arching of brows.

Julie laughed tremulously. "*Love.* I just meant..."

"I know, dear. I understand. And you can't understand how you could have done such a thing."

"How *could* I?" Julie whispered wretchedly, as if she really hoped for an answer.

"Well," Madeline said with a smile, "of course, you're probably asking the wrong person. I don't find it at all hard to understand how you might love my son. But, dear..." She reached across the table to cover Julie's hand briefly with her own. "Surely he must have done something to *make* you love him—in spite of being a smuggler."

"He saved my life," Julie said with a rueful laugh.

And Madeline exclaimed, "Oh, well, that's surely a good start!"

They laughed together while Julie's mind went back...back to Baja, to that stuffy camper...remembering. And before she had time to consider whether or not she should, she was telling Chayne's mother everything.

"You never really had a chance to get to know each other, did you?" Madeline asked thoughtfully.

They were in the living room, curled up at opposite ends of the couch with their feet tucked under them, wrapped in bathrobes. Julie's, as usual, was borrowed, it having been decided during dinner that she would have to spend the night. There was just no way they were going to say all there was to say otherwise.

It was dark and foggy outside, serene and golden inside; Jack had begged to be admitted, been rousted from the couch, and now slept sprawled on his side against the base of it.

"No," Julie sighed, raking her fingers through her hair. "We couldn't talk—that was the problem. He couldn't tell me anything at all for fear of giving himself away, and to tell you the truth, when I felt myself falling, I didn't want to know anything about him. I thought...I could hold off the feelings, I guess. Or maybe I was just afraid. I knew it wasn't going to go anywhere—whatever it was between us. That it could only bring pain. And I thought if I could keep from knowing him, it...wouldn't be as bad."

She looked at Madeline for confirmation that she understood, and the other woman nodded and whispered, "Yes, I see."

"But we did talk—once. It was almost as if we just couldn't help it. It was painful," she added, looking away. "Funny, from nothing at all we went straight to each other's most closely guarded secrets. Maybe it was a way of...I don't know. Giving to each other. A gift."

"Yes..." Madeline whispered, nodding.

"Chayne . . . told me about Vietnam. About how he got his scars."

Madeline made a soft sound of amazement. "That's something he's never told *me*."

"You said . . . that Vietnam had changed him," Julie said. "What did you mean?"

"Vietnam changed everybody—the whole darn country!" Madeline rearranged herself and cupped her chin in her hand. "Oh, Julie, I don't mean to be evasive; it's just so hard to talk about. When you have a child—or any loved one, really—and you see this wonderful, warm, loving human being become bitter and cynical…someone else altogether…a stranger…it's almost as bad as losing them. Every day you remember what they *were,* and you ache for what should have been. . . .

"Chayne was such a . . . well, a caring person. Even when he was small. He was an only child, you know, until he was seven, but he wasn't the stereotypical spoiled only child. Maybe it was all that traveling around in poverty-stricken countries, but he was always concerned about other people. Always wanting to take care of them. I remember once—" She stopped, shaking her head and smiling, and Julie caught the shine of moisture in her eyes. "He couldn't have been more than four years old. I had picked up some kind of tropical bug and had to stay in bed for a few days. I remember being so worried that Chayne would have to fend for himself, feeling guilty. And he said, in this grown-up voice, looking at me with those eyes of his, 'Don't worry, Maddy; I'll take care of you.'"

She stopped abruptly and wiped a hand across her face. "Oh, well," she said huskily, clearing her throat, "you get the idea. And after the girls were born he was just as happy as a clam, being big brother. They adored him—absolutely adored him. None of this meant he wasn't a typical rough-and-tumble boy, giving me heart failure at every turn, of course. He always did have a knack for getting into—and out of—dangerous situations."

"*That* hasn't changed!"

"No, and he usually manages to come through all right."

"Not always," Julie murmured, thinking of Vietnam.

Madeline nodded and whispered, "No." Julie saw her throat move convulsively, and then the older woman tossed her head back and laughed. "No, not always. He got that scar on his chin trying to ride an unbroken horse—I think he was about twelve. The horse dumped him in the middle of a barbed-wire fence."

"I always thought—"

"You thought that one came from Vietnam too, didn't you? No," Madeline sighed, "just the big ones."

"Tell me," Julie said softly. "Please."

Madeline threw her a quick smile of apology. "I'm sorry, I do seem to keep digressing."

"It's all right—I have a lot to catch up on. Did..." Julie cleared her throat hesitantly, remembering something Chayne had said. "Did he play football? Have a ... girlfriend? A special one, I mean," she added hastily. Of course Chayne would have had girlfriends—probably more than he knew what to do with!

"Oh, yes." His mother made a rueful sound. "He was quite the big man on campus, as you might imagine, but you know ... even that didn't really spoil him. Well ... maybe a little!" She laughed. "I suppose it's impossible for an adolescent male to be varsity quarterback, *and* have eyes that can light up Carnegie Hall, and not be a *tad* arrogant.

"But he ... had a girlfriend. A very nice girl, a neighbor of ours. She was—"

"She was a cheerleader, wasn't she?"

"Yes. How did you know?"

"Just a guess," Julie murmured, conscious of a dull ache in the middle of her chest.

"Yes, she was a cheerleader, and he was the quarterback, and they were just the world's cutest couple, and everybody assumed they would marry and live happily ever after."

"What ... what happened?" Julie held her breath, marveling that something that was obviously very much in the past could still hurt her so.

"Vietnam," Madeline said simply. "Chayne went to Stanford and enrolled in premed. Kelly went to Berkeley. Then Chayne got this idea he should be doing something that mattered. He didn't *have* to go to Vietnam; it was his choice. He was with the medical evacuation corps—"

"I know. He told me."

"Yes. Well, you know more than I do about what he went through over there. But I swear, coming home was worse, Julie. Maybe you don't remember what it was like—you're a little young. But he was . . . almost an outcast for having been a part of it. No one wanted to have anything to do with a Vietnam vet. And Kelly . . . Kelly had gotten very heavily involved with the antiwar groups at Berkeley, and she . . . just dumped him."

"Not . . . for chewed-up veterans of dirty unpopular little wars . . ." Julie remembered the pain and bitterness in his eyes and felt the pressure of tears in her own. Oh, Chayne. . . .

"But whether it was that or something that happened over there or a combination of things, he was . . . different. Harder, cynical, bitter, cold. His eyes used to make me feel as if the sun were shining on me. After that it felt more like he was stabbing me with a knife. He wasn't interested in medicine at all anymore, didn't really know what he was going to do before this government thing came along. He didn't seem to care."

She was silent, lost in sad and wistful thoughts. At their feet, Jack stretched and groaned and went back to sleep.

"I'm sorry," Julie whispered, aching for Chayne, for his mother, for herself.

"But," Madeline said suddenly, straightening to smile at Julie, "he seems to care about *you.*"

"He said . . ." Julie gave a little laugh that was very nearly a sob and put her hand to her throat. She looked away, unable to meet those eyes that were so full of compassion and hope. "He said I . . . healed him. I didn't know what he meant. Oh . . . Maddy . . ."

All of a sudden she was crying. Without a word Chayne's mother slid across the couch to comfort her, wrapping her arms around her and rubbing her back as she would a child's.

"Why are you crying, Julie?" she asked gently after a moment. "It sounds as though you may be the best thing that could possibly happen to my son. If he loves you . . ."

"He does! I know he does. . . ."

"Then what on earth is the matter? You love him. Is it this job of his?"

"Oh yes, partly. But, Maddy, I can't accept the fact that I fell in love with a criminal. I can't deal with it! Chayne can't understand it. It hurts him that I feel this way, but I can't help it. I keep thinking, what kind of person would fall in love with a criminal? What kind of person does that make *me?*''

"Oh, Julie, for goodness' sake," Madeline said severely, taking her shoulders and giving them an exasperated shake. "I think you're selling yourself awfully short!"

"What . . . ?" Julie gulped, blinking away tears.

"Here you are beating yourself to a pulp with guilt, when you ought to be crowing with self-congratulation!"

"I don't—"

"You saw what he really was inside, all evidence to the contrary! The trouble is, you didn't trust your instincts."

"Instincts!" A very small bubble of relief tickled up through her and erupted in a breathless little laugh. "That's funny, you know. I've always thought I had very good instincts."

"Well, you see? Your instincts told you who he was; you just weren't listening. You responded to the basic good in him, to his kindness and decency—and that makes *you* a good, kind, decent, loving person. And I love you to pieces, and I can't tell you how wonderful it is having you here, and how happy I am that my son found you!"

They were both laughing, both crying, hugging, patting and rocking, feeling a little silly, a little embarrassed and a lot relieved, two women finding mutual love, comfort and everlasting friendship.

"Oh . . . ," Julie sighed tremulously, sniffling a bit as she wiped at her cheeks. "Oh, Maddy. . . I'm so scared. What if he doesn't come back?"

Julie lay awake watching horses, brought to life by the play of light and shadows, cavort across the walls.

Chayne wasn't coming back. She was sure of it. He'd been gone for three days. If he'd decided to quit SAT, it wouldn't have taken him so long; and if he'd decided to stay and wanted her to face the hazards with him, surely he'd have called to ask for her decision.

So . . . he wasn't going to give her that chance. He'd decided that she couldn't live with his job, and thought he'd spare them both the torment of another parting. . . .

Already, at that very moment, he was off somewhere in a secret clinic, preparing to have his face and body rearranged. And even if she should some day run into him, just by chance, she wouldn't even know him....

You do have a tendency to be melodramatic, Julie. She could hear Chayne's dry rumble as clearly as if he had spoken. But what if she *had* lost him? Oh, Chayne....

She'd been a complete idiot. A fool. What was all this garbage about decisions and scruples and self-respect? Nothing mattered if she lost him. Nothing.

She had felt alone before, and frightened, but never quite like this. She wanted Chayne—wanted him desperately. Wanted the feel of his arms around her, the taste of his skin in her mouth, the scent of him in her nostrils. How could she ever face a life without him?

At last, giving up on sleep completely, she got up and padded across the hall to the bathroom. She washed her face, got a drink of water, and then, instead of going back to bed, found herself turning down the hall to Chayne's room.

Of course he didn't really live there now, and the clutter of mementos on the shelves and walls was from a long time ago—plaques and trophies, pennants and banners from high school, photographs of a younger Chayne, laughing, with "eyes that could light up Carnegie Hall." But they were Chayne's things. They had been a part of him, and they brought him closer, somehow.

Most of the things hanging in the closet were old, too. Julie recognized a letter sweater and a football jersey. But there was a pair of scuffed tennis shoes on the floor that looked as if he had just stepped out of them, and hanging on a hook inside the door, a brown terrycloth bathrobe. Julie buried her face in it and inhaled deeply. He seemed so near—as if any minute he would walk out of the bathroom mopping flecks of white lather from his dusky skin.

Taking the bathrobe from its hook, she folded it in her arms and sat down on the bed. Chayne seemed so close that when the bedroom door creaked slowly open, her heart nearly leaped out of her chest. But the eyes that peered at her with sad commiseration were liquid brown, not demon blue.

"Oh, Jack," Julie whispered. "Poor Jack. Do you miss him, too?"

The dog padded across the rug, nudged at her leg and then laid his muzzle on her knee. Julie leaned forward impulsively and buried her face in the silky fur. "Oh, Jack . . . he'll come back. He *has* to. . . ."

Jack was whining. . . . Probably wanted out. Darn. She'd have to get up and let him out. Served her right for falling asleep with a dog. . . .

She'd fallen asleep on Chayne's bed, wrapped in his bathrobe. It was warm, and she didn't want to move. Jack had jumped off the bed, probably he'd find his own way out. . . .

There were small scuffles and thumps, a smothered exclamation of surprise. A weight pressed down on the edge of the bed, and something warm brushed her cheek.

"Go 'way, Jack," she mumbled, pushing at it.

"Hmm . . . I'm gone three days and already you've got somebody else?"

"Chayne . . . ?"

"So who's this Jack, hmm?"

"Oh God . . . Chayne . . ."

"Shh . . . be still and kiss me."

Her heart, so electrifyingly roused, exploded and took off like a rocket. With an inarticulate cry, she threw her arms around his neck and clung to his mouth as if it were her only lifeline.

"Oh God . . . I can't believe . . . I thought . . ." she gasped when she could speak again.

"Güerita," Chayne growled, "I don't know what you're doing here, but you talk too damn much!" His mouth closed over hers, his tongue sliding over her lips, dipping in and out, not in haste but savoring. She felt his hands on her neck pushing aside obstacles to his searching mouth. "My old *bathrobe?*" A warm gust of laughter exploded against her throat. "Ah . . . Julie. God, how I've missed you. I can't believe how much I need you . . . need to touch you . . . taste you." His tongue fluttered into the hollow at the base of her throat, while his hands massaged her breasts through the thin fabric of her

nightgown and tugged with growing impatience at even that fragile barrier.

"Julie...get this damn thing off. I can't find the buttons!"

She sensed an urgency in him that frightened her a little because she wasn't sure what it meant. "Chayne..." she whispered half-fearfully, and reached up to touch his face. He caught her hand and pressed it to his mouth, kissing the palm with the same hunger he had lavished on her mouth. Then he tore it away, slipped an arm beneath her hips and lifted her, dragging the nightgown up over her body. She arched her back and raised her arms, writhing a little to aid in its disposal, and then lay still, quivering with the sudden chill and with anticipation of his touch.

But now that she lay open to him he seemed content for the moment to feast on her with his eyes, devouring the pale outline of her body, caressing its dusky hollows with an oddly touching kind of wonder.

"You are a miracle," he whispered. "A miracle..."

His hands spanned her waist, and he watched with fascination the dark patterns they made on her silvery skin. As they slipped upward over her ribs, her body arched into his hands, her breasts swelling with yearning, the dusky areolas an offering. His hands humbly accepted her offering while his eyes lavished praise upon it.

Julie lay with her arms still stretched above her head and watched him from beneath eyelids grown heavy with love. Her breathing quickened, thrusting her breasts against his warm, encompassing touch. A thumb and forefinger captured each hardened nipple and rolled it slowly, tugging gently, and she gasped, shivering with the urgency of her own need.

"What is it?" he growled when she made an inarticulate whimpering sound of frustration. "Tell me what you want."

"You...just you. I love you. I thought you weren't...coming back! Oh God...Chayne...*love me!*"

"Sweet Julie...don't you know I do? How could I not come back to you? You saved me...gave me back my soul. God, Julie...I came back and you weren't there. No one knew where you'd gone. I thought you'd decided—and then I came *here* and found you in my bed. That's a miracle, and I'm still shaking. I just want to look at you...touch you...taste you...love you."

His words were warm moist puffs against her skin, and then his mouth joined his hands in worshiping her body. His lips and tongue teased a nipple, and then he drew it deeply into his mouth. She groaned as the fierce, drawing pressure caught at the secret center of desire within her and made it throb and ache. One hand stroked down over her belly, then slipped under her thigh to encourage it gently upward. His fingers cupped and then parted her, fluttered lightly over her womanhood like a butterfly caressing the petals of a flower, then dipped inside the honeyed chamber, tantalizing, coaxing, urging her to a breathless, shuddering passion.

"This is me loving you, Julie.... I love you. Feel my love!" His lips and tongue feathered across the quivering flesh of her belly. "I love you—all of you. My sweet . . . sweet love . . ." As his mouth brushed soft feminine down, his hand slipped under her, lifting her to him. And then his mouth cherished her, his lips and tongue adored her, while she obeyed his wordless request and became molten and pliable in his hands. She felt herself being molded to the heat of his mouth, reshaped by his loving hands to become, now and forever, a part of him.

Again and again Chayne took her soaring to the heights of ecstasy, and then each time eased her skillfully back from the precipice, keeping her trembling on the brink of fulfillment until she was all but mindless with the sweet agony of it.

She sobbed his name when he left her, but it was only for a moment. "I'm here, angel . . . I'm here," he growled, his voice thick with passion. "I'm not going to leave you, ever again." He slid over her body, grafting her to him with one swift, sure thrust. She arched upward against him, and he caught and held her tightly locked to his body. "Never again!" he growled fiercely, and took possession once and for all.

Much later, when Chayne's breathing had slowed and deepened, Julie roused herself reluctantly from her own languid doze and stirred in his arms.

"Where are you going?" he demanded, instantly awake.

"Just back to my room, my love." She kissed him, a tender promise. "Your mother..."

"Forget my mother. Stay! You're mine, and you belong in my bed!"

"Chayne! Don't talk like that. I adore your mother!"

"So do I. And I adore you. And I'll bet anything *she* adores you. Stay."

Julie sighed contentedly and snuggled back against his chest. "Do you really think she won't mind?"

"Mmm? I don't know...but I'm sure as hell not going to ask for *permission*."

The idea struck Julie as funny, and she laughed breathily into his neck. He laughed too, a warm rumble of pure contentment. "We'll wait and confront her in the morning with, as they say, a *fait accompli!*" And he stilled their laughter with a deep, drugging kiss.

"Well, you were right," Julie said, her voice husky with happiness. "Maddy didn't seem to mind our being together."

"I told you, she adores you. And so do I." Chayne tightened his arm around her, pulling her even more securely against his side.

They were crossing the pasture, striding in step and without haste through grass still wet with morning dew. They had gone for a walk after breakfast and had turned by mutual and unspoken consent to retrace the path by which Chayne had first brought her to his home. There were no lingering ghosts of that terrible night. The sun was just burning through the morning fog of summer, bathing the pasture in golden warmth.

"How did you and my mother get to be such good buddies?" Chayne asked suspiciously. "You two seemed pretty thick this morning for a couple of people who just met."

"Oh...," Julie said, smiling, "we have quite a bit in common."

"Hmm." They had reached the barbed-wire fence that bordered the road. Chayne held the strands wide for her to crawl through, and she did the same for him.

"It looks different in the daylight," Julie mused, gazing up at the adobe church. "Smaller."

"Come on." Chayne dusted his hands and started up the hill. "I'll show you where I spent Sundays in my wicked youth."

Julie glanced at him in surprise. "You were *never* wicked, but I didn't know you were Catholic."

"I'm not. Probably why it fascinated me so." They saved their breath for the last few steps of the steep climb. Chayne pushed open the massive, dark wooden doors and they went inside.

"I was right—the walls *are* three feet thick," Julie murmured in an awed undertone. She stopped to tip her head back and peer up at a peaked ceiling that was painted with roiling tilt-edged clouds and fat pink cherubs.

"They still held services here when I was a kid," Chayne said moving down the center aisle, his feet crunching on a litter of plaster and mouse droppings. "The congregation was mostly Indian. I don't know why they closed it down."

"It's too bad. It has a kind of simple charm, even like this, without all the trappings."

"There," Chayne said, stopping at the kneeling rail and pointing. "I used to sneak into the vestry after Mass had started and watch the altar boys going about their business. I don't know why. Maybe it reminded me of when I was very small, in Mexico. There were churches just like this in the little villages I grew up in." He thrust his hands into his pockets and glanced at her, ill at ease suddenly. "Do you have a church, Julie?"

"What? Oh. Well...actually I haven't been very active since I left home, but...yes, I guess I do. Why?"

"I'd like to get married in a church." She was silent, and he turned to her with a touching note of doubt. "You will marry me, won't you?"

Julie felt her heart fill to bursting, driving tears into her eyes. She reached for Chayne's hands. "Yes...of course I'll marry you."

"You...haven't asked about my trip to Washington. You don't know what I decided."

"*I* decided," Julie said fiercely. "I decided it didn't matter."

"So," Chayne said, watching her with wary eyes, "no more doubts and hang-ups about loving a criminal?"

"None," Julie said serenely. "It's something I'll tell our grandchildren with pride."

"And...the fear?"

"I'll always have that," Julie said with a little shudder, sober again. "I'd be afraid even if you worked in an office or a grocery store. I'd be afraid you'd get hit by a bus, or have a tree fall on you, or catch pneumonia. It's what comes of loving somebody so much."

"I know," Chayne growled, his eyes electric. And then, clearing his throat, he said, "I've resigned from SAT."

"Oh." Julie held his hands tightly and looked into his eyes. "Because of my fears?"

"No. Because of mine. Ah, Julie..." He gave a sigh and pulled her into his arms, as if he were finally bringing her home. "I'd have been no good at all to them. Life has become too precious to me. I'd never be able to face the risk that I might not get home to you." With his cheek pressed to her cotton-fluff curls, his voice hoarse with emotion, he went on, "Julie, I'd given up believing in anything, caring about anything. God, country, mom and apple pie—I'd believed in all of it once upon a time, and in a big way. But then, for a long time there was *nothing*. And then I had you dumped in my arms, this tiny little spitting kitten—so vulnerable and so damned defiant—and I was the only person who could protect you, get you out of that mess you'd stumbled into. I was *responsible* for you. Do you have any idea what it did to me, when I tore off that cap of yours and saw those big scared eyes staring up at me? It was like getting punched in the stomach...."

Julie couldn't answer, so she just held him tightly, listening to the erratic thumping of his heart. After a while she stirred and sighed into his chest. "Oh, Chayne...what are we going to do? Neither of us has a job, and neither of us is a nine-to-five person. I can't see you behind a desk; I just can't."

"Well," Chayne said carefully, clearing his throat, "that might depend on the desk."

"What?"

"I...uh...I spent some extra time in Washington, and I just may have come up with a solution to this little dilemma of ours."

"Chayne!" Julie cried, pounding on his biceps. "Stop sounding so smug, damn you! Tell me *what!*"

"Trust me, Julie...it's going to be all right."

"*Chayne!*"

"Ah-ah, *Güerita*...remember what happens when you don't trust me? Now then . . . just be still and kiss me."

"I thought it went well today, didn't you?" Julie added a log to the fireplace and sank onto the couch beside Chayne. Outside, the Charleston night had turned unusually nippy, even for December. "Was Davidson suitably impressed?"

"Knocked out," Chayne said, lifting her feet into his lap and taking off her shoes. "He was so impressed that he's talking about keeping at least one instructor on the training center's staff pregnant at all times. Or is it keeping one pregnant instructor on the staff . . . ?"

"Stop that," Julie giggled, poking him in the stomach with her toe. "Seriously, he's going to let me stay with this class of rookies? Even now that I'm beginning to show?"

"Seriously. You demonstrated today that you can handle it physically, and the trainees obviously like the little extra insights you give them. There are some things a male instructor just can't teach a future undercover operative, which is what the center had in mind when they took us on as team instructors in the first place."

"I know, but—"

"And your pregnancy just adds a—pardon the expression—a new *dimension* to the program."

Julie laughed and kicked him smartly in the ribs. "You're really in fine form tonight, aren't you?"

"Um-hmm. So are you. God, but you're gorgeous!"

"Chayne . . . what are you doing?" He had pushed up her sweater and unzipped her slacks and was kissing the gentle swell of her abdomen.

"Gorgeous...and delicious. Umm, I'm glad I married you." He hooked a finger in the elastic of her panties and drew them down past her navel.

"Oh, sure, you say that *now*," Julie said with mock severity. "But will you still love me when I'm huge and ugly and covered with blue veins?"

"Didn't I ever tell you? I've had this secret craving for a huge wife with blue veins." He rubbed his cheek against her belly, chafing gently with the roughness of his jaw, and then began laving the spot with his tongue. "Did you feel movement again today?"

"Yes," Julie murmured, beginning to melt.

He placed his hand reverently over the growing mound. "Do you suppose I could feel it?"

"No," Julie whispered, stroking his hair. "Not yet." She smiled a secret smile. For a while yet it was hers and hers alone, this tiny being she and Chayne had made. Just a tiny fluttering deep, deep inside, like butterfly wings . . .

"Chayne . . . I love you."

He lifted his head and smiled at her with cobalt eyes . . . and Julie felt as if the sun were shining on her.

* * * * *